"When it comes to decency, you haven't a leg to stand on."

Lady Brocknell's smile of triumph was unmistakable.

Joss turned to face his mother, his movements so precise and slow he appeared to be a mechanism rather than a man.

"And what, exactly, do you mean by that, mother dear?" His polite control quivered with sarcasm. "Are you insinuating that my wife is indcent? And if so, in what way, pray tell? As her husband, I really think I ought to know."

"You don't really want me to tell him, do you, Yvonne? Why don't you go and get dressed and go to the party, and then we can forget all about this unpleasant little scene?"

Yvonne, dizzy with fear and bewilderment, looked blankly down. "I don't know what you mean . . . truly I don't . . . I never know what to expect from you or what you expect of me."

Lady Brocknell said, "I certainly did not expect an illegitimate child."

A Woman of Two Continents

Pixie Burger

BANTAM BOOKS
TORONTO · NEW YORK · LONDON · SYDNEY

A WOMAN OF TWO CONTINENTS
A Bantam Book / July 1982

Lyrics from "Adios, Buenos Aires, Goodbye," "Arroro Mi Nene,"
"Caminante," and "Gabriela;" copyright © 1981 by Pixie Music
Co. Reprinted courtesy of Pixie Music Company.

ISBN 1-553-20833-0

Published simultaneously in the United States and Canada

Bantam Books are published by Bantam Books, Inc. Its trademark, consisting of the words "Bantam Books" and the por-
trayal of a rooster, is Registered in U.S. Patent and Trademark
Office and in other countries. Marca Registrada. Bantam
Books, Inc., 666 Fifth Avenue, New York, New York 10103.

PRINTED IN THE UNITED STATES OF AMERICA

0 9 8 7 6 5 4 3 2 1

I dedicate this book
With all my love
To those I love
And the lands of my heart

I

Edie
1896–1907

1

Edie sat, stiff-backed, on the edge of the dining room chair, her chubby legs itching against the horsehair stubble sticking through the velvet upholstery and her feet dangling above the floor. Her arms ached from the strain of best behavior and the big, grown-up knife and fork that were too heavy, too long, and all the wrong shape for her small, sweaty hands. The silver, cool and smooth when she had first picked it up from the damask-covered table, was now greasy with heat and effort and slipped within her palm at every move.

She could feel a trickle of perspiration beginning a path down her back, underneath her Sunday camisole and petticoat. The waistband of her bloomers was already beginning to press against her stomach, and there was still the Yorkshire pudding to finish before getting to the cream-covered sweet she knew was waiting in the pantry.

The high heat and light of early afternoon slanted through the slatted wooden shutters of the dining room's tall windows. There was no breeze at all, only the slight movement of air induced by the room's several openings—the windows, the door to the corridor leading to the front hallway and entrance, and the double doors with the glass inserts on their upper halves leading into the main sitting room, the front *sala*, as the servants called it, but Edie was mindful only to give it its English name when her parents were around. Because of the heat, all the doors were open today, including the door to the pantry. Edie could hear the clash of pot against stove in the kitchen beyond and the servants' low voices, talking constantly. Usually they talked much louder, but with the door open, they knew better than to risk Papa's ire.

In the dining room, the click of cutlery on china sounded in counterpoint against the sideboard clock's metronome. Tick, tock, click, click. Edie's grasp slipped, and the heavy fork lost its load of stodgy yellow, the pudding falling back onto

3

the plate with a soft plop. She struggled with the knife and loaded the fork up again, her forehead creased in concentration to do it the way she had been taught. Over the scraping, ticking rustlings, the room's silence mingled with the thick midsummer air of January.

Edie's mother sat at the end of the table nearest the door to the pantry, absorbed in her meal. Directly opposite, to the right, Edie's father occupied his habitual chair. Edie heard it scrape against the floor in movement; she turned to watch her father as he rose and went to the sideboard. Was he going to cut some more of the roast? Yes, he was.

Please-God-don't-make-me-be-made-to-eat-any-more...

The Deity, ever watchful, even in the midst of a Rosario heatwave, apparently heard and granted her wish, for the metal-on-metal sharpening of the carving knife, followed by the snicker-swish slicing of the roast itself, was not interrupted by any spoken question or command. Mr. Moore helped himself to more vegetables and potatoes from the dishes grouped around the roast-platter and came back to the table. The silent meal continued.

There. That was the end of the pudding. With a stifled sigh, Edie placed her knife and fork next to each other in the middle of the plate. She wiped her mouth on her napkin and looked at her mother, who smiled faintly and reached for the silver bell. Its tinkling note caused an immediate change in the mingled sounds coming from beyond the pantry. The voices stopped, and Rosa's footsteps came across the tiled floor.

The plates and dishes were cleared, fresh ones were brought in, and the sweet served. Cream in a silver jug was placed in front of Mrs. Moore, in case anyone wanted a second helping. Edie brightened; apart from preferring sugary foods, she also liked the smaller spoons and forks used for dessert. Her interest in eating was renewed, and she forgot about the heat.

She was so immersed in thought and blancmange that her father's voice made her jump.

"Edie, my child," said Mr. Moore, "kindly tell Mrs. Moore to pass the cream to you. I would like to add some to my sweet."

"Yes, Papa." Edie turned to her mother. "Mamma, may I have the cream, please?" But her mother was already handing it to her.

"Please tell Mr. Moore to pass it back to you when he has finished with it, as I, too, would like some additonal cream...."

Stretching toward the other end of the table, Edie gave her father the silver pitcher.

"Mamma wants it back, Papa."

"Thank you, my child."

Mr. Moore concentrated his attention on pouring the cream over the contents of his plate. When he was finished, he handed the jug back to his daughter.

"You may now return it to Mrs. Moore."

It was only recently that Edie had begun to wonder about her parents' behavior toward each other. Earlier than that, she had not questioned it. In all her life she did not remember ever having heard her father address her mother directly.

The home into which Edith Ida Moore was born in the late 1880's, that of a respected and well-to-do resident of Argentina's second biggest town, was composed of two worlds, superimposed. The first, an immediately visible world to a small child, was one of English language, habit, and style, with duties, behavior, and functions, and weekly, yearly, and seasonal patterns inflexibly laid out. There was church on Sundays and schoolroom on weekdays and special lessons on Saturday as she got older. There were birthdays and Christmas and special collections for the heathen, and honoring thy mother and father but especially Papa. Edie came to think of that world as Mamma's world, and almost everything in it was neat and tidy and constantly being cleaned.

The other world was bigger and almost everywhere outside and somehow underneath everything even inside the house, although you couldn't see it when you woke up every day. It showed in the kitchen, because there one spoke Spanish, and the things brought in from the market were definitely part of the other world. But Edie did not question life's duality, for that was all part of the way things were, like God and lessons in the schoolroom and learning the times table forwards, backwards, and jumping, and nighttime with the lights out even if you were afraid, and not playing with the street children.

"But Rosita plays with them."

"That's different. She's one of them."

Edie was puzzled. "Why is she one of them if she lives here in the house with us?"

"Rosita is a servant's child," Mamma had said, as though Edie didn't know it.

"But she doesn't live in a dirty *rancho* or wear torn dresses or not wash her face..."

"That's enough, Edie."

Sensing danger, Edie did not go on to mention that Rosita, Rosa's daughter and born on the same day as Edie, although in a different, earlier year, seemed to have the best of the two worlds that formed life in Rosario and privileges Edie herself was always denied. Rosita could run over to *Doña* Pancha's house any time she wanted to, there to spend the day amid the steaming tubs of boiling water and strong soap that washed away all the dirtiness of life that got into the sheets and towels and pillowslips and tablecloths, many of which had been brought out from England by Mamma when she came to the Argentine and married Papa.

Papa.

He was much more difficult to understand than Mamma. Papa was king of her world, and probably of the other one, too. Papa was a very important man; he was never to be disturbed, and children were not to make too much noise when he was home. Nor were they ever, ever to touch any of his books; they were not, in fact, allowed to go into his study at all. Edie had a vague memory of Little Brother lurching around on his unsteady toddler's legs and going through the doorway toward the heavy desk before she could stop him. Nana beat her for that because she had been left in charge of Little Brother while Nana went to see whether Baby Maude had woken up yet. But all Edie remembered was the feel of the moment rather than exactly what happened, that heavy, blanketing feel of Papa always there even when he wasn't. Very soon after that came the days of being sad when God took the other two Moore children back to Heaven, and then of Edie being very ill herself, and everything being different, and so the incident was never ever mentioned again. Nana only said she should thank God she got well again, and so Edie added a line to her nightly mumbled prayers.

When it came to God, Edie had a problem. For one thing, he did not always grant the requests you would expect Him to grant if He were a true Friend; He hadn't spared Little Brother or Baby Maude when Mamma had prayed for them so hard. For another, she knew that Papa did not believe in Him. And since Papa knew everything...

On the other hand, her best friend Dollie had told her that if a person did not believe in God, they could never go to Heaven but would end up in Hell with the Devil, for ever and ever, and have nothing but fire instead of heavenly peace, whatever that was. It made Edie feel sick and uncomfortable, and frightened her deep inside where she knew she couldn't tell Mamma. Besides, Mamma would only have chastised her, as she believed in God most fervently, even though He hadn't granted any of her prayers; He certainly hadn't done anything about Mamma going back to England. Edie had heard Mamma mention that it would take a miracle to get Papa interested in the notion, but miracles were what God wrought, weren't they?

Edie loved hearing Mamma talk about England. Mamma had told her when she grew up to be a big lady she would be able to travel to England and see how lovely things were there and how nice life could be. Mamma would tell her all about England when they were alone together, and those were the times Edie liked best, but they didn't happen very often.

Usually, Nana was in charge, and much of Edie's life was spent in the schoolroom. Weekdays, she also ate there with Dollie and Dollie's older brother, Robert, with Nana presiding. Nana did not allow much conversation, and it was mostly "Elbows off the table," and "Sit up straight," and "Gentlemen do not eat with their mouths open, Robert." The day Edie mentioned that Papa sometimes did, Nana yanked her out of her chair with a flesh-biting grip, dragged her into the bedroom, and ordered her to bend over the bed and lower her bloomers. Edie cried before the beating even began; this time it was with the bristle side of the brush, and it had left blotchy marks on her for days. They had changed color from red to scab-spotted blue and then to yellow and green before fading away. After the beating, Nana made her spend the whole afternoon standing in the schoolroom corner, but just before teatime Edie had vomited all the way down the front of her frock, and so Nana had slapped her and put her to bed early without any tea, and no supper later, either.

It was better to think twice, even thrice, before saying anything to Nana. Edie was much happier sitting at her place at the schoolroom table, practising her penmanship and writing *Edith Ida Moore* with care and precision on the inside cover of all her copybooks. She liked doing sums, too, and was much better at them than either Dollie or Robert, both of whom were older than she was. Edie found she could do lots of the sums in her head, without having to write them down, but when she had tried to tell Nana, she had been warned that pride goeth before a fall and then made to write out the phrase ten times in her copybook.

Dollie and Robert were Canon Thaxter's children. He conducted the church services and taught the older children's confirmation class. Edie attended the Sunday school lessons given by his wife, Aunt Bessie. Dollie also went to them and, although she was older and taller and fatter than Edie, and her mother's favorite in class besides, Edie knew Dollie was stupid. She took so long to understand things; Edie was always losing patience with her friend. But friend she remained, for Dollie was part of Mamma's world.

Edie's own world was a constant dividing and recognition of Us and Them, We and They. We were right, upstanding, responsible, clean, hardworking, honest, and, above all, British. With the Theys, it was rather more difficult: some of Them were clean, responsible, hardworking, and reasonably honest, but not all of Them. And They were never English; They were always Argentines.

Or natives, as some people said. This was one of the confusing bits, because the Theys were not Indians like the native Indians who had been so wicked and fierce and killed off so many people who were only trying to help them in the colonies they had formed. Mamma had told Edie that Papa had once wanted to go and live on a colony, but the bad Indians had swept down and killed almost everybody and stolen the horses and set fire to all the houses, so Papa had not gone to the Chaco region at all, but had stayed in Rosario instead and gone to work for the railway.

It wasn't always easy to tell who was good and nice and one of the Us, and English. Of course, you could tell easily enough that they weren't if they spoke only Spanish: then they were definitely Argentines. With the British, it was much easier. They always spoke English unless they were talking to the servants or somebody who was Argentine and who did not speak English.

Edie was gaining confidence in her perception of the different categories when the blow came from Dollie.

"My mamma says you're Argentine."

That was impossible. Edie always spoke English unless she

was talking to Rosita or Rosa or someone like that. Besides, they were all English, she and Mamma and Papa.

Dollie shook her head, making her cheeks wobble under her sausage curls, which her mother pinned up nightly in soft strips of rag.

"No, you're not. Your mamma and papa are English, but you're an Argentine. You were born here. My mamma said so."

From then on, it was understood Dollie had an edge on Edie, for she had indeed been born in England, whereas Edie had entered the world in Rosario.

It did not seem to interfere too much, Edie found, except in her dealings with Dollie. Whenever Edie managed to get the better of Dollie in anything, and the occasions were frequent, Dollie—after tears or a show of temper—would flounce off, saying, "Well, at least *I* was born in England," as though that settled everything in her favor.

Secretly, Edie liked Rosita far better than Dollie. She was dark-haired and quick and knew all sorts of forbidden and fascinating information that she would whisper to Edie when they got together in the cool and musty-smelling storeroom at the far end of the patio. Its tamped-down earth floor and high-piled sacks, some empty, some fat with flour, were safe witnesses to the secrets of little girls. Rosita did not join Edie in the schoolroom with Robert and Dollie. She did not need to learn the times table or English history lessons or any of the subjects Nana taught. Once, when Edie had asked why, Nana had slapped her and told her not to be impertinent, but later Mamma explained that Rosita was going to be a servant like her mother Rosa and would need to learn other things, like cleaning and dusting and scrubbing and ironing and how to polish the silver so it shone like the moon.

"And I don't have to learn all that?" asked Edie, knowing the answer by heart but wishing to prolong the delicious moment of having Mamma all to herself and in one of her happy moods.

"You have to learn to know how it is done, so you can supervise your servants," was the well-loved reply. "You're going to grow up to be an English lady and have a beautiful house with lots of lovely things in it. And you'll have to know how to have them cared for and looked after."

"I'm going to be an English lady when I'm big," Edie confided to Dollie later, in a burst of overexuberant friendship. "Mamma says so, and Mamma says I'll have lots of pretty things, and..."

"I'm English already," was Dollie's response, whose mood did not match Edie's at that moment.

"That's not the same as growing up to be an English lady."

"Yes, it is."

"No, it isn't."

"Yes, it..."

There were tears within minutes, and Nana bounding through the door, and the end of any fun or confidences for the day. Edie swore to herself she would never let Dollie play in her house when she grew up to be an English lady, and she paid extra attention to her lessons the next day, in an effort to speed up the process.

Not all lessons were easy. Music was one of the terrors. Edie knew from Mamma that all nice little girls knew how to play the piano and how to sing, but so far she had only been able to master a few scales, and the sounds she heard when she listened to music were not the same when she tried to sing them. Only the words came out correctly; the musical notes all went in opposite directions.

To make it worse, Mamma always sang so prettily herself, and Edie longed to grow up to be just like Mamma. She loved hearing Mrs. Moore sing, particularly when she entertained company.

"You'll be able to do it too, when you try hard enough," promised Mamma, but try as she might, Edie could not do so. A pale young woman came in twice a week, on Saturday mornings and Wednesday afternoons, and sat with Edie at the piano that had come all the way from England on a boat, ordered expressly for Mamma by Mr. Moore, shortly after their marriage.

Edie hated it. She hated sitting on the cushions piled on the bench that was too low for her; she hated doing the finger-stretching exercises in the hope of increasing the reach of her small, square hands; she hated not understanding why the notes in her ears never corresponded to those in her throat; and most of all she hated the way her pale teacher made everything about music, every move, look so easy and simple—when it always turned out to be hard and tricky and often impossible when it came Edie's turn.

Everything came to a halt the day Papa returned home early. Edie was at the piano, her teacher standing beside her, and the notes were going wrong both under her fingers and in her throat. She heard a door bang shut and the *sala* door burst open.

"Stop that abominable noise!"

Edie jumped in her seat at the sound of Papa's voice and snatched her hands off the keys.

"Yes, Papa."

"Mr. Moore..." The pale teacher was facing Papa, and she looked even paler than before.

"Enough of this nonsense. The child has a tin ear. Any fool can tell that. Or should." He glared at the young woman. "There will be no more lessons."

He left the room as abruptly as he had entered it, and that was the end of the music lessons, right then and there. Edie knew better than to mention anything about the subject to Mamma, who was tight-lipped the next day, but said nothing either. Edie noticed her mother did not play or sing at all for a while, until some visitors who came to tea begged her to do so.

"Oh, do, Mrs. Moore, do play for us... we always enjoy it so...."

And Mamma had played again, and things went back to normal, except that the pale music teacher was nevermore seen in the house.

Even though Papa did not believe in God, he did believe in church attendance for his wife and daughter. Perhaps it was because Mamma's papa had been a clergyman and in charge of the church before he died; Edie sometimes visited his grave with Mamma, who let her place the bunch of flowers next to the solid oblong stone with the neatly carved letters and different-looking numbers with XXs and Vs that Edie had to learn before she could turn them into proper numbers and know what date they said.

She remembered her grandmother as a soft lady with a damp face and a black hat with a veil on one side; she had sailed back to England with Mamma's sisters, Muriel and Beatrix, after Grandpapa had died. But Grandmama hadn't lasted long at all once she got there, and had gone to her eternal rest, too.

The flat-facaded, flat-roofed house that was the Moore home stood on a quiet street where *paraíso* trees gave speckled shade during the summer and dropped their squashy, harsh-smelling, yellow, clustered berries in the wet of winter. The road, rutted by cart and carriage wheels, powdered to dust in the long hot months, and most houses remained shuttered against its gritty invasion whenever a drought prolonged the problem. Front doors, flush with the front walls, were often flanked by a tall carriage entrance, leading to the rear of the dwelling, the inner patio and, beyond, the stables.

So it was at the Moore home; the carriage entrance, with its arched top and iron-grille gate, led beyond the house's central patio to an open-ended area the other side of the servants' quarters, where stables and storerooms enclosed two sides. At one time there had been slave quarters back there, and Edie dimly remembered a very old man with tight white hair around his dark face. He was bent over, he was so old, and he was the last man to live there. Mamma had said, left over from the time when all the slaves had been freed. Most of them had gone away or died, but he had stayed. When Papa bought the house, he had said the old man was to be allowed to live there for the rest of his life, even if he did no work but simply sat in the sunshine. And then one day he was not there any more.

Part of the house was old, built in the days when the Spaniards had colonized the country. Rosario, thus called from its original dedication to the Chapel of the Rosary of the Streams, built upriver from Buenos Aires and serving as a second and busy port, had been a frontier town from its early beginnings, for the *pampas* stretched from its river banks out to the distant west. Colonial houses, dating from the early 1700's, sat around open squares that served as marketplaces or were tree-planted and embellished with statues of heroes and politicians.

The entrance to the Moore house was the original entrance, with its one room upstairs over the front door. The room had a balcony, with a curved iron balustrade bulging out; this was the traditional *balcón mirador*, the looking balcony, as Millicent Moore always called it. A long time ago, the *mirador* balconies were used by the ladies when they watched a festival procession going through the streets. Or the ragged return of a regiment from battle; both Indians and independence had been fought nearby.

"But there isn't much to look at, is there?" Mamma would

12

sigh, and Edie had to agree. The view showed little other than the flat rooftops around them, the trees of the street and those of the square beyond, the plaza where Nana would take her and Dollie and sometimes Robert for an afternoon walk.

The upstairs room was used for storage; the living quarters of the house were all on the ground floor. Most of the rooms encircled the inner, tiled patio; only the front *sala* and Papa's study had windows onto the street. The main current of household life circulated around the covered corridor that bordered the inner patio and, other than the two front rooms, all rooms had windows or doors giving onto the corridor itself, and most of them had doors leading from one into the other.

Whenever Edie saw her mother's big plain muslin mobcaps hanging out to air on the line strung across a far corner of the patio, she knew spring cleaning was close at hand. On ordinary days Mamma would wear morning caps with tiny dots or sprigged flowers in their pale designs, but once a year, as the wet cold of the Rosario winter warmed toward spring, the large plain caps came out of the cupboard and onto the line, the signal that the Moore household was about to be turned inside out.

The hubbub of change took the better part of a week, a week during which Mr. Moore always absented himself. He took the opportunity to travel to Buenos Aires for the duration, and the combination of his absence and the flurried activity guaranteed gaiety and unaccustomed laughter in the home. During this period, Papa's traveling portmanteau would be lying open on a bench in front of his dressing room; starched linens and shirtings and collars would be placed in it by Rosa, who brought the freshly ironed clothes over from *Doña* Pancha's every afternoon. Sometimes Rosita would go to the washerwoman's rancho with her mother, also returning laden, and Edie felt left out of the fun and deserted by her friend.

"But I have to go."

"No. You could stay here and play with me."

"But when my mami says I have to help her..."

"What *my* Mamma says is far more important than what Rosa says...."

The truth scorched the bonds between them; each burned child retired, the one to the kitchen, the other to the nursery, where further bullying took place.

13

"Dollie's penmanship is far superior to yours, Edie, and this whole page has to be done again. . . ."

Edie passed on the insult.

"My papa's much richer than your papa, and that's why you have to come and have lessons in our house, because it's bigger than yours. . . ."

Dollie, in tears, told her mother when she got home. Mrs. Thaxter's rivalry with the pretty and wealthy Mrs. Moore was a lost battle before it ever got started. She spoke to her husband, who sighed for many reasons; on Sunday, he approached Millicent Moore after the services were over.

With spring cleaning set for the week ahead, Edie's mother had little interest in paying more than cursory, polite attention to Canon Thaxter's latest admonition regarding her child's behavior toward his daughter. She would murmur apologies and change the subject, leaving the Thaxters deeply dissatisfied but without further recourse. Monday would arrive. Mr. Moore would leave. Spring cleaning began.

Every window in the house exploded open; chill drafts swept through and slammed doors right and left. The washing lines in the patio were solid with garments and upholstery being aired, beaten, shaken, and aired again. Baskets of laundry were sent off to be soaped and boiled; then the tide turned, and the summer garbing began. The light curtains, the summer covers, the pale bedspreads, and all the slipcovers were thrown and patted and stretched and pinned into place, and then Mrs. Moore would begin to say, "Now we're almost done, aren't we?" to Edie, who would be carrying a box of pins or a soft clean polishing cloth for her Mamma, delighted to be an assistant at this special time.

The best part came on the very last day; by then, a lightness of spirit prevailed. The monumental task was done for another year, and the cleanliness gave shine to solid surface and spirit alike. The sole remaining task for the mistress of the house was the selecting and placing of objects and ornaments, crystal, silver, and china, taken from their wrapped shrines of storage and placed, changed, or put away again according to the seasons and Mrs. Moore's whims.

This was the part Edie loved best; it was the world of a grown-up's box of toys, the beautiful things that she, too, would have when she grew up to be an English lady like Mamma. There were china figures, beautiful ladies in wigs or dainty animals, grouped; there were porcelain bowls, transparent in their delicacy. Silver dishes, bonbonnières and salvers, heavy and ornate, were set near branched candlesticks, green baize beneath their bases so they could not scratch or be scratched. There were vases of all shapes and sizes, some cut, some tinted, some decked with gold. All the beloved belongings bore the stamp of England somewhere, either in lettering Edie could read, or in hallmarks she knew had their own language.

Different sections of the storage cupboards held the linens, the cutlery, and the treasures. On other shelves, full sets of china with patterned plates and dainty cups and saucers lay waiting to be used. But Edie's favorite was a small dark corner, half-forgotten in the rest of the splendor: this was the shelf that held her mother's possessions from her own early days. Here were tucked the talismans of youth, the mementos of Millicent's childhood in the soft reaches of the Sussex countryside: the remains of a rag doll, worn and washed to pale remnant, but still the solace of a little girl now grown to unhappy, womanhood; a seashell, more perfect in its opalescent curlicues than any china piece; a miniature, given her by one of her father's past parishioners, who took a fancy to the clergyman's three delightful daughters in the long ago, and painted tiny flower pictures for them during an English summer. The one treasure discovered during a spring cleaning that was allowed out on special occasions, no matter what the season, was Mamma's flower album.

It was Rosa who had come upon it, dusty and paper-wrapped, in the forgotten reaches of an old trunk.

"*Señora*, the trunk you wanted moved is not empty. Look what I found in it..."

Mrs. Moore took the rumpled package to the dining room table and there opened the crackling paper with patient care, layer by layer. Edie watched each move. Then came the book itself, unlike any she had ever seen. It was loosely tied together and had thick, dark pages; the front was flat and stiff, and a cord held it to the rest of the volume.

"What kind of book is it, Mamma?"

"It's not a book. It's an album. My flower album. Look—I picked and pressed these flowers when I was a little girl, just like you...."

Thus was born a ritual between them. For Edie, it was a time of closeness with her mother, a private bond. For Millicent, it was an escape from the present, a freedom from the

15

bondage of being a wife and mother in Rosario, Argentina, the harsh and foreign river city she had to call her home, but which she despised and feared and loathed in the silence of her soul.

Millicent lifted the cardboard cover and turned the dark, colored pages.

"Oh, look, Edie, that's a primrose... and this one's a buttercup... they say if you hold a fresh one under your chin, and it gets reflected, it means you love eating butter...."

Edie watched, enchanted. Millicent turned page after page, naming the blossoms as they appeared. She relived her youthful happiness, enchanced by time, in the faded, desiccated flowers, their brittle forms as fragile as youth's illusions, but more lovingly guarded and preserved.

Millicent loved looking at her album; she saw reflected in its pages the pale sun and gentle hills of her childhood's spring days, and remembered, with each flower, the way life had been when she had picked it in the garden, on the lea, over the Downs, in the meadow with her sisters, by the river with her parents on a special summer outing. Life had been happy then, happy and kind and good. She sighed for it, and she sighed for England, and she longed to live there again or at least to see it again, to see and hug her sisters, but Mr. Moore did not share her views at all, and she knew his word and wishes were law.

Thinking of him, she sighed her millionth sigh. He was a good husband, propriety and duty told her; he was the most difficult man on earth, answered her heart. It was all her fault, of course; she was too limited, too ignorant, too stupid to understand the vast knowledge he held in his head. He always knew everything. He was always right. In the early days of their marriage, when she had been groping her way through a new language, in a new country, tending to her married duties and, within a year, to her first baby as well, Millicent had cried herself to sleep nightly, bewildered and overwhelmed in a lonely, alien world.

But all anyone else saw was that Mr. Moore was a provider without peer. Gowns, hats, the latest of silks and satins arrived from France, embroidered linens, sumptuous silver, the piano, a carriage—all were hers, without the asking.

"It's all too grand," she once sobbed to her mother, in a rare display of her inner despair.

"Hush, Millie, you're a very lucky girl, and you know it. Every girl in Rosario had her cap set for Mr. Moore—and many in Buenos Aires, besides..."

It was all true, and none of it helped the young bride understand the inner workings of her husband's mind. She celebrated her eighteenth birthday shortly after their marriage, and on that day she told him she was with child.

"I see." His facial expression did not change. "In that case, it is time we move to a more accommodating house, and I shall engage a responsible person for the nursery."

That was all he said before leaving the house and going about his business for the day. That evening he informed her letters would be written to England, and a woman of good character and full training engaged to come out to the Argentine and care for the child.

She arrived the month before little Edie was born, and was known as Nana or *señorita* Nana to her face. A despot of the nursery and a terror to the servants, she was called *la bruja* behind her broad and meaty back, for witchlike she was in her bursts of fury, and her temper was feared by everyone except Mr. Moore, who never saw a demonstration of it in all the years Nana served him. Temperament was best left out of meetings with Mr. Moore, a tactic all who worked for him learned, either quickly, or to their cost.

Two more babies followed, and the young bride Millie matured, growing more accustomed to her married role. Taken up with the nursing duties of her babies' early infancy, she was protected from some of Mr. Moore's distance and dogmatism. He was present; he provided; between births, he visited her room by night. The unguent of habit began smoothing and soothing her days, and her children were pretty little things, animated replacements of her childhood toys.

Then in one terrible and terrifying month, her two younger children were taken from her in swift and usurping illness and death. Her oldest trembled on the brink, and pulled away; then Millie, too, was struck by the diphtheria. Still weak on her sweat-drenched sickbed, she learned her father had died also, taken by the fever. Collapsing back to the shrouding bed linens, Millie drew a veil between herself and the world, and long, anguished months passed before she returned to everyday life and the household became normal again.

Normal, but changed. Only Edie tiptoed by. And Millie's mother was leaving, returning to the England of the golden, lost days. Millie longed to join her, fully knowing she could not; Mr. Moore and her remaining daughter were her duty and fate.

"God's will be done," were the words her mother offered, and Millicent, aching for the warmth and tumble of her sisters' affection, kissed her mother on the cheek, wished her Godspeed, and waved good-bye. It was to be the last kiss; when the news of her mother's death reached Millie in one of her sisters' joint letters, written the following year, she felt protected by the endless miles, as she did from all distant catastrophes.

"It's all so far away... perhaps it didn't happen... perhaps it isn't even true, after all...."

In the long sad months following the diphtheria epidemic, Edie hardly saw her mother at all. At first, it was because Mamma was very ill. Then one morning there was a flurry of sudden activity, and people dressed in black came to the house. Dr. O'Connor, who had been visiting daily since the time of the sickness began, stayed for much longer than usual and had a special conference with Papa in the study with the door closed. Edie was not allowed to play or make any noise anywhere in the house, and everybody spoke in whispers, looking extra solemn and sad.

In the evening, Nana told her that her grandpapa had gone to his eternal rest and that Mamma was very sad about it and would have to stay in bed even longer than had been expected before. It turned out to be weeks and weeks, during which time life for Edie was strange and frightening; she was sure she could hear Mamma cry at times, and then, at others, she heard her cry out, as though calling for someone who was not there.

At last Dr. O'Connor told Edie her Mamma was getting stronger and better, and that very soon Edie would be able to see her and say good morning to her from the doorway.

"You're not to go into the room, or be loud, or make any sort of fuss," he explained, his tone soft and kind enough so that the strict rules being laid down did not upset Edie at all. When the big morning came Nana took her by the hand, and for once, Edie was glad of her presence, as she could feel her

18

heart thumping so hard she was almost afraid to approach the doorway.

"Good morning, Mamma. . . ."

Mrs. Moore was lying amid a billowing of pillows, half-hidden by them in the shaded light of the shuttered room. She looked almost as white as the bedclothes around her, and only her hair, loose and lank over her shoulders, held any color or contrast.

"My dearest little Edie . . . I hope you're being a good and sweet girl. . . ."

Her voice sounded as thin and weak as she looked; the image of her Mamma haunted Edie all day. She longed to dash into the room and clutch her mother's hand, the hand she had seen lying there, pale as the pillows; yet the thought frightened her, and she derived some comfort in knowing she would not be allowed to do anything of the sort.

The days grew better; Mamma strengthened. Presently she was allowed to get up and sit in a chair, and Edie was allowed to accompany her, as long as she promised to be good. Edie promised, and Mamma called her "my little angel," and smiled as she stroked her head, not talking about anything much at all. Just to be with her was comforting, and Edie spent the treasured moments standing close by the chair, hoping no one would remember to call her away until Dr. O'Connor came. He still visited daily, but his visits had become jolly, and his friendly, cheering voice boomed out instead of hiding the words in undertones, and Edie noticed his smile showed more of his teeth than it had before. He had a brushy gray mustache and wiry side-whiskers; they were different from Papa's, whose whiskers, though thick, were not quite as luxuriant as the good doctor's and a paler gray.

Mamma got well enough to get up and dressed every day; at first she only went from her bedroom to the front *sala* and back again, but soon she was allowed to sit in the sun, out on the patio corridor, as long as she did not get tired. At last she was able to go out for a short ride in the new carriage Papa had bought; the doctor's wife, Mrs. O'Connor, accompanied her that afternoon. From then on, Mrs. O'Connor began paying regular calls, and Edie got to know her quite well.

Mrs. O'Connor was nice. She was friendly and cheery, and her ever-ready smile tucked into the half-moon curves of her round, mottled cheeks. Her plump hands always felt warm when they held Edie's or patted her face, a gesture they did gently and not objectionably as some people did. Mamma liked her, too, Edie could tell; Mamma's voice sounded happy when she spoke to the doctor's wife, even though Mrs. O'Connor was more like a grandmother than a mother and had lots of gray in her hair like the doctor and Papa.

The day Edie heard Mrs. O'Connor was coming to tea with her sons, she was both interested and surprised; she had not known there were O'Connor children, too. They might be fun to play with, even if they were all boys; perhaps they'd be nicer than Robert, and not tease and push. Edie was eager for teatime to arrive.

But it was all a big disappointment; they weren't children, they were grown men. There was Vesey, who had a thin mustache and winked at her when they met; there was Edwin, who was fair and blue-eyed just like his mother except that he was very tall and very thin, and then there was Maurice, who was shorter and square-shaped and darker in coloring, and who didn't tease, the way Vesey did, but talked to her as though she were a grown-up, too, saying his father had often mentioned her, and did she know that her Papa and his were very good friends?

Edie wriggled off shyly and went to sit next to her Mamma, where she listened to all the grown-up talk going on around her. Mamma poured tea from her second-best teapot while Rosa, in a bib and apron from the latest sets sent out from England, handed around slices of cake.

It was mostly Mrs. O'Connor who spoke, and, of course, Mamma. Edwin sat silent most of the time, staring dreamily into space and eating so much cake Edie thought he should be roly-poly like his mother instead of long and thin. Vesey fidgeted in his chair, his small brown eyes darting about, his quick glances taking in every move made, every word spoken. Even his voice was quick, darting in and out of the conversation between his mother and Mamma.

Talk revolved around the trip Edwin and Maurice were about to take: they were going back home on the next boat to England. Maurice was beginning his university studies; Edwin was in his last term.

Mrs. Moore said wistfully, "Oh, how I'd love to go, too...."

For an instant, Edie was struck by joyous hope.

"Could we, Mamma—oh, please, could we?"

Everyone suddenly seemed to be looking at her. Mamma,

her voice shadowed, said softly, "No, Edie, I'm afraid not. Not this time," and Edie felt tears sting her eyes, embarrassed by her forward behavior and her mistake.

It was Maurice who spoke next, addressing her.

"If you're a good girl, I'll take you to England when you grow up," he said, and his smile felt kind to Edie, who nodded and smiled back but did not reply and began recovering her composure as the others, ignoring her, went on talking.

When it came time for the O'Connors to make their farewells, she whispered, "You will remember, won't you?" to Maurice, and he smiled again, and said, "Of course," and patted her cheek good-bye. Edwin offered her a limp hand, and Vesey pinched her on the arm, but Mrs. O'Connor gave her a warm hug and said she would invite her and her Mamma to luncheon the very moment she got the boys off on their trip.

That evening, at bedtime, Edie told Nana she was going to England.

"Children who tell untruths . . ." the threat began.

"It's not! It's *not* an untruth! He promised! You wait and see, Nana . . ."

Mrs. Moore, hearing the outburst, came into the night nursery.

"He promised, Mamma, didn't he?" Edie flung herself at her mother, clinging to Mrs. Moore's long, heavy skirt. "Maurice said if I'm good he'll take me to England when I'm big. . . ."

"We'll see, Edie, we'll see," her mother murmured, while Nana sniffed in disapproval.

"But he *promised* . . . Mamma, d'you think he will? He *said* he would . . . it *will* come true, won't it?"

Mrs. Moore put her slight hands on her daughter's tousled head.

"It's possible, Edie, but not very probable."

It was one of Mamma's favorite sayings, and with that, Edie had to be content. After all, she had said it was *possible* . . .

Papa, when he heard about it, said it was poppycock.

"Mrs. Moore is allowing you to fill your head with nonsense. Kindly remember who you are, where you are, and let me hear no more foolishness about trips to England."

Edie, mindful of Papa's orders, considered the matter and thought her whole name through in full: *she was Edith Ida*

Moore. *And she was in Papa and Mamma's house in Rosario, Argentina.* England faded back into the mists of imaginings and hidden dreams.

Bliss.

Nana recovering from a nasty cold and still staying in her room, taking her cough syrup and having her meals on a tray carried in by Rosa; Papa away in Buenos Aires; and Mamma in a happy mood.

Edie had her all to herself.

"Mamma."

"Yes, child."

"It won't squash."

"What won't squash?"

"The flower. It won't squash properly."

"Edith, what are you doing?" Alarmed, Mrs. Moore put down her sewing and came over to the table.

"I want to make an album, like yours." Edie's short fingers were struggling with the spray of jacaranda blossoms in her hands. The purple-shaded bells twisted unevenly as she attempted to place them between the pages of her copybook.

"I don't believe they'll work very well, dearest. You need thin, delicate flowers, not juicy ones."

"They're *not* juicy."

"Edie, don't contradict. You know perfectly well what I mean."

"But what can I use?"

"Something thin, something that lies flat on the paper."

"There *aren't* any flowers like that!" Edie's eyes were beginning to moisten.

"I know, dearest, I know. The flowers are different here. In England..."

In England.

It was always different in the Argentine and better in England. In England, the sun was not as hot, the grass did not burn down brown in the summer, and the cows gave rich and creamy milk from which you could get clotted cream and have it on buns for your tea. They didn't have the proper sort of buns here in Rosario, either. England was the distant, unknown Downs of Sussex and the pearly mornings with a heather haze, the long ago place where Mamma and her sisters had played and been happy when they were little girls. Edie loved hearing all about Mamma and Aunt Muriel

22

and Aunt Beatrix when they had been small and exactly her age. Her image of her aunts as children was more vivid than her actual recollection of them, for they had returned to England with their mother and only blurred memories of them remained.

They both lived in London now, Mamma had told her. Aunt Muriel had married, just like Mamma, and had two little boys, Dick and Peter, who were Edie's first cousins. Aunt Beatrix was not married yet, but perhaps she would soon; she was a schoolteacher, Mamma said. The two sisters wrote joint letters to Mamma, covering several pages in their strikingly different hands. Aunt Muriel's handwriting was thin and spidery; she wrote in great detail and always told the serious news. Aunt Beatrix was more given to exclamation marks and telling about birthday parties or festive outings.

Mamma would spend long hours writing letters back, and sometimes Edie was allowed to add kiss and hug marks at the bottom, along with her name. Then Mamma would put it in an envelope and make sure it was ready to leave on the next boat home.

Home.

"Mamma, doesn't Papa have any sisters or brothers at home in England?"

"No, dearest, he doesn't. He never had any, and his mamma and papa went to Heaven a long time ago."

"Before I was born?"

"Long before you were born. Even before I was born."

That took it so far into the past, it hardly existed.

"Mamma."

"Yes?"

"Did Papa ever tell you about being a little boy?"

"No." There was a measured pause. "He was born in the north, you know. They're never chatterboxes up there." Mrs. Moore softened and smiled. "You take after me, Edie."

"But he never says anything about how it was when he was still in England."

Mrs. Moore snapped the thread of her sewing and put the needle into her needlebook with care.

"Perhaps he doesn't remember it," she suggested. "Your Papa has so many important things on his mind, there probably isn't any room for the things that happened so long ago."

That made sense to Edie. Papa, she knew, was a very busy

man. Why should he be bothered to remember the days when he was a little boy?

2

He remembered everything.

He remembered so much, with such acute clarity, that it all poured together in an overflow of substance and detail whenever the past returned to his mind. Usually he kept it at bay, but there were times its rush returned, unbidden, overwhelming. Those were the times he would sit in a chair, silent, glowering, seeing the past and sensing its imprint on the present, feeling its force surging within himself. Of it, he never mentioned a word. He could not; he remembered too much.

Most of all, he remembered the cold. Cold that never went away. Not of feeling cold; that came later, when things were already better. But of being cold, all the way through, all the time. While the inside coldness was filled with aching, the surface cold was raw and grazed, sore from exposure, running wet from the suppurating chilblains covering his legs. They rose in dark red welts and swelled in pain.

The hunger, too, was part of the cold, though there were brief times when it was assuaged. The terrifying times alone were followed by his mother's return, bringing bread or more; once there had been a cake, sweet and soft, and he had been sick after eating it whole.

When he learned about fathers, he knew he did not have one, but by that time life was too tiring for him to care. There was huddling for shelter, and being chased and screamed at, and the blows if he did not move quickly enough or failed to hid in time. There were snowdrifts taller than he was and ice glazing the streets. Knowing what was expected of him he risked the blows to beg from tall-hatted gentlemen descending swept steps. There was a paper his mother needed, a paper that would allow them entry into the gaunt gray building that was the home of the shuffling figures of the poor, the rejects of Victorian England, where debt and penury and wasting illness ruined and ended lives never given a chance to start.

The paper was not yet obtainable; the authorities told his mother she would have to wait. Then came the long night in the stinging sleet that turned back to snow before the dawn. He awoke beside his mother's collapsed form; when he rose, her skirt, frozen to his leg, tore away a breadth of skin along his inner thigh.

The poorhouse admitted them late that day. Once inside, they were separated. He cried for his mother for days, and then he simply cried, but the tears did no good and he learned to stop them; finally he lost the art completely. Sudden blows smacked out at him from dark corners of the day and large shadows of the night, and he began to understand that the less noise he made, the less he was noticed, and the less he was noticed, the fewer blows came his way.

Within a fortnight one of the matrons sought him out, seized him by the arm, though not too unkindly, and guided him to a part of the building he had not known before.

"She be in there. You be good with her. Your mam's not long for this world."

The rough hands pushed him, and he stumbled through a doorway, the room he entered stretching into far reaches of dark. A hand motioned to him from a nearby bed. The whisper held no words, only recognized tones, and he went to his mother and sat by her side.

She looked different, and the sounds she made soon faded into silence; she lay still and staring for a long time, and finally closed her eyes. He sat next to her for hours, not knowing what was expected of him, but after his mother had become quite cold and her fingers stiff and unmoving, the matron reappeared at the door and took him away.

He ran away from the gloomy poorhouse, and no one followed to seek him out. Joining a pack of ragged urchins in an abandoned warehouse, he was beaten and bullied but accepted as one of the number. They begged and stole what they could, but the larger boys stole it away from the smaller. Then news of food being given away reached young Moore's ears, and he crept away alone to seek out a place.

It was a school belonging to the Ragged School Union and presided over by the local vicar, a man of modest means and an incurable faith in the betterment of man. An admirer of Lord Shaftesbury, he recognized the need for education as a path toward enlightenment; the Ragged School Union, pledged to convert incipient criminals to Christianity, dovetailed with the dire needs of his industrial parish.

The strays and starvelings came to eat and stayed to learn. They read from the Testaments and studied their numbers, and the meals received built their meager strength. Little Moore, barefoot and ragged as the rest, joined and stayed and began to learn. Neither quick with words nor captured by the Prayer Book, his was the method of the plodder, the determined.

A crowded bed in the school's shelter was found for him and, shortly thereafter, work in a mill. At that same time he discovered the world of numbers and, in it, logic and sequence. Best of all, there were the machines.

From the moment he first saw them, he loved the machines, even though they appeared as gigantic iron gods, objects of wonder not to be touched by the likes of him but altars only to be attended by those who knew them well. But, as he began to learn, everything about them made sense: their parts, their movement, their noise, the goods they produced. They had purpose and logic, sequence and rhyme: if something went wrong, if a machine stopped or slowed or jammed or turned out false product, there was a reason somewhere, and if you looked long enough and carefully enough, you were bound to find it, clear as day. Then, with matching clarity, it could be put to rights, as long as you knew how it should be working in the first place. All that was needed was knowledge.

The boy learned: he learned with an all-absorbing passion that obliterated hours, days, exhaustion, pain, as nothing ever had before.

At the mill, he ran and fetched and cleaned and carried and wiped the endless dirt and grease and waste, was shouted at, cuffed and abused in the manner of the times. But the mill meant life, because of the machines: they were the logic and sense of existence, as opposed to the chaos of people and life itself, where he saw only cruelty and abandonment and, still, the cold.

The cold never left him. Even in summer, its aftereffects lingered until the chill of autumn came upon him again. Sore troughs from the salty discharge of his nose furrowed his upper lip; the stinging winter winds etched them deeper. The mill offered him the only warmth he knew. Even the noise was a source of comfort, blocking out all other sounds and allowing him to experience an oblique privacy.

Young Moore came to the vicar's specific attention during

one of the many disputes that arose in the parish over the enactment of the Ten Hours Bill, an early attempt on Lord Shaftesbury's part to curb the abuses of child labor. Deputations from the authorities, the local mills, the workhouse, and the parishes in the area met to clash over the subject; the vicar, stubborn in his ideals, delved deeper than most men of the cloth. It was during one of his inquiries that he discovered the stocky child's aptitudes; from then on he encouraged him in his mechanical talent.

The rough hands at the roaring mill were beginning to recognize him, too.

"Nowt wrong wi' young Moore...."

"Tha's the lad for the job...."

"Call Moore—he be the one we need...."

Isaac Browntree was a man of exceptional height, heavy visage, stentorian voice, and total power. Universally hated and feared, he held the fate of his ill-paid, ill-treated workers in his oversized, dark-mottled hands. His gigantic frame cast a long shadow before him, and a savage delight in bedeviling others appeared to be his only diversion. Ruthless, vengeful, he spent his days prowling the mill, seeking out the mistakes of the hapless, then retiring to his office, where he devoured savoury pies sent over from the inn and harassed his bent-backed bookkeeper, who stood at the high desk piled with ledgers checked by the owner, daily, himself.

Browntree was sole owner and master of the mill. He was a widower with one married daughter, who had fled father and region and lived in the south. A distant nephew, seldom seen, was a longtime Londoner; the two cousins were said to be united in their hatred for the man.

Little of his attracted young Moore's interest. He worked, he walked, he ate when he could, his places of dwelling changed with the years. A bed crowded with other bodies gave way to a mattress merely shared. On occasion, it might be his alone, but the occurrence was rare, somewhat like Christmas, though more fleeting.

Time passed; Moore grew to a stocky lad and into early manhood and a measure of independence. With the vicar's continued encouragement, he found lodgings of his own in a dingy dwelling with grime-caked rooms in warrenlike sequence.

His room was little more than a cupboard, but the mattress on the floor was his alone, the blanket meant to cover only him. And when he shut the door and slid the squeaking bolt across the splintering wood, the world in which he enclosed himself was his, and he felt its damp and moldy smelling air to be the first air of freedom he had ever breathed. No blows, no shouts, and no commands came to him from within it; he knew he could continue to survive.

The passing years did not improve the mill owner's character; he took to carrying a heavy cane, and its slashing strokes hit flesh, factory, or fabric with equal force and intent. He grew to delight in setting traps: a pie left near the hungry, a coin near the poor, an extra rag by the shivering, an unlatched door, an open drawer.

Then blows would rain down as he sprang from his hiding place, and the trapped victim had no recourse but to confess full guilt. The penalties grew more and more brutal until the rumors and the whispers reached the vicar and the law, and potential victims learned to avoid most of the traps Browntree continued to set. This only served to madden him more, and his cane whistled down with ever-increasing frequency in the mill where his word was law and his habits accepted as part of the misery endured for the work.

He began turning gray of a winter; his parching skin started matching his hair. A shadow fell over his face, though his eyes still glittered from deepened hollows, and his temper continued to burn. The former fleshiness wasted away; his skin pulled against his heavy bones. But still he raged through his mill every morning, his breathing noisy and his steps somewhat slowed. New rages fueled his fury: a mill recently opened claimed his best people. Moore, standing near when Browntree learned of the changes, saw his employers' face turn livid, then drain white, and the cane sliced the unresisting air time and again and yet again, while the mill owner's ranting went out of control.

"I'll kill 'em ... have 'em hanged ... strung up, every last one ... thieves ... scoundrels and thieves ..."

The rag boys cowered away in terror and even the oldsters kept their distance. Moore stayed out of cane's reach all morning, finding work and safety within the carapace of his protective machinery.

Shortly after the incident, the workers heard Browntree had taken to his bed.

"He be dyin'. Good riddance," was the general attitude, and the mill went on working, at peace for the time. The future appeared uncertain, other jobs called. Those who could, left; young Moore was not among them. He awaited his majority to be free from all past bonds, for there were obligations to the workhouse authorities and official debts besides. Moore plodded on; it was his fate and his character to do so.

Isaac Browntree died on a dull summer day a week after young Moore's twenty-first birthday. He was said to have risen from his sickbed to see whether the sounds coming from below meant that one of the servants had indeed succumbed to temptation, scattered coins on the entrance hall table. When Browntree got to the top of the stairs, he perceived the noise to be the footsteps of the vicar, come to call on the dying man in the hope of offering him some comfort.

One final burst of rage suffered Browntree's face, and he toppled down the full narrow flight of stairs, to land dead at the vicar's feet, his veins and heart exploded at last.

Or so said the servants; the vicar never added confirming comment to the event. After having summoned the doctor he chanced upon young Moore on his way to the vicarage and told him the news. Funeral arrangements, the advising of next of kin, and the closing of the mill were all to be undertaken.

Moore helped the foreman close down the mill, stilling the boilers and covering the shafts. Later, he went over to the church hall to run errands; it had long been his habit to do so in exchange for being allowed to read the books on mathematics and engineering the vicar unearthed and kept in his study. This man of God was the only person Moore trusted in the world.

With the mill closed down, Moore had little to do but wait. He ran the errands and roamed the town; fond of neither company nor drink, the alehouses held no attraction for him, and he was uncomfortable with the sudden stripping of his hours of work. He woke at his usual predawn time and rose as always; the day of the funeral he dressed with extra care and went to the church.

He was early. The church was empty, the service not yet

begun. He waited, cap in hand, on the steps outside. Presently the vicar appeared, and one of the gravediggers, who announced that all was ready.

"Let us wait for the others," said the parson, so he and Moore waited. But, though they waited a long time, no one else joined them.

In the end it was young Moore who stood by the open grave and heard the words spoken and the first earth fall.

"...ashes to ashes, dust to dust..."

He walked away alone, thinking of loneliness and seeing its advantages; what did it matter, since Browntree had been dead? Logic necessitated an absence of need under the fresh-flung earth on the box. Only the living were affected, not the unlamented dead.

Twenty-four hours later, he learned to what extent.

He stood in the vicar's study, unsure of what to say or do, still puzzled by the surprise of being sent for at all. The room was stuffy and close, the window still shut against the morning sun. When Moore entered, the vicar was at his desk, while two men, unknown to the youth, were sitting in chairs nearby, their backs stiff, their countenances impassive, a generation stretching between them in age.

"Ah, my lad, there you are." The vicar rose. "Come in, come in. Gentlemen, this is the young man."

Introductions were made. Messrs. Blake and Tatley represented the firm of Blake, Tatley and Smith, Solicitors, who had long been in charge of Isaac Browntree's legal affairs. Moore's heart thumped in warning; solicitors meant the law and the law meant trouble. Was he to be accused of some horrendous crime? Had Browntree planned to lay a trap he could trigger from beyond the grave?

Mr. Blake selected a document from the sheaf of papers lying near him on the vicar's desk.

"I wish to read the late Mr. Browntree's Last Will and Testament to you in full," he said to Moore. "We shall then discuss any possible aspects and problems involved."

His manner implied there would be many. He cleared his throat, adjusted his spectacles and began reading.

"I, Isaac Matthew Browntree, being of sound mind, do hereby declare this to be my Last Will and Testament..."

The vicar, leaning forward on his elbows, looked fixedly at the reading solicitor. Young Mr. Tatley stared at nothing and cracked his knuckles. Mr. Blake's voice enunciated on; Moore grappled with the legal terms and phrases.

After the opening technicalities and generalities, the late Isaac Browntree's bequests began.

His pocketwatch to his daughter, "to be given to her firstborn son, whensoever he should appear"; a ring in his possession (Moore had never seen him wear it) "to my nephew, Jonas Browntree, of London, whose father's it once was..." A few more minor bequests followed. A sum of money was to be set aside for the tombstone to be placed on Browntree's grave.

Then the solicitor's voice stopped. He looked up from the document and around the room before clearing his throat again and returning his attention to the Will.

"All other worldly goods and monies in my possession at the time of my death are to be apportioned in equal measures among whomsoever attend the last rites held for my earthly body, and it is understood that the officiating clergyman is to hold no part herein, but is to be paid his fee as is regular and fitting to him in his parish.

"To all of the above, I do hereby set my hand and seal...."

Having finished reading, the solicitor offered the document to the vicar, who beckoned to Moore. The youth rose and went over to the desk, taking the paper and looking at it without seeing anything at all. Then his glance sharpened on the signature he had seen so many times, the dark, sloping hand that had been Isaac Browntree's. The Will was dated the previous year, shortly before the old man had taken to his bed.

A silence settled thickly over the room. Moore became conscious of the three men gazing at him.

"The gravedigger..." he began.

"He did not accompany us," the vicar reminded him.

Another silence. The boards creaked under Moore's feet as he returned to his chair. They were all still looking at him. Mr. Blake coughed.

"I think, Mr. Moore, we will all be agreed that you were the only person present, were you not? And therefore, according to Mr. Browntree's wishes, you are the main beneficiary of his Will. You must understand that it is a properly executed document, legally binding and correct. However..."

He paused to remove his spectacles and wipe them with his pocket-handkerchief.

"However," he repeated, "if I may say so, we do expect certain difficulties to present themselves. There are problems that may arise..."

The first to arise was a female scream, a daughterly tirade of anguish and rage. It howled at home and it howled across England and, rapidly disguised in mourning weeds and cloth of grief, it moaned in the offices of Blake, Tatley and Smith, Solicitors.

The daughter was soon joined by Jonas Browntree, arrived up from London posthaste at the news and none too happy about it, either. He fingered the ring with apparent distaste; it was not what he had expected from his departed uncle.

Nor was the sham grief a private family affair. The whole town buzzed with the news, and many a jug of ale was warmed over the details. The mill stayed closed and was likely to continue thus until all was settled, reckoned the hands. Due to an economic turn that had encouraged the building of other mills in the area, finding work was easier than it had been in years. It truly seemed as though the old man's death had signaled the advent of better times for all.

Well, almost all....

Young Moore found himself alone, unemployed, and afraid. Afraid, on the one hand, that his sudden good fortune would be snatched away from him before he had ever been able to enjoy it and, on the other hand, that it would not. If he got it, how was he going to handle the intricacies that prospects promised? Run the mill himself? He was not sure he wanted to; machines were one thing, business another. Take in a partner? Private and uncommunicative to his very roots, he shrank from the idea. Sell everything? He could not begin to imagine selling something he did not yet, and might never, own.

In the meantime he plunged into the world of books, steered to new byways by the vicar. Engineering was interrupted by forays into astronomy; physics attracted and then took hold. Literature bored him, poetry he discounted. The vicar's study became his personal schoolroom; he was there the day he heard of a missionary's lecture and gathering to be held shortly at the church hall.

"He's a third cousin of mine," explained the vicar. "His path took him to far places many years ago. I believe you might find his talk interesting. He has just returned from South America."

America was little more than a name to Moore. It was a distant and savage land, another world, the New World. But once at the lecture he found himself first interested and then fascinated. The Reverend James Mott was a chestnut-bearded man of enthusiastic manner and, apart from a few generalities of a spiritual nature, he confined his lecture to the solid practicalities of his mission.

"The country I am going to tell you about is called Argentina," he began. "Many of you will never have heard of it. Others, who know its name, may imagine it as wild and untamable, full of danger and Indians."

He paused, looking around at his audience with measured intensity.

"Danger, like temptation and the pitfalls of evil, is present everywhere in the world. With the help and grace of God, we try to overcome it and continue to strive toward the Light."

Thereafter, Moore noticed, God got left out of the missionary's explanations and the material advantages of joining the movement came to the fore. It all had to do with colonies already started in the Southern Hemisphere land; the church, established in the Argentine capital of Buenos Aires, had set up an autonomous colony in an interior province of the country and was now planning a second. The government of the country was Roman Catholic, explained Mott; this meant that proselytizing had to be of a guarded nature.

"We must teach by example, by ministering to those in need. We must care for those of our own church and nation, for there are already many families from these isles who are established there. And we must, as always, extend our way to those of other breeds and creeds."

It became apparent that what was needed were able-bodied young people willing to break away from Old World tradition and help build the new. Moore could hardly believe the facts Dr. Mott began citing, the vast stretches of open land, parceled not in tidy acres but in sprawling leagues, the varied range of climatic zones from snowcapped peaks to deep green jungle, the distances, the space, the endless scope for work. Employment was a virtual certainty; indeed a new world. . . .

There were, naturally, some problems to be encountered;

33

Dr. Mott smoothed over them with another reference to the ever-present evils in life throughout the world. That Argentina was at war with one of its neighbors and times had been bad in the northern provinces were none of the colonists' affair, and in any case the new territory they had been granted lay far enough from the direct scene of hostilities. Their land was farmland, not jungle, with excellent soil; there was hill country nearby, and a navigable river close at hand. Dr. Mott concluded his talk with the information that two groups would be leaving for Argentina under the auspices of his mission.

"The first will go with me. We shall be sailing before year's end. The rest will follow to join us early next spring."

After the lecture, the vicar introduced Moore to Dr. Mott, explaining briefly the young man's unusual circumstances and possible inheritance. The lecturer's eyes sparkled with interest. There were, he said, so many diverse opportunities in the Argentine. . . .

"I have no farming knowledge," Moore confessed. "Only the machines."

"Mills will be needed, too. Mills of all kinds. Machines will be our future, for all of us, everywhere. But in some places it is far easier to start than in others. There is room for everything and everyone in Argentina."

As Moore walked back to his room through the damp night air, long leagues and space and the machinery of the future formed revolving images in his mind. They spun with the stars he could see overhead, those bastions the reference points for astronomical calculations. Those were the markers of the heavens to be relied on for direction.

Later, lying on his mattress, he continued to think over all he had heard. There was so much about the scheme that intrigued him: the chance to start a life of his own, the facts and figures and distances involved, the abundance of virgin land, the freedom, the challenge to prove his mettle against the unknown forces of the new in the New World. There was nothing in the Old World that claimed or held him.

If the Browntree Will held . . . if he were declared the rightful inheritor after all . . . if he could sell the mill . . .

Dreams, yes, but dreams beginning to move toward the realm of possibility. The South American venture was still

34

months away. Much might be resolved by that time.

Argentina. A new life in a new place, with no ties to the old. It sounded possible and it sounded promising.

Above all, it sounded warm.

3

Young Moore grasped the sides of the greasy rope ladder and lowered his weight onto its swaying rungs. The masts of many ships spiked against the sky around him; the port of Buenos Aires was busy, and the air raucous with shouts and cries. Below him, a high-wheeled cart stood in the water waiting for him, its two soaked nags snuffling the wind. He reached its rough boards and let go of the ladder, noticing, with satisfaction, that his portmanteau, bags, and strapped leather trunk were already standing in the front half, near the driver.

A couple more passengers clambered down; a deckhand, arguing, joined them. The driver waved his whip and argued back; everyone, it seemed to Moore, demanded payment. There was a cross-barrage of confusion and vociferous energy.

Small sailboats moved between the anchored ships, as did smaller rowboats and the many carts. It was low tide; the shoreline and the jutting quay were several hundred yards ahead, beyond the stretch of mud-churned water. Gulls wheeled overhead, the high, strained cries answered by the calls of other seabirds swooping through their ranks.

"*Vamos....*"

The driver of the cart shouted at the horses, and the wagon lurched forward, heading for the wharf; Moore braced himself against the side. He narrowed his eyes against the brilliance of the morning sunshine and observed the wide stretches of the River Plate. It had been true to its name somewhat further out, where its waters had shone as burnished silver in the dawn air. But here, the *Río de la Plata* was muddy and garbage-filled and choppy with movement.

A breeze was blowing, its ocean tang not yet lost in the mixed smells of life around the port, and he thought of a phrase he had learned on the long journey: *la tierra de los buenos aires* ...

The land of the good airs.

He thought back to the good vicar's parting words.

"It is fitting that you should leave. God's opportunity may not knock again."

The official words returned to him once more.

It is the opinion of this court, that inasmuch as the late Isaac Matthew Browntree stated in his Last Will and Testament that it was his desire . . .

The past receded. Rather than allow for years of litigation, a bargain had been struck with both daughter and nephew: the mill had been sold, the total assets gathered, a sum of money was his, and he was here.

Dr. Mott himself was on the crowded wharf to meet him.

The minister took Moore's bag, shouted *"Changador!"* to a passing carrier. The horse-drawn vehicle took them to the parish house in the city, and Moore's entrance into his new life and world began.

He did not stay long in Buenos Aires, but traveled with the Reverend Mott further upriver to Rosario, a thriving river port and the second largest town in the country, where ships took on cargoes of grain, tallow, and hides, brought from the west-stretching *pampas*, before returning down river and sailing across the ocean to the markets offered by the European continent. Rosario was a raw town, peopled by a rough frontier collection of hard-driving and ambitious men. The sophistication of Buenos Aires was nowhere to be seen, and Moore was instantly at ease in the rough-and-tumble atmosphere. Here he felt he could learn his way: of immediate need to him was a knowledge of the language.

To his surprise, he found Spanish easy; it was a relatively simple tongue, limited in its vocabulary and straightforward in its construction. He set himself to the task at once.

The plan was for Moore and Mott to travel to the new colony with a new shipment of stores. Tools, supplies, books out from England, seeds, and tea were among the packages and bales accumulating for the journey. Another ship, expected to dock within the fortnight, held further cargo for the group. The two men awaited its arrival, after which they were to set off, a caravan of three covered *carretas* and an extra team of horses, set for the colony and long months of life and work there once they arrived. While waiting, Moore learned details of the war going on to the north: Argentina, Uruguay, and Brazil were still battling the power-mad dictator of landlocked Paraguay. Nor was that the only scene of conflict in the Argentine: marauding Indians and bands of *gauchos*, led by insurgent *caudillos*, defied governmental authority and ruled locally by terror. There also appeared to be a long-standing animosity between the main city of Buenos Aires and the rest of the land. The *porteños*, the city's residents, clashed endlessly with the *provinciales*: tariffs, laws, government, range of power, trade policies, and legal philosophies all served to start or spark the ever-smoldering animosity.

Moore heard the talk and absorbed the facts; still forming his opinions, he said very little. Through Mott, he met the town's forces at large: the men building the railroad through from Buenos Aires to Córdoba, the planners of commerce, the buyers of grain. The day the expected ship from England arrived, Moore went down to the wharf with the minister and helped him get the bales unloaded and up to the gathered stores. They would be ready to leave within the week, Mott calculated, and glad to go. Moore said nothing, but strapped up his trunk and bags. He would be ready whenever the caravan left.

He was woken next morning by Mott and the news: Indians had attacked the colony and killed almost all its members, setting fire to the buildings and driving off the cows. A few injured survivors had managed to escape them and, riding to the nearest settlement, had sent on the word.

The colony was never rebuilt; Moore stayed in town. He went to work for the railroad and found his life's direction. The country's habits suited him, its rawness hiding his own past. He soon gained the respect of those who worked with him and for him. There was nothing, it seemed, that *Meester* Moore could not work out about anything to do with machinery, nor was there any work he directed others to do that he could not do himself, and often better.

He could shoulder his share, and more; he took second place to no man, British or Argentine. He adapted to the country's ways, drank *yerba* rather than tea, held his own and proved his stocky, barrel-chested strength against the dark-moustachioed men who challenged any foreigner to the test.

The Paraguayan war ended; a new stability for the country began. Despite this, Mott's first colony failed; like so many other ventures in communal living, it did not keep its fervor past the early stages. The Reverend Mott returned to England; Moore never even considered it. He had, in the interim,

37

bought a house; the roots were beginning to dig in. And then there were the windmills, gaunt creatures of metal and movement, come to change the face of *pampas* farming and refresh the soil.

Moore recognized their power from the beginning; soon an expert in their installation, he saw a changing land. The railroad, transportation, windmills, irrigation, grains, yes, but now beef, too, began to show signs of developing for the future. There were not only windmills in the air, there were changes: they came rapidly and from all sides, influencing one another and the lives of all.

The year Argentina began importing barbed wire from the United States, a sister republic celebrating its centennial, the raising of cattle became a new source of wealth. Gone were the roaming herds only controlled by unpredictable *gauchos* on the enormous plains; barbed wire meant business, and business meant money, and both meant the beginning of serious, controlled stock breeding.

Early experiments in the freezing of meat took hold; a specially installed French ship carried the first ten tons to Europe. Early public reaction was skeptical, but time proved the test; the preservation of meat by refrigeration began.

Trouble with the Indian tribes waxed in various regions; reprisals, some led by colonists, started to take hold. Then came a dedicated campaign to wipe out desert Indians, led by an army general and successful in the main. Once more the settlers set forth to form farms and colonies; the outposts of civilization formed in the wake of massacre. The railroads stretched out fingers of track over the land.

Politically, the age-old animosity between *porteño* and provincial came to a head; after a rise to arms, it was equitably resolved: Buenos Aires was made the federal capital, a headquarters for the republic at large, while the provincial area bearing the same name was given another city, La Plata, as its nominal head. It was a solution suiting everyone, making the provincial voices equal and giving them a seat of power all could equally share. A new president was elected, peace returned to the nation, and the boom times came rushing in all across the land.

Over a hundred thousand European immigrants began pouring in per year; corn and alfalfa joined the crops reaping money for the sowers. During the 1880's, there were more than thirty thousand British residents in Buenos Aires, less in

Rosario, but still a powerful influence on the country's economy as a whole. A community within a community, they were by no means segregated but, enjoying the best from both worlds, chose to contain their own. English language newspapers were respected and of record, the British hospital celebrated for its medical service: trade with England reinforced the privileges enjoyed. Home was still the place across the seas, but money was being made here and, if the years passed and the people stayed, traditions held them fast.

By the time Moore reached his fortieth birthday, he was a man of substance, a well-respected citizen of the city of Rosario. His chance inheritance was now solid investment; his connections ran the full spectrum from foreign investors to local police chiefs, British importers to Argentine ministers. A leading figure in the British community of Rosario, he was also known in the circles of British residents in Buenos Aires. Moore was, by all criteria, a man of circumstance, and as such it had come time for him to take a wife.

Moore thought the prospect through with measured method, eventually asking for the hand of Millicent, eldest daughter of the parson who had replaced James Mott as pastor of the church in Rosario.

The seventeen-year-old Millicent's acceptance was an inevitable submission to her parents' wishes. To be a clergyman and have three daughters to marry off was no easy prospect, and the unexpected choice of their oldest by a man of fortune and excellent reputation filled the church couple with happiness and relief. It might even enhance the chances of their other daughters, too. Truly, the match was one made in heaven.

As with so many marriages made in heaven during the Victorian epoch, the Moores soon became a veritable hell on earth. Mismated from the start, surrounded by inequity, hypocrisy, and envy, they stifled in a straightjacket of fear on the one side and increasing isolation on the other.

Moore, at first surprised, then irritated, and finally exasperated by the inexperience of his young bride, allowed his impatience to grow into an increasingly silent distance. He had married a fool, an incompetent; unable to rid himself of her physical presence, he drew away. He saw no need to further exacerbate his mistake by paying even cursory attention to her fluff-headed foolishness. He ignored her more and more, listened to her less and less, found decreasing occasion to address her directly until, at last, he ceased to speak directly to her at all.

Few men understood Moore, and women not at all, least of all his pretty, bewildered, cowed wife. Nor did he keep a mistress as did many of his peers; his physical fires, distorted early, never flamed high. He had no wish for female company, especially not the young, and his physical pleasures, warmth and the table, were amply catered to in his everyday life. Warmth of a personal manner was not within his character.

One of the few people for whom Moore manifested a guarded degree of friendship was the family physician, Dr. O'Connor. He respected the man's medical acumen and trusted his word. Moore also like Mrs. O'Connor; she was his contemporary, a sensible woman with grown sons and nothing fancy about her. She was, he felt, a good influence on his wife and, if nothing could be done to change Mrs. Moore's folderol foolishness, at least his daughter Edie might develop some sense if he exposed her to people of her sex who were not as flibbertigibberty as her mother. He placed some faith in the nurse's training, too; Nana had managed to knock both manners and learning into Edie, who could do her sums quite prettily for a girl and was reasonably well-behaved. Mrs. Moore would never have been capable of bringing up the child on her own; with all her sighing and dreams of England, her household accounts were pitiful in the extreme, and her lack of ordinary common sense frequently alarming. He hoped against hope that Edie would not grow up to be a total fool, like her mother, but, knowing women, she probably would.

"Perhaps you are too impatient of Mrs. Moore," Dr. O'Connor once suggested. "She is, after all, very young. . . ."

Moore grunted. At her age, he had already been on his own for the better part of his life, and had forged his way alone across the world to lay the base of his present position in a new and unknown land. He had not wasted his time dreaming of the distant past, or sighing for other scenery.

Mrs. Moore, on the other hand, had gone from the bosom of her family to the shelter of his name and home, never suffering deprivation or hunger or the damnable cold. From the moment she had become his wife, every comfort and luxury available had been provided. Moore prided himself on his carefully appointed household; Mrs. Moore had never wanted for anything. If he was impatient with her, then his impatience was more than justified.

Dr. O'Connor let the subject drop, and they turned their discussion to stock breeding. Both men had invested in land and cattle herds, and they liked to keep pace with developments and innovations. Deeply engrossed in the vast potential of their adopted land, they both recognized the value of its very earth, particularly of the *pampas* that stretched west from where they lived in Rosario on the river's border, the *pampas* of untrammeled freedom and unbroken land.

The terrain itself was rich and flat—a flatness unbroken for miles and miles, leagues and leagues, land where a lone *ombú* tree, sentinel-still, could stand on the far, heat-hazed horizon that marked the edge of the pale *pampas*-grass covered land against the overhead bowl of dark azure sky. There had been a time when only savages saw its colors change with the moods of weather and hour.

When the first of the Spanish *conquistadores* arrived, the savage cannibals sealed the invading leader's fate and ate him, fighting with primitive ferocity across the plains to retain their natural freedom. But even their indomitable will could not stem the tide of greed and guns over the next three hundred years.

There were times when the Spaniards gave up and left, leaving only their horses and the smoldering ruins of their Indian-ravaged forts. But they always returned, in increasing numbers, until at last the native tribes were decimated, and the *pampas* were won.

The horses and livestock, luckier than the Indians, multiplied and roamed in wild herds, later to serve the emerging generations of mixed-blood men, born to the region, who tamed and teamed the beasts into the servitude of men.

Despite its flatness, the land was not barren; rivers softened its severity, and trees less lonely than *ombues* grouped in watered places. Nor was it uninhabited, the Spaniards' horses being only a late addition to the fauna, the first challenge in racing speed to the *ñandu*, whose ostrichlike build and habits hinted of ancient geographic heritage. Within the clumps of *pampas* grass, the tailless quis burrowed and gnawed, watched by solemn ground owls standing in the entrances of their dusty tunnels, while ants built hills the size of boulders, stripping the land to feed their armies. Armadillos ate the

41

ants, only to be a *comadreja's* prey themselves, while high above a hawk might wait to seize the polecat's progeny, dropped in an incautious moment from the hanging pole of her tail.

It was the *gauchos* who began to know the land, that proud, cruel, indomitable breed of men whose mixed ancestry of Indian and Spaniard made them masters of their world—a world where freedom meant life led on horseback in rhythm with the seasons and under no law save their own traditions. Often, they roamed in bands, sometimes under the auspices of an antigovernment *caudillo*, sometimes as an autonomous group seeking its own way. Some were loners, linking to others only in temporary ways. Much of the early *gauchos'* time was spent in fighting—another *caudillo's gauchos*, a border dispute, the government, or each other. Merciless in battle, their methods of revenge matched the ferocity of their breed. Common practice was to sew a man in rawhide and leave the shapeless bulk lying under the summer sun until the shrinking skin strangulated the last vestiges of life that remained in the dehydrated man's body. Failing a fresh supply of hides, other cunning came into play; staked out naked by a seething anthill, a victim lasted little longer than his sewn-up counterpart.

No *gaucho* worth the silver coins studding his broad belt would deign to till the land. His work was from the saddle. He could rope cattle, or *ñandu*, with the three-headed *bolas* lasso. He could break a wild horse, herd cattle across long leagues, butcher a steer and cure its hide, ride with a *patrón*, silence an enemy. A *gaucho* moved when he wanted to move, left when he wanted to leave, roamed as far and free as the land itself, and bowed low to no man.

To till the land was to become its prisoner, not its master, a slave to the seasons, not their cohort. Long, thin strips of beef *charqui*, sun-cured and dried, and ample drafts of *yerba* were all a man needed for food; both were simple to carry on the saddle. But if the womenfolk wanted to plant and harvest by a parked highwheeled *carreta* or a ramshackle *rancho* on the edge of a small camp town, the *gauchos* let them, returning to the place when the mood hit them, and leaving it again at their will.

Their loyalties lay purely in the *pampas*. Whenever a new *estancia* was rumored to be starting, *gauchos* would appear in the area, sometimes led by a *capataz*, sometimes on their own. In the earliest days, the men slept out under the starlit nighttime sky, wrapped in their ponchos and stretched on the ground, their horses tethered to a stake nearby. Then came the first of the *carretas*, bringing with them the *gauchos'* women and the rudiments of sheltered living. A settlement would begin forming; a couple of lean-tos would be erected, some chickens penned at the back, the first seeds of corn planted nearby, and the dark-haired *chinitas*, their long braids hanging down their backs and their knotted kerchiefs bright around their necks, were there to tend the food and the fire and their men when they came in, saddle-weary, as the long dusk closed in on the working day.

Both Moore and O'Connor had invested, and invested well. Their nascent properties were shaping well and solidly along with the growing knowledge of the times. Of an age, both men were at their maturity's prime, the peak of their hard-earned, successful years, where experience gained had not yet been slowed by advancing age.

And yet, Moore was uneasy; he had not felt himself to be in form for a long while. Quite apart from the dark moods that assaulted him on occasion, pinning him to his chair for tight, haunted hours, there were discomforts he could not dismiss, even though he might ignore them: the fleeting pains that flashed in his chest, a shortness of breath, the heavy feel in his legs. All his boots had become too small, leather pressing against his flesh and leaving deep red gouges overlapped by pale, swollen mounds. Moore knew, in the misty edges beyond the disciplined route of his thoughts, that all was not well with him.

The first attack he was unable to ignore came at the office. Managing to reach his chair, he sat in it until the blackness passed. After it was over, he hardly remembered any details; he had been standing by the window, yes, and had turned to get a book, and then came only glimpses of memory, and the chair, and that was all.

But his legs were heavy all the way home, and he did not finish his meal that night, retiring to bed far earlier than was his wont. As he rose from the dinner table, his savoury untouched before him, he caught a glimpse of Mrs. Moore's face, a questioning expression forming on it. Frowning, he turned away; his feet felt like lead as he forced them across the floor.

4

The year Edie celebrated her tenth birthday was the year the real changes began. Signs of them had been there before, but many had not been noticed; now they began to manifest themselves in ways impossible to ignore.

For one thing, Edie herself was changing. With two numbers to her age instead of only one, she felt she had achieved a big step toward being a grown-up. She was taller and she was bigger; her summer frocks from the year before were hopeless, Mamma had said. Even her winter ones had to be let down, and were tight under her arms.

Another difference was school; gone were the nursery days. Edie attended classes given adjacent to the church. Dollie and Robert also attended the school, but were in other forms: Robert was in the boys' section, which was quite separate from the girls', and Dollie, despite the Thaxters' urgings, had stayed back in the other form and was now a year behind Edie.

Nana was still part of the household, but with her duties curtailed. Edie had overheard her mother telling Mrs. O'Connor that Nana might be going home soon.

"She's getting on in years, you know, and her eyesight isn't what it used to be. . . ."

It certainly was not, as Edie well knew; she had made the discovery the day she presented her washed hands for Nana's inspection, saw to her horror one of her nails was still black-tipped and rimmed with ink, resigned herself to the inevitable crack across the palm with a biting wooden ruler, then heard Nana say, "Very well, Miss Edie, you may run along to luncheon with your papa and mamma."

More changes. Edie often took her meals with her parents, rather than with Nana as in bygone days. And Nana called her Miss Edie, and sometimes even Miss Edith. It was all part of growing up and learning how to behave.

The privileges like being able to stay up later, especially in the summer, were nice; the duties, like longer lessons, were hard work. And then there were the in-betweens; they were hard to place or understand. The widening gap between

44

herself and Rosita was one of them. Edie could not remember how or when it had started, but suddenly, it had been there, making their games difficult and their confidences impossible to continue. Somebody was always calling or interrupting them; it was usually Rosa, seeking Rosita for work. Occasionally it was Mamma, needing Edie to accompany her on a social visit or a company tea.

At first Edie accepted Mamma's explanation, that Rosita's tasks around the house were comparable to Edie's proper-school lessons. But that did not feel like the full truth after a while; the real reasons, Edie became sure, were quite different. The changes were in Rosita herself, and the day she called Edie *niña* Edie, just like Rosa and Juana did, instead of Edie as she always had done in the past, Edie felt a silken barrier descending, invisible and impenetrable.

"It's not like Nana calling me Miss Edie! It's not!" she had later cried, seeking her mother's comfort.

"Yes, it is, Edie. I ordered Rosa to tell her so," was the reply. "We all have our rightful places, and Rosita and you each have to learn how to behave in your own."

It was the first year Edie did not share her birthday celebration with Rosita, but had a party with her friends from school in to tea, with a decorated chocolate cake and games in the front *sala*, and Mamma led them all in song before they went home.

Another anniversary, thousands of miles away, touched Edie's life and fired her imagination: Queen Victoria's Diamond Jubilee.

"Just think of it, Edie—sixty glorious years!" Mrs. Moore took the slogan to heart. "Oh...all the excitement there must be... and the pageants...the ceremonies..."

Edie, who had seen pictures of the small, dumpy woman who ruled the British world, was far more interested in the crown Victoria wore than in the Crown itself. The queen's diminutive headpiece, made for daily use atop the lace and cambric square, seemed to Edie to be the most special ornament she had ever seen. Jewelry had begun to fascinate her, and many of Mamma's pieces were pretty. But to wear a crown...

"There are other crowns too, you know," her mother told her. "Crowns of state, worn for important occasions. They have huge jewels in them and are worth thousands of pounds.

They're kept in the Tower of London, and we would be able to go and see them, if we were in England. . . ."

Meanwhile, there were Jubilee celebrations in Rosario and special church services for the queen's continued health and prosperity. Edie had a new dress made to go to the children's party at the church hall, where there were Union Jacks all over the place and red, white, and blue bunting decorating the walls.

The British community in Buenos Aires was also celebrating the event: there were official government ceremonies, various church services, parties, and gatherings. Papa, having been invited to attend most of the events, caused another big change in Edie's life: he took his wife and daughter to Buenos Aires. It was Edie's first trip.

The excitement began right from the packing; she was to have her very own bags. And no, Nana was not coming with them. Edie and her Mamma would be together most of the time. There would be sights to see and shopping to do and parties to attend. Edie thought the day would never ever come, but eventually it did and they got up bright and early, had all the baggage sent off to the station, and then went off in the carriage themselves.

Edie had been to the station before but never in such anticipation. They had a reserved compartment, all to themselves, and everyone knew Papa and treated him with deference. Mamma kept fidgeting and saying, "Oh, Edie, isn't this fun?," but when Papa joined them she fell back into silence, and they settled down in the plush-covered seats, waiting for the train to start.

A scream of whistles announced their departure; they were off and moving across the land. The buildings of Rosario disappeared behind them; scattered *ranchos* showed through the train windows, with chickens and children running and scattering at the train's noise. Edie, who was next to the window, saw some of the children wave, and waved back. Mr. Moore frowned, but said nothing, opening up a newspaper and retiring behind it to read. Mrs. Moore, next to Edie, was fussing with a little cushion, placing it first in one place and then in another, seeking greater comfort.

Edie gazed at the land unfolding before her as the train jogged along. There were fenced fields and then open stretches and all sorts of greens with the differing grass, from the lush

46

dark tones of small alfalfa patches to the pale, brown-splotched areas of unused land. Trees in clumps or lines generally meant a river, she discovered; otherwise, there were few of them, and everything was flat. Presently she grew bored with staring and then hungry and then sleepy: sugar-dusted *alfajores* with sticky jam between their biscuity layers were a treat, and the jolting carriage was close and warm. She put her head in Mamma's lap and drifted in and out of slumber.

Retiro Station in Buenos Aires was huge, a vast cavern to Edie's gritty eyes. Not only sleep but dust had invaded them, and the confusion of arrival dismayed her until she saw how Papa set everything in order with a few quick, curt orders and a tip to the conductor. *Changadores* appeared and took their bags, and soon they were on their way to the hotel in a carriage that looked just like the ones in Rosario, but nicer.

Everything, she soon discovered, was nicer in B.A.

It was cooler, too, and she had to wear her jacket every time she left the hotel and went outside. But Buenos Aires was beautiful, with big important buildings and long, tree-lined avenues and lots of parks. And so much to do: she and Mamma went shopping in the mornings, and Mamma ordered a whole new range of dresses. That meant ordering the material and the styles at the dressmaker's, and after that the fittings took place at the hotel, in front of the tall wardrobes with the long looking-glasses in their doors that you could open so as to see yourself all the way around. Edie delighted in standing in front of them, seeing the back of her head.

They had a suite, with a sitting room, where Mamma received; they didn't see much of Papa, who was out most of the time. But they did see the O'Connors and the Thaxters, all of whom were also in town for the Jubilee celebrations. There were other ladies who came, too, and sometimes they would take Mrs. Moore and Edie riding out to the Palermo parks in their carriages, and Edie would look at the children bowling their hoops along the pavement and wish that she, too, could live there and go for walks with Nana in Palermo every day. She and Dollie were taken to several parties, given by church groups; Mrs. Thaxter would accompany them, leaving Mamma free to do grown-up outings on her own or with other friends. And on one very important occasion, Papa took Mamma to an evening gathering; Mamma spent hours getting ready and dressed.

"Ohhh...you look much nicer than the queen!" Edie gasped when she saw her, just before Mrs. Moore left the hotel.

"Thank you, dearest. Now you be a good little girl, and if you want anything, you simply pull the bell..."

But Edie, entranced by her mother's cloaked, bejeweled figure, lulled herself to sleep with enjoyable thoughts on growing up to be a lady lovely as Mamma and always, always dress in satin clothes with embroidery and laces and cut velvet and sparkling stones and a jeweled crown....

It was all over too quickly and they were back in Rosario, but the impact of the journey had taken full hold.

"When can we go to B.A. again?" Edie asked, soon after, but her mother's reply was vague and unsatisfactory; it did not sound as though they would be going for a very long time. Edie sighed with impatience and got told to do her lessons.

"They're all done."

"Then go and play."

"There's no one to play with."

"You can play on your own, can you not?"

No, she couldn't. She was bored. Bored, and inwardly uneasy; there were tides within beginning to trouble her. Eventually, she went to her room, and cried for no reason at all.

The biggest changes of all had to do with Papa's camp.

He had owned the land for a long time, but now it was his main interest, and he and Dr. O'Connor, who also had a camp, spent most of their time involved in camp affairs. Papa's had cattle on it, and some milk cows, and bulls brought specially out from England, and *gauchos* looking after the cattle and the horses. There were also several *ranchos*, with families in them Edie learned to call *colonos*. They grew fields of alfalfa and wheat on Papa's land; instead of paying him in money, they paid their rent in crops, and the alfalfa was fed to the cattle, and the wheat was sold for making into flour.

Edie listened to Papa talking about it whenever Dr. O'Connor came for luncheon. This was becoming an increasingly frequent occurrence, and it changed the whole atmosphere of the household while he was there. Apart from enlivening meals with their camp discussions, the two men would spend hours in Papa's study, books and papers all over the desk, figures and calculations filling the air. And Papa's old interests, windmills and water systems, both entered into the development of the camps.

Water was already being sent through all the big pipes they had built for the houses in Rosario; Edie knew her father had been one of the engineers responsible for the plan. And his ideas about windmills had long been considered important, too; she knew this because Robert had made up a verse he used to chant out of the adults' earshot.

"Oh, Mr. Moore, the windmill man
Send me a wind as fast as you can."

Edie thought it was very rude of Robert, and she hated the way he sniggered at her and called her the Windmill Girl.

"I'm not, I'm not!"

"Yes, you are, and when you're big you're going to flap your arms and whirl around with every breeze. . . ."

But now she was big enough not to care what silly Robert said or did, and whenever he started being horrid she would stick her tongue out at him. Nana couldn't see if Edie did it quickly enough; ever since the incident of the grubby nail, Edie had been charting her nurse's failing perceptions. There was a lot Edie could get away with now.

Often her triumphs were quite unexpected; the day she forgot herself at table brought undreamed-of results. Dr. O'Connor was present and, as usual, the camp was being talked about, and a trip to see about new fencing under immediate discussion.

"Oh, Papa—can't I go with you?"

The words slipped out before she could stop them; thunderstruck by her own boldness, Edie blushed bright red. She heard her mother's sharp intake of breath, saw her father's face turn toward her.

"And why not?" It was Dr. O'Connor, jovial and smiling. "The fresh camp air will do her good. . . ."

Edie held her breath. A short adult conversation followed. Dr. O'Connor won the day; Edie could hardly believe her good fortune. A trip with Papa . . .

It turned out to be the first of many; Papa, away from the house, was different from the way she had known him before. Or perhaps it was because he was away from Mamma; it was hard to tell, as the differences were subtle, not easy to define. He did not talk much to Edie at all, no more than he did at home. Eventually she decided it must be that he glared less, at least in her direction. She did not feel she had to watch her every step and move.

Visiting the camp also meant a ride by train, but in the opposite direction from Buenos Aires. They would rise before dawn and be at the station before it was fully light. Smoke and coal smells would fill the dawn-damp air, and the engine's hoot would sound fierce and demanding in the hollow of the station, ordering man and machine to attention so the day might start.

They would descend at a water stop on the northern line; a horse-drawn cart would already be there, waiting for their arrival. Often a *gaucho* would escort them, riding horseback next to the *carreta*; sometimes Papa would ride a horse brought for him by the man.

"*Buenos días, patrón. Buenos días, niña* Edie. . . ."

She was a princess, the daughter of a king, riding in a carriage to the royal lands. The wind was fresh and heady after the train's enclosure, and the sun hot in a rising sky of clear, dark blue. They drove along the rutted, pale earth, raising dust clouds that blew straight across the flat land, undisturbed. The wind sometimes came close to stinging Edie's face in its fierce insistence, but its touch was bracing, too, and she loved the smell.

Usually they drove directly to the main *rancho* where the camp's majordomo lived. Sometimes they visited *colonos* on the way. The sharecroppers always had a gift for Edie, or something to send back to the landowner's wife: a basket of eggs, a live chicken, a sun-dried sunflower. These would be placed into the cart as Papa talked crops and weather and harvest; Edie would glimpse barefoot children hiding behind the mud walls or the piled hay, peeping out at her, dirty, dark, and ragged, then disappearing again, out of the *patrón's* sight and way. Pangs of envy would hit her; it would be so nice to take off her own shoes and peel off her stockings, run free the way they did, and play in the dust.

At the majordomo's *rancho* there would be food and *yerba*, and lots of talk between Papa and the man running the camp for him. The times Dr. O'Connor came along on the trips, the talk would go on for hours, and Edie would fall asleep on the bed that was always kept ready in Papa's room.

Once, when the train to return them to Rosario was delayed, Papa and Dr. O'Connor had decided they had better eat a small meal at the town's only tavern. There had been spicy *chorizo* sausages and a hunk of smooth-topped bread, and Papa had allowed Edie to have some wine mixed with water. When the train came they found their carriage and Edie snoozed on a seat to herself; from time to time she woke and heard snatches of the conversation going on between the doctor and Papa.

The first time she woke, Dr. O'Connor was saying, "No, he isn't interested. He far prefers B.A. and, knowing Vesey's proclivities, I can't say I blame him."

He gave a short laugh. Papa murmured something but Edie did not catch it.

"Oh, no. Edwin's married," was the doctor's answer. "Maurice hasn't. I suspect he's his usual dull self. Does well in business, though. I believe he's on a Continental trip at the moment... expected back in London next month or so..."

She slept again, to reawaken, the buzz of talk still going. "... hard to tell, of course, but then, you never really know, do you? Look at Vesey. All the advantages. And yet, I don't mind telling you..."

The words blurred, and then Edie slept so deeply she had to be shaken awake when they pulled into Rosario, and she hardly remembered anything of the carriage ride home. All she wanted to do was crawl into her own bed, where her dreams returned her to the freedom of the camp and the cool feel of the *pampas* wind.

The end of the century was reached and, with it, the close of Edie's childhood days. Nana sounded many of the dirges.

"Don't run like that, Miss Edie! Young ladies stroll, they do not rush."

"Miss Edie, stop whistling at once! When girls whistle, the angels sob."

"I'm not whistling, Nana, you know I can't whistle properly. I'm only blowing...."

"A quick retort is not the mark of a gentlewoman, miss. And don't answer back...."

From Mamma: "We'll have to let all your hems down again, and I really think the bodices *must* be altered...."

Then a different knell-note: Nana was leaving. Nana, with her failing eyesight, her steadily increasing girth, and her trouble-ridden, aching feet, was going home to England to live with her brother and look after the household for him

51

and his wife. Edie, exultant when she first heard the news, was surprised, then frightened, and eventually rendered helpless by her own tears, so that all she could do was cling to Nana's arm and cry, "Nana! Don't go! Don't leave me, Nana, please... I promise I'll be good...oh, please, don't leave..." until Mamma had to pull her away and hold her until Nana left. It was only afterwards that Edie realized the tears soaking her face when she had kissed her nurse good-bye had not all been her own.

After that came the morning when, frightened by the bloodstains yet unable to find their source, Edie sat shivering in strangeness and fear until her mother discovered her, swollen-eyed, within the darkness of her shuttered bedroom. When at last the truth was sobbed out, Mrs. Moore sat next to her daughter on the rumpled bed and, in time-honored tradition, whispered out the bleedings and the facts of female life with its attendant rites and restrictions, monthly paddings and pinnings, the private launderings, the kept-away tubs and scrubs of the womenfolk throughout the ages. Edie had become one with the women of the household, never again to play in free innocence as a child. The difference had arrived, and with it, the early gathering of its adult burden.

Across the ocean, an old queen died, bringing to an end the era bearing her name. The British Empire mourned, greeted a king, shouldered its duties and believed it carried on.

5

The second attack was impossible to hide.

He was rising from his chair at the dining room table when the pain flashed fire throughout his chest. Its searing made him gasp; he grabbed the table, leaning over it.

"Mr. Moore! What is it?"

His wife was rising, talking, calling.

"Rosa! Juana! Come quickly! Quickly..."

He thought of countermanding her cry for the servants, but his voice was not there. The pain flashed again, its spasm causing him to lurch across the floor. The sideboard struck him in the ribs. His wife was still screaming.

He wanted to tell her to be quiet, to stop all her fuss at once, that if she did not do so he would . . . he would . . . The words had gone, along with his speech, and he could only grunt his own amazement at the void, hearing his breath's heavy gasps sounding as air rushing through a grating.

"Rosa . . . run to the doctor's house! Quickly! At once! Oh, God . . . please, somebody help me . . . get Dr. O'Connor at once . . ."

She was . . . he couldn't . . . his vision grew distorted until the voices also faded and everyone disappeared.

He lay at death's door; he came close to crossing its threshold, time and again. The house was dark and tense, vivid with fear. Sleepless faces, hollow-eyed, spoke to each other in low tones, and Millicent Moore, strengthened by clearly defined duty and role, followed the doctor's every instruction and remained, steadfast, by her husband's side.

Time lengthened, the immediate crisis eased.

"You're a marvelous nurse," O'Connor told Millicent. "Your husband is rallying, largely due to you."

She blushed, and didn't believe it, but stayed at her post, dozing fitfully on the canvas camp bed set up in the room, waking at the slightest change in Moore's breathing, the faintest sound, the smallest creak of the door. Dr. O'Connor's visits, akin to those when she had been ill, gradually lessened to twice a day. The household's windows and shutters could be opened once more.

Moore's convalescence was difficult and long; for months he was a morose and mostly silent figure lying in the wide four-poster bed, only occasionally rising to sit in a chair for a brief respite and then shuffling back to the pillowed bed again. Time passed, the seasons changed, and so did Mr. Moore. Despite his slowly regained strength, despite his ability to rise and spend his quiet day at home, much of it in his study, despite Dr. O'Connor's cheery encouragement, Edie could see her father was different.

He looked different; he behaved in different ways. There were times when he would stare at her as though he had never seen her before.

"What is it, Papa? Would you like me to bring you a cushion for your back? Are you comfortable, Papa?"

No answer. No change of expression. Edie was almost certain he had not heard her speak. Then the light in his eyes

53

would alter, and if he then chose to speak, which was not always the case, he never acknowledged her question, or even that she had spoken. It was puzzling and it was frightening when it first happened.

But as it went on happening with increasing frequency, Edie realized that, whatever it was, it held no threat of anger or outburst from him at all. He was fading; far more than his flesh had been lessened by the devastating attacks. The strictures his presence now placed on the household were applied because of him, and not imposed by him. The general effect was less oppressive, though not necessarily less hampering.

Mrs. O'Connor greeted her husband and looked questioningly at him.

"He's out of danger," the doctor reported, taking off his coat. "I think he'll last a while."

"Poor Millicent. She must be absolutely exhausted."

"She is. Brave little thing, when it comes down to it. I was surprised."

Later, at dinner, they talked of the Moores again, and then Mrs. O'Connor broached the subject she had been waiting to open since the doctor's arrival.

"Vesey's coming up on tomorrow's evening train."

"Oh, is he?" Dr. O'Connor's soupspoon descended back to the plate. "Wonder what he wants this time. More money, I suppose. And how, may I ask, did you receive this fair news?"

"Bessie Thaxter called on me today. Vesey sent the message with her. She and the children are just back."

"And our son sees fit to send messages . . ."

"Really, there's no need . . ."

Dr. O'Connor pushed his plate away. "Elizabeth, if I have tried to make one thing very clear of late, it is that Vesey must make his own way in life. It is high time he . . ."

"I know, I know, and I'm sure he's trying his best to . . ."

"No, he isn't!" thundered the doctor. "He keeps sneaking back, hiding behind you and your kindness and your generosity—to say nothing of your habit of shielding him. You spoiled him from the moment he was born, and . . ."

"Oh, I don't believe that's . . ."

They were words of long-known family anger, well-worn phrases between parents despairing over their eldest son.

" . . . and I have spent a veritable fortune covering his debts and trying to help him get started . . . cannot even take advantage of all the connections . . . ruined his chances time and again . . . must not be allowed to go on like this . . . a disgrace to the rest of us . . ."

After her husband left the room, Mrs. O'Connor wept silently for her favorite child.

The end came at the height of summer, shortly after Christmas. The holiday decorations had been taken down and were lying in a box on the *sala* sofa; Edie had spent the morning folding the paper garlands with care. After luncheon, the long *siesta* had gone on until the evening, when the early shadows lessened the day's high heat and the briefest of breezes moved the air again.

Papa was in the study; Edie had seen him make his way slowly to the chair behind his desk instead of the one by his reading lamp and table. Perhaps he was going to pull the desk drawers open and go through their contents aimlessly, as he sometimes did these days. Mamma joined her in the *sala*, bringing Aunt Muriel's latest letter with her. It had arrived only the week before, and an answer was due.

Mamma read parts of it aloud as Edie went on folding down the garlands.

"*. . . and of course, the boys hope to have a snowman of their own in the garden. The one they built last year melted rather fast and lost his carrot nose . . .*"

Mamma put down the letter, her eyes dreamy.

"To think you've never seen snow, Edie . . . it can make the whole world turn white. I remember waking up once and hardly recognizing the view from our bedroom window."

Edie fastened down a garland and picked up the next.

"I remember hearing Papa say he hated snow," she remarked conversationally. "He was talking to Mrs. O'Connor."

"Did he?" Mrs. Moore sounded puzzled. "How strange."

"He said it was nothing but trouble and cold, and he hoped he never saw any in his life again."

"Oh, dear. What did Mrs. O'Connor say? I do hope it didn't upset her."

"I don't think so, but I don't remember what she said."

"Well, anyway, perhaps he didn't really mean it. I'm sure your Papa appreciates the beauty of snow as much as . . ."

"You're a fool, Mrs. Moore."

His voice, unexpected, and stronger than it had been in

ages, made them both jump. He was standing in the doorway, his eyes lit with anger. Both women were so startled neither said a word. As his words faded in the quiet evening air, Moore turned and made his way toward his bedroom. They were the last words he spoke; after lying down, fully dressed, on the wide poster bed, he dozed on and off until shortly after midnight, when a final spasm seized his heart. Thus he died at the close of his fifty-seventh year, leaving a pretty widow in the early part of her thirties and a daughter blossoming with beauty on the dawn of fifteen.

Moore's funeral was the biggest that Rosario had seen in years.

The cortege stretched for close to a mile, moving slowly through the heat of the day. Threatening skies hung with heavy rain clouds gathered over the day's oppressive atmosphere, and many a mourner glanced up from time to time, fearful of a sudden downpour. The pace was solemn, measured, sad, the horses' muffled hoofbeats sounding their own passive note.

A black pair, plumed and dark-bridled, pulled the canopied front carriage, bearing the coffin in full view. Carved posts and ornate scrollwork framed the heavy, fringed curtains draped on all four sides. The coffin, visible between the folds of tasseled velvet, rode on a raised platform within, its brass handles burnished to reflect the gilded segments on the inside of the canopy.

The bereaved widow and daughter followed in a carriage directly behind; next came a string of dignitaries of Rosario, come to pay their last respects to a citizen of stature. After all the officials' carriages came one with the O'Connors, their eldest son up from Buenos Aires especially for the event; they were followed by numerous members of the British communities of both cities. All the pallbearers had been chosen from among their number.

Then came the procession of people on foot, led by the household servants and massed by the many to whom *Meester* Moore had been a long known and long respected figure. The railway men Moore had supervised, the camp *gauchos* he had hired and admired, the office underlings in trade employ, the dock workers who had offloaded his imported shipments and supplies, the flotsam and jetsam of the working world he had understood so well and had treated in fairness—all were there to accompany him on this his last and lonely journey.

Millicent and Edie stood close together at the graveside, enveloped in the mourning clothes and veils swiftly sewn and expertly pinned for the occasion, their pale faces misty behind the gauze.

Later, in the evening, when the storm had broken and the funeral was long over, the sleepless hours of the sad days showed on their drawn features, the finality of the funeral having drained the last of their strength. Only the O'Connors and the Thaxters remained; the servants hovered in the background.

"My poor Millicent," Mrs. Thaxter kept saying over and over again, imprisoning the widow's hand in hers. "What ever will you do now? You poor, poor thing . . . remember we are always here to comfort you . . ."

She cast a quick sidelong glance at Mrs. O'Connor, whose return smile was bland and unrevealing.

"Such a tragedy . . . so young . . ." Bessie Thaxter alternated her phrases with puffed sighs. "You must be very, very brave. You poor little thing . . ."

Their carriage came, followed by the O'Connors'. As they were leaving, Dr. O'Connor said, "Try to get some rest, Millie, and you, too, Edie. I shall call on you tomorrow to see whether you are following doctor's orders. . . ."

Mrs. O'Connor did not say anything, but merely hugged mother and daughter in her farewell. Vesey took Millicent's hand, bent briefly over it in parting gesture and murmured his condolences once more. Turning to Edie, he again expressed his sorrow, after which he joined his parents at their waiting carriage.

Edie watched him assist Mrs. O'Connor into her seat. Vesey was taller than either of his parents, and deft in his movements. She went on looking at the carriage as it rolled down the street until her mother's voice called to her from inside and she went back into the house and closed the front door.

"Mamma, what are we going to do?"

The house felt hollow and huge. Shuttered in mourning and against the heat, its rooms echoed the absence, mirrored the irreversible change. Meals were light, informal affairs.

"*Señora,* a nice roast for Sunday...."

"No, Juana, I don't think so. Let us have a boiled chicken instead."

Heresy. The Sunday roast had been law. But the law-giver was gone....

"Mamma, I really, truly don't want any more."

"You should finish it, you know, Edie. You should eat what you're given and be thankful...oh, well, never mind this time. But don't let me see you waste food like that again."

"No, Mamma."

But the change was there. Hence the eventual question:

"Mamma, what are we going to do?"

They were sitting in the patio on cool wicker chairs, enjoying the privacy and the after-dinner breeze. Mrs. Moore ran her fingers over the stiff black fabric of her dress, flicking at an invisible spot on it before giving an answer.

"I don't think we're going to do anything right away," she eventually replied. "We must wait and see what...what Papa left, and how we are to go on, and..." her voice faltered. "There is so much I don't know...he never told me. And of course, I never expected..."

"Never expected him to die?"

Mrs. Moore sighed. "Yes. I mean no—no, I didn't think he...I didn't think he would ever die," she blurted out. "I mean, I thought it was my fate..."

"Mamma...you're crying...."

"Yes, dearest, I'm crying, and I think I'll go and lie down. When I'm stronger, we'll talk about all these things, but I'm afraid I'm still rather weak from all that has happened."

Within the official mourning, there were duties and demands. Dr. O'Connor was not the only man who called with regular precision; Canon Thaxter accompanied some Buenos Aires callers, and legal matters were brought to the house by the executors of Papa's will. Edie was not privy to its details, but she could see that Mamma was rallying well; there were papers to sign and people to see, and Mrs. Moore, pale but persistent, struggled nightly to understand the documents handed to her by the lawyers and her late husband's bankers.

The young widow found herself to be far wealthier than she had dreamed. There was money, there was property, and there was land. The camp, valuable in itself, also gave a reasonable return; her income would be generous, her worth considerable. There was also Edie's inheritance, fully provided for under the law. Because she was still under age, her portion had to be safeguarded by a second adult; after some thought, Mrs. Moore chose Canon Thaxter for the part.

The formalities were concluded, the period of change underway. A year's mourning was traditional, recognized even by the secular as a time for retirement from the everyday social interchanges of the world. It gave the bereaved time to reconsider both the lost past and their future paths. For Millicent, the surfacing realization was even more profound: she began to discover she was free at last.

"... but I *need* it ..."

"It's out of the question, Vesey." Mrs. O'Connor was adamant. "I'm sorry, but I simply cannot. I've already managed to give you ..."

"You don't seem to understand." Vesey closed his eyes in taut impatience. "I'll be thrown out of the club if I don't pay. ..."

"And what you don't seem to understand is that if I take as much as one single solitary *peso* more out of the household expenses, your father will discover it anyway."

"Then what do you suggest I do?" Vesey's tone was icy.

For a moment, his mother felt herself weakening. Poor Vesey ... his luck had been so hard. ... But no. Her resolve firmed; she had heard all these stories before.

"I don't know that you have any other choice but to approach your father directly."

Vesey's face registered disgust, and he made no reply, turning on his heel and leaving the room. His mother heard the front door slam behind him and, despite herself, felt relieved. He was so tense, so angry, so difficult to handle these days; never an easy child, he had grown worse, she realized, with the years. His delicate nerves, no doubt; it was all such a shame. Her other two sons had never given her the trouble her first son had—nor had they ever given her the joy. ...

Within herself, she knew his faults, knew and recognized the lies, the subterfuge, the evasive ways. Vesey was not only difficult, he was dishonest. As always when he was home, there was money missing from her purse. The first time she had noticed a discrepancy, she had sacked a servant recently hired, but now she knew better, to her heart's cost, and tried to keep her purse away from harm. It was always useless; she was no match for her son, and she knew it. She also knew he was sure she would never tell Dr. O'Connor; the doctor had, after all, so many other things to worry about in his daily rounds. . . .

The shadow of mourning grew paler through the obligatory year. After the first period of welcome seclusion, mother and daughter became accustomed to the new feeling of freedom. Still within the strictures of custom, they traveled to Buenos Aires; there were formalities connected to the inheritance requiring their presence there.

But once these were concluded, the capital city continued to claim their interest. Millicent, still young enough to yearn for life's enjoyment, still pretty enough, despite her somber widow's weeds, to attract attention, felt the stirrings of excitement and anticipation of a happy future. Freed by death from wifely duty, by inheritance from want, she saw her beloved England beckoning, and planned to return.

Not immediately, however; now able to make her own decisions, Millicent found herself wavering. Another year or so, perhaps, while she grew used to handling her own affairs. . . . Besides, Buenos Aires was increasingly enjoyable— and, she would always remind herself hastily, Edie enjoyed it so.

Time passed. Millicent began shedding the trappings of widowhood; emerging from the dark-gowned chrysalis was a pretty woman who was easy to please, easy to amuse, eager for friendly, lighthearted company, and quickly responsive.

The British community of Buenos Aires, now well over fifty thousand strong, was a welcoming place for the pretty and wealthy widow. Her daughter, too, was eagerly met, for Edie was a developing beauty. Still shy and retiring in company, still unaccustomed to her increasing freedoms, she stayed close to her mother's side, seldom uttering her own opinions.

Edie, seeing life from her own youthful perspective, did not see herself as a valuable commodity, nor did she dream in marriage advantage terms. Her pounding heart signaled her cherished secret whenever Vesey O'Connor came to call.

Both the O'Connor family and the Thaxters introduced the Moores around Buenos Aires. The doctor and his wife often traveled to the city; Canon Thaxter, on the other hand, had recently been transferred to the capital, much to his bustling wife's delight, for she welcomed the wider social circles there. Vesey O'Connor, long a B.A. resident, had called on Millicent and Edie while they were still in Rosario; he had heard they were going to Buenos Aires, he said, where he would only be too happy to escort them wherever they might need or want to go. . . .

And, through the months, he did just that, courteous and dutiful whenever they came to town. He invited them for carriage rides through the parks during the early days of their mourning, and later escorted them to social gatherings and events. He made it plain he considered it both a pleasure and an honor to accompany them wherever they might wish to go, whenever they felt the need for masculine protection.

"He's very good-looking, isn't he, Mamma?"

"And he has perfectly lovely manners, which is so very much more important . . . oh, it is so reassuring to be able to rely on Vesey. I don't know what we'd do without him here in B.A., Edie, I really don't."

The horse stood, impassive, a straw hat on its head, ears protruding through the holes cut for them, shifting its hoofs from time to time and swacking its tail against the occasional fly. Mamma, unwell, had sent her regrets, but Edie, invited to the same afternoon concert, was to be escorted there by Vesey.

"Ready? That's a good girl. Up you go."

Vesey took her hand and she stepped easily into the hansom.

"It won't take us long to get there. . . . It's a shame Mrs. Moore is unable to come. . . ."

Somehow, her hand was still in his. Edie felt herself trembling. Vesey smiled, sitting beside her on the seat, their clasped hands concealed between them.

"You know, I don't think I can call you Edie any more," he told her, a light, bantering tone in his voice, a searching expression in his eyes. "You're too grown-up, and far too pretty for me to treat you as though you were a child. A beautiful young lady, sweet-natured and rare . . . Miss Edith . . ."

Edie felt her blush rising from the top of her high lace collar and burning into her cheeks.

"But that feels so distant," Vesey was saying, still looking at her but apparently unaware of her mounting confusion. "I remember dandling you on my knee, when you were little more than a baby. I'll have to find a special way of addressing you. Should it be Miss Edie? No, I don't think that suits you. Perhaps... Little Edith...?"

Edie did not recall sitting on Vesey's lap, although she remembered their first meeting quite clearly. But he was squeezing her hand, still closed in his, tucked between them in the intimacy of the rhythmic, moving carriage, and her flush was flaming to the roots of her hair. With emotions she did not fully understand and over which she knew she had no control, she felt the new title as a mantle that caressed her.

"Little Edith," he said again, murmuring it low, raising their interlaced fingers to his lips and brushing so lightly over the back of her hand that she hardly knew what had happened until it was all over and they were pulling up at their destination, and he went back to being the casual, gallant Vesey of before, helping her down and finding her seat at the concert hall and greeting all the people there, some of whom Edie also knew.

But late that night, lying wakeful in bed, she relived the interlude over and over, still feeling the light caress of his mustache, a silken whisper against her skin.

"...but surely you must have guessed my real intentions?"

Mrs. Moore looked out of the window, avoiding Vesey O'Connor's gaze. She was uncomfortable, unsure of herself and her ground; there had been some remarks made to her over the past weeks she felt she should take heed of and yet, now that she was facing Vesey, their weight wavered and did not hold.

She tried again.

"I do not mean you have been rude, or forward. It is simply that... well, my daughter is still very young... people may misconstrue... people might talk..."

Oh, dear... why had she started this? It all sounded so silly when she tried voicing it aloud. She should not have paid attention; it was probably nothing but idle gossip. A sigh of exasperation escaped her: truly, it was difficult to guard the best interests of a growing daughter when one was so alone.

Vesey was looking at her intently, his handsome, narrow face a study of concern.

Millicent took a deep breath and said, "My responsibility as Edie's mother is..."

Vesey rose. "But Mrs. Moore—no! I cannot, shall not call you that any longer!" he burst out with unexpected vehemence. "Millicent—Millie . . . in my heart, in my dreams, I have always called you Millie, little Millie, dainty, beautiful little Millie, ever since I first saw you. . . . Surely, *surely* you must have guessed . . ."

Millicent rose from her chair, alarmed.

"Mr. O'Connor . . . Vesey . . . I . . ."

"Millie." His voice turned quiet. "You knew. I knew. Look at me."

He took her hand. She did not resist. His eyes flashed deep and unmistakable meaning, but this time she held her gaze steady, and did not look away. His smile, gentle in its beginning, grew warm, then bold as it shared its secret with her acknowledging response.

"Let us not pretend to one another any more, my beautiful little Millie," he said softly. "There's enough pretending we'll have to do to the world at large for a while. I know the time is too soon, right now, this year. But in another year—think of it, little Millie! By that time . . ."

Late into the night, Millicent lay wakeful in her bed, reliving the enchanted hours of that day's afternoon, her youth recaptured, and love hers to hold. *Little Millie.* No one had called her that for years and years.

But that was who she really was: little Millie, young and carefree and in love. And loved. *Adored.* Vesey had used the word time and again: adored. Little Millie in love. For the very first time, and for the last. The one and only time, true love for life. They would be married and live happily ever after, she and Vesey, Vesey and she. Mrs. O'Connor. Mrs. Vesey O'Connor. Another thrill of pleasure rippled through her. Such a lovely name. And what difference did a few years make? They would be friends, companions, not distant spouses bound by marital obligation, but man and woman as one, united in love. And he was only three years younger—two, really, for part of the year anyway, because his birthday came earlier than hers. . . .

Vesey had spoken so beautifully that afternoon; she would never forget it. And the day would come when they would be able to declare their love for one another, and their intention to marry, to the whole wide world. Vesey said that what he wanted was to sing it from the highest rooftop. . . . Such a gloriously romantic notion, such a heavenly romantic man. . . .

Meanwhile, of course, Vesey was right: everyone would

believe he was calling on her because of his parents' long-standing friendship with her, and their continued interest in her well-being. It was only natural that their oldest son should be attentive; he was, after all, only carrying out his parents' wishes, possibly even their stated request.

And, despite all this, should there be any speculative glances, they would, as Vesey pointed out, fall on Edie, not herself. Since Edie was still so young, a child still, no problem could pose itself there, but if gossip's tongue were to waggle at all, it would waggle in the wrong direction, without effect, totally misled.

She smiled to herself in the darkness of the bedroom; happiness was hers at last. It needed only time for it to be perfectly fulfilled; only one more birthday would she let pass before everything became known. By then, all the details of the *sucesión*, the complicated legalities involved in the Argentine's strict laws of inheritance, would be completed. There would be no more ties to keep her here.

She and Vesey would marry, and sail home to England....

Time...time...one more birthday...she was still so young looking, far younger than her years. Vesey had told her so, stated it strongly. Two years was a mere nothing...a mere wink of time....

Edie, sitting at the dressing table, tilted the looking glass to get a better angle. Was she really, truly pretty? She checked her image with care. Vesey had told her she was a beauty, but it was difficult to believe; she was not soft and round and plump, the way Dollie Thaxter had become, nor did she have large luminous eyes like Dollie's.

Edie looked at herself with increasing dissatisfaction: everything about her was too slight, too small. Taken feature by feature, her face had nothing to recommend it. And, try as she might, she appeared unable to put her hair up in an attractive manner; something was always falling down, or wisping away, or going awry.

Removing the pins, she took it down, brushed through with extra care to get all the knots out and started once more. Being almost grown up, but not quite, had so many problems. Mamma said she could have a personal maid when she was eighteen, but that was two years away, and in the meantime, she had to learn to dress her own hair properly.

Two years. A lifetime. Edie sighed, then remembered, and

brightened with her secret and a smile. By that time, life would be completely different... why, she'd probably be married to Vesey by then, not just engaged. After all, the day was drawing closer every day... the day Vesey would no longer say it was not yet the right time, or that it would only ruin their chances if they broke the news too soon, the day that they would become engaged....

Edie attacked her hair with accelerated vigor. Perhaps if she made herself look older, Vesey would forget her age and ask Mamma for Edie's hand right away. Or, at least, soon. Otherwise, two years...

A lifetime.

Two years.

It was time enough. Only just, but still enough. And perhaps, with a bit of juggling here and there, even of eventual advantage. Meanwhile, the signature had been obtained and the money was forthcoming. Vesey leaned back in his chair. It had been a close call.

But now, he had all the time in the world if he played his cards properly. And he would. He flicked the ash off the end of his long, thin cigar. Horses, cards, gambling, and women... those were the things he understood and knew how to handle. Especially women. They were the easiest, the simplest to use, to play with, to foretell.

What he could neither understand nor abide were stuffy prigs like his father, his righteous, skinflint medical pontificator of a father, who had criticized Vesey all his life and never even so much as listened to his son's point of view. Dr. O'Connor, the great medical genius.... Vesey snorted. Great medical quack was more like it, with all the time in the world for everyone except his own family. Or certainly his oldest son, who should, by all rights, be first in line for favor.

Well, Edwin and Maurice were well out of it. Smart buggers, both of them. Not that he admired either of his brothers; neither had style or spark. Edwin was all higher thought and brains, while Maurice had always been pudding-stolid. Ah, well, they were both in England, well out of the way.

He could look forward to the future with confidence, enjoy the eventual fruits of his clever, careful planning. He smiled: he had done so well, it didn't really matter which way it worked. Millie or Edie, Edie or Millie: the intervening months would provide the answers. And Moore's money was there, either at firsthand, or second; it could not be drained away from his direct heirs.

No; from husband to widow, from parent to child, the laws of inheritance held money secure. Vesey stretched and smiled and poured himself more whiskey. His luck, as he had always expected, was finally coming in.

6

Vesey grabbed the crystal decanter and hurled it across the room. It shattered against the far wall, scattering shards and splashing whiskey over his father's desk.

Where had he gone wrong?

It had taken every ounce of control on his part not to leap out of the chair when Edie had told him. He was so taken by surprise, he could hardly speak at first. Luckily, Edie had been prattling on, supplying certain insights and oblivious to his state of shock.

"No, Mamma is not in this afternoon. She went boating. Dr. McIntosh and some friends came to fetch her. I doubt they will return before dinner. Mamma said..."

Confound whatever Mamma said—but most of all, confound Dr. McIntosh. Where had he received such entree into what Vesey considered to be his own private preserve? He might have known...

"... and I heard Aunt Bessie tell another lady she wouldn't be a bit surprised if Mamma married him, too." Edie was obviously most pleased at the idea. "They make such a handsome couple, she said, and he's just the right age for Mamma. Oh, Vesey..." Her eyes were sparkling with delight. "It would be so wonderful for us, too. If Mamma were to marry, then, we, I mean, you and I, could, I mean there'd be no reason not to tell anymore, would there?"

A horrid moment in an appalling afternoon. Somehow, he had extricated himself, pleading a sudden malaise. Millicent marry Dr. McIntosh: why, the scheme was rotten, through and through. It ruined everything Vesey had planned. How dare the fates flaunt his efforts in so vile a manner? There had to be a way to save the situation. And himself.

And just when everything had been going so swimmingly,

too.... Well, perhaps not lately. Everything *had* been splendid, until... Until when, exactly? When had the first of the upsets begun?

Pacing up and down in his father's study, Vesey tried to recall. It had been in Buenos Aires, he was sure of that, because he remembered one of the first small fusses had been there. They had been strolling in the park, he and Millicent; she had mentioned a minor annoyance that had occurred at the hotel.

"You really should start looking at houses here in B.A.," he had told her. She had been amazed at the mere notion; what on earth, she had asked, should she do that for? He had reasonably pointed out that, nice as the hotel might be when it was fulfilling all its functions, it could never be a home.

"I have no intention of ever having a home here," was the astonishing reply.

Where on earth did she think they would live? Was Rosario in any way dear to her heart? It seemed unlikely—nay, impossible; she had never known happiness there.

"My one true home could only be in England. . . ."

In *England*? She might as well have said *Siam*, for all the sense it made. Vesey tried to reason with her, pointing out the ease of life in the Argentine, the advantages, the freedoms, the pleasant days and ways.

"For you, perhaps, but not for me," was the reply.

Vesey had let the matter drop. It would take time, but he would bring Millicent around to his way of thinking. Besides, once they were married... And even long before, she would no doubt change her mind, once she saw it was a question of choosing between England and him.

He had never dreamt in terms of a rival. . . .

A doctor. A *doctor*. A curse on all doctors, starting with his stingy, stiff-necked father. And now a Scot... when had this scoundrel McIntosh taken the lead? Vesey had met him when he'd first arrived out, not too long ago, even gone out of his way to be civil to the man, introduced him around, that sort of thing. Not that he had introduced him to Millie; until recently, Vesey had not known that she even knew the wretched man.

And now this. Could Edie possibly be mistaken? He feared not. Edie was quite bright in some respects, for a young girl, especially when it came to gauging her mother's moods and desires.

It would mean his ruin. Total ruin. He had no other way out of his debts. The breathing spell afforded by the loan, commanded, luckily, before Millicent had turned so skittish, would eventually run out of time; he would need solid backing thereafter.

And now . . . this Scot . . . this blasted Dr. McIntosh with his ginger beard and his ginger mustache and his Scot's accent and homeborn advantage. Vesey could gladly kill him with his bare hands. Millie marry the doctor . . . no, it was unthinkable. The prospect rendered all his plans absolutely useless. Had she proved impervious to Vesey's advances—and, until recently, she most certainly had not—then he would merely have concentrated on Edie. A widowed mother-in-law posed no threat; as for the rest, it would merely be a matter of time. But a remarried widow . . . that changed the whole picture. She might have more children; Millicent was still young enough and stupid enough to do so. Edie would stand to get only a pittance by comparison to what Millie had right now.

To think that everything had been safe, plain sailing, until the disastrous doctor had appeared . . . he would like to strangle this popinjay of a medical buffoon, get his fingers round that red-bearded throat . . . wrench his neck . . .

The crystal goblet in his hands snapped at the stem, dousing him with its contents. Vesey snarled in rage and flung both fragments across the room to join the decanter's pieces.

The Buenos Aires Ladies Society Annual Picnic Outing was high on the list of popular events for the British community at large. For Edie, invited for the first time, it was the most exciting thing she had looked forward to in years; the day-long excursion to the island-filled estuary in Tigre was planned and talked about for weeks ahead.

The excursion boat took them from the station to the island where the picnic had been prepared. Pennants decorated the railings and the sides; the boat chugged by the first big islands rimming the tributary before turning off into a complex of smaller channels into the heart of the estuary. The journey did not take long; Edie spotted their destination before Mrs. Moore.

"Look, Mamma—over there! On the right! That must be it. . . ."

Indeed it was; pennants fluttered over the wooden landing. Members of the Society's Welcoming Committee were waiting on the open stretch of grass beyond. In greeting, the boat gave a loud and sudden hoot, causing gasps and then general laughter. The vessel pulled slowly alongside the landing and soon began to discharge its chatting, festive passengers. The babble of their voices echoed across the water.

When the passengers were all off and accounted for, the boat gave a second hoot, in signal of leaving, and pulled away. It circled around in midstream and returned the way it had come; Edie saw it disappear around the bend, making its way back into the main water passage.

"Come along, Edie . . ."

Mother and daughter descended from the landing onto the island's clearing, where most of the people had gathered. A thick background of trees sheltered the opening; at its far end there was a building and, in front of the building, long trestle tables set up with all the picnic fare. On seeing them, Edie realized she was very hungry; breakfast, and only a small one at that, had been a long time ago.

It seemed to her that everyone she knew in the world was there. Everybody who was anybody, and a lot who weren't besides, was strolling and laughing and talking in groups, admiring the island, the flowering trees, the river view, in loud holiday voices. The Thaxters and all that church's group were there, and coming over.

"Dear Millicent, how lovely you look! Edie, child, how are you?"

The church people and the railway people and the import-export business group, who were always much in view, and a sprinkling of schoolmasters and rising young bloods, and fathers of sons who would soon join them in shipping. And everywhere, young girls and wives and mothers, some with toddlers at their sides, others with nannies supervising their brood. Schoolgirls giggled in huddles, glancing at school lads who wandered by; a team of men, resplendent in striped bathing costumes, announced their intention of going bathing on the beach the far side of the island.

"Oh, Mamma, mustn't that be fun. . . ."

"If one knows how to swim, dearest."

"But we could paddle. . . ."

"Not now, Edie. Perhaps later, in the afternoon. . . ."

And there was Dr. McIntosh, tall and courtly with his bright red beard, going up to greet Mamma. You could see by the way he looked at her he thought she was the very nicest thing on earth. She liked him, too; Edie could tell. Mamma had said Dr. McIntosh had decided to return to England, rather than stay out in the Argentine, but just when he was going back was not clear yet, as it was a complete change of his original plans, which had apparently been to settle down in B.A. It all seemed to have come about since he had been seeing so much of Mamma, which made Edie suspect Mrs. Thaxter was probably right.

Oh—there, at last, was Vesey, more handsome than ever, talking to the people who had come from the district of Hurlingham. They were all interested in horses; several of them played polo, and the games' championship matches were a popular subject of discussion.

A bell sounded; the picnic tables were declared open, and all the visitors gathered at the spread: the ladies of the Society had spent weeks planning and getting everything in order, and the results on the tables were splendid to see. There were platters of beef, and cold, sliced pies, and sausage rolls, and steak and kidney puddings; there were Cornish pasties, and potted meats, and cold croquettes, and cold roast chicken. There was also a lavish layout of cheese, imported Stilton king in the center. As for the sweets, they covered a table: towering blancmange, shaped summer pudding, sliced fruits and cream, a rolled spotted dog pudding with sauce poured over.

There was fruit punch and lemonade and stronger fare for the gentlemen, many of whom tilted their boaters back on their heads in exuberance and warmth. To begin with there were toasts and a few speeches, and much general laughter, and then the serious business of eating began. Household servants, brought along to fetch and carry, scurried among the guests with plates and table linens and cutlery. After the inevitable initial confusion, everyone settled down: small children with their nannies or their anxious mothers, older children in friendship circles; a stranger rarely allowed or scornfully tolerated if already there. Small tables and seats and benches stood within the encircling trees of the island, a few in the sunshine of the clearing; most of the ladies chose those in the shade, for the sun's noon force was considerable and there was scarcely a breeze.

Edie lunched with Dollie, who was full of gossip, most of it gleaned from Aunt Bessie, Edie surmised, not really listening at all, for little of it interested her; what she really wanted to do was stroll around the island and see it all with Vesey. But Vesey, after having greeted her when she arrived, was busy with other people and groups he knew. Vesey knew everybody, Edie knew, and he was always so polite, and friendly; but still...

Never mind. Later there would be games and races, and no doubt she would be able to stand chatting with him then. Or perhaps he was going to race in the men's events, too, and she would be able to watch him beat all the others, for there was no doubt in her mind but that Vesey would win.

When the postprandial lull set in, and the older men leaned back against tree trunks and pretended they were only resting, their betraying snores making children laugh, only heat and somnolence hung in the air, joined in hum and murmur by an occasional eddy of flies. Millicent came looking for Edie; Dollie went off on her own. Mrs. Moore, flushed with the heat and the luncheon, fanned herself with a paper fan.

Edie was about to suggest they walk down to the waterside, when she saw Vesey approaching them.

"It's so hot here," he began.

"Yes, indeed. Quite stifling."

"... which is why I thought I'd come over and suggest a boat ride...."

"Oh, Mamma—let's!"

Edie saw her mother cast a glance over the scattered crowd. Dr. McIntosh was standing on the other side of the clearing, deep in conversation with a group of men.

"Well," Millicent hesitated.

"They won't be running the races until quite a bit later," Vesey offered. "It's far too hot now, and everyone's far too full. We could take one of the rowboats and enjoy a cooling ride, and still be back in plenty of time to see the fun."

Edie watched indecision play across her mother's face. It was out of the question for her to permit Edie to go alone with Vesey, but there was no excuse for Millicent not to accompany them. And it certainly would be fresher on the water.

"Oh, Mamma—do let's!" she pleaded again.

"Very well, then—but not for too long...."

They went down to the landing where a cluster of rowboats

71

swayed in the gentle movement of the water. Some, already occupied, were pulling away from the shore; others, still moored, rocked and wobbled as eager but nervous young women were assisted in by young men who wanted to show off their rowing skills. Parental chaperones got in last, steadying both the boat and mood with their presence. Oars splashed, ropes were untied.

"Very bad form," observed Vesey as water splattered from a boat next to them.

"Do you row well?" Edie wanted to know.

"You'll see...."

He got in first, dusting off the wooden plank seats before giving his hand, first to Millicent, then to Edie, and helping them into the small rowboat.

"Supposing you two sit there, opposite me.... Yes, that's right. It'll keep the boat balanced properly. Ready? Good. Anchors aweigh, and let's push off."

He handled the oars with expert movements, slipping them into the dark cloudy water with only concentric ripples to show where they had broken through the surface. A pull here, a twist there, and they were midriver, gliding along between the tree-covered islands on either side. Edie wanted to know how many islands there were.

"In the whole of the Tigre? I don't think anyone's ever counted them, there are so many. Big ones, little ones. Some are hardly islands at all, just swampy outcroppings of reeds. And then there are the islots, the floating islands. Nothing but reeds, really, all tangled, like a woven raft. They eventually float all the way down the river, past B.A. and out to sea...."

He slid the boat into a narrow side channel between two islands, emerging into a swifter-moving breadth of water on the other side. Never losing control for a moment, he sculled across it and around another island.

Millicent looked alarmed.

"Oh, dear . . . I do hope we don't get lost...."

"Don't worry. I know the Tigre like the back of my hand." Vesey smiled, shipping the oars for a moment and letting the water move them unaided. "Tell you what: I'll prove it to you by giving you a local tour. You can't see it now, but just ahead of us there's a big island with a lovely house. It has topiary bushes on either side of the path leading up to it, and..."

Taking the oars again, he went on describing the house

they were to see until, after another hundred yards, he again changed the rowboat's direction and they came upon the house, exactly as he had described it, and Edie noticed her mother smiled in relief and renewed interest.

The house stood back from the river; it was shuttered against the afternoon light. The island itself was surrounded by a low stone wall, mossed and stained from the restless water. Both women admired it.

"There are lots of others. I'll take you to look at all of 'em someday. Right now, what we're looking for is a cooling breeze, and I know where to find it. . . ."

More skillful sculling, another series of channels and bends, and they came out onto the open water.

"But it's still so hot. . . ."

"That's because we're still too close to the shore. Wait until we get further out into the river, away from the islands. . . ."

Vesey headed the boat out into the open, silver-glinted stretch of the River Plate, pulling swiftly away from the clustered islands of the Tigre. Once out on the open water, the breeze was fresh and clear. Millicent stopped fanning herself; Edie trailed her fingers in the water and flicked a drop into the wind.

"That's Uruguay over there," Vesey remarked, gesturing across the water but, peer as she might, Edie could see nothing on the horizon.

"No, it's not always visible. Depends on the weather," came the explanation.

"Can we row over there?"

Vesey laughed. "Of course—but it'd take us rather a long time."

"I think not— not today." Millicent's tone was sharp.

"I meant it in jest." He was quickly contrite. "It would take far too long. But it can be done," he went on to explain to Edie, who was still looking for a glimpse of the Uruguayan shore.

"Have you ever been there?"

"What, to Uruguay? Yes. Lots of times. But not by rowboat. The steamer's most comfortable."

"Is it nice?"

"Not a patch on B.A."

"I'd love to go there. . . . I'd like to travel all over the world, and go everywhere, and see everything . . ."

Edie chattered on, ignoring her mother's restive mood.

Vesey's rowing was smooth; they went past the last small outcroppings in the shallow river until all around them there was the glinting water and the breeze-brushed air, the trees of Tigre and its thousand islands visible as a variously shaded green cinch around a section of the horizon.

There were other boats, too; in some, people were fishing, the long poles sticking up like spiders' legs from the sides, their lines plummeting into the water, sharply angled at the top. Voices and sounds began reaching across the water; the breeze had dropped, the sky gone overcast; it was darker, grayer, lower on the horizon. A hush fell, a hollowness of sound. A bell from distant miles rang across the river.

"Will the sun come out again?"

Vesey slowed his rowing and looked up at the clouds.

"I expect so. It's hard to tell."

"Wouldn't you like to go back, dearest?"

"Oh, no, Mamma, it's so nice out here."

"Perhaps you two would like to try your hands at rowing," was Vesey's suggestion.

"No, thank you." Millicent clasped her hands in her lap, a handkerchief between them, as though to keep them safe. Edie, however, rushed at the idea.

"Oh, yes! Do let me try. . . ."

It was hopeless, but fun, and made Edie laugh till she felt weak; the oars wouldn't do anything she wanted them to, once they were in her hands. They were heavy, and hard-surfaced, and appeared to have a will completely of their own; they splashed and slipped and moved in opposite ways. Strain though she might, she had no control.

"Why won't they go in the same direction at the same time?" she puffed.

"They would, if you were doing it properly," said Mrs. Moore.

Vesey was kinder about it.

"Ah, you have to be very strong, and it takes quite a lot of training. Here, let me show you. . . ."

Vesey took one of the oars, letting her keep the other.

"Now, if you copy exactly what I do . . . no, you're not holding it correctly. Hold it like *this*. . . ."

There was a great deal of splashing on Edie's side of the boat, a graceful swirl of water around the blade of the oar Vesey was handling, and the rowboat suddenly swung around in a semicircle.

"I don't think..." Millicent began, only to be interrupted by another burst of splashing. "Edie! Stop that at once!" She patted her face with her handkerchief. "I don't want to be soaked to the skin."

"I'm sorry, Mamma."

"Here—try using both your hands to hold the oar. That way, you might be able to..."

"Vesey, I think you'd better take the oar back yourself. Don't you think it's about time we returned?"

"Oh, Mamma, please let me try just once more...."

"Come on, Millicent, don't be a spoilsport...."

The hushed lull was over. A slight breeze had picked up, enough to freshen the still air. Edie had another try at making her oar move in tandem with Vesey's. It provoked a burst of splashing that sent Millicent scrambling to the small bench at the far end. The boat rocked under her sudden movement.

"Oh, don't..." Edie squealed.

"It'll steady," Vesey said. "There. See. Just don't move around too much, or too suddenly."

"Then don't you two splash so much."

"I'm not." Vesey reached around Edie's back, placing his hand over hers on the oar. "Here, let me..."

Edie, who had been looking at her mother, jumped at the unexpected touch of his hand.

"Oh—you frightened me! Quick! Oh, dear... it's..."

But it was too late; her startled movement had flung the oar into the water.

"You *fool!*"

"Oh, Edie..."

Edie burst into tears, and leaned over the side of the boat to try and reach for the oar. It bobbed inches out of arm's length on the shifting waters.

"Perhaps I could..."

"Millie, for God's sake... Edie, hold this oar for me while I try. Hold it with both hands and *don't let it go.*"

Vesey stood up, Edie shifted over on the seat and clutched the other oar. Vesey leaned over the side of the boat; the floating paddle moved further away. As it was over near Millicent's end, she made a futile attempt toward it, too. A sudden gust sent her broad-brimmed hat whirling off into the water.

"Oh, my hat! Vesey, please..."

"Confound your blasted hat! The oar's far more important!"

"*Really*, Vesey, there's no need to..."

Vesey, who had been crouching over the side, stood up, his expression grim. He glanced at the horizon, then up overhead.

"Look, there's a storm coming. I want to get that oar. Edie, stop sniveling! It doesn't help. Let me have that again...."

He took the oar from her and, making her move to the middle bench, did all he could to single-scull toward his objective. More wind rose; the darkening sky hung with rain. Beneath, the water grew more and more agitated; Edie saw flecks of white foam fly from the choppy tops of the shallow, clashing waves. Mamma looked pale, afraid.

The rain began, cold and slanted, stinging against them with added force from the wind. The oar disappeared beyond a row of foam-turmoiled crests.

"It's no use.... I'm going to start back...."

The fishing boats, so numerous and close before, had all disappeared; even the estuary islands were almost invisible through the curtain of wind-driven rain. Edie began shivering from unhappiness and cold. A sudden lurch of the boat pitched her forward, sending her toppling against her mother. Mrs. Moore grabbed her and helped her sit back down.

"You're getting soaked, child. Here, put this on." Millicent took her shawl and swathed it around Edie's head and shoulders. Then she braced herself against the side of the boat, closing her eyes.

Edie wept in silent misery, clutching the shawl with one hand and the plank seat with the other. The boat slammed around in the angry water, the waves chopped, changed color, foamed furiously around, sending plumes of spray flying with the wind. All shades of dark and grayness whirled in a tumult of rain and wind and water, convulsing the river world.

A sudden series of heaving motions shook and tossed the boat, sending all images crashing into chaotic disorder. Mrs. Moore grabbed the edge of the boat and stood up.

"Vesey! For God's sake...we're going to..."

"Sit *down*, you fool! Sit down!" he screamed.

Millicent scrambled past Edie, over the middle bench.

"Damn you—sit *down*, I said."

Another lurch. The boat pitched and rocked.

"Vesey—help!"

"Let go! Let me go!"

"Vesey!"

Screams. A crash. The slam of surface against water, then everything turning over. More screams and splashing, a hideous cry. Edie was wrenched aside, tumbled against wood and hurled into the water. The stinging impact of her plunge was covered by froth and bubbles and cold churning all around her, and then the water engulfed her and pushed her down and around into the river's billowing dark.

Edie struggled and surfaced, gasping for air, choking on the water punching into her mouth and closing off her throat with wave after wave. Her clothes, soaked and leaden, pulled and bound her legs, the shawl dragged raw ropes across her face and neck. A foam-crested swirl crashed over her; she broke through on its other side. Her arms struck something; she grabbed for it, blindly. Her hand slithered across slime, found an edge, lost it, and grabbed again. She dug her fingers against the hard, unyielding rim.

Choking and gasping, she clung on, reaching for the overturned boat with her other hand. Buffeted by water, blinded by rain, she coughed her voice clear as best she could, and screamed "Mamma!" into the wind. Then her free hand met wood; as she grabbed, the boat swung sharply around. A jerk, a slam of waves, and the motion tore everything out of her grasp. Water closed over her head again, and blackness.

With desperate effort she fought against the drag of her clothing. Her face came up through bubbles. There was air . . . she gulped . . . pain fought, lancing, inside her chest. Suddenly an object jammed itself up against her neck. It jerked her chin backward, pulling her through the water . . . it was moving . . . it was pliant . . . There was something beneath her . . . a kick . . . a blocking form . . . alive. . . .

She tried to struggle free and grab hold.

"Don't struggle, Edie. . . . I've got you. . . . Try to float. . . . Try . . ."

Vesey's arm pressed against her, pulling her through the water. She could feel his legs kicking against hers, his hoarse grunts and spluttering breath only inches from her ear. Her own breath was sharp with pain, but there was air between the waves of water washing over them both, tossing them together.

". . . a bit more . . . can see land . . . must be shallow . . ."

The motion changed; the pull was not as great. Vesey's arm loosened, his harsh breathing louder through the storm's

77

roaring sounds. Her feet touched bottom, dragged along it . . . sank once more, touched again . . . Motion stopped. Vesey was standing, pulling her upright, his hands lifting her arms, heaving her forward.

"We're safe, Edie. . . . you can walk. . . ."

She clung to him, buckling with every step, falling against his side, stumbling to her hands and knees in the shallow water as they slipped and Vesey fell beside her. They dragged themselves onto the silt and rasping reeds, gaining their feet once more, pushing ahead, through the sinking quagmire further onto the island, until the ground firmed under them, and they were beyond water.

There Edie collapsed, retching and choking over and over until her strength was spent and all she could do was lie there in the pelting rain, shivering and helpless, moaning into the empty wind, "Mamma . . . Mamma . . ."

The search party found them long after nightfall, but Millicent's body was not recovered until the next week, when it washed up on a stretch of river beach beneath the sloping *barranca* cliffs south of the myriad estuary islands on the shore close to the city of Buenos Aires itself.

A gash across the dead woman's forehead contained wooden splinters embedded in the empurpled skin. At the inquest that followed, it was decided the blow might have been suffered as she fell into the water, striking her head against the boat at the very moment of the accident itself, or in the immediate turmoil that ensued. An autopsy confirmed that death had been by drowning; when the full formalities of the inquest had been completed, the incident was declared closed.

Speculation and gossip, however, remained wide open.

"D'you think he did it?"

"Hard to say . . . always was a bounder . . ."

" . . . knew the Tigre like the back of his hand . . . should've seen the storm coming . . ."

The River Plate, for all its width, and precisely because of its shallows, was long known as a watery grave when storms blew its waters to frenzy, their very suddenness their trademark.

" . . . been sniffing and licking after Millicent's fortune ever since old Moore kicked the bucket. . . ."

"Might have done it, too—until Dr. Redbeard caught her eye. . . ."

"Oh, did you think so? Thought it was young Edie he was after, meself. . . ."

"Coast's clear now, isn't it?"

The talk grew darker, the whispers and murmurs went the rounds.

"They say her skull was split wide open. . . ."

"A terrible temper he had, that O'Connor. . . ."

". . . and always in trouble . . . the debts alone . . . that unfortunate affair at the club . . ."

Nor was the talk confined to social circles. Behind the bland barrier of officialdom, an investigation began.

Dr. O'Connor, hearing of it unofficially from a grateful patient who had connections, knew what he had to do. That night at dinner, he looked across the table at his eldest son, and smiled in grim satisfaction.

"You're leaving for Uruguay at dawn tomorrow," he announced, pulling his chair closer to the table. "The passage is booked, the fare paid. Once there, you're to be on the next sailing for England."

What?

Vesey's face drained white. Mrs. O'Connor gasped and dropped her knife and fork onto the table.

"You heard what I said. You're to sail for England. From Montevideo, and as soon as you can."

The two men stared at each other in a silent, tense battle. Mrs. O'Connor put her hand to her mouth, hardly daring to breathe.

"I see." Vesey's voice was low, even. "And might I ask why?"

"Because there's an official investigation underway!" the doctor exploded. "You don't stand a chance once they . . ."

"But I didn't . . ."

". . . and they'll hang you higher than the moon, my boy, given half a chance. What you may or may not have done will be neither here nor there. You know as well as I do what your reputation is like—and that your word means nothing. *Nothing.*" The older man's eyes blazed contempt. "It never has, and it won't now."

"Are you trying to . . ."

"I'm not trying anything. You're finished in this country, Vesey, do you understand? And the quicker you get out of here, the better it'll be for all of us. You've been nothing but trouble since the day you were born, and your mother and I..."

"Oh, please, do stop... I... I can't bear it...." Mrs. O'Connor was crying.

"Elizabeth, I'm sorry, but there's no alternative now." Her husband's voice softened in addressing her. "If Vesey stays, they'll pin this ghastly tragedy on him—whether or not he caused it. And we'll all be ruined. None of us will survive. The one chance he has is to start afresh elsewhere." Turning to his son again, he said, "The arrangements have all been made this end. Once you get to England, your brothers will no doubt give you a hand. The rest will be up to you, and whatever may be your abilities. And I can only pray to God," he emphasized, "you'll have sense enough to stick to the straight and narrow at last...."

Vesey's disappearance set every tongue a-wagging, Argentine and English, social and official alike.

"... dropped out without a trace..."

"Probably went over the river..."

The investigation got as far as a riverboat passage, then was shelved and lay dormant but not forgotten and not closed. From his friend, Dr. O'Connor heard that the files would be kept waiting; writing to Edwin and Maurice in London, he made the message clear.

Under no circumstances is Vesey ever to consider returning to the Argentine. My advice would be to change his name and forget South America completely. Nor do I ever wish to hear from him again; his mother and I have suffered enough at his hands. I pray you both are well, and that your lives are in good order, so that your example may inspire your brother to mend and remake his ways.

Edie, confined to her hospital bed and guarded, day and night, by attendant nurses, struggled with her grief and her breath and her pain, hardly knowing where the borders were between life and death. Faces came and went, images faded to darkness; her mother's voice echoed in a stillness beyond grasp. There were times the choking tears left her exhausted and she would sleep, only to awaken to the waiting grief that time might soften but never take away.

More faces appeared, and spoke, and vanished, but never

the one she so wanted to see. The truth came to her by accident: Vesey had vanished. Other voices denied it, but the impact was real. And then there was nothing, only haziness and sorrow. Edie closed her eyes and made herself breathe.

Then came a hand to cling to, out of the darkness. She knew it when she felt its warmth, the shape of its hold.

"It's me, *niña* Edie . . . I'll be here for when you need me. . . ."

The bonds of trust sustained her and Edie slept, deep and dreamless, her wounded self protected in Rosita's care.

7

Edie rubbed the last gritty traces of sleep from her eyes, and sat up. She glanced across at Dollie's bed; the silent mount of blanket and counterpane rose and fell in barely perceptible, even motion. Sometimes Dollie snored; she also talked in her sleep, and Edie had taken a long while to get used to sharing the room. Even now, she did not like doing so.

There were so many things she did not like these days, but there was nothing she could do to change any of them. Not until she was twenty-two, and of age . . . and today was only her eighteenth birthday. Four more dreary years. Four more twelve-month stretches of life with the Thaxters. The mere thought of it was enough to make Edie cry, but she wasn't going to. Not this morning.

She had cried before. A year ago, after Mamma had died and Vesey disappeared and everything was so painful and terrifying, she had cried so much she thought the hot gushing tears would never stop. No matter who came to see her, no matter who tried to console her, no matter what they said, everyone had always managed to make her cry all the more. Except Rosita. Rosita, who had sat by the hospital bed hour after hour, holding her hand and saying nothing at all, doing the dirty jobs the nurses forgot, dozing in a chair at night, awake if Edie so much as moved or turned over in the bed, until Edie had summoned enough strength to insist another bed be brought in for the maid.

As time went on, the tears began slowing, and then they stopped. They would return in sudden hot overflowings, sometimes because of a direct cause, such as the time she came across Mamma's bead necklace, the one she had always coveted from the long-ago days of spring cleaning, and sometimes for no reason at all. If Rosita was near, Edie would cling to her and cry, and often Rosita's eyes were wet, too. But if Rosita was busy elsewhere, Edie had no one at all—and all the decisions about her immediate future were to be made for her by her legal guardian, Canon Thaxter.

Having visited Edie at the hospital during the afternoon, Bessie Thaxter was still visibly upset.

"That poor, unhappy, orphaned child..." She handed her husband his nightly cup of warm milk. "It's enough to break one's heart...."

"Thank you, m'dear. Ahh..." He took a sip. "Unhappy she no doubt is, and orphaned, without doubt, but poor is a misnomer. Edith Moore is a rich young girl." He returned his attention to the milk.

His wife, attuned to his habits of interrupted speech, waited.

Several sips later, he began again.

"A *very* rich young girl. Yes, indeed. She has inherited a veritable fortune—or will have, by the time all the legalities are satisfied and everything has been put in order. It can take as long as two years, you know." He looked at his wife over the rim of the cup, milk-steam brushing a film over his spectacles.

There was a pause.

"Robert should be here again by that time," Mrs. Thaxter ventured. The sips were resumed, signaling she had taken the correct tack.

"Indeed."

"...always fond of her..."

"...and would be so suitable..."

Sips interspersed assenting nods.

"...close since they were wee ones...so much in common...nursery schoolroom days...closest friends she's ever had...only *real* friends...owe it to poor dear Millicent...Christian duty..."

Thus did they each help spin their mutual web of dreams.

"Of course you'll come and live with us," Canon Thaxter had told Edie while she was still in the hospital but well enough to get up and sit in a chair for several hours a day. He had come in early that morning, brimming with smiles and self-confidence.

"You know you have always been as close as a second daughter to us. Dollie has looked upon you as a sister ever since the first day..."

Edie had been too unhappy to think about it, too unhappy to care. She knew she would be leaving the hospital soon, and she had to live somewhere.

The clergyman continued to outline the plans. There was all the room in the world at the Thaxter house, he said; she could share Dollie's bedroom, and the two girls could use Robert's room as their dressing room for the time being. Later on, when Robert returned from England after he finished school, everything could be rearranged. Robert would not be back for another year; by that time Edie would be eighteen...

Well, she was eighteen now, today, and Robert was due back soon, and really nothing had changed. More than a year had passed since she had moved in with the Thaxters; what had been unfamiliar and uncomfortable at first was now the dull routine of Edie's hampered, boring, uncomfortable life.

Four more years.

Four more years of being pushed around by the whims and wills of others....

On one occasion, Edie had fought back. It had been right at the beginning, and was about Rosita. The Thaxters had told her she was to return to Rosario.

"Where is she going to live?"

"With her mother," was the answer. "Rosa is going to work for the O'Connors."

"I want her to stay here in Buenos Aires with me."

"Edith, you're far too young to have a personal maid.... It's out of the question."

It was *Edie* when everything was running according to their way of thinking, *Edith* when it was not. Edie-Edith set her jaw and tightened her resolve.

"Either Rosita stays here with me or...or...or I'll go and live with the O'Connors in Rosario!"

The spontaneous outburst was a well-chosen threat. The Thaxters reconsidered: perhaps it could be managed...the servant was young; she could work for them as well as assist Edie...it would be Edie's money paying her wages...

Rosita stayed, and Edie discovered that digging in her

83

heels could sometimes—not always, but sometimes—bring about the formerly impossible. It helped, but did not solve, Edie's present position: Dr. Thaxter was her guardian, and that was that.

How could Mamma have appointed him? Edie pondered the question, realizing that Mamma had been a fool about certain matters, just as Papa had always maintained. If only Mamma had chosen Dr. O'Connor... Edie was sure he would have been her father's choice. And the O'Connors were so much nicer....

Edie had seen little of them since she left the hospital, and the few meetings had been awkward, filled with silences and unsaid words. She could not ask about Vesey; they never mentioned him. Mrs. O'Connor always had tears in her eyes when she said good-bye.

Four more years.

Edie shuddered, and drew her knees close to her chest where her barely perceptible bosom ended in two pale pink points. Her body was so different from Dollie's hourglass shape and rosy, ample roundness.

"You're a scraggy little thing," Dollie had said on more than one occasion and, although Edie hated her for saying it, she had to admit it was true. She would never be round and soft and cuddly; she would never be a proper woman, never be able to catch a husband, never get away from the Thaxters, never.

Her birthday... eighteen years old today...

Edie brightened. It might not mean freedom, but the birthday was to bring certain change. From today on, she would be allowed to attend the social events of the season, the teas and receptions and dances Dollie had been going to since the year before. Instead of only hearing about the fun, Edie would now be able to participate in it, too.

Despite herself, Edie wriggled in anticipation.

The succession of inheritance was more complicated than had been expected: there were sums of money missing, property unaccounted for, changes without reason. The late Millicent Moore, never adept at figures and believed amenable to any advice on financial matters, had apparently made moves without mentioning them to her advisers. She had also spent far more money than anyone had realized.

Worse: she had mortgaged both the Rosario property and

the camp. The house would have to be sold, its profit forfeited to the mortgage. The camp mortgage would be continued.

Jewelry was also missing: some rings, an especially valuable lavalière, a ruby pin, a brooch. She had been wearing a couple of the pieces on the day of the accident; it was generally accepted they had remained in the river that killed her, for her garments were bereft of any ornament when her body was found. Still, a ring...

"Perhaps it was ill-fitting, and slipped off when she drowned...."

Perhaps.

Some thought otherwise, and said so, privately. They also wondered about the other pieces of jewelry, the sums of money, the mortgage, the sale... Tawdry and tatty, the whole affair. Tongues wagged again.

It was Mrs. O'Connor who first came upon her husband's body, crumpled sideways over the arm of his favorite easy chair. There were papers scattered all around him, some torn, one sheet still folded between his stiffening fingers. They appeared to be letters and notes, written in one hand, annotated in another. Mrs. O'Connor instantly recognized both; she gathered up all the scraps and tearings, stuffed them into a hastily removed cushion cover, fleeing to her bedroom, where she hid the bundle beneath the heavy counterpane. Smoothing the bed to its former condition, she retraced her steps to the study.

After holding her dead husband's head against her for one last farewell, she closed his staring eyes. Only then did she call the servants for aid.

In the late hours of that night, when everybody had gone home, she was able to close the bedroom door and have complete privacy in which to move the hidden letters to a safer niche. They stayed in the false bottom of her dressing-table drawer until after the funeral was over, and the callers had all paid their respects, and she was left to the hours on her own. Then, still behind locked doors, she removed the pieces and torn sheets of stationery and read them all with care.

Some, ripped by an angry hand, needed piecing together in the manner of a jigsaw puzzle; others, though torn, were still linked by crumpled stretches. All needed smoothing out;

all were legible. And all were starkly revealing: the whole horror was there.

Even the hastily written, undated notes were easy to put into sequence, once Mrs. O'Connor had read everything through. Millicent's growing infatuation shone plainly through the early letters; her declared love followed, the mortgage mentioned thereafter. Then began the first of the notes; they were most of them unhappy. Calmer letters came again, then more notes, then pleadings.

And in the margins, Vesey's hand: numbers, sums of money, reminders for further demands, a pawnbroker's address . . .

Mrs. O'Connor wept and read on, saw the shadow of blackmail in Millie's last notes, the counterplay of her mention of a doctor, her possible change of plans . . .

No. That was enough. Carefully Mrs. O'Connor gathered everything together again, this time placing all the papers in the grate of her bedroom fireplace. She watched the flames dance up and high; she watched the blackened pieces curl and turn gray. When she was satisfied only ash remained, the doctor's widow went heavily to her wide and lonely bed, lying there awake till the crowing at dawn.

Robert was on his way.

The Thaxter household was in an uproar. Edie was reminded of her mother's spring cleaning days, only Bessie Thaxter was nowhere near as effective in her approach. She was hopeless with the servants and was given to sighing that some people had all the luck. . . . She, instead, suffered through an endless succession of useless, hopeless maids and cooks who were either sluts or thieves and frequently both.

And then there was Rosita . . . Rosita was a thorn in Bessie Thaxter's amply padded side. . . .

Not that the girl was a slut or a thief; even in her most perturbed moments, the clergyman's wife could not accuse her of that. But a thorn she was, difficult and distant. She was never openly rude, and yet Mrs. Thaxter felt uncomfortable in the girl's presence. There was always that flick of contempt in the dark eyes; the too-quick, "Yes, *señora*, of course, *señora*," of her nominally polite answers. No doubt the girl felt safe behind an unseen barrier: her wages were paid by Edie, not by the Thaxters. Canon Thaxter handled the sums, and Edie's part was never visible, but behind the routine lay the truth: Edie and Rosita were a team, opposed to the rest of the household in unfathomable ways.

Bessie had caught them talking and laughing together on more than one occasion; the moment they saw her, they fell silent, or continued talking, but in low tones. Now, why on earth would Edie want to chatter to a servant girl, when she had Dollie, her closest and best friend, right there all the time, and her hostess besides?

But meanwhile, Robert was almost home, and the thought was enough to make Bessie Thaxter push all her problems aside. She had already spoken to everyone she knew about his return: how he would be accepting a position at Bateman Company, how Horace Bateman himself had insisted, positively insisted, mind you, that Robert work for him and absolutely no one else in B.A., and yes, of course, she could not help but be proud of her Robert, he always had been outstanding, and...

H. Bateman Co., Ltd. was a long-established import-export company in Buenos Aires. Both the company and its owner were powers to be reckoned with in the British community, in the city, and in the economic structure of the republic of Argentina.

The Thaxters were in their glory.

"Yes, only a few more weeks..."

"...called on by Mr. Bateman himself... most promising, indeed..."

"...must come to tea when Robert arrives... though I'm afraid he's going to be terribly busy... you have no idea how many people..."

"...always showed interest in international affairs... import-export's the coming thing... right connections..."

But there were other implications in Robert's return.

"I'm being pushed into a corner," Dollie whined, resenting the return of a wardrobe into the bedroom she and Edie shared. Robert's room was being restored to its original purpose; the girls were now being restricted to their own quarters.

"There, there, dear, I'm sure you don't mind too much," Mrs. Thaxter said to her pouting daughter. "Besides, perhaps it won't be for very long...."

Edie, who was rearranging her clothes in a chest of draw-

87

ers, saw mother and daughter exchange furtive smiles. Late that night, when both girls were already in bed, Edie asked Dollie exactly what had Mrs. Thaxter meant.

"Well," Dollie began, "I'm not supposed to tell you..."

Edie waited in silence, having discovered long ago it was the best way of getting information out of Dollie.

"...but, as we're best friends...well, I'll tell you if you promise you won't tell anyone I told you...."

"Cross my heart." Edie's answer was mechanical. She began smoothing her long springy hair into three wide ropes, preparatory to plaiting it for the night.

"All right. I'll tell you. But remember, it's a big secret, and you're not supposed to know anything about it."

"I promise."

"They think Robert might want to marry you," Dollie confided. "Everybody says it'd be a very good match."

Edie's fingers stopped weaving her hair into the thick braid.

"Of course, we don't know whether he'll have you," came from the other bed: "Mamma says he's such a good prospect, he'll have the choice of any girl out here. But perhaps you'll be lucky, and then we'll be sisters-in-law!" Dollie finished on a note of triumph. "Just remember—not a word to anyone that I told you...."

Edie lay awake for a long time that night and when sleep came at last, it was not for long, for she woke, whimpering and gasping for breath, her heart pounding from the vanished nightmare, her throat dry from a silent scream. As she looked around the room, regaining equilibrium, she saw it was still the darkest hours of the middle of the night.

The wharf was crowded with carriages and people; Edie pushed her way through the jostling crowd, staying as close to the Thaxters as she could. The spring sunshine was already warm, but she was glad of her new fur-edged tippet, worn especially for the occasion and a good shield against the spanking breeze blowing onshore from the River Plate waters. Dollie, decked out in her latest finery, had been bossy and overbearing ever since they had woken before dawn.

"No, it's my turn first today.... He's my brother, not yours, and I don't care if you did know him when we were small...."

Dollie, the laggard, the lazy, the slowcoach, had insisted on being first with everything all day, thereby delaying Edie in all her preparations and occasioning one of the scoldings at Canon Thaxter's hands.

"Edith, if you cannot be ready on time the very day my son Robert returns home after his long absence . . . truly cannot understand such ungratefulness . . . the very least you could . . . and should . . . Mrs. Thaxter and myself . . ."

Edie gritted her teeth and heard him out without a murmur, not mentioning Dollie's constant obstruction and demands. Tempers were high all over the house until the carriage arrived. Then they were off and down to the *dársena*, and the excitement of the moment carried the ill feelings away. They descended from the carriage and walked along toward the passenger jetty; the ship was already in full view.

"Oh, I wonder where Robert is. . . . D'you think he'll see us?"

"Look at all the people standing out on deck. . . ."

As the ship neared, they tried to see the people's faces, comparing impressions with friends standing around also waiting for arriving passengers.

"Hullo, Mrs. Hamilton, lovely day, isn't it? Who? Oh, your sister . . . how nice . . . I'm sure you're longing to see . . . . Yes, my son . . . finished school now, you know . . . . will be joining Bateman's shortly . . ."

"I saw Mr. Bateman arrive a while ago," was the unexpected remark offered. "See? Over there . . . he's just getting out of his carriage. . . ."

Bessie Thaxter swelled with pride; was Mr. Bateman actually coming to meet their Robert? She tugged at the Canon's sleeve and whispered to him behind her gloved hand. A smile spread across his face.

"Indeed . . . well, well . . . how nice . . . how very gratifying. . . ."

The noise of chains and shouts and clangings was punctuated by several whistles and shrill hoots. The ship slid alongside, and movement was everywhere, ropes slung, sailors swarming, *changadores* wheeling their waiting handcarts to place, and the air filled with halloos and hurrahs from deck to wharf and back across the narrowing slip of water, everyone waving in the glee of triumphant encounter.

"Ohhh, there he is!" Dollie suddenly squealed. "Look, Mamma, Edie, Papa—there's Robert, over there, near the gangplank! Robert, Robert!" Her brother saw her, his smile beaming down at them all, and he waved both his arms over his head.

"Goodness... hasn't he changed? Isn't he grown-up? And how handsome he's become...."

With the gangplank finally in place, the passengers began coming down onto the jetty. The Thaxters and Edie pressed closer, but the stream of disembarking people made their progress imperceptible.

"We'd better wait here," Canon Thaxter conceded. "Robert'll find us easily enough."

He did, with the aid of youth and height, moving from the bottom of the gangplank to his waiting family in few and easy strides.

"Hullo, Pater... Mater, it's marvelous to see you.... Why, Dollie, how pretty you've grown... and little Edie..."

As Robert greeted and hugged them in turn, Edie became aware of a stranger standing right behind him, waiting, it seemed, for Robert himself.

Then Robert was saying, "Come on, now, Edgar, don't be shy.... They don't bite, any of 'em.... Mater, this is Edgar Waring, Old Man Bateman's nephew. It's his first trip out here, and we're going to be working together for his uncle. Have you seen him around, by the way? He's supposed to be meeting Edgar...."

As everybody was introduced, Edie looked up at the newcomer's face and found herself staring into the steady blue eyes of the handsomest man she had ever seen in her life.

"Yes, it was a stroke of luck, wasn't it?" Robert was saying, helping himself to another slice of cake. "He's a jolly decent chap, too. We had a marvelous time on board...."

The members of the Thaxter household were hanging on Robert's every word. He had returned so tall, so grown-up, so *guapo*, as Rosita whispered to Edie. No wonder Horace Bateman had picked him out on his trip to England of the year before.... You could see he had the makings of a man of the world.... The Thaxter family fairly burst with pride.

Robert told them all about his chance meeting with Edgar Waring at dinner on the first night out on board ship; the two young men met and discovered they were destined to work together, the one as Bateman's nephew, the other as his choice, both in the main offices of the long-established and prestigious firm that spanned the ocean they were about to cross. Edgar, it turned out, had worked in the Bateman

90

offices in London, but had never been out to the Argentine before.

"I've promised to show him the ropes, introduce him around, that sort of thing. You'll be seeing a lot of him. . . . And by the way, Mater, I've asked him to have dinner with us next week. . . ."

Mrs. Thaxter, pouring her son another cup of tea, murmured it would be quite all right, and what did he think Mr. Waring would like?

Robert waved a generous hand. "Oh, anything, Mater, anything. . . . I'm sure you'll do us all proud. . . . And you two girls are not to frighten him by being forward or too pert."

The idea sent Dollie into a fit of giggles and Edie into a brown study after teatime was over. Then there was more chatter about England, and all the things Robert had seen and done while in London, and both the girls sat, listening raptly, to the tales he told.

Everything became more lively for them with Robert back in B.A. Invitations poured in, friends called and were called upon in turn, and, everywhere it was possible, Robert took Edgar Waring around, so that the young foursome became a frequent social unit in the events of that spring's season. As Robert had predicted, Waring tended to be reticent during the early days of his introduction into the British community of Buenos Aires, standing back and listening far more often than offering comment.

But if Edgar Waring proved quiet on first meeting, it was this very quality of well-mannered reticence that endeared him to the community at large. There was nothing brash about him, nothing that grated on even the most susceptible of sensitivities. Old and young alike soon pronounced young Waring to be a highly welcome addition to their ranks. His standing as Horace Bateman's nephew was indisputably in his favor, but he never used it in any way that might be termed forward.

He never mentioned his horsemanship either and then, that day at the Hurlingham gymkhana, everyone was flabbergasted to see him hold his own with the best equestrians of B.A., trotting away with several ribbons no one had even thought he would challenge, and earning his place for one of the future trophies as well.

The ladies soon discovered he was a superb dancer, too, and more than one heart fluttered in his direction. He appeared unspoiled and unaware of the stir he was causing, and continued polite and charming to all, favoring none.

Robert, well-known from the days before he went to finish his education at home, was equally in demand. The days lengthened and warmed as spring changed into early summer, and the cricket matches, picnics and dances held out of doors opened up whole new vistas of social enjoyment.

Life in B.A. blossomed for Edie; gone were the dreary days with nothing to do. There was tennis to try—though she preferred watching—and rides through Palermo's bridle paths. Also amid the Palermo parks of the city of Buenos Aires were the lakes, and the lake pavilion where one could seek refreshment. There was boating, too, safe and guarded, all within the confines of the formal lake in the park, and ducks to feed at the water's edge, and balloons from the vendor strolling by, and the company of the young and eager, like herself, though always chaperoned by someone reliable, of course.

A parent or a companion or a governess: there was always a sobering influence around. Edie tried to persuade the Thaxters that Rosita could be adjudged reliable, but her argument proved fruitless.

"Absolutely out of the question. . . ."

Not because she was young, but because she was a native servant, Edie was told.

Arranging for chaperones was all part of the social fabric, and Mrs. Thaxter often accompanied the girls on their outings. She and her husband were also in demand for many of the balls and parties, and at one, given out under Japanese lanterns and an early December sky, Canon and Mrs. Thaxter watched with pride and enjoyment as their son, their daughter, Mr. Bateman's nephew, and their charge danced and changed partners and danced again, the girls filling the programs hanging by slender gold chains from their wrists, the two young men courteous and dashing and much in evidence as leaders in their crowd.

Robert waltzed by with Edie, smiling at his parents over her shoulder as he saw them. Shortly thereafter, Dollie's blond curls bobbed into view; Edgar was leading her with practised ease through the dancers. Mrs. Thaxter caught her daughter's eye and waved; Dollie disengaged her hand from Edgar's and waved back.

Mrs. Thaxter gave a satisfied sigh. Dollie was such a pretty girl. . . . A thought struck her and she turned to her husband.

"Do you suppose it might be a double wedding?" she whispered.

"Hush, Bessie. Someone might hear you." But Dr. Thaxter was beaming.

His wife lowered her voice still further, and continued her dream.

"Would you be allowed to give both brides away?"

"What? One on each arm?" His tone was jocular. "No, I'm afraid not, m'dear . . . what strange notions you do have. . . ."

"Think how . . ."

"No, no, Bessie, it simply isn't done. Of course, a double ceremony . . ."

"It *would* be nice, wouldn't it?"

"Indeed." He took out his pocket watch. "I think it is time we think about going home."

"Oh, don't interrupt them now. . . . They're all dancing . . . so nicely . . . and I *would* like . . ."

"Well . . ." He replaced his watch. "Perhaps a few more minutes. . . ."

Far be it from him to rush things if plans were going well.

Christmas Day. It had dawned hot and clear and would no doubt be a scorcher.

"*. . . and unto you a King is born . . .*"

Edie shifted in the pew and thought she might explode with heat and impatience. Dr. Thaxter was droning on and on. There was no point in listening to what he was saying; she had heard it all before, over the past week, as he intoned the sentences at mealtimes, preparatory to delivering them officially. The best escape was to let her thoughts wander; if she did that, perhaps she would forget about the stifling air in the church.

"*. . . a King . . .*"

God—but the Pater was a windy old bore . . . even worse than the headmaster at school. And this heat . . . Robert edged a finger between his neck and his collar. If it went on much longer, he'd have a rash all the way up to his chin from the chafing.

He saw Edie fidgeting in the pew in front and wished that he were sitting next to her, so he could catch her eye, and wink, and perhaps make her start, or at least blush. She was such a pretty little thing, and so easy to tease; with a little

93

shaping up here and there, he knew he could turn her into a good wife. He was fond of her, too; they would make an excellent match. Both his parents said so, and for all that the Pater was a bore in the pulpit, he certainly knew what was what when it came to Edie's financial affairs, being one of her trustees and fully aware of all that her fortune entailed.

Another six months, and Robert would propose. His parents had agreed the timing would be perfect. Then he would be set for life, and an eventual partnership in Bateman's was sure to be his.

In the meantime, there was lots of fun and games to be had palling around with Edgar. Gad—but he was a devil of a fellow! Dreamed up larks like nobody Robert had ever met before. Paid for 'em, too. Most generous fellow—always looking for a good time. And none of the stuffed shirts would ever suspect it, either; he was so quick about it. Why, it'd set the Pater's head spinning if he as much as suspected some of the things Robert had been up to lately, led and mostly financed by Edgar. Old Man Bateman was also in the dark. Just as well, too. . . .

"... *who taught us to pray and to say* ..."

The congregation's voice joined the minister's as one, and Edie, her murmur mechanical in the Lord's Prayer, gave mental thanks for the sermon's end, noting simultaneously that the things to be truly thankful for were so often in total contradiction to the precepts preached by the likes of Dr. Thaxter.

A month into the new year, Dollie was asked to be a bridesmaid, so pinnings and fittings got underway when the seamstress arrived at the house.

"Three times a bridesmaid, never a bride," observed Edie, standing by with the pincushion, while Mrs. Thaxter busied about, assisting the dressmaker.

"It's only the second . . ."

"*And* you were a flower girl . . ."

"That doesn't count, does it, Ma?"

"Yes, it does," Edie said, enjoying Dollie's discomfiture.

"No, it . . ."

"Girls, girls," admonished Mrs. Thaxter. She and the seamstress were circling around Dollie like wary wolves, the pins lined along the hem of the dress their immediate target of inspection. "*Do* stop pecking at each other." She pounced on a pin and moved its position. "Turn around, dear. Let me see the back. . . ."

The discussion moved to the betrothed couple.

"She's marrying very well, isn't she?"

"Yes, indeed. His father has a big camp up in Misiones."

"I heard someone say they think she's too young. D'you think she is, Mamma?"

"I was already married when I was her age," came the smug reply.

"My mamma was even younger when she married Papa."

"So she was, the poor dear." Mrs. Thaxter gave Edie a commiserating smile before turning her attention back to the pins and fabric.

"*I* think nineteen is a very good age to get engaged or married," said Dollie, who had recently celebrated that birthday.

"Well, I was eighteen, and everybody said I was a lovely bride..." Mrs. Thaxter's voice faded into her efforts at correcting the silk's fall over her daughter's hips, and the conversation went no further.

Its content, however, fell on furrowed, fertile ground; one seed bore its fruit of fantasy that evening.

"Do you know," said Mrs. Thaxter to her husband, "I think our Dollie sees marriage on the horizon?"

"Does she, indeed?"

"Yes." And Bessie Thaxter proceeded to repeat the conversation of the morning. ". . . and there was something about the way she said it that made me think about it later . . ."

"I suppose it is young Waring?"

"I don't see who else she could be thinking of. It *would* be nice, wouldn't it?"

"Yes, indeed." A pause. "Yes, yes . . . most suitable. *Most*. And now, my dear, since it is late, do you think I might have my customary cup of milk?"

Apologizing, Mrs. Thaxter scurried off to get it; her husband leaned back against the pillows of the bed, smiling and satisfied with the ways of life.

"Edie, do you feel all right?"

"Yes. Why?"

"Because I've asked you twice to pass the gravy, and I don't think you've as much as been aware that I spoke at all."

Edie blushed and passed the gravy boat to Mrs. Thaxter.

"I'm sorry, Aunt Bessie. I must have been woolgathering again...."

"She's been like that for weeks. Months. Ever since about Christmas," Dollie observed. "I'd like another potato, please."

Edie gave her a sharp look along with the dish of vegetables. The meal continued in momentary silence. Then:

"When's Robert coming back?" Edie wanted to know. "He promised me he'd go and visit Mrs. O'Connor while he's in Rosario, and I do so hope she'll send me a letter with him...."

The Thaxters exchanged amused glances, which Edie affected not to notice. After the girls had left the table, Canon Thaxter observed to his wife that he felt sure Edie's absent-minded malaise was nothing more serious than a case of love.

"You mark my words, Bessie, all her woolgathering will be over the moment our Robert pops the question...."

The light tap on the door made Canon Thaxter look up from his desk. Edie was standing in the doorway.

"May I come in?"

"Yes, of course, my dear."

"There's something I wanted to ask you... if you're not too busy."

The clergyman rose and pulled a nearby chair closer to him. He had long finished his work for the day, but his evening ritual of repairing to the study after the meal had been sacrosanct ever since the first days of his marriage.

"I am sure whatever you want to talk about must be most important indeed," he said, putting papers together with great show and emphasis, closing a ledger with elaborate care. "My business matters can wait until I have heard all about it. Sit down, my dear, sit down. Tell me all about it."

Edie did not sit down, but came close to the front of his desk, moving slightly from one foot to the other as she began to speak. Poor child; she was so nervous. Dr. Thaxter sat down again and waited for her to gain a modicum of composure.

"It's about... about... well, it's because my own Papa is dead..." she started off, twisting the handkerchief she held in her hands. "And as I have no family of my own at all... my aunts are too far away, and anyway, I don't think an aunt is the proper person to... er, I mean, if I had an uncle... but..."

"Go on," the clergyman encouraged.

"Well, I wanted to ask you, is it all right ... would it be ..."
Then, all in a rush: "I think my secret intended is going to
ask you to grant my hand in marriage."

Canon Thaxter looked up at her and beamed.

"Well, well—this is indeed a lovely surprise! What marvelous news ... our little Edie to be a bride ..."

The blush tinted her whole face, her downcast eyes fring-
ing halfmoons against it.

"And I shall be delighted to perform the happy task of
granting your hand, one in which I know your poor father
would have taken much pride ..."

"Thank you ..." It was little more than a whisper.

"... and now we'll have to start thinking of making all
sorts of plans, won't we?" He rose, still beaming, and made
his way around the desk to take Edie's arm and escort
her to the door. "A nice wedding—nothing ostentatious, I
know, you wouldn't like that, but with all the details properly handled ... you can trust Aunt Bessie to take care of
that ..."

At the door, he said with a conspiratorial smile, "... and I
know that you and Robert will be ideally happy. ..."

Edie stepped backward into the passageway, her eyes
round and wide, her expression blank.

"Robert?" she puzzled. "It's got nothing to do with Robert....
It's Edgar who wants to marry me ... Edgar Waring ... and
he's coming to call on you tomorrow, for my hand. ..."

"... but why didn't you tell any of us? You didn't even tell
it to Dollie ... your closest friend ... or me ... haven't I been
as close to you as though you were my own daughter...?"

"Because," Edie started explaining again, patience under-
lining every word, "because Edgar made me promise not to.
He had to speak to his uncle, first. It's all very complicated,
and I'm sure he'll tell you all about it if you ask him when
he arrives, but you know what a difficult man Mr. Bateman
can be ... and how he paid Edgar's passage out here, and ..."

The Thaxters did not want explanations. They wanted
divine justice, blood, revenge, a backtracking of time, a
change of scenery, a holiday, air, to forget, to wipe out—
anything but this prostrating turn of events none of them had
bargained for.

Dollie's nose was a round red blob from crying.

"Not even *me* ... why didn't you tell *me* ...? Me sharing

my bedroom and everything with you..." sobs choked her. "You're a sneak, and horrid, and I hate you!"

"But why?"

"Because—oh, you've made me look such a fool!"

"No, I haven't..."

"Yes, you have—everyone in B.A.'ll say that they knew, and I didn't..."

"No, they won't." Edie stood firm. "*Nobody* knew."

"That's a lie!"

"No, it isn't."

"Yes, it is—I'll bet Rosita knew...."

Edie said nothing. Dollie stopped crying in her triumph.

"*There*. You see? I was right. Rosita *did* know—all the time. You'd rather tell your biggest secrets to an Argentine, an Argentine *maid*, than to me or my Ma..."

The clashes continued.

"But you're so *young*..." Mrs. Thaxter wrung her hands.

"I'll be nineteen very soon."

"That's what I mean..."

"You told us eighteen or nineteen was a perfect time to get married," Edie said, her steady gaze level.

Mrs. Thaxter looked away.

"...and you were already married when you were my age..."

Mrs. Thaxter changed course.

"You hardly know each other..."

"It was love at first sight..."

"What nonsense!"

"Ask Edgar!" Edie's temper flashed. "He says the same thing! And I *am* going to marry him—I am! And what's more, Mr. Bateman says..."

Not all the clashes occurred in Edie's hearing.

"A fine kettle of fish! And all because you wanted to bide your time...."

Robert, sullen in his anger, said, "I had no idea..."

"Well, you should have!" exploded his father. "He was supposed to be your friend..."

"He was. Is. Er—I mean..."

"You don't know what you mean, and you certainly didn't know what he was doing, did you?"

"Not about Edie, no sir, I didn't. But—well, you know, Pater, Waring's not all he's cracked up to be... there are certain things..."

"What things? And how do they affect this most unfortunate state of affairs?"

Robert considered before replying.

"They... well... no... no... I don't suppose they matter..."

"Then for heavens' sake, don't waste my time about them! I've had to listen to quite enough nonsense today..."

Robert stormed out of the study, only to bump into Edie in the front hall. He took her by the arm and pulled her toward the dining room.

"Listen, Edie—I've got to talk to you. You're making a huge mistake. Take it from me... think of me as a brother... Edgar is not the man for you..."

"Oh?"

"No, he's not... he's... he's not really a very nice chap at all..."

"I thought you considered him a good friend..."

"I do, I do... it has nothing to do with me.... I'm thinking of you...."

Edie pulled away from him and laughed.

"Don't laugh, Edie—he's pretty underhand... I know..."

"You mean he fooled you by not telling you he's in love with me."

"No, not that... there are other things. Edie, I beg of you, don't marry Edgar Waring. He's not..."

"I *am* going to marry Edgar. And what other things are you talking about?"

"Edgar has... does... Edie, it's impossible to talk to you about such matters..."

"Then I'm sure you'd like to talk to his uncle about them." Edie smiled sweetly and walked toward the door. "Mr. Bateman has his office just down the hall from yours, I believe? Edgar told me he did. Perhaps you'd like to go and complain to him..."

"Edie! You know I can't... my job... my whole future..."

"Then why don't you—and your whole family—simply mind your own business? You're such nosey-parkers, all four of you!" She flounced out the door.

Robert, recognizing defeat, kicked the leg of the dining room table.

Canon Thaxter also knew when he was beaten.

"... there was nothing else I *could* do, Bessie—nothing. The rotter had already spoken to his uncle before he came to

99

see me—to say nothing of spreading the word all over B.A. What on earth was I to do except be as gracious as possible and accept the whole thing..."

"Perhaps you could...perhaps there's still time..."

"To do what?"

"Speak to him..."

"Speak to whom? Waring?"

"No, no...suppose you have a talk with Mr. Bateman..."

"And what in Hades do you expect me to say to him?" roared the irate minister. "Tell him I want Edie to marry my son instead of his nephew? After he's told his cronies he's most pleased with the affair? Oh—a pretty fool I'd look, wouldn't I, my dear? A pretty fool..."

Mrs. Thaxter sobbed into her handkerchief.

"I don't think I can bear it...just as I thought everything was going to work out so nicely..."

"Well, you'll have to bear it—and quickly, too. I don't want to be made a fool of by my own family...although I must say I think you're trying rather hard..."

"Ohhh...don't..."

"And stop that confounded blubbing! Pull yourself together, Bessie, you're an absolute disgrace! And bear in mind that Horace Bateman is our son's employer. Robert's future rests in his hands. Perhaps that thought will keep you from spouting a lot of rubbish. And now, if you'll bring me my cup of milk..."

Dabbing her eyes, Bessie Thaxter complied.

Canon Thaxter, having capitulated, turned his clerical coat with ease, seeing the many advantages and exactly where they lay. To be closely linked to Horace Bateman...now, there was an interesting proposition indeed. Edie's age might allow her to marry, but she still could not have full control of her financial affairs. The law was the law, no matter what the country. There would still have to be a certain amount of legal maneuvering and financial accommodation until she reached her majority at the age of twenty-two.

No doubt Edgar, already in his mid-twenties and about to become her husband, would take a full share in the administration of her capital and property. But there were laws and bylaws to be explained, legal niceties to be followed.

The bride's guardian should certainly discuss all these matters with the bridegroom's uncle, long before the young couple tied the knot. The more he pondered it, the more Canon Thaxter recognized the sagacity of the approach: two men of mature judgment would be of immeasurable aid to the youthful pair.

He would arrange to see Horace Bateman privately as soon as he possibly could.

Canon and Mrs. Thaxter are pleased to announce the betrothal of their ward, Miss Edith Ida Moore, to Mr. Edgar Geoffrey Waring, son of Mrs. Gerald Waring of London, and the late Mr. Waring, and nephew of Mr. Horace Bateman of Buenos Aires....

"...and I understand the wedding's to take place before the winter's out. They *are* rushing things, aren't they?"

"You'd think there'd been a scandal..."

"...*was* trouble of some sort in London...never heard anything definite...just rumors...Old Man Bateman's eager to see Waring settled..."

"Money can hide anything..."

"Still, it's a surprise. I'd always thought little Edie had her cap set for Robert..."

"Perhaps it was the Thaxters who'd set their caps for Edie's fortune..."

"...just goes to show...the best laid plans of mice and men..."

"Especially church mice..."

The tongues of the British community rattled in enjoyable speculation.

None of it touched Edie at all.

Her splendid secret published at last, she basked and glowed in the warmth of love, community attention, and total success. Edgar was wonderful, the future was rosy, all would be well in her own private world. The clouds and tears were gone and spent; life and happiness lay ahead. There was nothing to stop her any more and, with Edgar at her side, there was nothing to fear.

Everybody said they were a marvelous match, even Edgar's cantankerous uncle. Mr. Bateman had pronounced her charming; a perfect choice, he had said, for his nephew. He had then gone down to the vault at the bank and picked out a sapphire ring, once the property of his late wife, a lady

101

deceased so early in their marriage that no one in Buenos Aires could remember her at all.

Edgar slipped it on Edie's finger and both were delighted with the perfect fit. At night, Edie refused to take it off, waking in the dark hours to feel it pressing on her finger, a token of safety, of a journey done. It hadn't been easy, keeping the secret until Edgar had deemed it safe to reveal; if it hadn't been for Rosita delivering notes back and forth between them, and being the perfect confidante to both, Edie didn't know how she would have managed.

Not that life with the Thaxters had been pleasant since the news had shocked them into tears and exhortations; the men had calmed down about it relatively soon, but Dollie and Mrs. Thaxter were still edgy and cool. Well, it would soon be over, and she and Edgar would have a house of their own, and a splendid life starting: Mr. Bateman had already promised he would help them find the right place to live.

As to Edgar, he was almost too good to be true and yet true he was, right there before her, the embodiment of her dream. His blue eyes, the gentle wave of his pale russet hair, sweeping back from his thin white forehead, his courteous manners, everything about him was enough to make any girl swoon. Edie was sure every girl in B.A. envied her, either openly or in secret; she knew Dollie did, no matter how much Miss Thaxter tried to deny it, but Edgar would never have looked twice at Dollie. Never. He had told Edie he thought Dollie looked remarkably like a porker in frills.

"Edie!"

"Yes, Aunt Bessie?"

"The dressmaker's here."

"Coming..."

There was so much to do, so much to prepare....

Floating on happiness, Edie sailed out of the room to be fitted for her wedding gown.

8

Her wedding gown lay, carefully folded, over the stand in the hotel dressing room beyond the closed door. Edie, pale with emotion and exhaustion, lay back against the pillows and closed her eyes. Edgar had said he would be in any moment;

she so wanted to talk to him and ask him what he'd thought of it all. They'd scarcely had a moment of privacy in the hours since they had exchanged their vows; it had all been toasts and speeches and dancing and congratulations...

The sound of the door made her open her eyes. Edgar was in the doorway, looking at her. Edie smiled and blushed; he was going to come over and sit next to her, and hold her hands in his, and kiss her fingertips, one by one, as he had the evening he had proposed, and...

"Take it off."

Edie's eyes widened. He had not moved, and was still looking at her, almost sternly, she noted in surprise.

"I said, take it off." Edgar waved a gesture. "Your nightgown. All those frills and furbelows. I want them off. Let's have a proper look at you."

She sat quite still.

"Well—go on."

Her throat was closing. "I—I can't," she whispered.

"What d'you mean, you can't?"

"I haven't anything on underneath..."

Edgar laughed.

"No, of course you haven't, you silly nincompoop. We're long past the days of chastity belts and chain mail. Now, do hurry up and get a move on. Get out of that confounded shroud."

Shroud? Her beautiful nightgown, made especially for her wedding night, with all the lace and embroidery, a shroud? What on earth had come over Edgar?

He strode over to the bed, and as she saw his hand stretch out toward her, she shrank back, suddenly afraid. He grabbed the froth of lace at her neck.

"Would you rather I ripped it off?" He said it pleasantly enough, which made her all the more confused. Tears were beginning to well into her eyes.

"No, Edgar...please...what's the matter? I don't understand..."

"Don't be silly, Edie. This is what marriage is for." Another laugh. "At least, that's what women are for. Now: are you going to do as I say, or do I start pulling...like this...?"

"No...no...I'll do it..."

Edie fell back against the pillows the moment he let go. She pulled the bedsheet up to her neck and fumbled for the tiny buttons on her bodice. Her fingers would hardly do

103

as she bade them, she was shaking so. If only Edgar would stop looking at her...

He began rubbing his hands across his lower abdomen, where his dressing gown had fallen open, and all of a sudden Edie became aware of the bloated red protuberance sticking out from between the material and looking for all the world like a monstrous drumstick, bereft of its chicken skin, and raw. Edgar noticed her staring.

"Nice one, don't you think?" he remarked conversationally. "Better women than you have gone mad over it. You will, too, once you've had a taste of what it can do for you." He held it loosely, sliding his hand up and down as he talked. "Ahh... that's better..."

Not knowing where to look, Edie began pushing her nightgown down off her shoulders with one hand, bunching the sheet up under her chin with the other. Edgar reached over and pulled the sheet to one side. The uncovering felt like a slap.

"Well, they're small, but I always knew that."

His hand was startling against her breasts; they hardened and sent their pink points against the palm of his hand.

"There. You see? You like it already..."

She did *not* like it... she didn't like it at all... if only Edgar would stop rubbing her like that... rubbing himself like that.... She was trembling so violently she could hardly breathe.... It was useless to try and say anything... this all had to do with the horrid side of the way things were, the awful secrets Mamma had hinted at all those long years ago when Edie had bled for the first time and Mamma had told her it was going to happen once a month for all her life until she was very old except when she was going to have a baby. Edie did not want a baby, but she knew she might have to have one because she was married. And Edgar was tearing at the sheets and at her gown and smearing his wet mouth all over her body and—oh, the horrible shame of it!—he had uncovered her completely... was putting his hand *there*...

"Ah! You *have* got a quims... I was beginning to fear you were unnatural..."

He was laughing at her again with that peculiar, high-pitched laugh she had never heard before.

"Oh! Ow! Don't..."

His teeth nipped at her breast, her arm, her breast again.

"Oh, for God's sake, Edie..."

"Edgar . . . stop . . . please . . . you're hurting . . ."

"You'll get used to it, my girl. All women do. You'll soon be at the point where you can't have enough of it. Here. See?"

He pushed his swollen member against her.

"Isn't it magnificent?" he crowed, crushing down with his hand.

Edie shuddered.

"Ahhh, there's a good girl . . . you're getting the idea. . . . Hot as a whore, I'll bet, once you get started . . . wonder if you're even a virgin . . ."

She gasped in pain. His hands were doing terrible things down there . . . down there where she had hardly ever dared look, in all her life . . . and now Edgar was pushing his fingers into her and pulling apart and digging so that the piercing of knives was biting . . .

"Stop . . . oh, please . . . do stop . . ."

Her sobs were open and loud now. She tried pushing him away, but he seemed to be everywhere, his hands, slimy mouth, biting teeth, his arms bands holding her down, constricting her, forcing her, bending her this way and that. . . . No words of supplication could get through the rising grunts and savage sounds Edgar was making; he mauled and tore at her all over her body, seizing her by the hair and pulling her head to one side, biting into her neck and shoulder, switching his mouth further down, then rising to pin her onto the mattress with the stabbing force of his full weight, his hands groping at her thighs, pushing, pulling.

"Spread them, damn you, Edie . . . spread 'em wider . . ."

Another rough grasp of his hands and then the simultaneous thrust of something piercing deeply into her and his body hammering against her. She shrieked in pain and fright. His hand clamped down on her mouth.

"Shut up . . . this has to happen the first time . . ."

A sudden fierce pain sliced inside her.

"Done . . ."

But the pounding went on, the tearing fire spread so far she felt her whole body being torn, abused. Edgar gave a high, harsh cry: he shuddered, collapsing over her to lie there, panting, spent. Presently, he coughed: heaving himself off with a push to the center of the bed, he lay next to her, but turned away, until the paroxysm had passed. Then he turned and lay on his back, his eyes closed, ignoring Edie.

She did not move, her pain and fright too great to do

anything but lie there immobile. As the searing sensation abated, she realized there was sticky wetness between her legs, on her thighs. The throbbing soreness that remained twitched sharp stabs upwards into her stomach when she tried to move in an effort to get away from the sodden patch on the sheet. Still and staring, she lay there, wordless, waiting for her breath to return, waiting for Edgar to say something, waiting for the end of the world, waiting...

Long after Edgar's breath had become snoring, Edie lay awake, her tears dried, her flesh bruised and aching, her skin crawling with revulsion and disgust. Blood pounded in her head; she would never be able to put up with this... never. The shame of it... the disgrace.... Every twitch of pain reminded her of the revolting assault she had suffered; surely Edgar could not like behaving so?

Perhaps he only did it that way because he had to do it; it had to be done. Because they were married. Because that was the way it had to be. He'd even gasped out something about a first time in the midst of his animal behavior. Perhaps it would get better for her later on... and perhaps Edgar wouldn't do it very often, anyway....

Exhaustion dimmed the many pains; the rising tide of sleep started to wash across her eyes. If this was the way marriage had to be... Her mother's words from a distant day of the past came to her: *expect the worst, but hope for the best*....

Hoping for the best did not help.

"Of course I like it. Everybody does."

"*I* don't. I *hate* it."

"You'll get used to it, my dear, and grow to like it, just wait and see. Now, come and bring your rump over here, let's see if you can..."

"But I don't want..."

"Edie, do I have to drag you...?"

"But I *hate* it..."

"That's unnatural."

"No, it's not... what you're doing is vile, revolting..."

Edgar laughed. "You're quite wrong there, my dear. Other women say I'm particularly good at it."

"Edgar! How dare you!"

His taunting of her knew no bounds. He took to pinching her secretly, suddenly, often when her gasp of surprise could

106

be heard by others; Edie accused him of behaving like a low-class servant.

"My dear, some servants do it rather well. Certainly better than you. I really should give Rosita a try. She looks as though she might..."

"Edgar! You wouldn't dare!"

He looked at her, his eyes glittering as they had begun to do so frequently since the wedding.

"I most certainly would... if she tempted me enough. But there's better to be had elsewhere, so perhaps I shan't bother. For the moment..."

In public, he was the perfect husband, courteous and attentive as ever.

Through her tears, Edie sobbed, "If you really loved me, you wouldn't make me do all these disgusting things..."

"Nobody's talking about love, you romantic ninny."

The shock transmogrified her mood.

"Then you don't love me." Ice touched her spine. "You never did..."

Edgar's answer disappeared into his habitual cough. Edie waited for him to stop, a vital question ready.

"If you don't love me, why did you want to marry me?"

"Why would anyone want to marry you? For your money, of course."

"But you didn't know. You started courting me the very first day we were introduced... no, don't say I'm a ninny, or imagining things, you did. I remember it very well. The way you smiled... the way you held my hand... longer than you should... squeezing it..."

"But I did know. I knew all about you and your fortune. Had it all planned how I'd court you and marry you, long before we met. Dear old Robert spilled the beans. He would, wouldn't he? No sooner had we set sail from Southampton than he started boasting about how he was going to marry an heiress and live happily and richly ever after. It was all set, he said." Edgar leered at her. "Or didn't you know he wanted to marry you?"

Barely perceptibly, Edie nodded.

"And I decided I'd see to it that I got you, and not Robert, no matter what you looked like. My dear, I'd have married you even if you'd turned out to look like the south end of a cow going north. Which, right now, you rather do. Splotched cheeks and all."

Instead of reacting as she usually did to his jibes, Edie went on looking at him without changing her expression.

"Robert's really a perfectly dreadful chap, don't you think?" Edgar continued conversationally. "No? Nothing to say about him? Well, I do. All piss and wind, and very little to back it. Like father, like son. Just think of it, Edie: if I hadn't turned up, you might have married Robert." After a pause: "No, you *would* have married him, I'm sure. You were just at the right age and stage." He laughed. "And the Thaxters swallowed it whole: my friendship, your loyalty ... The fools. They're all fools and, like it or not, Edie, you and I are quite a pair."

Edie acknowledged he was right about the Thaxters. They *were* fools, all four of them. But that wasn't going to help her now.

Later, Edgar informed her he was going to be absent from the house for several days.

"Use any excuse you care to, should anyone inquire as to my whereabouts," he said, adding, "but, in case you're interested ..."

"I'm not."

"... I shall be spending my time at *Doña* Gloria's, where the girls know how to ... er ... care and take care ..."

Still Edie said nothing.

"I am, in fact, going to take over the establishment. With *your* money, my love—now so delightfully mine to share." He bowed. "The place is to be mine, for the next few days, to do as I like. No customer allowed in, unless by my invitation. As you may guess, I'm to be most popular among the lads these days."

With another mock bow, he turned to go.

"And, oh, yes, I simply must tell you before I leave: our good friend Robert is sure to be there ..."

Doña Gloria counted the money, smoothing out each bill and placing it on top of the others lying next to her on the shiny pink counterpane of her bed. The coins she dropped into a leather pouch; it was a soothing routine of many years. At last, she folded the notes together, keeping out her usual nightly fee to the watchman and his cohorts. They would be coming by soon; she tucked the money into the top of her corset.

The rest was placed in the strongbox hidden beneath the floorboard under her bed. Grunting, she replaced the loose plank; the years made it increasingly difficult for her to get up off her knees. Pushing the bed back into place was also an effort: she was getting too old for physical exertion and unnecessary trouble.

The noise upstairs had dimmed; no doubt the *señor inglés* was sleeping. And about time, too; *Doña* Gloria had had enough of him for a while. It was a pity, because his money was good, but she did not want trouble.

Not that any of her clients were guaranteed to be trusted, to be without problems, to be honest or honorable. But there were different kinds of hazards in the trade, and sickness on the part of a patron was among the worst. If any man got ill while on her premises, the repercussions could be severe, and blood was blood, no matter which end it came from, and blood from a man was trouble.

The girls had told her; then she had seen for herself: smears, dark, brackish, and foul-smelling, on the pillows, on the sheets.

"Are you sure it was not you?" she questioned the little Yvette who was proving such an attraction to the free-spending Edgar Waring.

Evette swore up and down that it was not.

"Here, look, see for yourself." The girl bent forward and over, pulled up her skirt, and inserted her fingers. Then she held them out to the madam for closer inspection. "Nothing, *Doña* Gloria, nothing. No, it is *Don* Edgar, I am sure."

The watchman's whistle sounded in the distance, and *Doña* Gloria reached for her shawl. She would talk to him tonight because if *señor* Waring was beginning to break in health and in humor, they would have to find ways to discourage his visits. The easiest would be to pass him on to someone else, and the way to accomplish that was to send Yvette ahead, as bait. It would be a pity to lose the girl, of course, but she would probably be able to get her back afterwards.

The *sereno*'s whistle sounded again. *Sereno*; such a misnomer, *Doña* Gloria thought as she made her way down the narrow flight of stairs. There was nothing serene about the watchman's world of night. Perhaps the stars... They were too far away for anyone to tell. But life, whether by day or at night, was seldom, if ever, serene, in the madam's experience. If it was not one thing, it was another. She sighed,

109

reaching the last step, and crossing over the tile floor to the high front entrance.

She stood in the opening waiting for the *sereno*; through the arches of the covered sidewalk, she could see the false light of predawn reflecting in the night sky over the river beyond the docks and wharves. The air was cool with dampness; she pulled her shawl closer around her.

"Your name looks like you, Yvette, with the Y spread wide open, like your legs."

Yvette giggled, and moved again.

"Ah, *monsieur* Edgar, you make funny jokes about me always. So sweet, and so funny... and so clever..."

While she worked, Yvette's thoughts spun ahead in plan; her brief days with the traveling players had served her well. Not that she had trodden the boards in public: there were other shows connected to the troupe that had sailed from Marseilles to Buenos Aires. But her flair for mimicry and imitative powers gave her a wider range of appeal now, for it enabled her to play up to her favored client, Waring, and slip into the roles and poses he wished her to assume.

If she worked well enough, perhaps he would become a permanent protector; the house and *Doña* Gloria were not Yvette's end goal in life. If *monsieur* Edgar's pleasures bordered on *le malaise anglais*, it was only to be expected of him and his caste; they were practises she knew and understood well.

She only hoped he would not fall sick, for he could be useful, the handsome Englishman with the good position and the rich wife and the easy spending ways. With a little encouragement...

"...being far too extravagant and..."

Edgar tapped the paper in front of her with his finger.

"Suppose you let me be the judge of that, and simply do as you're told. Now sign it, Edie, and let me take it."

"But I don't think I should... I don't want to. You're spending so much money... and anyway, it's always for you and what you want."

"Ah, so that's it." He cupped her chin in his hand. "Little Edie isn't quite as generous or sweet as everyone thinks, is she? Well, what would you like? More gowns? Another hat? Rings for your fingers and bells for your toes?"

In the silence that ensued, Edgar began pacing the room.

"No, that's no way to strike a bargain with you. Your

110

wardrobe's bulging with silk and frippery. Come on, Edie, there's a good girl, tell me what your heart desires. Surely your heart desires something, even if the rest of you apparently does not? You cold little witch..."

He stopped in mid-room, a smirk touching his mouth, then widening to a full smile.

"Eureka! I have it!" He turned and faced his wife. "Suppose you sign ... and I promise not to touch you for—oh, let us say three weeks? Think of it, Edie: you can sleep undisturbed if you merely write your name ..."

An initial moment of confusion was followed by Edie's assent and signature. It set the pattern of bargaining between the young married couple from then on.

"Don't be ridiculous, Edie. Of course I'm all right."

"But your pillow was soaked through ..."

"If my natural inclinations were allowed free rein, perhaps my body would not accumulate so much heat," was the immediate reply. "Tell Rosita to remove some of the coverings from the bed. I will not be smothered ..."

Within the week, Edgar complained of the cold at night.

"It's this damned foreign climate making every bone in my body ache," he complained.

Edie glanced at the sunshine pouring in through the windows and suggested another blanket be placed on the bed. But her husband had lost interest in the subject and discussion.

"Do what you will," was his short answer; he finished dressing and reached for his hat. "I shan't be back for dinner."

Edie heard him singing long before she heard him at the door. By the time it slammed shut, thundering into the still night air, she was sitting bolt upright in bed, wide awake, trembling. For a brief instant, she considered locking him out of the bedroom, but it would be a futile move. He would probably break his way through from the dressing room; the double doors never held well in the lock.

There was a splintered crash, followed by a louder song. Edgar was offering "Auld Lang Syne" to the Buenos Aires night at the top of his lungs, his voice distorted by drink and effort, but still melodious and true. Another crash, and the singing stopped; coughing took over. The silence that followed became as threatening as any noise.

The singing began again, quieter, a lot closer. With a shuddered sigh, Edie stopped trembling; he was coming to the bedroom, and if she feigned sleep, he would only shake her until she could pretend no more, so she might as well wait for him as she was, sitting up and with her eyes open.

He fumbled the door handle several times before releasing its catch and swinging it open. He swayed with it, rocking to and fro, the lamp in his hand moving shadows across his face from beneath, distorting his features, making his grin grotesque.

"Good morning, Mrs. Waring." He leaned against the frame of the doorway, dangling the lamp from a still-swinging forefinger. "I have come to bid you a bounteous New Year. Or do I mean Christmas? Ah, yes, that's it . . . Christmas. Since it is summer in this godforsaken country of yours, I find it hard to tell . . . hard." He snickered. "Hard . . . so many things are . . ." He fumbled the front of his trousers. "Ah, well, perhaps not this very moment. The climate again, no doubt."

Keeping her voice level, Edie said, "I didn't expect you home so soon . . . so early . . ."

"Quite so, quite so." Edgar nodded in agreement, over and over again. "Didn't expect to be here myself." The mocking tone vanished, and he straightened up. "I was thrown out, Edie. Slung out on my arse. . . . I'll have her neck broken, the slut . . . that whore . . . slung out on my arse, Edie—do you hear me?"

Convinced that all the neighbors could hear him, too, she merely nodded.

"Dismissed . . . by a fat and ugly whore . . . my little girl sent away . . . Yvette . . ." his voice sank to a mumble. "Tried to find . . . somewhere else . . ."

He began moving, lurching toward the bed and grabbing the post at its foot to save himself from falling down. Edie sprang out of bed to take the lamp from his hand; he gave it without argument and slid down onto the floor, where he lay, gasping for air and then half-sobbing.

"Edgar! What is it? Are you ill?"

"Damn you, Edie, no!" He thrashed away from her concerned touch. "You and that slut . . . what a pair . . . . sent my girl away . . . must find her . . . no relief . . ."

Edie began pulling at his arms.

"Here, I'll help you . . . why don't you lie on the bed? That's right . . . lean on your side . . ."

He offered no further resistance, but allowed Edie to

struggle and pull until she had got him onto the edge of the bed, where he sat, his torso still swaying, his eyes half-closed. She had seen him in this stage before; it meant he was on the verge of sleep. There was no danger in him now.

Edie helped him lie back against the pillows and heaved his legs onto the bed.

"I'll get you in the morning," he mumbled. "And by God, you'd better perform... tomorrow..." Heavy breathing closed his sentence; within moments, there were snores.

Edie returned to bed beside him. There was no harm left in him tonight, and tomorrow he would sleep.

She soon slept again herself, unafraid.

When she woke, it was in panic, fighting against the weight pinning her down in the terrible dark. Edgar was on top of her, pounding, insisting, the hideous smell suffusing everything, slime smeared across her face. She gasped and fought, trying to push him away.

"Edgar! You promised... gave me your word..."

He wrenched her shoulder to one side, turning her over.

"Damn you and damn all women and damn all promises..."

The more she fought, the stronger he seemed to become, the more violent and vile his actions, his blows. Stunned, too exhausted to do more than let her tears roll freely, Edie closed her eyes and prayed.

Please-God-let-it-be-over-soon...

The room was light; the housekeeping sounds of early morning reached through the closed doors, but still Edgar kept on, attacking, groping, grabbing for her, pushing her across one way, around another, his grunts and cries and snarled abuse an endless torrent of violation until at last his frenzy spent its energy into her.

There was a brief stillness. Then he withdrew and rose, going through the doors to the dressing room without another word. Sick with shame, her stomach churning in disgust, Edie waited for a long while before pulling herself slowly over to one side.

When, later, she finally arose, she saw and examined the dark patches on the sheets and pillows. Knowing Edgar had left the house, she called for Rosita.

"You did *what*?"

Edgar was pale with rage, shaking, two bright pink spots forming on his cheeks as he spoke.

"How dare you, Edie... how *dare* you..."

She dodged behind a chair, avoiding his path. He paced back to the window, yanked a curtain shut, then open again. Turning to Edie, he suddenly changed tone and announced, "I'm going out."

"It won't help, Edgar. You *must* see the doctor. If you avoid him today, he'll only come tomorrow again. He said..."

"I don't want to hear what he said, the quack! There's nothing wrong with me. How can a man tell what's wrong with me by looking at a pillow?" His voice rose hysterically. "A *pillow.*"

"The sheets were also..."

"And sheets!" He broke off into high-pitched laughter. "My God—the next thing you know, he'll be saying the *bed* needs dosing! You make a fine pair, you and your medico."

"He's the best in B.A. And what's more, your uncle..."

"Don't tell me you told..."

"Yes, I did. I had to. There was no one else I could turn to."

A knock on the door interrupted them.

"*Señora* Edie, the doctor is here."

Edgar shouted, "Tell him to go away."

There was silence from Rosita on the other side of the door. Edie moved towards it, opened it and went out, telling her husband as she left, "You might as well wait for him in here..."

"Yes, Mrs. Waring, I'm afraid it is. Both you and your husband are going to have to be very brave and make a number of changes in your life."

Consumption.

Edie felt her world crumble away beneath her. Edgar was indeed terribly ill, much more so than she had even feared. He himself had taken the news very badly, the doctor informed her, had refused to listen to advice, to reason, to anything.

"...which is why I must talk to you, dear lady, and, although you are very young, I can see that you are a highly intelligent and perceptive young woman, and I am sure you want to help save your husband's life..."

There was no question of staying and living in Buenos Aires. Edgar needed a dry climate, mountains, fresh air.

114

Above all, he needed rest; bed rest at first, the doctor told her. Later, when he got stronger...

"Will he get better? Can he be cured?"

Edie surprised herself in her questioning. Her words seemed to come to her from somewhere else, from some other source. The doctor's answers were difficult, not reassuring, uneasy.

"He can be cured insofar as it is possible to combat consumption and become healthy again. Sometimes. Whether he will or not... is very much another question." The doctor sighed. "I wish I could be more definite, more positive in my views... but I do not believe in lying to those who will have to help a patient. It might make them complacent where they must be alert. Not that I am suggesting your husband's cure is entirely up to you and in your hands, of course. There is a specialist in the north..."

There were meetings, consultations, gatherings, rows. Other doctors were called in to give their opinions. Edgar wished to hear none of them. Had it not been for Horace Bateman, the furious denial might have caused even more delays, but the one person able to reach Edgar's ear and hold his attention was his uncle.

It was Bateman who applauded the doctor's suggestion of the north; he, too, had heard of the specialist.

"He's a Spanish bloke. Came out here about twenty years ago," was his comment. "Lot of newfangled ideas, and some success, too. You'd better face up to things, my boy. It's either that, or push up daisies."

Edie was glad she had gone to Horace Bateman and poured out the hideous problem. There was no one she could turn to, and no one else must know. Only Rosita knew the full story from her side. At home, the two young women stood fast against the helpless rages of the sick and struggling man; elsewhere, no outward sign was given to indicate anything was amiss. Edgar's absences from work were explained away as confidential business dealings for his uncle, while Edie busied herself with routine affairs and presented an unchanged appearance.

But word seeped out; the rumors started. Glances were cast, questions implied. Edie, pretending not to see, not to hear, found staying home easier; it was hot, she was tired, she felt exhausted from the strain.

115

Nonetheless, speculation filled the summer air.

"...shouldn't wonder at all, considering the establishments he haunts..."

"...looked a bit thin, perhaps, but then, he always was...and mark you, only the other day I saw him at..."

"...more likely her than him...mental, I'd be willing to wager."

Neither charity nor kindness blossomed for the Warings; the scoffers and the scorners were having their day.

The Spanish doctor was contacted, the arrangements made; the Warings would go and live in the foothills of the *cordillera* of the Andes until Edgar's lungs were cleared and his health regained. There was to be the packing up of the household and the opening of the new one, miles away in the northwest, where the climate, the terrain, and Dr. Ibañez would help effect the cure.

It became impossible to hide the calamity. Having dreaded the move, the departure, the journey, Edie now longed for it to be over so that she might be far away and not have to face all the eyes, the looks, the half-hidden, sorrowing smiles, whether of insincerity or genuine concern she neither knew nor cared. To get away, to fight and be free...

She and Rosita were packing household linens when the doctor, unexpectedly, came to call. She sat with him in the living room, taking note of his instructions: Edgar's diet until they were to leave, the hours he should rest, the care...

"I doubt he'll pay heed," she observed. "Nothing I say makes any difference."

The doctor shrugged. "Try. You'll be leaving soon. The train journey will tire him, and by the time you arrive, your responsibility will be over."

She promised she would do her best, rising to see the doctor to the door.

"Just a moment, Mrs. Waring..."

Edie sat down again.

"There were some questions I wanted to ask you...about yourself..."

"About me?" Puzzled, she wondered what the doctor might further demand of her; if only Edgar were easier to cope with...if only she were not so tired...

"Yes. You've been looking rather pale lately. I want to know how you've been feeling."

116

"Very tired," was the spontaneous answer.

"Yes, I would suppose so. Not sleeping well, perhaps?"

With surprise, Edie realized she had been sleeping far better of late than she had since she had got married, and for longer hours. Well, of course, she now knew Edgar wouldn't approach her, but still...

The questions continued. Edie's eyes grew round with apprehension as she heard her own answers and began recognizing the path they were tracing. Then she and the doctor both started counting. He smiled as he reached the total and a conclusion.

"...next October, I would say. Certainly before November..."

But it was not possible... Edgar hadn't... she had been on her own... Then she remembered the time he had not held to his bargain....

For the second time in as many months, Edie's future lay shattered before her.

"But what am I going to do?" Edie, heavy with the bloat of early pregnancy and despair, leaned on the kitchen table and buried her face in her hands. It was early afternoon; only Rosita remained in the kitchen, the other servants having gone to have their customary *siesta*.

If marriage had made a further distance of formality between Edie and Rosita, it had pulled them closer together in the bonds of women.

"Does it hurt very much?"

Rosita shrugged. "Marta says it is worth it. She always says that she would go through it all again, even twice, if necessary, for her Miguelito."

Edie frowned. She saw no special grace in the cook's dark-eyed boy, now learning to walk and growing steadier by the day. The thought of a similar being in the house, belonging to her, gave Edie no sense of anticipation at all. Instead, the sick feeling, the early changes in her body, the beginning distortion—above all, the heavy fear and the sprung trap weighed on her every moment and movement. Only sleep was an escape; she was tired all the time.

"Only a few days more, *señora*," consoled Rosita, putting the last of the lunch plates away. All the good china, the silver, the vast assortment of household ornaments and artifacts Edie had both inherited and been given for her marriage, everything was already packed away, and only a few everyday utensils remained. There was to be a whole new household set up in Cosunzué, the foothill town for which they were leaving the next week.

"I don't think I have the strength."

"Don't worry—I'll be there." Rosita sat down next to Edie. "You know I'm strong—and you will be too, you wait and see, *señora*. All your strength will come back when we get to the good mountain air."

The train left at night; it would take more than two days to travel to the distant province, and even then their journey would not be over. At the station, they would be met by a patrol of *carretas*, to carry them and their household goods to their abode.

With each tug of the engine, Edie felt her insides lurching back against the seat. She was sick through and through, sick inside her heart, her stomach, her soul. There was no end to the misery, no hope of any sort. Edgar, sullen on the seat in front of her and refusing to say a word, was her fate.

They would be stopping in Rosario on the way; Edie saw her path as strewn with unhappy remembrance. She closed her eyes and leaned her head against the window, too heart-sick, too tired and far too defeated to be able to loosen a tear and cry.

A bitter taste began seeping into her mouth; she was afraid that, before long, she was going to vomit again.

II

El Naranjal
1911–1914

1

Yvonne plunged her chubby fist into the water and watched it change the pattern of wiggling shadows on the rippled, pebble-scattered riverbed. From her squatting position on the slight outcropping of rocks, their surfaces already warmed by the sun, she could reach into the water without getting her shoes wet. Her hand not only changed the shadow patterns; it changed the noise, too; the bubbles' song was different. The river noise, as a whole, remained the same; it took bigger things than her four-year-old fist to alter it.

There was a splash further out. Yvonne squinted, catching a glimpse of something silvery dropping back into the water. Could it have been a fish? She could almost hear her mother's voice saying, "Well, I don't know, Yvonne . . . of course it's possible, but not very probable." Mami often said that, and it confused Yvonne, because possible and probable were so close together she couldn't see any difference. But perhaps it *had* been a fish . . .

Tiring of the shadow game, Yvonne moved ahead to look at the pools, the water-filled crevices where the snails were, a few yards further on. She glanced back at Ña Conce, sitting near the other rocks, the washing rocks, where on other days the women congregated to slap the clothes clean against the flat, smooth surfaces. Ña Conce, her red poncho tossed aside and her cheroot puffing smoke past the rim of her round-topped hat, was sitting on the bank with two baskets and a sack in front of her, plucking chickens. She put the feathers in the sack every time she got a handful off a dead bird. Later, Yvonne knew, Ña Conce would divide them up, and some would be made into *plumero*-dusters and others would be used to stuff pillows after they were washed.

If she wanted to make different ripples in the water, Yvonne could always go and ask for a long wing feather; the current made it vibrate in her hand, and she could trace patterns both in the water and on the surface below. But right now, she wanted to see the snails.

There were knots of them on the flat-bladed reeds, tiny bunches like opalescent berries clinging to the gently swaying plants. Everything moved much more slowly in the pools, where the river's rush was toned down to the occasional eddies sent through the side channels and into the protected places behind the rocks.

Yvonne bent down to take a closer look; she loved seeing the transparent snails. Their shells had colors like rainbows when the light shone through them, they were so thin. Carefully, she moved the reeds so as to catch the sunlight in the right position.

"Yvonne!"

The call came over the river noise. Yvonne scrambled to her feet. Ña Conce had heard the voice too, and was looking over her shoulder toward the house.

"Your mami's calling you, *niña* Yvonne..."

But Yvonne was already on her way, trudging through the clumps of grass. She reached smoother ground under the orange trees and began threading her way through them. Sometimes she ran a zigzag course, making her path to the house almost twice as long, but today was a straight to the house day, she could tell from the sound of Mami's voice.

"Yvonne!"

"I'm here, Mami..."

She broke into a trot and reached the kitchen door, where her mother was standing, a bowl in her hand.

"Lunch is almost ready. Go and say good morning to your father, then wash your hands and go to the table..."

There had been a time, when Yvonne was not as big as she was now, that she had thought Papi's name was Yourfather, all in one, and she had not understood why he had always laughed when she called him that. He never laughed when she called him Papi, and one day she had asked him why.

"Ah, my little heart—you're such a solemn child, Yvonne," he had said. "I hope you learn to laugh when you grow up."

But stubbornly, insistently, she had wanted to know.

"But why...?"

He had capitulated, nodding.

"You're quite right, my little heart—you should know all these things, shouldn't you? Very well. We'll have a name lesson, shall we?"

And Yvonne had smiled, and sighed with pleasure, because Papi's lessons were very interesting, no matter what they were about. And so she began learning all about names.

There were real names and nicknames and surnames and English names. There were Spanish names, and names that went into both languages, like Mary and Maria. But her name, Yvonne, was all different and all special: it was French, Papi said, and always stayed the same, no matter who said it or in what language.

And Papi was her father, but she could call him Papi if that was what felt most comfortable, and it did, but from then on she knew how to separate the *your* from the *father* in Mami's voice. And Mami was her mother, and had several names of her own, besides, plus a married name plus a shortened name, plus *señora* when the servants spoke to her, just as Yvonne had *niña* as a name for the servants, too.

Another one with a shortened name was Ña Conce, Yvonne discovered. She had started off as *Doña* Concepción, the *doña* part being like Mami's *señora*, except Ña Conce was older. Much older—she was a wise old Indian woman with a lot of grandchildren and a collection of plants called *yuyos* that made tonics and medicines for everybody when the seasons changed or when you had to rush to the potty the whole time because you had eaten something bad.

Now that she was bigger and could understand more things, Papi had even given her a lesson on the alphabet and how to count up to a hundred. When he was well, they would sit together on the chairs kept specially for them on the sunny patio, the one where the wind did not reach and they could look at the brown hills and sometimes see the high ones beyond. Papi told her that many of the Indians came from over there, the ones with the round hats, who wore one hat on top of another to show they were richer than somebody who only had one hat. Papi thought that was very funny, and laughed; Yvonne thought it was interesting, and smiled.

"Ah, my solemn little heart..."

And the very best of all was when Papi taught her songs, and they would sing together. There was "Sing a Song of Sixpence," and Papi showed her a coin that wasn't at all like a *centavo,* and she would hold it in her hand as she sang. There was "Ring a Ring o' Roses," which had a little dance to it, Papi said, but he never got out of his chair to dance. There were other songs, too, and Yvonne loved them all. Singing them with Papi were the best times.

The worst was when he was not well, and didn't come out onto the patio but stayed in his room with the door closed and only Mami was allowed in with special drinks and the doctor. Yvonne liked Dr. Ibañez. He was kind when he spoke to her, and sometimes brought her *alfajores*, but Mami said she was only to eat them outside and after lunch, because they made a mess of crumbs all over her pinafore and the floors.

If Yvonne went to eat them in the clear part between the orange trees and the river, the birds would come and find the crumbs. Yvonne would watch, from a distance, her mouth still sticky and sweet with the *alfajores'* last traces; the birds would peck away at the place she had been standing, finding the crumbs amid the dust and stones. Those stones were tiny and jagged, not like the smooth river pebbles she liked to collect.

She had some now in the pocket of her pinny; she would show them to Papi and see if he liked them.

She found him sitting in his chair by his bedroom window, and he had on his favorite pajamas. They were Yvonne's favorites, too, the ones with the stripes in two different kinds of blue coloring. Blue was her favorite color, as it was Papi's.

Papi went everywhere in his pajamas. Not that he went many places; apart from his room and the sunny patio, he very seldom went anywhere else in the house. Occasionally, he would accompany Yvonne down to the river, but for that, he put his dressing gown over his pajamas, and changed his slippers for some black boots he never wore at any other time. He hadn't done that for a long time, though, just as he hadn't come into the dining room for ages. Before, when he sometimes joined them in there for lunch, he also wore his pajamas, and so Yvonne thought it was all right to wear nightclothes in there. But the day Mami found her wandering around in her nightie, playing under the table with her small tin tea set, Yvonne got a smack on her bottom and told never to do that again.

Papi didn't smack; he very seldom even scolded, and when he did, it was more telling Yvonne what she should do, rather than what she should not. He always explained, and she always listened.

"Ah, there's my little heart," he greeted her as she entered the room. "The only girl I've ever loved. How was the river today?"

Gravely, she told him all her findings, and the snails, and the perhaps-fish, and the sounds of the river song, and how she could change it, but only a little bit, at the sides, and about Ña Conce plucking chickens, and the feathers.

"Next time, ask her for a long feather with a strong quill. We'll let it dry, and then I'll show you how to make a pen."

That sounded so very interesting, Yvonne said, "Shall I go now?"

"If you can be quick about it. . . ."

But even though Yvonne rushed out over the patio and round the back and over to the other side of the house, Ña Conce, her baskets and her sack were nowhere to be seen. Panting with warmth and exertion, Yvonne returned to her father.

"I looked everywhere, but she's disapappeared," she reported.

Papi laughed and said she was his funny little heart and did that mean that Ña Conce had vanished into even thinner air than if she had merley disappeared, but Yvonne didn't understand what he meant, and when they began talking about words again, Mami came and said lunch was ready and why weren't those hands washed, so that was the end of it. Later in the afternoon, when she went in to see her father again, he was tired, so they didn't sing any songs together, but she sang one for him, very softly, and then saw he was asleep.

"I wish you wouldn't encourage her to go to the river. . ."

"I don't encourage her, Edie. She likes it."

"It's dangerous."

"Not necessarily. The banks won't bite her. And Ña Conce's reliable."

"Oh, Edgar." Edie continued tidying up the room. "You know it makes me nervous."

"Don't be so idiotic. Simply because a knave with his eye on the Moore money managed to capsize a boat. . ."

Stung, Edie reacted. "I wouldn't talk about money-minded knaves, if I were you. . ."

She regretted her outburst the moment the words were out. Edgar, his thin face dark with sudden emotion, pushed himself forward in the chair.

"Don't goad me, Edie, or I'll. . ."

"I'm sorry . . . please, be careful . . . you mustn't strain . . ."

But he was already sinking back against the pillows stacked behind him, the fluttering of his striped pajamas against the caved-in contours of his chest signal of his heaving effort.

When he had regained his breath, Edgar muttered, "I think I'll get back into bed."

"Then I'll go and get you your tray..."

While he ate, Edie gathered the days' debris—the clothes and basins, the packs and medicaments, the discarded linens, some glasses, a towel. She took them from the room and deposited everything in the scullery, returning to wait until Edgar had finished his meal.

He had become even more haggard in the past weeks; his nose had gone all beaky, thin and angular, and his head jutted forward on his chicken-scraggy neck, the flesh quite wasted away. Even his hands had developed talonlike features, with the knobby joints grotesque in the skin-and-bone fingers that ended in bent, distorted nails.

Edgar was hunched over the tray on his bed, his shoulder-blades two sharp wings behind him. Edie was reminded of a haggard fowl poised over a morsel of food, too weak to make the effort to peck down and eat.

"Have another spoonful, Edgar."

His mouth moved into the beginnings of his old sardonic smile.

"You're trying to fatten me up."

"It'll help you get better."

He put the spoon down on the tray and leaned back, looking exhausted, the faint mocking smile fading.

"It's not worth the candle."

His voice was so hoarse it made Edie want to clear her own throat.

"Edgar, please try."

He shook his head.

"No, it's useless. I don't want to. I don't feel like it. Please take it away."

She rose and reached for the tray.

"Perhaps if I brought you something else? Some more warm milk instead of the soup?"

Edgar closed his eyes.

"No, no. Nothing at all. I think I'll sleep a bit now...."

Edie slid the tray off the bed and removed it to the scullery. All Edgar's receptacles were cleaned and washed in there, a special basin being kept for the purpose. Dr. Ibañez was insistent on such measures; everything used by Edgar had to be kept away from the rest of the household as much as possible. It was all an enormous amount of work and desperately tiring, and Edie only hoped it was as effective as the doctor claimed it to be. She washed her hands and dried them on a clean towel before going up the brick step and walking into the kitchen.

Rosita stirred the *dulce le leche* with a wooden spoon and watched Edie, who had come into the kitchen looking white and drained of all energy and thought, and was now sitting at the table, her face buried in her hands. Rosita knew she was not crying; there was nothing, in an immediate sense, over which she needed to shed tears. No; what Edie was doing, Rosita knew, was restoring her strength. In a little moment, the talking would start, and Edie's courage would return.

Rosita thought of Edie as Edie, varying her form of address from *niña* to *señora* depending on mood—hers or Edie's or the presence of others. The formal *usted*, instead of the familiar, childhood *vos*, remained immutable on her side; Edie varied from time to time, and Rosita was able to gauge her disposition by her choice of pronoun.

Edie's head drew away from her hands; her color had begun returning. She was much thinner, though, even thinner than she had become in the months after the *niña* Yvonne was born. Those had been difficult days; there had been so much to do, Rosita was afraid she would not be able to manage. The saving grace had been the arrival of Mrs. O'Connor with Rosita's mother, Rosa. They had stayed for a month, and when they left to return to Rosario, El Naranjal was functioning as a reasonable household should.

It was a pleasant *quinta*, with its orange grove and the river running close by and the hills rising behind. There was sun and good dry air for poor *Don* Edgar who, after seeming to get better the first year, had deteriorated steadily ever since. Ña Conce, who came with the place, and lived in a *rancho* on the property, said he would not last much longer. Rosita believed her; Ña Conce knew about things like that. She did not go by Dr. Ibañez' medicines, but was versed in plant lore and the ways of the weather—a *curandera*, one who cured with infusions and pastes made of natural ingredients.

Thank God the little *niña* Yvonne was a healthy child, and Rosita always dosed her with Ña Conce's special brews when the seasons were changing. Edie was too busy with *Don Edgar* to pay much attention to her daughter.

The child was beautiful and sweet, good-natured and easy to please, but the *señora* seemed at a loss whenever she was faced with the child's needs.

It was as though Edie herself had not yet finished being a child when she had been called upon to be a mother to a daughter herself, Rosita reflected. If only there had been brothers and sisters to stand by her . . . if only the poor *señora* Millicent had not been drowned in the Tigre . . .

Rosita stifled her sigh. Those were tragedies of the past; there was another one at hand. *Don* Edgar was taking another turn for the worse; she had seen it plainly the last few days. His eyes glittered like wet glass now, never still unless he was sleeping, and she had noticed the fever burning bright red spots on his cheeks.

"I'm going to send Yvonne to stay with Mrs. Ibañez," Edie said, her hands pushing a few loose strands of hair away from her face. "She's underfoot. I cannot have her clinging around my skirts when I'm busy. Besides, Edgar tires himself out talking to her, I'm sure. . . ."

The *dulce de leche* began making plopping noises as the bubbles rose more energetically, and Rosita stirred with greater fervor, to prevent it from scorching on the bottom of the pan.

"A few days of rest would help," she agreed, leaving unsaid her conviction that Edie resented Edgar's interest in the child. It was true that he seemed to adore her; when he had still been well enough to sit outside, father and daughter had shared hours of sun and silence, or sun and conversation, depending on his mood. Yvonne was uncanny in her intuitive understanding of what the dying man needed, whether another blanket to place over his thin legs or a time of undisturbed quiet.

Rosita had watched Edie try and join in the companionship, but her presence only succeeded in breaking its previous mood. Her husband either mocked her or complained of physical discomfort; with his daughter, he was another person, truly another soul.

At the far side of the stove, the kettle boiled. Rosita removed the pan she had been stirring, and turned her attention to making a jug of *yerba*, pouring it out into two mugs and lacing both servings with sugar.

"Here, *señora* . . ."

"Thank you." Edie sipped, closing her eyes. "I'm so tired, Rosita, so tired . . . you cannot imagine . . ."

"I'll tend to the *señor* tonight. You sleep in Yvonne's room. That way, the noises won't disturb you, and you'll be rested tomorrow, and feel better."

"Yes." Edie offered no resistance, which indicated the extent of her exhaustion, for she had tended to *Don* Edgar's every need since the first moment they had known of his sickness. Only in the months when she was so big with child she could hardly move around had she first allowed Rosita to help her, and in those days there had not been nearly as much to do as there was now.

Now it was unending: pans and cloths and more pans and more covers and sheets and changing all the bed linens and starting all over again. He coughed, he vomited, he bled, his stomach was all in disorder. It took a staunch will to face the stench and mess at times.

"If the *niña* is to be away, we can take it in turns. You must get proper rest, Edie. You need your own strength."

Edie sighed. "I know . . . but it's so strange . . . sometimes he helps me. Like today, for instance: I had to change him again, before he could eat. And he behaved as though everything I did for him was wonderful, and perfect. It makes it so much easier to do."

She drew imaginary circles on the table with the bottom of her mug.

"And then at other times, he fights me, every inch of the way. Yesterday, he was fearful . . . and who knows which he'll be tomorrow. . . ."

"It is the illness, *señora*."

"I don't think so . . . I think it is Edgar. Oh, some of it's the illness. I know that. But Edgar himself . . ." She stopped with a sigh. "Anyway, what's the use . . . it's all too late, now."

She drank down the rest of the *yerba*, and when she started speaking again, her voice was different and she talked of peripheral things, avoiding the central subject presently filling the household's life.

Yvonne reached the kitchen door and saw that Mami and Rosita were alone in there, talking together in that special way that meant they were busy with each other's words and would not pay too much attention to her if she went in and joined them. Mami might hold her close to her side, or if she went and stood next to Rosita, perhaps she'd get picked up into her lap.

It was best just to go in and not ask any questions or interrupt. Yvonne had discovered that, if she asked something, or butted into the conversation, Mami's mood would change at once, and that often made the niceness go away. Then it would be back to ordinary times, and Mami would get up from the chair and Rosita would start sweeping or cooking or being busy without talking, or shouting to one of the other maids to come and help her prepare the food. And Yvonne would be told to run off and play, sometimes with Ña Conce to watch where she was, sometimes on her own.

"Oh, there you are, Yvonne. I was just going to go and look for you."

Mami was rising from her chair. Puzzled, Yvonne stood still. It was not like her mother to seek her out at this time of the early afternoon. Had she done something wrong? But Mami did not look cross.

"How would you like to go and stay at the doctor's house again?"

Her momentary fear fallen away, Yvonne was enchanted with the idea. The first time, she had not wanted to go, and she had cried and made a big fuss and been afraid. Mami had smacked her hard on her bottom for being a naughty, rude girl and made her go anyway; she had gone alone with Dr. Ibañez, on his horse. Yvonne had cried until they had lifted her onto the saddle in front of the doctor, who had told her to hold onto the leather rise if she wanted to. He had carried her little bag inside his, and put his arm around in front of her so she could not fall off.

Then he had jiggled the reins and the horse had begun walking and soon Yvonne was laughing and happy and enjoying every bit of the ride. She had recognized the doctor's house when they arrived, having been there with Mami once before, and the nice smiling lady who was Mrs. Ibañez, but whom Yvonne was allowed to call *tía* Adele. She was not a real aunt, only a pretend-aunt, but she was specially nice. Even Mami said so.

The house was fun to stay in, too, and quite different from El Naranjal. For one thing, it was not a *quinta*; it had a much smaller garden and no stables or donkeys or barns or *ranchos* with people living in them, the way Yvonne's house had. For another, the house itself was much smaller, and had little rooms, all of them filled with lots of delicate, pretty furniture quite unlike the sturdy furniture at El Naranjal.

And there were plants and flowers everywhere. Not just outside in the ground, but in pots on the windowsills and in the patio near the well. There was a trumpet vine growing over the railings, its long red flowers tumbling over the wrought iron among the shining leaves. In the corner, where the railings met the roof of the house, the vine got mixed up with the bougainvillea that rose on the other side of the white wall, and red and purple and orangey tones cascaded together in tangled profusion.

On the other side of the patio lay the path to the chicken run with the woodshed backing up against it, and there Yvonne spent long happy hours among an assortment of animals and their young. There were usually little chicks or ducklings in some stage of fluffy development, and cats and their kittens could be found in among the corners and hidey-holes of the stacked wood. Mother animals could be fierce: Yvonne collected scratches and pecks along with knowledge and hours of enjoyment. Then *tía* Adele showed her how to sit quietly and not make any sudden moves, and only watch, until they were not afraid anymore. Another way to make friends was to take them something to eat, and Yvonne got up extra early to help carry the pail of food and mash, steaming and sloppy, out to the chicken run in the waking dawn.

There was no river, the way there was at home, and there was no cook, either. Instead, it was *tía* Adele who did all the cooking, and she made special dishes for Yvonne to try, and little gold cakes that melted the moment you put them in your mouth and tasted sweet even without putting butter and sugar on them.

Best of all, there was Pepe, the tame *coatí*, who slept a lot during the day but liked to play around the house at night; once Yvonne woke to find him burrowing into her pillow with his funny wobbly nose and his pretty dark paws. He clung to things with his tail, which could squeeze, but not so hard it hurt, and Yvonne liked it best when he climbed up on her shoulder, wrapping his tail around her arm to steady himself. She fed him little bits of cake, and he also ate fruit. When he was small, *tía* Adele told her, Pepe used to go to sleep in Dr. Ibañez' pocket, but now he had grown too big to fit, so she had made him a special sleeping place in a box with old rags.

131

You could never tell, just by looking, whether he was in there or not, because he always burrowed right down under all the rags when he wanted to sleep, and you couldn't see anything of him at all, not even the end of his squeezy tail.

Yes, going to stay with *tía* Adele would be nice. Yvonne wondered whether there would be any new kittens in the shed, and whether the broody hen had hatched out any more eggs yet.

"Dr. Ibañez will be coming today, after tea," Mami was saying. "You can ride back with him after he's seen your father..."

Adele Ibañez stood in the doorway and watched the cart approaching. She could see the small figure of Yvonne Waring sitting next to her husband on the plank seat; their voices began reaching the house, the child's piping and intense, her husband's comforting rumble a blur of tones on the vague breeze.

Yvonne had caught sight of her and was waving, bouncing up and down on the seat with excitement. Adele waved back and began walking toward the weather-blanched hitching bar. The evening air was mild; dusk's shadow, already lying in dark pools at the bottom of the valley, had not yet seeped up to where the house stood on the sloping side amid the early hills. Behind her and to her right, rose the *altiplano* and the distant *cordillera*, whose snow-capped peaks were sometimes visible when the air was clear.

As it was now; clear and still, with the early evening birds' calls echoing through it from time to time. The afternoon wind had dropped to the barest of whispers; by nightfall, there would be total calm, and a fine, hot day promised for the morn.

That would make it even easier to have Yvonne staying; the child could spend hours entertaining herself out of doors. Adele took special pleasure in her little guest; she was such a beautiful child with her huge round blue eyes reminiscent of those in china doll faces Adele remembered from her own childhood in her native Auvergne. The soft hues and sharp smells of the French countryside were always tucked away in Adele's memory, along with the images of early days and toys. Even though it had been decades since she had married the young Spanish doctor who had courted and convinced her to join him on his outbound path, she always sensed the pres-

132

ence of her faraway background through the veil of present life and days.

The horse drew up to the accustomed bar and stopped.

"Hullo, Yvonne, here, give me your hand and I'll help you down . . . How pretty you look! And a new dress, too . . ."

"I held the reins! I held the reins!" The child was flushed with pleasure and triumph. "And the horsey did what I said him to do . . ."

"Aren't you clever? There! There you are . . ."

Yvonne waited to be handed her toy suitcase and doll, then scampered ahead. Dr. Ibañez removed his battered bag and a case.

"Here, let me take that . . ."

"No, there's another one also. It's smaller. Suppose you take that one instead."

Adele complied. They walked along the path to the house; Yvonne was already waiting in the doorway.

"How is he?" asked Adele.

The doctor shook his head. "Not well. Let's leave it till later."

"Are both these bags Yvonne's?"

"Yes."

"Oh. I see."

By the time they reached the child, Adele had removed her frown of concern and was smiling again.

"You'll never guess, Yvonne, what Pepe did yesterday . . ."

Later, after she had given Yvonne her supper, and put her to bed, and promised to show her the new kittens the very first thing in the morning, Adele Ibañez joined her husband in a glass of wine and the evening's lull. As was his custom, he recounted the events of the day.

". . . another knife fight down at the *boliche* last night . . . twins born over on the Hernandez place . . . patient from Buenos Aires arriving next month . . ."

When he fell silent, she said, "Now tell me about the Warings."

"Yes." He sighed. "Edgar is dying. He gave up long ago, as you know. The end is very close."

A few minutes passed. Adele said, "And Edie?"

"Thinner than ever, and holding tight. She knows, and is braced for it."

"It's so much for so young a woman to bear," Adele sighed, her hand reaching for her husband's. "Is Yvonne to stay here until everything is over?"

133

"Yes. That's why Edie packed two bags."

"I rather thought so."

Glad as she was to have the child staying with them, the doctor's wife knew there would be moments of unease. After the immediate novelty had worn off, Yvonne always missed her mother, and Adele had found her in uncomplaining tears on more than one occasion. The first time it had happened, it had taken quite a while for the truth to emerge.

"I . . . I want my Mami . . . but she said I mustn't . . ."

Adele had held her tight.

"You mustn't what, Yvonne? Try to explain to *tía* Adele . . ."

"Mustn't say I want to go home to my Mami . . . only silly babies do that, Mami says . . . b-but . . " The tears overcame the voice.

It was a pity, Adele mused, that Edie had so little patience with her daughter, and so seldom seemed to want to have her around, no matter how Edgar was feeling.

"I don't know what to do with a child—any child," Edie had said candidly on one occasion. "I'm not used to them. My brother and sister died when I was so very small, I hardly remember them. There never were any other small children at home."

She had later added she thought Yvonne was a difficult child anyway.

"So secretive and stubborn . . . you have no idea . . . and Edgar spoils her . . . sides with her every time . . . it might have been different if she were a boy . . ."

To Adele, though, she had unusual qualities, this beautiful little girl who never laughed and was slow to smile. There were depths to her Adele found easy to see, but difficult to understand; her love for her father was understandable in itself, but her strong protection of him was beyond her years. In her childlike way, Adele realized, Yvonne understood Edgar Waring better than his wife did.

But, of course, she loves her father . . . her Papi is the center of her life and her world. . . . His death is going to hurt her terribly . . . she is going to miss his presence for ages —for a lot longer than Edie will, after the shock dies down . . .

Edie stood, small and straight and still, waiting outside the bedroom door until Dr. Ibañez emerged. He put his arm around her shoulders and led her gently away; she felt his warmth as a protection, but there was no emotion left in her. Rosita and Ña Conce were already doing the laying-out, and Edie was not going to return to the room at all. She had done her part.

She had been there till the end, seen the shadow fall and transfix Edgar's face. She had known the exact moment without having to be told. It was over, and she felt cold and empty inside, with no tears or words or regrets or feeling. It was over.

In the past months, from the day she had known it would be definite, she had thought ahead, about her own life and future and what she would do when she was free. It had been easy to decide: she would go to England, fulfilling the dream she and Mamma had shared all those sad years ago. She would go and stay with her aunts, whose names and memories and anecdotes and letters had filled some of her happiest childhood hours.

Now she would go and visit them, and take Yvonne, and enjoy it all.

Mami was waiting at the gate, dressed in a black dress Yvonne had never seen before, and her face looked very pale, like it did when she was not feeling well. But when she smiled and kissed Yvonne hello, she didn't say she was ill, or anything, but took her hand and began walking toward the house with her while Dr. Ibañez drove the cart around to the back as usual.

They went inside.

"Is Papi sleeping, or can I go and say good morning?"

Mami sat down in one of the entrance hall chairs, took Yvonne's other hand and drew her close.

"We have to be brave, you and I, Yvonne," she said. "You see, your father's gone away. . . ."

This was unexpected news.

"Where'd he go?"

Mami said, in a very soft voice, "He's . . . he's gone away to Heaven, and . . ."

Alarmed, Yvonne reacted. Had he gone alone?

"Mami—did Papi go to Heaven in his pajamas, without getting dressed? Won't he catch cold?"

No, the soft tones went on, Papi wouldn't catch cold. . . . He would never be ill or uncomfortable again. . . .

135

And then suddenly Yvonne understood: Papi had disapappeared. Not just for a little while, like other people did.

Papi had disapappeared for always.

2

"I don't believe it!" Edie forced the words out between gasps. "It's not true! You're lying to me..."

"Edie, Edie... you know I'm not. I've never lied to you about anything. Please... please... Sit down, Edie.... Listen to me." Dr. Ibañez took a deep breath. "I'm afraid, my dear, that it *is* true: one of your lungs has been touched. Slightly. It is only the faintest of shadows. And it can most certainly be cured. I would stake my life on it. Naturally, it will take time, and you need to rest..."

"And stay in this hellhole of a place for life! Just when I thought I was free at last! Oh, it's too horrible... horrible..."

The sobs of rage and fear tore through her words. The doctor waited for the first force of her desperation to abate.

"It is *not* for life," he said after a while. "Be reasonable, my dear. Try to think more clearly. I know it's a shock for you, and that after all you've been through in the past years, it seems too much to bear. But you've always been so good about facing up to facts—and it is a fact that now you, too, must be cured. A few more months... A year at the most. Then you'll be well again, your whole life before you."

"*What* life? My life has been ruined... *ruined* by Edgar..." Edie was sobbing and shivering at the same time, hysterically out of control, clawing at the world. "After all the horror... and now he's left me his illness, too... so like him... so vengeful... even in death, he ruins my chances...."

The doctor let her rave for a while. When the worst of her rage began to subside, he tried again.

"For your own sake, Edie, try to see that you need to care for yourself for a while. And allow yourself to be cared for by me, by Rosita, by everybody." Letting his tone become conversational, he went on, "This often happens, you know. Nothing very unusual about it at all. A family member gets ill, and the person who does most of the caring and nursing uses up all strength in doing the work—and then easily picks up the illness...."

Edie's sobbing was calming down.

"What's more, your life has *not* been ruined—no, don't interrupt me." He put up a hand to ward off the words she was about to say. "I know it's been made difficult. Very difficult. And you're very young to have had to battle such enormous problems all by yourself. But Edie, listen to me, believe what I tell you: your very capability shows how quickly you'll mend, if only you'll give yourself the chance. And I know you will."

She raised her head and looked at him. Gently, he smiled. "I promise you that, on my word as a doctor."

She held his gaze steadily for a moment. Her shoulders rose and sank in a capitulating sigh.

When all his instructions had been given, she accompanied him to his tethered horse.

"Remember," he said in parting, "the most important thing is your desire to be cured. You *want* to get well. A person's will makes all the difference in the world. And you have so much to live for: your lovely little daughter, your many youthful years ahead..."

...and my long-promised trip to England, Edie thought, watching him as he rode away.

The rain beat steadily against the dining room windows. Edie pushed the ledger to one side and turned to Yvonne.

"*Now* what do you want?"

The child was getting more impossible by the day. It was bad enough that the rain was preventing Edie from having her required hours of sunshine out on the patio; desperate to finish healing, she resented the wet and chilly day. But it was even worse to have to share the boundaries of the house with her bored and whiney daughter.

Yvonne was always clinging to her skirts and asking questions. If Edie heard the word "Why?" once a day, she heard it a thousand. If only the child had the gumption to go off and play like a normal little girl... But no. She had to pester underfoot until Edie thought she would lose her reason.

"Haven't you got anything else to do?"

"No, Mami."

"Why don't you go and play in the kitchen? But don't get in Rosita's way."

"I can't. She's washing the floor. Mami, can't you play with me?"

137

"Oh, for heavens' sake." Edie gave up. She swung around in her chair, away from the table. "What do you want to play? But only for a little while..."

"Can we sing a song?"

"No." Brusquely.

"Papi used to..."

"That was Papi, not me. Hurry up, Yvonne. Make up your mind."

Tears began welling in the child's eyes. Edie's temper snapped.

"I'm certainly not going to play with you while you blub. Crybabies don't get played with. Now, run off to your room, and don't bother me again, do you understand? Because if you do, I'll really give you something to cry about."

Yvonne ran off, and Edie returned her attention to the books and papers in front of her, spread out on the table, some in neat, designated piles, others still to be sorted and categorized. Writing paper lay to one side, several envelopes already filled and finished. Her lengthy correspondence with the Buenos Aires lawyers was unending. What a mess Edgar had left!

They were still unearthing debts and financial frauds he had initiated, liens against her property, monies never deposited, income intercepted between source and bank, double-dealings and bribery at the banks themselves. The moneylenders had known their business: Edgar had been an ideal customer—unconcerned about the capital, eager to enjoy anything money could buy, and when he considered the income insufficient, borrowing and mortgaging where he could.

In the first years of their northern exile, as Edgar used to call it, Edie had celebrated her twenty-second birthday and thus become legally of age. Because of her husband's illness, it became permissible for her to take over all financial affairs. Canon Thaxter had accompanied the two lawyers who had come up to Cosunzué to see her; an unpleasant week's worth of double acrimony had ensued.

On the one hand she had had Edgar, ailing, bitter, and peevish, venting his acrid resentment at every opportunity. On the other, she had the three Buenos Aires visitors, privately dismayed at having to hand over the financial reins, publicly puzzled at her former actions.

"But Edie—why on earth did you sign?"

It was a question asked over and over again. And what

138

could she say, she kept telling herself—that she had bargained away the greater part of her fortune merely to obtain a few nights of rest and peace and freedom from fear? That she had ransomed herself from assault? From her chosen husband... the man she had defied those very men to marry...

"Edgar made me," was her eventual and only answer. True as it was, it explained nothing, and did not make it easier for anyone present, least of all for Edie herself. She had stuck it out, though, and it had been worth it. By the time Thaxter and the lawyers left, Edie had her own financial reins in hand.

Little as she knew, she was determined to hang on; there was no one she trusted, no one she could turn to. The very people who had been supposed to safeguard her money had first coveted it and then ignored her husband's abuse of it. She would have to learn how to manage by herself.

"But Edie—that's ridiculous... why worry your pretty little head about it... with so many other problems right now..."

She had looked Canon Thaxter straight in the eye and not even bothered to say a word. The lawyers had limited their version to murmuring that their firm was always at her service. Edie had been relieved to see all three of them go.

And yet, all these years later, she still struggled with the books and the bills and the debts. Dr. Ibañez had recommended a firm for the legalities; Edie kept all signatory rights for herself alone.

She sighed, and pulled the main ledger toward her, the one in which she kept all the figures from everywhere, entered and ordered in her own personal way. As she began entering the information from the latest letters received, her brow smoothed and her mood calmed; her neat numbers flew into place in the correct columns.

It was still raining; Yvonne stared at the gray wetness outside; there was no hope of going to play by the river this afternoon. Not that there was much to see or play with there at this time of the year; all her favorite river places, and the pools, and even the washing rocks, everything was under water. Even the banks were completely covered by the swollen river, now no longer a singer of bubbling songs but a slow, wide, gray snake, engorged on all it had swallowed, almost silent in its course. The water's edge was at the orange

139

trees; when the waters went down again, the grass would be all squishy-sludge, and pale. Yvonne remembered it from the year before.

She also remembered finding differently colored stones amid the mud, brought by the annual flood waters from a different region. It had been interesting collecting them; perhaps there would be some this year, too. It was something to look forward to, when the river went back to normal.

Pleased with the thought, Yvonne turned to her toy shelf and decided she would take Pearl, her doll from England with all the changes of clothes, into the dining room and dress her in another costume. She would change Pearl into her nightie with the lace and the pink ribbons, and then she would make her a bed in the big corner chair with all the cushions, and sing her a lullaby. That way, she could be with Mami and not be a nuisance and everything would be fine.

"Please be quiet, Yvonne . . . you're disturbing me . . ."

Yvonne stopped humming and went on playing with Pearl. Perhaps if she kept singing the lullaby in her head, Pearl, being a doll and therefore magic, would be able to hear her anyway. She busied herself with the doll's clothes, smoothing the creases and folds the way she had seen Rosita tidy clothes when she was going to iron them. The song kept running through her head; it was warm and comfy in the big chair. She put Pearl on the corner cushion.

"Yvonne!"

"Yes, Mami?"

Only as she answered her mother did she realize she had been humming out loud again.

"Come here."

When Yvonne reached her mother's side, she could see the anger coming. But it was too late to do anything about it now.

"Didn't you hear me tell you to stop making a noise?"

"Yes."

"*Yes, Mami.*"

"Yes, Mami."

"Then why did you deliberately start singing again?"

"I didn't . . . I wasn't . . . I was only humming in my head . . ."

"Don't talk rubbish! You've been singing and humming loud enough for the hills to hear! Do you do it on purpose to upset me? Can't you see I've got all my books in front of me? Haven't you been told time and again by Dr. Ibañez that you've got to be a good girl so I can get well?"

140

Yvonne felt herself tightening up; she made no reply. The unanswerable questions insisted on, but the longer they continued, the tighter she became, until she felt like a clenched fist. If she closed her eyes and her ears and herself, the pain wouldn't reach inside at all.

The slap caught her by surprise; for an instant, the pain bore through. Then only the burning on the left side of her face remained, and that didn't matter; nothing mattered out there; she closed her impenetrable protective shell around her inner wounds.

Edie stood in the back doorway; Ña Counce, several paces ahead in the sodden grass, looked at the flood waters reaching close to the house under the orange trees and shook her head.

"They are all bad signs, *señora*, bad signs. The water is gray...."

Native lore judged the annual floods by the quality of the water itself: when it was clear, it was greeted as beneficial for man, beast, and plant. But this year the swollen river was a surly gray, and opaque.

"Perhaps it's because the clouds are gray," Edie suggested. "They get reflected in the water, and..."

"No, *patrona*." Ña Conce was polite but adamant. "There is earth in the water; that is what makes its color. And this color means the floods will be bad this year...."

She had seen it that way many years ago, the Indian woman went on. She would never forget the disaster that had followed. Whole *ranchos* had been swept away, babies torn out of their mothers' arms by the sweeping water, whole families drowned, their corpses discovered miles distant and weeks later, livestock scattered and lost, crops flattened and ruined by the engulfing mire. It had been a terrible time.

"... and the waters were gray that year, too..."

Edie frowned, and went back inside the kitchen. Ña Conce followed her, closing the door behind her.

"This house held then, and it will hold this time, too—as long as the river doesn't break over the Punta de Lobos..."

Punta de Lobos, thus called because of the wolf-gray of the rocks' color, was an outcropping less than a mile away, upriver, and visible from the house itself. El Naranjal, built on a slight rise in the ground, was the highest point in the area.

"*Señora* Edie!" Rosita's voice called out. "Dr. Ibañez is here...."

141

Edie walked through the house and greeted the doctor at the front door. His medical visits, grown less frequent as her health had improved, were welcome to her now. Her questions this time concerned Ña Conce's gloomy predictions; the doctor listened to them as well as to her pulse and chest.

At last he put his stethoscope away.

"You're much, much better, my dear," he told her, smiling. "Very close to being completely healed. In fact, I might be tempted to say you *are* cured—except I wouldn't want you rushing off and dancing to celebrate..."

"Then I can leave..."

"Very soon now, but not immediately—and don't go dancing jigs at midnight in the meantime, or you'll risk a relapse."

"Don't worry, I won't. There's no one to dance with here, anyway." Edie looked up at him. "But afterwards—I'll be able to, won't I? I do so want to enjoy myself again...."

"You will, Edie, you will. Just have a little more patience." He snapped his black bag shut. "I'll come by again early next week. Then we can talk about your plans once more."

When he left, it was near lunchtime. Edie went looking for Yvonne. The child was playing on the north patio; Edie could not approach without seeing in her mind's eye the reclining, wasted figure of Edgar in his last days, still mocking her memory, so pitiful and yet so abusive in the short years they had shared.

As she had so often before, Edie again reflected on the proportion of harm possible to life in a short period. Life was so easy to destroy, so difficult to rebuild. She would never again take her health for granted; everything else came second to that.

Health and money. Without them, life was unbearably hard. She had fought desperately to regain them both—was, indeed, still fighting, for neither was yet secure for her. But she was going to recapture them both, and she was going to keep them, for the rest of her life. Nothing, nobody, was going to stand in her way.

By the next morning, the river was bigger than Yvonne had ever seen it; the water had crept closer and closer through the night until it was almost touching the kitchen door. And it was raining—hard, insistent, slanting rain that made a drumming noise against the windows and even drove the river water along in little lines as it pelted down.

Everyone was very busy and Yvonne had to finish dressing herself, which meant all her buttons were wrong and her pinny all sideways, but Mami didn't seem to notice, which was strange. But there was so much movement, perhaps she didn't see it, and after a while, Yvonne forgot about it, too, as there were so many interesting things to watch, things that had never happened before.

The animals, for one thing. All the donkeys and the cart horses and even the chickens from the chicken run at Ña Conce's *rancho* were brought up to El Naranjal and either shut up in one of the barns or tethered outside in the north patio.

There was a sudden flurry of talk and excitement in the kitchen; someone had arrived, and was telling Mami and Rosita what had happened further down the road.

"...even the table is floating...can't risk it any longer..."

A *carreta* filled with people splashed through to the front door and disgorged its human load into the house.

More people arrived; Yvonne knew most of them by sight, as they sometimes came to work at El Naranjal, or lived at a house where Dr. Ibañez would stop on his rounds when he took Edie and Yvonne along for a ride. Then even the children from Ña Conce's *rancho* came wading through the water up to the kitchen door, and this puzzled Yvonne greatly, for they had never been allowed in the house on ordinary days.

On the contrary; contact with the *rancho* children had always been discouraged, and the only times Yvonne had played with them had been on washing days. Then, when their mothers were scrubbing clothes in the river, she would sometimes manage tø join in with their running around games, but never very easily or with any true confidence in her ability to keep up with them, for they never welcomed her presence, and would change course, or the rudimentary shape of their game, so as to confuse her. Sometimes they would huddle, whispering and casting glances at her, and then giggle and make her feel terrible and want to go away. And yet she was curious about them, attracted by their presence; she also knew they would laugh if she turned and walked home.

In the summer, all the smaller children ran around with ragged cotton shirts on the top and nothing on the bottom, and that was how Yvonne found out little boys were made

143

differently from little girls, because in the place down there where she could put her fingers between, the boys had a little thing hanging out, and they wee-weed through it and made it work like a hose, and didn't even have to sit down on a potty, but wee-weed standing up. The bigger boys held their hoses and splashed their wee-wee wherever they wanted, onto the rocks, into the river or, if they got the chance, onto one of the other children.

One of them had once splashed Yvonne, but she hadn't told Mami anything about it because she was too ashamed, and didn't know how to explain. And Mami had warned her about the *mestizo* children.

"I don't want you playing with them. You'll get *piojos*."

Yvonne knew all about *piojos*. They were little black dots that lived in hair, and many of the women would sit by the riverside on calm evenings and comb their long black hair over the water, flicking through the strands with their fingers or a comb, getting rid of all the *piojos* they could. Rosita sometimes looked through Yvonne's soft pale curls, just in case, but none had ever been found. Because of the *piojos* fuss, Yvonne had never told anyone about the toe worms. They were white and fat and made a bump next to your toenail, and you could get them out by squishing against the bump with something pointy and hard, like a stick. Some of the boys were very brave about opening the skin with a knife, and then pulling the whole worm out in one piece from the tight round circle it had made in their flesh.

Yvonne had inspected her own toes very carefully many times, but she had never seen any worm bumps anywhere. Perhaps that was because she was always made to wear shoes, whereas the other children never did unless it was very cold, or for a special occasion like going to their church far away in the town for their first communion, and then Ña Conce made them sandals, either from strips of leather or from old boots that Mami gave her.

The flash flood waters broke over Punta de Lobos shortly before sundown, engulfing all of El Naranjal and sending streams rushing through the doorways into the house itself. In the kitchen, a step higher than the rest of the rooms, the water came in ankle deep, and went on rising.

"Put the children onto the table," was Edie's order the moment the flood came through. Yvonne was lifted up with

144

the rest, sitting next to the ramshackle basket with a baby inside, the latest of Ña Conce's grandchildren whose mother, little more than a child herself, crouched, shivering, on top of one of the chairs.

Shouts from outside announced the arrival of yet more drenched safety seekers, each bringing a few saved possessions and worsening news as the dark hours continued.

"... bridge shattered by the crest..."

"... no *carreta* can pass through the current now..."

They were cut off, in darkness and, Edie knew, in danger. The only thing to do was wait out the night.

Outside, the elements raged in their storming, the rain still pelting, the wind on the rise. The wind first whined, then screamed through the gorges and down the river, adding destruction along its path. A crack, a snap, and another tree branch splashed down, borne away by the rising force of wind and water. Some, torn loose and flung by the wind, slammed against the walls of the house, or struck the roof, ripping tiles away and sending them cascading into the muddy maelstrom below.

Rosita was crying.

"Ay, *señora* Edie, I'm so afraid..."

"Don't be an idiot, Rosita. We're going to be all right."

"But all that water... and if the walls collapse?"

Ña Conce muttered, "Then we will all be drowned in the flood. It was that way last time, *señora*, the time the children were swept away. We cannot let that happen again."

Another swell of water pushed against the door with the dull thudding of the flood's insistent pressure. Her skirts dragging in the seeping flow, Ña Conce took a blackened ring from the iron stove and made a mark with it on the wall.

"If the water comes in over the windows and to here, everything will be finished...."

A huddle of adults congregated around her.

"... safe on the table unless it reaches here..."

"... avoid the horror of being swept away..."

"... hold the table under until we get swept away ourselves..."

"... roof sure to cave in when the walls go..."

"... at least save them the terror of dying alone..."

Outside, the wind howled, and another branch crashed against the window, shattering the glass.

Yvonne stared at the mark on the wall, and the tightness inside her was colder than the air and the wind blowing through the broken glass and the water and everything put together. Shadows leapt with every flicker of the lamp swinging from its hook in the ceiling, and the whispers she heard, from Mami, from Ña Conce, from the people standing near the stove, made ghost noises against the wailing of the sounds outside. The baby began to cry; Yvonne peered at his tiny face, centered by the howling oval of his mouth.

"Here—have this..."

One of the girls pushed a chewed breadcrust into the infant's mouth; his lips closed around it and he suckled for a while. Other children were crying, not loudly, but sniveling in fear.

"They're going to drown us...hold our heads under the water till we die..."

So whispered the older boys, the ones sitting nearer the end by the stove, and no one rose to challenge the message, believing it to be too frightening to deny. Ribbons of water were threading through the sides of the door, above the sacks of grain placed as bolsters against it, and slithering down to swell the splashing wetness underfoot. Yvonne could see it making higher marks on the chair legs, and then it reached the little wooden bars with the roll-pattern between the legs. She was shivering with fear and cold and she wanted to wee-wee but had no voice to ask, and she could not say anything to anyone at all.

She was sleepy, too, and wanted to lean against something, or lie down, but there wasn't any room, until she leaned against the other children, even though they smelled funny, but she had no more strength to sit up or try to care, and the waves of tiredness made the shadows darker still. Something was warmer, and it was Mami putting a coat over her and then another coat and they were all huddled together, she and the boy who had wee-weed on her long ago and she didn't care.

"That's a good girl, Yvonne, you go to sleep..."

Yvonne smiled, and wanted to hug Mami but she was too sleepy to move, and then Papi's face smiled at her in the shadowy figures instead, and she smiled back at him and let her sigh make her sink down to where everything was dark and warm and she slept.

146

Edie stared out into the raging darkness and thought: *it wouldn't dare*. Nothing would dare to destroy her now. She had not battled for all these years just to see everything swept away by a stupid river temporarily flooding with the seasonal rains.

No. She clenched her hands into determined fists. The danger had to pass her by. Whoever else might get harmed by it—she was going to be free. Safe and free; she could feel it in her bones.

She looked around the crowded kitchen; most of the children had fallen asleep, huddled all over each other on the wooden table. Rosita was sniffing in a corner, on a chair; Ña Conce, impassive, was watching by the other door. The gardener had barricaded the doorways with flour sacks; he and several others were dozing on chairs, their heads nodding down toward their folded, crossed arms. The women-folk, by and large, were the ones who were awake.

Edie knew she would not sleep until all danger was passed. She looked at the walls, and knew they would hold. Was it her imagination, or was the wind dying down? Whatever it was doing, she knew she would beat it, win against the odds, once again survive.

Let the others be afraid, or sleep, or shiver. She would stick it out, and wait till the dawn. By then, she felt certain, the worst would be over.

Expect the worst but hope for the best....

Well, this *was* the worst. It could only get better....

At the gray light of dawn, Edie was still by the window, watching the destruction by the water outside. The bloated body of a cow, grotesque in the distortion of water-logged death, floated into view, rising and falling in the moving waves along a gravely sedate path, now floating left, now pulled right by a sudden eddy. The stiff angular legs rolled in an arc from side to side until they caught on one of the orange trees, straddling it horizontally across the trunk. Then a change of current disengaged it once more, and the drum-taut corpse proceeded down the flood path until it disappeared.

But the rain had stopped, the wind diminished, the height of the storm faded into scudding clouds. Edie watched the water, both inside and out. She watched for the darkened, giveaway gaps...

"It's going down..."

There was immediate reaction.

"Are you sure?"

"No, it's not..."

"God be praised..."

"Where's the mark?"

Everyone was suddenly moving, talking, gesticulating, trying to find proof positive of the changing tide.

"No—it's rising again..."

But the swell went down, only an eddy of the moment, and every further swell rose only to fall further, subsiding more each time than it had the time before, until the water-soaked patches above the level still flooded were clear indications that the danger had passed.

"*Señora*—we are saved..."

"Thank the good heavens..."

"We had better check the livestock..."

Edie, her skirts hoisted and her spirit high, was already ploughing through the water and on her way.

It took weeks to clean up the debris and clear the damage the flood had caused, and through it all Edie was indefatigable. The crisis had proved her mettle, forged her will; everyone spoke in awe and praise of the *señora* Edie, whose courage and spirit had never failed, who had comforted and sheltered everyone she could during the blackest hours of the devastating storm. And now she was out and working, ordering and directing, knowing what should be done.

Thanks to her efforts before the worst of the flooding, the animals of El Naranjal were, for the most part, safe and sound, and the *quinta* itself, although awash in mud and silt, had been lucky in contrast to other properties nearby, where loss of life, both human and among the livestock, had compounded the desolation. It was days before Dr. Ibañez was able to get to the *quinta*; when at last he arrived, he found Edie astride one of the horses, directing the clearing of the mud-caked barns and outbuildings.

"My dear...are you sure...? I must beg you...don't overtax your strength...."

But even he could see by the healthy tone of her radiant face that his words of caution were useless.

"I *know* I'm well," Edie insisted, back inside the house

once more. "I couldn't have done all I did—am still doing—and not be perfectly all right. . . ."

There were crumbled walls to be rebuilt, barns swept away that needed replacing, wandering livestock found far afield that needed returning to rightful owners. And everywhere, from everything, mud had to be removed, mud and silt and the sticky, glutinous coating that dried and hardened as the waters receded. Everyone helped everybody else, and when at last the main part of the work was over, a party was given in Edie's honor, with a sizzling outdoor *parrilla* of meats and sausages and big bloated demijohns of lusty local wine and long speeches filled with flowing words of praise and acclaim for the *señora's* courage, and toasts to her good health. Even Yvonne was allowed to stay up late for the occasion, and eat more *alfajores* and *dulce de leche* than had ever been permitted.

"*Que viva la señora* Edie!"

"*Que viva!*"

The *vivas* and cheers rang out through the clear evening air over the now-normal river to the boulders beyond. Edie curtseyed and thanked everybody, and the *bandoneón* struck up for some dancing. Edie waved and retired to the house with her daughter, Rosita following closely behind them; she was the only one who knew there was further cause for celebration, because Edie had confided in her earlier that day.

Dr. Ibañez' words still rang in Edie's ears.

"Yes, you are well. Completely cured. Just don't overdo it."

"When can I leave?"

"Wait another month or two. That'll give you time to decide what you want to do. And then—yes, I'll allow you to go and travel whenever you desire. . . ."

Long after the *bandoneón* music had died down into the insect whirrings of the quiet night, Edie moved silently around her bedroom, unable to sleep, hardly aware she was tired, knowing only that her life was turning around. The bad days were behind her; she would not let such misery ever happen to her again. She knew so much more now, was better prepared. It would be far more difficult for anyone to fool her, ever again: she knew what was important, the things that really counted. Health and money. Never mind what anyone might burble regarding love, or loyalty, trust, or

149

faithfulness. Marriage was supposed to be full of all those things—and it was nothing of the sort. Ever. Except in books.

Look at Mamma and Papa; what a life they had led. Well, it had been all right for Papa, of course. It always was, for the men. And the Thaxters. Robert was going to be exactly like his father, selfish and grasping, and Dollie was turning out as dim as Aunt Bessie. Robert was going to be a pompous bully, too. At least she hadn't married *him*. And she wasn't going to, either—despite some hints there had been in letters from B.A. disguised as sideways allusions to "our old childhood friendship."

It wasn't their shared friendship Robert was after: it was her money. What was left of it. No, one had to be extremely careful; Edie knew that, to her sorrow, now that she was older. Older and sadder and wiser, and a child's mother, besides. A widow with a small child was not much more than a drug on the market; Edie was certain where any attraction she might hold still lay.

For those who know about what money I have, she reminded herself. And there isn't all that much left anyway. But even if there were—I don't want to be trapped any more. I want someone to marry *me*, not my money. I'm going to be much more careful when I pick and choose.

If I get the chance, a small inner voice whispered, after which the day's tiredness took over, and Edie went to bed and slept.

Adele Ibañez opined differently.

"You'll turn heads, my dear, I am quite sure of it. You must try not to lose yours."

"Oh, I won't," Edie promised the doctor's wife, and she promised herself the very same thing almost nightly as she sat in front of the mirror and brushed her curled and tangled hair before going to bed. Even after the years of solitary sleeping, the horror of Edgar and the crudities of sex made her feel sick in memory.

Love would have to have another face if she ever met anyone she wanted to marry. Now that she was of age, there would be no more hopelessness; she was never going to let anyone force her to do anything she did not want to again. Never, ever, ever again.

3

Everything was packed and the house was hollow and empty, the few remaining crates and boxes waiting for the *carreta* outside. Everyone had gathered to say good-bye, and Dr. and Mrs. Ibañez were there, too, ready to take them to the train station, the first step in the long voyage that was going to take them to England.

Not immediately; there was to be a stay in Rosario with Mrs. O'Connor, and Rosita was going to stay there and work for her with her own mother, Rosa. It had never occurred to Yvonne that Rosita had a mami, too, and she wondered what Rosa would look like.

"Do get out of the way, child. Can't you see the men want to bring the boxes through here?"

Mami looked so pretty, all dressed up in clothes Yvonne had never seen before, and with a special hat on her head which made her look wonderful. Rosita also had a new dress, and Yvonne had two, in case one got dirty on the train. She was going to sleep on the train, Mami told her, and when she woke up they would be in Rosario, and Mami would take her to see the house Mami had lived in when she was a little girl like Yvonne.

It was all very interesting and very exciting and then suddenly it was time to get into the cart and leave the house and go. Yvonne felt a burning coming up in her throat and blazing into her face. Tears began to pour from her eyes.

"*Tía* Adele, *tía* Adele—I don't want to go! I want to stay here with you and the doctor and Mami and Rosita and Pepe and . . ."

She sobbed and clung to the doctor's wife, feeling the soft protective arms around her and hearing Mrs. Ibañez murmuring, "There, there, don't cry, there, there . . ." until Mami's hand grabbed her shoulder.

"Yvonne! Stop that crying at once! A big girl like you—you ought to be ashamed of yourself! Now blow your nose and pull yourself together. I thought you weren't going to be a crybaby any more. . . ."

151

"She'll get over it, Edie, once you get on the train. She's just upset, that's all."

"Well, it's high time she learned to control herself. . . ."

"There, there, Yvonne, don't cry . . . here, take my hankie and wipe your eyes. . . . There, that's better, isn't it? And just think of all the adventures you're going to have, and all the things you'll be able to tell us about. . . ."

"But Mami says we're never, never, never coming back. . . ."

"Then we'll go and see you, wouldn't that be nice? Blow your nose, there's a good girl . . . that's better now. . . ."

But the handkerchief was sodden and heavy in her pocket as she stood at the moving train's window, holding Mami's hand and waving a last good-bye.

In Rosario, there were tumultuous greetings and tears of recognitions and joy and reunion. Mrs. O'Connor, white-haired and much aged, seemed to lean on Rosa even when she walked.

". . . so wonderful to see you . . . and little Yvonne . . . what beautiful blue eyes . . ."

Rosa and Rosita embraced in a sobbing of Spanish and splashy tears. Moments later they were all energetic efficiency, getting bags to bedrooms and baskets stowed in the pantry and a meal laid out on the dining room table.

". . . lots of letters waiting for you . . ."

"Oh, yes. . . . I told my aunts to write to me here . . . what with El Naranjal being sold. . . ."

Edie turned the envelopes around in her hands. Both aunts had written from London; so had Mrs. Thaxter, from Buenos Aires, and Dollie had enclosed a note. There were stiffly formal letters from the B.A. lawyers, and one from the bank. And then there was one, in an unfamiliar hand, from London.

"Oh, yes. . . . I wrote and told Edwin you were thinking of going home. . . . He and his wife will be so pleased to see you. . . . Maurice is in London, too. . . ."

The ghost of Vesey's name flickered in the room, but remained unspoken. Mrs. O'Connor sighed and poured out more tea; Edie busied herself with the accumulated correspondence.

My dear little Edith,
The letter with all your splendid news arrived in the first

post last Friday morning. Your Aunt Beatrix and I will only be too happy to accommodate you and dear little Yvonne. It seems so sad your poor dear Mamma was never able to make the voyage home with you.

We are all well here, and no doubt you will find our lives very different from those led by you and your Argentinian friends out there. Still, I feel sure you will enjoy living in London, and we all look forward to your visit with great anticipation.

Your ever affectionate
Aunt Muriel

The letter from Aunt Beatrix was far longer and far more untidy, full of exclamation marks and uneven lines.

I am so excited to think we shall be seeing you at last that I fear I have become even more scatterbrained than before! Do sail home as soon as you can. Just think of it: we shall be celebrating Christmas together!

Her signature was surrounded by kiss and hug marks, and Edie, in a surge of good humor, showed them to Yvonne.

"... and when I write back, you can put kisses and hugs from you, if you like..."

"Mami, what was it like?"

"What was what like, child?"

"*You* know... when you were a little girl...."

"Very dull, Yvonne. Very boring and dull. I never did anything and I never went anywhere. And I got so tired of going in through the same front door all the time..."

"But then you didn't any more."

"That was when I was bigger, and we moved down to B.A., where you and I are going to go to, tomorrow, on the train. But I didn't move there until... until after my father passed away."

"Oh—did your papi go to Heaven, too?"

"Yes. Just like yours. Now run away and play, Yvonne, and don't get grubby. We have to keep that pinny for you to use on the train...."

Buenos Aires was full of comings and goings and new things to listen to, and watch, and observe. They stayed at the Thaxters' house and shared the big bed that Mami said was in her old room that she once had shared with Aunt Dollie, many years ago before Yvonne was born.

Yvonne didn't like this new aunt, Aunt Dollie, too much, and she didn't believe Mami did, either, although they called each other *dearest* and did a lot of laughing and talking together. It looked like the times Mami and Rosita used to laugh and talk together, but it sounded different, not just the language being English instead of Spanish, but underneath, in the way they said things to each other.

The Spanish in B.A. was different, too, with the same words made to sound harder, and a bit draggy. Yvonne noticed it was more the way Mami had always spoken, so different to Ña Conce and all the other people at El Naranjal. Here in Buenos Aires, people made comments about Yvonne's northern singsong, and so she paid a good deal of attention and tried to say things the way they did in Spanish.

The English, however, was all the same, except there was a lot more of it all the time, and many of the people who were English first and Spanish second made lots of mistakes when they spoke to the maids. At first, the silly things they said made Yvonne smile, but then Mami noticed her and said not to be a rude, nasty little girl or she would get a smack, so Yvonne stopped smiling and pretended she didn't hear.

It was difficult, though, because people like Grannie Thaxter, who was Aunt Dollie's mother, made so many mistakes it was sometimes hard for the servants to understand. Mami said Grannie Thaxter was not all there, but that was puzzling, because she did not seem to have anything missing; Yvonne looked at her very carefully. If anything, there was a lot of her, and she certainly had legs and arms like everyone else. She was usually smiling and often chattering, but the things she said did not always make sense, and were not proper talk.

The best times in B.A. were when Mami took her out for a carriage ride, or a nice walk to look at the shops and sometimes have tea in a *confiteria* where they had lots of different cakes and a band making music in the afternoon. The worst times were when she was left in the house with Grannie Thaxter and the servants, when Mami went out with Aunt Dollie and Uncle Robert. Then Yvonne would feel the pain inside of missing Rosita and Ña Conce and Dr. Ibañez and *tía* Adele, and she would go and lie on the big bed upstairs and hope that Mami would come back soon.

154

But usually Mami and Aunt Dollie would be out for hours, sometimes so late Yvonne would be asleep when Mami came back. If they had been on a shopping trip, then it meant there would be boxes delivered the next day, and hats and dresses unfolded from them, made by a special dressmaker for the long voyage home.

At home, in England, they would need pretty clothes, for Yvonne had more new dresses, too, and a thick blue coat with a soft bunny collar. There were dresses for daytime and a special party dress, with lace and ribbons and a big broad sash. Yvonne liked the coat best of all.

"That's because it matches your big blue eyes," teased Uncle Robert.

Yvonne shook her head.

"No, it isn't—it's because I like the collar. . . ."

"Of course you like the color—because it's blue."

"Not the color—the *collar* . . . the bunny collar . . ."

"You women are all the same—vain as vain, and you won't admit it. You'd rather tell a fib than say it's because it's blue. . . ."

"But it isn't . . . that isn't . . ." Yvonne tried, her eyes filling with tears.

"Of course it's blue. Don't contradict, Yvonne, it's very rude of you to answer back." Edie took the coat away and hung it on a chair.

"Come now, let's not have any tears. I don't like to see a little girl cry." Canon Thaxter had unexpectedly entered the room, and Yvonne wanted to run away upstairs and out of his way. His eyes frightened her, even though he pretended to smile when he talked, and he always seemed cross about something without saying what it was, and she didn't think he liked her or Mami at all.

Yvonne sat on the big steamer trunk, her legs dangling over its smooth, cold side, watching her mother move around the disordered room. Everything was packed, but Mami was looking in all the drawers, just in case. Yvonne felt very serious and was trying to be as good as possible, to suit the grandeur of the occasion. They were sailing for England in a big new steamship. Mami had pointed it out to her the day before.

Without meaning to, Yvonne started crying, not loud tears that made har gasp, but the spilling, slidey kind. She hoped

Mami wouldn't see, and took *tía* Adele's handkerchief out of her pinafore pocket. Voices sounded from the foot of the stairs.

"Are you ready, Edie?"

"It's almost time to go...."

"Coming..."

"Ah, there you are, my dear..."

"And wee Yvonne, such a little precious..."

Nobody noticed her sodden hankie in the ensuing hustle and bustle, and as the departure got underway, Yvonne felt no need to cry anymore. It was easy to say good-bye to these Buenos Aires people; there was no one there who meant anything to her at all.

Inside the ship a man with lots of buttons up and down the front of his jacket led them to their room, where there were flowers and more people, and then more came, and there was a crush of friends and stewards bringing bags and Mami smiling and people giving her boxes of chocolates and kissing her and saying "Bon voyage," until the voices were blurring together and loud with laughter, and then a hooter made such a loud noise Yvonne could feel it in her chest and someone was shouting, "All ashore's that's going ashore," and there were more kisses and good-byes and everyone was leaving. Mami picked her up and they went out on deck to wave to everyone; the people lining the wharf were waving handkerchiefs and paper streamers and hands, and everyone was calling out, "*Adiós*, good-bye, have a good trip, bon voyage, *adiós, adiós*, good-bye..."

The hooter hooted again so loud that Yvonne put her hands over her ears and buried her face in Mami's shoulder until the hooting stopped and they were moving away. Then Mami put her down and they both waved and waved at Mami's friends, who were shrinking smaller and smaller on the edge of the pier. It was getting cooler and breezy and Yvonne began to shiver until Mami said it was time to take a turn around the deck to begin getting their sea legs, and after that they would go to their stateroom and settle in to sea.

For Edie, the sea voyage was simply splendid. After a dreamless night's solid sleep the first night out, she woke to the bracing breeze and rhythm of a sunny day on the open waters, and she went out onto the deck to begin discovering the enjoyments of life at sea. There were hot broth and biscuits served at eleven, and shuffleboard games for those so inclined. Introductions were effected, and shipboard friendships began to form; knots of conversing passengers grouped both out on deck and in the salon.

At lunch she was seated at the captain's table; by dinner, it was apparent she was the belle of the ship. Within days, the first officer was madly in love with her, while the second glowered, planning his intentions.

The captain, a married man who knew his junior officers as well as he understood the sea, took the pretty widow under his wing, basking both in her company and the jealousy it easily engendered, quashing rumor and tension by assigning a different officer to escort Mrs. Waring at each port they reached.

Then it was out to the open sea again, and parties and merriment and shipboard camaraderie; when the brief storms came, Edie loved every minute, never knowing discomfort, never seasick at all.

"A born sailor," was the verdict, and her popularity rose even more.

Crossing the Line saw her crowned Queen of the Gala, and she danced and laughed and coquetted to her heart's content. She was happy and safe and alive to her fingertips, safe, she knew, as never before, escorted by the captain, flattered by everyone, dancing every dance and loving every minute, the ship's darling, the beautiful young widow with the sweet child.

Not that Yvonne appeared very often. The poor child seemed to turn green at the mere sight of a wave. But the crew was used to such matters, the cabin stewards coped very well. No doubt Yvonne would grow out of it eventually, and the quicker the better; it was such a pity to waste so many days in bed.

The rough seas began north of the equator, after the hot calm weather was left behind; the wind picked up, and the waves rose from the sullen sea as it changed in color and movement until the plumes of spray hissed in the wind over the churning water, streaked and bubbled in gray-green anger. The ropes went up and the hatches down, porthole covers were clamped and closed; the dining room became less and less frequented by all, but Edie was steadfast, never missing a meal.

As the ship neared its destination, Edie knew that, eager as she was to get to England, she would remember this, her first ocean crossing, in glowing and perfect detail, the rest of her life.

For Yvonne, the boat trip was frighteningly horrid. When she woke from her exhausted sleep after the excitement of the departure, everything was rocking and moving about and her whole world was unsteady. A sour, sick feel lay in her tummy, working its way up and down toward her throat. She was not hungry, but Mami said she should eat something, so she did, and sicked it up again and had to go back to bed.

Then a steward came to look after her because Mami was going to be busy all day. From then on, she didn't see much of Mami at all, only to say nighty-night and sweet dreams when she went to bed, and sometimes in the morning, but not always.

She was just getting used to the motion and beginning to eat almost normally again when the sunshine went away and the clouds got dark and there was a storm that made Yvonne want to stay in the cabin all the time, no matter how much the steward told her she would feel ever so much better if she went up on deck.

Not until it was calm again did she creep outside, gripping the steward by the hand; eventually, Yvonne got bold enough to go over to the railing and look at the sea. The water was far below and unfriendly, so big and huge you couldn't see its end. It was lonely and frightening, being out there in the middle; there was no land to step onto, to hold her firm and safe.

It was still calm when they came to the place everyone said was an important line, and they were going to cross it, but stare as she might at the moving water, Yvonne never saw it, even though they had a big party and splashed her with water because it was a ceremony, the captain said.

After that, the sea got dull-looking and the sky went gray and the weather got so bad Yvonne had to stay in her bunk all the time, even after she had been sick so many times there was nothing left inside her. Sometimes she saw Mami's face, and sometimes it was the steward holding her hand, and then there were the times there was no one there at all, everyone had disappeared and Yvonne couldn't even cry out in the choking darkness around her.

It was a nightmare so total, so undivided in waking or

sleep, that the moment the ship slid into the calming shelter of the river leading to London, Yvonne's thoughts pulled the curtain of darkness around the voyage and hid it from her mind for the rest of her life.

4

England was gray shapes shrouded in mist that thickened into fog in the low-lying parts. The ship, slowed to a soothing, almost silent glide, slid closer and closer to the fog-wrapped shore. Bulky shapes began emerging from the billowing, opaque swirls; bells sounded out hollow across the water below. Yvonne held on tight to Mami's hand, trying to feel warmth through the barrier of gloves. It was cold; not the roaring, windy cold of a few days before, but quiet cold, and Yvonne felt cold inside.

"Never mind, Yvonne, we'll soon be there. . . ."

They went back inside, and soon the shape of all the noises changed, the rumbles and clankings sharp in the air.

"There—you see? We've docked. . . ."

It took quite a while, but even when everything was ready and all the good-byes were being said over and over again and they walked slowly down the sloping gangplank down to the side, even then there wasn't any sun and everything looked shadowy and gray. Then Yvonne became aware of two shapes waiting in the mist-swirled morning, ghost-lit by the haloed gas lamps amid the moisture-hollowed sounds of the dawn-dark docks. One figure was tall and thin, the other short and wide; both were wrapped in folds of protection, dark hats on their heads angled against the gray of the air.

Hesitantly, they came forward, the tall one leading. It was she who was the first to break the curtain of time.

"Is it really Edie? Our little niece Edie—it's Millicent's dearest daughter, come home to us at last. . . ."

Everything was different in London, in England, just like everyone had always said it was, but it was different from what they had said, too. The great aunts were totally unalike, too—"as different as chalk and cheese," as Edie and Yvonne soon learned to say, acquiring the phrases and opinions and ways of their new surroundings, their new life and home.

Aunt Muriel was tall and thin and serious; she sometimes smiled but seldom laughed, even though she was kind and good and respected by everyone who knew her or even met her. There had been sadnesses in her life, Edie told Yvonne, and that probably explained why she was serious most of the time. Her husband, the Reverend John Barnes, had died very young, and Aunt Muriel had been left a widow, with two small boys to bring up on her own.

Aunt Beatrix, on the other hand, was short and round and fat and jolly. She bounced when she walked and she smiled all the time, and she not only laughed with frequency: she giggled. She had no children because she never married, and had always lived with her older sister, the contrasts between them balancing their lives.

Where Beatrix was jolly, Muriel was kind; Beatrix bounced and rushed, Muriel held her head high and moved in stately fashion. Muriel enjoyed reading; Beatrix loved to sing, and was a longtime member of the local church choir. Both sisters always attended church as a matter of course, but Muriel paid far more attention; it was Beatrix who brought the gossip home, to which Muriel would listen, frowning. Devoted to each other, the two sisters could spend hours bickering in apparent discord.

" . . . and when we were little girls your age, Yvonne, we lived in Sussex, and we used to have a dog called Spot, and . . ."

"That wasn't Spot, Beatrix, that was Tootoo. Don't you remember? Spot was the big dog we had later, after we came home from South America after poor Papa died . . ."

Or:

"Mamma always liked Millie to have the pink ribbons for her hair, and I always had the blue ones . . ."

"No, you didn't, Muriel, I did, and what's more, Millie always wore green. Your mother loved the color green, Edie, my dear . . ."

Muriel said sharply, "She did not. She hated it, and thought it unlucky. Millicent favored pink; I remember it clear as clear . . ."

Nonetheless, they all lived comfortably together in the London house, Muriel and Beatrix and the two boys, Peter and Dick, with Great-Aunt Muriel the nominal head of the family. The household ran smoothly, Muriel handling the finances and bills and Beatrix in charge of the day to day duties and tasks. She also taught music at a local school, and Sunday school at the church they attended, her many paths well suited to her bustling personality.

The boys were away when Edie and Yvonne arrived, but would be coming home for Christmas. Peter Barnes was studying for Holy Orders, as his father had before him, and Dick Barnes was in his last year of school, up in the north.

"I just hope the weather turns fine when they arrive. It has been terrible for weeks," said Beatrix.

"We may be in for a hard winter," was Muriel's rejoinder.

"Yes, I know. Ah, well, we must expect the worst but hope for the best. . . ."

As Edie heard the words, time and place blurred and the tears almost came but subsided in calm. Rosario and Mamma had been a long time ago.

Two more members completed the household, Gladys the maid and Bronner the gardener. Gladys lived in, but Bronner only appeared, hardly seen except as a shadow in the far potting shed. The great-aunts confessed they knew little about him, acknowledging the garden flourished as no other in the neighborhood under his wide, thick hands.

"My dear late husband found him somewhere," Great-Aunt Muriel told Edie. "He never told me where, and I was a bit afraid to ask. Bronner followed John around like a puppy dog in gratitude, and when he had finished his tasks at the church, he'd come and garden here. When John died, Bronner simply kept on coming."

"Goodness," said Edie, not very interested. But Yvonne was intrigued, and kept watching for him through the kitchen window, because Gladys had piqued her curiosity before.

"Got green fingers, 'e 'as," she had mentioned, and Yvonne wanted to see them up close. But the day she managed to do so, his hands were caked with earth at the time, and it was difficult to see what color they were underneath.

The great-aunts' house was tall and narrow, with a winding staircase that went up four floors. It also went down a flight, to the scullery and the cellar, and from the first day she arrived, Yvonne loved every room and corner and felt safe within its walls.

The house stood on a tidy, tree-lined street near one of the bridges stretching across the Thames. Identical houses stood on either side, jammed up together and joined at the edges, all the way up to the corner of the roof. Each tall house had a small front garden, with a wall and a gate and a path to the door. Then came two stone steps leading up to the doorway with its porch and a slot for the letters in the door.

The weather was so cold and nasty when they first arrived that Mami didn't let her go outside very much, but they had been on a quick walk to the local shops one afternoon and had only just got home when a commotion at the front heralded the arrival of two tall men. To Yvonne's amazement, they turned out to be "the boys," Great-Aunt Muriel's sons; one of them had a beard, and both were thin like their mother but friendly and jolly like Great-Aunt Beatrix, so Yvonne decided they were going to be fun, after all.

It was from them she discovered, that very evening, the names she was to associate with the aunts from then on. Dick Barnes gave the show away, during supper; Yvonne having been passed a plate of pudding, said, "Thank you, Aunt Beatrix."

"Good heavens! Aunt Beatrix indeed—hasn't anyone spilled the beans?" He looked around the table.

"Now, Dick, really..." His mother looked stern. Across the table, Beatrix giggled.

He turned to Yvonne.

"No, I see no one's told you. Well, the truth will out, I always say." Leaning toward her, he whispered conspiratorially, "She's been masquerading under false pretences and an assumed name. She's not a Beatrix at all." Then he winked.

Yvonne, ill at ease, tried to draw closer to her mother, and wanted to ask what Dick meant. But the next moment, it all became clear.

"We call her Aunt Boo," he was saying. "And you'll hear other people call my mother Aunt Moo."

"I didn't know that," Edie interjected.

"They were nicknames applied to us when we returned," Great-Aunt Muriel explained. "I think I got mine first, and then someone said Boo rhymed with Moo, and..."

"No, it wasn't that way at all," came from the other side of the table. "One of our cousins called me Boo because he was small and couldn't say Beatrix, and then, because your name is Muriel, someone said Muriels are always called Moo, and..."

And the sisters, off and bickering again, were transformed into Great-Aunts Moo and Boo.

Although she soon grew to love both of them, Yvonne liked Aunt Boo best; she was easier to play with, to talk to and understand. Aunty Boo, celibate maiden forever, had a child-like link to Yvonne's moods and joys; the love of singing also bound them close together in common voice.

"She's exactly like a child herself," Muriel observed, talking to Edie about her sister one day. Edie felt more on a level with her older aunt, despite the distance of years in their ages. Both Muriel and she had married, experienced child-birth, been widowed, known the sorrows of sickness and the valley of despair. Both had been left to bring up their children alone, defend themselves as best they could singly against the world. All these facts gave them the basics of their lives in common; they were the only two true adults, each felt, under the London house roof. Beatrix, the boys, Yvonne, and even Gladys, were all in another group, all children, in a way. Bronner didn't really count, being both an independent outsider, and a man.

Edie loved London. The city, swirled with damp and fog, slashed with heavy rain, whipped by wind, was everything Edie had ever dreamed it would be, and more besides. Everything was there, all the sights and palaces and places and parks she had heard of all her life.

Everything was exciting: the famous buildings, the familiar names, the shops and shoppers, the multitude of goods known to her from previous times as imported luxuries. But here, they were not imported at all. It summed up the paradox: everything was familiar, yet everything was strange. She knew the names and places, never having seen them in her life.

And to be surrounded by the English language was the strangest part of all, although Edie would never admit to this out loud. She had to keep reminding herself that everyone, even people employed in the shops, could understand what she said.

Yvonne, unhampered by social custom, piped up one day and voiced the thought.

"Mami," she said, tugging at Edie's skirt, "why do the shop people speak English here?"

They were at the draper's, where Edie was matching silk for a dress. She flushed with embarrassment, noticing the looks on customers' faces.

163

"Because we're in England—and don't tug at my dress like that, Yvonne."

"But why do people like maids also . . ."

"I just told you."

"Oh—are the maids English, too?"

For Yvonne, the strangeness and the newness all blended: chestnuts and double-decker buses and motorcars and wearing woolly things all the time because it was always cold and usually raining. For her, the difference started with sounds: the sounds of London were quite different from the sounds of the other places she had known. Even the street cries were different from the ones she had heard in Buenos Aires; they sold different things here, called out other names, offered other wares or services, chair-caning, knife-sharpening, buy old rags and bones.

And then there was the food.

"Nice people don't eat in the street." Yvonne discovered that even sweets had to be brought home to be consumed.

They were wondrous to see in the shop, though, hundreds and hundreds of different kinds, all sorts of colors and shapes and tastes, some to suck on and others to chew, long ones and square ones and ones that looked like round rainbows and others that changed color and tasted different as you sucked your way through from layer to layer.

The memory of *alfajores* and *dulce de leche* dimmed; toffee and gob-stoppers slid sweetly, easily into the breach.

Christmas was coming, and there was present buying and carol singing and making paper garlands for the church hall. Aunt Boo took Yvonne to the Christmas party there, and there was a Father Christmas, all dressed up in red, with white fur around the edge of his hat that matched his long white beard. She lined up to speak to him with the other children, and when it was her turn, he asked her whether she had been a good little girl all year.

"Mami says . . ." Yvonne began, but her great-aunt cut her short by saying, "She's the best little girl in all the world," and so Yvonne was allowed to tell her wish for Christmas.

Yvonne swallowed hard before replying. She could see the dolls' tea set as plain as plain could be, the way it had been in the lighted shop window when she and Aunt Boo had walked by, then stopped to take a look at it. There were cups turned sideways in the bottom of the box, and six little saucers standing beside them, each in a slot to hold it tight. There was a sweet teapot, with round pink roses painted on its side and a matching milk jug next to it. There was even a slop bowl and a wide pink ribbon all around the box, and it was clearly the most beautiful thing Yvonne had ever seen.

Still, she hesitated.

"Come along now," Father Christmas was saying, "surely there must be something. Mustn't take too much time, you know. I have to talk to all the other boys and girls here, too."

Yvonne felt her throat tightening up.

"Can I whisper it?" she whispered.

He bent his ear towards her.

She cupped a protective hand around her mouth.

"The dollies' tea set," she managed.

He straightened up, smiling.

"Ho, ho, ho! Well, well! A dollies' tea set, eh?"

"No, *no*," Yvonne said desperately. "Not just any tea set . . . *the* tea set . . ."

But he wasn't listening any more, and was saying good-bye and pushing her aside, and then he began talking to the boy behind her. Yvonne's eyes filled with tears.

"What's the matter, lovey?" Aunt Boo asked. "Does something hurt? Perhaps you had too many little cakes . . ."

But Yvonne could only close her eyes and shake her head in denial, and when the tightness had left and she could speak properly again, the tears had left, too.

There it was. Under the tree. A real tree, too—not like the spikey, dusty one she remembered from Cosunzué, with the branches that had to be pulled down and were a funny green, with hard red points at the end Mami said were supposed to be holly, but holly was another kind of plant that didn't grow at El Naranjal.

This was a real Christmas tree, and today was a real Christmas, and even the wish she had made had come true: the dollies' tea set was there, its wide pink ribbon standing up in a beautiful bow, the box leaning against a wrapped package at the base of the tree. Yvonne could hardly believe her eyes.

"Careful, lovey . . . we're going to light the candles now . . ."

Great-Aunt Moo lit each one from the special taper, and everything looked like fairyland, with the tinsel glittering silver lights and the ornaments shining against the dark green of the branches. There were glass birds and golden bells and silver-and-gold chains and tiny houses painted in bright colors, and there were stars and trumpets hanging on thin silver cords. Right at the top of the tree sat the special Christmas angel, almost touching the ceiling.

Everyone was oohing and aahing and saying wasn't it lovely? and Merry Christmas! and shall we put the candles out now, and open our presents? There were lots of people in the front parlor, not only the two great-aunts and Mami and Dick and Peter, but also visitors Mami had known a long time ago, Uncle Edwin and Uncle Maurice, who were big men, and brothers, and Uncle Edwin's wife, Aunt May, and their two little girls, Maisie and Jeannie, who were both bigger than Yvonne, but who would probably play with her, Mami had told her in a whisper, if she was a nice, polite child. It was a shame, really, that they had come today, because Yvonne only wanted to take her tea set off to her room and play with it on her own; she wanted to get to know the tea set before she played with it with other people.

"Nonsense, Yvonne, don't be selfish...run along, girls, and play upstairs..."

Yvonne heard the one with the mustache, who was called Uncle Maurice, say, "She doesn't look a bit like you did at that age, Edie," and she heard Mami answer, "No, she has Edgar's eyes—and he used to say she took after his mother. But, tell me, Maurice, what news of Vesey? Oh, it's so nice meeting old friends from Rosario again..."

It was May O'Connor who eventually told Edie the truth about Vesey—thin, pale-haired May, with the long nose and the distracted air, who looked remarkably like her husband in coloring, without his multiple chins or reddened, shiny pate.

"Edwin and Maurice never mention him if they can help it," she said. "I'm sure all they'll tell you is they think he's in Hamburg."

Edie nodded. "...and then Maurice changed the subject. I thought it a bit odd, but I didn't like to pry. After all, I didn't want to spoil Christmas..."

It was May's turn to nod.

"Quite so. You see, they're dreadfully ashamed of Vesey."

"What happened?"

"He took some money. Edwin never would tell me the whole story. I think Maurice covered the debts here in

166

England, and then got him a job in Germany with a company they know."

"A shipping company?"

"I think so. After all, that's what he did here, just like his brothers. At first, they all worked in the same firm, but there was a fuss there, too, and Vesey was sacked."

"Did he not marry?"

"No—and I pity the poor woman who lets her head be turned by him. Oh, he's a flatterer, all right—but a liar through and through. I hope we've seen the back of him forever." May spoke with unusual force. "And I know Edwin hopes so, too."

5

The bad weather continued; the New Year saw swans swimming over the flooded pavements of low-lying London areas along the swollen Thames. In mid-January, the heavy snows arrived, and Yvonne woke to an enchanted, white-covered world.

The snow changed all the sounds, made them soft and muffled and kind. Even when it was still falling, it was quite different from rain, and the wind sang different songs through the snow, until it stopped altogether, and everything was quiet in a gentle hush like a deep winter lullaby.

She couldn't go outside very much because Mami was afraid she would catch a cold, even though Mami herself went out quite often. Yvonne didn't mind; there were so many things to do in the house, many of them introduced to her by Aunt Boo. Making fudge was one of the favorites.

Making fudge meant being wrapped up in a big white apron and helping to squash the butter and sugar together in a big bowl with the long wooden spoon. Yvonne always stood on the kitchen chair when she worked, because otherwise she could not get the spoon to push in the proper way. Then Aunt Boo would take over, and when all the chocolate had been added, she would let Yvonne lick the spoon. Watching the fudge bubble in the pot was fun, too, and then Aunt Boo would say, "I think it's just right," and pour the rich dark mix into a long buttered pan.

The worst was waiting for it to cool, watching the top begin to glaze and shine in that special way. Once it was ready, and cut, and cold, Yvonne delighted in placing it on the silver platter with a pretty lace doily, and neat fudge squares piled just so.

"It would never have turned out so well if Yvonne hadn't helped me," Aunt Boo always announced, and Peter and Dick took an extra piece each, agreeing that it was a better batch than the one before.

"But I helped with that one, too..."

"Well, then, there you are—practice makes perfect," they would chorus with a smile.

If Edie found her aunts' home to be welcoming and congenial, perfect for her under the circumstances prevailing, for Yvonne it was even more perfect: it was a solid home. Routine was reliable, soothing, nourishing; no sudden drama, no harsh fatality stabbed through the tranquility of order and content. Meals were served at regular intervals; expected dishes turned up on time. Monday there was always cottage pie, the natural follower of Sunday's roast; porridge could be counted on to appear at breakfast, with thick cream waiting to be poured from the silver creamer. Tea and bread and butter and slices of cake made their appearance at half after four; supper in front of the fire, before the grown-ups had their evening meal, closed Yvonne's day.

And then there were her privileges, like the toasting fork. She learned to use it with Aunt Boo's aid, and making toast became her special job.

"I don't ever want to leave," Yvonne declared with passion when mention was made of an eventual return to the Argentine.

Edie, whose mood had been set by the increased number of her social outings and her widening circle of friends, consoled her by saying, "Don't worry—we'll always come back home to England," and Yvonne was content.

Her English adapted to the accents around her, her likes to the local views and tastes. When spring came at last, a visit to the country led to her discovery of the Sussex Downs so loved by the grandmother she had never known, and while her great-aunts reminisced about their own childhood long ago, telling Edie stories about the mourned Millicent, Yvonne ran in the sunshine and played by a stream.

The Andes faded; a condor Ña Conce once showed her flying high, soaring back to his *cordillera* home, was replaced

168

by a sparrow hawk seen near the sea. The indigo blue of the Argentine sky paled to English countryside pastels; the scent of the jacaranda was overshadowed by the earliest hyacinths, perfuming leftover snow. The passing weeks and the easy adaptability of childhood worked swiftly to transform the blue-eyed child from rarity to the norm: Yvonne became, to all intents and purposes, an English child.

What disparities there were became hidden deep below the surface; she took her manner and her mannerisms from the strictures of her class. Her ear heard, her memory retained, her throat and tongue reacted, imitated: her accent and intonation changed.

"No one would ever guess she wasn't born here. She's English through and through," said the great-aunts to Edie who, partially pleased and peripherally annoyed, changed the subject.

With winter gone, the London garden sprouted, budded, bloomed behind the tall house, and became Yvonne's favorite haunt. She would dart out as early as possible, running to the overgrown tangle near the potting shed, feeling the light threads of spiders' webs, woven overnight from branch across to branch, brush her lightly as she sped down the path. She inspected the new leaves growing pale green tips out of formerly bare branches, checked the budding raspberry canes behind the shed, watched blossoms open overnight.

One bright and breezy day, she caught up with Bronner at the compost heap; he was handling a rake, and she could see his hands and fingers grasped around the handle.

In her disappointment, she voiced her thoughts out loud. "Oh—they're not green..."

Bronner looked up, said nothing, returned his attention to his work. Yvonne edged closer, getting a better view. A smudge of green raised her hopes, but then she saw it was only a leaf, stuck to the side of the gardener's hand.

"I wonder why Gladys lied to me.... She said your fingers were green... that's why plants grow for you.... It was naughty of her to tell a taradiddle...."

"It's no lie."

His remark, so unexpected, made Yvonne jump.

"But she said they were green...."

"Ay."

"... and they're not."

169

The rake stopped moving. Bronner rested the handle against his shoulder, stretching out his gnarled hands, palm upward, toward her.

"They be green inside, where it counts. The plants know."

Yvonne considered this, then looked at her own small hands.

"Are mine green inside, too?"

Bronner only grunted, taking up the rake.

But the next day, he presented her with an old garden hand-shovel and cleared a patch near the vegetable beds to call her very own.

In Edie, the changes tended to be more visible and were all superficial; the blossoming that had begun on the trans-Atlantic voyage continued in London as the months went by. Her tastes and interests, primed by her childhood, took to English ways and habits with enthusiasm, but she was already capable of quiet discrimination when anything did not suit her own immediate needs. A holiday trip to Paris with May and Edwin O'Connor convinced her of the excellence that France had to offer; back in London, she swore she would return to the Continent at the first chance. Privately, she knew she wanted to travel everywhere and see the world.

In the meantime, there was London, and the headiness of living there; Edie's life was mostly centered on herself, and her own enjoyment. Relieved of household responsibilities by her aunts' established home, cosseted and protected by the two doting sisters, Edie had only herself to think about, her own time to occupy and enjoy. She was only too glad to leave Yvonne to her own happy devices in a household equally glad to look after the child, leaving Edie free to accept the ever-increasing invitations to parties and dinners, excursions and theater parties, outings and, once in a while, a really grand ball.

It was at a theater party hosted by Maurice O'Connor that Edie met Harry, a brother officer in Maurice's regiment, and a friend since university days. He was a tall and distinguished man, white-haired, with a young-looking, ruddy-hued face, but clearly a good twenty years her senior, a man of gentle manner and straightforward mien. He was, Edie discovered, a member of the Royal Corps of Gentlemen at Arms, a group usually referred to as the King's Bodyguard, and frequently at court, fulfilling his honorary duties in court circles.

During the course of the evening, she also learned he was a recent widower; Edwin told her, in a quick aside, before seating Edie at the after-theater supper table with the newcomer next to her.

The delight of the evening was marred only later when Edie overheard another guest saying, "...oh, yes, of course, very pretty indeed—but, my *dear*, such a colonial...have you ever heard anything like her accent in your *life*?"

"Mami, can I have..."

"For goodness sake, Yvonne—*will* you please learn to speak properly! If I've told you once, I've told you a dozen times; it's *Mummy*, not Mami. Say Mummy, child."

"Mummy."

"There. That's better. Now what is it?"

"Mami, can I..."

The slap stung Yvonne to silence.

"Naughty little girl! Go to your room! Why you persist in being so stubborn is quite beyond me! Upstairs, at once! And don't you come down again until I tell you to...."

Aunt Boo offered to give Yvonne lessons.

"She's such a bright child, I'm sure we'll do splendidly...."

And so they took to having lessons on the dining room table after Gladys had done the room before mid-morning. Lunchtime would be upon them before they knew it, and Aunt Boo would say, "Goodness! How time flies!" and Yvonne readily agreed; books and reading and writing were all exciting and new. Sums were not as much fun, and took more effort and work, and they always got harder and harder, instead of the other way around. But she managed to keep up with the exercises Aunt Boo set for her, and the best part of all was the afternoon session, held once a week, at the upright piano.

"Mummy, look! Come and listen to me play! I can do a whole scale!"

"Yes, Yvonne, very nice, but I'm in a hurry now...."

"Oh. Are you going out, Mummy? Will you be back in time to say nighty-night?"

"I don't think so. Not tonight. You be a good girl and don't make a fuss about going to bed...."

"I won't, Mummy, I promise. I'll kiss you nighty-night now...."

Mami/Mummy went out a lot, Yvonne noticed; she had also overheard the great-aunts talk.

The big bathtub was white, with feet like a lion, and when it was filled with lots of water almost to its top, Yvonne could float in it.

"Look, Mummy—look! I can swim!"

"*Do* hurry up, child. It's late, and I have to change."

"But I'm *swimming*."

"Yes, dear. Very nice. You can swim some more next time. Now—out of that tub. Here's a nice big towel..."

Bath times were fun, even if Yvonne did have to get out before she really wanted to.

"Are you going out to supper again, Mummy?"

"Yes, darling, with Aunt May and Uncle Edwin..."

"And Uncle Harry, too?"

Edie rubbed her back warm and dry.

"There you are. Ready for your nightie?"

"Will Uncle Harry be there?" Yvonne persisted, slipping the nightdress over her head and pushing her arms into the sleeves.

"I expect so." Edie handed Yvonne her dressing gown. "You like him very much, don't you?"

"Oh, yes."

"Do you like him best?"

The question came as a surprise, and Yvonne considered it for a moment before answering.

"I like them *all* best," she decided finally. "Uncle Harry and Uncle Edwin and Aunt May and Uncle Maurice. After Aunt Moo and Aunt Boo, of course."

Then her expression changed, and she flung her arms around her mother. "But firstest and bestest of all, I love *you*, Mami—I mean, Mummy...."

Strangely, Edie did not correct her, but stood quite still, absently stroking Yvonne's damp, silken hair.

"But still, you *do* like Uncle Harry very much, don't you?"

"Oh, yes. Don't you?" Yvonne drew back and looked anxiously at her mother's face, to be visibly relieved at Edie's nod. "I'm glad, because I heard Aunt Boo telling Aunt Moo she thought he was your best beau. Is he, Mummy? What's a best beau?"

Edie smiled, and went on stroking her daughter's head.

172

"It means a very good, a very special friend, darling—a *very* special friend..."

Late that summer they went to the seaside with a family of cousins on the Barnes side. The great-aunts and Edie sat in deck chairs with parasols while Yvonne played with the Barnes children and their nannie by the water's edge. Peter and Dick spent most of their time on the pier, at the amusements, but everyone gathered for the donkey rides along the wide stretch of sand. They all enjoyed themselves immensely, but even Yvonne noticed her mother's impatience to return to London.

Edie was, indeed, eager to get back; Harry's early attention to her had continued apace. His courtly ways had progressed to pronounced interest; at first she had merely wondered, then speculated, later become hopeful, and was now almost certain: Harry was falling in love with her, might well be about to propose. The signs were all there, though veiled by propriety: the longer glances, the wider smile, the extra phrase, the solicitous air.

Even as she sat on the Southcoast beach while Yvonne made sandcastles down by the water, Edie turned the matter over and over in her mind. Harry would be exactly the right sort of husband for her; she would love every moment of his court duties and attendance. It would naturally mean that she herself would have to be presented; the mere thought of curtseying to the king and queen was the substance of hours-long dreaming. If only reverie could become reality...and it might...it could...if...if...

Edie sat up in the deck chair, blinked against the sun and adjusted her parasol. She counted the days and sighed with impatience; another four days before they could leave.

The closing months of the year brought Yvonne's sixth birthday, unusually warm and mild weather, and the fruition of Edie's romantic dreams, which came with Harry's frank declaration of his love and intentions. His earlier reticence, he explained, had in part been because of the difference in age between them; also playing a role had been his recent period of mourning. But now more than two years had gone by since his late wife had passed away; not even the strictest moralists could possibly deny him the right to another partner in life.

173

All this he explained, and to all this Edie listened with joy in her heart; her own dream's achievement was coming to pass—even if, as Harry was saying, their plans for the future and many of their present meetings must still remain secret. The reason, he told her, had nothing to do with them.

". . . but I must tell you, in full confidence, there is going to be a war. . . ."

He did not wish to hide his privileged knowledge from her; he was already involved in plans being made by His Majesty's Government. War would not break out for about another year, and once it did, it would be over quickly; of that, Harry had no doubt. Therefore, the best thing for them to do was to wait until the hostilities were over; then they would be able to start their life together in peace and full happiness.

They could even use the intervening time to their advantage; Edie herself readily acknowledged she would have to make a trip out to the Argentine to rearrange her financial affairs. If she were to travel out soon, say, right after Christmas, at the beginning of the new year, Harry would go out to Argentina to fetch her when the war was won and over.

"We could then marry, and have a shipboard wedding trip home. . . ."

It worked out perfectly. With Christmas preparations already in the air, the added activity of planning the return to B.A. became all part and parcel of the change of pace. Yvonne, crestfallen on hearing they were going to leave, brightened at once when her mother said, "But we'll be coming back, you wait and see."

For Edie and Harry, life went on as usual, although they found it hard to disguise their feelings and keep their secret. Those who guessed were both diplomatic and discreet; the great-aunts made no mention of anything except their happiness at seeing Edie "look so well," as Aunt Moo delicately put it.

A sailing in early January was found, passages were booked, the steamer trunk and the traveling bags brought down from the attic and dusted off. On Christmas Day, the toasts around the tree ranged from "Merry Christmas!" to "Bon voyage," and all the O'Connors promised to come and see the travelers off when the time came.

The week before they were set to leave, Edie did some last minute shopping, walking home from the bus stop in the slate gray midwinter dusk. She rounded the corner into the residential street leading to the great-aunts' house, her thoughts on her purchases, and then on Harry, whom she would not be seeing until the day before she left, as court functions were keeping him at his duties fulltime.

A clattering disturbed the deserted road's hush; looking up, Edie saw a carriage coming toward her from the far end. To her surprise and delight, it was one of the state coaches, the gilded, ornamental beauties that carried royalty and visiting dignitaries to official functions and palace occasions. Harry had told her about them in detail. Edie stopped to watch the carriage go by, thrilled to get such a close and unexpected view. She could see the tall-hatted coachman, sitting high on the driver's seat.

He was drawing up the reins. The coach was stopping. Edie stared. The door flung open.

"Edie!"

"*Harry!*"

"Quick! Give me your hand! That's right...now up..."

She was up and inside and the door banged shut behind her, and she lurched clumsily into the seat as the coach started up and they were moving swiftly away. They were hidden inside, laughing in delight, she stealing a royal ride, he a passionate kiss, huddled and cramped yet free as birds, not minding the ancient, lumpy bench with its creaking frame and rattling boards beneath the uncomfortable padding.

"Won't the coachman...?"

"Don't worry. He knows what to do. I'll have you home, safe and sound, before you know it. I'm due at the Palace within the hour. But I had to see you.... I wanted to give you this..."

The heavy, wide chain folded its links into her hand, the gold smooth and cold against the warmth of her palm. The center of the elaborate bracelet was a solid disc, gem-studded..

"...been in my family for generations. May I fasten it around your wrist?"

"Oh, Harry, I..."

It glinted beneath the darkness of her velvet coat-cuff.

"It'll hold us together for the months to come, Edie, and serve to remind you, every time you look at it, that I shall go

175

out to the Argentine and fetch you the moment the war ends and I am free. Then we'll sail back together and live happily ever after."

"Here in England..."

"Of course..."

Golden dreams and the royal coach bore her to the aunts' front door.

They were not back in Buenos Aires many months when an Archduke's assassination broke into the news. The war clouds gathered, rumbled and grew dark. Edie, who received long letters from Harry regularly, felt herself privy to the secrets of the world. He had rejoined his own regiment, as had Maurice O'Connor. No one in their circles talked of anything but war.

As I told you would happen, my sweetest darling, the war clouds are overhead, very soon to burst. It will storm fiercely for a short while and, I trust, most healthily. The Continent needs a fresh breath of air.

The thunderclap came in the first days of August; the guns roared, cannon answered, men marched off to war.

It's all so far away, perhaps it isn't happening.

The phrase rang clearly from the lost long ago, coming to Edie in her mother's soft voice.

Unbidden, other tones answered.

...a fool, Mrs. Moore.... Papa's voice said.

Edie started to cover her ears, then smiled at her own foolishness. Harry was a man of the world and knew what he was talking about. She would leave the war and all the planning to him, and wait, exactly as he had told her to do, until everything was over and he came to B.A.

She was returning from church with the Thaxters when Edwin's telegram arrived.

REGRET TO INFORM YOU HARRY KILLED IN ACTION AT THE FRONT STOP LETTERS FOLLOW FROM ALL OF US STOP OUR SYMPATHY AND PRAYERS.

III

Palermo Chico
1918–1920

1

Yvonne fitted her pencil sharpener into the long wooden pencil box and wiggled it with her index finger to lodge it into place. It was a tight fit; she adjusted the contents of the box with care and picked up the cover. The dry smooth feel of the planed wood was silky under her fingers. It was her new pencil box, given to her for her eleventh birthday, and she wanted to keep it as nice and pretty as possible. Her old one had gone all splintery and was blotched with ink besides, but now her writing was much improved, and she was used to a pen and caring properly for its nibs, removing them and wiping them off on blotting paper before putting them away.

At the desk next to her, Lally Young was also tidying up her pencils. She had a leather case that opened out flat, with loops to hold everything in place. She and Lally were Best Friends and told each other everything.

When she and Lally had first met, Yvonne had only been seven, and she hadn't known how to spell properly, and had written it Best Freind. But now she knew better; spelling was among the many things she had learned in the years since she and Mummy had come back from England and Yvonne had started school.

At first, it was only supposed to be living in the hotel for a little while, until This Dreadful War was over. That was when Uncle Harry was going to come and fetch them and be Yvonne's new father when he married Mummy and then they were all going to return to England and be happy for always and live there forever. But then came the day when Mummy had cried and cried, and Uncle Robert had explained to Yvonne that Uncle Harry had Fallen at the Front, and she was to be extra-specially good because her poor Mummy was very upset. Yvonne, who didn't like Uncle Robert, said yes, she promised she would be, and got out of his way as soon as she could without understanding what had happened to Uncle Harry. For a long time afterward, she thought he had slipped on the steps leading to the great-aunts' house and died right there in the front garden.

Mummy had gone on crying for ages—not all the time, but on and off, and sometimes her cheeks would be wet and shiny with tears when Yvonne least expected them to be. Even after she stopped crying, when they moved to the house Mummy bought in Palermo Chico, she hadn't worn any of the pretty new dresses she had had made; they were all in the wardrobe, some hanging up and some folded on the shelves. It all had to do with Harry having died and now never going to be her father because, as Yvonne eventually discovered, he had been shot by a horrid German. The war kept on going, but it wasn't coming to B.A., Mummy said, and so life had to go on.

Lally was luckier; she did have a father. Her real name was Allison, she was a year older than Yvonne, and a little bit taller but not much, and she didn't have any brothers or sisters, either. Lally's hair was dark and straight, much darker than Yvonne's even though hers was not as pale as Rosita said it used to be when she was very small, but their plaits were almost the same length.

They both attended Miss Bowen's English Day School for Girls, which was quite near where Yvonne's house was, and even nearer to Lally's. There was also an English boys' school in the same district. All the Argentine schools had boys and girls mixed, but Yvonne and Lally did Spanish lessons on Wednesday afternoons, right at Miss Bowen's. The Spanish teacher was very boring, and there was often so much chattering in class that they didn't get any work done at all. Sometimes Miss Bowen herself would burst in when they were being noisy, and say, "Girls! Girls! Stop this at once! I want you to be nice to poor Miss Jimenez, and get on with your lessons."

If Miss Bowen heard them again, she would send in her special assistant, Miss Webb, to take over. That was the nicest of all, for Miss Webb, usually known as Miss Peggy because she was young and not a real teacher, was kind and understanding. Miss Webb knew how to get them interested in the lesson so that time flew by and they forgot about being mean to the Spanish teacher.

Miss Peggy's official job was secretary of the school, which meant she knew everything about everything, and you went to her for new pencils and fresh copybooks and if you had a pain in your tummy and wanted to go home. No matter what the problem was, she always said, "Never mind, we'll manage." It was a shame, really, that she wasn't a proper teacher, because Yvonne was sure it would be easier to learn things with Miss Peggy than with the teachers they did have, including Miss Bowen, who was all right, but sometimes very strict, and always impatient when Yvonne didn't understand arithmetic, which was most of the time.

There. The pencil-box top slid to an easy close. Simultaneously, Lally's case snapped shut. The two girls looked at each other and smothered giggles, saved from the teacher's frowned attention by the opening clang of the school bell. On being dismissed from their classroom for the day, the best friends walked to the front gate, where Rosita would be waiting for them.

Sometimes it was Mrs. Young who escorted the girls home, and occasionally Edie would come to fetch them, but usually it was Rosita who waited by the door and walked the familiar walk with them, first to Lally's house and then on to Yvonne's, along the ridge-tiled pavements and across the cobbled, treelined streets of Palermo, which was really Buenos Aires, but one of the parts where there were more houses than shops. It was one of the nicest parts, really, with the biggest parks with real lakes and boat rides and hundreds of trees, not just plazas with a few statues and some bushes, like other districts had. The Botanical Gardens were near, too, and so was the Zoo, and one could go for walks in all sorts of different directions to see different things.

Closer to the center of Buenos Aires the houses and shops were all jammed up close to each other, but in Palermo many of the houses had big gardens and there were open spaces and fields, too. There was a big one next to Miss Bowen's English Day School for Girls, and one section of it was used for marching and running, and games of rounders, and School Sports Day, when they had events like the egg-and-spoon race, and the sack race, and the potato race, all of which Yvonne enjoyed, because she was good at them, and often came in among the winners of her age group, flushed with exertion and pride. Lally was not as good as Yvonne, even though she was bigger and older, but she was better at throwing things and aim, like tossing hoopla rings over prizes when the church had a fete.

Going home from school with Rosita always meant hearing

her make a big fuss about crossing the road, because there were many more motorcars now, and Rosita was still afraid of them. Neither Yvonne nor Lally could understand why, especially after Mr. Young had taken everyone for a ride in his when he got it.

After leaving Lally at her house, Rosita and Yvonne would go down another street and round another corner, and then they would be home. The house where Yvonne lived was set back in the garden, and there was a high brick wall, too high for anyone to see over it, which was topped with broken bottles stuck in cement, to prevent robbers climbing over and getting into the garden. Further protection against intrusion ran about inside: the teru-bird, with his double "teru! teru!" cry and his thin, spikey legs, who spent his days strutting the lawn, his crest a feather-wisp curving out and back from his head. His pointy bill was always at the ready for insects, stabbing repeatedly into the turf like a sewing machine needle. He also ate little pieces of meat from Yvonne's finger, his bright eyes two tiny buttons set in the smooth-plumed head. He couldn't fly, because the lead-feathers on one wing were always kept cut, to prevent him from going away; Yvonne wondered whether he would leave, if he could, and if his flying would be as jerky and mechanical as the rest of his movements were. No other bird she had ever watched looked like a clockwork toy, and she enjoyed watching not only birds and the ducks and geese in the parks but also any kind of animal, even insects, nice insects, friendly ones, like crickets.

Yvonne knew far more about animals than Lally, although Lally liked them, and was interested when Yvonne told her about the cricket who liked peaches; she had found him in a corner of the kitchen, where Rosita didn't sweep too carefully, and as he chirped in such a friendly way, even Mummy said, all right, let him live there. Yvonne gave him a small piece of the peach she was eating one day, and he hopped over to where she had put it on the floor and leaned over it to lap it, cricket-fashion. Later in the summer he disappeared; Yvonne decided he had probably gone out into the garden to live with the other crickets who sang at the far end.

That was the summer she and Lally had made so many daisy chains, except not with daisies. They used the white and purple clover flowers, with the firm, splittable stems. They made long necklaces with them and garlands for their hair, and when they tired of that, they caught some of the yellow or white butterflies that came in clouds to rest on the clover flowers. Yvonne thought it would be all right to keep them in a jar, as long as there were holes punched in the lid for air. But Rosita said the next day that most of the *mariposas* had died, so the next time the girls used a birdcage with netting over it instead, hoping the butterflies would live on the flowers they also placed in the cage, and eventually lay eggs. Yvonne had already housed a caterpillar in a shoebox, and he had curled up in a leaf and become a chrysalis, but someone had thrown the box away. Caging the butterflies was no more successful; perhaps, Lally suggested, they were all boy-butterflies, and they let the survivors go and went back to making necklaces instead, and flower crowns.

Not all the girls at school were as nice as Lally.

"You think you're big and important just because you've been to England. . . ."

Yvonne flushed, stung by the taunt.

"No, I don't . . ."

"Yes, you do. You're always showing off about it. Little Miss Show-Off, that's who you are. And Little Miss Stuck-Up, too. . . ."

"That's not fair! And it isn't true!"

"Yes, it is—and Janie and Isabel and Moira think you are, too, and we're going to call you Little Miss Show-Off from now on. . . ."

"You're horrid . . . all of you are being horrid. . . ."

"Little Miss Show-Off! Little Miss Show-Off . . ."

Tears choked off Yvonne's desperation and she fled her tormentor. Allison found her later, still sobbing, at the far end of the cloakroom, where their games shoes and tennis rackets spilled over shelves and their coats were hung from individually labeled pegs.

"What's the matter, Yvonne? Aren't you going to come and play tennis?"

Yvonne sobbed out her unhappiness.

Lally put her arm around her.

"You mustn't let them bother you," she comforted. "They're only jealous, because they've never been anywhere."

Yvonne calmed down, and the two best friends eventually went out to the tennis courts at the back of the school, but Lally's words of reason, although consoling, never healed the cuts of cruelty dealt deep and early, indefensible for being targeted so well.

Yvonne had only been eleven for a few weeks when the news came through that the Great War was over at last. The cheering went up all across B.A. and the British community celebrated in full style. There were speeches and parties and holidays and celebrations, and tears of joy, of relief, of sadness in memory of the fallen, of happiness at the thought of a future without war. From now on, it would be ever onward and ever upward: life, happiness, and financial gain.

"Jolly good thing, cleaning up the Boche like that..."

".. shipping lines opening up for us, bound to be an advantage..."

".. starting a new office, old boy, can't let a good thing get away, can I?"

When Mrs. O'Connor died, the following March, Edie went up to Rosario for the funeral. At the cortege, she was in the family carriage with Mrs. O'Connor's sister, Anna Casey, and her sons Timothy and Kevin.

"So terribly sad none of her boys are here," sighed Mrs. Casey, and Edie nodded. Tim, Edie's contemporary, was solicitously at his mother's side, his ruddy features and shock of sandy hair lively contrast to the day's solemnities. Kevin Casey, younger, shorter and more slightly built, reminded Edie of Vesey; he had the same quick, nervous mannerisms. Tim appeared to stand taller and more secure in his ways. It was Tim who told her he had already sent word to England. After Edie returned to Buenos Aires, May's letter reached her.

Edwin and I feel it is useless our going out, she wrote. *The girls need us here. And Maurice can handle it on his own; we do not believe there is anything very complicated involved. Vesey is apparently somewhere out East; he left Germany before the War, telling Maurice he was going to Japan. Whether he is still there or not, I have no idea, as Edwin has not mentioned him, but I imagine Maurice knows.*

She gave the date on which her brother-in-law was sailing, and closed with fondest love.

184

Although we are all glad you missed the terrible war years here, all of us, including the Great-Aunts, long to see you again . . .

". . . and if Maurice is going to handle the inheritance, perhaps you can persuade him to give some of it—in his mother's memory, of course—to our new school."

Dollie Thaxter bustled about as she spoke, sorting out contributions for the next jumble sale. Edie handed her another woolen cardigan from the pile she was inspecting.

"I don't think I can do that, Dollie. Why don't you ask him?"

"Because you know him much better than I do—why, I hardly remember him at all."

"But I'm not even a member of the Ladies Society."

"Well, you *should* be."

Edie sighed, regretting she had as much as mentioned Maurice's imminent return, and went back to looking through the pile of used clothes. Dollie, fatter and more fervently involved in good works than ever, was forever pushing her to belong to any one or all of the church groups. Edie always managed to muster sufficient reason and enough excuses not to do so, but the tugging and pulling was always there. She compromised by helping Dollie, as she was now, as an unseen and unsung assistant whenever a *kermesse* or a jumble sale or a fete was underway. As always, her childhood ties to the Thaxters were a mixed blessing at best; tradition rather than affection kept everything going. Nonetheless, Edie knew that their usefulness to her, though limited, was real. Robert was well thought of in the business community, on his way to becoming a contender for the top spot in Bateman and Co. in future years. Canon Thaxter, thinner and more taut than ever, was still one of the British community's leading men of the cloth, although even the staunchest of his supporters would now acknowledge, if only in private, that old Thaxter was going a bit overboard in certain matters these days.

". . . spends his time delving into exorcism . . ."

". . . told me only the other day there's a house in Hurlingham haunted by a slug . . ."

"If he means in the garden, he's probably quite right! Mine's full of snails."

General laughter.

"No. He said indoors. And it isn't a real slug, but a gigantic shadow. He's conducting an exorcism ceremony next week...."

Cannon Thaxter was indeed growing increasingly strange.

"How is your father feeling?" Edie asked, knowing it would get Dollie's mind off its present path.

Dollie sighed and said, "You'd do better to ask how *I'm* feeling....It's very difficult, I swear...with Robert gone from the house. I have to cope with so much. And whereas Father's still much more sensible in some ways, he does get very difficult indeed, much of the time. As to Ma," she went on, without waiting for Edie's question, "she has become a terrible cross I suppose I shall have to bear...."

Edie knew for herself exactly how vacant Bessie Thaxter had become. It was one of the many reasons she had discouraged Rosa, now considering a change of work so as to be nearer Rosita in Buenos Aires, from working in the Thaxter household. Rosita, of tougher fiber, had always refused outright.

"It was different, *señora* Edie, when you were living there as a girl, but without you, I would *never* work for that crazy old woman...."

Rosita had rejoined Edie the moment she had returned from London, leaving Rosa in full domestic charge of the ailing Mrs. O'Connor's home. Even after Anna Casey was widowed and joined her sister's household, it was Rosa who ran it until Mrs. O'Connor's death. She was still there, awaiting Maurice's arrival and the settling of affairs; it was an anxious time for the aging servant, and Edie had promised to help her find other work.

"But not with the Thaxters..."

"No, *señora*. Rosita says the same...."

"Maurice..."

Edie rose from her chair, holding out both her hands to the man stepping through the doorway from the entrance hall into the living room.

"Edie, my dear..."

"I can hardly believe it..."

"And to see you...is almost a dream...to be here at all..."

Outside, the cold rain drummed against the tall french doors that provided a watery picture of the winter-bleak garden beyond. Its pattering sound filled the silence of the moment until Edie broke the spell.

"Let me ring for tea. We can have it here by the fire. You're probably chilled...."

Maurice smiled, then settled himself in the armchair facing hers. "That would be delightful," he said.

Rosita, having already seen Maurice when she opened the front door on his arrival, was still breathless with excitement and pleasure when she brought in the tea.

"I didn't think you'd remember me," he told her.

"Oh, *señor* Maurice, how can you say such a thing? I, who spent all that time with your sainted mother, and knew your poor father..."

"Ah, yes, yes. Of course." Maurice rubbed his forehead as though trying to brush away the years. "One forgets. Being away from the Argentine for such a long time, you see..." He left the sentence unfinished. "But you forgive me, Rosita, I hope?"

She blushed.

"But of course, *señor* Maurice, how could you ever think...?"

"Now she'll be impossible for days," Edie remarked, watching Rosita scurry from the room. "Bossier than ever, I expect."

"She's very good for you. Always has been."

"I suppose you're right. But she can be a tyrant." Edie turned to the tea trolley and removed the cosy from the silver pot. "Will you have milk or lemon with your tea, Maurice?"

The soothing ritual of serving and drinking tea bridged the intervening years. Maurice spoke, but little, of the war itself; all that mattered, he said, was that it was over. Nothing of like nature should ever be allowed to happen again. Edie, in turn, chatted about B.A., its growths and its changes, and brought him up to date about the people he had either heard of or known.

"...and Robert finally got married last year to a dim little thing from the southern suburbs....Canon Thaxter is getting very peculiar....We dread his sermons, they last forever and sometimes don't really make sense....Bessie? Oh, she has to be watched all the time now....No, Dollie hasn't married ...very involved in church and charity....Yes, you wait 'til you see Yvonne...a big girl now...school very near here...at a friend's for tea this afternoon..."

When they spoke of Rosario, she told him about his mother's funeral, and Maurice said he would be traveling north the following week to see what needed to be done.

Then he shifted in his chair, sat up, and leaned forward.

187

"I want to tell you about Harry," he began. The fire in the fireplace between them set off a shower of sparks as a log settled further into its own ashes.

"Yes. I'd like to hear . . . whatever it is you want to say. . . ."

Edie's voice was very low. Maurice reached into his pocket, drawing out a small package wrapped in rumpled, worn paper.

"He made me promise I'd bring this to you if he didn't return. You see, Edie, he was convinced—well, perhaps not convinced, but reasonably certain in his own mind that he'd not get back. He had a distinct foreboding about it, right from the moment war was declared."

Edie turned the package over in her hands, reluctant to open it immediately, trying to sense the past in its contours, and feeling only the worn surface of the paper and the thin ridge of string.

"Before that, he was most optimistic. In fact, the mood you knew him in was the way he believed. He more or less told me the plans you and he had made, and there was no doubt about it: Harry was sure, at the time, that the coming war would be a quick, clean sweep."

Maurice gave a short sigh, catching his breath. Then he went on talking, telling how Harry's whole demeanor had changed once the first campaigns started.

"He was very high up, you know—privy to information and decisions very few people ever knew about, or heard. And once the fighting started, he was dead set against some of the leaders' opinions. He felt they were assessing the facts very badly. It got him down, and that was when he became convinced he'd never see you again."

Edie opened the package slowly; under several layers of the thin paper lay Harry's regimental brooch. She looked up at Maurice then down again at the military insignia, knowing she should feel something—regret, sadness, perhaps a tear. But all she could feel was the gulf of time long distant and the silent memory of a man once known. Perhaps that in itself was the sadness, that it all seemed so alien, so very far away. Her only other thought was that the brooch needed cleaning. She looked up again; Maurice was still watching her.

"When you think of Harry," he said quietly, "you must try to remember that the happiest moments of his life were those he spent with you. Try not to be too sad, for too long, about his death. He knew deep happiness with you, Edie, and he

188

died for his country. I don't believe Harry himself would ever have asked for more."

Edie looked down at the brooch again and began wrapping it up in its paper.

"I'll try, Maurice," she said. "I promise I'll try. . . ."

2

During the weeks that followed, Edie saw Maurice O'Connor frequently. After his initial trip to Rosario, he came to the house for Sunday luncheon. To her surprise, he announced his intention of buying an *estancia*; he and his cousins, the Casey brothers, had decided it was time.

"The right time for us, and the right time to invest," Maurice said over Rosita's treacle pudding. "Tim understands crops and cattle, and there's good land going for a song. What estate is left of my parents' holdings might as well be reinvested in this country. There's future here, and enormous potential."

Edie sat and listened, interested, remembering her visits to Papa's camp, and the land. Maurice revived her faded memories.

For Maurice had changed. Edie had been struck by the differences in him from the moment he had walked into the living room, that first rainy afternoon. He seemed taller, was definitely gray at the temples, and the thick military mustache he now affected suited his face, giving it a grave dignity she had never noticed in him before. He did not look very much older than she had known him in England, but deeper, somehow, of more substance and force. His light hazel eyes, always so unexpected in his otherwise heavy features, held a new, compassionate expression, which underscored his kind nature, an attribute Edie had always taken for granted.

That was it. That was the difference; now there was no question of taking Maurice for granted. He was no longer a man in the background, but markedly a man to the fore. The war and his experiences had sharpened his presence, strengthened his approach, defined him. Having commanded men, he now instinctively commanded attention.

Instead of returning to shipping after the war, Maurice was dealing in grain. It all tied in, he explained to Edie.

189

"Knowledge of the market helps me see the advantages of an *estancia* on the *pampas*. . . ."

There was more to his company than business talk or discussions about *estancias* to the north. Maurice bought a motorcar, much to Yvonne's joy: now she and Lally were even on that score, too.

"Ay, *señor* Maurice—so dangerous!" Rosita cried the first time he drove up and parked outside the front gate.

"Perhaps if you come with us for a drive slowly around the square—only once—then you wouldn't be afraid any more," Maurice suggested, and although it took time and encouragement from both Yvonne and Edie, whose hand Rosita held tightly all the way on that brave first ride, eventually she became as enthusiastic as they.

Yvonne was fascinated. She had always liked Uncle Maurice. And now he not only had a motorcar, but he also allowed her to look at its engine, and sit in the driver's seat when the car was parked. Yvonne said she wanted to learn how to drive.

"Not until you're grown up, miss," said Edie. "Now run along and don't bother Maurice so much."

Maurice traveled back and forth between B.A. and Rosario; when in town, he was the perfect escort for Edie, safe and acceptable. They motored out on Sundays, and went to the races; Maurice, long an appreciator of horseflesh, was a shrewd observer. The horses he picked did well. Edie enjoyed the excitement of the crowd.

Then came the day when he returned from a trip to Rosario and announced, "Well, I think we've found it. Tim's going up to have a look next week, and I'm going to join him. It's out past Rosario, on the line to Córdoba, and the *estancia* itself is called El Ombú."

The property Maurice was interested in was no fledgling homestead. Originally staked out during the boom years of the 1880's El Ombú, though nowhere near the size of some of the vast *estancias* being set up all over Argentina at the time, was nonetheless immediately recognized as having great potential. Its soil and location insured success; only human frailties could dim its progress.

The first owners, a family of Spanish descent, Catholic loyalties, and shrewd instincts, were among the many cattle-barons building the Argentine oligarchy. Pious, political, and powerful, they wangled the best leagues in the immediate area in return for past favors and future commitments; most *estancias* established during the era were similarly obtained. But El Ombú, right from the start, had an advantage not possessed by all land holdings: it lay right next to the railroad only recently completed from Buenos Aires to Córdoba, with the river city, Rosario, and its port, at the halfway point on the section to B.A.

Next to the track lay the main road, which also linked the country's three principal cities. Argentina's main markets lay less than twenty-four hours away. Whether buying or selling, the benefits were obvious, and El Ombú's value unequivocal.

Early in the *estancia's* formation, the *patrón* himself had come from Buenos Aires to inspect the work being done on his politically-acquired booty. He rode out with the *capataz* during the day and dossed down in the backroom of the nearby town's best bar and *boliche* where, if the beds were not entirely free of lice, at least the food and firewater *caña* were plentiful. Before he returned to his home in the capital, he had laid out detailed plans of what he wanted done on the nascent *estancia*: there were more divisions to be fenced off, sharecropping *colonos* to be installed; a main house was to be built and, at the same time, a number of outbuildings were to be constructed.

Above all, trees were to be planted—the first of them in the area chosen for the family home. The *patrón* was a traveled man of cultured sensibility along with political astuteness, and he knew the value of woods and shade in the hot summer months of the Argentine year. He ordered the homestead center to be planted and built on the property's western boundary, facing the road and the railroad beyond. A lone *ombú* tree pinpointed the area, its bulging trunk and thick foliage heavy and brooding.

It was the tree that caused the property to be called El Ombú, which was duly registered and entered on all official documents, while an *E* superimposed on an *O* was designed as the registered brand for the property's cattle. The resulting mark was an oval with three lines across it.

Over the years, the *estancia* formed a worked and workable world of its own, possessed of its own limits and rhythms and pace and customs. Cows gave birth and wheat was planted; alfalfa fields grew lush and green. The stock was improved by the importing of bulls from Europe; sharecroppers came, men from camp towns and of immigrant stock, whose forefathers had tended farms far across the seas. *Peones* joined the original group of *gauchos*; hay was scythed and sheds constructed. Seasons, good and bad, left their imprint on the camp; progress was steady, and well rooted.

The main house rose within sight of the big *ombú*. The trees planted around the house grew and flourished. Once the homestead was occupied, additions sprang up: servants' quarters, chicken runs, an orchard, another well, a small plot of medicinal herbs, the traditional *yuyos* of *pampas* healing lore.

The *estancia* house started as a rim of rooms ringed three-quarters of the way around a big tiled courtyard; the central patio was closed off on its fourth side by an iron railing and a grillwork gate. All the rooms connected to one another by doors, and every room had a door that opened onto the patio, too, while windows on the opposite side of the room looked out to the property and its plantings around the building. Kitchen quarters were at one end, the owners' sleeping quarters at the other; between them, the rooms changed their purpose and furnishings as the needs of the *estancia* changed with family and time.

In subsequent years, the change was constant, and more buildings rose. A small chapel, simply built and exquisitely appointed, served the pious family's spiritual needs and the Church's spread of power. As on so many of the country's *estancias*, a priest formed part of the growing permanent retinue attached to the main house and catering to the *patrones*. By the turn of the century, the household staff rivaled the *gauchos* and *peones* in number.

Political changes, often swift and violent in the Republic of Argentina, also brought about changes on the *estancia* through the years. A government falling-out, a failing fortune, a sudden death, and a family divided all contributed; eventually the property passed into other hands. The new owners instituted new practices, ordering the building of this and the tearing down of something else. Developments in distant lands also played their roles as wars shifted balances of power, and inventions brought new methods of working the land. Presidential elections, economic failures, the spreading use of electricity, and the Great War in Europe all had their eventual effect on El Ombú. Then a profligate son gambled away what was left of his inheritance, and once again the *estancia* came on the market, its appearance coinciding with Maurice O'Connor's return and his search, with Tim Casey, for a property to buy.

The right price was found and the camp was bought, with Maurice holding a mortgage on his cousins' share. Then the moving and settling in began; Timothy Casey went up first, to get things running at the disorganized *estancia*. There were men to be hired and cattle to be moved, crops to be sown so as not to miss the spring. Kevin was meanwhile to oversee the moving of all their household goods from Rosario to El Ombú, and when things were fairly settled in the house, Anna Casey would join her sons, Rosa at her side.

Maurice pronounced himself well satisfied; both the purchase and the arrangement were much to his liking. He became very busy with the business and financial arrangements; Edie saw less of him during the next weeks, and her thoughts began turning to England again. Perhaps she could manage another trip to stay with the aunts without jeopardizing her finances too much. A talk with the bank, now managing her affairs, cleared the way, although it meant keeping a tight rein on expenses.

I'm so tired of pinching pennies, she thought as she returned home. If only Harry hadn't been killed...

But a trip to England would be lovely. And it would be something to do. She was sick and tired of Buenos Aires, bored by the people she knew and the life she had been leading for the past few years. As to Yvonne's schooling—well, the child could always make it up later. Or they could get a governess for her, if Edie could afford it, which she doubted. And, of course, in England, there was always Aunt Boo.

The next time Maurice came to call on her, she told him about her plans. To her surprise, he hardly responded to the news, becoming monosyllabic over tea, and refusing a second cup.

"Are you not well, Maurice? You seem so silent, so lost in thought."

He looked up.

"Sorry, m'dear. Didn't mean to be rude. But, yes—I was thinking. Hadn't meant to talk about this just now. However..."

A moment's hesitation followed. Then:

193

"I was wondering, Edie, whether—instead of planning your trip as a visit to the great-aunts—you'd consider sailing to England with me, as my wife... my bride...?"

A distorted oblong of moonlight patched the bedroom floor, patterned only by the window frame. Edie stared at it unseeing, sitting up in bed, clutching her knees to her chest.

Marry Maurice?

It seemed so absurd... to marry Maurice was like marrying a member of the family, an uncle, long trusted and always known. Maurice was leftover from the days and times of her parents, from childhood, innocence, from the dead long-ago. When he had suggested it, early that afternoon, so suddenly, so out of the blue, Edie had sat quite still, suspended in the surprise of the moment, unable to think of a single thing to say. She had seen him watching her intently, reminding her for all the world of the teru bird outside and the way he would jut out his long neck to watch her as she emerged from the house, hoping, perhaps, for an unexpected treat, a sliver of cake, a snippet of scone.

Maurice was watching, waiting for an answer. She had to think of something sensible to say. She got up from her chair and moved over to the window, sensing rather than hearing his similar moves.

"Maurice, I... to be truthful, I think... I need time to think it over." She kept her gaze fixed on the far trees. "I had not thought... have so much to consider..."

She knew he was standing a few paces behind her; she turned, and saw him nod in agreement.

"Of course, my dear. I quite understand."

The immediacy of the tension eased.

"I'm not pressing you for an immediate answer, Edie. Hadn't meant to broach the subject, actually, for another couple of months. But now that it's come up—well, do think about it, won't you? I fully realize there's much for you to consider: Yvonne, and her schooling, and..."

With a start, Edie realized she had not thought of her daughter at all. But, of course, Yvonne had always liked Maurice, and besides, who she married was not the child's concern.

She smiled faintly.

"Give me time, Maurice... I beg you to have patience with me...."

He had inclined his head in a bow to her.

"Always, my dear...."

Shortly thereafter, he had left the house, and now it was hours later, past midnight, and her heart was still thumping. She kept turning and churning the subject in her mind. Marry Maurice? Why?

Why not?

She was thirty-two. She was still pretty. She had enough money to live on in a reasonable way. Reasonable, but not lavish; she had to be careful all the time. An old saying came to her.

From birth to twenty, a girl needs her mother: from twenty to forty, she needs her looks—and after that, she needs her money....

Well, she still had her looks and she wasn't anywhere near forty yet; that was eight years away. Still, eight years could go quickly, if you looked at it in a certain way: eight years ago she'd been a prisoner in the north, tied hand and foot by Edgar's illness, and then her own. Eight years before that...

Edie shook the thoughts away. Going back was useless; the past was no more there. Only its lessons remained, or should. and eight years were eight years, no more and no less, and not an awful lot, at that.

Marry Maurice...

Well, now, she told herself, the good things first. He's rich, he's kind, he loves me. I think I've known that for some time; I just didn't want to think of it out loud. But anyway...

I know his family; he knew mine. He has no hangers-on, no dreadful friends, no ruinous vices. He comes from the right sort of people—well, acceptable, anyway.

A fleeting image of Harry went across the moonlit patch. Another ghost gone. Edie sighed.

Marry Maurice ...why not?

An inner dialogue began.

Because I don't love him. I never shall. The thrill won't be there.

The thrill—as there was with Edgar?

Edie shuddered. The other voice continued.

You see what rubbish you're telling yourself. Love—indeed. What love? There is no such thing, and you know it.

There was Harry...

195

Harry's dead.
Perhaps I should wait...
Wait for what?

To meet someone else—but even as she formed the thought, Edie saw its weaknesses. Would fate really send anyone else across her path? Time *was* running out, and never mind the old saying. Over thirty-five was hopeless from her point of view, and thirty-five was nowhere near eight years away, it was right around the corner, now.

Another thing: widows who remarried tended to marry widowers, who either had young children still in need of a mother or were very much older, and sickly, and needed care. Maurice, in his forties, was neither a widower nor in ill health. There were no remnants of a former family clinging to his coattails.

And remember, the other voice started up again, *you're not the only widow around. There's a selection here in B.A.—and there are thousands back home in England. So: what are you waiting for? What do you want? Not love; you know that. What is it?*

A cloud blocked the streaming moonlight, and in the sudden change, Edie changed, too. She suddenly saw what it was she wanted, and, in its definition, a path to pursue.

No, she didn't want to wait to meet someone else; she didn't want love. Love had nothing to do with the case. Like the flowers that bloom in the spring, tra-la, her mind ran absurdly on. Yet that was all part of what she wanted: *The Mikado,* the theater in London, being able to enjoy what she was meant to enjoy, exactly like Mamma had always told her.

London was what Edie wanted. London, not love. London and England and traveling and excitement and life. Life was enjoyment, not losing the years the wrong side of the ocean down at the bottom of the world. If Maurice would give her the life she wanted, was supposed to have, was brought up for—then, yes, she would marry him. She would most certainly marry him.

Even though she did not love him....
Sometimes, you have to strike bargains.

That's true. I may not love him, but I do like him. And he does love me, which is far more important. I'll be good for him, too. He thinks I'm beautiful. Well, I know I'm pretty, and people look at me, and if I'm with him, people will look

196

at him and admire him for having me as his wife, and that'll make him proud and happy.

But I'll be good to him, too. Even if I don't exactly love him, can never love him . . . can never love anybody because there is no such thing as that sort of love, not for me, anyway.

But I'll like him, and I'll know I like him. And that will have to be enough.

Edie did not see Maurice for the next several weeks; the taking over of El Ombú kept him going between Rosario and the *estancia* itself. When at last he returned to B.A., shortly after Yvonne's birthday, the weather had turned hot, signaling the arrival of the summer.

He took her to lunch instead of the races; after the meal, at Edie's suggestion, they left the car parked and went for a stroll through the Botanical Gardens, the lush plantings cool and refreshing in the heat of early afternoon. They were only a few paces in from the entrance when Edie began.

"Maurice, I've made my decision," she said, her hand resting lightly on his arm. "But I have to explain one or two things first, and then—then see whether you agree. . . ."

"By all means. Would you like to go on walking like this, or would you rather sit down? There's a bench over there."

"No, no—I'd rather walk. . . ." Her steps quickened, her former calm abandoning her. Maurice adjusted to her pace, keeping level at her side. "You see, my decision is—I *will* marry you. But on two conditions . . ."

She stopped walking, he stopped with her, the gravel ceasing to crunch beneath them, and only the traffic noises, screened by the park's foliage, mingled with the murmur of the hot summer day. Maurice looked enquiringly at her.

"Yes?" he encouraged.

"The first one is—I don't want any children. Any more children," she added with haste.

His answer was immediate.

"I don't either, my dear. Go on."

"The second is—well, it's about going to England. The wedding trip to England . . ."

Edie took a deep breath, and then the words came out in a rush.

"Maurice, I don't want to just *go* to England. I want to stay there. Oh, perhaps not there, exactly—but certainly not

197

here. I want to live in Europe, to see the world, to travel. I want to see and do *everything*, not just sit around B.A. doing nothing all my life until I die." She released her hand from his arm and turned to face him. "That's my condition, Maurice. I want to live over there. Permanently. Not here in B.A. with trips home only once in a while."

He took her hand in his, and she saw he was smiling.

"Then you don't remember?" was all that he said.

Edie was taken aback.

"Remember? Remember what?"

"An afternoon long ago when you were a little girl and I was on my way home, to university, I think. We went to your parents' house for tea, my mother, my brothers and I—and I promised to take you to England when you grew up. Well, that's a promise I'm now offering to fulfill—and yes, I mean to live over there, wherever you choose."

"You remembered that, all these years?" Edie's voice was little more than a whisper.

"I've remembered you all these years," was the simple reply. "You must have captured me then, even though you were only five. Such a pretty little girl you were then, too—and such a captivatingly beautiful one now...."

". . . and it's still a big secret, so you mustn't tell anybody. I wasn't supposed to tell you, either, but as you're my best friend..."

Lally absorbed Yvonne's news of her mother's forthcoming marriage with a serious and thoughtful expression. The girls had been playing in Lally's room, having been told to stay inside out of the hot sun until later in the afternoon. Edie had gone to the Thaxters' house, and Yvonne, invited by the Youngs, was spending the day.

"You know what that means, don't you?" Lally said at last. "It means they're going to do it."

"Do what?"

"The thing that makes babies."

"Oh."

There was a pause, during which Yvonne became busy with the tassel of the curtains, knotting it and unknotting it with intense concentration.

Lally watched her. "Don't you know about them?"

"About what?" Yvonne didn't even look up.

"The facts of life."

Yvonne shifted position in her chair.

"You don't know, do you?" Lally persisted.

"Yes, I do."

"No, you don't."

"Yes, I do."

"I don't believe you."

Yvonne shrugged, and did not answer.

"Well, if you know them, why don't you tell me what they are?" It was an open challenge.

"I don't want to."

"There!" Triumph rang in Lally's voice. "You see? I was right. You don't know anything about it at all." Then: "D'you want me to tell you?"

Yvonne shrugged again. "I don't care."

But Allison, her superior knowledge and advantage established, was ready to talk.

"Well, you know how little boys have a thing hanging down there? That's their *poronga*, and when they grow up and are men, it sticks straight out, and when they marry they put it into their wife's tummy-button, and it makes a baby."

Yvonne was horrified. "I don't believe it."

"But it's true," Allison insisted. "Maria told me." Maria was the Youngs' maid. "And anyway, I've seen it."

Yvonne could hardly breathe. "You mean you've seen someone doing that?"

"Not exactly," was the frank admission. "But I've seen a man's *poronga*. You mustn't tell anybody, but the gardener at school always shows his if you go to the back of the trees near the fence, and he finds you there alone. It sticks out of his pants."

"But I've never seen..." began Yvonne.

"Oh, I expect men strap them down to their leg, or something, when they put on their trousers," Lally declared, dismissing the problem. She got up from the table and squinted out of the window. "Let's see if they'll let us play outside now. We might even be allowed to have tea outside."

Yvonne considered the possibility of having a little brother or sister, and the thought intrigued her enough to want to clarify the matter. One evening, after her supper, when Edie came up to hear her prayers, she asked, "When Maurice is my new father, are you going to have a baby?"

For a terrible moment, she thought her mother was going

to strike her. She seemed to freeze in fury, standing quite still. Then she blinked and said in a tight, strained voice, "No, I am most certainly not. Just who put that absurd question into your head?"

"Nobody, Mummy—I just wondered..."

"Well, don't you wonder any more, miss." Edie's tone, though still sharp, was normal once more. "Now tuck down, and nighty-night and go to sleep. And let's not hear any more rubbish like that."

But Yvonne lay awake for a long time, wondering why her mother had been so angry at her.

3

The whole *estancia* was agog: one of the new *patro´nes*, *Don* Mauricio, had chosen a bride, and was bringing her to El Ombú to celebrate the engagement in the company of his aunt and cousins, the other *patrones*, and to present his bride-to-be to everyone there. Word went around with lightning speed, from the main house to the *capataz* to the *gauchos* to the sharecroppers out in the fields. There would be a celebration, an *asado*, a big festivity. It was an event to look forward to, and there was work to be done.

The *capataz* called his *gauchos* together. In the blunt, unvarnished phrases of their kind, they all agreed that *Don* Mauricio, being the best of the three new *padrones* and—as local scuttlebutt already knew—the major shareholder and real boss, deserved the best the men could do. If he was bringing his future bride to show her the *estancia*, then it had better be a property worth showing. The *capataz* made his aims clear: woe betide the man whose responsibilities were not fully undertaken. No fences were to be down, no cattle astray, no fighting until the visit was over. One flash of a knife against another man and the *capataz* would see to it the aggressor never worked in the region again.

Another warning: the midnight races of Saturday nights might have to be suspended. A groan went through the group, and boots shuffled in the pale brown dust. Racing and betting and the game of *taba*, all illegal, were their traditional enjoyments, and the races at El Ombú, run in the long field behind the work road near the barns, were among the best in the district.

The *capataz*, knowing his men, sensed their borderline mood. He'd decide on that later, were his final words; he went on to mention that it was a well-known fact *Don* Mauricio was an appreciator of horseflesh, a frequent visitor to the official hippodromes...

The boots moved again, this time into easier stances. There were many *estancieros* who protected the illegal racing; when it was done on their camps, the authorities, adequately bribed, always stayed clear. If *Don* Mauricio could be persuaded...

There was also, said the *capataz*, the question of a sensible wedding present. He would confer with *Don* Casey and let the men know.

Work at the *estancia* geared up from the moment the meeting ended. Fencing was fixed, gates mended, the main entrance road cleared of fallen boughs and leaves. Stirrups were shined, English saddles polished, reins braided and ready, should the guests wish to ride. And a special *recado*, the wide *gaucho* saddle, was spruced up and brought into readiness, in case *Don* Mauricio preferred it to the others. The saddle room had not been so clean and orderly in years.

Up at the house, preparations were also underway. Wines long stored in the musty, rat-harboring cellar had been brought up to lie on the pantry shelves; in the same room, wicker-covered demijohns stood on the floor. Vintage for the guests, *tinto* for the *gauchos*, wines from across the ocean, from the best vineyards in Europe, and wines from across Argentina, from the vineyards at the base of the Andes mountains. There were even bottles of wine pressed out from the harsh red grapes that grew as best they could in the *estancia*'s region.

Then came the making of the *empanadas*, the kneading of pastry, the cooking of meats, chopped and spiced, and the long line of varied ingredients placed along the center of the kitchen table, so that each circle of pastry, cut with a sharp knife and practised flair around its soup plate marker, could be filled with the required selection. Waxy potatoes, hard-boiled eggs, sharp peppers, vinegary olives, and the crushed seeds of cumin were grabbed, placed and sprinkled before the pastry folded over everything, to be quickly secured by the pressing tines of a fork, sealing the pocket ready for baking.

Far from the kitchen, over in the north wing, the guest rooms had been cleaned and aired, lace bedspreads, long in the Casey and O'Connor families, dug out of trunks and placed over the beds, their folds softening the spare furnishings of the long-unused rooms, whose proportions were nonetheless cool and serene, and whose tall windows gave onto the shaded verandah and, beyond it, the dark green depth of a *gomero* tree.

Edie and Yvonne arrived late one evening; they had been accompanied by Maurice from Buenos Aires, and had Rosita with them. The Casey brothers were at the local water-stop station to meet them in a horse and trap; two saddled horses were standing by.

"You drive, Maurice. We'll ride alongside. Much more comfortable that way. . . ."

Maurice took the reins, Edie by his side, while Yvonne and Rosita sat at the back, bags at their feet. The Casey brothers started off, cantering back to the carriage and racing off again as the mood took them. They went along the road next to the train's track, seeing the train disappear into the distance on its way to the Córdoba hills. When they reached the gates of the *estancia*, they found a welcoming group standing by the pillars on each side, and at the end of the straight stretch leading up to the house, Anna Casey stood, with Rosa, ready to receive them.

"*Dear* Edie . . . such wonderful news . . . so happy you are here . . . welcome, my dear, welcome to El Ombú. . . ."

While Edie was being driven out and around by Maurice, seeing the *estancia* and visiting neighboring *estancieros* and being feted as *Don* Mauricio's future bride, Yvonne, after the first excitement, found time hanging heavy and oppressive; there were no other children, and Rosita could not be spared. She had teamed with her mother, the moment of arrival, disappearing into the kitchen and the servants' quarters beyond. Mrs. Casey, although kind, was not much of a companion; Yvonne roamed around the gardens, the orchard, the immediate environs of the house, and grew increasingly bored.

Not that there wasn't anything to look at; there were animals and insects and the whole *estancia* world. But there wasn't anyone to look at it *with*. If only Lally had come to the *estancia* with her... Even long ago in England, she'd had Aunt Boo, or sometimes Gladys.

"Can't I go with you, Mummy?"

"No. Certainly not. Maurice and I have grown-up things to talk about with the other grown-ups..."

It was almost as bad if she went looking for Rosita.

"Now, *niña* Yvonne, you mustn't get in the way here. You know the fiesta is tomorrow night, and we have so much work..."

It was Maurice who saved the situation.

At the dinner table he said:

"You know how to ride, don't you, Yvonne?"

"Oh, yes. I remember from when I was small. At El Naranjal, I had a pony and a donkey and I also rode on the horses, and..."

Edie looked up, annoyed.

"Don't chatter so, child."

"That's all right, my dear. I understand what Yvonne means. And I think it would be good for her to go riding with us—I mean with Tim and me, early in the morning." He turned back to Yvonne. "If we do that, d'you think you can keep yourself busy for the rest of the day?"

Delight was shining all over her face. "Oh, yes! Oh, that'd be *lovely*..."

"Mind you, I mean *early* tomorrow morning. Before breakfast. Will you be ready?"

She was. At six the next morning, she joined Maurice in the main room. A steaming pot stood next to three mugs and a sugar basin on a tray at one end of the long dining table.

The *yerba* poured out hot and green. Maurice added sugar to Yvonne's mug and handed it to her.

"That's all we get for now. You can eat lots at breakfast when we get back."

Yvonne nodded. While they were sipping the drink, Tim Casey entered the central room, his puffy eyes still bleared with sleep, his white kerchief tied *gaucho* style around his neck.

"Top o' the morning to you, Maurice. Ah, Yvonne—coming with us, are you? The horses are already here...."

They were waiting, with the mounted *capataz* in attendance, near the front door beyond the low garden wall.

"I chose the palomino especially for the *niña*," he explained, getting off his own horse to help Yvonne mount. "He is gentle, but still a good horse, not a plaything." The *capataz* handed Yvonne the reins, and she managed to get her left foot into the stirrup. With a swing and a push, she was up and astride, the wide *recado* saddle comfortable beneath her.

"We could put a sheepskin over that, if you like," Tim Casey offered.

"Oh, no. I'm fine. Look!" Yvonne nudged her knees against the palomino and the riders began making their way around the main house to the road at the back, where the fields began and the morning's ride was set to start.

It was a morning Yvonne was to remember for the rest of her life. Clear and mild, fresh with an early breeze, the scent of early growing crops, of earth and dew-damp ground still lingered. Once past the *gauchos'* quarters and the *estancia's* main interior road, the riders crossed grazing fields flanked by planted sections, aiming, Maurice explained, for a windmill that needed checking. As gates were reached the *capataz* would heave the iron loop up over the gatepost, freeing the barrier and pushing it open with a booted kick, closing it again after the other three had ridden through.

"That's one of the laws of *estancia* life," Maurice told her. "You never leave a gate open behind you."

They went on through the field and the open land, galloping over the last dusty stretch to the windmill standing at the corner meeting-point of four fenced sections. There, its water served a trough in each of the four fields, and salt-lick slabs, gray and rough, stood nearby.

"We'll be here for a while, Yvonne. You can gallop around the field if you like. . . ."

The men, talking technicalities, dismounted to inspect the wind-operated structure; Yvonne, heeding Casey's suggestion, turned her horse parallel to the fence and galloped along in joyous freedom. She felt as one with her mount and the wind, free to move through the rising dawn and race with the light of the starting day. Presently she wheeled her horse around and turned back, cantering first, then trotting and walking him to a stop near the field's trough. The men were returning to their horses.

The sun was beginning to get hot, and the thought of breakfast suddenly appealed. Yvonne trotted behind the men, who were still deep in conversation, but as they neared the *estancia* buildings they rode four abreast.

"The *niña* sits a horse well," the *capataz* observed.

"Indeed she does. You ride very nicely, Yvonne."

"Thank you, Maurice."

"It is more than that, *Don* Mauricio," the *capataz* corrected. "Some ride well, and others not so well—but the *niña* Yvonne is a born rider."

The day of the fiesta dawned bright and cloudless; the whirring sound of the *chicharra* augured a hot and rainfree celebration. By noon, the *asado* pits were already dug and being tended by the men over near the *peones'* quarters, and trestle tables had been set up under the trees behind the main house. *Gauchos* and household servants combined their preparations for the evening's event; only the essential chores of *estancia* work were tackled, as the occasion was deemed worthy of a full holiday.

Up at the house, a private celebration took place: Maurice placed a ring on Edie's finger, and the cool green fire that flashed from the emerald caught everyone's eye.

"Oh, Mummy, isn't it pretty—do let me see it . . ."

Anna Casey kissed Edie on both cheeks and then, wiping away a tear, murmured her wishes and hopes for the forthcoming marriage.

"I only wish my dear sister had witnessed this day. . . . She would have been so proud. . . ."

The Casey brothers were jovial: Tim pinched Edie's cheek and said she must promise him a dance that evening.

"Oh—is there to be music?"

"Heavens, yes—didn't you know? They're even going to dance the *pericón* for you. . . ."

By nightfall, everything was ready, the tables set with plates and utensils, the wine bottles placed at regular intervals down the center. The overhead canopy of the trees moved intermittently with a slight evening breeze, soon joined by the increasing chatter of arriving guests' voices. On one side there were the neighboring *estancieros* and their families; on the other, the *gauchos'* womenfolk and men from the train-stop camp town. The focal point for the evening was the *asado* itself, the split steer, sizzling at its inclined angle over the large glowing fire pit, the sausages and *chinchulines* at the smaller one. Surges of spice-laden smoke rose from both as the men in charge basted the roasting meats with liquid held in old wine bottles; nearby, a collection of honed knives glinted in readiness for the meal to begin.

In front of the workers' quarters, *chinitas* in fresh kerchiefs giggled and whispered in bunches, while the *gauchos* themselves—their black hats slung behind their heads on the holding cords, their studded belts polished, their silver knife-handles stuck through the leather and gleaming—poured *tinto* from the demijohns into waiting glasses. A *bandoneón* player conferred with his guitarist over by the well, then tuned up and commenced playing when they saw the *padrones* coming towards them from the main house.

"*Que comience la fiesta*... let the festivity begin...."

A full moon rose; lanterns hanging from posts added light to the proceedings; candles on the tables, stuck with their own wax to the rough wooden surface, did the rest. Plates were fetched, carried, filled; large platters of hot baked *empanadas* were brought from the main house kitchen. More wine flowed; the guests intermingled. The barrier between owner and worker, *patrón* and *peón*, became blurred. All gathered around the *asado*, toasting and laughing.

"Long life and happiness..."

"*Vida y alegría*..."

The *bandoneón* struck up the quick-paced *milongas* of the Argentine plains.

As the slices of succulent meat piled up on plates, and the serious business of eating got underway, the groups separated again, each to its own set of tables. More toasts rang out under the trees; Maurice rose from his seat to thank his guests, and answer in kind. Speeches followed, more wine flowed. The servants, led by Rosa and Rosita, cleared plates and brought out others. When the last of the toasts faded under the trees, the *capataz*, who had been waiting near Maurice, advanced to tell the *patrón* that the dancing was about to begin.

"Come along, everybody—they're going to do the *pericón*..."

The guests rose, and as they approached the cleared portion of the *estancia's* inner road behind the buildings, the *gauchos* and *chinitas* were already responding to the deliberate beat of the *pericón's* repetitive melody, their kerchiefs, undone from their necks, now waving from their hands, as they danced face to face with their partner, broke away to form a circle, regrouped to make a chain, an archway of waving cloth, a huzzah of whirling figures, then sedately back to the chain until they reached their partner and new patterns formed. The *bandoneón* puffed away next to the guitar player, both musicians humming as they played.

The *pericón* dancers whirled to their finale.

"*Que viva la Argentina...*"

"*Que viva...*"

They circled around Edie and Maurice.

"*Que vivan los novios...*"

"*Que vivan...*"

And then away again into the quadrille complications of the *pericón's* final salute, all kerchiefs high in the air, all voices answering the cheer.

"*Que viva la Argentina!*"

"*Que viva!*"

After the cheers had died away, and the *chinitas* curtseyed, and the *gauchos* bowed, the *capataz* approached Edie and Maurice, one of the men by his side.

"*Don* Mauricio, we want to give you and your lady a reminder of us, your faithful followers...."

The *gaucho* handed the *capataz* the object he had been carrying. The head man moved forward to present the gift.

"Wherever you go, wherever you travel, may you always remember El Ombú..."

The *yerba* gourd, inlaid with silver, resting on a silver mounted stand, held its own sipping *bombilla* in its opening. Maurice accepted the gift, holding it high for everyone to see.

"...it will be our talisman, our link with the *estancia*, its people, its land..."

When his speech of thanks had ended, the *capataz* spoke once more.

"We have another memento—this time for the *niña* Yvonne. May she, too, always recall us, and her own special gift...."

Yvonne, who was standing next to her mother, received a quick push from Edie.

"Go on, darling... they want to give you a present....You mustn't be shy...."

The expression on the man's sun-worn face, creased into a smile, helped Yvonne forward. Then she saw the *rebenque* and, seconds later, it was in her hands, its ornate silver

207

handle shining, the rawhide width of whip stiff and new. She tried to say thank you, but no words came, only it didn't matter, because someone behind her started clapping, and general noise took over, and everyone cheered.

On Saturday, at midnight, the races were run as usual. Far from forbidding them, *Don* Mauricio was there, and not only did he place a bet: he won.

Edie sat, quite still, in her upright bedroom chair. Beyond the pale patch of light from the waning moon that was shining through the window, she could hear the *sereno's* lonely whistle sounding through the hush of the sleeping Palermo streets. The traveling case Maurice had given her only hours before lay in her lap, its leather glowing in deep patina of luxury and worth, the initials soon to be hers gold and clear in its center.

She snapped the locks open; the key still hung from a gilded cord attached to the handle. Lifting the top, she smoothed her fingers over the soft grain and solid clasps.

Inside, the *nécessaire* was lined with green watered silk; fluted compartments held silver-stoppered crystal bottles and jars. There were shirred silk pockets, ready to hold toiletry essentials: hairpins, powderpuffs, the paraphernalia of beauty and care. At the bottom of the case lay a silk-covered, stiff square; a buttonhook and a shoehorn were fastened to it by flat, narrow straps.

Edie picked up the fitted objects one by one, turning them slowly in her hands, entranced by the total significance of the case. It meant travel and luxury and being Mrs. Maurice O'Connor, cared for and safe at last. At last she was going to have all the wonderful things she had always longed for; within days, she and Maurice would be married and sailing for England. Maurice had promised to get her some furs the moment they arrived in London.

"You'll need them, my dear," he had pointed out. "You're not used to European winters, so you'll need them earlier in the season than anyone else. We might as well order them when we get there. . . ."

It was heaven to know he was in charge, to know she was safe, to be secure in his knowledge of what to do and where to go and how to handle everything in their lives.

It was going to be marvelous for Yvonne, too; she was going to be sent to a really good English boarding school. Edie would confer with the aunts and May O'Connor on this; they were sure to know and recommend the most suitable establishments there were. The child was reasonably bright and should do well; during her holidays, she could join Edie and Maurice on their travels, while term-time would see her safe at school, and Edie free.

A slight noise made Edie look up. Yvonne was standing in the doorway.

"Mummy—are you all right?"

Tousled with sleep, the child came into the room. She's growing taller every day, Edie thought.

"I woke up, and saw your light because your door's still open, so I wondered."

Edie put down the jar she had been holding and stretched out her arms.

"Yes, darling—I'm quite all right. Just sleepless. I expect it's excitement... because everything's going to be simply perfect from now on...."

IV

The Tango Years
1924–1928

1

Yvonne considered the choice of butter or jam and chose the latter. It was plum this week; she could see its rich purple glistening on the edge of the container. It was also out of her reach.

She moved her knife over her dry toast in the accepted, time-honored tradition, but nothing happened. The trouble was that Hilary, sitting on her left and nearer the jam pot, was a New Girl. It was her first term at Crestwood Close, and she hadn't yet reached the point where the school's rules and traditions, commonly known as the Regs, were second nature. She was being a bit feeble, too, if you came right down to it: you'd think she'd twig to the knife-scrape signal. But no.

Yvonne sighed. She'd have to apply more obvious measures.

"I say, Hilary—may I pass you the jam?"

Hilary's round glasses caught the window light, and flashed patterned reflections as she turned to Yvonne.

"No, thanks. I've already got some."

For a moment, Yvonne thought she still wasn't going to catch on, and despaired. Then Hilary reacted.

"Oh—oh, I see . . . I mean, would you like some jam? May I pass it to you?"

"Yes, please," Yvonne nodded, accepting the china container. She glanced to her right, checking the table to see whether there was anything she could offer Hilary. "Would you like some sugar?"

"Thanks awfully—but you passed it to me before."

Yvonne smiled at Hilary, having made her point. The new pupil blushed.

"Oh, I say . . . I *am* sorry."

Yvonne said, "That's all right. We all go through it at first. You'll catch on," and turned her attention to the jam. She had

213

been right; it was plum, and jolly good. Last week's had been watery strawberry, and a big swizz.

Not that one would dream of complaining. One could grouse and grumble with the other girls, but no pupil at Crestwood Close would ever complain officially about the food. Or about anything else, for that matter. It was all part and parcel of the school system, like the Regs. Everything was there for a purpose; the reason you were never allowed to ask for anything at table was to keep you on your toes about offering things to people. The school's motto was "Be Thoughtful," and was meant to be interpreted in the broadest terms. Thoughtfulness in study and thoughtfulness of behavior were insisted upon; a Crestwood girl was to be intelligent and well brought up.

The curriculum included mathematics, science, literature, and sports. There were full courses of trigonometry, biology, literature of all times and lands, and hockey. There was also a well-equipped gymnasium, and a full-size swimming bath. It was all a far cry from the hitherto accepted form of education for girls. Crestwood Close had caused—was still causing—quite a stir. It afforded a modern education within traditional bounds.

It was also expensive, somewhat snobby, and partial to picking what the headmistress called "a leavening mix" in the pupils it accepted. Aristocracy was yeasted with a dash of foreigners, some new money, and a solid base of upper- and upper-middle class. Dukes' daughters dormed with the heiresses of newspaper barons; the only darling of a foreign despot sat next to a girl from Kent. Everyone wore the same uniform; all pupils were addressed by their surnames; no taking of social precedence was allowed. Merit and seniority were all.

Scholastically a success, the school's social credentials were also impeccable. Crestwood Close was, in effect, the safe avant-garde.

It was Maurice who came up with the suggestion of Crestwood Close—Maurice, whose club connections always knew everything about everything. Female education included.

"Lord Bracken's daughter is there—I've mentioned him to you, Edie, old Bumps, who was with me at Arras. And I understand the Chilean attaché's girls are down for next year. Why don't you ask Aunt Boo about it, from the educational point of view? She must've heard of it."

She had.

214

"Oh, my dear—I think it'd be absolutely marvelous. They treat girls like human beings with proper brains. . . ."

Tea was the only meal from which one could rise without waiting for the mistress on duty to ring the silver bell at the staff table. Yvonne wiped her mouth on her cloth napkin, rolled it, and slipped it through her numbered ring, leaning forward to catch the table prefect's attention.

"May I be excused?"

The older girl nodded. Yvonne rose, pushing her chair back into place without making too much noise. Then she made her way through the long refectory tables toward the door, where she popped her ring into its numbered pigeon-hole in the wall. The tuck cupboard was right outside the dining room; Yvonne waited in line to get her tuck-box from Matron. Jill Edwards was in the queue in front of her.

"Is the list up yet?" Yvonne wanted to know. Jill shook her head. Both girls, fond of singing and eager for parts in the school's yearly production of a Gilbert and Sullivan operetta, had been haunting the Notice Board for days, hoping to have been assigned featured parts after the tryouts of the week before.

The line moved up.

"What's your number, Edwards?" Matron wanted to know.

"Seven."

"Here you are."

"Forty-three," Yvonne said automatically as Jill moved away.

Matron handed her the closed tuck-box, her number clearly lettered on its metal lid. It felt light and unpromising; opening it, Yvonne surveyed the lone bag of leftover fudge. There were very few pieces left, not enough to offer around. It was a good thing Mummy and Maurice were coming up for Visiting Sunday the following weekend. She'd have to send off a letter tomorrow asking for the things she needed. New bust-bodies, for one thing. And definitely some more fudge.

After popping a piece of it into her mouth and returning the tuck-box to the cupboard, Yvonne went upstairs and walked along the corridor to the Common Room. She entered it, as she always did, with mixed feelings; today, there was no one in it, which helped.

The day's newspapers were lying on the long table under the windows; the month's periodicals, neatly stacked, stood

215

on a lectern nearby. A sofa, cretonne-covered and worn, was in front of the empty fireplace; unmatched armchairs were ranged on either side. It was in this room Yvonne had first learned of her election to the Quad Game Team, a moment of elation and high triumph. Here she had also discovered many of the secrets of school life's true vein, one from a conversation overheard.

She had been ensconced in one of the high wing chairs, its back to the room, facing the windows, trying to get a better light to read by on a rainy Saturday afternoon. Yvonne was absorbed in her book; the sound of other girls entering and leaving the room was no more than a blur in the background; murmurs and giggles blended with the beating rain outside.

A phrase knifed its way through the buzz.

". . . simply because she comes from the Argentine . . ."

Yvonne became instantly aware, electrified.

". . . always showing off with her swimming . . ."

"*And* her riding . . ."

". . . swanking about all the land her stepfather owns, too . . ."

". . . probably not true anyway . . ."

That was Anthea's voice, clearly, Anthea, who had once asked her what an *estancia* was, and Yvonne, eager to please, had done her best to describe the land so far in distance and way of life. But Anthea had *asked* her, had even appeared interested. Why now this?

The voices lowered, giggled out of reach, rose again.

". . . simply N.O.S. Even Daddy says so."

Yvonne's heart pounded on a surf of pain, the waves of tears beginning to spill, first one wet drop and then another and another, splotching the pages of her book.

N.O.S. The dreaded imprimatur.

Not Our Sort.

". . . nothing but a bunch of dagoes, anyway . . ."

"That's why we call her Deedee. Didn't you know?"

"No. Why?"

"D.D. The initials. For Damn Dago."

Stifled laughter bubbled beneath another voice cautioning, "Shh . . . shhh . . . there's someone in that chair. . . ." and the conversation dropped down into unintelligible murmurs again. The pages on Yvonne's lap swam into unreadable blurs.

Why, oh, why didn't they like her? That had been Podge Bartlett leading the talk, Yvonne was almost sure. And Podge

216

wasn't even particularly keen on swimming, so why was she always so beastly about Yvonne having won the Junior Championship?

Yvonne reached up and fingered the medal pinned to the yoke of her tunic; the Regs required all honors achieved to be worn, whether Colors—soft felt badges awarded for general proficiency—or medals won in competition. Perhaps she could hide it, not wear it, and then they'd forget she had won it, and like her. But that meant risking an order mark the moment the medal's absence was noticed by a member of the staff. One order mark for not remembering to wear it; if she pretended it was lost, Yvonne dreaded to think how many order marks might be meted out.

Even if she did take it off and risk official trouble, it wouldn't really change anything or stop the jeering. They would always find something to laugh about, to mock in her. She would never ever be one of them.

At first, it had been her accent that set her apart. It didn't always show through—her years with the great-aunts had set a good base—but it was sometimes the way she said things that gave it away. Expressions, phrases, things the grammar books didn't tell you about. Yvonne had had to discover for herself that to say *a lost case* wasn't English: the proper phrase was *a lost cause*. And more ridicule had been heaped upon her for asking someone to *wait a little moment*.

"What barmy things you say, Yvonne. Can't you speak English?"

She learned to substitute *wait a minute*, but not before the wound had been inflicted.

That had been ages ago, of course, when, as a New Girl in the Junior Division, she had had to struggle through the subtleties of British boarding school life and pick up the passwords and sayings the other girls had known since their nursery days. Now it was all quite different: she was in the Senior Division, and next year would be her last year at school. In the meantime, she had been swimming champion for three years running, and a valued member of the Quad Game Team for her House. Next term she would probably be a prefect, too, with a table of her own in the dining room and the authority to dish out minor punishment to the Junior girls—lines of poetry to be learned by heart, the number of lines depending on the severity of the rules' infraction.

217

Over on the far wall of the Common Room, the Notice Board appeared to have some additions pinned to it; Yvonne went over to read through them: the lower hockey field was to be out of bounds while the new goal posts were being installed; chapel services would be earlier than usual on Sunday because it was a Visiting Weekend; the usual timetable for the weekend was also up.

Mummy and Maurice would arrive at lunchtime and take her out for a jolly good meal somewhere. Any change from school food was always marvelous, even if it was only a stodgy rissole in the saloon section of one of the pubs in the village. But Maurice always insisted on going somewhere special; there was a good choice of inns in the vicinity, and as they always had the car, there was the fun of driving there, too.

She must get that letter off to them. Perhaps she could manage to write it during Prep. You weren't really supposed to do anything but homework, but once you were a Senior, the teacher seldom checked to see what you were doing.

Mentally, she began compiling a list. Bust-bodices. More fudge. More tuck generally, in actual fact. She had been out of cake for weeks; another gingerbread would be nice, and some more jam, also. Twice a week, they were allowed their own jam at tea; Sundays you got everything: a go at your own tuck-box after lunch and your own jam or cake for tea. Weekdays were more sparse: tuck sweets after lunch twice a week, after tea once a week, your own cake on Wednesdays, on the table at tea. Everything at Crestwood Close was in sequence, in order, numbered, regulated; from fish on Fridays for High Churchers and Catholics to Assembly in the Main Hall every morning before classes to sewing and mending on Saturday mornings and Dorm Inspection Saturday afternoons.

A bell sounded in the distance: time for Prep, which would last until a half-hour before dinner. Yvonne went downstairs and outside to the Quadrangle. A group of leaping girls practising goal shots clustered at the double-looped target on the far side, probably the new ones going out for the Quad team this term. Yvonne watched them for a moment, then continued over to her form room in the other wing. There was no teacher at the podium desk when she arrived, although most of the girls were already there.

"Hullo, Yvonne—did you go and see whether the list . . . ?"

"Nothing yet. Perhaps there isn't going to be an operetta this year."

"That'd cheese everyone off."

"Anyone seen the atlas?"

"Who's done the algebra? I need some help. . . ."

"*Guten Abend, meine Damen.* . . ."

Inwardly, Yvonne groaned. If Miss Strauss was going to take Prep, that meant all questions would have to be asked in German. The strict Reg of talking to a language mistress in her own tongue was as immutable as all the other rules; Yvonne far preferred Madame Dupont. But no: old Last Straws and all her gerunds and declensions. Yvonne had told her parents about old Last Straws and her stiff-necked attitudes, and Maurice had said what could you expect from a bloody Hun anyway, and Mummy had said Maurice be quiet that isn't very fair. Maurice had said the Huns weren't very fair, either, but that he supposed Edie was right, and that had been the end of the matter.

Still, Miss Strauss was not liked, no matter what anybody said, and besides, she smelled on warm days, and Yvonne didn't like that, either.

". . . *and some fudge,*" Edie read aloud over the breakfast table to Maurice. When she finished Yvonne's letter, she said, "I think I'd better go shopping before we go to see her."

"Why not do it this morning?" Maurice suggested. "I'm going out myself. Have to see a man about a horse."

It was one of his regular phrases, signaling that whatever he was going to do would be of no interest to Edie, whether it was a business transaction, a visit to his London club, a meeting, or any other of his activities outside her sphere. Maurice never burdened Edie with mundane details that would only bore her; everything else they shared. Sometimes, the phrase meant he was organizing a surprise, or getting her a present, but it was no use trying to guess, and Edie didn't want to anyway, because that only spoiled the fun.

If Maurice himself was a bit of a bore sometimes, well, that was all part of the bargain. In all other respects, everything was close to perfect. Maurice saw to it that the best of everything life had to offer was hers, and theirs, to enjoy. Deciding that travel would suit them best, they had begun touring the moment Yvonne had been safely ensconced at Crestwood Close, starting off with a leisurely peregrination around the Continent. As the months went by and Edie's experience widened, they grew more selective, until a general pattern of life and travel began to emerge. They wintered in London and summered in France, went shooting in Scotland and skating in St. Moritz, enjoyed the spring air in the mountains of Bavaria, broke the cold months with a stay in Cannes.

The Riviera became a favorite; there was so much to do there, so much to enjoy. It was a gathering place for their own traveling kind, the international rich with a penchant for self-indulgence, who clipped coupons, owned racing stables, collected celebrities, arranged marriages for their progeny, and basked in the sun and self-assurance. Minor titles and major fortunes blended into burgeoning new dynasties during the tango years, the time the dance and tempo of Argentina captured the attention of the European elite. The *thés dansants* at the top hotels throbbed with the haunting strains, and many a fortune-hunting male practised the steps in the privacy of his lodgings, hoping to sweep an available heiress off her feet.

The war to end all wars had made the world safe and enjoyable. Edie and Maurice traveled to all the European playgrounds, doing the season. They strolled in Deauville, gambled at Monte Carlo, bathed in the waters of Biarritz, drank the waters of Carlsbad. Chic was beginning, glamor was all; life was rich, it was fun, it was sound, it was gay. In one of the phrases of the epoch, it was all very mad.

Edie, dazzling and decorative at Maurice's side, loved every minute of it. Wherever they went, she was complimented and courted, cosseted and admired. Everyone said they were a marvelous couple, what with her looks, his money, her gaiety, his solid ground. They were right for the mood of the age; the style was theirs and theirs was the hour. If midwinter dragged, they dashed south for some early spring; if Berlin became dreary, Vienna awaited only a few waltzes away. They danced to the rhythms of the time and the bands, Edie light on her feet, secure on Maurice's arm.

True to human habit, men and women speculated.

"Sure to be her money..."

"Bags of it, you know."

"Mind you, he's no pauper..."

"... must be worth a packet..."

"No doubt. But still, the big share's hers..."

"... otherwise, why stay?"

"... treats her like a ruddy queen..."

"You must admit she's lovely."

"But too, too selfish..."

"... simply impossible... don't see how he stands it."

"That's why I said... only explanation..."

"... her face *and* her fortune..."

Those who believed the hypothesis were satisfied with its answers; those who knew its falsity could only puzzle on. Had Maurice heard the rumor he would have been aghast at its presumption and speechless with surprise that such a question should arise.

For Maurice never dreamed the case was not completely obvious, that his love for Edie was not a fact for all the world to see. It was still incredible to him that this dazzlingly beautiful woman, this gossamer creature by his side, was his wife, had consented to bear his name and share all his days. She, who could have chosen anybody, had chosen him, plain, dull, stolid Maurice, whose face and manner and very air were all a far cry from those of the dashing charmers who filled the social world.

Edie was the crowning achievement of his life, the jewel at its center, unique and precious. He wanted no more than to protect and shield her, and set her in the luxury he knew she deserved.

The truth was far simpler than all speculation: Maurice loved and respected Edie for all the things he knew her to be, far beyond anything anyone else knew or saw in her. No one he felt sure, understood her as he did; no one else knew her invincible strengths, and the desperate battles that had forged their steel.

Only he knew how she must have suffered at the hands of his conniving, treacherous, despicable brother Vesey; only he understood the horror that Edgar had been to her. Maurice knew Edie as no one else could, not even her daughter.

His only regret was his mother had not lived to see him now.

Motoring was the thing to do, the way to travel, the smart way to go. Maurice, true to his own particular style, was a cautious enthusiast: enthusiastic enough to purchase the newest and the best of whatever took his automotive fancy, the cautious side of his nature counseling for a chauffeur. On the Continent, Yves was duly found and hired; in England, Bert took over.

Life was as it should be, was meant to be, Edie smiled at her reflection in the center panel of the dressing table's looking glass. With practised care, she brushed her hair into place; it was short now, expertly bobbed. As she moved, dozens of Edies moved with her in mirrored image; she turned a side panel fractionally, getting a better view of the nape of her neck, then picked up the hand mirror for closer inspection. It matched her brush and the comb and powder jar lying in front of her; she had wanted a silver-backed set; Maurice guessed better and gave her one that was gold. The pieces gleamed in the quiet room's light; of all the hotel suites they stayed in across Europe, Edie always enjoyed the one in London best, and it was always ready, with fresh flowers in every room, for their arrival.

One last flick to her hair, and Edie rose, satisfied. She would go shopping, meet Maurice later for lunch, then they were meeting friends for an afternoon game of bridge. Edie had taken to it immediately. The aunts' occasional game of bezique had never attracted her, but bridge—ah, that was different.

Thought of the aunts made her frown. She really should go and visit them soon. Perhaps when Yvonne's summer holidays started, before they left for France; the aunts always enjoyed seeing Yvonne, and that way they could make it a family affair. It was useless having Moo and Boo over with the O'Connors' contemporaries and friends; they were worlds apart.

The aunts formed one of the few awkward spots in Edie's life; she sometimes felt she should do more in their direction, without knowing quite what. Luckily, Maurice got on well with both of them, as he always had, and family gatherings with the aunts, and May and Edwin, and all the children, usually solved the problem. Maurice was very good at handling things like that, anyway; Edie always let him take charge.

Her dressing case lay open on a stand near the table; from it, she took a small perfume flask and applied a drop behind each ear. She had been right; she *was* good for Maurice, and he in turn had proved to be the husband she needed, a man to depend on, to give her all her due.

Not even sex had proved much of a problem; far less, indeed, than she had steeled herself to bear. Maurice seldom demanded it of her and, when he did, he was gentle and kind. She had never confessed the full horror of Edgar, but had given Maurice to understand a measure of her suffering.

Fortunately sex with Maurice was nothing like it had been with Edgar. He was discreet in his approach and it was always quickly over. Sometimes he would fall asleep at her side, only to disappear back to his own bed during the oblivion of the night; more frequently he would rise and kiss her on the forehead, bidding her a fond good-night and retiring to his own bedroom.

Edie would then read in bed until sleep came and, with it, far dreams.

"I thought you said the car was here, Maurice."

"I did, my dear, and it is."

"I don't see . . ." Edie began, only to stop short as she recognized Bert behind the wheel of the sleek and shining touring car parked right in front of the hotel steps.

"Oh! *Maurice!* You've done it again. . . ."

A smile twitched beneath his military mustache.

"Thought it'd be a nice surprise for you . . . and Yvonne. . . . She enjoys cars. . . ."

They drove through the quiet of the Sunday morning, elegant in the almost deserted streets of/the West End, stared at by motor enthusiasts and small boys when they reached busier neighborhoods on their way out of the city headed for Visiting Sunday at Crestwood Close. As they went Edie oohed and aahed at the new car's interior appointments being pointed out by Maurice.

"It's really very grand, Maurice—and you're right, the seat *is* more comfortable for me. . . ."

Mechanical technicalities, however, did not interest her in the least, and once Maurice and Bert began discussing the engine and its properties, Edie's attention wandered off to her own set of thoughts. She enjoyed being driven, and she liked the ride; settling in against the well-padded back seat, she looked out of the window and admired the passing scenery along the route to the school.

Crestwood Close was a little more than an hour's drive from London and set in the rolling richness of the English countryside. It dated from Tudor times; the old manor house and its attendant buildings rose from a wooded hilltop looking west. Modern structures had been discreetly placed, screened by trees, and housed the gymnasium, the swimming bath, and the sanatorium. Tennis courts and playing fields had been leveled on the other side of the hill. The school's entrance and driveway led directly up to the Tudor mansion itself.

It ranged around three sides of a paved quadrangle, its two-storey structure housing the school's main assembly hall, the dining room and kitchen, the library and the senior classrooms, all on the ground floor. The upper floor on one side was all dormitories and staff bedrooms; over the dining room, the Common Room served as a main gathering point for the girls during their free time.

"Not that they have very much of it," the headmistress had said to Edie and Maurice when she showed them around the school on their first visit.

Along with the building and the grounds, the school had also its very own game: the Quad Game, played in the school's entrance, was a fiercely competitive affair.

"It teaches them team spirit along with tradition and self-discipline," explained the headmistress, going on to say that the pupils belonged to one of four Houses, one for each cardinal point, and all honors or demerits accumulated not only to the girl receiving it, but also to her House. "Again, the same values are emphasized."

New Girls were assigned to a House on the day of their arrival; Yvonne found on entering the premises that she was a North. It was customary for the House teams to play an exhibition game for the new pupils' benefit during the first week of every term.

No doubt an Elizabethan version of later basket games, Quad was played with an elliptical, handled ball. To score, it had to be thrown up through an iron goal loop so that it then descended through a second. Skill, speed, aim, and the knowledge of precise rules of position were all needed to play on a Quad Game team. It was a coveted honor.

Yvonne had watched her first game with fascination; it had been East House against South House, and South had won.

"Doesn't any other school play it?"

No, she was told. It was unique to Crestwood Close.

"How strange. . . ."

"Not really. It's like the Wall Game."

Yvonne looked blank.

"The Wall Game," repeated her informant. "Eton, you know. . . ."

Yvonne didn't know, but did not dare ask, realizing her ignorance was a gap of some kind. It had been her first moment of specific social discomfort, the first of many, a small but perfect example of the gulf between her background and that of the English girls.

"Milk jam? What bunk! Never heard of such a thing."

Patiently Yvonne tried to explain—the taste of *dulce de leche* so strong in memory she could almost recall it to her tongue's delight.

"It's delicious stuff, really it is, a bit like custard, I suppose, only not really. . . . It's like very thick sweet cream, only sweeter and smoother than cream could ever be, and . . ."

The girls in the dorm didn't believe her.

"Utter bosh!"

"Sounds beastly to me. . . ."

"What a peculiar place South America must be . . . full of milk jam and jungles. . . ."

Yvonne's face flamed as laughter overtook the girls.

I must remember not to mention things like that. . . . They never understand, no matter what I say. . . .

"Oh, Mummy . . . how ripping. . . . It's a Hispano, isn't it. . . ? Hullo, Maurice . . . when did you get it . . . ? Guess what happened yesterday! I've been given the best singing part in . . ."

"Please stop knocking me over, child, and *do* try to be a bit more ladylike. . . ." Edie, flustered in the general confusion of arrival, readjusted her stance and took Maurice's arm. Yvonne, standing a full head taller than her mother, flushed and stepped back.

"Sorry, Mummy. Here, let me take your coat for you. That's a new brooch, isn't it? How lovely. Did you get it in Paris? How was the crossing?"

"Very rough. You would have loathed it. Where are the parcels, Maurice?"

"Here, my dear. Bert, you'd better wait for us while we leave all this inside. We'll be going to lunch shortly."

225

"Certainly, sir."

Yvonne walked between Edie and Maurice, towering over her petite mother. An awkwardness of movement still caused her frequent embarrassment, and inevitably brought on her mother's acerbic comment. She tended to fall over her own feet, or other people's, or bump into things, small tables with bric-a-brac, door frames, open windows. The moment she stepped onto a playing field, however, or a tennis court, or the Quad, or slipped into the swimming bath, Yvonne's movements went from coordination to grace to excellence, her muscles responding to training and self-assurance.

"If she can do exercises without knocking things over, why can't she get up from the table without spilling something?" Edie wanted to know, unconvinced by Maurice's attitude that it was "just growing pains, m'dear, and she'll get over it."

The hubbub of Visiting Sunday calmed to conversational level once they reached the dormitory.

". . . and here are the underclothes. No, we'll have to take that box downstairs—it's the fudge. . . ."

"Oh, ripping! Thanks most awfully, Mummy. . . ."

". . . and I got some chocolates and toffee, too, so we'd better hand it over to Matron. . . ."

At lunch, Yvonne regaled her parents with school news, the biggest excitement being the preparation for the Gilbert and Sullivan production now underway.

". . . and if I do well in it this year, I'll probably get one of the leading roles next year, too, and then perhaps, when the D'Oyly Carte people come, they'll notice me and . . ."

Edie put down her knife and fork.

"And what?"

"Well, they come every year, you know, and last year Mary was taken on, right after school and . . ."

"Yvonne, are you trying to tell me you think you're going to join a *theatrical* company?"

Yvonne looked up at her mother and saw danger there. She cast a glance of appeal at Maurice, and tried to explain.

"I don't know if they'll choose me, Mummy, really, I don't. But our singing mistress says my voice is developing nicely, and I *do* enjoy it, and anyway, D'Oyly Carte isn't just any old company, and all they do is Gilbert and Sullivan and . . ."

"And I take it you are planning all this for next year when you finish school?"

"Oh, yes, not before then. . . ."

"And that's precisely the year you are going to be presented at court, and do the season, and . . ."

"I don't see why I can't be a deb and sing at the same time."

"Don't be rude, Yvonne, and stop being so silly. You do want to come out properly, don't you?"

"Yes, but . . ."

"Then there's no question of fooling about with fluff-headed ideas of going on the stage. I do wish you'd try to be a bit more sensible about things. You know perfectly well I was presented last year so I could then present you. Maurice has already begun making arrangements to take a house in London. It'll be easier for us when you're a deb. You can have your parties there, and all those lunches and teas. So let's not hear any more D'Oyly Carte nonsense."

Edie picked up her knife and fork again, and the meal was resumed in awkward silence until Maurice broke it to tell Yvonne an anecdote about the new car, and talk became more general and flowing again.

That summer, they motored through Arras, stopping to spend the night in lodgings on the cobbled main square, where the beams crisscrossing the house fronts were stained by centuries of smoke and conflict. Next morning, Maurice took them on a tour of the nearby battlefields.

". . . must have walked every inch of this . . . It was nothing but mud . . . mud and dead men . . . over a million gone before we were through . . . mindless carnage . . ."

Yvonne had never heard her stepfather wax so eloquent before. She listened in surprised wonder at his reminiscences of war and death and total devastation, his words vivid and surreal against the birdsong and breeze of the early summer day. They walked over the war-scarred land; there were tree trunks, shattered by mortars and shells, standing gaunt and gray against the calm blue sky, the fresh green tendrils of growing vines winding around them. Tall-growing weeds had softened the deeply gouged lines of the trenches, and the cratered pits were covered with summer grass.

"Plenty of unexploded shells down there," Maurice observed, pointing to a frond-filled crevasse near them. "It'd be more than your life's worth to walk through any of these trenches."

Edie shivered and said she'd had enough, turning to go

227

back to where Yves was waiting with the car. But Yvonne stayed on with Maurice and listened to his words and the background birdsong and the echoed bombshells of the past.

At half-term that autumn, Yvonne joined her parents for the long weekend stay at the London house they had taken. The first surprise was the flurry of fur that rushed at her the moment she came in, barking and wagging two plumed tails, eventually separating into a pair of Pekingese.

"Oh, Mummy—they're gorgeous!"

"Aren't they precious? This is Taitai, and that one's Ming, and they're almost a year old..."

The second surprise was Lally.

Lally, grown almost as tall as Yvonne herself, but with a bigger bosom, and her dark hair bobbed and gleaming, the straight fringe low over her laughing eyes. Her father had been transferred back to the London branch of the bank, and the Youngs were now living in England permanently. Lally was attending a finishing academy and having what Edie later told Yvonne was "a little season."

"Not a proper one like you're going to have, darling, but you mustn't say I said so. I wouldn't want to hurt the Youngs' feelings, and Maurice says he's rather useful at the bank from time to time."

The girls giggled and talked for hours, catching up on each other's lives and taking the Pekes for a walk in the brisk autumn air. Lally was still full of news of Buenos Aires, having only arrived in England the month before.

"... and—oh, yes, I knew there was something else to tell you. Remember Miss Peggy? From school, I mean."

"Yes, of course."

"Well, she left. Took a job in an office—and then there was a big scandal of some kind, and she got *married*."

But Lally didn't know the details, which was rather disappointing, so Yvonne went on telling her about Crestwood Close.

"You'll have to come and see it with Mummy and Maurice, either for a Quad Game, or a Visiting Sunday."

"I'd love to."

"Come on—race you to the end of the square."

The two girls, each with a bounding Pekingese at her side, ran laughing over the carpet of autumn leaves.

The blossoming mimosa smudged duckling yellow against the Côte d'Azur's sparkle as the car drove into town with Yves at the wheel. In the backseat, Maurice snapped the double-lead onto Taitai's collar; Ming was still curled up in Edie's lap.

"I think you'd better get her ready, my dear. We're almost there."

Edie said, "Come along, Ming. Walkies time," and both dogs responded to the phrase, thumping their tails in anticipation. Another snap of metal, and they were leashed in tandem, sitting on the floor and waiting for the car door to be opened.

They drew up at the hotel, its broad yellow facade bathed in the morning light, its opulent interior rich with the aura of wealth and comfort and service. Calm efficiency permeated the atmosphere; only the manager was flustered.

"A thousand pardons, M. O'Connor... a minor but most regrettable delay... if you and Madame would care to enjoy the terrace for a while, the sun is splendid... breakfast, perhaps? Or an aperitif... as M. O'Connor knows, our barman makes an excellent Horse's Neck...."

Maurice was not to be mollified.

"... absolutely absurd... never heard of the suite not being ready before... been coming here for years... will not put up with..."

He rejoined Edie, who was walking the Pekingese outside.

"Come, my love. Let us go and look at villas. I think it's about time we had one of our own."

By mid-afternoon, they had purchased La Maison.

They had been shown over several before they came upon it, and had rejected them for size, for ugliness, unsuitability, poor location.

This one was different.

For Edie, it was love at first sight.

"Oh, look, Maurice—what a perfect drawing room! Think of the parties we could give here...."

"... room for this car and another besides, and I *do* like the idea of staff quarters above the garage, nice and separate..."

The villa, a two-storey stucco structure, stood against a hillside, its ascending driveway cut through boulders. Tall, airy rooms led off the marble-floored central hallway, from which rose the wide staircase leading to the upper hall and the bedroom suites upstairs. Double drawing rooms and a chandeliered dining room, connected by glass-paned french doors, all opened out onto a vast graveled terrace bordered by a white marble balustrade, and overlooking Cannes and the sea beyond.

The Pekes, let off the lead, rushed about everywhere, sniffing and inspecting everything and then dashing back to prance around Edie's ankles. She walked, enchanted, around the terrace and between the high palms at its far end and then back into the waiting house.

"Oh, Maurice . . . it's magnificent. . . ."

They went upstairs, the dogs bouncing at their heels, making their way through the bedrooms and dressing rooms. The large square room on the southeast corner captured Edie's attention.

"It's got a looking-balcony . . . and *what* a view . . ."

"A what, my dear?"

"A *balcón mirador*, like the one in Rosario. Don't you remember? Mamma always called it the looking-balcony, and lamented there was never anything very much to look at. But *this* . . ."

Her arm swept out in a gesturing arc; the panorama was the same as from the terrace below. The slopes down to Cannes were faintly hazed in the sun of the late afternoon, which glinted sharply on the water of the Mediterranean beyond.

"Then that's it," said Maurice. "We'll buy it. You shall have your *balcón mirador*."

That night, Edie smiled at Maurice across the orchids and champagne sent by an abject management and said, "You'd get me anything I ever wanted, wouldn't you?"

He looked at her gravely before replying, "I'd certainly try to, m'dear—I would most certainly try."

Since the villa had never been officially named, and because Edie's French continued to be minimal, they called the house as they referred to it: quite simply, La Maison.

The sudden change from several years of hotel living to the running of two households altered the pattern of the O'Connors' lives.

"We can always go back to traveling after Yvonne has come out," reasoned Maurice, and even Edie admitted she was enjoying the change. La Maison was more fun, in a sense; it

230

was theirs to do with what they wished, their plans and ideas carrying into the future. On the other hand, the place they had rented in London needed a minimum of attention, as the resident staff came with the premises and needed little direction.

Yvonne joined them in Cannes for the Easter holidays, spending most of her time at an indoor swimming pool practising for her last chance at the school swimming championship.

"I hope you'll tackle your exams with as much pluck," observed Maurice, after watching her dive in and thrash through the water for the umpteenth time.

"Don't worry. I'll get through," was the rejoinder, and the next day she made a point of mentioning the good marks she had been getting that term.

The three of them traveled back to London together, Yves leaving them at the French Channel Port and Bert waiting for them at Dover. Within days, Yvonne was back at school, starting what would be her last term at Crestwood Close.

2

She could hear her name being shouted above the tumult of the watching crowd.

"Come on, Waring! You can do it! Swim for North!"

Distorted as the sounds were through the tight bathing cap and the bubbling water churning around her head, every syllable added impetus to her force. Yvonne scissored through the water, hands and arms slicing forward, legs kicking out and closing in: thrust, arms out and push, and in, and thrust once more. The pool's end was right ahead of her now . . . one more stroke . . .

Her fingers touched the side. Curling her legs under her, she brought her knees level with her chest, turned and pushed off from the wall with a smooth, all-in-one change that sent her back down the length of the pool again. Only one more lap, and the relay race was over . . . one more length . . .

She was beginning to tire badly, having been in and out of the water all afternoon. The relay race was the closing event of the Swimming Sports Day, and the drain of her earlier

231

efforts was beginning to tell. She had won the butterfly and backstroke races. Winners of the diving, floating, and general style competitions would not be announced until the prize-giving at the close of the afternoon, but she felt reasonably sure she had done very well in them.

But the relay race was the most important of all, pitting the swimming teams of the four school Houses against each other. Each House always put its best swimmer in the last position; they were expected to overcome any loss of time accumulated by the earlier swimmers of the team. Anthea had bungled badly for North this year, in her lead position, showing confusion at the starting whistle and losing precious seconds before diving in. Nerves, of course, but still...

Yvonne could see the rail now; only a few more strokes, thrust, push, kick again, never mind the knifelike stitch in her side, thrust...

"Come on, North! Keep on going!"

One last lunge, and her hand struck the rail. Yvonne sank slowly down, her hand still clutching on, her energy spent. The noise roared; her head dipped below the water. Then she raised her other hand to the rail, momentarily too tired to do anything but hold on.

Hands reached down. Her grinning teammates hoisted her out of the water and onto the side of the pool. Yvonne sat with leaden weight, heaving for breath, her tears indistinguishable from the water, her heart pounding with victory and effort. The audience was clapping and cheering wildly.

"Hurray for North! Three cheers for Waring! Hip, hip..."

When the tumult died down, the Games Mistress announced that tea was now being served in the refectory.

"Prize-giving will then take place in the Main Hall...parents and girls are asked to take their seats before the staff arrives...."

In the changing room, Yvonne was a center of attention.

"Congrats, old bean—you did it again!"

"Good show, Yvonne..."

"Jolly good, Waring..."

Smiling her thanks, Yvonne finished dressing and began tearing a comb through her hair. Her ears had blocked up. Probably water in them. She went into the bathroom to try and wipe them out. Returning to her locker, she was in time to hear Podge Bartlett saying, "Well, of course, if you think the D.D. can *always* swim like that..."

Yvonne tightened. They were at it again.

"Oh, *do* shut up." It was Anthea's voice. "You're just jealous."

"Jealous? Me? Don't be so feeble. Why should I be jealous of the D.D.?"

"Because she's a lot prettier and a lot more popular than you are," was the answer. "And because your brother thinks she's smashing, and that cheeses you off..."

"He does nothing of the kind!"

"Oh, yes, he does. He told me so. Says he's potty about her. Come on, hurry up, or we'll miss tea...."

They vanished through the door. Yvonne watched it swing shut, the glow of victory dimmed. Then she, too, left to join Lally and her parents, who would later witness her receiving the treasured championship as her prize.

As Yvonne's schooldays drew to a close, the house in London became the focal point for the O'Connors and their immediate plans. Its Belgravia location was excellent, and the house itself perfect for the entertaining that would all be part of Yvonne's debutante season. Her name, already on the official lists, was noted by longtime hostesses involved in the traditional launching of young girls into society; they called on Edie, who in turn, called upon them. The seasonal structure was quick in building.

As with all debutantes, the traces of an invisible web began being woven around Yvonne. Edie's aspirations for her daughter, well in keeping with the manners and mores of the times, helped develop the pattern. For if the debs themselves saw the season as their emergence from schoolgirl chrysalis to social butterfly, it was not the true view as seen by their parents or society at large; the safeguarding of tradition, privilege, family, and future all came into play. Social eligibility on the one side and solid lucre on the other had long been deemed suitable for marital unions; old names and new fortunes had blended through the ages to build continuing strength into the upper crust.

Yvonne Waring and the O'Connors had been scrutinized and passed muster; the girl was lovely, her stepfather had money, and she had certainly gone to one of the right schools and met and mixed with the right people. The South American background could be overlooked and forgiven, even if never entirely put aside or forgotten. Invitations poured in for both Yvonne and her parents.

The smaller parties began first: tea gatherings, introductory get-togethers, and the smaller of the charity affairs. From each event attended came invitations to more; Yvonne's circle of acquaintances widened and the season got underway. Individuals began standing out in the crowd; opinions started forming.

"I say—have you met Yvonne Waring?"

"Rather. Stunner, isn't she?"

"Jolly good sport, too. My sister was at school with her."

"Really? Got an in, have you? The pater says her step-father's worth millions."

"Chap in the City told me the same. Tin, you know. Or is it land? One never knows with these dagoes."

"Argentinians, actually."

"That's it. Probably beef, in that case. Or is it mutton?"

It did not make the slightest difference; what counted was that it was money in a marriage market where beauty and money had long been valuable commodities.

Edie finished reading the list of engagements in *The Times* and said to Yvonne, "Weren't you at school with a girl called Jill Edwards?"

"Of course I was. She was Head Girl, don't you remember? She left last year."

"Well, she's engaged."

"Oh—do let me see."

"A very suitable match," Edie commented, handing the paper over. "Her mother must be pleased."

"You mean he's rich."

"*And* very nice family."

Yvonne finished reading the notice and looked up at her mother. "Which d'you think is more important?"

Edie fussed with a piece of toast. "Darling, really... what a question..."

"No, I mean it seriously," Yvonne insisted. "Should one marry for money? Would you want *me* to, fr'instance?"

Edie considered the question for a moment before replying.

"Well, you know the saying: *Don't marry for money, but try to fall in love where money is.*"

"But supposing I fell in love with a penniless poet?"

"It seems unlikely, doesn't it, darling? To my knowledge, you've never even met a poet, penniless or otherwise."

"But *supposing*..."

234

"Supposing you stop talking a lot of nonsense and get ready to go to the hairdressers'? Maurice wants Bert to drive him to the club in a little while, and he can drop us off on his way."

Lally Young flopped down onto Yvonne's bed.

"I'm absolutely bushed," she moaned. "And my foot still hurts where that oaf stepped on it. . . ."

"Must've been a marvelous party." Yvonne opened her chest of drawers to get out yet another handkerchief.

"Oh, it was. We danced reels most of the time, with a few fox-trots in between, and the pipers were tops. Lots of people asked where you were, including Stuffy Bartlett."

"Oh, him."

"He's jolly handsome. . . ."

"If you like that type."

"And you don't."

Yvonne sneezed. "No, not really. Besides, can you imagine having Podge as a sister-in-law?" She sneezed again.

"You mean the Lady Patricia . . ."

Both girls laughed, Yvonne's laugh turning into a cough that suspended conversation for a few moments.

"You'd better get rid of that filthy cold by next week."

"I'll say." After another sneeze, Yvonne added, "Are you coming to help me dress?"

"Wouldn't miss it for the world. I'll come over in the morning. What time's the actual presentation?"

"About eight—but we have to be there hours before. Maurice says we have to leave the house shortly after five. *Do* come and spend the day. . . ."

Yvonne ducked her head and climbed into the limousine with care, the footman hired for the occasion standing, resplendent and immobile, holding the door for her. Once in, she sat on the edge of the seat while she gathered her train around her. The footman shut the door. Yvonne's hands went to her headdress, feeling the soft veil and then the three regulation feathers. Nothing had moved; everything was in place. With a faint sigh of relief, she settled herself more comfortably, trying not to crush her veil or her train or her dress and placing the fan she would be carrying in the chiffon folds of her lap.

Edie, still outside, was clucking last-minute worries.

"Are you in, darling? Do be careful of your train. Are the

sandwiches here? Where's Mr. O'Connor? It's getting late. Is my tiara crooked? It feels as though it's slipping."

"The sandwiches are in the hamper on the front seat, Madam." Thus the chauffeur, who formed a team with the footman, his calm manner bespeaking many presentations in the past.

Yvonne spoke to her mother through the rolled down window.

"Maurice said he'd be out to see us off, so don't worry. He'll be here any minute. And what's more, we're early."

Edie got into the car. Her motions of care, like Yvonne's, were dictated by her garments; the ostrich feathers rising from the back of her tiara brushed against the top of the door as she got in.

"*Do* straighten my tiara for me."

Yvonne touched the band of diamonds with a light finger.

"It's fine, Mummy, really it is. It looks lovely—and so do you. What did Maurice say when he saw your dress?"

"He said he liked it. Now—let's have a good look at you. . . ."

Yvonne turned in the seat to undergo her mother's token scrutiny, feeling that all of London had been doing nothing but take good close looks at her ever since the deb season had gotten underway. The feeling intensified in regard to the presentation: dressmaker's fittings, the curtsey she was to make before the sovereigns practised over and over again under tutelage, today's dressing and getting ready for the big occasion itself—it was all rather like being on display, she reflected, realizing simultaneously that indeed, that was exactly what it was.

And today, today was the biggest day of being on display in what would eventually be a full season of balls and dances and parties and outings, all with the aim of introducing her into society and all the members thereof to her. Or, at least, as many as possible. Especially the eligible ones. It was the proper way to start off one's path into adult life, the right way to meet the right people and, eventually, the right man. The dream prince. Prince Charming, the perfect husband-to-be. Then she would get married and live happily ever after—the perfect Englishwoman with several children and a house in the country and a place in town from which she would one day leave in a limousine with her debutante daughter to present her at court. . . .

She shivered with excitement and pent-up nerves, all of which seemed to be knotted in a fluttering ball somewhere in her solar plexus. Although it was only late afternoon, Yvonne had already been dressed and prepared for hours, every inch of her gown and train inspected and admired by her parents, Lally, Mr. and Mrs. Young, and every member of the staff in the house. The actual dressing had taken place in the mirror-lined dressing room that was usually Edie's domain so that Yvonne herself could see every detail of her presentation gown.

The silver-tissue train, its sheen shot with blue, fell from the shoulders of her draped chiffon dress and trailed the regulation eighteen inches on the ground. The three white feathers in her hair, also required garb, had been the crowning touch, and from them hung the traditional three-foot tulle veil, in a sheer curtain behind her head.

Silver shoes and long white gloves, reaching to her elbows, completed the picture. As all debs either carried flowers or a fan, Maurice had given her an antique fan, remarking that it could be a memento of the occasion.

"Nothing much you'd be able to do with a bunch of flowers, once they'd faded," he had pointed out.

"You could press them," Edie said unexpectedly. Yvonne had felt there was more her mother was about to say, but then attention had been returned to the present she had just received, and she practised carrying the fan so that it looked graceful in her hands.

Lally, who had been there since the early morning said, "You *are* lucky, Yvonne—and you look absolutely perfect."

"I think I'd better practise curtseying, now that I'm in full regalia. . . ."

"And remember you have to back out. . . . You must never, never turn your back on royalty. . . ."

"I know, Mummy, I know. . . ."

She practised curtseying and walking backwards in front of the mirrors, trying to avoid tripping on the train, remembering to stand straight, to move with grace, to hold her head properly . . .

"Suppose I trip on the train?"

"You *mustn't*, that's all."

"But supposing . . ."

"Yvonne, for goodness' sake . . ."

The nerves of the day tightened for the event.

Now, in the limousine, the splendor of the occasion began working its spell. Maurice emerged from the house to see them off, and he and the Youngs waved from the doorway as the car began pulling away. It slid smoothly along, rounding the corner at the end of the enclosed, tree-filled square, heading for Buckingham Palace.

As they approached the Mall, thickening crowds and choked traffic slowed their stately pace to a crawl. People peered in through the windows, which were now closed, rolled up tight; the faces of the curious were smiling, awed, fascinated by turn. All the way down the approach to the royal palace, onlookers gazed at the debs and their sponsors, the beautifully coiffed and attired ladies, both presenting and to be presented, in the long line of cars and carriages.

Yvonne said, "I feel like something in a zoo."

"Nonsense, darling." Edie smiled at the faces in the window and turned her head with a gesture calculated to display her tiara to its best advantage. "Let the poor devils enjoy seeing you. And think how much of this sort of thing the king and queen go through every time they leave the Palace."

"But they make me nervous."

"Well, you might as well get used to it. We're probably going to be here for at least another hour. I remember how long the wait was when I was presented. How about a sandwich, Yvonne? I think it's about time you had something to keep up your strength. . . ."

The hamper was opened; slowly, they neared the Palace gates. Cars and carriages at the front of the long line were those carrying members of the peerage, to whom precedent was given, and thus tradition obeyed. Eventually they got near enough to see one elegantly garbed figure after another descend and enter the Palace. Yvonne's heart began thumping again. Soon it would be her turn.

"We'd better start getting ready. . . . Here's your cloak, Yvonne, be careful as you put it on. . . . Remember to hold yourself properly when we get out . . . keep your back nice and straight . . ."

The limousine drew to a full stop. The footman got out and opened the door. The next thing Yvonne knew, she was going up a vast flight of stairs, her mother a scant step behind her, and when they reached the top they were swept into the midst of the mood of the hour.

Their cloaks were taken from them. An usher stepped

forward to escort them through the corridor to the Throne Room. Uniforms and pageantry were everywhere; Yvonne found herself gliding along a chandelier-lit way, and then the Throne Room opened before her.

The two thrones stood, in regal solitude, at one end of the room on a dais; near them were grouped the Gentlemen at Arms, members of the King's Body Guard, resplendent in their scarlet coats with enormous gold epaulettes. Tiers of seats, ranged at right angles to the dais, lined two sides of the chamber. The splendor of the occasion was everywhere: jewels, gowns, uniforms, military honors and decorations, beauty and power, peers and precedent, everything blended in glorious spectacle. There were duchesses and dowagers, tiaras and trains, helmets held at uniformed elbow-crook, feathers cascading, the golden glow of heavy tassels falling from swords, and everywhere, everywhere, the plumes of the presenting and those to be presented—the headdress designed after the crest of the Prince of Wales—waving and nodding in the movement of the coiffed and banded heads meeting and greeting, going to their designated seats on either side of the royal room to await the entrance of the reigning sovereigns themselves.

High above, in the musicians' gallery, an orchestra played soft waltzes and light music, the strains audible over the chatter of the crowd. Yvonne and Edie reached their seats.

"When the time comes, you'll have to go out of that door and then around at the back and..."

"But how will I know which way...?"

"Don't worry. An usher'll come to get us."

The orchestra struck up the first notes of "God Save the King," and everybody rose. Conversation died down; Yvonne stared at the dais. Yes—there they were. The king and queen entered in exactly the sort of stately, measured paces she had always imagined they would, moving with majestic dignity toward the two thrones.

Once they were seated, everyone sat down again. The presentation ceremony began, and presently an usher beckoned to Yvonne.

"That's us," Edie whispered to her. "Be careful with your train...."

Yvonne followed the usher to a side door, leaving the Throne Room only to double back to another entrance opening onto the dais itself. There she was grouped with all the other nervous and expectant young presentees, their sponsors close by, the ushers in their black coats and knee britches solid and reassuring, the buckles gleaming on their dark shoes. Everyone waited, tense and silent.

The ceremony started. Yvonne, shaking, moved into the forming line. As she neared the door through which entry to the dais was made, she could hear the names being called out by the announcing usher.

"The Duchess of ... presenting Lady ..."

"Lady ... presenting ..."

As each was called, movement stirred the line, and a presenter and a presentee walked out onto the dais to make their obeisance to the seated monarchs. Sonorously, the names continued to boom out; the closer she came to the door, the less Yvonne heard their content, the syllables blurring behind the thumping of her heart. Another step forward, more names, the resplendent thrones now in sight beyond the door. She was the fifth in line ... the fourth ... next ...

Yvonne felt a sudden push in the small of her back. She was out, beyond the door, walking onto the dais, moving in mechanical terror tinged with soaring delight. There was the king, only paces away.

"Mrs. O'Connor, presenting Miss Yvonne Waring ..."

She curtseyed deeply, her muscles easing her body into the low, swooping bow with the glory of the moment, every motion easy and graceful, a joy to perform. As she rose, the king's smile was an unexpected anointing of royal grace. Then another step, and Yvonne curtseyed again, her second obeisance directed at the imposing queen.

Rising once more, Yvonne observed the second royal face; not a hint of a smile anywhere. Impassive, unmoving and unmoved, the queen stared stonily at her as she came up out of her bow. Then the expressionless eyes moved, ready to watch the next tendered homage. Yvonne's moment was over in the royal glare.

Making her trained quarter-turn, Yvonne started to back, hoping she was lined up correctly with the exit on the opposite side, praying she wouldn't trip on her train. One careful backward step, another and another—and then it was over and she was through the far doorway and out of the Throne Room, safe and sound, presented and undisgraced by mishap or stumble. Her heart was still beating wildly, but it was light and free; she was floating with joy. There were low voices around her and an usher's arm at her elbow, and then Edie was there and they were once again being escorted along under chandeliers.

More vast double doors and their goal was reached; their places were found at one of the round supper tables in the specially appointed palace room. Joined by others, they were soon served supper and champagne; throughout the meal, Yvonne bubbled with the aftermath of the heady affair.

She compared notes with the other debs at the table, as their sponsors reminisced on their own first times. Everywhere, all over the room, the excited chatter echoed exultation and the high-keyed relief of having got through.

". . . and I was so sure my tummy would rumble . . ."

". . . shaking like a leaf until I actually got there . . ."

". . . nothing like last year, when I presented Pamela and two girls swooned away before the king arrived . . ."

". . . smiled at me—yes, he did, Mummy, he really did . . ."

Shortly after midnight, still glowing from the momentous occasion, Yvonne sat in front of the official photographer's camera eye and had the day captured with the chemical magic of silver on glass.

"You're sure you're not too tired, darling?"

Edie, aware of playing a secondary role, if only momentarily, was beginning to flag.

"Oh, no, Mummy, I feel wonderful. Please let's go on . . . you promised me I could . . ."

And so, in the time-honored tradition of the regal occasion and the anointed few, Yvonne Waring went to the private post-presentation party that was part of her debutante calendar and danced in the remembered glow of her royal encounter until the hours of dawn.

The season continued; sometimes Yvonne had invitations to several different parties and dances on the same night, and she saw the dawn time and again as she arrived home. Some of the dances took place in private homes, while the big balls were usually held at hotels or official halls. There were dinner parties beforehand, each deb attending with her escort chosen from the official register of carefully vetted men, who filled in their dance programs and saw them safely home.

Flirtations and friendships were the rule of the day; more

serious attachments were not encouraged at this stage. There would be time enough for lifelong decision in the years to come.

"Remember, you're only young once," Edie said to Yvonne, in unnecessary warning, for Yvonne, much as she was enjoying her social whirl, was restive for something she could not quite define; for the moment, she assured her mother, she enjoyed the company of her escorts as friends.

"Men talk about things that interest me," she explained.

"You mean cars."

"Well yes. Mummy, can I learn to drive?"

Edie was dubious. Maurice was all for it.

"Why not? Bert can teach her."

The lessons were a resounding success. Yvonne learned quickly, efficiently; "...like a man," said Bert proudly. Yvonne's movements at the wheel were sparse, secure.

"She's not one of your flippin' all-elbows types, sir," he explained to Maurice. "Miss Waring understands the car. Asks the right questions, too, she does."

Not only did she understand a car's responsive actions; she also learned to know its systems, and her conversation soon became peppered with mechanical terms. She and Maurice could spend a whole mealtime discussing the merits of a Hispano versus a Rolls, until Edie would become bored and complain.

"Can't you two think of anything else to talk about?"

"Sorry, m'dear. Must be dreadfully tiring for you. How about a game of golf this afternoon?"

Edie had recently started to play, and all three found they enjoyed it. On occasion, Lally Young would join them, having taken up the game several years before.

But Lally was not herself these days. Yvonne soon found out why.

"I don't care what they say. I love him, and nothing is going to make me change my mind. I don't care if I'm young, and I certainly don't care if he's been ill. He's all right now, and that's all that matters."

Lally, full of defiance and tears, poured out the story.

His name was John Bell, she had met him at a county dance, and he had come up to London, expressly to see her, the very next week. From then on, they had seen each other frequently and, at first, the Youngs had not minded.

242

Then the blow had fallen. Mr. Young, making discreet inquiries, discovered that John had only recently returned from a sanatorium in Switzerland. When he faced his daughter with the fact, she admitted knowing it all along.

"But what does it matter? He's all right now."

"Tuberculosis is not something to be taken lightly, Allison..."

The battle had raged from then on. The more her parents argued, the more determined Lally became.

"Have they forbidden you to see him?" Yvonne wanted to know.

"Not quite. But it's all very awkward. Oh, how I wish I were already twenty-one... then they'd have nothing to say. I'd be able to do as I pleased...."

As she had yet to celebrate her twentieth birthday, coming of age was out of immediate reach. Yvonne sympathized and said she only wished she could help; parents, she knew, could be so difficult about things.

"But at least you only have your mother to contend with. Maurice always takes your side, doesn't he? I like him. He's awfully nice."

Yvonne partially agreed.

"He *is* nice—but he doesn't exactly side with me all the time. I think he'd like to, but he never really contradicts Mummy's wishes."

"You can't blame him, can you? She's your mother, and he isn't your father."

It was at a gathering at the aunts' house, a rare family reunion, that Vesey's name was mentioned for the first time in years. As usual, it was May O'Connor who spoke in private to Edie first—May, grown paler than ever. But later that same day, Edwin mentioned his brother's name at the dinner table.

"Forgot to tell you, Maurice—letter from Vesey arrived the other day. Out of the blue. Hadn't heard a word in years. Says he's been ill."

"You haven't answered yet, I trust." Maurice's voice was quieter than usual.

"No."

"Good. We'll talk it over later." Maurice shifted in his chair. "Aunt Moo, do you think I should do some more carving? Plates look a bit empty...."

Talk turned to other topics, other family members not

present: Peter, who now had his own parish in the Cotswolds, and had recently become engaged, Dick in the Navy, bearded the last time he was home, Jeannie O'Connor, spending a year with friends in Scotland to get over "... someone most unsuitable, I don't know how it happened, but we caught it in the nick of time. ..."

Yvonne excused herself from the table and went out into the garden to say hello to Bronner. There was no guarantee she'd get anything more than a grunt in return; old and bent with the passing years, the gardener was more taciturn than ever.

Yvonne reflected that everyone seemed to intensify with age: Aunt Moo was thinner, Aunt Boo fatter. Edwin had become so vague as to be almost translucent; May was milky pale. The aunts' house, on the other hand, had diminished in her eyes; it appeared smaller than when she had first seen it, the scullery shadows less deep, the raspberry canes less spikey, not so towering into the sky. She still loved it, though, particularly the garden. Bronner's green fingers were still working their magic, she noted, admiring his work as she wandered along the path.

She found him down by the ancient toolshed and got the expected grunt in answer to her greeting, but it was satisfying in its way; she returned to the house with her mission accomplished, and as she entered the hallway, she came across the two O'Connor brothers deep in private conversation.

Maurice was saying to Edwin, "He wants money, I suppose. Well, we'll have to send him some. But only on the condition he steers clear."

Then he noticed Yvonne, and said, "Ah, there you are. We were just about to call you. It's time to leave. Your mother's in the kitchen saying good-bye to Gladys," and after that a general leave-taking took place, with promises made to send postcards and write, for the O'Connors and Yvonne were leaving for the Continent and La Maison the following week.

"... and if Jeannie still hasn't got over that fellow, you can always send her on to us. ..."

"... think of it, Muriel, motoring to the Mediterranean, the sort of trip poor dear Papa would have enjoyed. ..."

"Nonsense. He'd have hated it. You know what a fuss he made whenever we had to travel anywhere. ..."

It was nice to know, Yvonne thought as she waved from the

car till the aunts were lost from sight, that some things never changed, no matter how much time went by.

3

Ming stretched himself out along Yvonne's lap, sphinxlike and patient, regally ignoring the other animals in the waiting room. A panting terrier fidgeted by his owner's feet; two kittens grappled in a netted cage. An elderly Pomeranian, asthmatic and rheumy-eyed, surveyed the world from its position on a chair. A white mouse twitched in and out of its exercise wheel.

Yvonne, stroking Ming's silken head and tracing her fingers over his long-fringed ears, noticed yet again how many pets resembled their owners.

The door opened and a young woman came in, carrying what appeared to be a bundle of fabric in her hands. She sat down in a far seat, two cats and the white mouse away from Yvonne. When the vet entered to call for the next patient, she rose to speak to him.

"Madame said she rang you up. About Coco."

"Ah, yes. Let me see."

The doctor pulled aside the top layer from the bundled fabric and gave its contents a quick look. Then he covered it again.

"There's nothing I can do quickly, mademoiselle. This parrot has been very badly mauled."

The girl nodded.

"The dog that attacked him was very big. Won't he live?"

The vet shrugged. "It's hard to say. Probably not—and in any event, trying to save him will mean constant attention."

"Madame told me to tell you that, if that was the case, could you put him to sleep?"

The vet nodded and the girl handed him the bundle, saying good-bye quickly and leaving through the front door. The doctor looked over at Yvonne.

"You and Ming are next, I believe, Miss Waring?"

Once inside the surgery, Yvonne said, "May I see the parrot, please?"

The vet again unfolded a corner of the cloth. The bird was

crumpled against the gathered rags, his bright green feathers twisted, oddly awry. Darkened splotches of drying blood were spattered all over him, and a deep wound showed on his side. One of his wings lay awkwardly against him; his eyes were closed.

"Is he alive?"

"Barely."

"Poor little thing."

The vet covered the bird over and put him aside.

"Would you put Ming up on the table, please? We'll have the injection done in no time."

He pressed the buzzer for his assistant, and in that moment, Yvonne made up her mind.

"Can I have the parrot?"

The vet looked at her, then shrugged.

"If you wish, Miss Waring. But I would counsel you against it. He's badly injured, and there's not much you can really do. . . ."

"Well, what *can* I do? Tell me so I can try. . . ."

An hour later, Yvonne arrived back at La Maison with an inoculated Ming, a barely breathing parrot, and a sheet of hastily scribbled instructions.

"He needs to be kept warm and quiet, and I have to try and get some food into him, and I must check on him all the time, and . . ."

A small open basket was found to accommodate the bird, with a layer of soft clean rags placed inside it to cushion its surface. A hot-water bottle was filled.

"No, I'd better have another one, so I can put one each side of the basket."

Yvonne cleared the top of a small table in her room.

"That way, I can keep setting my alarm during the night, and get up and check on him without disturbing anyone else. . . ."

She waited and watched and waited again, testing for the bird's breath by holding a thin wisp of cotton to the parrot's upper beak and withdrawing it, relieved, when she saw it move in the faintest of responses. Once, during that first night, she saw he had opened his eyes, but the next time she checked him, he had closed them again, and she feared the worst.

Next morning, however, he was still there, and his eyes opened when she lifted the light cover.

"Hullo, Coco....You're going to get well, aren't you...? and be my very own parrot...for years and years...."

He blinked and made a slight movement, as though in response to her voice. Yvonne reported on his progress at the luncheon table, her optimism growing, but by nightfall he seemed worse again, and at midnight, hardly alive. She spent the small hours until dawn cradling the basket in her arms as she lay in bed, dozing fitfully, her bedside lamp on all the time, so that she could check on the bird without causing him undue disturbance. At daybreak, she saw to her relief that he was still breathing.

For the next few days, the pulse of the house beat in time with the parrot's battle to survive. Every day gained caused renewed hope; even the staff asked about Coco when Yvonne arrived downstairs.

"I think he's really better....He opened his eyes again....Yes, I need some more clean cloths....Thank you, Mummy, for sending Yves to get that medicine....I think I'd better go and check up on Coco again...."

It took a week before the battle's outcome became clear, but the day Yvonne saw Coco struggle up to wobble on his feet, she knew the parrot had won. The vet told her the bird would probably never fly again, but that would hardly matter. Coco next started to peck down food on his own, and Yvonne no longer needed to pry open his beak to insert small pellets of nourishment.

Then came the day he perched on the edge of his basket. He watched every movement Yvonne made; she reached her hand out toward him. Cautiously, the parrot moved over, gripping his toes around her index finger. She brought her hand, bearing the parrot, close to her side; he nestled against her, making barely audible throat sounds.

"He's going to be perfectly all right," she reported. "But we'll have to get a proper parrot stand for him. I don't want him in a cage."

"The garden room'll be the perfect place for him," Edie added. "And won't he look splendid there, with all the plants...."

The garden room, a glass-enclosed section of the terrace at the back of La Maison, offered a profusion of leaves and flowers at all times of the year. During the summer months the doors were left open to the outside, allowing the breezes to cool the enclosure, as did the overhanging trees. In winter, the sun reached the garden room through the bare branches, giving a tropical touch to the living room that adjoined it inside. Tubs and pots were changed discreetly with the changing seasons, and Edie often ordered informal meals to be served there. White-painted wrought-iron chairs and a matching round table stood at one end, banked by a ceiling-high stand of ferns; toward the other side, flower-patterned cretonne covered the sofa and some easy chairs.

The parrot stand was placed halfway between the two furniture groupings; there, Coco preened in the streaming sunlight, steadily regaining his strength.

He also, suddenly, regained his voice.

The first clear phrase Coco ever uttered at La Maison caused the new parlor maid to cross herself and flee to the kitchen. The cook reported the event to Yvonne.

"But what did he say?" Yvonne wanted to know.

"Ah, no, *mademoiselle*—I cannot say it. It was a terrible *grossièreté*." As she spoke, the cook was smiling from ear to ear.

The next day, Yvonne heard it for herself. Giggling, she told her mother.

"How amusing," said Edie, who did not understand a word of it. "I do hope he says it at cocktails tonight."

He did. The several French-speaking guests present roared with laughter.

Coco squawked, "*Ta gueule!*" and began whistling.

"Where *did* you get that parrot, Yvonne?"

"*Espèce de con!*"

"At the vet's. I think he used to belong to someone who owned a bar."

"*Fils de put'!*"

"I'll say he did. And it wasn't the one at the Ritz, either. . . ."

More laughter and more squawking followed. Coco was on his way to being a local celebrity.

Lally came out to Cannes for a visit; having turned twenty, her defiance was growing.

"All John and I have to do is wait another year, and then it won't matter *what* my parents say . . ."

In the meantime, there was fun to be had, and if John Bell, staying with friends at Cap d'Antibes, managed to attend the same parties to which the two girls were invited, no one was officially the wiser. Life went on, with all its subterfuges; Yvonne found Edie more lenient when Lally was around.

"Yes, of course, darlings—off you go and enjoy yourselves...." Edie seldom questioned their specific plans, being busy with her own social engagements. Life had resumed a predictable pattern, the seasonal sojourns spent as before. Yvonne, now launched, was expected to join many of the calendar's engagements, but impromptu outings with her own set were also expected, wherever they happened to be.

Thus, the younger set partied in Paris and Edinburgh, London and Vienna, while the parental group gathered in the same spots. Yvonne gained experience and self-confidence and aplomb; there was much in the opulence cushioning her life that she enjoyed, but it did not hold quite as much for her as it did for her mother and Maurice O'Connor. There were pressures that hampered her, restraints imposed. If life was lovely, it was never entirely her own. There were engagements she had to attend, whether or not she enjoyed them, social obligations she had to fulfill; if scheduled events and invitations clashed, it was Edie, and not Yvonne, who had the final word.

"... but they've invited me to stay next weekend, Mummy, and I'd far rather..."

"I'm sorry, darling, but Maurice wants to drive to Paris on Monday, and from there we're going on to..."

"I could stay here by myself...."

"Don't be absurd, Yvonne."

Lally offered the perfect solution.

"You'll simply have to fall in love and get married," she said. "I find it's much easier to put up with my parents now that I know John and I will be on our own in a year's time."

"It's easy for you to talk. You *did* fall in love."

"You will, too."

But as yet, Yvonne had not.

Oh, there had been flirtations and several proposals, all turned down. Some, she felt sure, had not been sincere, but in any case, it didn't matter, because she hadn't wanted to marry any of them. Yvonne had made up her mind about one thing: she was going to marry for love. She could see how much it meant to Lally and John.

In the meantime, she still had to toe the mark.

"But I wanted to go riding, Mummy...."

"You can go tomorrow, can't you?"

"Yes, but..."

She went riding the next day.

It remained one of her passions: riding, galloping free, sensing the power and the speed of the animal beneath her, the rushing breath of the wind in her face. Whether on the winding paths in the hills behind the Riviera or over the green reaches of the English countryside, riding was a joy and an outlet to freedom, and Yvonne rode whenever she got the chance, her silver-handled *rebenque* kept at La Maison, a proper English crop hanging beside her riding jacket in the London house.

She had been riding in Hyde Park the day she came home to find a strange man waiting for Maurice in the morning room.

"I don't know who he is, Miss Yvonne," the parlor maid told her anxiously. "Said he had to see Mr. O'Connor, and insisted on coming in."

Just then, Maurice walked in through the front door. On hearing of the visitor's presence, he walked quickly over to the morning room door. As he entered, Yvonne heard him say, "What the devil are you doing here, Vesey? I thought I told you..." and then the door slammed shut behind him. Later that day, strict orders were issued against letting anyone unknown into the house.

"And if you ever see that particular man again, you are to get hold of me at once." Maurice looked so stern he was almost forbidding; Yvonne had never seen him anywhere near as angry as that before.

"I would also like to spare Mrs. O'Connor any unpleasantness," Maurice told the gathered staff. "There is no need to mention this unfortunate affair."

When Edie returned home that evening, after a long shopping expedition, conversation centered around their planned departure for Cannes the following week, and no further mention was ever made of the day's visitor.

Edie woke and heard the fan-tailed pigeons cooing their good-mornings on the dovecote below. They were pretty little things, with their gentle murmurings and their lifetime faithfulness to their partners. She had wanted a pair the first time she'd seen them, and Maurice had duly had the dovecote installed on the terrace at La Maison.

That had been for last year's birthday. Today was her fortieth. Sitting up in bed, Edie reached for the big down-filled pillows she had cast aside the night before, preparatory to sleeping. She piled them up behind her, sinking back into their receiving comfort to consider the day.

Forty.

Fingers of sun were probing through the early morning haze; soon the warmth of Riviera summer sun would bathe La Maison. There was to be a party that night: cocktails followed by a buffet dinner and then dancing, with a band out on the terrace, and probably a mad whirl through some of the night spots until dawn, when bacon and eggs would be waiting for them on the terrace again. Edie loved parties, particularly those given for her or at La Maison. Still, forty...

She could see herself in the dressing-table mirror directly across the room between the two french doors leading out onto her bedroom balcony. Each was half open, the long voile curtains moving slightly in the incoming freshness of the new day. The oval frame of the looking glass encircled her image.

She did not look forty. Her small-featured face was still heart-shaped, her jawline firm. Her hair, attractively touched with silver, was as vibrantly springy as before. Time and the practised scissors of the best hairdressers London and Paris had to offer had tamed the childhood frizz and made it frame her features, while its abundant volume made it easy to adapt to changing fashion.

She rose, slipping on the peignoir waiting on the chair. Her figure, unfashionably short, was still slight and wiry, despite the few extra pounds it had gathered in the last years. They did not show in any marked way; she probably had golf to thank for that. It was good exercise for her, along with being good fun, which was just as well, for otherwise she might risk getting far too broad in the beam. Some of her friends went to the most appalling lengths to exercise, standing on their heads and sitting cross-legged and going in for all sorts of sweaty physical exertions, but Edie would have none of it, and Maurice quite agreed. "Just enjoy yourself, my love," he always said.

Edie walked out onto the balcony and looked at the world below. The fantails, hushed on first seeing her, soon took up their billing and cooing again. The sun glinted on the distant sea, while on the sweep of terrace directly below her, the tall palms over by the balustrade cast long shadows over the raked gravel. Footsteps sounded; the gardener was carrying a ladder toward the palms. Maurice had ordered lights strung across, to accommodate the evening's dancing, and the household's preparatory work for the party was already underway.

A faint knocking came from the room behind her.

"Good morning, my dear—and many happy returns..."

Maurice joined her on the balcony; as they stood looking over the familiar view, breathing in the calm of the morning air, his hands rested on her shoulders.

"You and your *balcón mirador*," he smiled. "Shall we have breakfast here? It's going to be a perfect day...."

Their *café au lait* and pannier of croissants were already half-consumed when Yvonne appeared.

"Happy birthday, Mummy!" Yvonne greeted her mother effusively and hugged her. "Here"—she thrust a package into Edie's hands—"I made it myself...."

"Well! Aren't you clever?" Edie unfolded the sleeveless pullover from the tissue paper wrapping and admired its jacquard pattern. "How on earth did you find the time? Thank you, darling...."

"Did it at night, most of it. Wanted it to be a surprise. Maurice"—she turned to her stepfather—"is it all right if I take one of the cars? I know I said I'd be home all day, but I'd like to get in at least an hour's riding, and..."

Maurice looked at Edie, who said, "As long as you get back in time for luncheon. I don't want to keep our guests waiting for you."

"Oh, I'll be back in plenty of time. I promise."

With a swinging of curtains and a slamming of doors, she was gone. Edie sighed.

"I do wish she'd be a bit more ladylike. I know she's tall, but is there any need for her to..."

"It's just youth, m'dear. They all rush about like that."

"When I was her age..." Edie began. Maurice immediately put up a hand to cut her short.

"My love, when you were her age, you were a very different sort of young lady. You had suffered great tragedy, you were of an entirely different nature, and life itself had forced you to grow up far beyond your years. And you must take into consideration that she's far taller than you are. You move differently. You don't even look alike, you know."

Edie acknowleged Maurice's points, adding, "All the same, you'd think she'd have the sense not to stamp around so

252

much. Why—she strides almost like a boy! And she *is* going to be twenty quite soon."

Maurice said nothing; neither the theme nor the tone were new to his ears. Instead, after a moment's pause, he produced a long, narrow box.

"For your birthday, my dear...."

The dull patina of the blue leather box was broken by the bright point of its metal catch. Edie pushed it; the domed lid sprang open. Inside, on its dark velvet bed, the bracelet's diamonds sparkled rainbows on either side of the square-cut sapphires that ran like a faceted ribbon along the entire length.

"Oh, Maurice—it's marvelous! And I can wear it tonight. It'll be just right with my new frock."

"I know. That's why I chose it...."

At lunch, it was much admired, Edie explaining she had been reluctant to take it off "even while I had my bath after breakfast." Yvonne, arriving late, found it a deflecting point of her mother's reprimand.

"...yes, Mummy, I know....I'm very sorry....What a magnificent bracelet....Maurice, I'll bet...Aren't you lucky...?"

Later, in an aside to her stepfather, she said, "You'd give Mummy anything she wanted, wouldn't you?" busying herself with her salad as she spoke as though trying to cover the edge in her voice with physical activity.

If Maurice noticed, he gave no sign, for after he finished patting his mustache with the white linen serviette, he answered in his customary, measured tones and said, "I would most certainly try."

A network of Japanese lanterns bobbed over the terrace, the accordion-pleated shapes pink and gold in the day's fading light. Music came from the band set up near the door to the garden room, the instruments resting on the raised and paved section of the front terrace. Down the two shallow steps to the wider arc of its graveled expanse, the guests strolled in groups and couples, cocktail glasses in hand.

Inside the house, Edie wove her way through the crowd of chattering guests, her gestures highlighting the presence of the bracelet on her arm. In the wake of her path, the currents of cocktail party talk closed in.

". . . spoils her rotten. Still, she *is* lovely, even though she must be forty if she's a day."

"Didn't you know? Today *is* the day. It's her birthday."

"Well, I must say, Maurice does her—and himself —proud. . . ."

There were also the less kind.

"Paste, probably. I'll bet she wishes they were real."

"I'll bet you wish they weren't. O'Connor's never bought paste in his life. Wouldn't recognize it if he tripped over it. Now, buck up, my girl, and look pleasant. I don't care if you loathe her. He's the bank's bread and butter these days."

Yvonne, caught up in the lavish mood of the party, was humming to herself as she circulated among the middle-aged guests. Her own crowd would turn up later, after dinner when the dancing began; until then, she was playing her part as the dutiful daughter. Actually, she was enjoying herself. It was a perfect evening, Mummy hadn't criticized her all day, and she had even approved of Yvonne's dress and general appearance.

One of Maurice's cronies approached her.

"I say, Yvonne, just *entre nous* and on the q.t.—how old is your mother?"

Yvonne told him. "Doesn't look it, does she?"

"I'll say she doesn't! Damned good-looking woman, for her age. . . . Mind you"—his tone changed—"she hasn't got your beauty . . . never did have, I'll wager . . ."

Yvonne edged away with a polite smile. She was finding it an increasing bore having to keep Maurice's friends and contemporaries at arm's length. Dirty old men, the lot of them, always trying to sidle up to her or invite her to tête-à-tête drinks and lunch in town, or how about a naughty weekend in Paris, no need for her parents to find out, surely she can think of some alibi or other . . .

When it had first started happening, she had summoned up enough courage to tell Edie, giving a censored and name-free version of the latest instance to have occurred. Edie had brushed it aside.

". . . only after the money, darling. I wouldn't let it worry you. Once they realize it's not yours, they won't stick around anymore."

Yvonne felt her throat tighten, and had given up. Thinking it over later, she wished it were only the money; getting rid of them would be so much easier. But it wasn't, so she kept on trying to keep them at bay as best she could.

If only she could get away. Be independent. Go and live on her own and be free of this cloying atmosphere in which she lived. She had everything she could possibly wish for, as her mother kept pointing out, but she was still being treated like a little girl. The conflicting style went on no matter where they were; *you're old enough to know better* and *of course you can do nothing of the kind* were driving her to a silent form of inner despair. Any time there was something she really wanted to do, those phrases were sure to come into play, as they did when she announced she wanted to learn how to fly. Having been taken aloft by friends with flying licenses, Yvonne knew she would take to the air with as much enjoyment, and perhaps even as much ability, as she had taken to driving a car.

Edie had at first scoffed at the idea.

"Don't be ridiculous. Girls don't fly."

"Yes, they do." Yvonne cited a few well-known cases. Edie brushed them aside.

"You can't set down rules by a few eccentrics. You're really old enough to know better, Yvonne. It's high time you stopped indulging in these childish ideas...."

But Yvonne, truly taken with the idea of flying, tried to convince her mother.

"You didn't think I'd be able to drive, and then you finally saw I was quite capable of doing it. What's more, you say you think I drive quite well...."

"Flying isn't driving."

"No, but it's similar. And more and more people are doing it, and..."

"I don't care what other people are doing—you are not going to do it, and that's final." Edie dismissed the subject by laying down the law. "And I don't want to hear any more about it, miss, as long as you are under my roof...."

It was useless to appeal to Maurice; Yvonne knew quite well he would not side with her against her mother. In discussions, he always stuck up for Edie. He did not fight Yvonne, but he never interfered, other than to try and smooth the rough seas between mother and daughter. Yvonne had once tackled him about his defense of Edie and her points of view.

"Don't tell me you think she's always, always right, Maurice."

"That's not the point, Yvonne. We're all allowed to have our opinions."

"But she's so unfair at times."

"You must keep in mind you're her daughter, and still under her roof."

"It's your roof, too."

"But you are not my daughter. We're discussing a question that has arisen between your mother and you. Do try, Yvonne, not to muddle things, though I quite understand it's all rather hard on you. Growing up *is* hard, you know. . . ."

Sometimes, Yvonne got the feeling there was more he would like to say, that, in his gentle, awkward way, Maurice truly wished he could smooth her path as he smoothed life everywhere for Edie. He was that sort of man, and Yvonne loved him for it, but it did not always help her in her current problems.

A waiter came by her, bearing a tray with champagne. Yvonne took a glass, and walked out to the terrace to listen to the band. They had just swung into the new melody of the season, and a favorite of hers. Softly, she began singing the words.

"*Adiós*, Buenos Aires, good-bye . . ."

Maurice was leading Edie out onto the dance floor, and Yvonne had to admit her mother looked exceptionally beautiful that night. They danced their way slowly around the terrace, joined by other couples.

". . . though my heart stays here
Now the time draws near I must go . . ."

Yvonne watched her mother and thought: *she almost looks like a bride at her wedding . . . and Maurice looks so proud of her . . . as he always does . . .*

". . . I shall miss your sky
And the sun, golden eye, radiant glow . . ."

She repressed a sudden stab of jealousy. It must be so wonderful to be loved like that. Yvonne reached the side of the bandstand. One of the musicians leaned over toward her.

"Why not sing the song with us, mademoiselle?"

She smiled, and he caught up with the words of the tune. Together, they sang and blended their voices.

> "And I weep as I wave as I sigh
> That you never took me to your Latin heart
> Though I love you deeply you will never know
> You disdain to know, you refuse to know
> So I turn away and with a tear-filled eye
> I say *ciao*
> And good-bye
> And *adiós* . . . good-bye. . . ."

A medley of fox-trots followed, and dancers flocked to the floor. Yvonne thought: *it's going to be a very good party*, and made her way back inside to the buffet she knew would be starting any moment now.

There were people already gathering around the sumptuously laden table, filling their plates along with their gossipy knowledge.

". . . drove down with David, and he was simply awful—tight as a tick all the way. . ."

"Darling Elsie was there, with her swami . . . so amusing, you know . . ."

". . . and then Cole and company turned up, and you cannot imagine . . ."

". . . and Syrie will have it all white-washed p.d.q. . . ."

". . . put the kibosh on her hijinks at once, in true archduke style . . ."

Edie's birthday party was well underway.

Hours later, as the colors of a new dawn tinted the sky, Edie and Maurice stood on the terrace, waving good-bye to the last of the guests. The only car left in the driveway was theirs; some time earlier, Yves had been dismissed to bed after they, and guests, had arrived back from the last of their stops in Cannes, to find the little round tables set up on the terrace with champagne and orange juice and breakfast, waiting for the hearty who had lasted the full length of the celebration.

"A most successful party—one of our best," Maurice was saying. "And, as always, you were the loveliest woman present."

On the terrace, the servants were clearing the party's debris.

"How about a nightcap, Edie? A last sip of champagne. And let's take a look at the sea before we go to bed."

They strolled over to the balustrade and leaned on it, their glasses drawing wet circles on the marble's cold surface. Maurice took the long jeweler's case from his pocket and put it in front of Edie.

"Oh. Shall I take it off now?" Tired as she was, Edie still did not want to remove her bracelet. "I suppose I'd better, and we can put it in the safe on our way upstairs." She reached for the box and pushed the catch; the top flew open on its spring.

The band of stones inside did not glitter; being rubies, they glowed. Their shape was similar to that of the sapphires on her arm, their setting the same.

"The two fit together," Maurice was saying. "Here, let me show you. I thought they would be so suitable for an Englishwoman. . . ."

The red, white, and blue blaze linked together in a wide cuff, the weight noticeable, the beauty of the jewels surpassed only by their worth. As she kissed Maurice and thanked him for giving her such a memorable birthday, Edie secretly wished he had presented her with the second bracelet before the guests had left.

4

The Honorable Jocelyn Nigel Anquetell Dancourt, elder son of Baron Brocknell and six foot two in his stockinged feet, cautiously laid his splitting forehead against the cool pane of the train window and hoped that neither he nor the glass would shatter once motion began. The *Golden Arrow* was due to leave the gloomy Paris station within the next five minutes. He might, of course, not live as long as that. It had been a splendid weekend and a damn fine party, what he could remember of it, and now all the pigeons were home to roost, cheerful as buzzards, clawing inside his cranium.

The position ceased to be comfortable; the armchair seat was too far away from the window. He pulled back, the tom-toms in his head stepping up their wild beat. Even his eyelids hurt—God, what a marvelous bash it had been. . . .If he could just manage to live through the next hour. . . .

With extreme care, he opened his eyes. A white jacketed vision swam from side to side in front of him. He blinked, cursing inwardly at the pain. The figure cleared. Salvation. A waiter.

Feeling better at once, he ordered, then leaned back to await his drink. There was a commotion in the doorway of the carriage; people were coming in, hurrying in the last minute rush. Outside, whistles began blowing to warn of the train's imminent departure. Dancourt winced; did they really have to blow their infernal torture instruments with such relish? Closer to his seat, a babble of voices gave disjointed advice.

"...remember to ring up Mrs. Young when you get to London...."

"...quite sure Bert will be waiting for you, my dear...."

"...and Mummy, *please* don't forget Coco's sunflower seeds....Bye-bye, Ming, be a good boy....Let me kiss Taitai once more...."

"...*so* kind of you..."

"Not at all, Mrs. O'Connor. I'm sure we'll have a very nice trip together. Yvonne, I think those are our seats over there...."

More whistles, the bustle of baggage, a flurry of Pekingese trotting along the floor. Then the dogs were picked up; the couple holding them descended while two passengers accommodated themselves at the far end, across the aisle.

The tall girl waved a last good-bye from the window before sitting down. She was quite the loveliest sight he had seen in ages; apparently unaware of his scrutiny, she talked to her companion—a middle-aged woman with her back to Dancourt—in a low, musical voice. Gone was the confusion and the fuss and the flap; they settled into their armchairs with the set table between them.

The train lurched, then began pulling its way steadily out of the station, emerging out of the dark cave that was the Gare du Nord. The waiter served Dancourt his drink; he sipped it, pondering his present dilemma: how was he going to meet the girl? Alone, it would have been easy, but he hadn't the foggiest who the old battle-ax was. And he couldn't very well saunter over and spill his drink at her feet.

He was still mulling over the problem when the far door opened and voices he recognized reached him over the quickening rhythm of the train's noisy wheels. He looked up and saw his fellow survivors; both Stuffy and Charles appeared

259

to be in far better shape and spirits than he was. The old adage was true: the years did tell.

Charles was leaning over talking to the girl's companion. The fates had smiled; Dancourt did, too. He braced himself to sit up and lift his glass to the arrivals. It was Stuffy who saw him first.

"Hullo, Joss! Didn't think you'd make it."

"Neither did I, Stuffy, old sock—neither did I. Do sit down. Join me in another?"

The younger man flopped down in the chair opposite and signaled to the waiter.

"How about one for Charles?"

"Rather. He needs one, badly."

Joss looked down the carriage. Charles was still talking at the far end.

"He seems to be doing all right for himself. Who's the looker?"

"Yvonne Waring. Don't you know her?"

"Never seen her before."

"Your fault, old boy. Shouldn't have stayed abroad so long. She was at school with my sister—came out the same year, too. Want to meet her, do you?"

Joss Dancourt frowned.

"Stuffy, you are talking to an infirm laddie. A chap who has suffered. Do try to be kind."

"Righto."

"And for God's sake, try to be less convulsively *cheerful*." Joss shuddered. "My eardrums...somebody sandpapered them while I wasn't looking...."

"It really was a top-hole do, wasn't it?"

"Please." Joss held up a restraining hand. "I'm not strong enough for memories. Later, perhaps...after some more liquid, or a spot of nourishment. Ah, I hear the encouraging sounds of cutlery....there is yet hope...."

At meal's end, all introductions were effected.

"Won't you join us for coffee?"

"That's very kind of you, Mr. Dancourt, but I think you young things would do far better on your own. I expect you to take good care of Yvonne while I enjoy my book."

They chatted all the way to the French coast. As they boarded the cross-channel steamer Joss Dancourt made it clear, in an aside to young Bartlett, that he wanted the field to himself. Then he turned his full attention to Yvonne.

". . . quite understand about not liking the Channel. . . . Used to feel a bit queasy myself. . . . Champagne and fresh air's the best thing for it. . . . Let's go up on deck. . . ."

Joss Dancourt kept Yvonne Waring out on deck all the way across the Channel on one of the smoothest crossings either of them had ever known. He bowed when she mentioned it.

"A mere nothing, I assure you. . . . All I did was telegraph ahead and order the day. . . ."

Yvonne laughed, as she had laughed many times in the hours since they had met. She was delightful, unaffected, marvelously straightforward; he hadn't met anyone like her in years. And she told him, quite unselfconsciously, what pure chance her whole trip had been.

"Mummy and Maurice had a fit at first, but then when they found out a friend of theirs would be traveling too, they calmed down. You see, we were all supposed to go back to London together until Maurice said he had to stay for a meeting, and Mummy decided she'd stay with him, and . . ."

"And if it weren't for the fates," Joss pointed out, "who provided you with a suitable traveling companion and me with Stuffy Bartlett, all in one go, it might have been years before we bumped into each other. Though I must say, the thought of Stuffy as fate personified does strike me as rich and strange. . . ."

This time, they both laughed.

"Now you've done it—introducing them. *And* giving in, letting him shove us out. He'll be nibbling on her ear before you can say knife."

"She'll probably love it."

"No doubt. But I'd imagine her parents . . ."

"Oh, bugger her parents. Besides, they're not here, are they?"

"No, but still . . ."

"Joss wouldn't dare pull one of his tricks on the *Golden Arrow*."

"I wonder."

"Stop worrying, old bean. We'll be in London soon enough. The boat docked right on the nose—I happened to notice the clock—and we're moving nicely now. Nothing's going to happen."

"You sure?"

"Well, not in broad daylight while they're serving tea."

261

"Mmm. Well, I hope you're right."

"Tell you what. Let's go and join 'em for tea. That'll queer his game—at least till we get into London."

"Jolly good idea. Come on, Stuffy."

Shouldering their tennis racquets, they walked along the train. Beyond its windows, the rolling countryside of Kent scalloped contours against the evening sky.

He was charming, he was funny, he was suave, he was sophisticated, he knew all the right places and the right times to go. Joss turned up at whatever party she attended, was always known to the hosts and most of those present. Dances, balls, weekends in the country, he knew all the ins and outs, everyone there was to know, had entree everywhere. He was older, nearly thirty, and therefore a far cry from the young men who had formed Yvonne's circle before. But his friendships seemed to spread out to all ages; he had the unaffected polish of upbringing buffed by experience. Maurice and Edie liked him at once; Lally thought he was simply too marvelous for words.

"And what's more, Yvonne, I think he's serious about you."

"He hasn't said anything."

"I bet he will. You wait and see."

Yvonne waited and secretly hoped, falling more in love with Joss every day.

"But why didn't we meet before?" she had asked at the very beginning.

"I've been out East. Got tired of things here."

But he didn't seem tired of anything now.

Was he serious about her? Yvonne waited and dreamed. The Hon. and Mrs. Jocelyn Dancourt...wouldn't it be grand? And one in the eye to all the Podge Bartletts of the world, who thought the D.D. would fall flat on her face. It would serve them right if she could sweep right by them with someone who, apart from being out of the topmost of top drawers, was also handsome and charming.

At a dance one night, breathless from a frantic Charleston and sipping restorative champagne, Yvonne heard a masculine voice behind her say, "Hullo, D.D. It's been years," and in the second it took her to whirl around, she felt the shock of hopelessness, of being trapped with no escape.

But the man standing there, ruddy-faced and smiling, was

a total stranger. Only then did she realize he was greeting Joss, who, in the next few moments, introduced her to the newcomer, adding to him, "And hands off, old boy, whether or not I'm around, but I usually am," which added to her intense confusion.

At supper, she asked Joss, "Why did he call you D.D.?"

"A nickname from long ago—my gambling days. They said I was a lucky dog, and then someone said no, just a dirty one, and Dirty Dog Dancourt became my sobriquet. Rather tiring in its full length, so it got chopped down to initials. Haven't heard it in years." Joss speared another oyster with unconcern.

Yvonne swallowed hard, and said, "You know, I used to be called D.D. at school, too."

"Really? What a nice coincidence."

"I'm afraid it wasn't. They only used it behind my back."

"Why?"

She told him.

"Typical school rot," was Dancourt's only comment, his manner banishing the years of pain. "Have some more oysters. They're excellent for all D.D.s in sight. . . ."

Later in the evening, as they danced, he said, "You are going to marry me, aren't you, Yvonne? I've already told the family that you were. . . ."

Everyone agreed a long engagement was pointless.

". . . not as though Joss were a mere stripling. . ." Thus Lady Brocknell, thin, taut, austere, and a head taller than her husband, whose pale blue eyes were a faded reflection of his son's.

". . . marvelous to know Yvonne has found exactly the right man." So pleased was Edie at the match, her manner implied personal responsibility for it.

"Damn' fine gel. Lucky chap, Joss." It was one of the only remarks fully expressed by Baron Brocknell the first evening both sets of parents met for dinner, but, as Joss explained to Yvonne afterward, his father was a man of few words.

Lady Brocknell made up for it, proclaiming her delight.

". . . always wanted a daughter . . . no need to wait . . . both of you old enough to know what you want . . . I'm sure, Yvonne, you're the sort of girl who'd never let Joss down. . . ."

Yvonne, aghast at the thought of ever causing Joss even the

263

slightest discomfort, was vehement in expressing her loyalty and her love. She was in seventh heaven, floating on air; everyone was pleased with her, she could do no wrong.

Their engagement announcement appeared in the London *Times*, Joss slipped the family sapphire, reset, onto the fourth finger of Yvonne's left hand. She kept looking at it all the way through their engagement party, making sure it was still there, hardly believing the joy of the moment every time she saw it. Guests, congratulations and champagne flowed throughout the London house.

"... Yes, very soon, in the autumn... No, we haven't decided on the actual day yet...."

"... but of course, he's always been everybody's favorite. ...Joss was never shy, not even as a child... takes after my side of the family... not like Cedric..."

"...not here today...Joss says he's very busy in Paris...but I'm sure his brother'll be best man....No, I haven't met him yet...."

"Rum do. Pretty gel. Brazilian, I think."

"... and Lally is to be my only bridesmaid, which will make it a bit different, I think...."

Joss, at Yvonne's side, smiled his agreement.

"Make a nice change from all those gangly cousins with big teeth one tends to see loping after brides these days...."

It was not being mentioned in public that Lally herself needed something to look forward to, something to hide her present unhappiness. John Bell had been obliged to return to the sanatorium in Switzerland, ruining their elopement plans. His doctors had been reassuring, saying it would only be a matter of time before he was completely cured; Lally, swearing eternal love, vowed she would wait. But Mr. and Mrs. Young were being obvious in their efforts to get her to forget John once and for all.

As the engagement party drew to a close, the great-aunts kissed Yvonne good-bye and were charmed when Joss kissed them.

"It really is wonderful, isn't it, Muriel?" said Aunt Boo as they were driven home by Bert. "Our little Yvonne... and that delightful young man... truly a match made in heaven, I swear...."

In point of fact, it was a match greatly assisted by two sets of parents whose motives reached farther than the immediate desires of their offspring. In the short months that followed, all stumbling blocks were pushed aside, any discrepancies swiftly explained and wedding nerves were frequently cited as the only cause of upset or tears.

". . . don't let it worry you for a single moment. He always was an impetuous boy. . . ."

". . . sure to calm down after it's over and you start your lives together. . . ."

". . . no, I don't think anything of the kind, Yvonne. I'm sure you're exaggerating. Besides, you're tired. Too many fittings yesterday, I'd imagine. Perhaps you'd better rest after lunch today, darling. . . ."

The wounds of lovers' spats were quickly healed. Yvonne dreamed forward to her wedding day.

As in a trance, Yvonne moved up the aisle, her hand secure on Maurice's arm. Beyond the organ music that enveloped her she knew there were people sitting in the pews, yet she saw nothing. Only the brilliant stained glass light coming from the high windows reached her; she moved in her shell of scent and sound toward the altar where Joss stood waiting for her.

Gone were all the tears and the tremblings, the fears and the tensions of the months recently passed. She was hardly aware of walking, so perfect was the moment; she was gliding, moved by magic, guided by a star.

She could see Joss; she reached him; they stood side by side. The music's pounding eased, quieted, ceased. The vested cleric stood before them.

"Dearly beloved, we are gathered here today . . ."

The guests in their pews followed the service, some more closely than others. In the front, the families sat attentive, their faces socially set, reflecting the ceremony, masks.

Thank heavens she didn't galumph. . . . Poor Maurice, he's beginning to look old. . . . She'll be Lady Brocknell one day . . . fancy that. . . . Still, I'd rather not have to live in England all the time. . . . The pearls he gave her are quite nice, but mine are far better. . . . I wouldn't give much for that ring, either, even if it is an heirloom . . . glad I decided on my diamonds for today. . . .

. . . about time we got a new one . . . didn't like that knocking noise . . . Bert says . . .

. . . perfectly amenable, if not quite what I wanted in the way of background, but there it is, one can't have everything,

265

though I don't see why not ... won't upset things ... luckily the mother spends most of the year abroad ... vulgar ... typical nouveau riche, of course ...

... damn fine boy ... close in here ... mustn't snore ...

Emerging from the church under a Guard of Honor formed by regimental swords, the bridal pair went down the steps in a crossfire of rice and slipped into the waiting limousine. Passersby stopped to watch the fulldress glamor of the occasion. Long gowns swept the rice aside, chauffeurs closed car doors.

At the reception, the long line exchanged wishes, handshakes, kisses, thumps on the back. The tried and true words, the banalities, the expected phrases ran their course. The champagne began flowing, the cake towered, awaiting the sword; music started up, the receiving line finally disintegrated into individual groups. The ceremony was over and the celebrating could begin. Chatter and laughter rose everywhere as great-aunts and grandes dames, titled English and *le tout Riviera*, business friends and social foes talked and toasted and stabbed hors d'oeuvres and each other's reputations against the backdrop of flowers and food and festivity. Joss, tall and handsome, led Yvonne to the dance floor and into the waltz. The moment others joined in, the party began, and the comments.

"Fancy wearing *pearls* at her own wedding ..."

"... don't envy her Lady B. as a mother-in-law ..."

"Iron fist in the velvet glove, eh?"

"Without the glove ..."

"... silly old dodo ... hasn't finished a sentence since the relief of Mafeking ..."

"Wonder how long it'll last ..."

"Suits all sides, I'd say. ... She wants the title, they need the money. ..."

"That's not all they need ..."

"New blood may help ..."

"I doubt it ... but perhaps she won't notice. ... They're colonials ..."

"That won't change *him*. ..."

"... must want an heir."

"Of course they do. And you know *Cedric* ..."

Laughter.

It mixed, indistinguishable from its counterpart of enjoyment, into the general sounds of music and celebration.

V

Changing Places
1930–1931

1

Yvonne leaned her folded arms on the casement of the open window and wondered whether it hurt very much to jump out and kill oneself. She gazed down at the moat two storeys below, gray green and opalescent, summer lazy, clogged with lank water plants straggling in the lighter patches, the water-darkened stone thick with slime on either side.

Beyond it, the tended lawns of Raedmor Hall stretched thickly to the herbaceous borders, and the hedged-off rose garden was a mass of bloom. Behind her lay the morning disorder of her marital bedroom and, deeper within the ancient house, her demon mother-in-law. Yvonne shivered in the hot summer sunshine; between the Dancourts and death, what choice was there?

She would never understand them, not if she lived to be a thousand. None of them. Either they were all mad, or she was, or . . . or . . . But her thoughts refused to follow the path so often haunted in the year and a half she had been married to Joss; during that time, her thinking had become so hopelessly entangled she now no longer knew what to believe, and could only despair.

The superstition about pearls—never wear pearls at your own wedding, for every pearl will mean a tear—told to her shortly after she returned from her honeymoon, had proved to be only too true. She had shed more tears than she would have believed possible, and all of them to no avail. She was stuck, stuck—trapped in a marriage of little convenience, less advantage, and no happiness at all.

And yet, when you came right down to it, what did she have to complain about? She had everything she wanted and would be Lady Brocknell and in charge of Raedmor Hall and all its gardens some day. Joss had been the catch of the decade; their suite of rooms in his ancestral home was the nicest of all, and they could afford to do all the things young married people did, without a second thought.

Perhaps. But...

She had tried confiding in her mother the last time Edie and Maurice had been in London, prior to their trip through France and their return to Cannes. They had given up the house in Belgravia, preferring La Maison as their only home; the rest of the time they traveled where they wished, staying in London at the hotel when they came to England at all.

Edie had not let her say very much.

"All young couples have some difficulties at first, Yvonne. I've heard it said that the first year is the worst...."

"But we've been married for more than..."

"Yes, I know, but it takes time to get used to each other. If you think your father was any prize..."

"That was different, Mummy—he was very ill. Joss isn't. You simply don't seem to understand..."

"Yvonne." Edie's tone cut her short. "Do try to pull yourself together and not be rude."

"I'm sorry, Mummy, but..."

"No, I don't want to hear any more about it. I've been listening to your tale of woe ever since you arrived, and none of it seems very serious to me. Of course the Dancourts are different in many ways, with all their tradition behind them. It's up to you to fit in. You're quite grown up enough to behave properly...."

Yvonne fell silent, for her mother's point held true. There was enough tradition and history in the Dancourt family to fill tomes of genealogical worth.

Raedmor Hall was named after an early ancestor who, fighting with Henry V at Agincourt, and having covered himself with mud, glory, and royal favor, was awarded with both recognition and the lands upon which the manor hall stood. Raedmor d'Agincourt died in later combat; two generations spanned the change from d'Agincourt to Dancourt; the baronetcy had been bestowed by a later crown. But, with precedent and privilege set, the family grew and prospered, changing loyalties when necessary and building as it grew.

The hall, a heavy rectangular building with a moat around, had been ravaged by fire on several occasions, rebuilt and added to on many others. The central hall's massive fireplace and defective chimney were eventually bricked off to reasonable and safer proportions by Joss's great-grandfather, who had also caused a permanent bridge to be built over the moat, doing away with the previous wooden relic and its untrustworthy chains. It was the same baron who, shortly before his unfortunate demise on one of the early unicycles, cleared additional space near the Elizabethan maze for a rose garden; here his widow sat amid the scented summer bloomings before succumbing to dropsy and laudanum during Victoria's reign.

Portraits of varying worth hung on the walls of all the main rooms and along the high corridors of Raedmor Hall. Some of the paintings were small, some were vast and massively framed, but all, all were of ancestral heritage—a younger brother; a hapless Dancourt attainted and beheaded; female members, painted as children before being bartered off at the best price they could command; heirs; wedded wives. Many Dancourts had died young for, along with the usual ravages of disease to kill them, the family had the aristocratic bent for armed combat in the service of the crown.

There were exceptions, the fourth baron having lived for over a hundred years. Or so the documents had it; local legend held otherwise. A younger brother, it was said, poisoned his way to the coronet with the aid of a biased family retainer and a strong family likeness, heightened by artifice and a flair for mimicry.

The drains of Raedmor Hall had been rebuilt, after the prince consort's death at Windsor Castle, in the 1860's; indoor plumbing arrived before the turn of the century. An uncle of Joss's, before reaching his majority, had experimented with the new bathroom and the electricity, also recently installed, electrocuting himself in the process and thus shifting the burden of being a baron onto his younger brother, the present incumbent and Yvonne's father-in-law.

Of all the Dancourts, Yvonne decided, her father-in-law was the easiest, even though he was, in some ways, the strangest of the lot. Only yesterday she'd met him on the staircase on her way down to dinner, and he'd asked her what her name was, and whether she was his wife's niece or his son's guest for the weekend.

"I'm Yvonne," she had answered quietly, slipping her arm through his. "And the croquet game this morning was great fun, wasn't it?"

The curtain lifted; Baron Brocknell smiled in warm pleasure.

"Was, wasn't it? Jolly good show. Glad you like croquet.

Good game, that. No one played with me before. Glad you married Joss."

They had walked together all the way into the long dining room, where Lady Brocknell, Joss, and a quivering, tasteless aspic awaited them in the customary atmosphere of tension and rising damp.

The baron often reminded Yvonne of a sleepy walrus, with his drooping mustache and his eyelids at half-mast. He did look a bit like Joss if you looked at him carefully, a shorter, tubbier Joss, much gone to seed, and long past his prime, if, indeed, he had ever had one. In his way, he was kind, and Yvonne was used to him; even Lady Brocknell acknowledged Yvonne was very good at handling him—"Especially when he is tired, don't you know... I think it's your voice...."

Tired was the only word ever used. Joss also remarked on her ability to cope with his father.

"He always likes your singing."

So Yvonne sang and played the piano and tried to while away the hours. But there was no substance and too much uncertainty in her everyday existence; she always felt uneasy and she often felt very tired, if not exhausted, herself.

And then there was Cedric.

She had first met Cedric in the week before her wedding; he was thin and slight, like his mother, but short like his father, and did not look anything like his brother at all. By the time she and Joss returned from their honeymoon, Cedric had gone back to Paris; he apparently spent most of his life either in Paris or in Venice, appearing at Raedmor infrequently and only for short periods of time, his visits having coincided, for the most part, with weekends she and Joss were spending at other country homes. Thus it was she learned far more about Cedric over an incident that occurred when he was away than she ever had while in his presence.

It had been the arrival of a letter; as it was addressed to Mrs. C. Dancourt, Yvonne had opened it, being the only Mrs. Dancourt on the premises. The handwriting was unfamiliar to her, the Parisian postmark a puzzle, as none of her friends was there at the time, and her mother and Maurice were sightseeing in Spain.

The pink notepaper was thin and perfumed.

Dearest Chichi, Yvonne read, after which she began blushing. By the time she came to the signature, *Your adoring Babette,* she had glimpsed, between the garish sen-

272

timents and the atrocious spelling, a sordid, searing, and distant world, only linked to her by the true nature of her brother-in-law.

She had shown the letter to Joss that night; he had reacted with frightening fury.

"Why the hell did you open it?"

"Because it was addressed to me—at least, I thought it was."

"Well, you shouldn't have."

"But how was I to know? I *am* Mrs. Dancourt, after all. . . ."

"Mrs. *Jocelyn* Dancourt. . . ."

"Well, that writing is so peculiar, I simply didn't notice."

"Don't be silly, Yvonne. That's obviously a C, not a J."

"But Cedric isn't married. There *is* no Mrs. C. Dancourt."

Joss slammed the door behind him. Yvonne later heard his voice rising and falling in counterpart against his mother's. As usual, they were arguing in Lady Brocknell's bedroom, behind closed doors; the storms that raged there were seldom mentioned and never explained. Any criticism of Joss in front of his mother was tantamount to treason.

The next morning, Lady Brocknell informed Yvonne that in future she would receive her post in her own suite of rooms, delivered there by one of the maids. From that day forth, letters were no longer laid on the table in the room off the great hall, as they had been for decades. No one challenged the change; no one asked why it had occurred. It was all done in what Yvonne judged to be the typical Dancourt manner: sudden, secretive, and seemingly insane.

Yvonne sighed, straightened up from the window, and brushed her hair away from her neck. It was unseasonably warm; the early summer air was heavy and still. Perhaps she would go riding later, in the evening; the woods would be lovely. That was the one nice thing about living at Raedmor Hall, the grounds and the land. And, of course, the animals. The dogs were all jolly, and the wild animals—deer, rabbits, all sorts of birds, moles and voles, squirrels, all so English— were a delight to watch. She had even seen foxes, had come upon them playing in a clearing, until they had sensed and seen her, and flashed away.

Yes, Raedmor Hall wouldn't be at all bad if it were inhabited only by animals and no people. Even the servants were an uneasy lot, living in terror of Lady Brocknell. Lady Bitch,

273

Yvonne knew they called her, having overheard a conversation in the servants' hall. Yvonne had vowed then and there that when she and Joss took over, things would be very differently run.

But that would be years and years in the future, and sometimes Yvonne doubted that it would ever happen. Even if her father-in-law were to die, she suspected his wife would never go. She'd kill Yvonne first, Yvonne felt sure.

Another sigh escaped her. If only she could get away. . . . If only they could get away, she and Joss, and live in a house of their own, and lead a normal, young-married life, with the husband tending to his business affairs, whatever they might be, and the wife in charge of the house and its staff and the two of them enjoying their lives together, on their own. But no; to be a Dancourt meant one had to be different. One had to be a Dancourt. One lived on a different level, with different views. Joss was going to be Baron Brocknell one day and had to live accordingly in the meantime.

"You'd think you were the Prince of Wales!" Yvonne had cried out in an early argument. "The way your mother . . ."

"In a sense, I am," Joss had interrupted. "If my mother over-emphasizes certain things, it's because she has always wanted the best for Raedmor and the family traditions."

It all sounded so worthy, so noble, when he spoke of it, yet the currents of unease still swirled.

"Couldn't we be more . . . more normal? In the way we live, I mean."

"Depends on what you think is normal." Joss finished adjusting his tie. "A bungalow in Surbiton, I suppose, and a steady job in the City . . . How utterly dreary. . . ."

"Well, not exactly, but . . ."

She couldn't explain, she merely knew something was wrong. To single out any member of the Dancourt family, however, never helped her cause; not even the baron and his tiredness proved the point.

"Everyone has eccentric people in their family, Yvonne."

"But there are so many in yours."

"We're a big family." Joss was being logic itself. "And then, you must bear in mind we know a lot about the previous generations, too. Families that form part of history get recorded, warts and all. It's easier for plebs. Most of them pass from life and mind without a trace."

"That doesn't make them any less worthwhile!" She felt stung, goaded, her eyes filling with tears.

He shrugged. "Perhaps not. But their potty habits get forgotten almost right away."

That night at dinner he had drunk far more than usual, and it had been one of the first times she had seen his darker side emerge. He was abrupt, rude, loud, and downright vulgar, and then slammed his way out into the night, with no explanation, only a curse at the kicked front door. No one else at the table appeared to notice anything was wrong. His father looked glassily into space, as he did much of the time, whereas his mother merely finished her meal as though nothing untoward had happened.

Yvonne shivered again. His mother. Lady Brocknell. Her mother-in-law. The demon.

She ruled everything. She was everywhere. Nothing escaped her gimlet eye.

She can probably see around corners, Yvonne thought, hear through walls, feel beyond darkness, see at night. With the passage of time, Yvonne had come to the conviction that Lady Brocknell was always present, even when she wasn't there. Talking to Joss, there were many occasions Yvonne sensed the shade of his mother's presence between them, her influence a shadow falling on every step they ever took. Even in bed, at night, she sometimes thought Lady Brocknell was watching, and the ludicrousness of her own thoughts helped upset her all the more. But there was something in the older woman's behavior that was like a warning flicker seen in the dark of the unknown.

It's just my imagination, she had told herself over and over again. Her mother-in-law had never been anything but kindness itself to her, a fact Joss pointed out to her on numerous occasions.

"I don't see why you want to find another house, Yvonne. I've lived here all my life. We'll have to live here eventually—and you must admit my mother has been kindness itself. . . ."

But it was kindness with an edge to it, a cutting edge, an edge that could chop down in a trice and have its steely way. There was no warmth at Raedmor, no peace, nothing but the unease of waiting, listening, waiting for something to happen, to go wrong, to be blamed for, accused of, *something*. And yet . . . nothing appeared to be there.

If she were to have a baby, of course, then things would be different. And a baby was what everybody else seemed to be waiting for. But as yet, nothing had happened.

"It takes time," Lady Brocknell had soothed, her smile disconcerting. "And after all, you're very young ... perhaps not yet quite formed ..."

Alarmed, Yvonne had resented the implication. She was no child; many brides her age became pregnant with speed and ease. Perhaps Joss ... ?

"Jocelyn had one of those tests some time ago," his mother informed her. "There's absolutely nothing wrong with my son. Quite the contrary, Dr. Guthrie said. Perhaps you should go and see him yourself, my dear. ..."

Yvonne went to the Dancourt family doctor, who spoke to her gently about time and patience.

"Sometimes nerves play a big part in these things, you know. And you *are* rather nervy, Yvonne. ..."

She returned to Raedmor Hall feeling depressed. Her mother-in-law's patronizing manner did not help.

"There. You see? I told you so. You're young, and time will tell."

Joss, who was in a good mood, tried to lighten hers by telling her about his sperm test.

"... little bastards wriggling all over the place under the microscope, old Guthers told me. Enough to father an army. ..."

But still nothing happened.

Sometimes Yvonne thought it would be better to wait a while. On the other hand, a baby would be something to do, someone to be with and talk to as it grew older. The work part of it all would be done by a nannie, so it should be rather fun. Also, Joss was keen: "a boy for the title and a girl for beauty" was the way he had put it, and, seen like that, Yvonne supposed it was a good idea.

She wondered where Joss was; he had left the house before she had woken and had not left word about where he was going or when he would be back. He had seemed all right the night before, but that, she had learned, didn't mean a thing; the Joss she was married to was a very different man from the Joss who had courted her and to whom she had been engaged.

And yet ... that wasn't right or fair either; that was all part of what made everything doubly difficult. Sometimes he was

276

exactly like the Joss of before, charming and delightful and affectionate and ready to tear off on a lark to London or a game of tennis or a trip in the car with her, cheerful and carefree, the perfect husband and companion, the man she had fallen so deeply in love with and who had appeared to be very much in love with her.

It was the other times Yvonne dreaded, and there seemed to be more and more of them. Certainly their proportion rose here at Raedmor Hall. His mood could twist and turn in a second, the change unheralded, as far as she could tell, by any visible mark or event. He would suddenly be different, withdrawn, unpredictable, short-tempered; and then, if the rage was given fire to develop, absolutely beyond control.

It was in these moods that he drank himself into a stupor, or, conversely, into frenzied activity. It was also in these moods that he headed for the gunroom; if he emerged, it was to brandish any one of the hall's collection of firearms, ranging from an ancient blunderbuss to rifles and hunting gear. Like all else in the Dancourt family, these incidents were never mentioned after they had occurred, but Yvonne could not forget them. Terrifying in themselves, they were usually triggered by the most innocuous and insignificant events, rendering them even more frightening. The Jordan water bottle had been one such starting point.

A new maid had come across a small bottle, silver-stoppered, on a table in the pantry, where cutlery and other silver objects had been placed to be cleaned. Judging, correctly as it turned out, that the bottle held only water, she emptied it and dried it, thus completing its cleaning.

When all the cleansed silver had been returned to place, it was Lady Brocknell who noticed the bottle's emptiness.

"The Jordan water—where is the Jordan water?"

The facts were discovered, and another one emerged: far from being ordinary tap water, the bottle had contained holy water from the River Jordan, always used to christen members of the Dancourt family. Lady Brocknell recounted the outrage at dinner that night. Joss, who had been in a fidgety mood most of the day, listened with his face darkening. Yvonne felt her stomach twinge in fear.

"You sacked her, of course."

"Of course. She leaves tomorrow."

"Tomorrow?" Joss stood up, pushing his chair back so hard it fell over with a crash. "She leaves tonight."

"Now, Joss . . ."

Lady Brocknell did not bother to finish her sentence as her son stormed from the room, but returned her attention to the plate in front of her. The meal continued. Shots were heard out in the garden. The bell was rung for the next course; dishes were removed, fresh ones brought in. Shouts and cries, muffled by distance, reached the dining room along with dessert. Then there was silence. Joss did not return. Yvonne escaped upstairs to her bedroom as soon as she could.

"She left last night," was all Joss would say when Yvonne asked him what happened on the following morning. No more was ever said about the incident, by anyone. A new maid was found; the hall went on as before.

Yvonne's thoughts were beginning to blur with the confusion she had learned to dread and fear. Perhaps if she went for a stroll with the dogs until lunchtime, her head wouldn't feel so heavy and dull. And perhaps Joss would be back by then; perhaps he'd even be in one of his nice moods.

Perhaps.

The guests made their way to the dining room from the drawing room, their footsteps and laughter echoing along the marble-columned halls. Yvonne walked miserably in the crowd, holding back the tears that had poured forth earlier, trying not to be conscious of her reddened nose and puffy eyes, sure that everyone else had noticed them and therefore knew she had been crying her eyes out all afternoon.

Joss had been at his very worst ever since they had left Raedmor on Wednesday afternoon. He'd driven like a maniac, terrified her and other motorists besides, then decided he wanted to stop off at a country inn for the night, instead of going, as previously arranged, directly to their destination.

"But we're expected for dinner . . ."

"I don't feel like any."

It was useless to argue.

They had arrived in mid-morning the next day; Joss had left her in the front hall.

"They'll take the bags upstairs for you. I'll be back later." Whereupon he had driven off.

It was now Saturday, and he had yet to reappear. Her host and hostess, distant relations of the Dancourts, were not people Yvonne knew well; she had only met them briefly at her engagement party, and then again as they greeted her from the reception line at her wedding. Her embarrassment at Joss's behavior was almost more than she felt she could bear.

". . . said he'd be back . . . I really don't know . . ." Yvonne found her throat and voice closing down with shame.

"Yes, well, Joss has been known to be a bit difficult before," murmured her hostess, a bland mask of manners. "Luckily, we've got a lot of young people with us this weekend, and I'm sure you'll find plenty to do. I understand you're keen on swimming. The river . . ."

And the river was where Yvonne had spent most of her time. Flowing past the far end of the mansion's historic gardens, the river had been beached and jettied for the convenience of boating and swimming enthusiasts. Here, Yvonne found it easier to mingle with those members of the house party who shared her enthusiasm for the water; few were people she had met before, although all of them either knew Joss well, or had met him from time to time through the years.

"Oh, D.D.'s wife—well, I never! Didn't know he'd taken the step."

"I didn't even know he'd returned from wherever it was he was. . . ."

"Not around, eh? Never mind. He'll be back. Bad pennies, y'know."

The laughter that followed was too hearty.

But at least in the water or on the nearby tennis courts, Yvonne could hold her own. It was the times indoors, the cocktail hour, dinner, the talk and laughter of the evening that she dreaded. She felt alien, alone; the house party spoke of events she did not know, experiences she had not shared. They conversed in social shorthand, acquired through years of social ties and connections. Passwords, catchphrases, nicknames known since their nursery days peppered their conversation and left her out in the cold.

If she could get through dinner tonight without bursting into tears or making a fool of herself, she would then plead a headache and go up to bed instead of to the dance being held at a neighboring estate. She could not stand facing yet another group.

The dining room, famous for its classic proportions and the intricacies of its gilded ceiling, glowed in the light of the table's candelabra. Yvonne, thankful for the flattering illumination, eased into comfortable small talk with her companion to the left, with whom she had played tennis the day before. After their conversation dwindled, she centered her attention on the food.

"I don't think we've met," said a voice to her right, "but I was admiring your swimming after I arrived this morning. I'm Philipe van Landen."

Yvonne turned and introduced herself.

"Do tell me—where did you learn to swim like that?"

The question took her by surprise. She had expected a remark about her being Joss's wife, a reference to the Dancourt family, a question as to her husband's whereabouts. Instead, a direct question relating to her, from this friendly looking man with hazel eyes that crinkled with interest at the corners.

Usually, Yvonne defined her sports education by her days at Crestwood Close. This time, she told the truth.

"You'll never believe it. In the River Plate." She waited for the habitual incomprehension.

Instead, his smile widened.

"In B.A.? But how amazing. I was there only last year. . . ."

He knew B.A., his inflection told her he wasn't English, and Yvonne found herself flowing into easy conversation. He knew Paris better than she did, had recently returned from Cannes. They talked skiing and train stations, a few words of Spanish, current dance melodies.

"Let's hope tonight's orchestra is up to them," said Philipe. "Last time I went to a county dance, it was all reels and waltzes."

Yvonne smiled. "They're fun, too."

"Ah, now you're being very English. . . . I prefer a wider variety. . . ."

He was Belgian.

"Oh—I thought perhaps you were an American."

"My mother is. Tell me, when you lived in B.A., did you like *dulce de leche?*"

"We used to have a servant, Rosita, who made it specially for me. . . ."

280

Hours later, in the middle of a frenetic Charleston, Yvonne remembered she had not intended to come to the dance at all.

Joss turned up on Sunday, shortly after lunchtime, full of charm and anecdotes about a gambling spree. His host and hostess appeared to take it in their stride as though it were an expected part of his character; they listened and nodded and laughed at his tales, and handed him another drink. Soon, he was the center of attention.

By dinner, he had taken over, and even Yvonne found it hard to realize he hadn't been there all the time. They played charades, and his team won, and then he organized a scavenger hunt.

"Everyone back here by midnight, and a bobby's helmet is worth double points. . . ."

They divided into groups and piled into cars, roaring off through the summer night's velvet; ripping up a signpost here, picking out a live duck there, searching for the items on the duplicate lists. In the end, it was the team under Dancourt's direction that won the prize: they brought back not only a policeman's helmet, but the policeman as well.

"He was just getting off duty, and I persuaded him for a fiver . . ."

Clearly, the house party had been a splendid success, and its grand finale was due to Joss. Yvonne, overshadowed, protected, back in her niche, fell into pattern and smiled with the rest, and, in true Dancourt style, never mentioned the previous days, not even after they got back to Raedmor Hall.

Yvonne sat, hunched and miserable, on the end of the hotel bed. Her mother's dressing case lay open beside her. Across the room, at the dressing table, Edie experimented with another pair of earrings.

"There. I think these look better, don't you?" She twisted her head appreciatively.

"Let's see, Mummy. Oh—aren't they pretty. . . . Where did you get them?"

"Paris. Maurice chose them."

Edie patted a finishing touch to her hair. In Yvonne's opinion, the hairdresser had put too much blue in the rinse, but she knew better than to voice her thought aloud. Besides, she was too upset; her mother and Maurice were off to Egypt, and it would be months before they would travel to London again. On first hearing the news, Yvonne had been engulfed in desperate loneliness; no one close to her was going to be around for ages. The Youngs were all out East; Mr. Young had gone out to the Singapore branch of the bank and had insisted on Lally accompanying her parents, making sure she was not in England and thus in contact with John Bell. Yvonne had since heard he had come out of the Swiss sanatorium, apparently cured, and had returned to London, looking for Lally. But the Youngs had left word for him, gossip had it, that they would prefer to see their daughter dead than Mrs. Bell, and the next thing Yvonne was told was that John had left for South Africa, seeking sun for his health and solace for his heartache, and cutting all ties with the country of his birth.

And now Maurice and her mother were leaving.

"How I wish I were going with you. . . ."

"Well, darling, I'm sure you and Joss will go and see the pyramids some day." Edie surveyed her image, giving herself an imperceptible nod of approval before turning away from the glass.

"Oh, but I don't mean that. . . . I'd like to go now . . . with you . . . even if you weren't going to Egypt. . . ."

Edie looked at her daughter with the beginnings of a frown.

"Yvonne, don't be so mizzy. You've done nothing but whine since you got here this morning, and . . ."

Maurice appeared in the doorway.

"Ready, my dear? The car's downstairs."

"We won't be more than a minute. . . . Yvonne, do pull yourself together and help me. . . . Yes, close the dressing case. . . . I think my hat's up there. . . . Go ahead, Maurice, and we'll meet you downstairs. . . ."

In the rush and bustle, Yvonne's tears receded, her composure holding even after the train began to move. She waved and waved, watching the carriages pull away under the dark arches of the station until they shrank into the distance outside and disappeared from view. Then the cloak of misery descended and her tears began to flow; she walked back along the platform, hardly aware of her surroundings. If only she could have gone with them. . . . If only she could get away. . . . Joss was being awful, the past weekend had been a nightmare, and only that very morning, before she'd taken the early train in to London to see her parents off, he'd managed to start a pointless argument and reduce her to tears.

And now the tears were here again, distorting her vision as Joss distorted her life. She reached into her purse for a handkerchief and dabbed at her eyes.

"Well—what a surprise! Hullo, Yvonne. . . . How nice to see you. But you look a trifle forlorn. Something's wrong. Can I help?"

The mild face with a kind smile swam at her through her screen of tears.

"Oh—oh, dear . . . Philipe . . . how are you? I'm sorry . . . I'm afraid I'm being very silly. . . ." She had no control over the tears, and she blushed beneath them, embarrassed, awkward, helpless. "I've just seen my parents off. . . . They're going to Paris and then to Egypt . . ." Her voice stopped and the tears took over.

She felt Philipe's hand firm at her elbow.

"What you need is a drink. Come on . . ."

He propelled her through the crowd and into a taxi, handing her his large handkerchief to cope with her tears. Not until they were comfortably installed in the saloon of the pub and she was seated with a drink in her hand did he allow her to offer any further words of explanation.

"There, now." He smiled over the rim of his own glass at her. "You're beginning to have some color again. Drink up, like a good girl, and I'll order another round. Then you can tell me all about it. If you want to, of course. If not, we can talk of other things."

Yvonne started by talking about her parents' departure, but somehow it led to other topics almost immediately, and her gloom lifted. It was such a change to talk to someone with whom she felt so at ease, with whom neither accent nor catch phrase nor intonation mattered, to whom foreign birth was all part of life and the world. They talked about racing, and horses, and riding.

"You like it, do you?"

"I love it. . . ."

And she told him about her rides with Dr. Ibañez in Cosunzué, and the *rebenque* given her by the *capataz* at El

283

Ombú, and he knew what she was talking about and she didn't have to explain. Philipe countered with anecdotes about polo games in B.A. and on the Riviera, and told her about a pony he had had as a child. Then he told her there was a delightful spot for lunch very close by, and how about a bite to eat as it was lunchtime?

"Oh, I don't think I . . ."

"Then don't think about it at all, but just come along. . . ."

A split of champagne matched their mood, and they laughed over lunch and had several coffees. After a walk in a leafy square nearby, Yvonne suddenly realized it was later than she had thought.

"Don't worry. I'll get you to the station in time for your train. . . ."

On the platform he said, "It was marvelous. I'm so glad I bumped into you. We must do it again sometime."

Meeting at another country estate not ten days later, they played tennis while Joss disappeared for hours on end; Yvonne managed to persuade her husband they should return to Raedmor, as she could see his moods were going from bad to worse, and she feared a public scandal. In the moments before she joined Joss in the car, another lunch with Philipe was set, and that lunch led to another, and eventually to bed. It was all so casual and relaxed, so uncomplicated and natural, it was almost as though it hadn't happened at all, and Yvonne found it easy to dismiss her London meetings from her mind the minute she returned to Raedmor Hall in the evening. Most of the people she knew in the young set had affairs, anyway; it was the smart thing to do, and no one really cared, as far as she could make out, as long as there was no scandal.

Postcards began arriving from Edie and Maurice, and then a letter, describing their trip and suggesting it might be a good idea for Joss and Yvonne to enjoy a stay at La Maison during the O'Connors' absence.

It will do you both good, and then we can tell you all about the pyramids when we get home, Edie wrote. *We should be back by mid-September. I do hope you can arrange to be there. We don't like leaving Taitai and Ming alone with the servants for so long.*

284

Beneath Edie's signature, a short postscript written by Maurice also encouraged the scheme.

Yvonne mentioned it to Joss, with little hope. With the grouse season open, he was sure to head straight for Scotland. He always went shooting.

To her surprise, he said he thought it was "just the ticket."

"Are you sure? I mean, I know how much you enjoy Scotland at this time of the year."

"No, I'd prefer the Riviera. . . ."

They left a few days later; it was not until they reached Paris that Yvonne discovered Joss had needed to get out of the British Isles for a while. There had been some unpleasantness over gambling.

"But what happened? What did you do?"

"None of your business."

All she eventually got out of him was that the trouble would be over in a few weeks—"our bank manager'll take care of it"—and that she needn't worry about it being dangerous to return.

"But right now, I'm better out of the way. And that's all I intend saying, so stop badgering me."

"But. . ."

"Never apologize, never explain, and I do not intend doing either. Therefore, either you shut up, Yvonne, or I'm going down to the Riviera without you. . . ."

He'll be better once we get there, she told herself. He's always happier by the sea. . . .

For once, Yvonne was right. Cannes was warm and sunny, the beach and sea glorious. Joss shed his ugly moods the moment he arrived. La Maison was perfect, the Pekes delirious to see them. Coco screamed obscenities incessantly and Joss began teaching him English equivalents.

"You know the mark of an English gentleman, Yvonne—must be able to swear for ten minutes without stopping and without repeating himself. Now, let's see whether we can turn this filthy foreign parrot into a proper British bird. . . ."

They swam, they played golf, they basked in the sunshine, they made love with renewed relish and the vigor of their young years. They drank and danced away the late summer nights with the early autumn warnings, joining their friends at the gambling tables, entertaining and being entertained. Yvonne could not remember ever having so much fun or being so happy, and she could see Joss was as happy as she was, too. He was amusing, he was charming, he was the Joss who had courted her, the man who swept her off her feet, the husband she loved. If only they could always live this way, on their own, independent, everything would be perfect. This was the way life was supposed to be, the life she'd dreamed of and felt sure should be hers with Joss.

The days sped by; Edie and Maurice returned, full of stories about Egypt and the curse of the pharaohs and a scarab bracelet for Yvonne that shimmered iridescent green. They all golfed together, and the idyllic time continued. Yvonne, conscious that her body's tides had not flowed with the moon, went on a secret visit to a doctor in Cannes, and he confirmed her hope. She told Joss that evening, and he was visibly overwhelmed with joy.

"Come on—let's go and tell your parents—yes, right now...."

Hand in hand, like two children, they ran down the stairs to the surprise of the O'Connors, and the best champagne in the laden wine cellar was immediately brought forth.

A week later, the young couple returned to Raedmor, radiant with their news.

The Pekingese lay at Edie's feet, Ming using her shoe as a chin-rest, Taitai curled beneath her chair. Across the bridge table, the woman in the dark brown cloche was talking, her eyes barely visible beneath the hat's low brim.

"She's absolutely extraordinary, my dears—you'd never believe it. She's the one who told Margot she'd be on her own very soon. Of course everyone thought Luther'd drop dead on the golf course..."

"Or the nineteenth hole," cut in the player at Edie's right.

"... until he ran off with that bit of fluff from the cabaret, and refused to listen to all reason. She's also told Margot he'll eventually be back, though not for long. But that's by the by. What I mean is, she's an extraordinary fortune-teller, and you really should..."

Madge Petersen chattered on. The bridge foursome finished its game. Edie ordered tea brought in to the garden room, and the four women sat talking, awaiting the return of their golfing husbands. Coco, preening and practising his trills, moved up and down on his parrot stand near them.

Conversation returned to the soothsayer.

"Why don't we get her to come here next week and tell our fortunes for us?" Edie suggested. "You say she needs the money. . . ."

"Yes, poor thing. She's not a bit well off. I suppose that's why she started doing it."

"All right, Madge, why don't you arrange it? Bring her over. I'm sure it'll be great fun."

"Okay. You must all give me your birth dates. I know she needs them."

Far from being a flamboyant gypsy, the fortune-teller that Madge Peterson introduced turned out to be a mousy little woman, middle-aged and sweet faced, a gentle, soft-spoken American from that country's south, who had seen better days before her French husband had fallen on bad times and out of a top-storey window near the Place Pigalle. No, she explained, she had not learned her mysteries from a mammy in bygone days; it was a gift possessed by many women in her mother's family.

"Do you use cards?"

"Some. And I have your horoscopes here, the ones I did with the information you sent me about when and where you were born. And also, I'd like to see your hands. . . ."

The sessions got underway.

When it came Edie's turn, the fortune-teller looked at the chart in her name, said, "Oh, yes, I remember—now let's see whether it's reflected in your hands, too."

Edie was immediately intrigued.

"Is there something special?"

"There is change due, according to the stars. Not immediately, perhaps, but soon. But let me look at the other things first. . . ."

She spoke of the past, of Edie's young years, of early unhappiness.

". . . you were alone . . . no one to help you . . . early loss and tragedy. I also see an illness, but then it went away."

There had also been people working against Edie's interests, the woman continued.

". . . and they harmed you . . . you lost many things . . property. Then your stars and your strength rose. . . ."

It made sense, Edie reflected, but much of it might have been told the woman by her local friends. On the other hand, she had never mentioned her own bout with consumption,

287

and she seldom referred to Yvonne's father at all, except that he had died.

"... and nowadays, you are a supremely contented woman...."

Edie smiled; that was self-evident, she thought, looking around the long drawing room of La Maison with its tasteful appointments and magnificent view.

The fortune-teller laid out a block of cards, face up.

"Yes, it shows here again. I saw it when I did your horoscope, I see it in your hands, and now the cards tell the same story: quite soon, there is going to be change."

Edie looked up, suddenly alarmed.

"Is something dreadful going to happen?"

There was a long scrutiny of her hands again and the chart and then the cards.

"No—no, not in the general sense of the term. But there is going to be radical change. Total change. Things you never expected to happen are going to come about."

"Oh," said Edie, remembering. "I bet I know what it is. My daughter is going to have a baby, so I'll be a grandmother next year." She laughed a light, tinkly laugh. "Imagine . . . I'm to be a grandmother. . . . The very idea seems odd. But I suppose I'll get used to it."

The fortune-teller smiled. "I'm sure you will. But that isn't the sort of thing I mean. The change I see in your future is far more basic. And it takes place in several stages. There will be some difficulty far away which will begin to cause it, and then there will be upheaval for you, and change. Your life will take a new shape, one you did not expect, but which you'll enjoy once you approach it. Temporary conditions will turn out to be far longer lasting than foreseen."

"Dear me," said Edie. "It sounds rather ominous."

"It shouldn't, Mrs. O'Connor—yours is a long and fulfilled life. Not many people have that good fortune so clearly defined."

Over dinner, Edie gave Maurice a description of the afternoon's gathering.

"... and she said everything would change, but that it would all come out all right in the end."

"Did she indeed, my dear? I'm very glad to hear it." The supernatural never having been among Maurice's chosen spheres, he made no further comment. Besides, he had an announcement to make.

"I have booked our passages for a trip out East. It's about time we had a look at the Orient, don't you agree? And as I supposed you'd want to be in England when Yvonne's baby arrives next year, I thought we might as well travel now, so we can be back in plenty of time..."

2

Yvonne gripped the bannister and closed her eyes, all the happiness of the past weeks drained from her. At the foot of the stairs, Joss stood with his arms crossed, his legs apart, his face cold and unreasoning, immovable in his stance and attitude.

The lovely days in Cannes, the joyous news, the happy planning that had filled their time since their return, all were banished to oblivion by the thunderhead in the hall. He was in the depths of one of his moods, Yvonne knew; his voice, cold and monotonous, continued to drone.

"... and you will bloody well do as I say, Yvonne. Spare me the excuses of not feeling well. You're perfectly all right, and you know it. Now get dressed and meet me outside, and we'll drive over to..."

"No." It was little more than a forced exhalation, all Yvonne could manage. But she was not going to go. Nothing would induce her to step into a car driven by Joss in his present state. Yesterday had been bad enough, and her acquiescence had only led to endless vomiting through the night on her part and further tantrums on his. Shortly after dawn, Joss had disappeared downstairs. She'd heard his car roaring down the driveway, and he had not reappeared at Raedmor until a half-hour ago. It was now nine o'clock in the evening. Wherever he had been all day, and she had not the faintest notion of where it might have been, there had been ample alcohol provided.

No. She was not going to risk her life and that of her baby simply because Joss had decided he wanted them to drive over to a party in the next county, a gathering he had previously said he did not wish to attend.

Footsteps sounded, and her mother-in-law entered the hall from the passage leading to the library and the billiard room.

"What on earth is the matter, Joss, dear?" she asked. Then

289

she followed his gaze, looked up and saw Yvonne. "Ah—I thought I heard conversation."

"She's refusing to accompany me to the party."

"What nonsense. Of course she'll go. Won't you, Yvonne?"

"No. I won't."

A sharp intake of breath signaled Lady Brocknell's surprise; Yvonne had never spoken to her like that before.

"And why not, may I ask?"

Trembling, Yvonne reached out for the older woman's help.

"I don't feel at all well. . . . I was sick all last night . . ."

"She's perfectly all right now, mother," Joss broke in. "Look at her. Nothing wrong at all."

"I'm sure, my dear, if you just wash your face and put on a pretty frock, you'll be quite . . ."

"No."

"May I remind you, Yvonne, that your place is at my son's side. . . ."

"But the baby . . ."

"Joss is far more important. You must learn never to let him down."

"I don't see why staying home when I feel ill is letting him down in any way or shape or form. . . ."

"You are not, ill, Yvonne. Please do not overdramatize yourself. And your place is by my son's side. Now kindly do as you are told, and get dressed, and . . ."

Suddenly, Yvonne could stand it no longer.

"You're crazy, quite crazy, both of you!" she cried, too weak, too sick at heart, too desperate to care what she said. "You're bad enough apart, but together, you're mad . . . you're wicked, that's what it is . . . willing to make me risk the life of my unborn child just to please your drunken, irresponsible son. If you had any decency," she turned her full cry on Lady Brocknell, "any decency whatsoever, you'd be up here on the stairs with me, defending *me*, me and the baby, rather than sticking up for Joss just because he's your son when you *know* he's wrong, and . . ."

"I would not talk about decency if I were you."

Lady Brocknell's words were ice, yet a faint smile, a twist of her lips, played around the older woman's controlled mouth.

"What do you mean?" Surprise husked Yvonne's voice down to a whisper.

"I mean exactly what I said—that when it comes to decency, you haven't got a leg to stand on." Lady Brocknell's smile of triumph became unmistakable.

Joss turned to face his mother, his movements so precise and slow he appeared to be a mechanism rather than a man.

"And what, exactly, do you mean by that, mother dear?" His polite control quivered with sarcasm. "Are you insinuating that my wife is indecent? And if so, in what way, pray tell? As her husband, I really think I ought to know."

"You don't really want me to tell him, do you, Yvonne? Why don't you go and get dressed and go to the party, and then we can forget all about this unpleasant little scene?"

Yvonne, dizzy with fear and bewilderment, looked blankly down.

"I don't know what you mean...truly, I don't....I never know...what to expect from you...or what you expect of me...."

Lady Brocknell said, "I certainly did not expect an illegitimate child."

Life hung in space, time stretched into silence, hideous, hollow, and final in the seconds that followed. Yvonne's hand went slowly to her mouth, as though seeking her breath, which had become suspended, choking in her throat.

"How...dare...you...how...can...you...?"

Joss asked, "What was that you said, Mother?"

"That is not your baby that your wife is carrying."

"Indeed?" His tone was almost pleasant, conversational, but his gaze remained fixed, stonelike in its immobility, staring into his mother's face. "That's a fascinating statement, I must say. And just whose do you think it is?"

"I have no idea. But it cannot be yours."

His face went white, his jawline jutted.

"I have never struck you in my life, Mother, but I am sorely tempted...."

"You needn't be." Her calm was total. "I know what I'm talking about. It can't be yours. You're sterile."

"That's not what old Guthers said."

"Dr. Guthrie takes his orders from me." Contempt dripped from every word.

"But the tests," Yvonne whispered. "The tests Joss took..."

"Yes, Mother. The tests." Joss looked at the older woman, who looked aside.

"The good doctor does what he's told."

"You mean they were fake."

Lady Brocknell's shoulders straightened. "Certainly. I told him what I wanted. I didn't want you to know.... You see, it happened when you had mumps. If you recall, you had them very badly...."

Joss nodded. "Yes, I remember. I was quite a sight. Cedric used to come in and ask to have a peep under the blankets."

"That's enough, Joss. Please don't interrupt me. All this is quite upsetting enough."

"It has its interesting aspects, however. Tell me, Mother— what charm do you hold over the good doctor that he does your bidding? Your *illegal* bidding?"

"That's none of your business, Joss."

"At this point, I rather think it is."

Mother and son stared at each other.

"Abortions," said Lady Brocknell, breaking the tense pause. "He performs them regularly. I found out years ago."

"I see. And so you have old Guthers right in your pocket, falsifying tests..."

"I hadn't wanted you to know. And, under normal circumstances, you never would have. But Yvonne's behavior tonight has made it impossible."

Two pairs of eyes turned to stare upward, and Yvonne felt the two Dancourts had suddenly remembered her again. She was shaking too violently to move away, terror pinning her to the spot. She could not say a word, feeling she could hardly breathe.

"Shall I kill her?" Joss sounded speculative.

"No."

"Too risky, d'you mean?"

Lady Brocknell gave a slight nod.

"It could be an accident... cleaning a gun..."

In horror, Yvonne realized he was deadly serious. The walls swam; Joss's voice reached her across a huge and dark abyss.

"Tell you what, Yvonne... going to give you a sporting chance.... I want you to get out of here right away. Tonight. This very minute. Get dressed, get a coat, and go."

"But... but..." She opened her eyes with desperate effort. "I can't leave.... I have nowhere to go.... There isn't anybody... it's terribly late...."

"I don't give a good goddamn where you go or what you do

292

or when you do it." Joss struck the newel post with a clenched fist, his temper returning. "Just *get out*. You may take one of the cars, and either leave it at the station, or drive yourself to London. Or Scotland. Or Hades, for all I care."

"Joss, I . . ."

"You are not to sleep under this roof again. Never in your life." He stepped back and stood next to his mother. "I am now going to the gun room, where I shall remain for thirty minutes." He glanced at his watch. "And if you are not gone by the time I emerge . . ."

Yvonne looked imploringly at Lady Brocknell.

"Please . . . give me until tomorrow . . . I . . ."

The older woman's gaze was steady.

"You heard my son. He is the master of this house."

The two Dancourts stood together, staring up at her, in the chill silence of the cavernous hall.

Yvonne sat on the slatted bench of the waiting room in the small station. Unable to control her shivering, she clutched her fur coat tightly around her and stared down at the floor, waiting for the train. The few people around had looked at her oddly when she first arrived, half-stumbling up to the ticket window, her small suitcase a millstone, her steps faltering and afraid. But there was no turning back; Joss had watched her departure from the massive mouth of the open front door, a shotgun broken over his arm the silent signal of his intent. Somehow, she had managed to get to one of the cars, and get it started, and had driven off, but she knew that driving all the way to London was beyond her in her present state. The shame of facing the station was her only recourse.

The night man did not know her, and no one she knew turned up to take the train. She hunched at the end of the bench, beyond tears now, numb with fear. She had no one to go to, nowhere to turn. Her mother and Maurice were somewhere east of Suez. Lally was still in Singapore. The great-aunts . . . no, she couldn't possibly go to the great-aunts in this disgraceful condition. She had no one to turn to.

Except Philipe. She would have to go to him.

The London Set loved it: a freshmeat scandal. Tongues wagged over every cup of tea and many a cocktail hour besides. Social malice drew its bead and scored: everyone was guilty. It was the perfect match, the best in ages, and marvelous to watch.

None of it was official of course, and much was still unknown. Even more was speculation, imagination given free rein on previous incidents in Dancourt family history and scandal.

"... *never* would've allowed my daughter to marry into that family ..."

"... half of them are mental, and the other half spend their time trying to cover it up...."

"Very hard to work out which half is which, though...."

The known facts were sketchy: the O'Connors had rushed back from their voyage out East to be at Yvonne's side after her collapse; she was in a nursing home, discreetly screened from the world. Baron and Lady Brocknell were at Raedmor, anxiously awaiting her recovery and return. Joss, desperate over his wife's delicate condition, had gone off shooting in Scotland, to keep out of the way.

"I don't believe a word of it."

"Is she really preggers?"

"I heard he shoved her down the stairs."

"Probably. You know Joss."

"What *I* heard was that he kept firing into the air as she drove off."

"Lady B. won't be seen in town for quite a while, I'll wager."

"Don't know how Yvonne stood it as long as she did, myself."

"What about Philipe van Landen? Thick as thieves, those two, last time I saw 'em at the Fotheringhams'."

"But why do a bunk together?"

"They didn't. She bolted."

Even as the gossip swirled, the chatterers themselves sensed there were gaps.

Meetings between the Dancourts and the O'Connors took place only through their solicitors. Returning to the hotel from one such appointment, Edie flung her purse onto the hotel suite's sofa in exasperation.

"... and just when we thought we had everything worked out so nicely. I really believed Yvonne was set for life. *What* a mess. ... You'd think she'd have had more sense ..."

"All very unfortunate," Maurice agreed. "Still, you must remember, my dear, his family has behaved abominably."

"According to Yvonne."

"Well, I think we can safely assume they are the ones who've been lying, right from the beginning. A drink, Edie?" He busied himself at the waiting decanter.

"She should've handled things better."

Maurice did not respond, but handed Edie her glass. There were difficulties enough, without goading his wife's attitudes, and his present aim was to see the rough patch through, and resolved.

As it stood, the situation was a standoff, a total checkmate for both sides. Each had a secret it wished to keep hidden from the general public's view: sterility and adultery lay in perfect balance. A discreet divorce was the only answer, and if discretion was too much to hope for, then speed was essential, for the child, if a boy, would inherit the title.

The legalities were complicated; an accommodating judge had to be found to expedite the immediate process as quickly as possible. Fortunately, Yvonne's pregnancy was in its early stages, for there would be a mandatory six-months waiting period between a decree nisi and the final divorce decree. It would be touch and go, and all the parties knew it.

"We must do what we can—and as much as possible of it," Maurice insisted, dogged in his determination. Unmoved by either hysteria or emotion, he could see that the very nature of the case led to forced complicity for the benefit of all. "Let us get down to the financial aspects," he told his solicitor, and the law, aided and abetted by all means at Maurice's disposal, moved to expedite the case.

While her future was argued and planned and discussed and bartered, Yvonne lay on her bed in the private clinic's hushed room, listlessly turning the pages of novels and magazines brought to her by Edie, hardly reading the words and making no sense of them at all. At least she had stopped crying; she thought it was probably because she had no tears left inside. She longed for her parents' visits, yet dreaded every one of them; Edie's anger and Maurice's discomfort were hard for her to bear. But Yvonne knew he was battling her cause, a stalwart defender by her side, facing the Dancourts down.

Her only other visitor was Philipe; it was he who had rushed her to the exclusive clinic in the first place, knowing she could hide there from the prying eyes of society and the world until she felt stronger and had decided what to do. It had also been Philipe who cabled Edie and Maurice, and then he had gone to meet them when they arrived back in London.

Philipe had visited her daily, his repeated presence gradually lessening the acute embarrassment she had felt at first. Her hysterical collapse on his doorstep that terrible night was too vivid to cope with; she remembered his tousled hair and striped dressing gown and, incongruously, his bare, pale feet.

"Don't worry," he had kept saying, plying her with hot tea and brandy in an attempt to stop her shivering. "Don't worry. . . . It'll all work out somehow. . . . First we must get hold of your parents . . . and prevent the Dancourts from knowing where you are . . ."

When he suggested the clinic, he told her it was the best place he could think of for the time being.

". . . . simply won't list you on their official patients' list . . . used to doing things like that . . . I rather imagine royalty goes there when it needs a rest or, for that matter, anything medical . . . best care you can have . . ."

He had driven her there himself. Yvonne had seen everything through her screen of tears, doing what she was told, unable to make any moves on her own. The next day was grim and the following one worse; not even the doctor's bland assurances helped. Philipe came in the evening, gentle, reassuring. He held her hand.

"Don't worry." Over and over again. "No one knows where you are, except me. No one here will give you away. I certainly won't, you know that. You're quite safe here. . . . Your parents will be coming back soon. . . ."

She longed for the drugged drowsiness of sleep, and smiled at the nurse when she came in after dinner, bearing the medicine that obliterated the night hours until the next day.

Agitation and movement returned with the O'Connors' arrival, but it was decided Yvonne should stay in the clinic for the time being.

". . . you'll only be in the way, darling, and I must say, there's quite enough to contend with . . ."

". . . useless letting them attack you, my dear—you've suffered quite enough at their hands, and I don't intend to . . ."

The solicitor also felt it was the better part of valor.

"No need to expose yourself to any more of their tricks, Mrs. Dancourt—and besides, your health . . ."

The hard bargaining went on in paneled offices. Papers were drawn up; the legal processes began.

The letter from New York still in his hand, Philipe went into the bedroom of his London *pied-à-terre*. It was late; he was due at a dinner party within half an hour.

He left the letter on his bed and made his way to the bathroom. Of course his mother wanted him to return to New York; it was always easier to have him manage her affairs than make the effort herself. Not that there was all that much to do; his late father had set up his wife's inherited fortune in adequate banking hands. Philipe had always known his parents' marriage had been one of convenience; now it looked as though he would have to make a similar union, albeit for differing reasons. That did not matter; he knew where his duty lay. Had known, from the moment Yvonne had appeared in his doorway.

Of course he would do the right thing and marry her to give the child a name. They could always part and divorce amicably later on. But he was not even thinking that far ahead; it was the immediate that needed working out. For one thing, time was tight: everything was being done to expedite the Dancourt divorce as quickly as possible, but still, six months from decree nisi to decree absolute... Both he and Yvonne had counted as carefully as they could: there was a slim chance they would be able to marry in time.

Meanwhile, he had to go to the U.S.A. His mother, his business connections, the social climate that was beginning to bubble around him and Yvonne. The more he thought about it, the more he felt it might be a good idea for both of them to travel to New York and get married there. Maurice had told him the Dancourts were on the verge of settling their side of things. Once that was over, Yvonne would be able to leave.

Philipe cleared the last patch of shaving cream from his chin with the razor and suppressed a sigh. It wasn't exactly what he had planned for his immediate future, but on the other hand, he hadn't planned much of anything in his life. As he washed his face, a recent scene flashed to mind, and the eyes of the girl he had met recently mocked his memory and his undefined yearnings.

Remembering, he knew he had made no promise there.

There would be no need to explain. He simply would not ring her up any more.

A Mrs. Y. Dancourt sailed from Southampton on the latest of liners bound for New York. She was accompanied by a uniformed nurse, having been in a delicate state of health for the past few months. This was also cited as the reason her name did not appear on the official passenger list; Mrs. Dancourt needed absolute privacy, and the luxury ship, known for its service and opulence, was only too willing to accommodate her.

On another deck, in an equally elegant stateroom, Monsieur Philipe van Landen, too, was a passenger, traveling on his diplomatic passport, and thus also assured of the finest the line had to offer.

If neither of them chose to have bon voyage parties, no one felt it to be amiss. There was gaiety enough among the rest of the first-class passengers, with champagne corks popping left and right. Only a few of the eagle-eyed, on their way back to shore along the gangplank, spotted the potential social snippet.

"I say—isn't that O'Connor and his wife over there?"

"By Jove, so it is. And they're not sailing. Must be seeing someone off."

"Wonder if their daughter's doing another bunk..."

During the entire voyage, Yvonne hardly left her stateroom; Philipe, though freer, also behaved with caution. They did not dare risk complications until the decree became final. Once they landed, he arranged for Yvonne's hotel accommodations; the nurse was to stay with her until the child was born. He then braced himself for the confrontation with his mother.

"Please don't ask me to meet her now, Philipe."

"Of course not, Mother. But after Yvonne and I are married..."

She dismissed the end of his sentence with a wave of her thin hand.

"I do wish you'd straighten things out for me at the bank, Philipe. I seem to have less and less, every day...."

Snow fell, and the poor huddled in Hoovervilles, while the van Landens found they were still well able to maintain the Park Avenue apartment as before. Philipe visited Yvonne, who whiled away much of her empty time knitting little

298

garments. Both of them waited, sitting out the race between a legal paper and the first pangs of childbirth.

The six months were up; the decree absolute came through. Their marriage was private, a minuscule affair. After the ceremony, Philipe took Yvonne to the Park Avenue residence for the first time.

Yvonne's bulky discomfiture was not aided by Philipe's mother who, in an audible aside to her son during the evening, said, "If you had to make such a fool of yourself, you might at least have done so with a genuine English girl. . . ."

A week later, a midnight trip to the hospital took place, and there Yvonne was delivered of a small baby girl. Thus Meryl van Landen was born in New York, a brand-new American, with an Argentine mother, a Belgian father, a thatch of black hair that fell out within the month, and an open future all her own. It was the early part of the new decade, the depths of the Depression, and a deceptively mild, late spring day.

VI

El Ombú
1933–1939

1

Political rumblings and the shifting sands of social structures had begun to be heard and felt all over the world as the 1920's came to a close. If there were masses of people who chose to ignore the signs, there were also those who, cushioned as they might be by the comfort of their own lives, sensed the changes and pondered their meaning, wondering what the world had in store.

Despite the world's economic woes, the Riviera still glittered. Fortunes were as evident as before; those with wealth still valid continued to live as in the years gone by. But there were changes, real changes, in the international winds, and the perceptive knew it. Maurice O'Connor, physically comfortable at La Maison, was one of those who was ill at ease.

He had been vaguely troubled, then openly worried about the manner in which the Caseys were running El Ombú, so many miles away. His cousins' profligate habits, their reckless spending, their pleasure-loving aims and devil-may-care attitudes had become more and more obvious as the years went by. The results began showing in the *estancia*'s productivity, for the Caseys tended to spend more money on cars than on crops, on a tennis court instead of on tenant sharecroppers, on an airstrip marked by a wind sock in a field instead of on stock improvement. Maurice had hesitated to carp or criticize; he was himself enjoying a leisured life while keeping his financial hand dextrous in the grain market. But placing money shipments of wheat was one thing; getting wheat to grow well in a field quite another. Eventually, Maurice wrote at length and in detail, distressed at certain figures and plans sent to him in regular reports.

Answering letters from the Caseys had mocked his fears; they were making a fortune, Tim assured Maurice, not only on the *estancia*, which was doing reasonably well, but in the American stock market. If they had changed things at El

Ombú, well, they had modernized it, and if modernization included a tennis court, surely Maurice did not feel such a minor fact was excessive? Tim repeated: there was nothing to worry about; prices and harvests were excellent. If the reports were not showing the profits Maurice had expected, Tim felt sure that was due to the portion being sent directly to America for investment. Everyone knew that was the place to build *real* fortunes. . . .

Maurice wrote back, by return post, ordering his share to be removed from the New York investment scheme immediately. What the Caseys chose to do with their share was another matter, but he wanted his to be kept in the Argentine, reinvested, for the moment, in the *estancia* itself or in more land.

I've followed your orders, came the reply, *but I still think you are making a mistake. Let me know if you change your mind.* . . .

The tone of Tim's letters changed after 1929, but he insisted all was well at the *estancia*, largely thanks to Maurice's funds, of course, and he foresaw no local trouble. Maurice, not eager to return to Argentina, allowed his misgivings to be assuaged but, with the arrival of the Thirties and all the attendant problems, his unease grew.

If other, acute matters claimed his immediate attention—Yvonne's unfortunate divorce the most involved—the underlying discomfort always remained. He followed the tides of the time with growing concern, insisting on a daily newspaper even when he and Edie traveled in far lands. On shipboard, he waited for the wireless communiques; with friends, he exchanged views. There were straws in the wind, change in the air, National Socialists in Germany, economic strains all around.

Then, in 1933, news came that affected him directly, and the die was cast.

The Government of Argentina decreed that all Argentine citizens who were landowners in the Republic and who spent more than six months per calendar year out of the country were to have their property taxes increased by a staggering rate.

Despite the cries of expatriate outrage, the swift assertions the decree was illegal, would not hold water, couldn't last, the stampede south, particularly out of Paris, was awesome.

Enraged *estancieros* gathered in ships' salons and discussed the new set of tax laws all the way home across the wide Atlantic.

Within a few months, Edie and Maurice were among them.

"... nice to be going back for a trip ... put a lot of things in order ..."

"... fun to see people again.... I wonder if they'll recognize me?"

"... set Tim straight on a thing or two ... new laws sure to be accommodated after a while ..."

Maurice sat and talked with other solid men, and they all agreed there were too many vested interests holding political power for the decree not to be bent to the will of wealth. Yet, in part, he knew he welcomed the excuse to go back; in recent times, he had longed to see and oversee the land that was his, the properties he had acquired. La Maison was all very well, but he always thought of it as Edie's, a perfect setting for a lovely jewel, a showpiece of worth.

El Ombú was different; it was his, it was a lifeline. It produced grain and food and work and the seasonal cycles of life's years.

Edie, as always, blossomed on shipboard; what beauty had been lost to the past and youth was bolstered by wealth and confidence. The sea air was invigorating, the trip a welcome change. They had done the rounds of Europe so very many times, and she really didn't feel like going to New York and seeing Yvonne and Philipe and her grandchild, Meryl. That whole episode had been so unfortunate, Edie didn't want to have too much to do with its aftermath right away; she and Yvonne kept in touch by letters, as always, but distance, Edie felt, was a good thing for the time being.

As they made their way down the east coast of South America and neared their final destination of the port of Buenos Aires, Edie realized she was looking forward to their arrival, eager to see familiar faces and hear everyone's news. And wouldn't they be impressed, she mused, by all she'd seen and done since she last saw them....

With Ming and Taitai on their double leash, she walked around the promenade deck, anticipating the excitement and planning, down to the last detail, what she would wear for disembarking.

"...but I would *never* have recognized you! How time flies..."

Edie, sitting on a worn armchair opposite Dollie, felt a tightening of dislike and masked it with a noncommittal smile. Deliberately, she poked her manicured nail through a hole in the chair arm's fabric and played with the raveled edge.

"Ten years," Dollie was saying. Ten full years..."

"Thirteen, as a matter of fact."

"...and so many changes, so much accomplished here... You have no idea how much I've been able to do..." Dollie was waxing to her theme, and looking as though she might melt in the process.

Hardly listening, Edie looked carefully at her childhood friend sitting on the sofa of her suburban Buenos Aires home. Dollie had more than doubled in size. Trebled, Edie decided, and every ounce of it blubber. Perspiration oozed from the thickly fleshed rolls that formed Dollie's neck and cascaded down to the vast expanse of her bosom under which widened her hips and thighs, the whole mass returning to a triangular point at the reddened bulges overlapping her curiously small feet.

"...so many things have happened... Let me see.... You know all about Robert, of course..."

Edie nodded. Robert, grown prominent and portly, had dined with the O'Connors at their hotel the night before. He was now one of the top men at Bateman Co., and he and Maurice had talked import and export and numbers and shipping lore until Edie thought she would scream. Robert was bluff and hearty and far too loud.

"...and that terrible *porteño* accent of his," she had remarked to Maurice afterwards.

"Most people talk that way in B.A., my dear."

"But Robert was *born* in England..."

Now spending the day with Dollie, Edie was trying to catch up with the rest of the news, hearing an endless outpouring of mainly irrelevant detail through which the lives and deaths of the British community were being recited.

True, there were some unexpected nuggets. Apparently Dollie had found, and lost, love in the years between. She had been secretly engaged, she told Edie, her voice taking on a breathy hush. He had been a young clergyman, just out from England, and shortly before they were going to announce their betrothal officially, he was suddenly taken ill, and died.

Dollie dabbed an eye in memory.

"It was *so* tragic. Poor, poor Ted. And of course, I've never even *looked* at anyone since...."

Edie reserved both judgment and comment; Dollie did not notice, for she was already on to her favorite subject, her many-faceted good works and her high position in the field of charity.

"... of course I work far too hard, but I can't let anyone down, can I? My committees need me..."

Clearly, she was the driving force of the Buenos Aires Ladies Society.

"... we do so many things.... I'm on the board now of our Córdoba school... truly a haven for..."

"What school?"

"Surely you remember, Edie... It was started before you left.... I know I told you all about it when it began.... I distinctly remember..."

Badgered, Edie remembered, too.

"Oh, the orphanage thing."

Dollie nodded. "But it's not only for orphans. The children of poor English families can go there, too. We want to save them from growing up both Catholic *and* Argentine, of course. At least if they can have a proper English upbringing, there's a chance they can make something of themselves later on...."

A shrunken figure appeared in the doorway, shuffling and babbling to herself as she moved into the room. Edie realized with a start that it was Bessie Thaxter, leaning on a cane and talking to a world of shades. Dollie rolled her eyes heavenwards. The old woman reached Edie and stared vacantly at her.

"You must remember to give Dollie her breakfast," she said in thin, reedlike tones, ignoring her daughter a few feet further on. Then she turned and shuffled her way out of the room again. Dollie gave an exasperated sigh. At the door, Mrs. Thaxter spoke into the hall beyond.

"Yes, dear, I'll bring you your hot milk right away...."

Dollie sighed again. "Ma's impossible. Just *impossible*. Nobody knows how much I have to bear. She's always trying to warm up cups of milk. Spilled a whole bottle on the kitchen floor only yesterday. Quite, quite beyond the pale. She's been that way, you know, ever since we laid poor Pa to rest. . . ."

". . . and not a moment too soon," said Edie's dinner companion the following night, when Canon Thaxter's death was mentioned as an event of the preceding year. "He had become an enormous embarrassment to the Church with all his ghost-hunting . . ."

Returning to the hotel suite that night, Edie made note of all the things she wanted to tell Maurice when he arrived back the next day. He had gone up to the *estancia* on his own, leaving her to enjoy Buenos Aires while he took a good look at what was going on at El Ombú.

"Better that way, m'dear. When I see how the land lies, we can both go up. But I expect there'll be some trouble spots this time. . . ."

The trouble was worse that he had thought.

Maurice returned grave-faced and with serious news; he had no alternative, he told Edie, but to foreclose on the Caseys' mortgage, the mortgage originally set up so that they could become co-owners with him all those many years ago.

"El Ombú has been sadly mismanaged; I am quite convinced that both of them have been stealing, and I want them out of there as quickly as possible with a minimum of fuss. Tim's apparently managed to buy himself a small *estancia* in the region, so they're not really destitute."

"Couldn't you take over his *estancia* in payment?" Edie wanted to know.

"Yes. But I don't want to. I want the Caseys off our land."

His tone was so unusually harsh that Edie looked at him questioningly.

"Had a chat with the *capataz*. A good man, that. He told me a few things." Maurice splashed soda into the glass of whiskey in his hand. "No. No two ways about it, my dear— I'm afraid I shall have to foreclose, and throw them out. They're disastrous. What's more, until we find the right man to run it, I think I'll have to take over—so we'll be leaving for El Ombú quite soon, to see what we can do. . . ."

Maurice O'Connor took over El Ombú with a minimum of fuss and a show of family solidarity. The Caseys, in turn, played their part in the transaction, giving as the official reason Kevin's desire to enter the business world in B.A. rather than go on being an *estanciero*.

"El Ombú's too big for me to run it without my brother, so Maurice'll take over, and I'll move to the little place I have on my own..." explained Timothy Casey, whose smaller property was nearby, and whose family and familial obligations had grown. Tim had married during the intervening years, and his son Harvey was already six years old; his wife Estelita had recently given birth to their second child, a baby girl, still in swaddling clothes and called Anita, after her grandmother, Anna Casey, who had died before the child was born.

Leaving El Ombú with the Caseys was their cook, one of the women hired locally, and a couple of the *peones*. Everyone else was staying at El Ombú. Rosa and Rosita were both adamant.

"Ah, no, *Don* Mauricio," they said. "We were here with the *señora* Anna, may God keep her."

Maurice, visiting on his own again, preparing the way for Edie's arrival, simply nodded and did not press the issue, sensing turmoil beneath the surface. The truth would come to light all in good time.

As the household furnishings had all been bought with the *estancia*, the Caseys only needed to pack their personal belongings when they were ready to go. The property Tim had bought, La Chata, had a house on it which they could inhabit immediately.

"It's smaller, but then, with Mother gone and Kev in B.A., we won't need so much room...."

Decidedly, Tim was putting a good face on it.

"And so he should. You're letting him get away with murder," said Edie. "He's been robbing you blind, bought La Chata with *your* money, lived high on the hog for years, and..."

"I know all that," Maurice interrupted. "That's why I want to run the place myself for a while. Then I'll find a good man to do it for me, and you and I will return to Europe."

The day Edie and Maurice arrived at El Ombú to take over, tears of joy spilled among the cries of greeting. Rosita could hardly wait to tell of all the wrongdoings and injustices of the Casey era.

" ... and you'd never even think they could be cousins of *Don* Mauricio's, *señora* Edie—not even of the same family, they are so different ... except *la señora* Anna, but she, poor thing, was so old toward the end ..."

"Never mind, Rosita," Edie consoled. "Now that we're

here, and *Don* Mauricio's in charge, everything'll be all right, you wait and see...."

It was an opinion—part wish, part prayer but also part conviction—that was voiced in no uncertain terms in the *peones'* quarters over the evening *yerba*-drinking around the fire.

By the time Edie and Maurice went to stay at El Ombú, the *estancia* had acquired the mellow air of the long-established, the dignity of the mature. The camp was now over fifty years old, its terrain long accustomed to the planting and reaping, herding and changing, grazing and growing that had been occurring on it for so many years. Despite the recent mismangement by the Caseys, progress had taken place; there were many more windmills filling the drinking troughs where grazing fields joined, the *colonos'* sharecropping sections had been developed and regularly brought in good harvests, and many of the *ranchos* built on them were somewhat more solid than they had been in the past.

As to the family dwelling itself, it, too, had changed with the years, and it bore the settled, established air of a place that belonged.

It was here, more than anywhere else, that the Caseys' profligate spending had produced both effect and comfort. They had widened the front drive, planted well, screened the tennis court with high hedging, added to the house, improved it inside, enclosed part of the verandah. To Maurice's surprised pleasure, Edie took to it right away.

"Well, it's not La Maison, of course—but it makes a nice change, and it's lovely being with Rosita again.... Rosa's far too old, we must do something about her, Maurice.... And the doggies *do* love running around after being cooped up in the hotel...."

The main entrance to El Ombú was from the road flanking the railroad. High double gates opened into the mile-long, straight as a die, poplar-lined drive that led up to the house itself. Behind the trees on either side stretched the *estancia's* front fields, all of them open grazing land. At the end of the driveway, thick hedges rose between the fields and the land directly around the house, affording a measure of privacy for the grounds immediately surrounding the homestead.

The house itself faced due west; a low white wall separated the end of the driveway from the planted garden, where flowering shrubs and grouped trees partially obscured the building itself. Two massive magnolias stood guard on either side of the flagstone path leading to the verandah that ran the full length of the front of the house. A grouping of wicker furniture, colorless with age, stood in the permanent shade near the main door.

Here, Maurice and Edie took to having their predinner drink.

"Simply because we're in the camp doesn't mean we have to forego everything we enjoyed in Europe," said Edie. She still changed for dinner, though not to a long gown; for Maurice, a change from *bombachas* and his riding shirt was an obvious courtesy. Routine evolved, the cultures melded.

"... even though we'll only be here a few months, of course ..."

Still, while she was at El Ombú, Edie felt she might as well set her stamp on the house. With Rosita at her side, it was almost like old times: the two of them and a house to set in order.

As the *estancia* had matured, so the house had grown through the years, and the original structure with its open patio and modest layout was unrecognizable now.

In its place was a sprawling, verandah-wrapped, multi-chimneyed establishment with north and south wings, screen-enclosed porches, and extended kitchen quarters. The once open central courtyard had long ago been roofed over; its floor, still tiled, was strewn with carpets and sheepskin rugs. A raised fireplace dominated one wall, and oblong windows, set high near the ceiling, were specifically engineered to let in a maximum of light without subjecting the dwellers to the full heat of summer. The sweep and scope of the huge room allowed for groupings of chairs, two leather sofas, an oversize desk surrounded by bookcases, a long dining room table seating twelve, built-in bookshelves on either side of the fireplace, a sewing corner, and a music nook, the latter displaying a table with a windup gramophone and albums with records piled on the shelf below.

A bookpress stood in the entrance archway leading to the front door; the thin leaves of the rectangular account books were held in its vise. Next to the desk, which was under one of the room's windows, a tall stand held the *estancia*'s over-size diary. Here, everything was entered daily: cattle sales, weather conditions, wages paid and income earned stood side by side with the world happenings as heard on the wireless, switched on every evening to catch the BBC broadcast on shortwave.

It was an improbable room of improbable proportions, a room that had never been planned but had merely evolved, like the *estancia* itself. The doors of all the rooms surrounding it had been left in their original state; they still opened and closed, with the turn of a key, as they had in the days when they opened out into a courtyard with the sky overhead.

"It's a comfy room," Edie remarked to Maurice. The Pekingese soon discovered they were allowed on the furniture for, unlike the delicate pieces at La Maison, the *estancia* chairs and sofas were built to withstand the rigors of *estancia* dwellers, and time. When the wet winter chill of early August was dispelled by blazing logs in the fireplace, Ming and Taitai hopped onto the sofa in front of it and curled into the cushions, while the smoky smell of burning *quebracho* wood mixed with the hearty meals brought in and served by Rosita at the long table.

With the *señora* Edie back, the Caseys' cook gone, and Rosa old and infirm, Rosita reigned supreme in the *estancia*'s kitchen quarters. Cooking was done on a black, wood-fueled stove with heavy, concentric metal rings that could be removed, one by one, with a thick wire hook whenever more heat was needed beneath the cooking pot, and whose oven was on all day.

From the kitchen, a swing door led to the *despensa*; here, stores were kept and the daily rations of household bread and *galleta* hung in floury white cotton bags from metal hooks on the far wall. On the unvarnished wooden shelves, tightly closed tins kept ants from the biscuits and cakes; in the center, a scarred wooden trapdoor led to the cobwebby depths of the cellar.

"No wonder Kevin wanted to work for Bateman," observed Maurice, climbing back up the narrow wooden cellar steps and handing the kerosene lamp in his hand to Edie before closing the trap door. "There's hardly a bottle of wine left down there. Must order some from B.A. Thaxter did mention something about Kev hinting."

Edie felt annoyed; once again, a Casey had taken advantage of them by getting them to find him a job in Buenos Aires and then behaving out of line right away.

"Never mind, my dear—he's far better suited to life down

312

there than being an *estanciero*. Tim at least has a feel for the land. . . ."

The two O'Connors had both heard enough stories about the Casey brothers' behavior at El Ombú to judge their differing characters, and whereas drink and gambling were traits they had in common, it had apparently been Kevin who had instigated the wilder brawls and high living, seldom spending more than a month at a time on the *estancia* he was supposed to be running, but traveling to Rosario and B.A. the whole time, appearing back with a crew in tow, ready for yet another *fiesta*, another week-long drinking bout, another carousal, another brawl. It had been Kevin, not Tim, who leveled the strip in the field for his wild friends to come in on an airplane.

"I don't think Tim's any prize, either." Edie found it impossible to dismiss from her mind his purchase of La Chata on what she felt sure was Maurice's money.

Her husband took the kerosene lamp from her again, and extinguished it.

"Now let's go and have a look at the saddle room," he suggested. "If I'm going to write to Bateman's for supplies, I might as well see what other things we need." And, leaving the lamp and ignoring the subject of Tim Casey, he opened the door out to the back patio. "Coming, my dear?"

Behind the house and beyond the patio, the regularly spaced trees that had canopied their engagement fiesta of so long ago had grown even taller, even leafier in the decade between. The O'Connors made their way to the *estancia*'s back road, the dusty width that was churned daily by the hooves of ridden horses, draught oxen, herded cattle, the wheels of small *carretas* and larger hay wagons, the occasional tires of visiting cars. More structures had been built along the *estancia*'s work artery and around the *peones*' quarters; a bigger corral and some cowsheds stood on the opposite side, while the hitching posts had grown white with rain and wear and age.

Outside the *gauchos*' bunkhouse, a handpump stood near a trio of *paraíso* trees. The men, back from the fields, were already lining up beside it, their short, dark, and time-creased boots in their hands, each awaiting his turn. No *gaucho* ever went to bed without running spurts of ground-cold water over his gnarled, stirrup-wise feet.

Without interrupting, Edie and Maurice went to the saddle room and on with their task of reassessing everything at El Ombú, preparing to set it on a safer, more profitable course before they returned to Europe.

The accounts book lay open on the desk; Maurice, frowning, checked down the columns of numbers. Edie, standing by his side, suddenly pointed.

"That's wrong," she said, indicating two rows of figures. "And so is the total, and that means the whole page...."

Maurice pushed his chair back and grunted, taking out a handkerchief to wipe his face.

"If you're tired, I'll do it," Edie offered, pulling up a chair and sitting down next to him. "I taught myself when I lived at El Naranjal...." But she was already pulling the book toward her, reaching for a sharpened pencil. Moments later, she was at work. Maurice watched her, bemused.

When Rosita came in, Edie looked up and said, "Goodness. Dinner time already?" And later, at the table, she and Maurice talked over the *estancia*'s business affairs. That night, it was Edie who made the entries in the diary.

"No, it's not too much for me. I like doing it, Maurice. After all, there isn't anything much for me to do around here."

It was true; *estancia* life, as such, held few activities for Edie. She did not ride for pleasure, only transportation, nor did she care to shoot; the house, now set in order, was run by Rosita, with little need for Edie to do much more than order necessary supplies and oversee.

The bedroom she had chosen as her own had already been transformed by her personal touches, its high dark wardrobes, unused to finery, taking on new life with her delicate dresses and gowns. To be sure, it was the tweeds rather than the tulle that came into use, but the general effect was still transforming. Her gold-backed brushes were set out before the mirror, the room and its adjoining dressing- and bathrooms scented with the powders and perfumes brought from France.

But she was set, her stamp imprinted on her surroundings, and so she eagerly accepted the opportunity to plunge into the spirit of *estancia* life through its productivity, its figures and its books. She began touring the camp with Maurice in the light trap, or sometimes the car, tramping across the fields with him in areas where a vehicle no longer served.

314

"You must teach me how to drive, Maurice. I can see that it's going to be most useful here...."

He looked at her in awe; a new side of her was emerging, one he had never witnessed, but which fascinated him nonetheless.

"Nonsense," she said, when he suggested it might tire or bore her. "You should've seen me in the days when I was at El Naranjal...."

To Edie, it was facts and figures again, and entries into ledgers. Nightly, she and Maurice sat side by side at the big desk, going over the day's production and events. Cattle, crops, prices, markets, harvesting and further planting—everything turned into numbers that had to be summed up. She took over the *estancia* diary, where everything was recorded, adding her own personal notes at the end of the day.

100 head of cattle sent to auction...wheat prices steady...capataz Braulio asking for more gauchos to be hired...rain stopped during night and pampero wind brought cleared skies...letter from Yvonne enclosing snapshots of little Meryl...Maurice going to Rosario for talks with bank next week...

She showed the snapshots to Rosita.

"Ay, *señora*, what a pretty little girl.... to think the *niña* Yvonne is a mother...it's hard to believe it...."

Edie, who found it rather hard to believe herself, made no comment and put the photographs back into the envelope. Rosita lingered by the desk.

"*Señora*, there's a little girl like that...perhaps a bit older, in the village.... I have been meaning to speak to you about her...."

"What little girl?"

"A little girl they want to give away as a *criada*...."

The custom of giving away unwanted children was not unknown to Edie. Customary in the region, the children, usually girls, were handed over to households where they earned their food and keep as best they could, depending on their age. The more fortunate were well treated and became family servants; for many, both fate and their future were sordid indeed.

In a sense, Rosita herself had been a *criada*, brought up in

315

the Moore household to serve Edie in her turn. The difference was that Rosita had been there with her mother. Most *criadas* were orphans, their parentage unknown.

"She's so thin, *señora*, that poor child. . . . You should see her . . ."

Edie asked, "How old is she?"

"About four years old, only a little bit older than the *niña* Yvonne's daughter. Just think, *señora* Edie, if your daughter and her husband came, for the two little girls, it could be like it was when we were children. . . ."

The two middle-aged women looked at each other, enveloped in the bygone days and years. For a moment, Edie almost thought she could sense the old house in Rosario, and the cool smell of the storeroom where she and Rosita had played.

Then she shrugged. "Who knows whether Yvonne and Philipe will ever come here? It's so hard to tell. . . . But never mind. Let's think about the *criada*."

Rosita vowed she would make sure the child was not a nuisance around the house.

"She'll be in my charge. I can teach her to clean and work properly as she grows older. . . . The *señora* will hardly know she's here. . . ."

"I'll have to speak to *Don* Mauricio. No doubt the people who have her want to be paid."

"A few pesos to the old woman who has been keeping her will be enough."

"Any idea whose child it is?"

"The old woman may be her grandmother," was the answer. "But no one really knows. In these cases, *Doña* Edie . . . well, you understand. . . ."

Edie nodded. "I'll talk to Mr. O'Connor about it tonight."

Maurice said, "It's up to you, my dear. After all, she'd be part of the household. Won't she get in your way?"

"Rosita says she won't let her."

"Mind you, I think it'd be a blessing for the poor child. . . ."

A week later, the diary entry ended:

The little criada arrived today. She is called Anatilde. A skinny little thing, very shy, big dark eyes. Is to sleep in old Casey cot in Rosita's room.

Answering Yvonne's letter, Edie wrote:

316

We all enjoyed the photographs you sent. Meryl doesn't look a bit like you. You were much taller at that age. I suppose she takes after Philipe's side of the family.

Maurice has gone down to B.A. again. The estancia is doing better, but times are still not very easy here in the Argentine. From what I can gather, things aren't very much better in America, either. I hope you're not being bothered by it too much. As far as I'm concerned, I'm very comfortable, and not at all averse to staying here a lot longer than we thought. The Government is being very pigheaded about the tax question.

Have you seen Madge lately? She wrote and told me they had decided not to go to Cannes this year, so I don't feel I'm missing much. She also mentioned Luther had gone back to his Margot again, very tail between his legs. I wonder where the floozie is this time? Madge says she's always somewhere, waiting in the wings.

2

Yvonne put the letter down on the table beside her and thought how typical it was of her mother to muddle Washington with New York. The only time she had seen Madge and Wilbur Petersen was when she went to Washington with Philipe, and as to the Grants, and Luther's floozie, she hadn't the foggiest notion what had become of any of them.

She leaned back against the sofa and lit a cigarette. Perhaps Philipe knew. He had been down in Washington for most of the month and, although he had said he would be back that night, she was not sure when to expect him. So much of his time had been spent in Washington of late that she had even suggested they move there, but Philipe didn't appear to be too keen. His work there wouldn't be lasting very much longer.

It was all so vague, Philipe's work, diplomatic linking at the trade level between countries. His unusual double-nationality, double-passport standing, tailor-made him for the field, of course, and it made their social life in New York pleasant enough, although she still felt hesitant to join him on all occasions.

317

At first, she had not accompanied him at all. She had been terribly weak after Meryl's birth—weak and fretful and desperately depressed. Life hadn't seemed worth living anymore. The nurse, Emily, had stayed, the only link to England, her flat, no-nonsense British tones curiously soothing to Yvonne.

"Now then, dear, none of that. We *must* get up and face life, you know. . . ."

Slowly, Yvonne had recovered, gone out of doors again, taken an interest in her new surroundings. Emily had continued to stay, was still with them, in fact—in the park with Meryl at that very moment—and life in New York was pleasant enough.

Of course, it wasn't London. . . .

Yvonne sighed and shifted on the cushions, tucking her legs up under her. If only things had been different; if only the Dancourts hadn't been so terribly unfair . . . The blur of familiar thoughts began trooping to mind, their attendant tears close. She missed England terribly, and longed to return. But not just yet; she couldn't face it yet.

And then, with Philipe, it wouldn't really be the same. . . .

Not that he wasn't sweet and kind and considerate, for he was all of that, and more. It was just that . . . just that . . . Yvonne could hardly explain it even to herself. She supposed it was the effect of all the fuss there had been; nothing would ever wipe away the effects of the long and terrible months they had gone through. Besides, there was always Meryl's presence to remind them of it, although Philipe appeared to enjoy the child, far more than Yvonne had thought he would.

Their original plan to get a friendly divorce a year or so after the child's birth had not been spoken of in a long while. In Yvonne's mind, it had been relegated to the faintest of smudges on the distant horizon of the future. She did not really want a divorce; Philipe was a pleasant enough husband, and now that she had a child, Yvonne did not know what else she could do with her life.

Yvonne put out her cigarette in the cut glass ashtray and picked up her mother's letter. She might as well answer it; there wasn't anything else to do, and she enjoyed getting news from Edie. *Estancia* life appeared to be agreeing with her, which had at first suprised Yvonne, and then amused her.

"I can't imagine Mummy pigging it out in the camp, can you?" she had remarked to Philipe.

"From your description of El Ombú, I don't think pigging it is exactly a fair description," was his only reply.

When Meryl and Emily came back from the park, Yvonne allowed her daughter to make a wobbly X mark on the letter, as a kiss to the grandmother she had yet to meet.

"Now run along and have your tea nicely with Emily, and let me finish my letter. Daddy may be home later. . . ."

She was still writing to Edie when she heard Philipe's voice in the hall. He came into the living room, and she rose to greet him.

"I've got a surprise for you," he told her, smiling. "How would you like to go back to B.A.?"

Edie had the pages of Yvonne's letter spread out before her.

"Here it is." She handed a page to Maurice who, still in boots and his riding *bombachas*, had just come in from a tour with the *capataz*. "She says Philipe has to set up a trade mission in B.A.—something to do with Belgium . . . You'll see when you read the letter. . . ."

After lunch, they discussed the matter further. Edie read other pages aloud.

"*. . . got another scare last month, and thought it had happened again, as though all Philipe has to do is hang his trousers over the end of my bed for me to get pregnant. . . .*"

Edie looked up from the letter with an expression of distaste.

"I *don't* understand where Yvonne picks up these vulgar expressions of hers. D'you think it's from Philipe?" She looked anxiously at Maurice.

"More likely to be the way young people talk these days. Wouldn't let it worry you, Edie."

"Well, if that's the case, I think Miss Smartyboots should confine it to her friends. I don't think it's at all clever."

Maurice ignored the comment. After a while, he said, "I suppose they'll be here before the end of the year."

Edie consulted the letter again. "I expect so. She says they're to sail as soon as they can."

Maurice seemed lost in thought, leaning back in his chair and staring up at the ceiling.

"You know," he said at last, "it might work out very well all the way around. By the time they get settled down, we should be in far better shape here, and just about ready to go to Europe again." He sat up and leaned forward, toward Edie, in his chair. "If they could keep an eye on things for us while we're in Europe, it'd make everything a lot easier, you know...."

"It's so strange to be back," Yvonne kept saying over and over again. "Of course I recognize everything—but still, it seems so different...."

They had docked at noon on the early summer day, the bright blue sky over Buenos Aires clear and cloudless. Yvonne had come down the gangplank first, carrying a birdcage; she was closely followed by Philipe with Meryl on his shoulders.

"Oh, Mummy—how lovely to see you.... You'd better put her down, Philipe...people are staring.... Maurice—look what we brought you.... I'm sure you miss Coco..."

Yvonne thrust the birdcage into her stepfather's hands. Inside, a small parakeet fluttered with the motion.

"Give it to a *changador*, Maurice.... He can bring it with the luggage.... How well you both look.... Were you seasick, Yvonne?"

"She did very well." Philipe stepped forward. "How nice to see you, Mrs. O'Connor. Meryl, say how-do-you nicely, and shake hands like a lady...."

The movement of the crowd covered the confusion of the moment, and the family group moved to the customs shed with the rest of the passengers. Two taxis took them and the luggage to the hotel once all landing formalities had been completed. Maurice had arranged for adjoining accommodations; they gathered in the sitting room of the O'Connors' suite.

"It seems so strange..." Yvonne began yet again.

"Well, it's been—what? Almost fifteen years, hasn't it, since you saw the place," remarked Edie. "And, Yvonne—I do wish you'd stop talking with an American accent. It doesn't suit you."

Maurice squirted the soda siphon into the drinks with rather more splash and fuss than usual.

"Cheers," he said, handing out the glasses and raising his in toast. "Here's to all of us..."

"Would Meryl like some orange juice, do you think?" Edie

eyed her granddaughter, who was still clinging to Philipe, sitting next to him and partially hiding behind his back.

"No, Mummy, not now. It'll only spoil her supper. I'll give it to her in a few minutes, and put her to bed."

"She doesn't look a bit like you, Yvonne. Isn't she very small for three?"

"No, not really. Philipe's mother is small-boned like that, and Meryl has her eyes..."

"Nonsense, child. They're just like mine. Aren't they, Meryl?"

Grandmother and grandchild looked at each other across the carpeted room. Then Edie extended her hand to Meryl and stood up. "Come, Meryl. Let's take the doggies for their walkies together...."

On hearing the word walkies, Ming and Taitai, who had been sleeping on cushions placed underneath a side table, raised their heads expectantly.

"If you say Walkies Time, Meryl, the doggies'll follow you...."

Hesitantly, the little girl looked from the adult talking to her, to the dogs, and back again at her grandmother. Then she pushed herself forward and off the sofa.

"There you go," said Philipe, helping her get down and giving her rumpled dress a tidying tug.

"Where's their lead...? That's right, now you hold my hand..."

"I'm surprised at Mummy," Yvonne said, after Edie and Meryl had left the room with the two dogs. "She's never shown any interest in children before."

"She's never had a granddaughter before," observed Maurice.

"I don't see why that should make any difference..." Yvonne began, but Maurice interrupted her by referring to the parakeet she had brought him. The bird was sitting on a perch in its cage, which had been placed on the room's side table.

"Very thoughtful of you. And you're right. I do miss Coco, although I understand he's very well looked after. We left Yves and his wife in charge of La Maison, you know."

"Perhaps this one'll learn to talk, too. By the way, she's female. At least that's what the vendor at the port in Santos said."

Maurice glanced over at the parakeet. "Then I shall call her Marina," he said, "since she came to me by sea. Now,

321

Philipe, let's hear about this trade mission of yours...."

Later in the evening, after Meryl had been put to bed and the four adults were having dinner, Edie said, "She's not at all shy, Yvonne. Chattered like a magpie while we walked the dogs in the plaza."

"Did she? I'm surprised..."

"Meryl often warms to people," smoothed Philipe.

"But she *can* be a very diffident child," insisted Yvonne. "And much more independent, Mummy, than children brought up in England. Right now, I think she misses Emily."

"Pity you didn't bring Emily with you."

"We wanted to, but she wouldn't come. Wanted to go home. I suppose we can find somebody here."

"Or you could get a nannie out from London."

"Surely there are nursemaids available in Buenos Aires..." Philipe began.

"Well, I don't want a native..."

"We'll have to start asking around. I'm sure that Dollie, with all her clubs and connections, will know of something...."

The van Landens moved into a large apartment in one of the new and modern buildings in the fashionable section near the extensive park of La Recoleta, its old trees and sloping lawns backed by the wall and crypt crosses of the cemetery of the rich.

"When I go back to England and then to La Maison and get all my belongings shipped out here, then we can look for a proper house with a garden somewhere...."

Thus Yvonne's reasoning and plans, amiably agreed to by Philipe. His office was a brief taxi ride away, and he had always preferred city life, but if Yvonne wanted to move to the suburbs later on, the train service, run by the British and noted for its excellence, would serve him admirably as well. Most of the British community members lived in enclaves in the outlying areas; even the station names reflected their influence through the years. City Bell, Ranelagh, Coghlan, Hurlingham, Temperley, their names were taken entirely for granted on the district lines leading out of B.A.

The apartment's rooms were spacious, the terraces wide, the view north over the street to the parks beyond cool and green.

"Meryl can play there, till we get a garden... but we must find someone for her...."

322

Yvonne turned her sights on finding a governess.

"Perhaps we really should get a proper nannie from England . . ."

Philipe looked dubious.

"Don't you think Meryl's past the nannie stage? After all, she's going to be four."

"Nannies in England stay until the child goes to boarding school. . . ."

"We're not in England, Yvonne. . . ."

"Well, I certainly don't want my daughter brought up by some Argentine . . ."

In the end, a compromise was reached in the person of Madame Benoit. French born, widowed, respectable to a T, she came highly recommended by the staff of her country's embassy.

"Meryl might as well start learning French right away. . . ,"

And, boring and pedantic as Madame Benoit might be, and was, Meryl did.

As soon as they had settled in to the apartment, the van Landens went on their first visit to El Ombú, taking Meryl with them.

"No need to bring the governess with you," Edie had told them. "Rosita can look after the child here." So Madame Benoit stayed in Buenos Aires and took charge of the new household, while the three van Landens took the train from the station Yvonne remembered clearly.

"I'm longing to show the *estancia* to you," she told Philipe as they chugged toward Rosario. "It's a lovely place, what I remember of it. Mummy says it's changed a lot—and it must have, for her to enjoy it. . . ."

"Perhaps Edie's changed . . ."

"Not much. . . ."

"What a daughterly attitude." Philipe smiled across the compartment. "Anyway, I'm looking forward to it. . . ."

They stayed overnight in Rosario, taking the afternoon train the next day, and arriving in the late evening. Maurice was waiting for them at the village station in an open touring car, and the dusty drive along the main road beside the tracks brought them to the *estancia*'s high gates, the wrought iron tracing elaborate designs in the pearly twilight. At the end of the long driveway, Edie and Rosita were standing by the low white wall.

"Ay, *niña* Yvonne!" Rosita wept with excitement and joy. "I mean *señora* Yvonne...it's so difficult to believe you're here...and the little *niña* Meryl..."

The soft darkness of the night rustled with summer sounds as the reunited family went inside.

"I didn't know Rosita had any grandchildren," remarked Yvonne at breakfast next morning.

"She hasn't. Rosita never married. What made you think she had?"

"The little girl. There's a little girl playing in the back patio."

"That's Anatilde, our *criada*. She was given to us last year."

Yvonne looked over her cup in surprise.

"A *criada*? But Mummy, you can't do that...you can't have a *criada* here...."

"Why not?"

"Because it's feudal, that's why. One doesn't go around accepting children as gifts in this day and age, Mummy—it's ridiculous."

"Rosita was a *criada*."

"That's different. She was born in your parents' house. And besides, that was ages ago."

Edie looked sharply across the table at her daughter.

"Not quite as long ago as all that, miss..."

"But the world has changed since then, Mummy."

"Apparently not, in this case."

"Well, I wouldn't..."

"Perhaps you wouldn't, but I did. The child's no trouble at all, I can assure you. Besides, she'll be a nice little friend for Meryl while you're here, she's only about a year older. And she's already beginning to learn how to do things. Rosita sees to that. They look after her very well in the kitchen."

Yvonne put her cup down with a clatter.

"You're as bad as they are—how *can* you do it?"

"Do what?"

"Push her off like that. Keep her in the kitchen. It's terribly unfair..."

"Life *is* unfair. Quite frequently. I..."

"Well, since you've taken the child, *I'm* going to see to it that she doesn't get pushed aside like that."

"Don't be bumptious, Yvonne. Nobody's pushing her aside. Anatilde is perfectly happy here. Now let's not have any more of this nonsense. I suggest you go and dress Meryl, and we'll get the two children together so they can play...."

The two little girls looked at each other, Anatilde standing in front of Rosita, Meryl clinging to her mother's hand.

"This is Anatilde, Meryl. You two can play together nicely in the patio."

Meryl edged closer to Yvonne's side; Yvonne gently disengaged her.

From her position behind the *criada*, Rosita was trying to encourage her, too.

"...and the *niña* Meryl came a long way, all the way from the United States, to visit us.... You can teach her Spanish...."

Edie, observing the encounter from the sidelines, grew impatient.

"Just tell them to run along and play," she advised.

Yvonne ignored her mother and spoke to her daughter.

"Meryl, don't be silly, and let go my hand. Now, let's see if you can say the little girl's name. Can you say Anatilde?"

Meryl shook her head.

Edie had had enough.

"Stop spoiling the child, Yvonne. Let's leave them here with Rosita. She can keep an eye on them. I've got lots I want to talk to you about, and..."

"All right, Mummy, but first, let me hear Meryl say Anatilde. You can, darling, can't you?"

"Lala," said Meryl in a sudden, clear voice, stepping forward and giving the *criada* a hard shove in the chest with both her hands.

"*Meryl!* How dare..."

"Never mind, *señora* Yvonne, I'll take care of them...."

But even as Rosita spoke, the *criada* had retaliated in kind. Meryl lost her balance and sat down with a bump.

"*Anatilde!*" Rosita advanced, her hand raised.

"That's enough." Edie stepped forward, seizing each child by a hand. "Come on, Meryl, get up. There now. Rosita—you take them."

Rosita marshalled the children out through the screened verandah into the garden beyond. Yvonne followed Edie back into the main room, and it was not until almost lunchtime that the children were mentioned again.

"They're playing, *señora*," Rosita reported. "Earlier, I gave them some *yerba* and biscuits, and now they're feeding lunch

325

to the *niña* Meryl's dolls. They only needed a little moment to get used to each other at first."

That evening, when Meryl's bedtime came, Yvonne went in to say goodnight to her daughter, and hear her prayers.

At the end of her usual litany, Meryl said, ". . . and God bless Lala and make her a good girl, too. . . ."

The nickname and the friendship stuck.

Once Philipe van Landen had established his office in Buenos Aires, he began making trips to the capitals of other South American countries. Depending on the length of his absence, Yvonne either stayed in town or went up to the *estancia*, taking Meryl and Madame Benoit with her.

The chill damp of the B.A. winter set in; Meryl, past her fourth birthday, began attending dancing school.

"It's a good way for her to meet other children and make friends," Yvonne told Edie. "It's pointless thinking of sending her to school out here, Mummy. She can have private lessons and learn all she needs until she's old enough to go to Crestwood Close."

"Then you'd better put her down for it," her mother advised.

"That's one of the first things I intend to do when I go home."

Edie looked at her daughter. It was the first mention she had heard of Yvonne's intention to return to England.

"I thought I'd go with you and Maurice when you go back," Yvonne continued. "Philipe thinks it'd be a good idea, too. Then I can arrange to have my things shipped out here. After all, it was all such a rush when I left. . . ."

Talking to Maurice alone late that night, Edie repeated Yvonne's plans.

". . . and just as you thought we'd be able to go and leave El Ombú in her care. I tell you, Maurice, she's never been reliable. . . ."

Maurice grunted and sat down heavily in his chair.

"Then we'll have to find an overseer," he said. "God knows there are enough of 'em around. Tim might know of somebody, or . . ."

"Surely you don't want any friends of Tim's back in here . . ."

"No, my dear, perhaps not. You're quite right. But I'll start asking around. We'll see what we can find."

September came, and spring. Philipe returned from one of his trips, and Yvonne, contemplating the long summer months of heat ahead, told him she was thinking of spending the time on the *estancia*.

"Go ahead," was the answer. "Perhaps I'll be able to join you there for Christmas. . . ."

By mid-November, Yvonne and Meryl and Madame Benoit were at El Ombú.

"Maurice looks tired," Yvonne remarked to her mother shortly after her arrival.

"I think it's the worry about not having found a majordomo," said Edie. "He was in Rosario all last week, seeing applicants, but he didn't like any of 'em. And if we want to sail back next year. . ."

But in the meantime, El Ombú was flourishing, and a family reunion for Christmas would be fun; Yvonne took to riding out into the fields before breakfast every morning, and Madame Benoit, muttering beneath the faint dusting of her light mustache, tried to teach the two lively little girls that *"le bras* was *the arm* was *el brazo"* in the shade of the verandah every morning.

Hers was, for the most part, a thankless task.

For Meryl, now chattering fluently in Spanish, had a friend in the *criada* and an ally in Rosita, who resented the Frenchwoman's air of superiority in household areas where Rosita reigned supreme. If Lala joined the hour of lessons, the two little girls giggled and rebelled at every turn; if Meryl had her lesson alone, she fidgeted and squirmed, hardly paying adequate attention, until her plaintive, "Is it time to go now, Madame?" was given the answer it sought.

Far more successful were the music lessons, given at the old and out of tune upright piano, a relic from the Casey days, and relegated to the south wing. There, Yvonne would play and sing to the children eager to join in with their high, piping voices. There were songs in both languages, and do-re-mi, and the fun of singing scales and making music together. There was "Hushaby, Baby" and "Arroro, Mi Nene," both of which the girls sang to their dolls later in the day when they lullabied them to playtime bed. And then there were "Chopsticks," banged out with four hands and stubby energetic fingers, until both Meryl and Lala knew how to

327

play either side of the four-handed musical game, even if Yvonne wasn't there to guide them.

And then there were marching songs, which they could also sing when they played out of doors.

"*Caminante, no hay camino, se hace el camino al andar* . . . Traveler, there is no path; you make your way as you go . . ."

They sang it in English, they sang it in Spanish, they shouted it running around the garden with the Pekingese bouncing and barking at their heels until Edie came out and said for heaven's sake to stop all this noise because Granmaurice was trying to get a *siesta* and why weren't they sleeping after lunch, too? And then Madame Benoit got in trouble for letting them run wild, which wasn't really fair as she had tried to stop them.

Rosita stepped in, restoring calm and order.

No, most assuredly, Madame was no match for them at all.

Meryl lay on the smooth, cool surface of the rush mat rolled out over her bed, waking slowly from her afternoon *siesta*. The thick scent of magnolias from the tree outside was mixed with the grassy smell of the matting beneath her. She slid her fingers along the reeds, finding the ridges of string binding them together.

Would it be Madame, she wondered, who would come to dress her this afternoon? Or would it be one of the lucky days, which meant Rosita? Rosita always sounded fierce, but she wasn't really, and if she came at *siesta* time, Meryl knew Lala was also ready to go out and play.

It was hardly ever her mother who woke her in the afternoon. Besides, today all the grown-ups had gone to Rosario; from there, Daddy, who had been at the *estancia* for a short visit, was going home to the apartment, and only her mother and Grannie and Granmaurice were returning tomorrow. Daddy had work to do, he had told her; he would be back for Christmas. But Mother wanted to stay on with Grannie and Granmaurice, and it was nice for Meryl to be able to play with Lala, and go riding when Mother had the time to take her. Meryl wasn't old enough to go by herself, but she was learning on a pony borrowed from Uncle Tim's *estancia*. When she was bigger, she might get one of her own, and when she was really big, Mother said perhaps she would have a horse.

In the meantime, there was lots to do and explore right

around the house when Mother wasn't here to take her riding. She and Lala were allowed to go through the trees and around the windmill and along the building that was the water tank and the dairy, as long as they didn't cross the back road behind the *peones'* quarters, or get in the *gauchos'* way, and they must always remember to be very polite to the men with the white headbands and the black hats they only removed when saying "*Buenos días, niña* Meryl," or greeting anyone from the main house.

This afternoon would be a good time to go and play in the *gomero* tree. It was right behind the house, near the north wing, and once you stepped between the low-hanging branches, it was like being in a huge tent, all covered over with leaves. The sagging branches even made perfect seats, and she and Lala pretended it was their very own tree house. It was cool, too, and a bit spidery at times, but they were only little webs that could be brushed aside and didn't do any harm.

If Ming and Taitai came with her, they would like it under the *gomero* tree, too. They'd lie on the green patches of creeping plants, the ones with the little blue flowers that were so bright and beautiful in the morning hours. Meryl had tried picking them, and bringing them indoors, but they hadn't lasted very well, so she never tried it again.

Or else, she and Lala could go and talk to Marina for a while. Only yesterday, Granmaurice had let the parakeet go from his finger onto Meryl's wrist. Her claws had felt funny and scratchy as she had walked up and down Meryl's arm, and then she had hopped back onto Granmaurice again. When he didn't have her on his shoulder or next to him on the side of his chair, Marina lived in a big cage over in a corner of the main room, and when she was in there, Meryl liked talking to her, watching the little bird twist her head from side to side, her shiny eyes dark points against the pale green of her feathers.

The door connecting her bedroom to the day nursery opened.

"*Niña* Meryl, it's time to get up. . . ."

Meryl smiled happily at Rosita and asked where Lala was.

"Waiting for you on the verandah. And be careful when you go outside. It's still too hot to play in the sun."

The *estancia* chapel, long deconsecrated and originally abandoned to ruin, had been put to use during the Caseys' time. A cement wall had been erected inside it, a few feet from the entrance door and running up to the level of the now gaping windows, their stained glass removed many years before.

The tank thus formed had been filled with water, piped in from the windmill that stood not a hundred yards away. The overspill was carried to the drinking trough on the back road behind the building and, in times of drought, the makeshift reservoir had proved useful around the homestead itself.

Eventually, part of the roof rotted and was taken off, leaving the tank open to the heavens. In recent times, it had not received much attention, as new windmills and better pipe installations provided the *estancia* with adequate water sources.

It was Yvonne who had the idea.

"If we cleaned it up a bit, and built steps up to the top of that wall and its ledge, it'd be a lovely swimming pool. . . ."

The cement enclosure was drained and scraped; cement steps were built on either side of the retaining wall inside. Wooden drainboards were placed in the minuscule antechamber at the chapel's entrance, where the roof was still intact and secure; two wooden benches and hooks for hanging towels completed the change.

The refurbished tank was filled again; the swimming pool was ready. Even Edie came to inaugurate it, sitting on the top step and watching Yvonne and Maurice swim up and down.

"Why didn't we think of this before? It's marvelously refreshing. . . ."

The lace-leafed trees around the building could be glimpsed through the gothic-shaped apertures of the building's empty windows, and in the late afternoon, anyone swimming in the pool could hear the snortings and snufflings of the returning horses, their *gaucho* riders, through with camp work for the day, giving them their first stop in from the field at the long, fresh-filled trough.

"They've brought some *huachos* in," Edie remarked, looking up from the desk as Yvonne and Meryl entered the main room. "Why don't you take Meryl to see them?"

"What are they, Grannie?" the child wanted to know.

"They're calves that haven't got mothers, so the *gauchos*

bring them in and feed them milk from a bottle until they're big."

They were joined by Lala on their way over to the barn. Meryl skipped ahead, then ran back with a question.

"If they haven't got mothers, why can't their daddies look after them? Where're their daddies?"

Lala laughed and said, "Daddies don't give milk and that's what the *huachos* need," but Meryl looked as though she did not believe her, and walked quietly on next to her mother.

The milk-filled wine bottles, equipped with rough-sewn funnel teats made out of old inner tubes, were lined up on the ground next to the open stall. Meryl watched the *gaucho* in charge feeding the little calves, one of them so young and spindle-legged it seemed in danger of collapsing as it pulled against the rubber teat, milk dribbling down its sides.

On the way back to the house, Meryl said to Yvonne, "I s'pose Lala's a *huacho*, too, isn't she, Mother?"

There was a pony for Christmas, and Meryl loved him. He was a Shetland, and was called Sammy, and had a thick, shaggy mane. She rode him bareback around the garden, and then he was put in the field near the orchard, so that she could visit him every day and feed him through the fence.

Philipe arrived to spend a few days' holiday, and they even had a party, with the Caseys coming over from La Chata in a rattletrap of a car. They brought their own two children, Harvey grown sturdy and tall, already seven years old, and the dainty little Anita, and also a smaller boy, their cook's nephew, they explained.

"Raul and Anita are inseparable, so we thought you wouldn't mind..."

"No, of course not...."

"Just like Meryl and Lala..."

"They can all go off and play together. Can't you, darlings? Madame won't mind...."

Madame, who did, smiled uneasily at Edie, who had already turned to her adult guests and was leading the way into the house.

"I think it's about time we all had a drink.... Fancy having a family reunion for Christmas after all these years...."

It was Yvonne who, during the afternoon, saw Harvey chasing Taitai in the patio with a stick.

331

"...and don't you ever do anything like that again," she admonished, the panting Pekingese safe in her arms, her anger directed at the sullen boy.

At dinner, she caught him pinching his sister and pushing Meryl when he thought no one was looking.

"If I find you doing one more naughty thing..."

After the Caseys had left, she told Edie, "He's a nasty little bully, and I wouldn't trust him for a moment."

"I'm not surprised," said Edie. "Like father, like son—and you know what Maurice thinks of Tim. But all in all, I think our little Christmas gathering went off very well, don't you?"

3

Early in the new year, the van Landens returned to Buenos Aires, much to Meryl's open dismay and Madame Benoit's secret delight. The reason for the return was the arranging of travel plans and the booking of ship's passages; Maurice, having found an overseer for El Ombú, wanted to sail for Europe in March.

Philipe, meanwhile, announced he had to go north to Washington; if Yvonne went with her parents, he could then meet them over in England later on during the year. She was overjoyed.

"It'll all work out splendidly, won't it? I can get my things from La Maison, and the ones in storage in London, and have everything ready by the time you get there, and sail back to B.A. with you...."

Plans and enthusiasm bubbled away.

Philipe came back from the office with sailing lists and ship accommodations, and he and Yvonne began discussing their choices as they dressed for a reception they were to attend that evening. They were still talking it over when they went into the living room to have their habitual cocktail.

"...adjoining staterooms," Yvonne was saying. Philipe put down the cocktail shaker and poured the mixture into two stemmed glasses. Handing one to her, he said, "And what about Madame?"

"What about her?"

"Shall we have her on the same deck, or..."

332

Yvonne looked puzzled. "Madame's not coming with us."

"Oh?" It was Philipe's turn to be surprised. "Don't you think Meryl will be too much for you to handle on your own?"

"I'm not taking Meryl. . . . What on earth are you talking about, Philipe? There's no question of her coming, too. . . . She's at no age to be dragged halfway across the world. . . ."

"I see." Philipe put down his glass. "You mean you want to leave her here with Madame. . . ."

"Of course."

"Here in town—or on the *estancia*?"

"Oh, I think on the *estancia*'d be better, don't you? She'd be perfectly safe, for one thing, and have Lala to play with all day, and both Madame and Rosita to look after her, and . . ."

"Yvonne." Philipe's voice was so quiet it was hardly audible. "Might I ask why you want to leave the child behind?"

"Because . . . because it's no trip for a little girl. . . . She'd hate it, I assure you . . . and I know what I'm talking about. . . . Mummy dragged me along when I was that age and it was *awful*, I loathed every minute of it, and . . ."

Her flustered words were stopped by the maid, who came into the living room to draw the curtains and announce that the *niña* Meryl had almost finished her supper and wanted to come and say good night to them.

"Yes, tell her we're in here. . . ."

Moments later, Meryl appeared, and after having kissed her parents good night, she looked at her mother and said, "You'll be the prettiest lady at the party tonight, won't she, Daddy?"

"She always is, sweetheart. Now hop off to bed like a good girl."

As she left, Philipe turned to Yvonne and said, "There are times I don't understand your attitudes at all."

"I suppose you'd take her everywhere with you. . . ."

"I certainly wouldn't want to leave her with that old witch of a . . ."

"Philipe, you're being absurd. Madame's very kind to Yvonne."

"She's useless—and she's too restrictive."

"If you had your way, Meryl would turn into one of those horrible American children, always whining, and spoiled rotten. . . ."

Philipe glanced at his watch.

"If we're going to be on time, I think we'd better get going. We can continue this discussion after we get back. . . ."

But when they returned home from the reception that night, their earlier discussion became purely academic, as the telegram telling of Maurice's heart attack awaited them on the entrance table.

Yvonne went northward on the next morning's train.

The *estancia* telephone stood like a thick-stemmed black daffodil among the leaves of accumulated papers on the crowded desk. The cord from its earpiece hanging on the stem was looped toward the base. Yvonne, sitting in the desk chair, brought the instrument closer toward her, lifted the earpiece and waited with her mouth near the trumpet.

She wondered how long it would take the operator to answer her call; they were always so slow in the *pueblo*, and the long-distance connection was sure to be poor, if they managed to get it at all. But at least the operator wouldn't be vile, the way the men on night duty in the B.A. suburbs always were. Especially when they heard an English voice.

"Ah, the *señorita* wants to make a telephone call. Perhaps the *señorita* would like to make love first?"

And you were stuck, truly stuck, because if you hung up in disgust, you couldn't make your call. And to tell the operator you were a respectably married woman, in tones of dignified reproof, only provoked more disgusting, more graphic suggestions.

A crackling of static exploded in her ear. Behind it, the operator's voice was faint. Yvonne gave Philipe's office number several times before it was correctly understood. Then she hung up; there would probably be a long delay for the line to Buenos Aires.

Maurice was better. Definitely better. She would be able to take the train home after the weekend. However, Philipe would have to postpone the passages to London. It would be months before the O'Connors would be able to travel again.

She sighed. No doubt Philipe would go to Washington anyway. She didn't want to go with him; it would be better if she stayed. Then, when Maurice was stronger, they'd sail to England; all it meant was waiting a bit more for their plans to work out.

After the second attack, the doctor was firm.

"No, *señora* O'Connor, no traveling." He closed his worn bag with a definitive snap. "Not next month, and not the one after. We need some more time."

Once beyond the front door and far out of Maurice's hearing, the doctor spoke to Edie in urgent, low tones.

"I'm afraid, *Doña* Edie, you must be strong and face the truth. In that manner, you can help your husband most now. *Don* Mauricio is not to travel again. Ever. The strain would kill him. He needs absolute repose."

Edie closed her eyes and braced herself against the wicker table. The shade of the verandah was chilly and damp.

"And if he rests, and gets stronger...do you think...how long...?" she left the thought unfinished.

"Difficult to say, but it could be several years. The calmer his life, the less risk of further attack. But even then..." The doctor gave a slight shrug. "One cannot promise anything, *señora*, only see that he rests and is not disturbed."

Late that night, Edie wrote at length to Yvonne.

....so you see all our plans have got to change. We cannot travel now. However, since Philipe is in the United States, perhaps you could go to England and wait for him to meet you there? Then you could go over to Cannes for a stay, and see how things are getting along at La Maison....

She put down her pen and sat doing nothing for quite a long time. She was tired, very tired; nursing Maurice was exhausting. Good as he was about doing everything she told him to and taking the medicines left by the doctor, the nerve-wracking nights and long anxious days had drained her of all energy. And yet—she must keep going; the overseer had proved useless once Maurice fell ill, and she had let him go, preferring to manage on her own with the *capataz*, thinking, at the beginning, that Maurice would eventually take over once more.

But now...now...Everything was different. Exactly as the fortune-teller had said.

....many changes...not of your own doing...life very different...

The woman had been right. In the past few years, everything had turned out to be different. And now this.

335

Wearily, she finished the letter, sealing it up to be sent to Buenos Aires in the next day's post.

In Washington, D.C., Philipe sat in the innocuous government office, listening to the statistics and suspicions being recited by the man on the other side of the desk. The hot morning's sun baked down on the Capitol, visible from the room's wide window.

". . . and now that you have all the trade connections established, you can operate behind them with no further problems."

It was true; the setup served Philipe's assigned work so effectively that neither his travels nor his contacts need cause anyone to have second thoughts.

"We'll need a report from you on Bolivia as soon as possible. The Germans got in there via the airline, so we'll need influence, too. . . ."

Philipe nodded, knowing he would have to go straight back south again. There would be no question of going to Europe, not for the rest of the year.

"After that, it'll be Chile . . . coastline . . . possible agents there . . ."

While being briefed on his assignment Philipe reflected privately on the absurdities of the world that sent him spying in South America because of the European rumblings being set in motion by a vegetarian with a clipped mustache.

"But you've only just got back!"

"I know, but that's the way it's going to be for a while. Why don't you go and spend your birthday on the *estancia*, Yvonne? I'm sure Edie and Maurice would love to see you. . . ."

Yvonne shook her head.

"No, I can't. Everything has to be kept so very quiet. It's not fair to Meryl. . . . Mummy won't let her run around and play anywhere near the house. . . ."

She picked up the newspaper and handed it to Philipe.

"Did you see the item about La Simpson? She's going through exactly what I did—and she'll have to wait until April next year for the final decree. I wonder what'll happen . . . whether he'll marry her and make her Queen of England. . . ."

Political plans and romantic notions buzzed around the world.

"Ay, *señora* Edie, there's a *calandria* in the patio!"

"Where?"

"Now it flew away again. There it is! Up in that tree!"

The *estancia* shivered in the shadow of the bird's omen. Everyone knew a *calandria* hanging around a house presaged disaster.

Edie told Rosita not to be so silly and superstitious, and please to bring *Don* Mauricio's lunch at precisely twelve o'clock, after he came in from his morning walk.

He arrived, somewhat earlier than usual, Marina perched as always on his right shoulder.

"Bit too hot for me, I think. Rather spend the time inside."

Lunch was served. Marina rode on his finger, over to the table. She hopped down and began trotting among the plates.

"Maurice, I do wish you'd let me put her in her cage while you eat. It's not healthy."

His mustache stood away from his thin, tired face as he smiled. For the first time in ages, Edie noticed a gleam of amusement in his eyes, a light she had forgotten.

"She seldom eats too much, my dear."

Marina waddled, pigeon-clawed, over to Maurice's plate of soup. Deftly, he pushed a noodle out onto the edge beside her. With a swift bob of her head, she won her prize, dragging it away to the table's center to consume it.

"Really, Maurice…" Edie began, and then she let the subject drop. The bird, having finished the noodle, hopped onto the back of a chair where she preened her feathers and waited for Maurice to finish his meal and take her back to her cage.

Then it was *siesta* time, and Maurice retired for his usual slumber. Edie went to the books on the desk. She was still engrossed in figures, and Maurice was still sleeping when, in mid-afternoon, there was a loud thump against one of the living room's high windows.

Looking up startled, Edie saw a flutter of dark wings before the *calandria* sped off again, only to reappear against the netting of another window further along. Uneasy, and suddenly afraid, she got up to take a closer look at the bird, but her movement apparently frightened it away, for all she saw was its swift form disappearing behind the trees toward the orchard.

Maurice O'Connor died the next day, his last hours comatose, his life beyond recall, while across the ocean a short reign ended, and the news of abdication rocked the waiting world.

When Edie emerged with the doctor, to make the immediate arrangements, she found Marina's body, still and lifeless on the table, lying next to the waiting breakfast cup that would never be filled again.

Maurice O'Connor was buried in the small *pueblo* cemetery that lay on low ground next to the *estancia*'s southern boundary, and after the funeral Edie announced she was staying on at El Ombú.

"At least for the time being. Maurice would have wanted me to, and I shall run it."

"Are you sure you want to, Mummy? Won't it be too much for you?"

"Don't be silly, Yvonne. I've been doing it for years...."

"Yes, I know, but that was with Maurice..."

"Not after his first attack—and stop interrupting me. I'm trying to tell you what I'm going to do. I'll run it on my own for a while, and then perhaps I'll find a manager, and if he works out, eventually I'll go back to La Maison. But I don't feel like doing that right away.... For the moment, I want to stay here...."

In the weeks that followed, Edie kept her tears to herself and busied her time with running El Ombú. To her surprise, Tim Casey made her a substantial offer for the *estancia*; to his surprise, she turned it down. Word of the failed transaction soon spread; *Doña* Edie was indeed going to carry on in *Don* Mauricio's place.

Privately, the *gauchos* of El Ombú relaxed after the months of tense speculation. They had followed the *patrón's* coffin and honored his word. His widow had now proved she planned to do the same.

Over the next year and a half, Meryl came to know the *estancia* through all its seasons. Every time her father went off on one of his many trips, and sometimes even when he didn't, she and her mother would go to El Ombú to stay, reluctantly accompanied by Madame Benoit who, encased in her corsets and black bombazine, learned to suffer, in Gallic silence punctured by Gallic sighs, the self-contained world and its hierarchy. Madame retreated into her needlepoint whenever her duties to Meryl were done.

"You're paying that woman for nothing," Edie observed to Yvonne one day.

"No, I'm not, Mummy. Meryl must keep up with at least some of her lessons. . . ."

Edie conceded defeat. In Buenos Aires, a series of private lessons and tutors were preparing Meryl for her eventual enrollment at Crestwood Close; on the *estancia*, Madame conducted a three-hour school session weekday afternoons. Lala also attended, her village school hours being morning ones only.

But there were other lessons, information imparted by the *estancia* and its way of life, its terrain and its seasons, the rhythm of its days. As a toddler, she had discovered the clock flowers you blew to pieces to know the time and the thick purple thistles with sharp prickles in their leaves. Now, older, she and Lala pulled up stems of the *inojo* plant, chewing the white meaty portion for the strong aniselike taste, and lying like troopers when warned about its ill effects.

"No, we didn't—we were only looking at the leaves. . . ."

And they chewed *inojo* to no great effect but with renewed interest.

The *bicho canastos*, also discovered when she was small, still fascinated her, the basket-bugs that so deliberately wove twig and filament cones around their grublike bodies for protection, hanging like Christmas ornaments from the trees, eating their inexorable paths across leaves. There were other *bichos*, too; summer nights winked with *bichos de luz*, the fireflies blinking in the velvet air. And the *bicho feo*, a bright yellow-banded bird, whose cry sounded like a melancholy "*bicho feo*," although he was neither ugly nor a bug at all.

The *estancia*'s fauna was at times linked to major events; some unforeseen and unwanted, some deliberately planned. Locust plagues could change life overnight.

Word of the locusts' immiment arrival always preceded them as they approached from the north. Fire and noise being the only two weapons available against the expected cloud of ravaging insects, the *peones* would prepare for the onslaught, hoping all the while that the swarm would settle in another *estancia*, on another region, be wind-veered or rainwashed on another path.

"Nothing to what it was in '31 and '32," Meryl heard Uncle Tim Casey telling Grannie, and even Rosita hardly seemed to notice the thousands of grasshoppers stripping plants in the garden and laying bare some of the trees.

But not the *ombú*; it stood, proud and alone, watching from its solitary position in the front field to the right of the house, dark and still and somber as ever.

She and Lala were not allowed to play around the *ombú* for long.

"It gives headaches," said Rosita, and no camp dweller contradicted her. "Even the birds know better than to stay."

Which seemed to be true, for, much as she'd looked, Meryl had never seen a nest on its branches or among its leaves. And there were stories about the leaves, too, stories she knew she wasn't supposed to hear. But Harvey said the *peones* had told him about jokes they played, putting pieces of the leaves into someone's *yerba* to give him terrible collywobbles.

"Is it true, Rosita?"

"Don't you listen to the *niño* Harvey!"

But as she also forbade Meryl and Lala to pick or play with the *ombú* leaves, Meryl realized the story had validity, and gazed at the tree with intrigued respect.

Cattle dipping was more fun to watch. Meryl and Lala climbed onto the gray-bleached wooden posts and ties forming the side barrier of the *brete*, the long, narrow dip filled with dark, opaque water, and watched the cattle being sent through it, one by one, from the corral at one end. Each animal would be herded and hustled into the wired-off corridor leading to the slide. Reluctance earned them the stab of the electric *picana*, and they would jolt forward and slither down the ramp and splash into the *brete* itself, paddling and lowing frantically along it until their hooves made contact with the far end's rise; its extended, ridged slope allowing them to scramble up it to firm-earth safety.

Long ago, when Granmaurice was still alive, he had explained to Meryl how the dip prevented the cattle from getting ticks, thus keeping them healthy, and Meryl could see that, although there was a lot of jostling and mooing and lowing, the cows soon forgot their terrified scrambled plunge and returned to their grazing and staring at the horizon once the *gauchos* had herded them back to their fields.

But individual animals were more fun, like the skunk they had almost caught the time Harvey and Raul were over from La Chata, and all of them were walking Taitai and Ming through the woods behind the *peones'* quarters and the work road. It was Raul who had altered them.

Running around in front of the older children, he suddenly wheeled back and came to Lala, grabbing her hand and pulling her saying, "Come quickly, Lala... I hear a loud smell...."

By that time, the dogs had started barking near a fallen tree trunk; a skunk was prancing, tail high along its curved form. Harvey, who had a butterfly net with him, said, "Let's catch it!" and ran toward the animal, but the skunk scuttled over the log and disappeared. The Pekes bounded and barked until Ming suddenly yelped and backed away from the tree trunk. The smell grew far worse; Lala said, "I think we'd better not try anymore." And after a futile attempt to dislodge the skunk, Harvey agreed.

But even though they walked away, the smell seemed to travel with them. Ming kept sneezing and trying to paw his eyes.

"I think the skunk must've sprayed him," Harvey said.

Rosita wouldn't even let them into the kitchen.

"Ay, *niña* Meryl—what have you all been doing... ?"

It took weeks to get the smell out of all Meryl's clothes; her shoes smelled of skunk right up to the moment she grew out of them and gave them away. Everything had to be washed specially, including all the children and the two dogs. Ming got special drops in his eyes, and neither dog was allowed into the main room for days. Tim Casey reported his children and Raul had been scrubbed again on returning to La Chata, and everyone was made to promise never, never to try catching a skunk again.

With time, the incident turned into a humorous anecdote, and Raul's phrase of hearing a smell entered the lexicon of *estancia* lore.

However, not all animal incidents were funny.

"Ming's beginning to show his age," Yvonne said, noting the dog's white-frosted muzzle and increasingly rheumy eyes.

"They both are," said Edie. "Taitai's getting grumpier by the day. But then, they're very old doggies, aren't you, my precious ones?"

The plumed tails thumped the floor in appreciation. Yvonne rose, announcing her intention to take them for a walk.

"Yes, do. It's about time they had a run, and I didn't go out with them this morning because of the rain."

341

Choosing a favorite path across the garden and through the orchard, Yvonne walked briskly, enjoying the rain-washed air and wondering whether Philipe had returned and whether she herself should go back to B.A. soon. Busy with her thoughts, she nonetheless realized only one dog was at her heels; she saw Taitai sitting down several yards further back.

"Come along, Taitai, walkies. . . ."

But all Taitai did was wag her tail. Yvonne returned and picked her up, the move greeted with a flurry of grateful tail motion.

"All right, I'll carry you. . . ."

Ming, still in the lead, trotted back and forth across Yvonne's path, disappearing behind clumps of high grasses, reappearing again on the other side. He stopped to sniff at a fence post, then slipped under the wiring and ran into the field Yvonne opened the nearby gate and followed; she would go as far as the *ombú*, and then turn home.

Ming stopped in the path ahead of her, inspecting yet another clump of grass. Yvonne adjusted Taitai more comfortably under her arm, glanced at Ming and then gasped. Between her and the elderly Pekingese, a coil of patterned black and gray was straightening out into a silent, moving line. For one brief but everlasting second, she stared at the snake approaching the dog. Then she reacted.

A dash, Taitai grabbed to her side, a swoop with hand outstretched, and a final swing with her fingers scraping against the ground and clamping onto the snake's tail. A moment later she had it high above her head, the whirling motion of her arm keeping the snake wheeling as the radius of an invisible circle in the air. Round and round it went, the motion constant and frantic. Taitai struggled under her arm; Yvonne hugged her closer, her hold awkward but tight, her attention darting desperately between the wriggling Pekingese and the sinewy creature in the grip of her fingers. She could feel the snake's convulsive contractions and tried to tighten her grip. But the all-important movement, she knew, was to keep it whirling as fast as she could so that the force of its whirling made it unable to double back on the hand that held it.

Yvonne looked around for help, but none was there. The flat field held only *pampas* grass and the lone *ombú*, the tree farther away than the gate and the fence posts. They were her only hope. Arm beginning to ache, muscles straining, she turned and began making her way back.

"Ming... Ming... come along, Ming, there's a good boy..." she called out to the distant Pekingese.

Her arm was starting to burn like fire, and she could hardly feel her fingers at all. Yvonne knew she still had the snake in her grasp only because it had not fallen anywhere, and she could sense it rather than actually see it, but the pounding of her heart and her gasping breath, both fueled by action and fear, prevented her from being aware of any more detailed sensation of the snake. She knew she could release it with a final burst of force and hope that it would land far from her or Ming; but what if her fingers were to slip at the wrong moment?

She could try dashing its head against the ground...

Again, she knew the hazard to be too great. Suppose she did not stun the poisonous creature with the first blow, suppose the snake looped back against her arm...

She tried to whirl her arm faster. Her only hope was to reach the gate or one of the fence posts; but the gate offered more hard wooden surfaces to dash the snake's head repeatedly against. The glancing blows would stun it eventually, and meanwhile she would have to keep it whirling.

Just before she came within reach of the gate post, she saw something fly from the front of the snake, through the air and onto the ground in front of her. A step closer, and she saw it to be the remains of a large frog, perhaps a toad. The skin was gone, but the lower half of the body and the legs were clearly articulated and visible. It was all pale pink, delicate flesh exposed.

The snake's recent meal.

She reached the gate. Leaning forward, she swung the snake lower and felt its muscles recoil and then go slack the first time she slammed it across the post, above the wire. Taking no chances, Yvonne wacked its head against the wood again and again with quicker, shorter circles. The body relaxed, then became limp. Again Yvonne slammed it. But by then even she knew that everything was over.

Later, she was told of the belief that a snake's heartbeat does not stop until sundown of the day on which it is killed. The *yarará* was a full adult, over three feet long, and one of the *peones* got the task of skinning it and hanging up the patterned cylinder in the saddle room to dry.

Edie sat down at the *estancia* desk and placed the rumpled letter before her. It had arrived a week earlier, and she had waited to open it until she had been on her own. Vesey's uneven handwriting jagged all over the cheap, thin paper; he had heard of Maurice's death from a business acquaintance here in Barcelona, he wrote... knew Edie would help him now as Maurice always had. Bad luck had been dogging him; a Spanish scheme had failed him. He was planning to come home again... after all, Argentina was his native land, just as it was Edie's. He counted on her support... passage money was needed... he looked forward to seeing her...

Edie had taken the noon train to Rosario the very next day.

Now her hand struck out with its pen onto the paper, the official *estancia* stationery with the branding emblem embossed. Her few lines were short and terse, immediately to the point.

I have spoken to the authorities, she wrote in bold, clear writing. *They tell me your case is still open in the records. Should you ever return here, they will immediately begin following up on all the facts known. No closing of the dossier is envisaged for the future.*

In her second, closing paragraph, Edie went a step further, making it clear that his extradition would be considered should anyone decide to apply pressure on the case.

As she sealed the letter's envelope and wrote the address firmly, Edie knew, with deep conviction, she would never in her life hear from Vesey O'Connor again.

Edie's half-century having been spent on the *estancia* and marked by a quiet family gathering, it was decided that Yvonne's thirtieth birthday would be celebrated in B.A.

"I'll come down a week earlier, and do some shopping, and visit Dollie, and perhaps get some clothes..." Edie, emerging from the first isolated depths of her bereavement and aware of the several pounds she had shed, was looking forward to her first trip to the capital since Maurice's death almost a year before.

"It's just like Mummy to come down and hog the limelight," Yvonne said to Philipe. "After all, it's *my* birthday...."

"I don't think that's her intention, you know. She seems to want to give you a party..."

"Of course. At the hotel. Where everyone knows *her.* And with all *her* friends..."

Philipe did not deny Yvonne's points, merely adding, "And your friends, too. She told me to get hold of them....

Yvonne gave an exasperated sigh.

"Mummy's always right, you're always right, everybody's always right... except me. But you wait and see how the party turns out."

The party turned out to be canceled.

A few days after Edie had arrived in Buenos Aires, she was woken one morning by a telephone call.

"Kevin! What a surprise! No, that's all right.... I wanted to get up early anyway.... Had I heard what...? No.... Oh...oh...how *frightful*...no...of course...yes, you'd better come over right away..."

She placed a call to the *estancia*. By the time Kevin Casey arrived, she was dressed and had alerted Yvonne to the terrible news. Estellita and Anita Casey had been drowned the previous day, and Tim Casey, berserk with grief, had smashed up rooms at La Chata and was now nowhere to be found.

"Of course we'll have to go back.... My son-in-law will help us...."

Philipe was at the hotel within the hour.

"Yvonne's gone straight to Retiro to get the tickets. I told her we'd met her on the platform by the morning train...."

Bit by bit, the known facts of the tragedy were pieced together, forming an incomplete picture of the events and with conflicting accounts blurring much of it. Estellita Casey had taken the two small children, Anita and Raul, to play near the river some time during the fatal afternoon; at some point, Raul had returned to the servants' quarters on his own.

Why had he come back?

"The *señora* told me to," was the only answer the child would give.

"Probably sent him packing for behaving badly," offered Harvey, who had been riding with the *peones* at the time.

Raul denied this hotly; everyone watched the five-year-old boy struggle with his tears. The cook said, "My nephew's too small to understand.... We are all too upset..." and the authorities agreed. Harvey, older and therefore more reliable, was questioned more closely.

"I was riding all afternoon. Ask any of the *peones*. My father? At lunch, he had said he was going to the *pueblo*..."

Witnesses in the small village testified for Tim Casey who, haggard with shock and grief and the aftereffects of the

345

alcohol-soaked rampage he had burst into after the drownings, had been found in one of the *estancia* barns shortly after his brother and Edie O'Connor had arrived at La Chata to offer what succor and assistance they could.

The authorities continued compiling what information they were able to obtain, and forming their official opinion of the probable events.

". . . and because of the recent heavy rains, the currents in the river have been known to be stronger lately . . . it would seem most likely that the child, paddling in the rain-swollen river, lost her footing and was swept downstream . . . and that the mother, in her efforts to save her little daughter, also lost her life in the deeper waters further on. . . ."

The alarm had first been raised when Mrs. Casey and Anita failed to return to the house by nightfall; at dawn the next day, it was a *gaucho* on a neighboring *estancia* who sighted the bodies as he rode along the river's bank. Bruises and lacerations found on the corpses were proof of the river's brutal rush over the rocks and stones in its path, and it had been the sight of his dead wife and child that had sent Tim Casey into his uncontrolled rampage.

The funeral was simple, the cortege short, the words spoken at the double gravesite brief and moving. Harvey stood next to his father, frowning and looking down at his shoes; Raul, clinging to the cook's hand, stared at the coffin bearing his little companion into the forgotten depths of the ground. Edie, standing across from them with Rosita next to her, had a sudden flash memory of Little Brother and Baby Maude, and then the priest's words rolled over the past and brought her into the present again, and she glanced over to Maurice's grave on the far side of the camp cemetery.

For the second year in a row, the holiday spirit of Christmas and the new year were dampened by the sorrow of recent death. At El Ombú, another life dear to Edie drew to its natural close, as Ming slipped away at night in his sleep, leaving only Taitai to walk slowly at Edie's heels.

In February, a long letter arrived from Madge Petersen, its Washington postmark a surprise—Edie had thought her friends back in Cannes—its contents full of gossip and a tempting suggestion; that Edie travel to the States and join the Petersens and Margot Grant in a motor tour of the whole country.

Luther finally died last year—good riddance, I say—and poor Margot had a heck of a time clearing up the details. He kicked the bucket at his floozie's dump in Paris, so you can just imagine the problems and legalities involved, what with the Frogs on one side, the embassy officials on the other, Luther on ice in the morgue and Margot in the middle of it all. But she's okay now, and we figure a trip around the good old U.S.A. would do us all good. How about it, kid? Will you join us?

Edie took the letter with her on her next trip to B.A. and showed it to Yvonne the first day she arrived.

"Shall I order tea, darling, or would you rather wait for drinks?" Edie moved around the hotel suite as Yvonne leafed through the thin airmail pages.

"What? Oh—tea, I think, Mummy, Philipe said he'd come by later and take us to dinner, but he'll probably be late." She went back to reading the letter.

They discussed the plan as they drank their tea.

"I think it'd be great fun, and I'd love to see America. . . ."

"When d'you intend going?"

I'd have to sail in May, I suppose. . . . Madge says they want to start the motor trip in June, when the weather's nice . . . start in New York . . . over to California . . . perhaps sail to Hawaii . . ."

"That means you'd be away a good four or five months." Edie nodded. "At least."

"And what about the *estancia*?"

Edie smiled ingenuously at her daughter.

"I'm counting on you to run it for me."

4

Edie sailed for North America during the month of May Yvonne and Philipe, returning to their apartment after seeing her off, discussed their own plans.

"She'll be back here by October, and then you can begin planning your London trip," said Philipe. "You could spend Christmas with the aunts, go to La Maison afterwards . . ."

"And I must make sure everything's set for Meryl at Crestwood Close. . . ."

Meryl would be going to England to begin attending the English boarding school after her ninth birthday, still a couple of years away. But, as Yvonne insisted, one never knew: she might have to catch up on some of the subjects, although, under the private tutelage she was receiving, the child appeared to be holding her own.

"Of course, there are going to be all these months now..."

Meryl was to accompany her mother to the *estancia* in a few days' time, and they would be staying at El Ombú until Edie's return.

"...but Tim Casey's got a teacher for Harvey, so perhaps they can share lessons. I'm sure something can be worked out. When are you coming back, Philipe?"

Philipe looked at his watch.

"In time for dinner, Late dinner."

No, I didn't mean that. I meant from your trip to Brazil."

He shook his head slowly. "I haven't the foggiest idea, Yvonne, I'm sorry, but I can't tell until I get there, how long it's going to take me to unravel the miss...."

And as he went downstairs again and took a taxi to his office, he reflected on the double-layered truth of his statement, thinking of the complicated contacts he made. Would it be easier if he could speak frankly about it? A moment's thought made him decide it would not, in any way, gathering information was a solitary man's game.

June 8: Arrived in New York at midnight, Edie wrote in her diary. *Madge and Wilbur to meet me. Went to supper. Bed at 3 a.m. June 12: Motored all over Long Island. Lunched at Jones Beach. Margot arrived in evening. June 13: Left jewels and valuables in safe deposit box at bank. Left New York. Lunched at drugstore in Sommerville. Stayed night at Lee Meade Inn, Gettysburg.*

By the end of the month, the motoring party of four was in Texas. Events, sights, incidents, and scenery crowded Edie's thoughts. They drove so far, saw so much, and took in so many impressions all the time that she felt her days were a kaleidoscopic-blur, their contents in need of sorting out each night when she noted down the journey's salient features, in the special diary she was keeping of her American stay.

Its notations were dry, factual, and numberical rather than

348

emotional or descriptive in tone. But for Edie, they served as signposts along the way, the traveling echoes of the *estanica* entries she had logged in El Ombú's records for so many years.

It will help me tell you all about my trip when I get back, she wrote to Yvonne.

It also allowed her precious moments of privacy every day. Madge's constant chattering could get on one's nerves, and Margot, although as sweet as ever, wasn't much in the way of brains. Edie could see why Luther had preferred his floozie, scandalous as it had been.

And as for Wilbur Petersen, he really was getting to be a windy old bore. She wondered, sometimes, how Madge could put up with him.

Perhaps, Edie reflected, she doesn't hear half he says... and I don't think he's listening to her most of the time, either.

Not that any of it mattered. And the general enjoyment of the trip covered a multitude of truths.

We went over the river to Juarez, Edie continued writing to Yvonne. *It was nice to hear Spanish again, but it sounds very different from ours. The waiters asked me about B.A. and were really very friendly. I think Madge was rather annoyed; must have put her nose out of joint....*

Yvonne, who had spent the morning seated at the *estancia* desk writing letters, finished the one to her mother and addressed the envelope, leaving it open so that Meryl could add to it. The girls were in the playroom adjoining Meryl's bedroom. Yvonne rose and called through the series of connecting doors.

"Meryl! Is your letter ready?"

"Coming...."

Outside, the chill rain of winter was dripping off leaves, slithering down bare branches, running off the sloped verandah roof, soaking the garden and the fields beyond.

A scrambling sound of chairs preceded the appearance of Meryl and Lala. They were both the same height, despite Lala's year and half advantage, and both were light-boned, but there the resemblance ended. The *criada's* eyes were hauntingly dark, fringed with thick lashes, and her black hair glistened and waved. Meryl's pale eyes were hazel, green shaded and flecked with darker points, and her lashes, long but somewhat sparse, matched her arrow-straight, mouse-brown hair. Her bone structure was finer than Lala's.

She's going to have Philipe's nose, Yvonne thought.

"Lala and I wrote together." Meryl handed over the letter.

"How nice. When are you going over to La Chata for your lessons?"

"Not till tomorrow," was the reply. "Uncle Tim took everyone to Rosario yesterday. . . ."

Lessons at the Casey *estancia* were always irregular, but the system was better than nothing.

. . . and after all, my schooling was decidedly spotty until I went home to Crestwood Close, so I'm sure Meryl will do splendidly once she gets there. . . .

Edie had not commented on the subject in her return letters; Philipe, answering from Santos in Brazil, had only raised a peripheral point.

Whereas I agree Meryl is likely to do well at your old school, there is no need to limit the choice to Crestwood Close. If, for any reason, it does not suit her, or if circumstances change, we can always consider schools in the U.S.

Yvonne did not bother to reply to his remarks, skipping to his mention of his probable return date and suggesting he plan to take a short holiday so as to spend time with her and Meryl on the *estancia*.

For now her own travel plans were beginning to take shape; Yvonne had made up her mind that she and Philipe would go to England after Edie returned from America. After all, she was doing a good job of running her mother's affairs while she was gone. It would only be fair for them to enjoy a holiday, too, when Edie came back from hers. It had been such a long time since Yvonne had traveled anywhere by choice. She could not remember any such event since her honeymoon with Joss ten long years ago. . . . No, it simply hadn't been fair, all these years, and when Edie came back, Yvonne would see to it that she and Philipe got their due.

In the meantime, life at the *estancia* was at least reasonably interesting, and the saving grace, even on the worst of days, was the riding she was able to enjoy.

Sealing the letter to Edie, she decided to drive into the

pueblo herself with the day's mail and the list of needed supplies. She could be back in plenty of time to enjoy an evening ride across the fields.

Edie continued to record the details of her trip.

...motored through the Painted Desert (rather disappointed in it) and the Petrified Forest...Hopi settlements...trading post...got turquoise earrings...stuck in sand with car twice (Wilbur is a rotten driver)...Navajo indians in Mexican clothes tried to hold us up...suspected bandits.

July 2: Grand Canyon. Got up v. early and went off with Wilbur on the trail. Very good mules. Rode for 9 hours, descended 4,500 feet and rode 6 miles each way. July 3: Bryce Canyon. Marvelous concert, then community singing over a fire in the Park. Lovely moon. Very cold. State of Utah. Heard "God Save the King" sung in American! July 5: Arrived in Nevada State where we can get anything, even a divorce at Reno. Stayed in Las Vegas. Went to the gambling pubs and had a grand spree. July 6: Left Las Vegas in the morning. Very hot; had dry ice in the car. Arrived in Los Angeles. Letter waiting from Yvonne, saying Taitai died.

It was San Francisco, however, that captured Edie's interest, much fueled by her anticipation of the sea voyage ahead.

Sailed in late afternoon...not impressed by Golden Gate...lots of drunks on board and one had to be stitched up...calm voyage...a Clipper flew right over us, saw green and red light distinctly. Quite a thrill...deck sports most amusing, turtles racing, and shaving race for men. Great fun...bingo at night, and dancing...met a Frenchman from Cannes...such a refreshing change...Margot quite put out when he took me in to dinner...arrived in Honolulu and all passengers decorated with leis as Hawaiian orchestra played songs of welcome.

"Mummy's been having a marvelous time," remarked Yvonne, gesturing to the pile of letters in front of her. "I thought you might like to read some of these."

Philipe, having arrived at El Ombú the evening before was still in his dressing gown and sleepy at the breakfast table. He yawned and poured himself another cup of coffee.

351

"You can tell me about 'em. Or I'll read some of 'em later." He sipped appreciatively from the steaming cup. "Right now, what I need to do is wake up."

Yvonne was already leafing through some of the airmail sheets.

"She's been going to a lot of parties. I gather there's been an admirer or two on the way."

"It wouldn't surprise me."

"And they're going to see all the sights there are to be seen. Here: she says, *We drove to see the Japs' favorite suicide cliff, after which we went to a luau, which is rather like an asado, except that it's pig instead of cow, and they put hot lava stones inside the carcass*. Oh, I'd love to go to Hawaii, wouldn't you?"

"I've been."

"Years ago, when I was a youngster."

"I see." Yvonne bit her lip, shot a quick glance at her husband and decided that she might as well broach the subject on her mind. "Philipe, thinking about traveling—I think we'd better go to England after Mummy gets back."

Philipe put down his cup.

"What on earth makes you think that?"

"Well, for one thing, I need a holiday. And so do you. And before, every time we planned to go back to London, something always happened. But now—now we'll have the time. And there's all my stuff still sitting in storage, and the things I left at La Maison, and . . ."

"Yes, I know all that, but I'm afraid it's out of the question. I can't possibly go now." Then, raising his cup again, he added, "Perhaps after Christmas . . . early next year sometime . . ."

Yvonne's mouth was tightening.

"No, We're always putting it off. I want to go *this* year. As soon as Mummy returns."

He shook his head. "I'm sorry, Yvonne. I absolutely cannot go now. I have to stay in B.A. for at least the next six months."

"Then I'll simply have to go alone."

For a brief moment, they looked at each other, their eyes unmoving, gazing each other down. Then Philipe gave a slight shrug.

"As you wish. What about Meryl?"

Yvonne gathered up her mother's letters and pushed her chair back from the dining room table.

"Since you say you have to stay here anyway, I'll leave her

with you. That way, I'll be freer to get around, and it'll be easier to get things done. Since I've got to do it all alone.

After lunch, it was decided all three van Landens would go riding.

"Lovely. I'll send word to the *capataz* to bring up the horses—and while I'm at it, I'd better tell Rosita about getting more supplies..."

Yvonne disappeared through the door on her way to the *despensa* and the kitchen. Philipe smiled at his daughter.

I'm looking forward to seeing you on a horse," he remarked. "How's your riding?"

Meryl shrugged, her gesture imitative of her father's. "It's all right, I suppose."

"Not too keen, eh?"

Another shrug, and she avoided looking at his eyes.

"I see," Philipe tried another tack. "How about your studies?" How're the lessons getting on? Is that tutor—I forget his name—the one at the Caseys' place—is he any good?"

"Didn't Mother tell you?"

"Tell me what?"

"That we're not having any more lessons over there, Lala and me. There's going to be no more going over to La Chata."

"Oh?"

"It's because of what Harvey did to the cats. There were lots of them in the barns where the *huachos* are kept.... Well, there still are but..."

What happened?"

"Harvey caught some of the kittens, and put them in a sack. Then he took the cart and drove it over and over the sack until the kittens were all dead and squashy and..."

"... and I told that rotten little bastard he was never, *never* to show his face in front of me again." Yvonne's eyes blazed remembered anger as she came back into the room. "I've given orders he's not to set foot on the *estancia* while I'm here."

"Quite right."

Meryl said, "The sad part is that now Raul can't come over, either. Lala misses him, I know, and I'm sure he misses us, too."

"Well, it can't be helped, Meryl. I'm going to have that brutal lout here simply because a *criada* and a cook's nephew want to play together."

"I'm sure Meryl doesn't like Harvey, either," Philipe interposed.

"No, I don't. He's a bully. And he's always pestering."

"Then why didn't you tell me?" Yvonne demanded.

"He never pestered me, Mother. Only Lala."

"Well, he won't be pestering anybody here at El Ombú anymore." And with that, Yvonne closed the subject. "Now—how about getting ready? The horses'll be up as soon as they get them saddled. . . ."

Edie, the Petersens, and Margot Grant returned to San Francisco from their trip to Hawaii. They headed north, driving into Canada and staying in Vancouver, where Edie went on a buying spree, indulging in some fox furs and triggering yet another marital spat between the Petersens that lasted all the way to Lake Louise. After that, they calmed down, and by the time Minneapolis was reached Madge was fully in charge again, seeking out her longtime interest and finding a palmist.

"No, darn it, she didn't say I'd get married again, but she did say I should be thankful . . ."

"What did she tell you, Edie?"

"That November would be eventful."

"Remember that day in Cannes, girls? She was the best I've ever known. . . ."

The trip drew to a close down through New York State; then the city itself was reached, Edie's last week in the U.S.A.

New York again, and glad to be here . . . shopping . . . Macy's . . . bank for money and jewels out of safe deposit . . .

August 3: Went to ship by car directly from hotel. Joined by Madge and Wilbur, Margot and their friends. Consumed a magnum of champagne in cabin. All very mad. Boat left at midday. Sat at doctor's table for lunch, was moved to captain's table by dinner. Marvelous fun; made great headway in acquainting myself with passengers. All men. Bed at midnight.

Edie got back to B.A. at the end of August, refreshed, full of energy, enthusiastic about the continent she had just seen, physically trimmer, and loaded with presents for everyone. Moccasins for Meryl were an instant success, as was a grass skirt from Hawaii. The van Landens, who had traveled down

354

from the *estancia* to B.A. to meet Edie, filled her in on all the latest developments at El Ombú.

When all news had been exchanged, Yvonne told her mother she was leaving for England.

"How nice, darling. When?"

"In November. Alone."

"Alone? But I thought you'd always planned to go back to London with Philipe...."

Yvonne explained. Edie frowned.

"Don't you think you'd be more sensible to wait, darling? After all, only a few months more..."

Yvonne's mouth set.

"No. Every time I wait, something happens and then the trip is off. This time, I'm going."

Edie sighed. "I really don't see why you're always so stubborn. You'd have a much better time if you went together...."

Yvonne shook her head. "No, Mummy. I've made up my mind. And Philipe understands. Anyway, we've decided on how we're going to arrange it. About Meryl, I mean. She's staying here with Philipe, of course, but perhaps it'd be nice for her to spend time on the *estancia*, too...."

Yvonne sailed for England toward the end of November; she arrived in time for Christmas, which she spent with the aunts. Her letters were long and enthusiastic; London was more marvelous than ever.

...and you'll never guess who's here: Lally! Isn't that an amazing coincidence? She came back last year, and is getting a divorce from the man she married out in Singapore. An awful rotter, according to everyone, and she's lucky to be out of it, but the actual divorce is likely to take ages....

In Buenos Aires, the sun beat down with the heat waves of high summer; Meryl and her father visited the *estancia*, but returned to the city after a two-week stay. Meryl appeared to enjoy her city style of living.

"The child'll get terribly spoiled, mark my words," was the opinion of Robert Thaxter, but his advice to Philipe went unheeded; was, indeed, ignored.

In the new year, Yvonne's letters came from Cannes; La Maison was in perfect condition, Coco was as splendid as ever.

...and he's picked up some more bad language from somewhere. I suspect Yves has been priming him through the years....

She was packing up her things, and shipping them to London.

There, everything will be put together in the crate and sent out to B.A.

In March, she wrote to Philipe she was delaying her return journey.

I'm having such a wonderful time here....Went to Crestwood Close the other day ... met my old school chums ...am spending next weekend with Lally at a friend's country place ...everyone being so kind ...Anthea's invited me for a weekend down in Devon, I was at school with her ...so enjoying it all, I'm sure you and Meryl won't mind ...

It was Philipe who organized a party for Meryl's birthday; Yvonne, still in England, sent her birthday telegram. Another month went by. England's summer was Argentina's mid-winter, and Philipe, scanning the headlines, felt chilled to the bone.

More letters arrived from Yvonne, one for him and one for Meryl. She had again postponed her passage. Across the breakfast table from him, Meryl was decapitating her second boiled egg. Philipe watched her for a moment before breaking the silence.

Then he said, "You know, your mother once told me that her grandmother Millicent had a saying about 'It's all so far away, perhaps it isn't true.' The great-aunts say their sister said it whenever news of a disaster was heard. Well, I think perhaps Yvonne is very like Millicent in some ways."

"Why?" Meryl looked up from her egg-laden spoon. "What's happened? All Mother tells me in her letter is that she's not coming back till October or November. She doesn't say anything went wrong."

"It isn't exactly what's happened ... yet. It's what's going to happen. And your mother, who is right there, apparently refuses to believe it. Or even see it."

He picked up the newspaper again, reading the front page with a frown. In mid-1939, all news made him frown.

356

VII

La Criada
1939–1947

1

In her first letter to Philipe after war had been declared,
Yvonne explained her decision to stay.

*I belong here, I can help—and it probably won't last very
long anyway....*

She enclosed a letter for Meryl, who received it, along
with the news that her mother would not be coming back
right away, in expressionless silence. Philipe watched her as
she stood, holding the sheet of notepaper in her hand without
looking at it.

"Aren't you going to read it?"

"I think I'd rather read it later, Daddy, in my room,
when I'm alone."

He did not press her further, not knowing what to say and
feeling hollow in the silence that closed in between them.

Edie came straight down to Buenos Aires the moment she
heard the news.

"She's going to live with the great-aunts," Philipe explained
to his mother-in-law.

"I think she's totally irresponsible," Edie declared. "Her
place is here, with you and the child, not lounging about
London pretending it's in aid of the war effort."

"That's not quite ... well, what I mean is, Yvonne's reasons
are perfectly valid in their own way, you know," Philipe
mollified. "She says she feels Meryl is fine here with me—
which she is, I hope—and that you, too, will see to it
that ..."

"You sound just like Maurice," Edie interrupted. "He
always defended her. Of course I'll have Meryl at the *estancia*
whenever you like."

Privately, Philipe did not entirely agree with Yvonne's
dramatic decision, but he did understand it; probably better,
he reflected, than Yvonne did herself. It was the perfect

opportunity for her to demonstrate her passion for the country she valued most highly. She was, he knew, seeking acceptance from England, praise from it, absolution. And all this, despite not having been born there. Or because of it.

He sighed, and turned his attention to the tasks at his own hand: he would have to rearrange matters here at home. For one thing, Meryl would have to be enrolled in school; there was now no question of her going to Crestwood Close. And Madame Benoit's duties would have to change; either that, or she would have to find another job. The van Landen household would need a fulltime housekeeper to run it and the servants, not a French governess who occasionally helped out.

And so Philipe van Landen wrote back to his wife and outlined his own plans for the months immediately ahead.

I shall to go your old school tomorrow and talk to the headmistress about Meryl's scholastic future. Your mother agrees it's the best school in B.A., and Meryl should have no difficulty at all with the work involved. If she does, I shall of course have her coached privately until she catches up with whatever class they put her into, but something tells me our daughter will do okay for herself. As for the holidays, I shall send her to the estancia; my own schedule calls for more traveling, I'm afraid. In connection with all this, Madame Benoit has agreed to turn into a fulltime housekeeper; I personally think that she is more suited to that sort of work, and it will be a form of continuity here at home.

And so Meryl began attending the school where her mother had been a pupil years before. The original Miss Bowen had died, and the establishment's name had been shortened and updated to Bowen Day School. Its general standards of education and principles of comportment were unchanged; its premises, however, had both enlarged and evolved. The school, with several new buildings and a complex of game courts and playing fields, now extended over two full city blocks, and the neighborhood surrounding it was completely built up. Other than the school's sports grounds, there were no open fields to be seen anywhere anymore; neat houses and walled or hedged gardens surrounded the academy.

The school was now bilingual, as was required by law. A full curriculum was taught both in English and in Spanish.

Scholastically, Meryl had no problem fitting in.

"Imagine," she told Madame, "the French mademoiselle spent the whole class on *je suis, tu es, il est*. It's baby stuff." She started singing.

> "*Je suis*, I am a pot of jam
> *Tu est*, you are a fool
> *Il est*, he is the biggest ass
> That ever went to school..."

"*Meryl!*" Madame was scandalized. "That's not at all nice, *chère*.... I cannot imagine where you pick up such things...."

"At school, of course...."

"*Meryl!*"

Fitting in socially was another matter.

For the first time in her life, Meryl became one among several hundred, a child in a school uniform with a badge on her blazer pocket identifying her as a Bowen girl. It was also her first encounter with the concept of team spirit, an attitude that puzzled her.

Conversely, she also found herself in a spotlighted position as the only pupil whose mother was in England, actively engaged in the war.

Girls and teachers alike seemed unable to understand it.

"But isn't she coming back?"

"... very brave of her, of course, but still..."

"I told my mother about yours being in England, and my mother says..."

What other girls' mothers had said inevitably echoed what Grannie had already said on repeated occasions.

"... selfish nonsense..."

"... wife's place is in the... mother's place is with..."

"... taking advantage of... simply showing off..."

Meryl soon found that trying to defend her mother only made things worse. It was quite all right for fathers to have gone home to England to join the war; in fact, it was heroic. The young unmarried volunteers who went were highly applauded, too. But for mothers, it was unheard of, except in Yvonne's case, and considered all wrong. In fact, Meryl's family was all wrong, although of course her father wasn't English, so it wasn't quite so serious. America wasn't in the war. Besides, Philipe van Landen was away again, having gone to New York on a business conference as usual.

This left Meryl to grapple with the social ghosts of her unsatisfactory parents all on her own, and because of it she discovered the magic of saying "I don't know" to the difficult, often unanswerable questions. It became a refuge, a curtain of protection she could pull down between herself and the questioning world. Sometimes, when permissible, she indulged in the hostility of a silent stare, keeping a fixed gaze on her questioner until discomfort developed, as it inevitably did.

Sympathy made her feel uncomfortable.

"You poor little thing... all on your own... well, at least your *father*'ll be back soon...."

Actually, Meryl considered herself to be quite comfortable and content, with Madame and the maids to look after her at home, and the pleasant prospect of the *estancia* for the summer holidays directly ahead. At least Madame Benoit was French, and therefore an acceptable Ally; one of her schoolmates had had a German governess for years, until the day she had mentioned at school that "*Fraulein* has a picture of dear Adolf on the wall of her room." Her parents had been summoned to a hasty conference; the choice was a change of school or a change of employee. It was decided the latter was the better part of valor and tact, and the ripple of feeling was allowed to die down, but not before the story had made the British community rounds, and its content remembered for the annals of local lore.

As Meryl's life changed with her first term at school, so the world adjusted to its first months of war. In Buenos Aires, the British community set up committees and watched and wondered and worried about "home"; volunteers signed up and sweaters were knitted and memories of a past war were suddenly revived.

But it was still far off for most of the people, a war being fought far across the sea. And then, in December, two weeks before Christmas, it burst into life and flame and blazing gun battle right on the doorstep, slightly north of B.A. up the coast of Uruguay.

A German pocket battleship, the Graf Spee, a killer ship with nine ships sunk on its score, was chased and cornered by a trio of British cruisers. In the encounter that followed, heavy damage was suffered on both sides, and the German ship, unable to get away, had to make for the nearest port to try and effect repairs. The crew got the ship into Montevideo harbor.

The Uruguayan capital, hostile to the German cause, gave the battleship's captain a set time to leave. Rumors on both sides of the River Plate flew thick and fast and furious, while beyond the three-mile limit, the British ships waited.

Four days after the drama had begun, it ended just as dramatically. After telephonic communication directly with Berlin, the battleship's commander took his ship out and scuttled her, returning to the shore only to take his own life.

Their prey sunk the British cruisers limped to harbor and safety; they docked at Buenos Aires for extensive repairs. The British community went wild: their war, their ships, their heroes, victorious. It was the first big win of the war, and it had happened here. . . .

Official receptions, gala parties, homey teas and dinners, cricket at every pitch; for the ships' crews, it was a pause in the bloody business of warfare, but for the English-speaking denizens of the Argentine it was a time of triumph.

Argentina itself, technically neutral, kept citizens of all kinds and creeds in uneasy proximity under its blue and white flag, the official sun emblazoned and shining down on all sides alike. And if there were murmurs and mutterings, they were kept behind closed doors; the government of the country stood aloof from the war.

Philipe, arriving home for Christmas, found his daughter untouched by all the excitement and grappling with a problem of her own.

"I can't draw," she complained.

"Neither can I," Philipe admitted. "Don't let it worry you; lots of people can't. Why? They weren't difficult about it at school, were they?"

Meryl shook her head. "It's not that."

"Then there's nothing to get upset about, is there?"

"But you don't *understand* Daddy." She was close to tears. "I can *see* what it should look like, but when I try to do it, it won't come out that way. And I *want* it to. . . ."

And she bent over her drawing book again, each attempt only ending in frustration and tears.

He got her a camera, and two rolls of film.

"If you can see the pictures you want, perhaps the camera will draw the lines for you. . . ."

It wasn't as simple as that, Meryl soon discovered. But she liked taking photographs; her pocket money went on film.

"Very pretty," said Madame, simpering over some early results. "And perhaps your father can get you the special paints to use for photos, so you can color them."

"Oh, *no*." Meryl was horrified.

"But why not?"

Because it would mess it up."

Not if you colored them carefully, *chèrie*."

"I don't mean that kind of mess—I mean mess the lines."

Madame remained puzzled; Meryl clammed up. How could she explain to Madame that the whole point of the photos was the shapes and the lines made by the blacks and the grays against the white?

When it came time for her to go and spend the rest of the summer on the *estancia*, Meryl packed her camera with care and bought all the film she could afford.

Although Philipe took Meryl up to the *estancia*, he only stayed a few days and then returned to B.A. There were too many trips, he explained, too much work piled up for him to do; he would come back and fetch her, he promised, shortly before school began.

But that would not be until March, almost two full months away. Meanwhile, the summer heat and holidays stretched out before her, and Meryl took up her life with Lala as before. The girls roamed the homestead grounds, sometimes going farther afield than strictly allowed to, but frequently getting away with it, as long as Rosita didn't tell.

"Rosita always knows everything," Meryl puzzled.

"It's because she looks closer than your grandmother ever does," the older girl explained.

Meryl regarded her friend with an oblique glance.

"You do too, don't you?"

"We have to, people like Rosita and me. . . ."

They rambled to the end of the mile-long driveway and climbed up the gates, hanging on the rails. When freight trains rattled by, they counted the boxcars, quarreling loudly when the numbers didn't tally.

"Fifty-eight. I'm *sure* it was fifty-eight. I *counted* them."

Meryl shook her head. "No, it wasn't. I counted them better than you. Sixty."

"You must've counted double when it was really one wagon."

"No, I didn't. It was sixty."

"No."

"Yes."

"No, no no!"

Meryl swung down from the gate and began jumping around in the summer grass at the edge of the driveway, shounting "Yes, yes *yes!*" in time to her leaps. Lala, still suspended on the railings, beat her fist against the wrought iron and shouted back, "no, no, *no!*" until she, too, leaped down to the ground and both became breathless with effort and laughter and turned their combined shouts into a marching cadence as the trains disappeared into the flat distance on its way to the far hills of Córdoba.

Halfway down the drive they broke into imitative canters, galloping back to the garden and making neighing sounds. When they reached the low wall, Lala said, "Let's go and play in the *galpón* after *siesta*."

"You think they'll let us?"

"If we don't tell them anything, they can't say no, can they?"

The *galpón*, a huge hangarlike storage building at the far end of the *estancia*'s interior road, well past the *peones*' quarters, had sliding metal doors that grated on iron runners. The oblong structure, with its soaring arc of corrugated roof, could be entered on three of its four sides, but only the door at the end stood partially open, and the two girls slipped through the aperture, waiting for a moment for their eyes to adjust from the glare of the early afternoon sun outside.

The streak of brightness slicing through the *galpón*'s gloom filled with upswirling eddies when they walked in; silken particles glittered in the sharp shaft of light, every movement causing their direction to change.

The atmosphere was thick with heat and silence and dust, soft, thick dust, inches deep on the dirt-packed floor, soft for shuffling through. Every footstep caused whirlpools of powder to billow, patterning the air in lazily moving streaks that were tinted in harmony with the mountains of grain sacks piled, fat, tight, and high, along one whole section of the vast structure's interior.

Work vehicles were parked at the far end, a clutter of spokes and wheels and machinery standing in jagged, dust-coated groupings.

"Let's explore over behind the sacks." Meryl's voice sounded amplified in the hollowness of the building. In contrast, their footsteps made no sound at all.

They scrambled up the ledges of grain sacks, their climb sending more dust into the air and frightening a small mouse away from their path of ascent. It also disturbed an owl in his daytime hideout on one of the high beams, and he flew away to another, further over, a flutter of indignation in the beating of his wings.

Reaching the top of the heap, the girls sat for a while, legs dangling over sacking, testing their voices, calling "Coo-ee" across the central emptiness, first softly, then louder, hearing their tones muffled if they called down, enhanced when they aimed up.

"Let's sing. It'll sound like the gramophone...."

"All right. You start."

"No—you go first."

And so Lala's voice began, softly at first, then joined by Meryl's.

"Caminante, no hay camino ..."

When the song's marching beat started, they began climbing down, reaching the ground and marching, singing louder and louder all the while until they were shouting and strutting through the clouds of dust and kicking at it, making it more dense with every step. They reached the door's opening and the song's closing line and ran out into the fierce sunlight. They tried brushing the powder off each other's clothes, their sweaty palms streaking everything they touched.

Rosita started scolding the moment she saw them.

"*Look* at you! Both of you! Where have you been?"

Meryl told her.

"And who told you that you could play in the *galpón*? Can you tell me that?" Rosita's voice rose.

"Nobody told us we couldn't," chipped in Lala, and Rosita, arms folded, glared at her personal charge. Then her stance relaxed, and Meryl knew they would get away with it.

"But don't let me catch you going there again...."

Later, Lala pointed out she still hadn't forbidden them to go there.

"But that's what she means...."

366

"Naturally. So it's up to us not to get caught."

Decidedly, Lala was a *viva*. A live one. A clever spark. Something Madame said was not nice. Not that she ever said it about Lala, because Lala was too *viva* for Madame to have caught her out. It was one of the signals of the big difference between parental grown-ups and friends like Lala. On the one side, for anyone to be *vivo* or *viva* was naughty or wrong or downright dishonest; on the other, it was an accepted method of survival within the way of life.

They were very much left to their own devices that summer, and apart from the occasional scolding, managed to enjoy their freedom well. Their swimming was still under supervision; either Edie or Rosita accompanied them during their twice-daily dips. At lunchtime, before the midday meal, it was usually Edie who, in a flowered bathing suit and matching robe, went down to the pool house with the girls and sat on the cement steps or on the wide ledge of the retaining wall, cooling herself off with a dip from the second-last step before returning to the house. In the late afternoon, Rosita stood by, holding the towels. But otherwise, Meryl and Lala roamed alone.

They were even allowed to go out and see the dynamiting of the gigantic anthills that had been formed in several of the grazing fields. The hills, bare earth moved and packed down by millions of ants over the years, stood shoulder-high to the average *gaucho*, and were now at a stage where their destruction was mandatory. The girls watched at a distance; the *peones* rammed sticks of dynamite into the base of the hills. Then the order was given, the fuse lit and all men moved away.

"Be careful, *niña*....Go further back...behind the fence..."

And shortly the resounding *whump*! would send the pieces of earth hurtling skyward, to return to earth scattered in a circle and leaving a crater where the hill had been.

"It was very interesting, Grannie," Meryl reported at dinner.

"Was it, darling? Good, I'm glad. There's always something interesting going on, on an *estancia*, don't you think?"

Gravely, Meryl agreed.

Not all interesting events got reported to Grannie.

Lala came into the playroom one afternoon and said,

"There's something going on behind the *huachos'* barn. Let's go and see what it is."

They crossed the back road and went through the grouping of *paraiso* trees. In the far field, the remnants of a tattered wind sock flapped against a pole, a ragged memory of past, fleeting glory. Near it stood a group of *gauchos*, their wide circle encompassing something hidden from the girls' view. A smaller group of women stood on one side. As Meryl and Lala approached, the murmur of voices began separating into clear phrases.

". . . leave them alone . . ."

"She always was a wild one . . ."

". . . step back . . . don't interfere . . ."

Meryl and Lala walked up without being noticed; all attention was focused on the events going on in the enclosed circle. The two girls edged closer until they could see.

Surrounded by the ring of *gauchos*, two women stood squared off at each other, less than six feet apart, their bodies taut in semicrouching postures, their torsos jutting forward, hands braced against their knees. Their brown bare feet shifted and flexed against the ground.

A man's voice said, "They look like cocks in the chicken run," and there was the harsh cadence of masculine laughter.

"Perhaps they should learn from the hens to be more docile. . . ."

"Well said. Hens know the rights of the male. . . ."

The glances cast by the group caused Meryl to look in their direction. She noticed the group watching one of the *peones*, standing on the far side of the circle to her, and a few paces away. His hat was pushed back off his head, hanging down his back by its strap around his throat; his arms were crossed, one hand resting against the hilt of the knife he wore, as did all *gauchos*, thrust through the coin-studded belt, flat against his stomach. He was the only one not joining in the murmured talk. All he did was watch the two women.

They began to circle.

As they moved, the differences between them began to show. One was markedly older than the other; her wary, steadfast gaze at her opponent was matched by her slow, surefooted movements. She edged closer to her rival, stood briefly still, then spat in her face.

The younger *chinita* recoiled, then recovered her stance and glanced briefly at the crowd, acknowledging it with a bravado smile. She was less sinewy, more round-fleshed and firm than her foe; her movements were not smooth, and yet an arrogance of carriage was still there.

Suddenly, the older woman sprang.

A second later, they were rolling on the ground, their furied shrieks tearing the brief hush of a moment before. Their cries were incoherent, raging; over and over they rolled, legs kicking, arms flailing, lashing out at each other with feet and fists in the tumbling frenzy of their fight. The spectators burst into excited comment.

"*Arriba!* Hit her again . . ."

"Look at her fight!"

"She's a tiger, the old one . . ."

". . . but the girl is fire . . ."

"Look out! She has a knife!"

The cry came from a woman at the edge of the watching ring; in an instant, the crowd converged on the warring two. Booted feet flashed out.

"Enough! Enough! *Basta* . . . you whores . . ."

The watching women rushed in and skirts joined the baggy *bombachas* in forming a curtain around the grappling *chinitas*. Meryl could no longer see what was going on. As she turned away she felt a grip bite into her shoulder.

"This is no place for you *niña* Meryl . . . and you, Lala, are a shameless one to bring her here. . . ."

The capataz stood sternly between them, a firm hold on each; still talking, he propelled them back toward the *paraiso* trees.

". . . . and you will go straight back to the house and behave as you are supposed to. . . . Only if you do as I say will I not tell the *Doña* Edie. . . . Not a word to anyone, and I won't speak either . . . but don't let me hear of you two hanging around stupidities like this again. . . ."

Shaken by the fight and by getting caught, Meryl was glad to reach the tall, thick woods behind the main *estancia* house. Lala was less perturbed; she had been intrigued by the fight.

"I wonder which one he loves the best?" she mused.

But Meryl would not be drawn into a discussion; her mind was on the *capataz* and whether he would keep his word.

"But of course." Lala was scornful. "If he tells, your grandmother'll be furious with *him*."

"With us, you mean."

"No, *him*. He's not supposed to allow fights like that on the *estancia*." Lala swung herself around a tree trunk; Meryl followed suit, relieved.

Late at night, lying in bed listening to the chorus of frogs backdropped by the hoot of a distant passing train, Meryl thought of Lala's understanding of life's logic that went beyond the precepts taught within the confines of Meryl's own world.

On a rainy day shortly before Meryl was to return to Buenos Aires for the beginning of the school year, she and Lala carved their initials into one of the legs of the dining room table. They took turns to gouge out the hard wood, deeper and deeper, using at first some embroidery scissors and afterwards, an old nail. The L was easier than the M.

"It's the middle bit... it doesn't meet properly yet...."

When Rosita caught them by surprise, she smacked Lala with a slap against her leg and later told Edie, who lectured Meryl and then forbade teatime *alfajores* for a week as punishment. But it was the last part of the summer holiday, Rosita soon relented, and the two girls giggled and washed all signs of crumbs away from their mouths before leaving the safe recesses of the kitchen and their clandestine tea.

2

Meryl got back to the apartment in Buenos Aires to find there was a new maid. She was young and pretty, and she sang as she dusted; the previous one, Meryl discovered, had been banished by Madame, who caught her drinking from the whiskey bottle and then refilling it with water.

Otherwise, there were few changes; Philipe, who had collected his daughter from the *estancia*, was busy with his office and likely to stay a while. School started, the weather turned cooler, the weekday pattern became regular and established. The school bus came by to pick Meryl up in the morning, depositing her back at the building in time for tea. She had her lunch at school, at a table with five other girls and a teacher in charge. Not everyone stayed to lunch; it was among the school's extras, as were piano lessons, which Meryl took, and Saturday riding class, which she did not.

Letters from Yvonne arrived sporadically; they were enthusiastic, brief outpourings of set phrases, containing little information. She was fine, the great-aunts were well, everyone sent their love. She was very busy, as indeed everyone was; she was also very glad to know Meryl was going to her old school and hoped she would do as well as Yvonne knew she could.

Dutifully, Meryl wrote letters back, feeling the distance between her and her mother to be greater than ever before.

I got ten out of ten in Arithmetic the other day. A girl was caught cheating, and so her book was torn up. Nélida, the new maid, is very nice. I taught her all our songs. I took a picture of Grannie on the estancia, but it chopped her head off, and you can see my shadow on the ground . . .

There being nowhere in the vicinity of El Ombú where she could get her rolls of film developed. Meryl's interest in her camera had waned during the summer, and by the time she came back to Buenos Aires, she had only taken one full roll of film, with a second still in the camera, partially exposed. But once she got the results, her enthusiasm was rekindled; if the photo of her grandmother was none too good, the one of Lala sitting on the top bar of a gate was satisfactory, while a shot of Sammy loose in the field had drawn praise from Philipe.

There was another photo of the pony, a close-up of Sammy's head. Philipe said, "I think you like taking snaps of him better than you like riding," and Meryl hadn't answered, but she knew it was true.

Philipe, who played golf, would take Meryl to the country club with him on weekends, where she sometimes followed him around the course, getting bored and impatient before he was halfway through, or else stayed near the clubhouse on the children's playground, getting bored and lonely before he arrived back. It was easier, Philipe discovered, for Meryl to invite a schoolfriend along with her; as the system evolved, a succession of friends accompanied them.

They were not the only ones to join the van Landens; a series of young women, sports-minded and eager for a game, began to play golf with Philipe from time to time. They became a variety of vague aunts, as far as Meryl was concerned; they came and they went; some came closer than

371

others, and were all part of the new shape of life. There were dinners at the apartment, six or eight seated at the table; Meryl would go in to say good evening while everyone was having cocktails, then take herself off to a kitchen supper with Madame.

Occasionally, the aunt of the moment would beg to have Meryl stay for a while, and then Meryl knew that, in a funny sort of way, it was the temporary aunt who wanted to stay on longer. Usually, whoever it was disappeared shortly thereafter.

School let out an hour early because of the national holiday being celebrated the next day. Meryl arrived home, her gym shoes stuffed into her brown leather school bag, next to her homework; they needed cleaning for the special marching parade to be held the following afternoon. She took the shoes out, left her bag on the vestibule table and pushed her way through the swing door into the kitchen section. It was Madame's afternoon off, so Meryl would have to tell Nélida herself about the shoes.

The servants' rooms were to the left of the pantry; Meryl saw that Nélida's door was slightly open, so she knocked on it and pushed it further ajar all in one movement.

A frantic scramble of sheets and bare legs and tousled heads divided into two separate forms, the one that was Nélida darting from the bed with a grabbed dressing gown held inadequately in front of her. The other form contracted and disappeared from view beneath the sheets. Nélida barged over at Meryl, pushing her out of the room and closing the door behind herself, the robe still pressed to her chest with her left hand, one breast falling nakedly over her arm.

"You... you mustn't come in here... out... go, please go to your room *niña* Meryl.... Oh, this is terrible..."

"I'm sorry," Meryl apologized. "I only wanted to tell you..."

Nélida burst into tears.

"Please, *please* don't tell your father.... If the *señor* finds out, I know he'll sack me... and if Madame knows, she'll tell him, too, and..."

Meryl said, "Don't worry. I promise I shan't say a thing. I'm just leaving my shoes here. They need cleaning. I promise... I won't tell anybody...."

She did not find it necessary to tell the flustered maid that

372

she had seen her father doing exactly the same thing with one of the aunts in his bedroom.

Nobody ever talked about things like that. Not out loud, anyway. It wasn't nice, and it wasn't done. Only people *were* doing it. Meryl had seen them.

The only adults who spoke about it were the men in the parks, the ones who stood behind big trees or clumps of high bushes, who waited until you were on your own, and then came up to you and offered to let you touch it or kiss it.

"See how nice and long it is, little girl? Why don't you come closer..."

The warnings given by parents and teachers were only general, never specific, never saying why.

"Don't ever go in a car with a person you don't know...."

"Don't talk to strangers...."

"Don't stare.... He's just being silly... don't notice him..."

They didn't explain why not. Or tell you what to do when men suddenly came up behind you and grabbed your bottom. Or blocked your path and thrust their hand between your legs, pinching hard with their fingers and trying to poke inside.

No one talked about that at all.

Even when there was the fuss about the ice-cream man near school, no adult ever talked about the incident. He used to stand very close to his cart so that nobody could see his trousers were unbuttoned. When a group of girls gathered around, he'd give free ice creams to those who let him push up against them and rub himself up and down. Once he gave a girl in the Third Form a whole box of chocolate-covered ice-cream blocks, but that was because she had held his *poronga* when he asked her to. Later she told her best friend about it, saying it had made her hand all sticky and smell funny, and her friend told another girl, who told Meryl. Meryl didn't tell anybody at all, but there was a lot of whispering going on during the following week.

Then one day the ice-cream man wasn't there any more.

But nobody said anything.

The war news grew darker and darker; the fall of France was followed by Dunkirk, and then, in dreary August, the Battle of Britain began. As bombs were pounding England, so Meryl's problem about her mother eased: Yvonne's heroism for having chosen to stay ascended over her desertion.

"... so splendid of her ... if only I had thought to go ... but of course I can't, now ... besides, my children ..."

"You must be very proud of your brave Mummy ..."

"... by God, it proves the British mettle ..."

Letters were fewer, their news sparse. Yvonne mentioned Lally more often than herself; John Bell was around again, life was strange, if only Lally's parents hadn't been so intransigent, it seemed such a shame.... Philipe, reading between the lines, guessed two marriages were fated to die. But in wartime, anything could happen; Yvonne hinted as much, without giving anything away.

She seemed to be in direct and constant contact with all her old schoolmates and friends, mostly through the Crestwood Close Old Girls' Association, which appeared to be involved in organizing war effort schemes at all levels. Philipe asked no questions, and was given no details, but it was obvious that his original assessment of her self-imposed role in wartime England was indeed correct.

Philipe read and remembered and understood; increasingly, Meryl read and turned away. She read her mother's words through thickening screens of distance and time; they were the sentences and sentiments of someone whose image was fading, whose presence she could no longer instantly recall. Other voices, different faces, had soothed her life and fears for years, her father in some ways the closest, in others, ranking far behind. There was Madame, boring but reliable; Rosita— ah, yes, definitely Rosita, stern and sudden and of rocklike strength. And Grannie, who didn't say the things but understood the facts. Even Nélida, who was sweet, knew how to comfort hurts and tears.

And then there was Lala, close in ways the others couldn't be. Lala the *viva*, with her peasant shrewdness, her inborn knowledge of life's basics and survival, who knew the things not spoken of and whispered them to Meryl's ear, and Meryl believed, for nothing the *criada* said was proved untrue. She knew how to get around adults and fools, knew when it was useless to try, or when the coast was clear.

At year's end, with school over, Meryl rejoined Lala for the holidays and the summer they shared. But this year Philipe did not go away; he collected his daughter well before school began again and took her over to the beach resorts in

Uruguay where, by arrangement, the latest of the temporary aunts was also spending the month.

When they took the overnight steamer out of Montevideo to return to Buenos Aires, Philipe took Meryl out on deck to show her the hulk of the scuttled Graf Spee, still sticking up, gray and silent, out of the water, a monument to the war that was so far away from her, and yet right here.

It permeated everything, the conflict miles distant; social, charity, and school events all centered on its cause. Bazaars switched their sights to war relief, patriotic songs were heard at children's parties, and current favorites got new lyrics, sung by young and old.

> Whistle while you work
> Hitler is a jerk
> Goring's barmy
> So's his army
> Shove 'em in the dirt

And yet, the war had no connection to Argentina at all. The country was neutral; any organization smacking of national fervor was banned. The German Bund and Baden-Powell's scouting movement both came under the same banner, as far as the Argentine Government was concerned; since neither was allowed to function, the Brownie Troops at the Bowen Day School folded their tents and called it a day.

"What a swizz! Now I'll never get any badges. . . ."

"My mother says it's typical native nonsense; that's exactly what she said. . . ."

"*My* mother said it was a good thing, because I hardly have time, as it is, for lessons. . . ."

Since Meryl's mother had said nothing, she didn't either; she would take the manual up to the *estancia*, and she and Lala could form their own special troop.

Another school year began coming to a close; Meryl's swimming, much improved, earned her a second-prize ribbon at the yearly races. Then the news of Pearl Harbor crackled through the static of every shortwave broadcast Philipe listened to; before Christmas, he was on his way to Washington, with Meryl safely installed with her grandmother at El Ombú.

"You really should send your *criada* up to our school for a year, or two," pronounced Dollie, fanning herself with vigor and making the wicker seat creak beneath her. "The poor little thing would be grateful to you for life. Just think of it, Edie—a free bilingual education for her. It'd be such an act of Christian charity on your part." More creaking followed as she turned toward Tim Casey. "Don't you think so, Mr. Casey? I mean, one does have to do one's duty in this world."

The *estanciero* confessed his ignorance as to which school she meant. While Dollie told him, Edie turned her attention from the departing figures of Lala and Meryl, now walking along the low garden wall on their way to the swimming pool, and considered her guests in the cool shade of the verandah.

"...a God-sent opportunity for poor, unfortunate children..."

"Well, I don't know about Lala," began Edie. "I don't know whether she needs anything like that. After all, she *has* been attending the *pueblo* school, and..."

"But think of the advantages of proper British schooling!" Dollie exclaimed. "She already speaks the language anyway. And she'd learn proper manners...would no doubt be able to get a good position in a household in Buenos Aires...or at least Rosario....All it would mean would be a small donation on your part...."

So that's it, thought Edie. You're out for funds for your pet project. Aloud, she said, "I'll think it over—but in the meantime, Tim isn't this the sort of think you were looking for, for Harvey?"

Tim Casey nodded; his son, now approaching his fifteenth birthday, had failed to pass his examinations at the Rosario boys' school. The failure did not upset the older Casey; he himself had little truck with books and schooling. But the school board had asked him to remove his son, couching the de facto expulsion in a fog of phrases and thus enabling him to hide, both from himself and the two women seated around the table with him, the real reason he was seeking another school for Harvey.

"The Córdoba hills would be good for his health....All that damp air in Rosario got him down....A year or two...polish him up a bit..."

Dollie, sensing an easy victory, pressed her point home.

"It would undoubtedly be the very best thing you could do for your son, Mr. Casey. Nowhere else would he get all the advantages of British schooling *plus* the bracing, healthy air.

And—although I wouldn't want you to tell anyone I said this—I often wonder about the caliber of teachers in the Rosario and Buenos Aires schools...whereas those we chose, being devoted to the good of the children entrusted to them..."

"Perhaps I should send Raul there, too," Casey said, unexpectedly.

Edie expressed astonishment. Dollie said, "Raul? I don't think I..."

"Our cook's nephew," explained Tim. "But the thing is, he was brought up with my son—with my children.... He and my little daughter were inseparable, until...until, as perhaps you know..."

"Yes, yes, don't speak of it—a tragic loss for you," Dollie murmured.

"Yes, well, you see, after the deaths, the two boys always stuck together—used to come over here and play with Edie's charges all the time when they were younger...." He paused for breath. "So I don't think it'd be fair to send Harvey and not include Raul. He's a bright boy, for his age. And I'm sure he'll make a better *capataz* if he gets a couple of years of your school under his belt. That's what he says he want to be, you know." Tim turned to Edie. "The *capataz* at La Chata." He gave an amiable laugh. "Can't think of a better arrangement myself. He'll be trustworthy, being almost like one of the family."

Dollie was beaming.

"Well, I think it is an absolutely lovely idea," she said. "And I'll bring it up at the next committee meeting."

Tim pushed his chair away from the table, and rose.

"Thank you very much. It's most kind of you. And now, if you ladies'll excuse me..."

"Oh, are you leaving?" Dollie's face crumpled into a fleshy pout. "I thought you were staying to dinner...."

"I'd love to, but I'm afraid I can't...."

During the evening meal, Dollie mentioned Tim Casey several times.

"...such a kind and good man...Imagine the wonderful surprise it'll be for that little boy...what's his name..."

"You mean Raul."

"Yes, that's it. Little Raul." Dollie helped herself to more baked potatoes.

"I must say, I was surprised when Tim said he'd send him, too. Didn't think he had it in him."

Dollie composed her face into a reproachful smile.

"You judge people too harshly, Edie dear. If only you would try to see the truth of their souls. . . ." She sighed. "I'm sure Mr. Casey is much nicer than you think he is. . . ."

"I didn't say he wasn't nice . . ."

"Ah, but you imply it, and that alone is enough. You know how poor Papa used to teach us about having charity in our hearts . . ."

"Tim Casey doesn't need charity, Dollie. You're making a mountain out of a molehill. All I said was that I was surprised."

Dollie continued her praise of the *estanciero*.

"And do you know, I think he's sweet on me," she finally confided. "The way he kept looking at me all afternoon . . . and I'm *sure* he really did want to stay to dinner . . . probably *just* to be near me . . ."

Edie said nothing. Dollie was such a fool. Although she was quite right in her guess that the *estanciero* had wanted to stay; Edie had never known Tim Casey to pass up a free meal, especially not at El Ombú, where the wines were known for their worth. What Dollie did not realize was Tim's reason for leaving; he had not stayed, Edie knew, because of Dollie's presence.

She knew, because Tim had told her what he thought of Dollie Thaxter not long before, when Edie had announced she would be visiting.

". . . cannot understand why you invite that woman . . . talks the hind leg off a donkey . . . and don't tell me Maurice tolerated her, either . . . no one would, no right-thinking man, anyway . . ."

Edie had suppressed a smile.

"That's not fair, Tim, and what's more, it isn't true, either. Dollie has lots of friends and, in her time, even admirers, I'm sure. Why, she was even engaged, many years ago, but the poor chap died."

"I don't doubt it," Tim nodded. "She probably sat on his lap. . . ."

This time, Edie laughed.

"Oh, you *are* naughty. . . ."

"Though I can understand you like having an old friend visiting you." Casey had gone serious. "It must be lonely for you here, on your own . . . the responsibilities . . ."

Edie admitted she looked forward to Dollie's arrival, ". . . and she won't be staying very long, anyway . . ."

"And then you'll be all alone again, with nobody at your side. Edie"—he leaned forward—"why don't we get married, you and I? I'm sure we'd get on very well... and you would rid yourself of all the disadvantages of being a defenseless widow...."

Edie had very nearly laughed again, but common sense had prevailed. She had seen him to the door as soon as she decently could without making it apparent she wanted him off and on his way as quickly as possible.

Then she'd called Rosita and told her all about it.

"The old goat! To my benefit, indeed! What he wants is the comfortable life—and El Ombú in his name...."

"And money, too, *señora*, I'm sure that would come into it, too. *Don* Casey gambles... everyone knows it..."

Seated at the dining room table with Dollie, Edie made no mention of the recent past scenes. But as Dollie rambled on between mouthfuls of pudding, Edie listened and remembered, and secretly felt pleased.

In contrast to their outdoor activities of the year before, Meryl and Lala spent most of their holidays reading books and playing paper dolls. As always, they swam at the high heat of noon, and once in a while, they asked to have Sammy saddled and went off riding, two leggy girls astride the Shetland pony, trotting around the old *ombú*.

But by and large, they stayed near the house or actually indoors, off on their own in the south wing in the room where the piano stood ignored against one wall. Here they played their paper-doll games, giggled secrets, blushed unexpectedly, or shared new knowledge, out of the way of the household's adults, and beyond their prying questions and eyes.

"You can't spend all your time inside. Why don't you try playing tennis on the old tennis court?"

Edie had the court mowed and an old net strung across it. Lala and Meryl took racquets to the court, tossed a ball back and forth with little enthusiasm, and then lay near the hedge in the taller grass, reading the books they had also brought along.

For the *estancia* house was full of books and bookcases, layers of oddly assembled literature from the years gone by. There was a cache of romantic novels lining the shelves of the room in the south wing; the girls read and sighed and read again, inventing their own stories betweentimes, building on the characters they found in the books.

"If I ever have a daughter, I've found the name I'm going to call her," Lala announced one day. She was lying, stomach down, on the grass by the hedge; Meryl, in the same position facing her, looked up from the volume she was reading.

"It's Amelie. Don't you think that's pretty?"

"Mmhmm. Did you find it in there? I haven't read that yet." Meryl reached over for Lala's book.

"I've almost finished. You can have it tomorrow." Lala rolled over on her back and looked at the sky. "Amelie...what a lovely sound...."

"It's French," said Meryl, returning the novel.

"The whole book's about France, that's why. But it doesn't matter; I think a French name'd be perfectly all right." Lala sat up. "Amelie. I'll buy her lots of pretty clothes, and different colored ribbons for her hair. And I'll never give her away. To anyone."

"Not even to me?"

"You can have your own children. Besides, you'll be her Aunt Meryl anyway, won't you?"

"And my children can play with her—I think I'll have some girls and some boys..."

"And we can dress them in matching clothes..."

"And teach them all how to swim, in the pools..."

"And..."

And the fantasies of adult future billowed into the hot afternoon.

Edie wrote—as she did every evening—in the *estancia* diary:

Hot and muggy today. Yesterday's storm damage not as bad as expected. Dollie T. staying on an additional week. Letter from Philipe in Washington. He returns next month; Meryl to stay here until he arrives. Decided to send Lala to the Ladies Society school in Córdoba after all. Told her so. Dollie v. pleased.

Edie's last task for the day was the filling out of a check, her substantial donation to the charity children's school.

"I wonder if you'll have a school uniform like mine?"

"I don't know. She didn't say." Lala kicked at a stone.

"You'll have to write to me and tell me all about it. And then we'll be able to compare everything when we get back here after school breaks up."

"Mmhm."

". . . and you'll see what I mean about hockey being awful. At least you already know how to play tennis. . . . I wonder if your school'll have a pool like ours does? A proper pool, I mean, not like the one here. In proper pool, you can really swim, without being interrupted to turn around the whole time."

Lala said, "Let's go and take Sammy a carrot and some bread. He's not going to like us both going away."

"Dad—when's your wedding anniversary?"

Philipe looked up from his newspaper.

"I'm afraid I don't remember exactly. Why? Why do you ask?"

"No actual reason, really. But a friend at school—her parents recently had an anniversary party, so I sort of wondered."

Philipe grinned.

"Then I'm sure you know how they say men never remember, and have to be reminded by their wives. You'll have to ask your mother when she returns to B.A." He ducked behind the paper again.

"Dad . . ."

"What?"

"Dad—is she really coming back?"

He emerged from behind the newsprint, faintly annoyed.

"Of course she is. She's told you so. When the war's over, she'll take the first boat she . . ."

"I mean back here, to this apartment, as your wife."

Philipe stopped pretending to read and put the paper aside. He sat forward in his chair.

"All right, Meryl. Out with it. What are you really trying to ask me?"

"Well, on the *estancia* . . ."

On the *estancia*, people whispered; Rosita made allegations; Tim Casey had been overheard. Grannie had said; Lala had repeated.

". . . and at school, too . . ."

A friend reported her mother knew; another schoolmate said people had talked.

"...and it's hard for me, Daddy, it really is....I feel people know things about me, or at least about Mother, that I don't. So I thought I'd ask..."

After a long moment, Philipe said, "I don't know that I'm a very good parent, Meryl. I can't make up stories to make it easier for you, or make it easy for you to believe. Probably because I think the truth is, in the long run, easier than anything. But at times it takes a lot of explaining, and this is one of those times." He smiled ruefully at her. "It's going to take a while, too, because I'd like to tell it to you from the beginning. You see, your mother and I agreed to divorce each other long before you were born. Even before we were actually married...to each other..."

When he had finished, Meryl gave a small sigh and said, "So that's why mother doesn't really like me."

Philipe was taken aback.

"Oh, no, Meryl—that's not true. That's not true at all. She loves you very much."

"Oh, sure, she *loves* me Dad, because she's my mother. But she doesn't like me, not really...and I don't think she ever has...."

In her next letter to England, Meryl wrote:

Now I know all about it—how you were married before and how you divorced, and why. Daddy told me the whole thing, and I guess it's better knowing the full story...

Long months later, Yvonne's answer arrived.

I'm glad you understand, but I do wish you would stop using Americanisms like "I guess." Do at least try to speak and write proper English, Meryl, the way nice people do.

3

Lala struggled into the dingy checked dress, hoping the sleeve wouldn't rip any further before she could get hold of a needle and thread later in the day. Then she went around the dormitory, helping the younger girls into their uniforms. The smell from the peter pot, urine-filled and rusted, rose from the far end of the room.

"She's late unlocking our door today...."

"Shhh...she'll hear...."

"Let's hope it isn't another of her spanking days...."

The girls talked in whispers and finished dressing. Lala pushed her feet into her espadrilles; they had been soaked by yesterday's rain and were still damp, the rope soles stiff and leaden, but it would not do to ask for a new pair. The toes had not worn through completely yet, and Mrs. Price would only lecture her about waste not, want not.

"You, of all people, to ask for more...not even entitled to be here...not a drop of good British blood in you...only because of our wonderful Miss Thaxter...who pleaded...as a special favor..."

Lala had heard it a thousand times or more: according to Mrs. Price, she and Raul were the lowest of the low.

Not that any child had high standing at the Ladies Society Benefit School; it was made clear to them, on all possible occasions, that they owed their great good fortune to the largesse of the school's providers and the dedication of its teachers, and they must always keep in mind how exceedingly lucky they were to be there.

A key rattled in the lock. The door creaked open.

"Good morning, Matron," rose the duty-trained chorus.

"Good morning, Hurry up. Why isn't that bed made? Do it at once, after which you may start your duty for the week which is to wash the floors."

"But I did them last week, Matron. It isn't my turn..."

"*Silence*. Don't answer back. You have no right to be here, anyway. None of your relatives have paid a penny this year. You should be ashamed of yourself. Only the goodness of Mrs. Price's soul..."

The day had started. It was six forty-five A.M.

Lala picked up the stinking peter pot by its chipped handle and took it out to the toilet enclosure in the girl's bathroom. After she emptied it, she sat on the toilet for a while, observing that the cut squares of newspaper on the wire hook were in need of replenishing and wondering whether she would get a chance to talk to Raul that day. Next to her, the malodorous wastepaper can awaited emptying, too; by school fiat, no papers were allowed to be flushed, and on Saturdays the contents were burned, preparatory to Sunday's cleanliness.

Washing her hands and face at the long, troughlike sink, Lala winced at the biting cold of the water. A quick comb

383

through her hair, and she was ready, walking quickly to the dining room and the warmth of the steaming jugs of *yerba* she knew would be waiting.

The dining room, with its scrubbed trestle tables and wooden benches, linked the two squat main buildings of the charity school. Boys on one side, girls on the other; everything was separated. Other buildings included the chapel, Mrs. Price's bungalow, and another house for the staff, usually only two teachers and Matron. The cook was a local woman who came in by the day; all other work around the institution was done by the pupils.

Raul was already at the boys' table, hunched over his cup, the bread slices on his plate disappearing fast. He looked so thin, thinner than ever, with his black silky hair soaked and slicked over the bony planes of his head. Usually, it was useless to risk talking to him at meals; between the boys' table and the girls' section stood the square table with proper chairs around it where the teachers had their meals. Butter and jam were already laid out on it, with the complete settings, but no teacher had yet reached the dining room, so Lala took a chance.

To offset danger, she grabbed the broom propped up against the wall near the door before walking over to where Raul was sitting. If someone came in, she could always say something had spilled and that she was sweeping up.

"I need soap," Raul muttered as she came up to him. "Matron ripped my bed apart and found the biscuit I'd hidden under the sheet, so I'm to get a spanking tonight."

"I'll steal some when I take the clothes to the washhouse," Lala promised. "How can I get it to you?"

"Put it under the cabinet in the front hall, I have to polish the furniture in there today."

"It'll be there before lunch. Remember to coat it on thickly. Let it dry, and then put on some more."

Voices signaled the imminent appearance of staff members, and Lala moved swiftly away from Raul and the boys' table, leaving the broom back where she had found it before serving out her mug of *yerba* and going to her usual place at the trestle table on the girls' side.

During the classes the children were given between their endless tasks of household work and cleaning, lessons were learned almost exclusively by rote and memory. Long chapters had to be committed to memory, pages' worth of dictation were given. Both in Spanish as in English, the lessons were dull and difficult.

There were only two classrooms—boys sitting on one side, girls on the other, in each—and were known as the Junior and Senior rooms. Every morning, English was taught in the Junior room, grades one through three, while the Seniors, aged eleven and up, struggled with Spanish and mathematics.

In the afternoon, the teachers switched classrooms, and thus the bilingual curriculum was fulfilled. The Scriptures were taught only by Mrs. Price, and only in English; the headmistress blended God and country, Church of England and Church *and* England with unrelenting emphasis.

A ten-minute recess broke both the morning and the afternoon sessions halfway through. The children then ran to play outside in a fenced-off area divided down the middle, girls to the right, boys to the left. Those who wanted to talk to each other could do so through the dividing fence, but conversations that lasted too long were interrupted by any member of the staff who might happen to walk through the playground at the time.

After the morning class dismissal and before the lunch bell rang, Lala went by the dormitory, collected the laundry and took it to the washhouse. It was a shed next to the kitchen door, with a vast tub and several washboards waiting for the next day's washing hours and the girls' knuckles. At the top corner of each washboard, a square indention held the strong soap used for all school laundry; sometimes leftover slivers remained there, too small and slimy for Mrs. Price to bother locking away in the store cupboard for the next time.

Lala saw she was in luck; there were pieces on all the boards. She grabbed them quickly; it was always a good idea to have a secret store of them, easier to get at than risking being caught taking the soap, as she was risking now. She tucked the pieces into the elastic-held folds of her underpants.

Minutes later, a quick darting into the empty entrance hall of the school building completed her mission; the slivers of soap were hidden from view beneath the old cabinet near the front door. As she gained the dining room, safe and undetected, Lala allowed the selection of prepared alibis to slide from her mind. She discarded them automatically, without giving the process another thought; it had become second nature to her to compose adequate defenses for almost every move she made. This helped her avoid punishment and protect Raul, or at least assist him whenever she could.

She saw Harvey standing at his place behind his chair, smiling at her and giving her a wink. She ignored him, taking her place on the girls' side. She stood, in silence, as everyone waited for the signal for grace to be given by Mrs. Price, already in her chair, ramrod straight, at the staff table.

When all the pupils were present, the headmistress inclined her head.

> Thanks to Thee, oh, Lord, we give
> For Thy mercies we receive
> While we humbly seek Thy Face
> Fill our hearts with Heavenly Grace.

There was a rustle of movement.
"Amen."
At last, they could sit down and start eating.

Sunday.
On Sundays, the misery was different, with the bleak, cold hours of long church services, and wondering whether or not one could hold out without fainting. Someone always did, toppling over onto the stone floor from the wooden pew or the slatted kneeling ledge, only to get whacked across the head for the indiscretion.

Sunday clothes were also different, blue serge skirts for the girls, serge trousers for the boys: short for the under-twelves, long for those twelve and over. No one stayed in the school after the age of sixteen; that year, Harvey was the oldest pupil.

White blouses or shirts, and a blue pullover in the winter, completed the Sunday outfits. It was also the uniform worn for any formal occasion: a visit from Miss Thaxter or any of the other Ladies Soceity dignitaries from Buenos Aires who might choose to inspect their protégés.

But the Sunday shoes were the worst of all. Daily espadrilles were not allowed; Sunday footwear meant leather shoes—shoes donated to the charity, used and worn, frequently inappropriate, usually ill-fitting, often humiliatingly ugly. But to complain was to be beaten.

Lala suffered in silence, for Sundays held one consolation: the hours permitted in the library room. It was a small, airless cell in the school building, and it housed an untidy collection of old and musty books, mány difficult to read and sometimes worse to understand, books donated over the decades by people long gone, relics from the shelves of spinster schoolteachers, aged uncles, or elderly aunts whose possessions had been disposed of by disappointed relations. No one ever checked the volumes for suitability when they were sent off, nor did the school staff look at them when they arrived.

On Sundays, after the midday meal, the library room was open until the bell summoned everyone for the chapel's evening service. Here, Lala found refuge, and peace, and silence, and a translated version of *Das Kapital*.

It got to be July, and the brief break of the winter holidays; Lala and Meryl returned to El Ombú, both of them taller, Lala more subdued. Over the days, the confidence began emerging.

Meryl was shocked.

"But that's *terrible*. Is it always like that?"

"No," Lala admitted. "Sometimes it's worse. When Mrs. Price went to Buenos Aires last month, she left a missionary couple in charge. Suddenly, there were no funds, so there was not food to eat, just peanuts, peanuts and *yerba*. That was our supper for several evenings."

"Couldn't you have told Mrs. Price when she got back?"

Lala shrugged. "What for? Matron knew, too, and she didn't tell her."

Meryl bit her lip and looked away.

"And then this man, the missionary husband, he was such a pig. He always *just happened* to walk by our dormitory when it was time for us to go to bed. He'd stand by that one window we have, pretending to be wishing us a prolonged good-night." Lala gave a harsh laugh. "We older girls knew what he was doing. We'd undress under the sheets."

"Didn't his wife see or notice anything?"

"Who knows? She never said anything. Not even when he made us girls do exercises every morning. Gym, he called it." Again, the harsh exclamation cut through Lala's words. "One exercise consisted in raising one leg as high as you could, and then the other. I'll always remember him calling out, 'Higher, higher'... and then he'd bend down to see we were doing it right... a horror, Meryl—he was a real horror...."

The afternoon before Meryl was to return to B.A., they went and sat on the gate leading to Sammy's field. The long fingers of cold winter sunlight pointed across toward the main road beyond the *estancia*'s front fence and boundary; a freight train rattled along the parallel track, its wagons uncounted by the girls this time.

"You shouldn't have to go back to Córdoba, Lala. You must tell Grannie. Promise me you will."

"No, It's *you* who has to promise you won't tell her, either."

"But why not?"

"Promise first, and then I'll explain to you. Promise cross your heart and hope to die...."

"Oh, all right." Meryl sighed and promised. "But why?"

"Because that's the way things are when one is a *criada*. And Miss Thaxter, pig that she is, is a friend of your grandmother's. I know this better than you do. Besides, it won't be forever."

"I still think..." Meryl began.

"And there's another thing," Lala's voice took on sudden urgency. "There's Raul. I can't leave Raul; he suffers so much more than I. The boys all pick on him, and so do the teachers. They aren't quite so mean to the girls; we're more useful to them, I suppose. They're terrible with the boys."

"But he's got Harvey there. Doesn't he protect him?"

"Harvey?" Lala's eyes narrowed. "Meryl, don't be stupid. You know what Harvey's like. He's the worst of all...."

A year pased, and there were deaths again, deaths both close at hand and distant. On the *estancia*, old Rosa died, and Rosita moved into the accepted comfort of black clothes and mourning. In Buenos Aires, Bessie Thaxter faded from beneath her shadow of senility. Edie traveled down to the city to attend the funeral, driven by the ghosts of the past and the vestiges of childhood duty.

Then word reached Philipe through diplomatic channels: the aunts' house, bombed, had been totally destroyed. Aunt Boo had died with it and so had old Bronner; Aunt Moo was injured but recovering. Yvonne was fine, driving an ambulance.

"Boo's death will hit her terribly hard," Philipe told Meryl. "She was always her favorite. They used to sing together."

There had been another family death, also: Aunt Moo's son Dick had been lost at sea. Yvonne mentioned it in her next letter, which was brief and nondescript, the very blankness of its tone bringing the darkness close. After reading it Meryl pulled down yet more curtains of distance; with each letter, Yvonne became less vivid to her daughter.

There were changes everywhere, in people, in the war, in the news, in governmental circles in B.A. There were tides changing, tides turning, tides beginning to flow. In Argentina, a revolution changed the government. With little fanfare and less fuss, an Army triumvirate took over in Buenos Aires and, after some jockeying for position, settled down to law and reform.

At school, it was a three-day wonder. The glory was soon lost in the immediacy of the midyear examinations, a test where proficiency counted and witnessing local change did not.

When summer came, Meryl went to the camp. Lala had already been home a week.

"Let's go to the pool."

"I can't swim today."

"Oh," Lala smiled indulgently. "So you've started?"

Meryl nodded. "This winter. Have you?"

"Already last year, at school. It was awful at first, because they make us wash the pads and hang them on the line, and if the boys see, they say terrible rhymes. But then I learned to hang them inside the pillowcases. . . ."

Meryl made a sound of disgust. "And you still won't tell Grannie how awful it is?"

"It's better now. I manage. At least Harvey isn't there anymore."

Harvey, now working for his father at La Chata, had put his schooldays behind him.

Lala said, "If you can't swim, I don't really care whether I do or not, so let's go and read in the *gomero* instead."

Their favorite sitting branches, looped low like seats, awaited in the damp cool spreading shade. The girls settled down, each with a book in her hands, but after a while Lala ceased to read, leaning against the tree trunk instead and gazing into the wall of leaves around her.

Finally she looked over at Meryl on the opposite branch and said, "Promise me one thing."

Meryl looked up from her book. "What?"

"That if something were to happen to me—if I died . . . promise me you'll look after my children."

389

"Why say things like that, Lala? Nothing's going to happen."

Lala's face twisted into a brief smile and she said, "Well, something happened to *my* mother, didn't it?"

"Yes, but that was long ago, and..."

"And the thing is, you never know. Just look at me, Meryl—if it hadn't been for Rosita, and your grandmother..."

"Oh, all right, I promise. If it makes you feel better."

"Another thing, also," Lala continued. "Never, never allow them to be sent to a school like the Córdoba one...." After a pause, she repeated, "*Promise* me, Meryl. It's very important."

"Yes, I promise," Meryl nodded. "I'll make them go to the Bown Day School," she added with a grin. "That's bad enough. But you'll have to see to it you only have girls."

Lala's face softened. "I told you years ago...one little girl...my Amelie...."

For a moment, they tried to recapture their fantasy games of the past years, but the attempted conversation faded, Lala turned serious again.

"I mean it about the promises, you know," she said. "That wasn't part of the game."

Meryl nodded. "I understand. And I meant my promises. But I still think you're having a big worry for nothing. Nothing's going to happen to you."

"But if it did..."

"Don't worry. I'd be there."

After staring down at the periwinkle carpet by the tree, Lala said, "I probably wonder like this because I never knew my mother or my father. It's difficult, not knowing one's parents."

"I don't know my mother well either anymore."

"But I mean at all."

Meryl fell silent. At last she said, "I wonder if it isn't easier that way."

To return to Buenos Aires by the night train was the journey Meryl liked most of all. Not only were the hours and the meals and the carriage configurations different and somehow more exciting, but there was also the mystic joy of staying awake into the dark of the night, sitting at the end of the made-down bunk, next to the window, and keeping the blind rolled up except when they pulled into a station. For hours, she would watch the ghostly landscape go by, the rhythmic wheels clicking beneath her. Shapes and shadows and an occasional far light on a lonely road changed the window-framed scene in front of her all the time, and if the moon was full, or nearly so, everything took on the aspect of cardboard cutouts, stage sets edged in silver against the star-flecked backdrop sky. She looked for the Southern Cross, she checked for the three stars called the Three Marias, and the train rocked on through the gentle night, across the flat of the Argentine land.

Most mysterious of all were the small graveyards lying between the camp towns where, if there had been a recent burial, she could sometimes glimpse flickers of the *fuego fatuo* as the train whisked by, flashes of thin blue flame darting into the air, the gases of decaying matter escaping up through the freshly turned earth and gasping heavenwards in the darkness.

In the early morning, Retiro gained, and Madame waiting solidly on the station platform, Meryl always managed to cajole the Frenchwoman into a quick breakfast at the station's bustling restaurant, where the waiters poured the steaming milk and thick brown coffee simultaneously into the cups from tall, spouted pots, filling the air with steam and aroma, and serving the best cup of coffee in the world.

4

In 1945, everything changed.

In May, the Allies were victorious in Europe; two mushroom clouds in August finished the Japanese. Buenos Aires celebrated the faraway glories, the victors with services of gratitude and parties, the losers with the mourning of their unhonored dead.

Rumors ran rife amid the postwar speculations; Axis criminals were in hiding in the Argentine hills. There were plans for business ventures, now that the seas were safe for commerce; the boom of beef and import-export was once again at hand.

In October, a march of thousands solidified the political aspirations of an Argentine colonel, and when he married the tense blonde actress who had helped him gain the power, the reign of Peron and Evita truly began.

At Christmas, the celebration at El Ombú included both

the Caseys; Harvey, grown tall and polite, was welcomed once more. The quartet of adolescents eased back to guarded friendship; the swimming pool helped cover the breach and smooth the immediate way.

"Race you to the end..."

"That's too little—let's do it four times there and back, from the steps to the end window...ready, steady...GO!"

Harvey, now eighteen, and doing his military service, had his hair cropped off in regulation cut, which accented the long oval of his ruddy face. The likeness to his father was stamped everywhere, the heavy shoulders, the slight stoop forward, the light-brown eyes, heavy-lidded, inclined to look away. Surprisingly, Raul, the youngest, stood almost as tall as Harvey, a rail-thin contrast to the *estanciero's* son, but also stoop-shouldered, as though to withdraw. His face was all planes, high cheekbones, darkly colored, the deepset eyes a startling green, pale, unexpected. His arms and legs were skeleton-long, cord-sinewed, awkward.

"He'll have to grow into himself," observed Edie. "He's too young to be so tall."

The two girls had grown apace in height, but Lala's proportions and features were more developed, fully defined. Meryl still moved with adolescent gawkiness next to the *criadas* firm female step. Lala tended to take charge of things, order Raul around, stop Harvey's teasing with a sidelong glance.

Games linked the four together; they swam, they went riding; in calmer moments, they played croquet on the freshly mowed tennis court, changing the rules and playing to their own tempo and force, until the whole point was to cannon the opponent's ball into the field beyond the hedge. Bicycles provided their next game, turning croquet into polo and widening their scope for letting off steam. On a few occasions, they went to La Chata, but Lala told Meryl who told Edie that no one was at the house when Harvey had said his father would be there, and from then on El Ombú was again the gathering spot.

Meryl walked into the main room for lunch; Edie was still sitting at the *estancia* desk.

"Ah, there you are, child. I've been waiting for you." Edie picked up a letter. "From your father in New York. There was one for me, too. I'd imagine he tells you much the same thing he tells me, but he says he wants me to explain to you first."

She turned in the swing chair and handed Meryl the envelope, settling her glasses more firmly on her nose and sitting back in the chair.

"Your parents are going to get a divorce. All very quickly. In Reno, Nevada." She looked over her glasses at Meryl. "I was there, you know, when I motored around." She turned back to the desk and picked up several sheets covered in Philipe's handwriting. "It all sounds very modern and up to date," she continued. "I take it neither of them is unhappy about it. Just one of those things, Philipe says, to clear up an old matter, although I understand it was originally Yvonne's idea."

She swung the chair around again.

"Your mother's still in London, of course, that's why Philipe's getting it. He says you know all about the way their marriage happened, and he hopes you won't be too upset. Says he doesn't believe you will be." Edie leaned forward. "Are you?"

And Meryl, feeling nothing, slowly shook her head.

A letter with similar information arrived from Yvonne, giving her side of the story.

. . . such a long and complicated thing to get here, and so it's much easier for Philipe to go to Reno and get it all over with. I suppose we'd have done it years ago, if it hadn't been for the war . . .

Yvonne wrote at length about Lally and John Bell, both of whom were in London.

. . . and as much in love as ever. Lally was informed recently that her husband died, shortly after Singapore fell; he was listed as missing all these years, but now she knows definitely that he's dead. The trouble is, John's wife is not—and as she's very Catholic, it's all very awkward indeed. Of course, she's in South Africa, so at least they can be together here, but all the same, I think it's tragic, don't you?

She also answered her mother on the subject of La Maison. Edie, who had decided to sell the property, wanted Yvonne to go over to France, have some of the furnishings shipped out to the Argentine, and arrange to have the house and grounds sold. Yvonne agreed to follow her mother's instructions as soon as she could.

...but I can't go right now, Mummy...restrictions on travel...currency regulations...rationing...special permission...transportation difficulties...

There was also a human element involved.

...and I'm afraid Aunt Moo has not been at all well. She'll probably have to go into hospital for an operation very soon.

There was an initial awkwardness between Philipe and Meryl when they both arrived back in the apartment, he pale and tired from the U.S winter months, she tanned from the *estancia* and ready to return to school. The mood broke when, at dinner, Meryl suddenly said, "Well, at least you're still my father...." and they both laughed in a release of tension that left them smiling at each other, and calm.

"Where's she going to live, d'you think, when she comes back?" Meryl wanted to know, but Philipe was uncertain.

"Perhaps she'll stay on the *estancia*...."

Meryl's thoughts, however, had progressed.

"And what about me? Now that you and Mother are divorced, where do I get to live? I mean, do I have to go and live with her when she gets back?"

"Why don't we wait and see what she does, first, before you try deciding? If she goes to El Ombú, you'll be spending time there anyway. If she takes a flat here in town, well, then I suppose you can take it in turns...some months here, some months with your mother...."

After a while, Meryl said, "It's not really going to make much difference, is it?"

"Probably not—except that it'll be nicer for you, having your mother back."

"Mmm. I wonder what she'll look like...."

"Different. Changed. But nowhere near as changed as you." Philipe smiled across the table. "It's going to be a shock to her, you know, finding her little girl turned into a *señorita*...."

Meryl was coming up on her fifteenth birthday, more composed, in many ways, than her immediate contemporaries and friends, much her father's confidante and matured by her position in a motherless household where Philipe's girlfriends of the moment still dined but did not reign or stay. Philipe's frequent trips to the U.S.A. were also to Meryl's advantage, for the great Americanization of the younger set was taking place, as it was all over the Western world. Buenos Aires had begun feeling the effects early on: American movies, the hit parade songs, the inevitable hotdog, Coca Cola, and—highest prize of all—jeans had grown to be the symbols of the newly dubbed teenagers.

Meryl's birthplace gave her a clear advantage, boosted by Philipe's trips from which he returned with the latest of teen status items. In Buenos Aires, the clash between the generations was at its loudest in the British community; the parental group still spoke of England as "home" while their Argentine-born children gazed to the U.S.

It was America paying attention to them, not England, America that talked of the teen years, America that recognized them as more than children, as a class of their own, an age group with identity. It was an acceptance seldom granted on their own home ground.

"You're so lucky," her contemporaries told Meryl, time and again. "Your father really seems to understand..."

And Meryl heard about the endless battles: going out with boys alone, staying out too late, not being home in time for meals, too many parties, too much noise, music too loud, telephone conversations far too long, ridiculous clothing, cheekiness, badly brought up friends, unsuitable behavior. She realized, too—as did her friends—that much of the problem was removed from her life not because of her understanding father but because her holidays were all spent away from B.A.

For, despite her Buenos Aires schooldays and schoolfriends, her circle of acquaintances was limited in the city, and the teenage life relatively remote.

"If you stayed here all summer..."

"If you lived in the suburbs..."

But she did neither, and thus was spared many of the indignities of teenage life in B.A. or, for that matter, teenage life anywhere.

"There's a photographer here from New York," Philipe announced one morning. "He's come down on a magazine assignment, all to do with the elections. I've asked him to dinner, and I think you'll like him. I've already told him you're something of a shutterbug yourself."

"Oh, Dad...you know how that embarrasses me.... You shouldn't have said anything...."

"Well, I didn't want him to think you were a mere child...."

Sal turned out to be a personable New Yorker of short stature, rotund proportions, bounding energy, and genuine interest in Meryl's work.

"You've got the eye for it, kiddo, now what you need is practise. Practise and technique." his round face beamed pleasure as he picked up a photo showing a closeup of the Shetland pony's head. "In this one, for instance..." He turned to Philipe.

"Seriously, Mr. van Landen, your daughter has the definite makings of a photographer...."

Salvatore di Leo was in his late twenties; his shining dark eyes and the thatch of dark brown hair bespoke his Sicilian ancestry. So did his short-legged body, tough and muscular beneath the extra fat. A ruptured eardrum had kept him out of the armed forces, but he rode along with the Allied invasion for the news services and the magazines, landing on the island his parents had abandoned and continuing up the boot of Italy to Rome.

"They kept me there till the guys made it into Paris. I flew up with a bunch of brass, snapping pictures all the way...."

He was interesting about his work, but didn't dwell on it continuously. He and Philipe discussed local politics, after which Sal wanted to hear all about Meryl's school.

"...should be a feature, but who'd buy it? No one would believe an English girls' school here. Almost sounds like the British raj in India...."

He invited Meryl to join him on one of his assignments.

"Don't thank me, kiddo," he said, as she started to do so. "I plan on making you do all the carrying. Besides, you're good-looking—and I'm taller. Believe me, from where I stand, that ain't to be passed up lightly...."

Meryl soon found she could relax with Sal.

"It must be because he's older," she confided to her father. "The boys I know are such drips."

Philipe smiled and agreed.

Sal, it turned out, had been married. Twice.

"And I think I'll do it again when I get back home. She's

sure to be beautiful, blonde, about six foot in her stockinged tootsies, and . . ."

"Don't you *know*?" Meryl puzzled.

Sal shook his head. "Not directly. But the other two were, so I figure the next one'll be the same. You see," he went on, "those are the ones I marry. I have it all figured out. Smaller babes with brown hair, like you, I keep as friends. Strictly friends." He looked straight at her. "Take it from your Uncle Sal, kiddo—never mix friendship with marriage. You end up ruining both. It's worse than mixing business with marriage. I don't mind doing that."

His wives, he explained, had both been pinup models.

"That way, our careers sort of mesh, you see—even if the marriages didn't last forever. . . ."

Sal was a painstaking craftsman when it came to his work. The joking stopped; there was no clowning around, and even though the pleasant manner remained, Meryl sensed steel of purpose beneath the polite instructions.

They were working in a museum; Sal was photographing a series of nineteenth-century paintings of famous battles in Argentina's war of independence. The camera on its tripod was flanked by four standard lights. Sal, peering into the ground glass at the of the camera, spoke the commands.

"The lower right one, Meryl—two inches further out, please. No—that's too far. Back'er up a bit . . . hold it. . . ."

They spent all morning in the airless room; Sal did not appear to notice time or discomfort or the passing of lunchtime. Meryl grew bored, then restless, then hungry; by three-thirty, her stomach was rumbling and her temper rising.

"There!" Sal said, taking what seemed like the millionth exposure. "We're done for the day. . . ."

Over a restaurant meal that evening, he agreed with her.

"No, I didn't like photographing those paintings much myself, either. I'm better at action stuff, or pinups. That's where I've done some of my best work, pinups. But it's all part of the game. Every once in a while, I get a cruddy job to do. This was one of 'em. But it was worth it." He grinned. "The moolah's good—and the rest of the stuff here in B.A. was okay."

Before he left, Sal gave Meryl a list of addresses in New York.

"That's the magazine and that's the agency I've been working for and that's my second ex-wife's mother—I get on great with her—and this is my married sister. One of these numbers should know where I am. So if you ever get to New York—call me. In the meantime, get to work, kiddo. Learn the physical basics. Get yourself a darkroom. And tell your old man from me you need a decent camera. . . ."

On the *estancia*, Edie said, "Yes, of course, darling. Your mother will have her old bedroom back. Everything's still there, as you know, just as it always was. And when she comes back, she can have Maurice's dressing room as hers. She'll probably want to change things around, and put in some of the pieces coming out from La Maison. . . ."

More and more plans were being made for Yvonne's homecoming. No date had been set for her arrival, but in her letters she mentioned the possibility that she would be out by Christmas.

It'll be so strange to have a hot Christmas after all these years. I think B.A. must have the best climate in the world; I've missed the sunshine, and those lovely golden days. Oh, won't it be fun being together again? I'm longing to see everybody.

On a more sober note:

Aunt Moo returned to hospital yesterday. They said the operation was successful, but I'm beginning to wonder whether they were telling the truth. She's never fully recovered, and she's painfully thin now. I'm going to visit her tomorrow, and then maybe I'll know more.

The war had been over for more than a year, but there was still turmoil in Buenos Aires. For the british community, the rejoicing of victory was overshadowed by the harshness of political realities closer to home. If they had sniffed at the grand march of the shirtless ones during the previous October, and sneered when an actress became a wife, the mood turned to surprise and then frightened indignation as formerly unimaginable events began taking place, and the British grip on Argentina's internal running and ruling, trade and transport, was pried loose, finger by finger. Each digit was removed from the economic pie in a welter of historical and sometimes hysterical changes, accusations, class awareness, and the general struggle of human endeavor.

Vile changes rang in the air, many of them smack on target. Means both fair and foul were used, and bitterness blossomed on every side.

"Argentina for the Argentinos ..."

"The wretched ingratitude! And after all the things we've done for them...."

"Down with the foreigners and the oligarchs ..."

"... and never had any class hated here before—*that's* what he's stirred up and built his power on..."

"The chains of subjugation must be broken ..."

"Mind you, it'll never last..."

"...can't go on much longer, you mark my word..."

As was increasingly often the case. Anglo-Argentine opinion was wrong.

From Yvonne came the news she was over in France; she had sold La Maison; she was returning to England; Aunt Moo was still in the hospital. Time passed; Yvonne wrote again, briefly: she had canceled her passage.

...I'd hoped to be back for Christmas, as you know, but my plans have had to be changed. Aunt Moo is much the same; the doctors say she is holding her own. She sends her love to you, as always. I'm going to see her at the hospital this afternoon ...

In Buenos Aires, Meryl wondered, Philipe said nothing, Edie visited and planned.

"The three of us could spend Christmas at El Ombú together...."

The cable arrived as summer's heat began; Aunt Moo had passed away.

... PUTTING THINGS IN ORDER SAILING LATE DECEMBER LONGING TO SEE YOU IN THE NEW YEAR...

How many times, thought Edie, have I stood here, waiting?

The crowd jostled and pushed around her; the sounds of the docks filled the air.

Waiting to embark, waiting to meet someone, waiting to go to England...

A shrill whistle split her thoughts.

... waiting for everything to start, for life to begin. And it did, that first trip home...

A shuddering hoot interrupted her, its note reverberating through her chest. The ship was docking at last. Meryl, by her side, fidgeted impatiently.

"Can you see Mother, Grannie?" she kept asking repeatedly, craning her neck and squinting across the wharf to the approaching vessel.

Philipe, the other side of his daughter, remained calm and seemingly impassive; how strange it must be, Edie thought, to be meeting a woman who went away married to him and was returning divorced.... But perhaps it was all for the best; Yvonne hadn't been a good wife to him. Now she could begin taking over the *estancia*. It was high time she learned the ropes, the full intricacies of running El Ombú. Someday, after all, it would pass into her hands. Not that the day in question was right around the corner—Edie had never felt better in her life—but it would be nice to travel again when things straightened thenmselves out in Europe. It wouldn't take too long, Edie felt, now that the British were no doubt at the helm again. And she'd be able to leave El Ombú in Yvonne's hands when she went away....

"Oh, look, Grannie—the crane's swinging a gangplank over..."

How many times had she walked up and down a gangplank, up to a voyage, down to new or familiar ground? Edie felt the urge to travel tugging strongly within her, to sail out East again, perhaps go around the world...

Yes it *was* going to be nice having Yvonne home again; they would each be able to benefit their futures secure.

"There she is!"

It was Philipe who had spotted her.

"Where?" Edie shaded her eyes with her hand.

"There ... over toward the side ... can't you see her, Grannie?"

Suddenly, Edie realized she was looking straight at her daughter. She began waving wildly, and Yvonne was waving back, her hand making a wide arc over her head and back.

She looks older ... prettier, too, in a way, more mature.... Perhaps she's grown up at last ... got some sense into her head. A bit late, but better late than never ... time to face her responsibilities here ... be a proper mother to Meryl ...

Meryl was waving both her hands up in the air, flushed with excitement. Philipe was smiling, not saying anything, his hand resting on his daughter's shoulder.

They're very alike, those two, Edie thought. Meryl looks just like him. And a little bit like me, perhaps—nothing of Yvonne in her.

There were shouts and calls and cries of recognition; the changing of metal as the ship was moored in place. The gangplank descended, steadied in its position. Officials in uniform pushed through the crowd to board the ship; the hubbub of voices rose in peaks with each sighting.

Voices and more voices. Shouts. And tears. Tears of joy and tears of recognition. The crowd moved and parted at the gangplank: the passengers were beginning to descend. More tears and cries and helpless sobs of greeting; there were hugs and clasps and clinging arms, handshakes and thumps on the back. There were wives hugging husbands, and parents hugging children, children solemn and frightened and trying not to cry, holding out their amrs to fathers never known, and parents, clinging to the arms of the returned. Many were in uniform, some were in mufti, all of them changed for now and evermore.

Yvonne came down the gangplank, holding a large toy monkey. A man in uniform stood in front of her, smiling across the crowd. Behind her stood a tall distinguished-looking man who appeared to be leaning awkwardly; then Edie noticed the right sleeve of his jacket, empty and flat against his side, its cuff tucked into the pocket.

"Mummy!" Yvonne was pushing towards her "Mummy!" Their embrace was tight, salted with tears. A confusion of greetings followed.

"Meryl!" Another hug.

"Philipe . . ."

Turning back to her mother, Yvonne handed her the plush toy animal with an exaggeratedly casual air.

"Would you carry this for me, Mummy, please? She leaned closer and whispered, "Be careful with it. . . . Coco's inside. . . . It's my pajama case, and he's in with them. As long as he feels he's being smuffled, he won't squawk, so if you hold it close to you . . ."

Edie cradled the toy in the crook of her elbow and said, "All right, darling, I've got it. Now let's go over and see about your trunks, shall we, so we can get out of this crowd. . . ."

But Yvonne wasn't listening to her mother; instead, she was stepping aside to make room for the one-armed man to join their tight circle. She was smiling up at him, her hand placed on his good arm.

"I want you to meet Wilfred, Mummy." Yvonne's face was flushed, her voice vibrant. "Philipe . . . Meryl . . . this is Wilfred Hume-Hawley. . . ."

He was smiling hesitantly, his head acknowledging the introductions with a slight bow.

". . . you see, Mummy, I'm Mrs. Hume-Hawley . . . isn't it marvelous? We got married last month. . . ."

VIII

Anglo Jangle
1947–1950

1

Meryl sat on the high stool, her fingers under the lip of the enamel tray on the counter in front of her, watching the surface of the sheet of paper floating in the developer. Nothing was coming up yet; she tipped the tray, causing the faintly viscous liquid to move back and forth. The yellow glow of the safelight made it a strain, watching for the first signs of image. Meryl leaned closer, frowning.

There. A faint smudge was beginning, a second followed almost immediately, and suddenly two eyes were looking at her, Nélida's dark eyes, emerging out of the paper's whiteness and visible in the safelight's yellow glow. The outline of her face, framed by her hair, quickly followed; the image was no longer black and white, for the shadings between were toning the portrait.

It was almost ready. Meryl stopped rocking the tray and reached for the tongs.

With a swift movement, she jerked the photograph out of the tray and slid it into a second tray. The stop bath, its sharp, clean smell brought up to her by the movement, only served as a shock-stop for the darkening chemicals on the paper which, after its brief plunge, Meryl held up in the air, letting the drips fall back into the tray. Then she slid the photo into the third tray, image face down, releasing the tongs' grip on the corner of the paper and seeing the sheet move of its own accord as she gave the tray a slight tip to get the hypo into a gently rocking motion. She would leave the photo in the fixative bath for the net ten minutes, but after the first three would turn it over to have a closer look at the quality of the image she had obtained in the print.

Glancing up at the clock on the wall, she saw with surprise that it was almost time for dinner. That meant the end of printing for the day. With a sigh, she got off the stool and began putting away the other negatives she had planned to print; they would have to wait until the weekend. While the eight-by-ten-inch portrait of Nélida was still fixing, Meryl slipped the negatives, each in its glassine envelope, into a small file holder and shut the lid; then she covered the enlarger with its protective hood.

Turning her attention back to the work she had accomplished that afternoon, she scrutinized the last picture, adding it to the others already washing in the sink.

Checking to make sure all boxes of photographic paper had been covered and put away, Meryl flipped on the light switch. The room, originally Madame's bedroom, had been converted into a makeshift darkroom earlier in the year when Madame, in a surprise move, had announced she was returning to France to keep house for her brother.

"I thought he was fighting with de Gaulle..."

"He was—but now, no more. For all of us, *chérie*, comes a time when the work must stop."

It turned out Madame Benoit had been planning along those lines for many years; there was the little plot of land she had invested in many years ago, and a modest little house on it.

"... and the time has come I need to return home, is that not so? To my own people, and my land...."

"She's probably been saving it in a sock under her bed for years," Yvonne observed when she was told of Madame's imminent departure. "They're all like that—and it's just as well, too, isn't it, Philipe? You don't need her any more, anyway...."

They were having lunch together, Philipe, Yvonne, and Meryl; Nélida, as always, was serving, and Madame had gone out for the day. Edie was expected in B.A. the following week; Wilfred was at the country club, entertaining some wartime cronies. As family gatherings went those days, it was a quiet and pleasant affair.

Not that they got together very often; there seemed little reason to do so and, increasingly, less desire. In the chaotic weeks after Yvonne's return, they had all been thrown together constantly, in different combinations: Edie, Yvonne, and Meryl; Yvonne and Edie; Wilfred, Yvonne, Edie, and Meryl; or Meryl, Wilfred, and Yvonne. After the meeting on the pier, there had only been one other occasion at which both men were present, a brief cocktail hour at the hotel before Edie went off to attend an *estancieros'* dinner, escorted by Tim Casey, down for the occasion.

But if the weeks, and many of the meetings, had been chaotic, for Meryl the decision about her future had been crystal clear. She refused, pointblank to even consider living with her mother.

"... and besides everything else, Dad, she's made up her mind she wants a house and a garden. That means the suburbs, and you know most of my friends are here in town."

Philipe looked at his daughter and said, "That argument doesn't hold much water. You and that bunch you run around with are always roaring around in and out of the suburbs. Besides, what's a short train ride?"

Meryl looked back at him with much the same expression.

"It won't be a short one. I guarantee it. You know what Mother's like. . . . And anyway, I just don't want to live with her and Wilfred. It'd feel all wrong. I'm staying here."

It wasn't that Meryl objected to Wilfred as such. There wasn't anything about him to object to. In fact, there were many times it was hard to remember he was there at all. Wilfred was amiably vague and quietly polite, unobtrusive to a point verging on the unnoticeable.

But his original impact as the unexpected remained, and her unseen bruise still ached from the invisible blow.

"I'm not going to live with them, and that's that."

Neither Philipe nor Edie tried to change Meryl's mind.

Yvonne, coasting on what she saw as her triumphant return, complete with English husband and social approval, had chosen to ignore direct confrontation on any subject. She threw herself into a frenzy of house hunting.

"... you see, I've been virtually homeless for so long, I'm absolutely busting to have a place of my own. . . ."

There was little else she chose to talk about. If she spoke about England, her family audience was quickly bored. In turn, they had little to say that held her interest; only themes of immediate mutual concern held them together.

"... yes, Mummy, I *did* arrange everything properly, and the stuff from La Maison will be arriving any day. . . ."

"I'm sure nobody's using my old dressing table, Philipe, so I'd like to have it back if you don't mind. . . ."

"... of course I'm disappointed, Meryl, but I don't want to insist. Tell you what: I'll fix up one of the bedrooms for you, and then you can come to stay with us whenever you like. . . ."

The one story that had held everybody's interest was the

407

smuggling of Coco. Yvonne's explanation was ingenuously simple.

"But I *had* to smuggle him. There was no other way of getting him into England. I realized that before I went over to Cannes. So I got the monkey pajama case—saw it at Lally's, an American gave it to her—and took it over with me. While I was at La Maison, I trained him to sleep in it."

She was convinced Coco had recognized her.

"You should have heard the screaming and the fuss when he first saw me. Yves and his wife had him in the flat over the garage. . . . They lived there, all through the war . . . living on next to nothing. . . . At one point, Yves told me, they only had the peaches from the garden to eat. . . ."

By the time Yvonne was ready to return to London, Coco was well accustomed to his new sleeping quarters.

"I'm sure it all stems from the time I first got him, when he was so near death. All those nights I held him in his little rag basket . . . anyway, he was as good as gold when we got to the customs'. Not a peep out of him. I did the same thing getting him on board to come out here—and I saw no reason to risk an argument with the Argentine customs, either . . ."

The parrot, edging up and down the newly purchased parrot stand stationed near the window of their hotel room, cocked his head and began to whistle, encouraged by the sounds of traffic below.

"If you stay here long enough, he'll start hooting like the cars," said Edie.

"I suppose so—but I *do* hope we find a house soon. . . ."

The Hume-Hawleys found exactly what they wanted during the closing days of the long summer, shortly before Meryl returned to school for her last year there. It was a pretty place, within walking distance of the railway station to which service was reasonable and regular, almost an hour's ride from town.

"You see?" said Meryl in tones of triumph. "I told you so, didn't I?"

"You did, and you were right, and you win," Philipe said, smiling. "And you'll never guess what the prize is. . . ."

Puzzled, Meryl said, "I didn't think there was one."

"Neither did I—but I got a letter from Sal di Leo today. He says he got the photos you sent, and . . ."

Meryl looked around the darkroom, and for the umpteenth

time gave silent and mental thanks to Sal for his encouragement, his suggestions, his aiding and abetting of her attempts at a career. Not that her father ever needed much pushing to give her the things she wanted. But would she or Philipe ever have thought seriously about getting a darkroom installed if it had not been for Sal's cheery insistence on the subject when he wrote?

... having an eye isn't all there is to taking good pictures if you want to rise about the happy-amateur ranks ... even if you end up farming out the lab work, you'll do far better if you know how it works ... besides, it's fun ...

It was more than fun; it was spellbinding, magic.

Meryl discovered it was one thing to see a potential picture in real life and try to capture its light and mood and moment, all in one swift metallic click. But it was quite another to see the results emerging on the sheets of wet, white paper as they lay submerged in chemicals in the white enamel trays. There was the intense moment of watching the image come up, its darkest shadows first, starting as a hint, then spreading and deepening into shape and line and form, the grays next, and then the lighter lines, until only the whitest of white parts remained unmarked and the image was complete, a picture, sometimes the picture she had aimed for in the first place, sometimes not, but a picture of its own, nonetheless.

As she experimented further, she found she could alter a picture's mood and will, sometimes by jerking it out of the developer tray ahead of time, perhaps at the one-minute mark, thus cutting its emergence to a fleeting impression of image, with only the first and boldest of strokes visible, swift contrast captured, full dimensions only inferred. Or she could leave the sheet in overtime, cooking its chemicals until every last possible shade had been pulled up from the latent impression.

And knowing the chemical format and formulae did not destroy the illusion one whit. That's what I'm working in, Meryl realized—illusions. Images and illusions, things seen as I wish to see them, forms depicted as I want them to be.

She spent hours in the cramped, converted room, working in the shadows cast by the yellow light, switching to total darkness while she loaded or unloaded her cut-film holders, feeling for their code notches in the upper righthand corner, the stinging smell of acetic acid and hypo clean and clear to her, fresh and stimulating.

The first day she had every locked herself into the newly equipped darkroom and turned off the top light, Meryl had felt she was wrapping her own private world around her, safe and secure.

And, above all, far from so many edgy voices.

Edie, who decided to cut her B.A. sojourn short, made little attempt to disguise her disgust.

At lunch with Yvonne and Meryl, she said, "...so of course now I understand why you wanted the divorce. I thought at the time there was something funny going on...."

"No, there wasn't. You're quite wrong, Mummy. I think..."

"Don't tell me you didn't have it all planned...."

"I didn't even *know* Wilfred at the time. Do try to be fair to us, Mummy. We hadn't even *met*...."

The meeting had taken place in hospital, Yvonne explained.

"I used to go there almost every day, to visit Aunt Moo, as you know..."

"Why didn't you mention it in your letters? You could at least have let us know you were getting married...."

"I wanted it to be a surprise..."

"Didn't it cross your mind it might be a bit of a shock? That we'd be totally unprepared? That, if we'd known, Philipe might have chosen to be away, so as to...well, make things easier..."

"But I thought you'd all be so glad, that you'd be happy for me, for my happiness...."

They were all discussions that had no common ground. The realities of wartime life in England were alien and remote from both Meryl and Edie, for the latter, although she knew London well, only remembered it in other moods; the postwar atmosphere of a large hospital was distant from anything she had ever known. Besides, she wasn't interested, she told Yvonne sharply. The war was over, and this was B.A. The important thing was the present, and the planning of the future.

"...and as to your planning to get a house here, I think it's ridiculous."

"But *why*, Mummy?"

"There's the whole *estancia* waiting for you, and..."

410

Yvonne brushed the idea aside.

"It's quite out of the question. Wilfred still needs care. His arm... additional treatment... still having spasms of pain..."

"I'm sure he doesn't need care every day. He could go to Rosario every so often, and..."

"Certainly not! I wouldn't dream of letting him go anywhere but the British Hospital here...."

Meryl tried to blank out their voices and let her thoughts turn on her own problems and views. Her last year of school meant a certain amount of application to studies, but nothing she felt would be of monumental difficulty. No, it wasn't school that was causing her any problems. It was the rest of life.

And not all the changes were problems, exactly, but they were differences that needed absorbing and accommodating. For all the discussion that went on in school. the choices open to a girl leaving the Bowen School and entering the job market in Buenos Aires were limited to three: she could become a teacher, she could be a secretary, or she could enter nurses' training at the British Hospital. To attempt anything else was to risk ridicule, scorn, rejection, and sound condemnation.

A fortunate few planned trips "home" to England and domestic economy courses or a university there; some only saw the trip as a means of moving to another part of the world, the part they identified as their rightful heritage. Occasionally, a girl was heard to say she planned higher studies at a local university, but her heritage was inevitably mostly Argentine, and then, she was sure to be a "brain," too—aspiring to be a lawyer, or something equally unusual.

"You could go to college in the States," Philipe suggested. "Most of the kids from the American School will be going, I'd imagine."

"Then why wasn't I sent there so I'd have an American education from the start?" Meryl wanted to know, her question rhetorical, as she understood full well the circumstances that had led her to what would be a week's long series of examinations, the questions sent out from England in sealed, official envelopes. "The whole thing's so silly...."

"Look, Meryl, you don't have to make any decisions now. Let's see how you feel about things after you get through the Cambridge exams in November. Then you'll have the whole summer to think it over. Okay?"

And there the matter had rested, as far as Meryl and Philipe were concerned.

Not so for Edie and Yvonne.

". . . and since you're divorced you won't even be able to present her at court. I suppose I should go back to London with her and see if I. . . ."

"I don't think it'd work, Mummy. Meryl doesn't seem to want a season anywhere."

"Isn't she going to have a coming out party?"

Yvonne suppressed a smile.

"The whole attitude here in B.A. seems to dribble out long before the age of seventeen. . . ."

The next time Yvonne saw Meryl, she recounted the conversation with Edie, and Meryl also smiled and had to agree with her mother. The formality of a presentation season, hollowly imitated by a few Anglo community diehards, was neither honored nor observed; apart from the grind of school and exams, life for Meryl and her friends consisted of setup weekend surprise parties, dates in groups to go to the cinema, gropings in the backseats of ramshackle cars, and a few big formal dances, sponsored for the most part by community organizations.

There was also the easily available world of athletics. All the country clubs had at least one pool, and sometimes several, separating high divers from leisurely swimmers. Tennis courts were available, and there were the bridle paths in the parks of Palermo or the riding fields further out of town and the river itself, with its yacht clubs and beaches.

No; a formal season in London was far from Meryl's mind. There was no waiting; it was all going on already, the fun of planning the next surprise party, the next outing, the fun of fooling stiff-necked parents who insisted on staying up, bleary-eyed, to see that no one danced too closely, too intimately cheek-to-cheek in their hallowed living room with the furniture pushed aside, the arm of the record player being sneaked back, over and over again, to the beginning of the same record, the one the parents had said was going to be "the very last dance now, mind you, this is the last" and didn't know enough to recognize its repetition for ages.

There were the records of Tommy Dorsey and the dead Glen Miller and the new bebop emerging, which some liked and some didn't, but the music was there. And then there were the soft boleros, moonlight become music, and the open-air nightclubs out along the road leading to the suburbs, by the river, with the patio dancing and the dusky gloom, where one could sip Coca Cola and dance cheek-to-cheek and feel the thrill of the boy of the moment, pressing closer and knowing he'd grapple all the way back home, where parental lights would be burning with midnight disapproval.

Shortly after the Hume-Hawleys had moved into their house, Meryl was invited to a weekend surprise party at a home in the same suburb. It was decided she might as well spend the night at her mother's, thus breaking the ice in the new format of their family life.

She arrived out on a mid-morning train on Saturday, the crisp autumn air bright with sunshine and tinted with smoke. Yvonne met her at the station, and they walked back to the house together, their conversation swift and shallow, the exchange of pleasantries and the news of the day.

"Dad's leaving for New York next month...."

"Wilfred's a bit under the weather, so try not to make a noise when you're upstairs...."

"...beastly algebra test next week..."

"Lots of nice English people around here, you know, and the party you're going to tonight is right around the corner from us...."

The day was spent admiring the house, seeing the garden, meeting Yvonne's neighbors, ironing her party dress. Wilfred emerged after lunch, said a pale "Hullo. Nice to see you," and disappeared off to the country club. The party took care of Saturday night, and Meryl slept late the next day, but after Sunday lunch, when Wilfred once again excused himself and went to lie down for a while, mother and daughter sat in the living room with hours to spare and, suddenly, little to say.

"It seems funny, doesn't it... all those years... all the changes..." Yvonne smiled at Meryl as her words faded into silence once more. Leaning forward, she tried again. "Perhaps it's harder for me, in some ways. You were still a little girl when I left, and now..."

"That's what Dad said"—Meryl nodded—"he said you'd find me a *señorita* when you came back, and that it'd be a shock."

"Well, I wouldn't exactly call it a shock—not in the unpleasant sense, anyway. But... well... a *surprise*, I suppose.

413

You've grown up—and I know so little of what your interests are. . . ."

After a short pause, Meryl said, "Well, apart from the photography, which I've already told you about, there hasn't been time for much else. Life's been all full of school."

"Bowen is certainly very different from what it was in the days when I went to it," Yvonne observed. "More like Crestwood Close, in some ways. D'you play a lot of games? Hockey? Tennis?"

Meryl drew back in her chair.

"I detest games."

"Oh," Yvonne looked down at her outstretched legs for a moment. Then she looked over at her daughter again. "All games?"

"I think so. Yes. I hate jumping around with a lot of other people."

"But you like dancing."

"That's different."

Yvonne waited for Meryl to say more, but no more was forthcoming. She gave a last, despairing try.

"How about swimming?"

Meryl shifted in her chair and acknowledged, in a close to grudging tone, that yes, swimming was something she did like.

"I even got a few ribbons for it. Last year and the year before."

"Oh, good." Yvonne beamed with approval. "I was school champion, you know. I mean in England."

"Yes, I know."

The awkward silence closed in again. Yvonne felt a tightness rising in her throat, and then remembered.

"I've been meaning to ask you, Meryl—d'you still sing?"

"Not much." A shrug. "Only on the *estancia*, really. With Lala. We still sing from time to time."

"Isn't it a funny coincidence we both have close friends with such similar names? Your Lala, my Lally . . ."

"But their real names are quite different."

Yvonne ignored the abrupt brushing aside and returned to the earlier subject.

"Remember the fun we used to have singing together? Not only with Lala, but also the two of us . . . on the train coming back, in the compartment . . . what *was* that song we used to sing so often? I only remember bits of the melody. . . ."

414

Yvonne hummed the opening bars. After a few moments, Meryl, almost despite herself, joined in.

"*Caminante, no hay camino* ...traveler, there is no way..."

From the far reaches of hidden-away memory. Meryl saw and felt the days of childhood, the opaque veil ripped away. Her voice rose, Yvonne's blended in.

> ... first you're walking, then you're running
> Then you dance the whole day through...

Their voices grew louder, split in harmony, came together in unison on the last note. Yvonne reached out. Meryl rose from her chair and flung herself into her mother's arms, and the two women clung together, and wept.

Although such moments of closeness were rare, it got easier for them to be together as time went on. Meryl grew to enjoy going to stay with her mother and Wilfred, and by and large her sojourns in the Hume-Hawley household went well, though on occasion the unexpected caused friction.

Meryl was brushing her teeth when she noticed the silver object. It was on the bathroom shelf, standing next to Wilfred's military hair brushes. She picked it up, wondering what on earth it was. Mostly, it resembled a footed eggcup, with an elongated oval bowl instead of an egg-hugging round. Intrigued, she carried it downstairs to the breakfast table.

"What's this?" she wanted to know.

Yvonne turned bright pink.

"Wilfred's mustache cup," she said.

"His *what*?"

"You heard me."

"But how does he use it?"

"He places it over his mustache to shape it...."

"Like a *curler*?"

Yvonne hedged. "Well, more or less. Now," her voice strengthened. "you go and put that back at once, before Wilfred wakes up...."

But the next weekend Meryl stayed there, she was told she could use the little bathroom off the landing halfway up the stairs.

"... so much more convenient for all of us," Yvonne said in a studiedly offhand manner. "*Much* more private for you, and you can leave all your things in there, of course..."

The suburb itself, a bastion of the British community, had a sizable population of young Anglo-Argentines in their last years of school or their first in the business world. Meryl joined in their activities on the weekends she spent there; on Sunday evenings she would take the train and return to the city and the rhythm of city life and, on Monday morning, school and her school world.

"It's rather like changing gears," she told Philipe the night before he left on a flight for New York. "And no, I don't want to stay with Mother while you're away. Look, I've been here on my own before."

"Madame was still here."

"For goodness' sake, Dad, I've got Nélida, and the cook, and I certainly don't need a governess any more. But okay, if it gets difficult, I'll move to Mother's till you get back...."

Such a move did not prove necessary, but Meryl did spend a long weekend helping Yvonne unpack her crate of belongings that arrived form La Maison. The bulk of the shipment was forwarded to Edie at El Ombú.

"... but I put my own personal things in here, so I could get to them right away." Yvonne, festooned with excelsior and smudged with dust, took out each wrapped object with love and care. "Oh, look—this must be my *rebenque*... the old *capataz* gave it to me, years and years ago, just before Mummy and Maurice got married.... The handle'll need a good polish..."

There were photo albums and dance programs, souvenirs from her debutante days, each with its accompanying anecdote to be recounted. Meryl helped and listened and looked. and admired; the photos, in particular, held her interest, especially if they were official portraits.

".... and I think it must've been midnight before I got to the photographer—I was *sure* my feathers were crooked, but they weren't... and here's my wedding photo..."

Toward the bottom of the packing crate, there was an album of records.

"I only packed my favorites... there were dozens more at La Maison...."

Later that night they played the old tunes on the Hume-Hawleys' newly installed record player. Many of the songs were famous and still popular.

"... but the bands sound so funny," Meryl giggled, and Yvonne agreed.

"Now, this one is one of my favorite favorites," she explained, cleaning the dust from the black grooved surface and placing it on the changer. The needle descended and the melody began. Yvonne sang softly along with the vocalist.

"*Adiós*, Buenos Aires, good-bye..."

Meryl listened, intrigued, then enchanted.

"Oh, I must get the words down—it's very pretty.... No, I've never heard it before...."

"They're sure to revive it here someday...."

"Can I take it up to the *estancia*? I'm sure Lala'd love to hear it..."

"All right—but please be careful with it, and remember to bring it back. I wouldn't want anything to happen to it...."

"I'll take extra care, I promise."

And so, when the midyear examinations were over, Meryl packed the record with her clothes in the suitcase she always used when she went to the *estancia*.

"But of course I remember it. I remember it very well indeed," said Edie, turning around in the swivel chair at the far end of the room. "Play it again, darling. It reminds me of all the lovely times we used to have at La Maison. Pity you weren't born then—weren't there to see it. But there it is. Life's all different now."

She turned back and busied herself at the desk while Meryl wound up the gramophone again.

"*Adiós*, Buenos Aires, good-bye..."

"You must remember to play it for Lala when she comes home tomorrow...."

Lala, now attending a state school in Córdoba City where she would earn a teaching degree, arrived back the next night, more intent on books than music.

"If I study hard, I might be able to do two years in one," she told Meryl. "And the sooner I get my certificate, the sooner I can go to work."

"D'you think you'll like teaching?"

Lala shrugged. "I don't really now—not till I try it, anyway."

"Then why did you pick it?"

"Because I know I want to do something that'll help make things better. Teaching's a good place to start."

"Here in the *pueblo*?"

Lala shook her head. "No, Córdoba, probably, I—I like it

there. I like the city, and I like the hills—anywhere, really, as long as it isn't in the Ladies Society school."

"Perhaps you could take it over."

With vehemence, Lala said. "I'd love to." Then, with her voice back to normal, she went on, "But I think I'll start with something in Córdoba City itself. . . ."

"Sounds to me like you've made friends."

Lala smiled. "That, too. There's a good bunch. We share a lot of ideas."

"I'll miss you."

"Come to Córdoba and visit me."

"Why don't you come to B.A.? There must be lots of schools to teach at—the suburbs are growing, for one thing."

Lala shot Meryl a sideways glance.

"And just where d'you think I'd fit in?" she demanded. "With your crowd? Hardly. I have to find my own life, Meryl, my own group. It isn't that you and your family haven't been wonderful to me—but I have to find my own way. . . ."

"Lala, I didn't mean to . . ." Meryl began, but Lala's torrent of words drowned out her apology.

"It's like being a bird that doesn't belong to the flock—the others peck you to death. You have to find your own kind. Only I don't belong to any flock, anywhere. To be a *criada* fifty years ago, well, maybe it was slavery at times, but at least you belonged . . ."

"But you belong here. . . ."

"In what capacity?" Lala's voice had risen, was tortured, acute. "As a maid, when I work with Rosita? Then why the supposedly fancy education at the Society school? As a daughter? I'm not adopted. I have no rights, no parents, no hold. There's nothing *real* for me here, nothing legal, nothing that can't be blown away by other people's change of heart, or mood. Or death," she added in a quieter tone. "I hate to say it, Meryl—but supposing your grandmother died? What then?"

"I suppose my mother . . ."

Lala's gaze held a quality of pity within its slight smile.

"You don't understand, Meryl—and it's good that you don't. You'll never have to, and for that, you're very lucky. But for me, a *criada,* and for many others, *supposing* something is not only not good enough; it is dangerous."

After a while, she said, "Meryl—forgive me. I must sound so ungrateful, so unpleasant, so . . ."

"No—no . . . that's not true . . ."

"... but more and more, I realize that it is difficult for me, and all the others like me. I need to know who I am, where I belong, where I should go... what to do..."

Their talks were mostly serious that brief winter holiday at El Ombú, and after Lala left to return to Córdoba, Meryl packed her mother's record carefully and took it back with her to Buenos Aires.

For the next few months, Meryl saw little of her mother. Her last term at school and the final exams loomed too large, too all-absorbing to be shunted aside on weekends; what spare time she had, Meryl preferred to spend in the protection of the darkroom.

Yvonne, busy in her own sphere, did not press for meetings with her daughter, nor did she visit Edie up at El Ombú. The full focus of her life was captured by her enjoyment of being a returned volunteer, the war bride of a military hero, complete with a jangle of medals. Everything was splendid—except for the local political situation, of course. But what could you expect? Look at the caliber of the people...."

Yvonne couldn't understand the Labour Government in England, either, pontificating about politics in growing discontent.

"Lally says it's awful," she told Edie, when Edie, down for a week's shopping, asked her to lunch at the hotel. "Rationing just goes on and on, and everything sounds so dreary for her.... She's terribly unhappy: John's decided to do the decent thing, and go back to his wife in South Africa, of course...."

Yvonne's eyes were bright with sympathy and tears. She went on, "And it really is tragic. Lally and John were *made* for each other. It's all Mr. and Mrs. Young's fault...."

Later, she refused her mother's invitation to stay in town for dinner.

"No, Mummy, I can't. I must get back to have dinner with Wilfred."

"Pity. Meryl and Philipe are coming, and I thought it'd be nice if we all..."

At dinner, Edie spoke contemptuously of Hume-Hawley.

"... didn't even have the grace to come in with Yvonne. ... All that talk about his heroism is all very well, but now that the war's over, what's he going to do?"

"Perhaps he can't do very much, Grannie..."

"You mean because of his arm? Nonsense, child. There's lots he can do. Yvonne told me with great pride about his riding, and his bowling. Seems to spend his time on the bowling green at the club..."

Edie also repeated the news about Lally. Philipe nodded.

"Yes, I know. She rang to tell me about it yesterday. I get the impression Yvonne's terribly upset about it, too."

Edie gestured to the waiter, who rolled the pastry and dessert cart over to the table.

"Yvonne always did prefer living other people's troubles rather than facing up to her own. Now, darlings, what shall we have? And doesn't it all look scrumptious today...."

2

Meryl's final exams began in late November; for two weeks, she attended school for the required hours of the examinations, returning home to prepare herself for the next day's test.

When it was over, she told Philipe, "I feel as though I'm walking around in a haze."

"You're probably tired out."

"I am—but it's more than that...."

Much of the lassitude was the letdown after the examinations themselves. Results would not be forthcoming until the middle of the following year, as all the papers, sealed and locked in shipment boxes, were returned to the English university. The marking and grading and returning of results took months; it would probably be June before anything was known.

"It's such an anticlimax...all that work, and then... nothing...."

By Christmas, however, the mood was beginning to lift. Meryl spent the day in awkward, partial enjoyment at her mother's house, where they had champagne at lunch. Yvonne was in a sentimental mood, speaking of Christmases past; Wilfred, glassy-eyed, repaired to the living room sofa after the meal, whence soon came a series of snores. Mother and daughter conversed in low tones over the dining room table, as it was too hot to go outside, but by mid-afternoon there was nothing more to say, and Meryl took an early evening train back into town.

New Year, however held more promise. All-night outdoor parties were long a tradition in B.A., and all the clubs planned celebrations, with dance floors and music out under the stars and often a breakfast in the light of the new year's dawn. Meryl had an invitation from a friend to join her family and their group at a yacht club; she chose that over Yvonne's suggestion that she attend the country club.

"... and Wilfred's already reserved a table... of course there'll be room for you...."

Meryl declined, her previous invitation solid armor. The only problem was what to wear; a long dress was imperative, and her party clothes looked childish to her, unfit for the new mood she felt awakening within herself. Even her hand-holding boyfriends of the recent past were beginning to provoke stifled yawns, and surprise parties on Saturday nights had dimmed to boredom, too.

And then Sarita Estrada rang up.

Sarita was the latest in the long succession of Philipe's companions, no longer defined as honorary aunts. However, Sarita was different from most of the others—she had been around a lot longer than any of her predecessors.

Although she was in her early thirties, she was much like Meryl in size and structure, unaffected in manner and ways. With Meryl she was friendly, rather than patronizing, and there were no false barriers of affectation between them. Sarita genuinely liked Philipe's daughter, and her sincerity showed; she maintained an easy balance between father and daughter, able to confide in either, and move individually within each one's different world.

"She's so easy to be with," Meryl had remarked on an early occasion, and Philipe had wholeheartedly agreed.

Yvonne had asked Meryl, "Is he going to marry her?"

"I haven't the faintest idea. Why?"

"I just thought you might know."

"No, I don't—but if you want to find out; why don't you ask him?"

But Yvonne never did. As Edie pointed out when they mentioned Sarita Estrada: "He never married any of the others, did he?" a fact also often stressed by other people in B.A.

If the gossip about them ever reached her, Sarita never showed any signs of distress, nor did she ever place even the most subtle of pressures on Philipe, a habit frequently displayed by other companions in the past. She was highly independent, the widow of an *estanciero* who had died of appendicitis shortly after they were married. The property, now run by her brother-in-law, served as her official home, but she kept an apartment in the heart of Buenos Aires and a summer house over in Uruguay, her native land, where her father still practised medicine.

As always, Meryl was glad to hear her voice.

"I call to tell you your father sent me a cable. He'll be back from Peru in a week's time. Perhaps after that you'll come and spend some time at the beach with me? I'm going over to Monte next week."

Meryl thanked her for the invitation and then described her dilemma.

". . . so I don't know what to wear."

"That's easy. I'll lend you something of mine. Come and pick out what you want. . . ."

"Oh, I don't think I . . ."

"Then I'll choose a few and take them over. I was on my way over in your direction anyway—I'm going to play tennis. . . ."

A half hour later, she was at the door.

"Here." She thrust a large bundle of loosely-gathered clothes into Meryl's arms. "Have fun. . . ."

In the end, Meryl chose a simple, black, unadorned dress that she knew her mother would consider unsuitable but which was, unmistabably, the one that looked best on her. That night, when she called Sarita to tell her about it, and thank her, her father's mistress laughed and agreed.

"Of *course* it's unsuitable . . . but that'll make it even more exciting to wear if you feel comfortable in it. . . ."

And Meryl, walking in front of the mirror to admire her borrowed finery, felt a kinship with the dress she could not explain in words.

Feeling ill at ease and somewhat defiant, Meryl made her way through the crowded clubhouse dining room and to the bar, where she got herself another orangeade. She was not enjoying the evening as she had expected to and was beginning to feel increasingly out of place, lonely, bored. The raucous jollity that was the prevailing mood grated on her, making her want to withdraw. And if one more idiot tried to get her to wear a paper hat, she thought she'd burst into open anger.

Why couldn't everyone simply dance and enjoy the evening? The night sparkled with stars overhead. And on the river, its waters lapping at the yacht club's velvety lawned edges, the yachts and boats moved and rustled, their lights reflected in the River Plate's surface.

She turned and bumped into the person beside her. The jolt sent a splash from her drink onto the floor.

"Oh, I'm sorry. . . ."

Another jolt, from behind, made her spill some more. The young man next to her snatched the glass from her hands.

"Since you insist on pouring your disgusting drink all over me—come, let's dance. At least I'll be safe . . ."

"I *said* I was sorry. . . ."

But he wasn't listening, or waiting to hear what she had to say; instead, he pulled her along by the hand, breaking a path through the crowd to the dance floor. He was fairly tall, a narrow-shouldered man, with dust-colored, tightly-waved hair which was close-cropped, covering a neatly shaped head.

He slowed his pace as they reached the floor, leading her into the rhythm of the music as though they had been dancing together for years.

"Now, isn't that better than throwing your drink at me?" He was smiling down at her, and he had strangely pale eyes. She smiled back. They danced a few more steps and then the fox-trot came to an end.

The music began again in different rhythms. An undercurrent of disappointment made the dance floor's round: the legally required interlude of Argentine music was about to get underway. The crowd thinned out immediately; the usual comments were heard.

". . . so silly to run people's fun by Government decree . . ."

". . . nothing but dreary tangos—God, how I hate 'em . . ."

". . . just like the natives, my dear—always done up in pale black, and wallowing in emotion . . ."

The tango's opening bars thumped out. Meryl expected her partner to lead the way off the floor, but instead, he stood still, looking down at her.

"Is your name Gabriela?" he asked.

"No."

"It should be."

"Why?"

"That's what they're playing," he said impatiently. "*Gabriela*. It's a marvelous tango. Don't you know it?"

"No, I'm afraid I don't."

"Well, you can listen as we dance to it. You do, I presume, know how?"

"Well..." Meryl hesitated.

His grip on her hand shifted position, became more secure; he tightened his hold across her back. "Ready?"

"I really don't think I..."

"Why not?"

"Well, I so seldom..."

He whistled in exasperation.

"Don't fuss, woman. Here we go..."

It was all so effortless under his guiding hands. They led off in a firm swoop that led into a glide and a series of calm, easy steps dictated by the music's unmistakable beat. He sang the words softly into her ear, interrupting himself to say, "There. You see? You do it beautifully," after which he continued humming. Meryl didn't answer, concentrating on following him. What she had told him was true: she seldom danced tangos, as most of the boys in her crowd made directly for the sidelines, or their table, whenever the *bandoneones* struck up.

Meryl knew she was dancing well; there was no awkwardness, no feeling of strain. She danced, relaxed for the first time that evening, her body responding to the slightest signal given by the hand holding her back. Her partner tucked her into the figure-of-eight step, the *paso-de-ocho* she had so often admired, but never attempted before. Then they slid out, pacing side by side. The dance floor was wide open, few couples sharing it with them in the tango's beat.

They went into the *paso-de-ocho* again, this time a double one, their movements mirroring each other in perfect step. Meryl became aware of the floor clearing around them.

"I think they're watching us...."

Her partner grinned. "I should bloody well hope so. And when the music finishes, I'll sweep you off amid the applause, and get you a drink... if you promise not to spill it all over me, of course...."

424

At the bar, after he'd ordered champagne for both of them, he turned to her and said, "I'm Jimmy Casterán. Who the hell are you?"

She told him.

"Meryl," he repeated. "I've never met a Meryl before."

"I haven't either," she admitted. "I mean, I don't think there are many of us."

He took the glasses from the bartender and handed one to her.

"I'm sure there's only one of you." He was looking at her intently, his eyes narrowed, as though he were puzzled by something, looking for an answer. "Shall we go outside? It's cooler there. . . ."

They went out onto the tiered flagstone expanse that formed the front of the yacht club, overlooking the river.

Jimmy remarked, "Here come the first of the balloons. . . ."

Meryl looked up and saw the flickering light of the paper balloon's candle against the star-filled sky. Another was drifting close behind it, and then several more appeared over the tops of the high trees lining the top of the bank. Some of the balloons were probably almost as tall as she was, she knew, but tonight was a good, clear night for them to rise high on the heat generated by the thick, squat candles anchored at their base, and they seemed small and vulnerable in their steady course, the slight breeze aiding their journey.

"You know what they're doing, don't you?" Jimmy said. "They're all looking for a haystack to drop into. The decree never works."

"What decree?"

"The one issued every year." His voice changed as he intoned: "It is expressly forbidden to all citizens of this republic to light up hot air balloons during the celebration of New Year festivities." Jimmy held his glass up in a mock toast. "Marvelous way of reminding everyone there's only a week left to dash out and buy as many balloons as they can afford."

"If they don't want people to buy them, they shouldn't let them be sold. . . ."

"If you're going to be *sensible* about things, you'll take all the fun out of life and government. . . ."

Meryl laughed. Jimmy smiled and took her hand again.

"Never mind politics. Let's go and dance. . . ."

The rest of the night was enchanted; they danced, they

sang "Auld Lang Syne" at midnight, they talked, they danced some more. When the sun came up, they had coffee together, but Jimmy refused to let Meryl eat breakfast.

"Not here, girl—not with the peasants. Go and find the people you come with, and tell them I'm taking you home."

Meryl looked dubious. He seized her hand.

"All right—I'll tell 'em myself...."

They found Meryl's host, who apparently knew Jimmy by the way they greeted each other.

"All right, Casterán—just see that she gets back safely...." The face, too flushed, matched the slightly slurred speech. "And yes, don't you worry.... I'll tell the wife...."

As they walked across the gravel to the club's entrance, Jimmy said, "We timed that beautifully. Another half hour, and he'd have been out for the count. Blotto, as he always is, down to the balls."

Meryl giggled; Jimmy took her hand.

"Now, what'll it be? Bus or train?"

"It'll have to be the train," she answered. "The buses from here don't go very near my street...."

"Who said I was taking you there?" Jimmy demanded. "I said I was taking you home. I didn't specify yours. Acutally, we're going to mine—Miss Peggy'll make us tea or something. You wait and see."

"Who's Miss Peggy?" Meryl wanted to know as they boarded the *colectivo*, the stubby inter-urban bus that plied its route along the Bajo, the main road paralleling the river leading from the Tigre estuary all along the suburbs into the center of the city.

"You'll see. There's a seat, Meryl—grab it." He sat down next to her and paid for the fares. "And maybe *Don* Julio will join us, if he's up to it. My father rather old these days, but he's a good sort."

The ride was a long one, and Meryl grew drowsy, but she snapped awake when Jimmy said, "Up, girl—we're there."

A short walk along a cobbled street and then their journey ended. Meryl, nervous, said, "Are you sure we won't be disturbing your parents?" but Jimmy shook his head.

As they walked into the front hall, a woman emerged from a sun-filled doorway.

"I *thought* I heard the gate being opened.... Happy New Year...."

She was tall, and her gray hair was piled into a loose bun.

on top of her head, from which wisps had escaped, forming tendrils around her welcoming smile and face.

Jimmy said, "I've brought a guest, Miss Peggy.... Meryl, this is my mother. Meryl in full is Meryl van Landen—and I can't understand why I haven't met her before...."

Peggy Casterán came forward, her hands outstretched in warm greeting.

"But how delightful... you're Yvonne Waring's daughter, aren't you? I knew her when she was a schoolgirl. Do tell me all about her—I hear she's as lovely as ever...."

"Before we go into biography"—Jimmy interrupted—"are there any chances we could get something to eat?"

"But of course, Jimmy—let's all go into the kitchen. I don't know what we've got, and the maid's away on holiday—but I'm sure we'll manage...."

When Margaret Webb—Peggy to her friends and, indeed, almost everyone who knew her—left her position at Miss Bowen's English Day School for Girls shortly after the end of the First World War, she did so for financial reasons. Her widowed father, whom she had accompanied out to Argentina from their original home in Kent, was retiring from his job on the British-owned railways, and the pension offered was only barely adequate for them both.

"I'm sure I can get better wages in an office," she told her father. "Now that I know Spanish well. It was different when we first arrived out here...."

"But it'll mean you'll have to learn how to do shorthand...."

"Oh, I'll *manage*," she insisted. "Just you wait and see...."

Peggy had always managed, right from her early, motherless childhood; this quality of capability had always endeared her to everyone. At Miss Bowen's, staff and students alike had loved her, often seeking her help in weathering their scholastic storms. Peggy Webb enjoyed her work, and knew she would miss it.

"I'll miss the girls, too—and the teachers, but..."

Family finances had to come first, and so Miss Webb got down to business. She tackled lessons in typing and shorthand, learning not only the English version but the Spanish as well. Thus, by the time she had completed the course, she was a fully qualified, bilingual secretary, and she went out seeking a position in that field with high recommendation from Miss Bowen herself, who also gave her a silver sugar bowl as a token of her appreciation, and several letters of introduction to firms in the Anglo-Argentine business world.

One of these letters was addressed to the *escribania of Julio Casterán, whose office handled the school's everyday legalities. As was traditional for an escribano*—that halfway mark between lawyer and notary public in the Latin business culture—Julio Casterán dealt in accountancy and real estate, contracts and day-to-day business affairs requiring the knowledge and practise of his degree.

It was Casterán himself who conducted the interview.

"I understand, Miss Webb, you are looking for a position—while I am quite desperate to find someone who can handle English correspondence for me. . . ."

He gestured to a towering pile of envelopes on his desk, and Peggy found it difficult to suppress a smile. The *escribano* seemed so helpless in his confrontation with a few letters, yet the man himself appeared to be anything but a fool.

He was approaching sixty, a man of middle height and expanded middle girth. As the interview progressed, Peggy Webb found him to be mild in manner and of exquisite politeness, his thick, round spectacles giving him a somewhat owlish appearance. He had dark brown eyes, a trimmed mustache covering his wide upper lip, a short, blobby nose and a surprising mouth: it did not smile often, but when it did, the gesture radiated generosity and warmth.

". . . and I seem to be getting more and more work from the import-export firms here, dealing directly with England, which is very good indeed, except that here in my office we are incapable of dealing with it in correct English. . . ."

Within the month, Peggy Webb had joined the *escribania* as an employee; she soon fitted into its organized routine. Already in her early thirties, she was quickly considered as the eptiome of the "English miss"—*la mess inglesa*, as they called her behind her back, *la miss inglesa*, a spinster with a heart of gold, the type who could always be relied on and would never give any trouble. When women talked of her, their phrases inevitably started off, "Poor Miss Webb . . ." They found comfort in patronizing her; it was so easy to do.

Tall, slender to the point of gawkiness, her reddish-blonde hair always ready to curl in the damp B.A. weather, the English miss with the never-straight stockings and the slightly awry air was as well-liked at the office as she had been at the school. No one ever got to know her well; no one ever tried.

428

She was the English miss, soon a fixture on the premises. Even when her father suddenly died, only a brief period of mourning interrupted her steady presence, and after the required civilities of a small wreath and notes of condolence had been attended to, her loss was not referred to again.

It was during her second year of employment at the *escribania* that Julio Casterán fell ill. No one seemed to know the nature of his malaise, nor did anyone consider it fit or seemly to inquire.

"When he is better, he will return...."

And, in the meantime, there was office work to be done, letters to be revised, papers to be filed.

The whispers struck on a Monday morning: did anyone *know* what the English miss had done? It really could not be understood: to climb a wall and get into the garden of Mr. Casterán's house, because, it seemed, she had not been able to get an answer at the door, or, before that, on the telephone... but no, it was not *possible*... but yes, it happened to be true. Truly, this was scandalous... such disgraceful, disgusting behavior.... And in broad daylight, *on a Sunday*... one would have thought the English miss knew better....

... and into the house through a window, as well? This had to be exaggeration... alas, it wasn't; ragamuffin street boys, witnessing the incident, had shouted out their frenzied delight. This had brought the neighbors to watching posts behind window curtains, and so the shameful incident could not be denied. The urchins chanted of it for days.

"We saw the English miss climbing over.... I saw her pants when she lifted herself on the wall.... *La miss inglesa* went to see the *escribano* in his bed...."

Shameful. Simply shameful, and a horrendous disgrace. No one could get over it; no one could understand. What could *la miss* have been thinking about? Where was her decency of mind? The office and Casterán's sisters buzzed for days.... There was no question about it... they simply could not get over it at all....

Julio Casterán, slowly recovering from serious illness, had long days and even longer nights in which to get over and think over many matters in his mind. He thought back over his life, at its pattern from the beginning. And there were things, he knew, it had come time to change.

Julio had been the unexpected child of middle-aged parents who already had several daughters in their fold. All the girls were much older than the unplanned baby and, far from becoming a spoilt only son, Julio had grown up with the responsibilities of the world heaped on his shoulders.

His father's death during Julio's childhood brought matters of inheritance to the fore. It was discovered that the young boy had been left the one-fifth portion of the estate permitted to be bequeathed "at will"; the rest, as required by strict Argentine law, had been duly apportioned at all the members of the family.

Still, his older sisters saw Julio's inheriting of the extra share as cheating them out of money that could have enhanced their dowries; not all of them married in subsequent years, and the bone of financial contention continued to be picked and gnawed at through the decades. On reaching adulthood, Julio Casterán found himself saddled with all the burdens and obligations of his long-widowed mother and his quarrelsome, bothersome sisters. His was not a nature to evade or rebel.

He became an unassuming man, and quiet; he was painstaking in his work and self-effacing in his mode of life. He was totally committed to family duties, and his only personal indulgences were a passion for opera and the two vacations he always took every year, at which time Casterán, the total *porteño*, born and bred in the metropolis of Buenos Aires, would go away either to the seashore or to the camp, there to spend his waking hours out of doors, observing the local flora and fauna. He was especially interested in birds.

His business acquaintances and colleagues considered him to be unusually honest, unbelievably trustworthy—and a fool. No one should be so conscientious... besides, to be at the beck and call of his family... an honorable trait, to be sure, but... without any gain for himself whatsoever... no, it was unnatural.

And yet they could see there was nothing unnatural about Julio Casterán and so, knowing him to be considered invaluable by his clients, they wrote him off as a good-natured chump, the sort of man who could certainly be relied on and, possibly, used. Those who tried to do so, overplaying their hand, soon discovered they were wrong. Casterán proved stubborn; polite, but stubborn—truly an enigma to those who tried to delve deeper into the workings of his life and mind.

Few did so, preferring to accept the easier concept of the

good-natured chump, a concept bolstered by his immediate family's attitude.

All these and many more things went around in his mind as he lay, convalescing, in his family home. The points turned as he contemplated events and habits, both recent and past: his sisters' unreliability in the face of his recent illness; their basic indifference to his well-being; their carping and grubby natures, revealed in piercing spotlight by this incident—he had heard of their enraged gossiping, and their forays into his office.

Above all, he thought about the plucky behavior of Miss Peggy Webb who, flinging gossip and convention to the four winds, had battled her way through prejudice, over walls and through a window to bring him succor in his hour of serious need. He had only vague recollection of the time she had appeared; his high fever and wretched state had rendered him close to delirious. But he knew from the moment her face swam into his distorted vision that he was being saved.

"...please don't try to talk....I'll get a doctor...I'll manage...."

A cool cloth smoothed his face. Low voices filled the room. Sleep came, real rest...there was someone taking care. ...Later, he remembered trying to smile, but did not know whether it had been marked.

Having seen the shadow of his own morality, life and its verities assumed new perspectives. He considered them, growing stronger, gaining his health back again. Eventually, it came time to return to his office. He did so on a cold spring day in early September of 1921.

The first thing he noticed when he walked into his private office was the air: it was too still. The *escribano* had never noticed it to be that way before, so still as to feel almost solid, as though he had stepped into a place caught under a bell jar, motionless, lifeless, apart and forgotten by the steady hum of the outside world.

Of course...it had been weeks...no, more than that, almost two months since he had first fallen ill. Never before had he been away from his office for so extended a period. That was it: the place felt unused.

All the same, had no one entered here?

Of course they had. He could see the piles of work, all in neatly divided categories, waiting for him on his desk. That

431

was Miss Peggy's work, Miss Peggy who had kept everything up to date and sorted out, ready for his return, as though she had never doubted that he would.

Suddenly he realized that she had *not* doubted it. The only person who hadn't. . . . A filmy memory of his ghoulish sisters flickered; it was useless to brush it aside, unacknowledged. He knew them for what they were. Well, there was nothing he could do to change them; they were too old and set in their ways. But there were other things he could change, and the thought reminded him of several tasks he wished to get underway at once.

New purpose and energy echoed in his step as he walked over to a bookcase, pushed aside several volumes and reached for the knobs of the wall safe behind them. Carefully, he turned the dials. Minutes later, he was at his desk again, hard at work.

Throughout the rest of the *escribania*, life was proceeding along normal lines. A new office boy, all thumbs and confusion, was scurrying from room to room on a series of ill-executed errands; the bookkeeper, her temper as sharp as always, her winter cold still tinging her long, thin nose, and her black hat set, straight and implacably, down to her ears, harangued the newcomer at every turn.

"No, not *there*, you imbecile, the files belong *here*. . . . A tortoise would move faster . . . the youth of today is incapable of anything resembling decent work. . . . An idiot, that's what we've hired, a useless idiot. . . ."

The postman arrived, messengers came and went.

"Yes, Mr. Casterán has returned to the office. . . . No, he does not wish to be disturbed at the moment. . . . No, I really cannot tell you. . . . Perhaps this afternoon he will have some time . . . or perhaps tomorrow. . . ."

Her tone indicated the *escribano* might not see anyone for days to come—if, indeed, he ever saw anyone again. . . . The bookkeeper was in her element.

Peggy Webb came in late.

"I was at the printers'," she explained to the older, black-garbed woman. "Of course, nothing was ready. . . ." As she spoke, she hung her hat and coat on the stand by the entry, shaking the vestiges of the spring rain from her unruly hair. "Did Mr. Casterán get here all right? I mean, is he . . ."

The bookkeeper nodded toward the closed door.

"The *escribano* has been here for over an hour. He specifically told me that no one was to interrupt him. Absolutely no one. . . ."

Peggy nodded and went over to her own desk on the far side of the long room. Once seated, she methodically tackled the work awaiting her, appearing to be oblivious of anything else. But her thoughts kept reaching to the inner office. Poor Mr. Casterán. She wasn't at all sure he was ready to return to work. . . . He had been so desperately ill. . . . She would *never* forget what he had looked like when she found him almost at death's door and with no one looking after him, no doctor called. . . . When a medical man had finally arrived, at her frantic insistence, he had told her it might have only been a question of hours before it would have been too late. . . .

Even now, a chill ran through her, recalling how close the call had been. And it was such a terrible shame; Mr. Casterán was such a nice man. . . . Surely it was too soon for him to resume all his business engagements? She would so like to take him a nice cup of tea. . . .

When the buzzer on her desk signaled, Peggy hastily picked up her notebook, several letters needing the *escribano*'s signature and two freshly sharpened pencils. As she walked across to Casterán's door; she realized with surprise that she was trembling. Well, not really trembling—just a bit shaky. Too much coffee for breakfast, probably; pull yourself together, my girl. . . .

She did, and opened the door. Mr. Casterán was standing behind his desk, a pen in his hand, a double blotter open in front of him and a file Peggy had never seen before propped up against his desk lamp. Her surprise at seeing it was immediately overlaid by her concern for the man. He was *not* well enough to be at work yet. . . . He was still far too pale. . . .

"Good morning, Miss Peggy." His voice was its usual quiet pitch. "I see you already have things for me to sign. But they will have to wait. Please close the door."

Peggy did so; her employer remained standing as he continued to talk.

"I do not wish to embarrass either of us by belaboring the point of my gratitude for all you have done for me," he said. "Let it suffice that I know—believe me, Miss Peggy, I *know* —that I would not have survived had it not been for you."

"Oh, Mr. Casterán, I didn't . . ."

His hand went up, gesturing for silence.

"Please don't interrupt me, Miss Peggy. I know, because

433

the doctor confirmed all my thoughts. But I didn't call you in merely to thank you. I have more to say, something that is to the point." He indicated the papers in front of him and the folder by the lamp. "I am in the process of rewriting my testament. No doubt you noticed the folder—oh, yes, I know how quickly observant you are. It is unfamiliar to you, because it's the one with my personal papers, and is always kept in my safe."

The one behind the books, Peggy thought dully. But why is he telling me all this? And why doesn't he sit down? I must really insist...

Casterán's voice cut through her thoughts.

"In any event, as I was saying: I am changing my last will and testament to make you my sole heir. That is, apart from a few minor bequests, I wish to leave you the bulk of my estate. Now, to make this binding and irreversible after my death, I need to know your choice in this matter. Would you prefer that I marry you, or adopt you?"

Peggy Webb heard herself give a foolish, strangled giggle, and she thought, oh, no, this isn't real. . . . I mustn't laugh. . . . This is ludicrous. . . . Perhaps he's raving with fever. . . . Yes, that's it . . . he's delirious again . . . I must get a doctor . . . or am I dreaming . . . ?

Nothing made sense except the rushing, roaring sound in her ears. She could feel high heat burning into her cheeks, and she could see Mr. Casterán looking at her, his gaze steady, as though nothing unusual had occurred or been said.

Peggy groped for words, her thoughts tripping over her attempted phrases.

"I don't think . . . that is . . . you don't really . . . I mean . . ."

She heard her stupid sounding giggle again; it cut off her words, and she gasped in an effort to control herself and speak properly. Perhaps it was she who was feverish. . . . Yes, yes . . . that must be the case. . . . She had to go home . . . go home at once. . . .

"Take some time to think it over, if you wish," she heard the *escribano* say, but he seemed to be saying it from a great distance, and then she wasn't sure whether he had spoken at all. With a supreme effort, Peggy tried to take a step forward, and found she could not move; when she tried to say something to excuse herself, she discovered she couldn't find her voice, either. Then the room whirled round and round with a resonating roar, and with another soft giggle and a drawn-out sigh, Margaret Webb did something she had never done in her life. She fainted.

They were married in a Church of England ceremony after the legally required civil marriage had been performed, and the bride, who was nervous, stood a good half-head taller than the bridegroom, who held her arm with tender solicitude as they left the church. A discreet reception was held, the strained attitudes of some of its guests reemphasizing the unusual combination of the couple.

A suite of rooms on the second floor of the *escribano*'s house had been redecorated for Peggy, and the gloomy old mansion that Julio Casterán had lived in all his life took on a new mood in the cheerful cretonne that reflected his bride's coloring and brightened the rooms' sunlit hours. On their wedding night, the *escribano* offered Peggy his arm and together they ascended the wide, curved staircase leading to the upper floor. There he escorted her to the door of her suite, and bade her goodnight. Peggy kissed him on the cheek and disappeared into her new abode.

Julio Casterán turned and walked slowly past the top of the stairs again, a lifetime of habit guiding his steps to the bedroom and dressing room that had originally been his father's, in the years long before Julio was born. So much was methodical tradition, he reflected, closing the oak door behind him; so much in life was done without any alternative even being considered. Well, he had made changes, and was pleased with his choice. Then the lifelong familiarity of his own suite engulfed him in his own life and past, and the next half-hour went by in predictable pattern.

He was already in bed, reading, when he heard the light tap on his door. He sat up, surprised.

"Yes? Come in. . . ."

Peggy's white-ruffled peignoir whispered in its folds as she entered, clicked the door shut behind her, and came over to the bed.

"Is there something wrong?" Then he saw that she was blushing, and he began to feel heat rising in his own face, too. "Miss Peggy . . . we arranged . . . you know . . . I explained . . ."

She placed a finger over his lips. "Indeed you did, and I know, but still, I am your wife, and it is . . . well, it is *right*. . . . It wouldn't be right any other way. . . ."

435

"But I don't know..."

Again she silenced him, this time with a hand on his, its pressure seeking reassurance as much as giving it.

"I don't know either... but I'm sure we'll manage...."

He called her Miss Peggy for all of their days and never ceased to treat her with the Victorian decorum that had endeared him to her in the first place. he replaced the father she had loved and lost, while she was the lightheartedness of youth he had never been permitted to enjoy.

The unexpected product of this unexpected pair was duly christened Jaime Julio Federico, amended to Jimmy during his early years. As the only child of unusual parents, he grew up precociously bright and selectively indulged. Physically, he took after his maternal side, stretching up tall and thin with his mother's small features, pale coloring and curly hair, and his father's left-handedness. From his own father he inherited the love of music and a penchant for the law, taking his career a step further than that of the *escribano* and, in the due course of scholastic time, receiving his doctorate with full honors at the Faculty of Law in Buenos Aires.

3

"... so he's really Dr. Casterán; he's twenty three... and he's left-handed... looks a bit like his mother.... She's sweet... so was his father when he came downstairs, but he's very old, more like a grandfather, and..."

On the other end of the phone, Sarita said, "And it's love."

"Oh, no." But Meryl could feel herself blushing.

"Well, I suspect it is—and after all, why not? How old are you now, Meryl?"

"Going to be seventeen."

Hmm. Yes—well, in any event, you must keep the dress. I absolutely insist. It'll be a lucky one for you...."

She would pick up the others next time she came over, Sarita went on, and after Meryl had thanked her yet again for the dress, now a gift, they rang off. Meryl went back to daydreaming.

He was wonderful. Sarita was right. It was love. Meryl felt sick. Not ill-sick, but hazy-headed and strange, unable to think of anything but the past twenty-four hours. It was the way he looked, the way he spoke, his intense, rushed sentences, the suddenness in everything he did. She felt safe with him, safe and afire; with him, she could do anything. Now, all she could do was wait for his call. He had said he would. He hadn't said when. But he'd kissed her good night and good morning at the door, and told her to get a lot of sleep, and he'd call her later, and then they'd see.

She'd slept, but not much. It was mid-afternoon. The only person she had been able to say anything to was, of course, Sarita. And now there was only the waiting; her eyes were still scratchy from lack of sleep. She mooned around the house, too dazed to want to get into the darkroom and print some photos. Besides, she might not hear the phone. Of course, Nélida would hear it, and call her, but suppose Nélida didn't, for some reason? Or didn't reach the phone before Jimmy rang off?

Jimmy. Dr. Jaime Casterán. A lawyer at a big Argentine law firm but, he had told her, about to set up his own office that year. Serious and funny, and funny about the things that he was serious about, knowing exactly where he was going, what he wanted to do, already involved in getting there.

"... and then I'm going to make pots and pots of money..."

He'd thrown his hands up as though sending gold coins high into the air to cascade down again around them both. Then he'd laughed, and pulled her up from the lawn where they'd been sitting near the yacht club's main dock, and said, "Come on—let's go and dance again," and they had until the sky was streaked with sunrise.

The phone rang. Meryl rushed to answer it.

It was Yvonne.

Slowly, Meryl sank into the chair by the telephone table and wished her mother a happy New Year. Then, as she listened, she grew more and more uncomfortable until, when Yvonne stopped talking, she felt herself close to tears.

"He's not *some Argentine*...and I did not duck out of her rotten party!" Meryl finally burst. "As a matter of fact, you know his mother—and we asked, that is, Jimmy made a point of explaining he was taking me home...."

"Well, it was very rude of you. They were, after all, your host and hostess, and I really think you should ring her up and apologize...."

"I don't think Dad would say that...."

437

"Philipe isn't back yet, is he?"

"No, he's not."

"In that case..."

"Mother, how can you say this sort of thing? You don't even know Jimmy. He's very nice. He's Peggy Webb's son. She told me to tell you her name before she was married. You knew her when you went to school...."

There was a pause at the other end of the phone. Finally, Yvonne said, "Yes, of course I remember her," in a calmer tone of voice, and the conversation became easier. But it did not resolve the matter between them, and after she hung up, Meryl's fury rose anew.

It was so typical. Typical for the gossipy mothers of the British community. How dare the old bag call her mother and complain? And how dare Yvonne side with the old bat right away, without thinking she might be on her daughter's side first? And anyway, how did she think she could butt in now, and try to tell Meryl what she should do? Especially since Meryl knew Philipe wouldn't say anything like that at all...at least, she didn't think he would....

She considered the matter and then decided Philipe would like Jimmy very much. That did not exactly answer the question at hand, but it eased her mind. Besides, if there was one thing Philipe always brushed aside without interest, it was the quibbling and squabbling, the rumors and the gossip, that always ran rife through the Anglo-Argentine circles.

The phone rang again. Holding her breath, Meryl picked up the receiver.

This time, the caller was Jimmy.

They talked for an hour.

When Philipe returned, he said, "I have a surprise for you. Sal's here. He's coming to dinner tonight." Then he asked, "Did Sarita call you? I asked her to, in my cable."

Meryl nodded, without further elaboration. She spent the afternoon in the darkroom, wanting to have prints ready to show to di Leo, and able to concentrate on work to some degree as she had already spoken to Jimmy that day, and he had said he would ring her again the next morning.

Sal's opening remark was, "Meryl—how could you do this to me! You've grown taller...."

They stood back to back, and indeed she had.

438

"And prettier, too. Next thing you know, I'll be aiming a lens at you, kiddo, so watch out. . . ."

Over drinks, she showed her latest accomplishments. Sal examined each print with serious care before giving his verdicts.

"That's good. . . . This one's a slice of garbage, and you know it, kiddo. . . . Now *this* one's terrific . . . you're beginning to show style. . . ."

Then Philipe looked at his watch, and reminded them about dinner. As it was Nélida's day off, they were going out.

When they walked into the restaurant, the first person Meryl saw was Jimmy Casterán. He was sitting at a table near the entry, facing her; his companion was a dark-haired young woman, Latin-featured, soignée. Meryl stared, then tried to smile; Jimmy stared back, unblinking. Then Sal took her arm and they followed the gesturing maître d'hôtel, Philipe bringing up the rear. Their path led away from Casterán's table, and Meryl was thankful she had not had to say hello.

"You're very quiet," Sal observed, halfway through the meal. "You sure you're okay, kiddo? You look kind of pale."

Meryl said she was tired.

"Too much New Year partying," smiled her father.

For a moment, she wondered whether Sarita had said anything, but nothing more was mentioned by Philipe, and when they rose to go home, the Casterán table held other diners, all strangers, and unaware.

Jimmy did not call the next day.

She saw him at a wedding months later, and the shock of recognition across the flower-filled church was only slightly tempered by the time gone by, during which other interests and, eventually, other outings, had assuaged the brief, bursting hurt of the year's opening days. She turned her head, pretending she hadn't seen.

At the reception, he strode up to her.

"Why the hell didn't you at least nod hullo?"

"When?"

"Screw that, Meryl. You saw me. . . ."

She said nothing.

"At least we can dance."

She pulled away. "I'd rather not."

439

"But you will." His pale eyes were slitted, angry, colorless in their intensity. "Because if you don't, I'm going to raise my voice, and that'll embarrass the fuck out of you, and..."

On the dance floor, he asked, "Why are you angry?"

"Why didn't you ever call?"

"Because I'll be damned if I'll run after a chit of a girl who's playing with a dozen others behind my back..."

Meryl gasped. "How dare you..."

"...and doesn't even come over to say hullo in a restaurant...."

"You were with...with someone else...."

"Previous commitment. Unfinished business." He pulled her closer to him. "I wanted *you*. And besides, you weren't alone...."

"Jimmy—that was my *father*...."

"*Both* men?"

Despite herself, Meryl giggled.

"No, the other was Sal di Leo, the photographer I told you about. Remember? The one from New York...."

She felt Jimmy's arm relax around her, then tighten, shifting position, holding her possessively rather than in strain. She looked up at him and smiled.

"Dammit, Meryl...I believe you...."

"You should. It's quite true."

Jimmy lowered their clasped hands so that he was holding hers close to his chest, between them, kissing the top of her fingers.

"You're far too young, you're obnoxious as hell, you're a thorn in my side, and I want you." After a few more steps, he added, "Let me get you another drink," stopping at the edge of the dance floor.

"No, thank you."

"Clever girl. Not going to let yourself be seduced by being tiddled, are you?"

"Jimmy, I didn't mean..."

"No, of course not. Perhaps I did. But *I* want a drink. With your permission?"

She waited while he went in search of one of the waiters circulating with champagne. Why did he mock her so? She felt helpless; he could twist her words and phrases back at her with no trouble at all. But when he returned, bearing two glasses, she accepted the drink, knowing she had wanted one after all.

440

They danced again, staring into each other's eyes, oblivious of everything except each other. When the music stopped, Meryl was shaking. Jimmy said, "I trust you're not here with anyone impossible?"

"No."

"Fine. We're going. Get your coat. You don't have to kiss the bride good-bye."

He had his mother's car.

"Where're we going?"

He shifted into gear. "To bed. Where'd you think?" Then, before releasing the clutch, he turned to Meryl and said, "You knew that, didn't you?"

She nodded.

"Okay." He turned the wheel and they moved out of the treelined street into the main avenue. Meryl sat silently as he drove, her hands unsteady as she lit her cigarette and his.

Afterwards, they lay side by side in embracing silence for a while, and then Jimmy kissed her nose and drew back while his finger traced around her forehead and down around her chin. Finally he said, "This was your first time," in a quiet voice.

"Yes."

He shifted onto his elbow and looked at her.

"Why didn't you tell me?"

"You didn't ask."

"But still..."

Meryl turned to face him. "Would it have made a difference?"

"No... *Yes.*" He paused. "Well, maybe not... oh, hell, I don't know...."

"Then why..."

"Because if I had known, I'd have had the choice... of not bringing you here...."

Meryl feeling suddenly naked, turned over on her stomach and pulled the pillow under her chin. "I'd have thought you'd be pleased."

"Pleased?" He considered the question, then sat up, swinging his legs over the edge of the bed. "Not in effect... not for what has to be done.... I'm not that primitive." He turned to her, putting his hand on her shoulder. "I didn't hurt you too much, did I?"

She smiled and blushed, shaking her head, unwilling to trust her voice.

"Good." He got off the bed and disappeared into the bathroom. Meryl turned around to lie on her back and contemplate the room.

When they had turned into the innocuous-looking driveway with the cobbled circular courtyard at the far end, she had realized that it had to be an *amueblado*, that Buenos Aires specialty of rooms by the hour for assignations, always open at any hour of the day or night. Jimmy pulled the car up to the far wall, told her to wait, and reappeared within minutes, a key in his hand. A series of tall, shuttered doors were shaded by the thick ivy growing up the wall of the two-storey building.

"It's the fourth one over...." Jimmy's arm draped itself over her shoulder and drew her to him. They walked across in the chilly night air; when they reached the door, Meryl found it was the only one where the shutters were open, and she could see curtains through the glass, on the other side. Jimmy fumbled with the key, pushing down on the handle, and stepping back to let Meryl enter first.

Then she had been too nervous to notice anything much, too uncertain of what to do, where to look, what to say. She was aware of the big double bed centered on the opposite wall, its sheets turned down in readiness and stark white, even the protective intimacy of the low-lit room.

But now she took in every detail, her roving gaze noting the thick velvet curtains pulled across the window and hanging in heavy folds down to the carpeted floor. Curtains also concealed the door through which Meryl and Jimmy had entered. On the inside wall, a door led to the bathroom, from behind which came the sounds of water running, and some splashing. A standard lamp, shaded in deep red, gave the area a warm glow.

Meryl smiled to herself; an *amueblado*. A known fact about Buenos Aires life so often referred to and giggled about.

She pulled the sheet up under her chin, stretching beneath the fabric's taut surface. Overall, her body felt silken, the specific soreness more a badge of accomplishment than anything else. Meryl's smile widened; she felt enormously pleased with herself, grown up, irrevocably in love.

It soon became apparent that love, whether irrevocable or not, was intent on running a course neither smooth nor true.

"I understand you were at the wedding with the Casterán

boy," said Yvonne, when Meryl arrived out on the following weekend. Meryl mumbled "Not exactly," and tried to change the subject, but Yvonne would have none of it.

"Don't lie to me. You were seen leaving together."

"I'm not lying. We *did* leave together. I didn't *go* there with him, that's all."

"He's too old for you—and he's got a bad reputation."

"Oh—Mother..."

"... always did hang out with the Argentine crowd, I'm told, even though he did go to a decent English school here.... Of course, his father's Argentine, but still..."

Yvonne also let drop the information Jimmy Casterán was known to have a mistress.

"... been keeping her for years... a flat in the middle of town... a sort of *garconnière*, I suppose...."

Meryl finally got her mother off the subject of Jimmy Casterán by telling her the examination results had arrived at last.

"They rang up from the school office to tell me yesterday, but there's supposed to be an official letter being sent. And, of course, the certificate."

Yvonne looked questioningly at her daughter. Meryl grinned.

"Don't worry. I got through."

"I *knew* you would." Yvonne relaxed visibly. "We'll have to celebrate tonight. You must be so relieved...."

Meryl shrugged and smiled and promised to show her mother the certificate when it arrived; she did not want to go into any lengthy discussion about her feelings on the matter. It would only dismay Yvonne to know that Meryl had found the whole thing to mean little, if anything, at all.

So much had happened in the months between, she almost felt as though she inhabited another world. Getting through school was not a subject that had its place in her life with Jimmy. The next time she spoke to him, Meryl repeated a censored version of her mother's remarks. Jimmy's face went blank, expressionless.

"Yes, I have a flat. You want to see it? Fine. I'll take you there tomorrow, on the way to the theater. If, that is, you're going to accept my invitation to see an *Argentine* play." He looked at her with mock severity. "Remember, now, Meryl, this is *native* stuff....."

It turned out to be a back apartment in an innocuous building. Riding up in the elevator to the third floor, Meryl wondered about the supposed mistress, but there was no one in the place when she and Jimmy entered.

"Make yourself at home. Check the cupboards. Lie down. Anything you like, while I got you a drink." He disappeared into a minuscule kitchen.

Meryl walked through the small entrance into a wide-windowed room with a beige carpet and curtains. There was a bed, a desk, an old-looking coat stand with some coats hanging on it, a view onto an airshaft, and little else.

Jimmy returned, bearing glasses.

"I got it when I started working—well, no, the year before...." He handed her a glass and looked at his watch. "We haven't got much time, Meryl, so drink up, and let's get going...."

On the way down in the elevator, Meryl realized he had not as much as held her hand while they were upstairs.

Over dinner after the theater, she mentioned it.

"I don't believe in boiling water unless you're going to make tea," was the answer. "All that messing around is something I left behind years ago.... If you want to play games like that, stick to your ruddy club playmates...."

The tight look of annoyance had masked his features; Meryl found it impossible to gauge the topics that produced it.

"I suppose it serves me right, for cradle-snatching," Jimmy observed, looking at her intently. "Why, in God's name, did you have to occur? You're too fucking young...."

"Then why bother with me? Why invite me out?" In her rising anger, Meryl could feel her proximity to tears.

"Because you *fascinate* me...."

He leaned across the table, reaching for her hand. Suddenly, she wasn't hungry any more.

"Let's go back to the apartment—" he signaled to the waiter—"right now...."

What she had not learned from Lala, hearsay, the *estancia,* and the parks of Buenos Aires, Meryl leaned firsthand from Jimmy in the weeks that followed. Early on, he had asked her whether she knew how to take care of herself and when she'd confessed she didn't had said, "Oh, God," softly, and reached into the night table drawer next to his side of the bed in the third-floor apartment, fumbling briefly with a small square packet before sheathing himself. Meryl had watched with the

444

heightened clarity of the moment, fascinated and embarrassed, too acutely conscious to care.

Afterwards, they had talked, as they always did in the afterglow, and Jimmy explained and answered questions and made comments, and she was no longer embarrassed at all.

"I don't want any mistakes," he told her. "No pregnancies, no trouble. I'm not playing games with you, and I don't want you pulling any on me."

Sometimes, in the middle of their serious talks, his mood would change.

It was mid-afternoon of a late spring Sunday. Officially, they had gone to the cinema.

Jimmy sat bolt upright in the rumpled bed.

"That's it—finally, I've got it! They're fantastic!"

Meryl blinked. "What are?"

"Your toes. Just look at 'em. They're adorable... all round and fat and delicious-looking, like kernels of corn, to nibble on. . . ."

He was off the bed and at the end of it, swooping down.

"Ouch! Jimmy! Stop that! You're biting!"

He looked up.

"I am *not*," he said indignantly, "I'm *nibbling*. There's a big difference... don't tell me it's hurting. . . ."

"No, not exactly... but. . ."

"But *what*?"

"Well, it *tickles*, feels funny..."

"Funny-godawful or funny-ha-ha?"

"Funny ha-ha. . . ."

"Then be jocose—make sounds of jollity, woman, and let me enjoy my nibble. A nibble a day keeps my passion at bay. . . ."

After a moment he said, "Except that it doesn't. . . ." and the lightness of mood left as their bodies' intensity took-over.

After they'd shared a shower, Jimmy said, "I know—let's go to the zoo," and once there he took Meryl directly to the hippopotamus pool.

"See? The spitting image of you, Meryl—just look at those toes... larger than life, of course, but still... eminently nibbable. . . ."

On the way out, he bought her a balloon. The next morning, when she awoke to the hot and brilliant sunshine

445

pouring through her bedroom window, the helium-filled globe was outlined against brightness as it hovered in the air, firmly anchored by a string tied to the end of her bed.

Meryl had been correct in her assessment of Philipe's reaction; he liked Jimmy, and they talked easily together whenever Jimmy came to pick her up. As time went on, it became generally accepted, though unsaid, that Meryl and Jimmy were *going around*, in the parlance of the younger crowd, a phrase that somehow made it easier for Yvonne to pronounce Jimmy a likable young man.

"It probably gives us an innocence she wants to believe," was Jimmy's sugestion; he himself loathed the phrase. "*Going around*. At my age . . . for Christ's sake. . . ."

And he did not call Meryl for over a week, during which she fumed, then worried, then cried.

The telephone rang at four o'clock in the morning. She reached the instrument seconds before Philipe. Jimmy's voice said, "I feel like hell, and I'll come and pick you up in the morning," and when she put down the receiver, she could not control her silent tears.

Philipe, hovering in the doorway, said, "You're a bit too young for these shenanigans—and you can tell Jimmy from me I think he's a bit too old. . . ."

Meryl handed Jimmy the new camera Philipe had brought her from the U.S.

"You look down into it like this . . . hold it here . . ."

"Everything's fuzzy," he complained.

"Of course it is—you have to focus on something. . . . Turn the knob on the side. . . ."

"There isn't one."

"Of *course* there is. No, not *there*. On the other side. . . ."

Jimmy put the camera down on the table and pushed it away.

"It's hopeless, Meryl, hopeless. When I pick things up, knobs are always on the *other* side. I tell you—the world's against me. And the conspiracy starts right from the beginning—see?" He broke off in emphasis. "I fall into the trap all the time. Why isn't the phrase *left* at the beginning?"

"Because they'd sound as though something'd been forgotten."

"Exactly." Jimmy's clenched left fist thumped on the table. You're all against us—us, the talented, the extra brainy fabulous left-handers of the world. Just think, Meryl—there's

446

only fifteen percent of us. Geniuses to a man." Triumph rang in his voice. Then he lowered it to a tone of stage despair. "But are we honored? No. Are we acknowledged? No. We're not even *tolerated* most of the time. You self-satisfied right-handers—you even make bloody *doors* open right-handed-ly...."

After a pause he said, "And *corkscrews*. I ask you now: have you ever seen a left-handed corkscrew? *No.* And have you ever seen a left-handed genius struggling with a right-handed one? I tell you, it's *pitiful*. *Nothing* is made left-handed for us...."

A sudden memory rose, and Meryl said, "They make left-handed *tabas*. I know. I've seen one."

Jimmy looked at her in surprise. "And just what do you know, miss, about an illegal and officially immoral game?"

She told him of the times she and Lala had watched it out behind the *galpón* on the *estancia*.

"...and we noticed one of the *gauchos* was throwing with his left hand, and the *capataz* told us...and then showed us the special *taba*..."

"And probably weighted, too...."

Meryl shrugged. "Lala says most of them are."

When it was decided that Yvonne, Wilfred, and Meryl would go up to the *estancia* to spend Christmas with Edie, Meryl accepted the decision with mixed feelings. It would mean not seeing Jimmy for a couple of months, for she would stay on at El Ombú after the Hume-Hawleys returned.

On the other hand, Lala would be there, and she missed Lala, wanted to tell her all about Jimmy, wanted to confide and exchange views on her now-adult experiences. She felt sure Lala would understand what no one else could: that it was difficult, that it was real love, as real as love could possibly be, that it was wild and total all wrapped up in one. And that most of the time, she wasn't sure of anything, neither Jimmy, not herself, nor anything about them together.

The truth was that, for Meryl, the volcanic affair was almost impossible to handle; still in her teens, she was faced with emotions deep into adult depths of scope and range. Nor was she alone in her problem; from Jimmy's perspective, it was no easier. He had asked both Meryl and himself from time to time: what was he doing with a girl scarcely more than a child?

"I'm not a child!" Meryl had been furious, now into her eighteenth year.

"You're probably still *teething. . . ."*

Fast appraching the quarter-century mark, a practising attorney and a young man of charm, good connections, and easy sophistication, Jimmy Casterán had long had a wide range of women throwing themselves at his head. His involvement with Meryl did not prevent it from continuing to happen and yet, to his own vexation, he could not let go.

"I think it's a good idea," he said, in a moment of seriousness, on hearing about the holiday plan and the length of time Meryl would be away. "Now perhaps I'll get some work done," and from the time he knew she was going, he seemed to draw away.

"Will you write to me?"

He shrugged. "Depends. If I have something to say . . ."

Meryl didn't answer, feeling hurt, but later she made a point of writing out the *estancia* address for him.

Christmas was bearable, if edgy, but by the end of the following week tensions were on the rise.

"It's the heat, Mummy—he's not used to it. Poor Wilfred cannot stand these temperatures."

"Nonsense. He's simply bone lazy. Does he ever do anything other than doze or sleep? You tell me he rides at the club. Why doesn't he go riding here with you?"

"I told you, Mummy—the heat's too much for him. . . ."

Meryl did her best to stay clear; only at mealtimes did she join the rest of the family. Otherwise, she found it best to be with only one member at a time.

"The trouble with your mother is she's a fool . . . always has been and, I suppose, always will be, more's the pity. As to that useless husband of hers . . ."

"Mummy does nothing but criticize me and Wilfred. . . . I really don't think I can stand much more of it, Meryl. . . . We'll probably be going home in a few days' time. . . . Besides, all his friends are at the club . . . I'm sure he'd be happier back in B.A. . . ."

Wilfred, fortunately, seldom said very much of anything, limiting his conversational forays with Meryl to such remarks as "Jolly hot, isn't it?" or "Lunch ready yet?"

When the Hume-Hawleys left, everyone breathed a sigh of relief. Even Rosita.

448

"Ay, *niña* Meryl, it is such a pity . . . to think that the *señora* Yvonne didn't marry a husband more interested in things of the *estancia*. . . ."

Edie said, "I don't think Wilfred Hume-Hawley is interested in anything that isn't Wilfred Hume-Hawley," a remark she repeated on later occasion when Tim Casey was lunching at El Ombú.

With Yvonne gone, Harvey and Raul ventured over, joining Meryl and Lala as in the days gone by. Harvey offered to teach Meryl how to drive, and she accepted; a couple of lessons were all she needed, and even Edie was pleased.

"That's lovely, darling, and now you can do the driving when I need to go into the *pueblo*. . . ."

But if Harvey was friendly to Meryl, he was pointedly baiting with Lala, always ready to tease or jab at her, never letting an opportunity go by. He grabbed at her in the pool when the four of them went swimming, mocked her about her studies, predicted she'd certainly fail.

"You'll never make it as a teacher, Lala, and you know it—but never mind. You can always come over to La Chata and be our housekeeper. . . ."

Lala said in an even voice, "I'd rather die," and for a moment there was no conversation between the foursome, so vehement had been her message. Then Meryl jumped into the water, holding her knees to her chest to make a big splash, and the tension eased somewhat, although it did not disappear.

The quietest of the four was always Raul, now the tallest and most striking, tanned, lithe, his dark hair clinging wetly to his head, the green eyes more startling than ever, his smile hesitant, seldom seen. It was he, however, who predicted the bad weather.

"You sure? Dad said he thought it'd only be a few passing showers." Harvey squinted up at the sky, where clouds had been thickening over the past hour.

Raul climbed up onto the ledge by one of the pool's windows and eased his thin body through its opening, straining to see up and over the nearest *paraiso* tree. Then he ducked back in.

"No. You should see it over there. We're in for a long one."

He was proved right within the hour when the heavens roared their anger, and the fury of the pelting rain flattened the fields' crops and grass. Watching from the house, Edie said, "You'd better spend the night here," and she managed to ring through to La Chata and let Tim Casey know, just before the telephone and power lines went down.

That night, a bed was made up for Harvey in the south wing; a fold-out cot was found for Raul and set up in the passage off the kitchen leading to Rosita's quarters. Before dawn the next morning, Rosita, waking early, glanced at Lala'a bed and saw the forms lying there asleep.

She tiptoed over and stood, looking. Raul, vulnerable in his dawnlight slumber, was curled as though a snail shell in the curve of Lala's protection. Rosita pursed her lips, took a step forward and, after a spasm of hesitation, stepped back again. He was still a child, and Lala was what she was, and what would come later, if anything did at all, would not matter for the moment.

Let them seek the warmth and protection none of us ever had, Rosita thought, and turned away, walking by Raul's empty cot in the dim passageway. As long as she did not tell anybody, who would know? She stretched forward, and closed the door to the kitchen; the cook would be up soon, and there was no need for her to see.

Reliving their childhood haunts and pleasures, Meryl and Lala repaired to the *gomero* tree, to sit within its shady protection for hours, talking of their lives now grown distant with the years. But the friendship remained; each sought the other's interest and opinion, Meryl perhaps more than Lala, the same pattern of long ago.

"...but Lala, what I mean is, do you think Jimmy *really*...?"

"If he didn't, why would he bother coming back to you all the time?"

"...but he makes it so difficult...."

"It'd be more difficult for you without him, I think...at least for now."

Of her studies, Lala spoke with enthusiasm; of her friends in Córdoba, she said little, other than to refer to them as a good group, of similar interests.

"...and sometimes I think I'm even beginning to understand where we...where I belong...."

They also read in the tree, as they used to, although Lala's books tended to be textbooks, whereas Meryl read her grandmother's new book-club novels.

"Photography's not something you can read about much," she told Lala. "You have to *do* it. . . ."

But at the *estancia* she did little; with no darkroom, the exposed film collected and waited in her suitcase, no further work on it possible until she returned to B.A.

The letter from Jimmy arrived unexpectedly, after she had given up all hope that he would write at all. Also to her surprise, it was from Uruguay; she read it through several times, as though trying to absorb all of him from its scanty lines. He was in Montevideo in connection with a case undertaken by his law firm; since he was already in Uruguay, he planned to have a beach holiday there when the work was completed. Before he'd left, he'd seen her mother and Wilfred at the country club and, by chance, bumped into Philipe in a restaurant downtown. Sarita had been there; they would probably all meet over in Uruguay, too.

Meryl felt a pang of jealousy. If only she'd stayed with her father, she'd probably have gone over to Sarita's with him. . . .

She showed Lala the letter. Lala was interested in the envelope.

"Why?"

"Don't you see the stamp?"

"Yes." Meryl was puzzled. "It's Uruguayan, of course."

"No, no." Lala was impatient. "Don't you see? He's put it upside down. . . ."

And then it was that Meryl learned from Lala of the silent signal, the traditional message of love sent through the mail.

"Perhaps he did it by mistake."

But a second letter repeated the signal.

When she posted her answer, Meryl carefully placed the stamp upside down.

Meryl leaned her head against the *gomero* trunk.

"Remember the *chinitas*' knife fight we saw when we were kids?"

Lala looked up from her book and nodded.

"I've been thinking about it lately," Meryl went on, "and I was wondering—would you fight like that for a man, Lala?"

Lala considered the question for a while; finally she said, "I think it would depend. I might, yes—to defend him. . . ."

"But if it wasn't a question of defense . . ."

"I don't know."

"I wouldn't," said Meryl decisively, thinking of Jimmy, and Uruguay, and wondering, knowing.

Lala smiled. "Let's hope we never have to," she said, and both girls resumed their reading.

Harvey took Meryl aside and said, "Don't tell your grandmother, but there's a game of *taba* going on behind the *galpón*. Let's go and do some betting. I feel like getting my hands on some money...."

They went out of the house where they had been having dinner and joined Edie and Tim, who were already sitting out on the verandah, discussing cattle prices, over coffee and brandy. Harvey accepted a shot, tossed it back and announced he and Meryl were going for a walk.

"Take your time, lad," answered his father with a wink. "Edie and I have plenty to discuss here." He waved the sheaf of auction notices as though in answer.

"We won't be long," Meryl interjected, putting down her demitasse. "Ready, Harv?"

As they walked away, she heard the older Casey remark, "They make a nice couple now, don't y'think?" to her grandmother, but she did not hear Edie's reply. She'd have to tell Grannie she had absolutely no interest in Harvey Casey, even though his father's hopes were embarrassingly obvious at times.

They found most of the *estancia's gauchos* at the clandestine *taba* game. Lanterns hanging from fence posts illuminated the level patch of road. The participants, awaiting the next round, were tossing practise throws or flexing their hands around the metal-edged sections of shinbone with which they played the game. Each player used his own *taba*, a prized, though illicit, possession.

"You have to feel the throw before you start," Harvey said, producing a *taba* from his jacket pocket.

"I thought you said you were only going to bet...."

"I want to play, too...."

But the *capataz* wouldn't let him.

"... it would not be right ... not with the *niña* Meryl here.... If *Doña* Edie were to find out ... another time, perhaps...."

Meryl could see the man's discomfiture. She put her hand on Harvey's arm.

"Don't," she said. "It makes it too difficult for the men. If

452

you insist, they'll have to let you play, and I'd have to leave. And I don't want to. I want to watch the game. . . ."

The pitching started after all the side bets were placed, and the cries of *"Buena!"* and *"Mala!"* rang out with cheers and groans. Watchful eyes counted the turns the bone piece made in the air before falling to the ground, and if the required two and a half flips were not completed, then the throw was declared null and void. *Tabas* landing on their side were also discounted.

If the bone landed with the "good" side up, the player and the *buena*-bettors cheered and collected, but a *mala* landing brought success only to the bettors of that side. Bets and counterbets were placed and argued; the tosses continued, the game went on. Meryl watched with intense concentration, calculating motion and speed and light. With perhaps a few more lanterns, fast film and a wide-open lens . . . yes, it would be worth it, definitely worth a try. . . .

She was speaking to the *capataz* about it when she noticed that a player standing near them was holding a *taba* in his left hand, flexing his fingers and moving his arm in the motions players used to warm up before a throw.

"Oh, certainly, *niña*, they make the *taba* the other way around for those who need it. The metal pieces are attached in the opposite way. Would you like to see it?"

When she and Harvey walked back to the house, Meryl had the left-handed *taba* in her pocket. Harvey was still grumbling.

". . . and if only you'd let me play, I could have won it from him for you. You paid far too much for it, you know. . . ."

"Harvey, I told you—I don't care. . . ."

Meryl also had the *capataz*'s word he'd advise her when the next *taba* game took place. By now, Meryl knew enough to acknowledge her bargaining weapon: she would not give away the existence of the games if he allowed her to attend with her camera.

And she'd go with Lala. Never Harvey.

Lala said, "You know why the *capataz* wouldn't let him play? Harvey's got a loaded *taba*; it always falls with the *buena* side up. And so, of course, he never loses. But around here, they never let him play. . . ."

The political climate grew increasingly uncomfortable for the British community. The Perón regime, far from being a

453

passing aberration, broadened its power base and bared its teeth; early hostility on the part of English-owned enterprises paid back drastic dividends as time went on. The biggest single blow was the takeover of the railways, but no firm was immune to the changes in the air.

Nor were any individuals; unfriendly opinions voiced in the wrong company could have unpleasant consequences.

"... and you'll never believe what happened to Tony in town today. He was in a taxi, and the driver was complaining about some of the new decrees. Tony had some papers he was working on, and he didn't feel like talking, so he merely said he would have thought the driver would appreciate all that had been done for him and for the people, and got back to his work.

"Can you imagine Tony's surprise when the driver turned around, grinning, and said, 'You're a sensible and lucky man, *señor*, to say what you have said.' When Tony asked him why, he was only too happy to tell him. 'If you'd agreed with me and criticized, as many do—you'd have been the third person I've driven straight to the police station today. . . .'"

There were, of course, those who adjusted, but in the middle-aged generation, their numbers were very few and their accommodation often drew sharp criticism from others of their age group. And plans were heard, both muttered and open, about "pulling up stakes" and "going back home." The jangled community recoiled and reacted to every change and every new decree.

They lived on largely false premises, slender hopes, taut nerves. Above all, they lived on an endless succession of rumors, the wilder they came the better received, feeding obsessively on themselves.

"They say the chief of the secret police answers to *her*, and not to *him* . . ."

"They say he's got another mistress . . . that they'll flee the country . . . that it's only a matter of time . . ."

For the younger generation, the choices, though wider, were difficult to make among the mass of contradictions.

"I don't care what the old ones say, *che*, I prefer it here . . ."

There were also those who left, who went to England, the U.S., Canada, while others went to South Africa and the Australian shore. But leaving wasn't easy. . . .

"But, *che*, what can I do? I feel myself an *argentino*, and . . ."

"That awful *accent*!" Yvonne Hume-Hawley was vehement in criticizing the *porteño* mixture of English, Argentine slang, muddled syntax and intonation. "I simply can't bear it—and I'll thank you, Meryl, to speak proper English when you're here. And do not—and I repeat, *do not* use that dreadful *che* habit every time you speak."

"Sorry."

And Meryl made the effort around her mother, although it was not easy; around Jimmy and many of their friends, the two languages were used interchangeably all the time, and the Argentine specialty of saying "*Che*," a friendly, familiar form of address, was a verbal sign of intimacy appropriate to the place and times.

Meryl, too, had her own complaints about her mother's household.

"It's got to the point where there are only two themes of conversation: the cost of living if the maid's within earshot, and politics the very instant that she's out of the way or leaves the room."

"It's all well and good for you, Meryl, living with your father in the lap of luxury, but running a household is no sinecure with the prices rising as they are these days...."

Jimmy, on hearing from Meryl about the set-to with her mother, said, "If Wilfred were to be of more use..."

"You don't like him, do you?"

"No, I don't. Wilfred's a shit."

"How can you say that?" Despite herself, Meryl was shocked. "I agree he's a bit of a wet, but..."

"I say it because it's easy, that's why, and it's true, besides. He has your mother running hither and yon at his beck and call...."

"You have to remember he only has one arm..."

"Remember?" Jimmy laughed wildly. "How the fuck can I ever forget? When does he ever *let* one forget it?"

Meryl bit her lip; Jimmy went on talking.

"Let me tell you something, Meryl. I don't care whether a man has one arm or two heads or a profusion of peckers flourishing out of his arse. It doesn't excuse his behavior in anything and everything for the rest of his life. Wilfred Hume-Hawley is a shit—a one-armed shit, a sponger and a moocher. He's never tried to get anything better than that piddling little do-nothing job your mother got Robert Thaxter

455

to fix up for him at Bateman's. Wilfred's living off your mother, just waiting for your grandmother to die."

Meryl sighed and said nothing; she had heard similar opinions from Edie herself, although differently expressed.

"And what's more, he uses that nonarm of his like a club. It's bigger than lifesize, being invisible, and he sees to it that everyone pays for him and caters to him and looks after him...because of his arm." Jimmy snorted with disgust. "Arm, my arse. It's because he's a born sponger, that's why...."

The left-handed *taba* sat in its usual place on the cluttered night table. Meryl reached over it and extracted a cigarette from the pack beyond. She turned to Jimmy.

"You want one?"

He shook his head. She lit hers and then lay back against the pillows.

"You're smoking too much—far more than you used to."

"I know." Deliberately, Meryl inhaled longer and deeper than usual, secure in the drowsy aftermath of their contact. Jimmy's left hand drifted over her shoulder, his index finger drawing circles.

Suddenly, he withdrew his arm and reached over to grab her sunglasses from the night table. Rearranging his posture, he sat upright and crosslegged, pulling her feet close in to his crotch and carefully arranging his penis, now flaccid, so that it lay over his left ankle. Placing the sunglasses across its base, he ran his fingers through his pubic hair, fluffing it out around the frames.

Meryl giggled. Jimmy looked at her, frowning.

"It's no laughing matter, my girl. You see what happened to poor Filomena? She also used to smoke too much. Didn't you, Filly, old thing?"

He cupped his penis in his left hand and looked down at it with affection. Then he looked back at Meryl, his momentary smile gone.

"You know what they say about masturbation and going blind, don't you? Well, it's more or less the same thing with smoking. But Filomena wouldn't listen. Of course not. You females, you're all so stubborn. Naturally, one day, smoke got in her eyes, and the next thing you know—glasses!" He paused, glancing down again. "Such a shame, Filly, old dear...and you so young...if only you'd listened..."

456

"Why Filomena?"

"What d'you mean, why Filomena?"

Meryl hitched herself onto her elbow. "Why a girl's name?"

Jimmy removed the glasses, folded them with elaborate care and replaced them on the night table. Then he said, in tones of patience worn thin, "You don't think I'd want a little *boy*-penis hanging around inside my pants, do you? For chrissake, Meryl, *think* before you ask such asinine questions. Imagine: what would my balls say?" His voice took on an overly plummy English accent. "I mean, I say, after all, Meryl, dash it, I'm not one of your *British* chaps . . . rugger scrum every Saturday, arseholes nose to nose, buggering in there . . . you have to keep in mind I'm a *native*. . . ."

As abruptly as he had started it, the game was over; Jimmy's fingers began roving around Meryl's shoulders again, up her neck, into her hair, around her ear, tracing lines and fingers until his fingers roamed further and probed deeper and all the clowning had vanished.

"I want to corrupt you. . . ."

Jimmy's eyes were at their most pale, his face taut and drawn. But Meryl, gasping to catch her own breath, had no vocal reply. When the room stilled once more, and she again lay cradled in his arms, Jimmy murmured, "I take it back."

"What?"

"What I said about corrupting you. It's not true. I want to *have* you. Totally. Just for me. Corrupting sounds as though I want to do it all first, and then throw you to the wolves. And I think that'd be easier." He tightened his hold on her. "But what I want is you, dammit—you."

Meryl snuggled closer, but Jimmy seemed to be talking to some place beyond her, beyond her body, beyond their presence in the room.

". . . to have, to hold, to protect, to piss on, to give diamonds to, to cry with, to shake by the shoulders, to laugh with, to . . ." His voice stopped. In swift moves he was up and off the bed, pacing up and down the room, his ribs showing in pale ridges.

"I have you under my skin, like your smell on my fingers, in my nostrils, in my brain. Dammit, Meryl—it's *you* who's corrupting *me*." He paused at the end of the bed, seized one of her feet and banged it down against the mattress in a quick succession of blows. "Up, up! Let's get the hell out of here.

Get up! D'you want to eat something?" He didn't wait for her answer. "Because I do. Hurry up and get dressed and I'll take you to dinner. You can have the bathroom first."

After dinner, he took her home, saying he'd call the next day. Two weeks went by, and she did not hear from him at all. Late on the following Sunday night, Meryl heard the phone ring while she was washing her hair.

Nélida knocked on the bathroom door a few moments later.

"*Niña* Meryl, the telephone. It's the *señor* Jimmy..."

The argument started at once.

"...and I don't think it's fair, Jimmy—honestly, I don't. If you say you're going to call me, then call. If not—then leave me alone."

"All right, I will."

He hung up, and she did not hear from him for over six weeks, during which she cried herself to sleep time and again, angry at her own weakness. Then she caught a cold, ran a fever, and was put to bed. The telephone's ringing no longer disturbed her, and the first thing she knew of Jimmy's repeated calls and concern over her illness was his own announcement of them when he appeared in her bedroom's doorway, half obscured by the cellophane-wrapped roses in his arms.

"They said you were too ill to talk or see anyone until today...."

"They didn't tell me it was you on the phone."

"I told them not to." He tossed the flowers onto the bed. "You look like hell. And beautiful." He grinned. "I can't bear to look at death and decay. Get well quickly. Ring me when you're better."

He was gone before she could answer, and when she called the Casterán house a couple of days later, his mother told her Jimmy had left for Montevideo the night before.

"I don't know when he'll be back, dear, but I'll tell him you rang, and I'm sure he'll be in touch with you the moment he returns...."

He wasn't. The next time Meryl saw him was at the country club, where she and Yvonne and Wilfred had gone to have dinner after watching the bowling matches all afternoon. Jimmy was seated at a table with people she did not know. A dark-haired girl was sitting next to him; later, Meryl saw them dancing cheek to cheek, Jimmy's eyes closed, their hands held closely against the girl's neck.

Luckily, Wilfred wanted to go home early.

". . . and do you mean to tell me that, after all the upset of last weekend, you're going out with Jimmy tonight?" Yvonne was exasperated. "I don't understand you, Meryl, I really don't."

"I don't see why you don't understand. I've told you how it happened—I saw him last night when I was at the club with the bunch *you* think are so delightful, and he came over, and he apologized, and . . ."

"And so you're going back to him—until the next time!"

Meryl did not answer, not deeming it wise to describe the scene as it had actually occurred. She had been sitting at a table with the young English crowd, playing Liar Dice, the current craze. Someone had ordered martinis, and hers stood on the table in front of her. Jimmy had come straight over the moment he entered the room. With a sweeping gesture, he knocked over her glass.

"You can't drink martinis after dinner," he announced, taking her hand and pulling her up from the chair. "Come on."

"Jimmy . . . I . . ."

Ignoring her, he smiled at the table's other occupants. "Good night, everyone. Sorry we must be going. . . ."

In the parking lot, he kissed her.

"Jimmy—you're impossible. . . ."

"Of course." He held her face in his hands. "It's my stock-in-trade. . . ."

Now, avoiding her mother's angry gaze, Meryl knew only that she awaited his call. Nothing else mattered; everything else always worked out, one way or another.

". . . you're only going to get yourself hurt time and time again, Meryl, and you know perfectly well it isn't going to work out. You and Jimmy have nothing in common. You come from totally different backgrounds, and in the long run, you'll only have yourself to blame. I've told you all this before, and I'm not the only person who feels this way. Wilfred says . . ."

"To hell with what Wilfred says!"

"Meryl!"

"I'm sorry, Mother, but I don't see what right Wilfred has to stick his nose into my business. . . ."

"You only happen to be under Wilfred's roof, for a start. . . ."

"No, I'm not. This house isn't his—it's yours. Grannie paid for it, and it's in your name. . . ."

"Meryl, will you stop being so rude! And that's not the point, anyway. Wilfred's the head of this household."

459

"He may well be, but he's not my father, and I don't belong to his household, and..."

"But you *are* staying here..."

"Fine." Meryl started to rise. "I'll leave right now...."

The phone rang. She dropped back into the chair and picked up the receiver. It was Jimmy. Yvonne continued to stand in front of her, her arms folded in braced anger.

"At three? Fine. I'll be there." She glanced up at her mother briefly. "No, *che*, I don't know...okay. *Chau.*"

She was replacing the receiver as Yvonne burst out, "And don't use that damned *che* the whole time! Don't be Argentine!"

Meryl finished cradling the receiver. When she stood up, her gaze met her mother's.

"I'm not," she said, taking a breath as though about to say more, only to exhale slowly into silence. But her unspoken words glinted like steel through the stillness between them.

I'm not an Argentine. You are.

4

Late one summer evening, as the darkening light faded across the reaches of the *pampas*, Tim Casey rode carelessly along the dusty road. Turning across a field, he headed home, failing to see the burrow openings directly in his cantering mount's path.

The horse stumbled, throwing its rider; it was an unexpected pitch, an unfortunate, ill-fated fall. Tim Casey lay on the *pampas*, beer-bloated and corpulent, dead, at sixty-two, of a broken neck.

His riderless horse went home.

It was hours before they found him, but earlier succor would not have helped. Instantaneous death, was the medical verdict, pronounced the next day. By then, the neighborhood people had gathered, and the news was out to all corners of the area. Edie, advised of the death in the morning, waited to hear how best she could serve.

They'd need help, of course. Probably money. An *estancia*'s need for cash could come in unexpected ways. No doubt Harvey, who would inherit, would be over to see her shortly. And there would be the funeral and all the services, of course; there was plenty to do.

It was hot; she decided on a *siesta*.

"If the *niño* Harvey comes, let me know at once... wake me, Rosita, not later than four...."

Edie thought: but he'll be *Don* Harvey now.... We'll all have to get used to it... lucky he has Raul to help him... he was always fond of the land....

It turned her thoughts from La Chata to El Ombú. How ironic that Tim Casey, dead, had the makings of a *capataz* already on his *estancia*, whereas she—still alive, and hoping to remain so for many years to come—had to struggle on alone, managing El Ombú by herself, every day of the year.

Edie dozed fitfully, woke to hear Rosita knocking insistently on the door.

"*Señora* Edie... they've come to see you... from La Chata...."

Edie was surprised to see only the Caseys' cook and another woman, easily recognizable as the cook's sister, younger by some years. Both women were already in black.

"We have come to you, *Doña* Edie, because we need you to help us.... This is a sad moment at our *estancia*, and there are difficult times ahead...."

Edie spoke consolingly, sympathizing with their bereavement.

"... but you must not be afraid of the future. La Chata will continue to flourish, and your place there is safe. Harvey is grown now, and I am sure he will work as his father did, when these days of grief are over and he takes his place as his father would have wanted him to...."

The cook stepped forward and seized Edie's arm.

"Ah, no, *señora*... it is not so easy. That's where I know we need your help. Raul must share, too."

Edie patted the strong square hand clutching her arm.

"Raul will certainly be Harvey's *capataz*, as he was training to be *capataz* under *Don* Casey." She turned to the cook's sister. "As his mother, you must be very proud of your son. Why, only last week, *Don* Casey was telling me how pleased he was with Raul's work."

The woman started to say something, but the cook quickly interrupted.

"No, no, *señora* Edie, you don't understand. Raul must have his full share, his rightful portion, the inheritance he deserves."

"Inheritance?" Edie's eyebrows shot up. "But why?"

461

The cook removed her hand from Edie's arm and drew herself up to her full, solid height.

"Because Raul is *Don* Casey's son, *señora* . . . *Don* Casey's . . . and mine. . . ."

After the funeral, the whole story became public; the cook had in her possession a sheaf of papers to prove her statements, and the future of La Chata was thrown upside down. There were documents substantiating her statements in detail, letters officially notarized, certificates of acknowledged *parentesco*, documents signed by Tim Casey recognizing Raul as his natural son. A quick perusal immediately showed all the papers to be binding and legal; the only discrepancy as such was their date. None had been filed at the time of Raul's birth, but several years thereafter.

The cook was questioned, as was her sister, both having played roles in the deception through the years. Both answered without hesitation, and again the neighborhood reeled, as the full details of an old tragedy came to the fore.

"It was after the *señora* Casey drowned, and her little daughter. . . . I knew what had really happened . . . and I made him sign. I had to, to protect my son. To protect him from his own father. *Don* Casey was a monster, *señora* Edie . . . Only those living in the same house could have any idea. . . ."

In the dead, flat tones of the long-resigned, the cook told of Tim Casey's continual abuse of his wife and anyone in the household.

". . . he kept forcing his attentions upon me. . . . I needed the work . . . my salary was all that my parents, in the *pueblo* and I had . . . and if I resisted, he beat me. . . ."

He also beat his wife, Estelita, and the cook knew.

"I heard her cries, but what could anyone do? He was the *patrón*. . . ."

When she discovered she was pregnant, the cook told Tim Casey.

"Because I am fat, I was able to hide it for many months. At the end, I invented an excuse that my father was ill, and went home to the *pueblo*. Then I went to Rosario, to be with my sister until I had my boy. No one saw me, as I never went out. My sister came back to the *pueblo* with me, and we invented the story Raul was hers. But *Don* Casey knew the truth, of course and, because it was a boy, he allowed me to bring Raul to the *estancia* to bring him up as my nephew—which, as you know, I have done all these years."

Edie nodded, but was still puzzled. If Tim Casey had not signed papers then, why later?

"Because of what happened the night before the *señora* drowned, *Doña* Edie. *Don* Casey was drunk, drunker than he had been in ages. He broke up the furniture and hit his little girl and beat on his wife. She managed to lock herself in a room, to get away from him. It was then he shouted and screamed at her, telling her Raul was his son, boasting of it, telling her all the women he went with, how he despised her, that she was no good to him for anything any more. . . ."

Edie asked, "And in all this, where was the *niño* Harvey?"

Harvey, it appeared, had been in and out of the house.

"As he always was, during his father's rampages. *Don* Casey never touched Harvey. Nor, I must admit, did he ever hit Raul. It was only women . . ."

But that night had been worse than any of the countless incidents that had occurred in all the years before. There had been no sleep for the women; Harvey had spent the night in the *peones'* quarters, as he often did, while Tim Casey, after one last furniture-smashing spree, had collapsed into deep drunken stupor on the shabby sofa near the front entrance.

"Raul, who was only a little boy then, you must remember, had slept through everything. When the poor *señora* took her daughter down to the river, perhaps to try and collect her thoughts—who knows—he must have followed them, expecting to play with them, as he always did.

"When he returned, alone, he was crying, and he kept telling me, 'The *señora* was so cross with me, she told me to go away, that she never wanted to see me again. But I didn't do anything bad today, *tía*, truly I didn't.'"

The cook closed her eyes and sighed, the past momentarily too close, the square hands, clasped in front of her, tightening on each other to regain hold.

"I don't know what happened at the river," she told Edie. "Perhaps the little girl fell, perhaps the poor *señora* tried to save her . . . Who knows? Both were bruised—not from the rocks in the water, *Doña* Edie. Those bruises were from before. From *Don* Casey. I saw them. So afterwards, I told him . . . I told him I would tell, *tell everything I knew*, unless

463

he made official papers recognizing Raul as his son. It was the only thing I could do . . . to protect my own boy."

The silence that followed was thick with summer heat and heartache. Edie nodded, not trusting herself to speak right away. Eventually she said, "The lawyers will see to it that something fair is arranged for everybody."

But before anything further could be done, Raul disappeared.

Edie leaned her head back against the leather seat in her compartment and closed her eyes. The clanging sounds of the Rosario station were pierced by a succession of shrill whistles; in a moment, the train would start, and then she'd have only another four hours before her arrival in B.A.

She's got to come up to El Ombú and help me now, Edie thought. She can't possibly refuse. Perhaps Wilfred could learn to be useful, too . . . but even if he isn't, I must have Yvonne by my side. The last few weeks have really been too much for me. . . . I need a holiday and some rest. . . . If she were to run the place while I'm away . . .

A lurch, and the train began pulling into motion. Soon the handbell announcing lunch would be rung through the corridors. I'll have a nice lunch, thought Edie, and then tonight, when we're having dinner at the hotel, I'll bring the subject up, and we can start discussing the details. . . .

A white-coated waiter knocked on the compartment door. Smiling, Edie called out for him to enter.

"Ah, *señora* O'Connor . . . how nice to greet you again. . . . Lunch will be served in ten minutes. . . ."

" . . . and you'll reserve a nice table for me, as always?"

With a slight bow, the waiter withdrew. Edie took out her compact and touched up her lipstick, scrutinizing herself with care in the small, round mirror. She would go to the hairdresser's tomorrow; a fresh rinse, perhaps a slightly different cut . . . But above all, a rest away from the turmoil of the past weeks would do her a world of good, even though it would not be long enough this time. However, if she could fix things up with Yvonne, it would all work out for her next trip.

She rose and picked up her purse, ready to go to the dining car.

Meryl sat in the corner chair of the living room and listened to her grandmother and mother. She had been staying with Yvonne ever since Philipe had gone to the U.S.

the week before, called there unexpectedly by a cable informing him his mother was dying.

"I'll let you know when I'm coming back," he'd said, but so far no word had come and Meryl, glad of the club pool so close to the Hume-Hawley household, had stayed on at the suburban home, swimming and sleeping and doing little else. Her grandmother's arrival in B.A., however, had changed the tenor of everything. The Casey scandal seemed to have triggered a change in the plans Edie was determined to push through.

Having broached her ideas to Yvonne her first evening, Edie had said she would elaborate over a Sunday spent at Yvonne's home.

"Then we can talk without being interrupted. . . . If I'm here at the hotel, somebody always seems to be ringing up. . . ."

And so Meryl had met the mid-morning train, and driven Edie the few blocks to the house. She had then helped with serving lunch, it being the maid's day off till late evening, and the meal had passed pleasantly enough. After coffee, Wilfred had excused himself and announced he was going off to the club. The moment he left, the discussion started.

It had been going on, nonstop, ever since, the ebb and flow of family vituperation rising to new heights with each turn of the tide. Unresolved conflicts shot to the surface, the flotsam and jetsam of times long ago joining the stream of the subject at hand.

The clashing note had been struck by Yvonne the moment her mother had explained her proposal.

"No, I'm afraid I don't want to move to El Ombú. It's quite out of the question, Mummy. I'm sure you can get a good *capataz.* . . ."

At first, the discussion got underway in tones of reasonable force and meaning. But it didn't take long for the voices to take on inflections raking the past. Wounds were reopened, old fevers stoked anew, unrelated matters thrown into the pile. The afternoon light slanted in through the windows, coming from beneath the leafy fringe of the garden's luxuriant trees, until the sun dipped below the thick hedge beyond them and the living room grew darker as twilight drew near.

". . . and I've always had to do what *you* wanted, what suited *you*. Never mind about me, or about what I might want . . ."

465

"Yvonne, you're being absurd."

"Am I, Mummy? Am I?" Yvonne's voice rose. "How about the many times I've had to give up my ideas, my plans, my dreams—just because you wanted me to do something for you. Or you wanted me to do something different. Or because you didn't approve."

"Now, that's patently ridiculous. I never..."

"How about my singing?" Yvonne demanded. "I so wanted to do it. And I had a chance—I know I had—but you didn't approve.... You ruined all that for me, always telling me what I should do, or what I shouldn't. Even when I was a child..."

"Of *course* I told you what to do when you were a child!" Edie interrupted. "And a very silly little girl you were, too—stubborn as a mule. Stubborn and secretive. That's always been your trouble, and I suppose it always will be. Just look at you now! You should be ashamed of yourself! You're being selfish and stubborn and utterly pigheaded. I simply don't understand you...."

"You never have." Yvonne made the statement under her breath, but Edie caught it.

"That's where you're quite wrong—I can see right through you!" she triumphed, logic giving way to the thrust of the moment. "You seem to forget, Yvonne, that you're my daughter..."

"As though you'd ever let me..."

"... and there are times, many times, when I can read you like a book. It's always your mulishness that gets you into trouble. If you'd only *listen* and take my advice..."

"And I suppose if I always did things your way, everything would be all right...."

"Well, things certainly wouldn't turn out as badly as they do when you persist in being stubborn...."

But Yvonne wasn't listening. Tear-choked, she fought back.

"You've always, *always*, pushed and pulled me your way, to suit you and the way you wanted things to be. It's always been Yvonne, do this, and Yvonne, do that—and then, whenever I've really needed you, you've never been there. *Never.* I've never been able to count on you...."

"That's not true!" Edie was enraged. "How dare you speak to me that way? How dare you say anything of the kind? If it weren't for all that Maurice and I did for you when you got yourself into that disgraceful mess in England, you'd have been ruined. *Ruined*. You know perfectly well you were entirely to blame for the whole thing—and yet we rushed back and did everything we could for you. And the child."

Edie gave Meryl a sidelong glance, acknowledging both her existence and her presence in the room. Returning her full attention to Yvonne, she added, "And I can assure you that it cost a pretty penny too..."

"I know, Mummy, I know," Yvonne said wearily. "You've told me exactly how much it cost masses of times. I doubt you'll ever let me forget it. But there are other things I can't forget either—such as the way you encouraged me to marry Joss, practically *pushing* me into it, telling me how marvelous he was, and what a perfect couple we'd make, and how wonderful the Dancourt family was, and..."

"You didn't need any encouragement," Edie countered. "You yourself told me it was love at first sight, and you practically threw yourself at his head from then on. Besides, nobody forced you to marry him."

Yvonne, having paused for the interruption, ignored it and went on.

"... and then, when everything was so ghastly at Raedmor, and they were all being perfectly *beastly* to me, you never even *tried* to help. You weren't even *there*, most of the time...."

"And where were *you* for all those years while Meryl was growing up?" Edie shot back. "Certainly not by your daughter's side. Oh, no—you were disporting yourself halfway across the world, having a grand time. You simply abandoned the child and went your own way. At the time you accuse me of not being with you, you were already a grown woman, respectably married and moving in very good circles, I might add. But you—you more or less left Meryl to the wolves...."

"I would hardly call Philipe a wolf. And he *is* her father."

"So he is." Edie was ice itself. "And just *look* at the way you've behaved to *him*. The one decent man in your life, and you..."

"Are you trying to say that Wilfred isn't decent?" Yvonne's voice lowered dangerously.

"All I'm saying is that you are totally irresponsible. To me, to your daughter, to your ex-husband, to everyone. You are bone-selfish."

"Selfish!" Yvonne burst out. "Oh, I like that! Coming from you, it's priceless...." Her gasp of laughter strangled in
467

derision. "*You're* the selfish one, Mummy—you always have been, and everybody knows it. For you, the world begins and ends with you and what you want. Today's suggestion is a perfect example: *you* want to travel, so *I'm* supposed to get saddled with running the *estancia*." She leaned forward toward her mother. "Well, I'm not going to do it."

Meryl observed her mother's jawline squaring with tension and wondered whether her statement was one of conviction or desperation. The two older women went on glaring into each other's faces until Yvonne leaned slowly back in her chair, an air of finality about the movement, as though she had finished with everything she had to say.

It was Edie who broke the short silence, and when she did, her attitude seemed conversational rather than argumentative.

"Now look, Yvonne—let's try to be sensible about this. You know you'll be getting the *estancia* when I'm gone."

Meryl noted her grandmother was now talking about death and not travels, but one had to know her well to hear the change of theme. Edie never spoke of dying, but of going. Going where? Meryl wondered, having heard it so many times before. And there was never a question of Yvonne *inheriting;* she was going to *get* whatever it was. Had the conversation been held so many times that Edie now used a form of vocal shorthand? Or was it the way she thought, or refused to think, about the eventual certainties of life and death?

"... and now with all this terrible business at La Chata, and all the uncertainty..."

"I don't see why you're bothering to get so involved with it, Mummy...."

"It's quite simple, darling: I hold the mortgage on the place. *Now* d'you understand?"

"It hasn't got anything to do with what we've been talking about."

"Yes, it does—it's precisely the sort of thing you should know all about. Don't you think it's about time you learned how to run El Ombú? And whatever other business affairs there are?"

There was another silence, a longer one this time. Yvonne and Edie continued looking directly at one another until Yvonne's gaze drifted down to the floor. She said nothing. Edie tried to press her advantage, leaning forward in her effort to do so.

"After all, you and Wilfred could be very comfortable there, and..."

Yvonne's voice interrupted her, in flat, taut tones.

"Mummy, I've told you: I am not going to do it. Wilfred and I like living here in B.A. We need to, we want to—and we intend going on doing so." Her back straightened and she looked directly at her mother once more. "And I absolutely refuse to go and live on the *estancia*."

"But *why*?"

Something electric seemed to snap in the air, and Meryl wanted to run, to hide, to bury her head in a pillow and put her fingers in her ears. Instead, she sat rooted to the spot, watching her mother's face beginning to flush red.

"Because I'm sick and tired of having you dominate my life!" Yvonne rose from her chair, the floodgates finally burst. "Everything has always been done for *you*—your convenience, your comfort, your every whim, your health, your wishes! Now it's your travels! Well, I've had enough of it in my life—and I'm not going to let it happen again. During all the war years, I learned what freedom really is—despite the danger, despite the uncertainty, despite the blackouts and the bombings! Then, I was able to lead my own life and do what I wanted to do when I wanted to do it. And with whomever I wanted to do it...."

"And since you did so very splendidly for yourself then, couldn't you do something for me, now, for a change? But no, of course not. You never can. You couldn't even take the time to find a better buyer for La Maison while you were still in Europe—managing so beautifully, according to you. But when it came time to do something for *me*, you had to rush everything, not waiting long enough in France to..."

"Wilfred needed me."

"Wilfred is not a child, and what's more, he apparently had half the hospital at his beck and call. Again, according to *you*. He didn't need you so urgently that he couldn't have waited another few weeks while you got a decent price for La Maison...."

"Oh, Mummy, you still don't understand.... I've tried to explain it to you, so many times.... Everything was so different in France. The war had been on there, too, you know..."

"Don't be rude, Yvonne. Sarcasm doesn't suit you. Of

469

course I know—and I also know that you absolutely threw La Maison away...gave it away for a song..."

"*All* property values on the Riviera were like that. No one wanted to risk any capital there at the time. They kept saying the Communists were going to take over any day, and that everything would be expropriated."

Edie sniffed in disbelief. "At the price you got, we'd have been better off gambling on the Reds. And anyway, they didn't take over. You shouldn't have sold the place at all."

"Nothing I do is ever right...you're never satisfied..."

"Because you never do things properly..."

"Because *you* only judge on what you care about: money. Property and money. You don't give a damn about anything else. Love, other people's feelings, husbands, children, friends—none of that means anything to you. All you love and want is money...it's even the reason you married Maurice—for his money...."

"I *loved* Maurice..."

"You loved him *for his money*!" It was a wail, a cry, a scream wrenched and reaching. "That's all he ever meant to you—money, money, and nothing else!"

"That's not true!"

"*Yes, it is!*" Yvonne shrieked before her sobs broke through to obliterate her voice while she covered her face with her hands, her tears pouring between her fingers. Eventually she took a handkerchief from a pocket in her blouse, wiped her face and blew her nose and said, in a still unsteady voice, "Mummy, for once, just for this once, try to be honest. You loved Maurice for his money—not for himself, or the way he looked, or who he was, but *for his money*, for the comfort and security and luxury he could provide...."

As her voice faded into the room, there was a deep stillness; outside, the twilight was fading fast. Edie's head turned away; Yvonne, staring down at her mother, was motionless. Meryl could hardly breathe. When Edie broke the silence, it was with a feathery sigh.

"Yes...yes...he gave me all the things you say...and he did it because he loved me...." She was looking and speaking into bygone years and, momentarily, Yvonne joined her.

"That's true...he *did* love you. Very much. That was his undoing."

Edie's head straightened. "I never noticed him suffering because of it." Her tone sharpened. "Besides, miss—just where would you be today if I hadn't married him? You, with all your high and mighty ideas, and your English schooling, and your presentation at court, and the lovely London season when you made your debut—all of it paid for by Maurice, and made possible by me, because I married him!" She was back in the present, her energy returned, even angrier than she had been before. "You're an ungrateful, selfish, self-centered . . ."

"I no longer care what you call me, I'm sick and tired of hearing it all, I am not going to . . ."

The words, hurled in anger, clashed in rage, crashing amid the lacerations of familial ire. Every hurt and anger, each slight and rebuff and lie, assiduously stockpiled through the years, the formidable weaponry of a family's arsenal, roared out from under cover, exploding in mid-flight. Meryl shuddered in her chair, willing the screaming to stop, shivering against the chintz-covered arms and back until her thoughts were so shredded by the incessant screaming that they dispersed untidily in scraps, whirling through her mind, making her feel sick and dizzy and confused and terrified. Surely nothing could be worth these passion-ridden furies, no possession valued at so frightful a human rage. . . .

Meryl thought: they are my mother and my grandmother and they are tearing us to pieces, with jagged words and terrible phrases that now all never die. And for what? For all and nothing—for things that only exist in their own imaginary world.

When she could stand it no more, she tried to stop the trembling of her mouth, and in tears, cried out, "Why can't we leave it all alone, and say good-bye?"

Both the older women stopped to turn and look at her, blankly. Then:

"Meryl, don't be rude." "Meryl, don't interrupt."

Reduced to her place as the child in the room, Meryl could only feel her heart thumping against her throat. As her mother and her grandmother turned to each other again, Meryl's only remaining fragment of coherent thought was: *I must get out of all this mess. I have to go away.*

In the small, cramped room that she lived in, Lala said, "The best thing would be for you to go and work on El Ombú."

Raul, sitting hunched on the edge of the bed, stared down at the splintery floorboards, frowning.

"Or you could stay here in Córdoba," Lala continued. "But I don't think you'd like it. Besides, what would you do? Some miserable sort of work, cleaning streets or working in a garden? You know you'd hate offices."

"But the group..."

"The group will need people everywhere," Lala assured him, sitting up next to him and rubbing his back with affectionate resolve. "In the meantime, you go and talk to *Doña* Edie. I personally think she'll be glad to have you...from what Rosita says...."

They talked into the darkness, then dressed and went out to eat their dinner.

"You're always trying to stuff food into me." Raul said it with a smile.

And Lala grinned back, overjoyed at the first sign of relaxation in him; he was still overwhelmed by the news of his parentage, and the recent maelstrom of shock-filled events.

"I hope I always will be...have another *alfajor*...."

They took a box of the confections back to the room with them, and held each other close in loneliness and protection and love for the remainder of the night.

IX

The American Dream
1950–1959

1

"We'll probably be getting in quite soon, Meryl. I think you'd better start getting ready...."

Philipe's voice reached her through the incessant throb of the engines. Meryl wriggled up in her seat and rubbed her eyes; they were gritty with insufficient sleep and the long hours of flying all the way from Buenos Aires, in an endless series of hops and landings, first across to the continent's west coast at Santiago de Chile, and then north along that coast. Chile, Peru, Ecuador, Columbia, Panama... They had landed and taken off and landed again, and Meryl had gazed and stared and dozed and woken. At the airports, men came to confer briefly with Philipe, and he always introduced her, his daughter, with a voice of pride.

On the plane, the two of them had talked and eaten a jumble of snacks and meals, slept fitfully, waking to talk again.

"I think you'll like it...."

"I'm sure I will, Dad...."

And she was sure. Anything would be better than B.A., anyway, certainly for a while. Probably forever. She only wanted to think ahead, leave all the mess and unhappiness behind. Jimmy, her family, the terrible row—no. She would not, she could not cope with any of it any more.

The sky was beginning to show light toward the east. They were scheduled to land in New York shortly after dawn. New York and her future lay directly ahead; Meryl made her way along the aisle to the bathroom, where she splashed her face repeatedly with water, trying to wake up her eyes.

When she returned to her seat, Philipe was holding two small trays on the pillow in his lap.

"I didn't think you'd want much more than coffee...."

As she sipped the drink that did not taste anything like coffee to her, Meryl thought: that's the way it's going to be. Different. She was flying over the United States of America

475

now—not South America, where the last vestiges of her adolescent years lay abandoned in her recent past. There was no future there; not in Buenos Aires. So many of her friends and contemporaries had taken off for other parts of the world. The death of Philipe's mother, the grandmother she did not remember, had finally triggered the radical change for Meryl herself.

Meryl thought: the city I am going to is where I came from, and it is secure. She glanced at Philipe, who smiled back fondly.

"It won't be too much longer," he said. "We've begun descending. Can't you feel your ears popping?"

Meryl nodded, looking beyond her father out of the window; she saw the sky was now light with the promise of dawn.

"Let's swap seats again," said Philipe, rising. "Maybe you'll get a good first view of New York."

They changed over. Philipe busied himself with the papers in his briefcase, packing them away and snapping the case shut. Meryl stared out at the last vanishing stars, seeing and not seeing the landscape below. They were flying along the coast, the shoreline's contours clearly visible, the signs of civilization everywhere: huddled towns, ribbon highways, stretches of green, the lead-colored waters of a breeze-rippled bay.

And then, suddenly, there it was.

Rising out of the early morning mist, the towers of Manhattan reached up immediately ahead, just as sunlight appeared. The buildings glowed with its reflected summer warmth, floating, fairylike, magic, marvelous, unreal, a toy kingdom of hope beckoning to her, warm and shining in the fresh new sunlight. Pink and gold touched the tops of the buildings and the spires, which floated, disembodied, delicate, glowing in the spare blue freshness of the dawn, an oblong of clustered, uneven, delicate spires, their base hidden beneath the billowing haze rising from the waters all around.

To the east, the full sun rose. The plane banked and turned toward it, circling and turning in its descent toward Idlewild Airport. The beckoning spires disappeared from Meryl's sight, and she turned her attention to her seat belt, her hand luggage, the admonitions and messages from the stewardesses, all to do with their imminent landing.

But that first glimpse of her native city had etched its perfection into her mind, and she knew she would never forget the fairyland, fairytale sight of Manhattan, rising out of the mist at dawn, in the gliding sunlight of a clear summer day.

New York. Manhattan. Midsummer. Meryl was breathless. It was marvelous, mystifying, magnificent, breathtaking, puzzling in spots, wonderful fun, dizzying, different. Enormously different. And the biggest difference was the language.

"Dad, it feels so *strange*. I keep getting mixed up...everyone speaks *English*...."

"Funny you should mention that point.... Your mother told me, years ago, when we first met, I guess, that one of *her* difficulties when she was a small child and went to London was the very same thing...."

New York. Full of surprises. The old doorman who remembered her. The stairs in the entrance lobby that Meryl felt she knew.

"You should...you used to crawl up them, refusing to take Emily's hand...."

And the quick discovery that, having returned to the place of her birth, she felt more alien within it than ever before.

Alien—but glad to be there. There were freedoms within the American way of life that, surprising as they were to her when she first bumped into them, she soon discovered to be the norm, accepted behavior in every respect. An essence of all the implications were crystallized for her one day at a drugstore food counter.

To eat quick meals on her own, sitting on a stool among strangers, unmolested, inconspicuous—this in itself was a freedom Meryl had never experienced before. But its boundaries were stretched even further as, treating herself to the novelty of a dimestore breakfast, she heard the woman seated next to her say something and realized, with a shock, that the remark was addressed to her.

"I...I beg your pardon?"

The woman, middle-aged and mildly pleasant, repeated her praise of the dimestore's doughnuts.

"...and that's why I always come here...can't find another decent doughnut this side of Forty-Second Street...that's what I always say...."

As she answered, her words hiding the thumping of her heart, Meryl stepped further into her new world. It was okay to speak to strangers. It was okay to say okay. To think okay.

Nobody was going to jump down your throat for using Americanisms. This was America. Nobody was going to pull her up short on the usage of language or the pattern of her behavior. No need to remember who she was. And who was she, anyway? One of several million people now, most of whom believed, at least theoretically, that everyone was more or less equal.

And you better believe it, bub, Meryl told herself with a stifled giggle, mentally repeating one of the many phrases enchanting her in this new world of shattered syntax and grammatical grotesqueries that signaled a freedom from social chains. Snob and slob, it seems, moved with equal assertion through the everyday swim of life in the U.S.A.

So many differences, surprises, freedoms, innovations. Phoning in to radio shows. Music in the shops—stores, as she was learning to call them. Supermarkets: the rows and rows of food and goods and color. The first time she stood in front of a vegetable counter, she gasped.

"Dad—the potatoes—they're *clean!*"

The wealth of merchandise, the range of goods, the brightness, and the carefree air. She even found a place with specialized left-handed items and, looking at a corkscrew with its inverted spiral, felt a tug of anger and regret. She put it back on the shelf, forcing herself to inspect more conventional gift items in another section.

And the stark contrasts.

"I think the slums here are much worse," she told her father, after he had driven her all around Manhattan on a quiet, clear Sunday in his new convertible. They had had the top down, and had driven slowly, from one end of the island to the other, weaving through all the districts in between. From the Battery to the Cloisters, the diverse neighborhoods had emerged: Wall Street, Chinatown, the bridges and Fifth Avenue, the houses and apartments, Hell's Kitchen, Central Park. They had driven through Harlem, seen Spuyten Duyvil, the Empire State Building, the Hudson, the docks. They wound up with a short stroll by the ivy-covered houses overlooking the East River, a small enclave of shuttered luxury in the heart of Sutton Place.

Philipe questioned her opinion. "Think of all the shacks and *ranchos* you've seen. . . ."

"They don't stand next to skyscrapers," was her determined

reply. "You don't live in *rancho* and see a Fifth Avenue in the same town."

More impressions. Lights and colors. Times Square and the gaudiness around it. The smell of popcorn. And, in people, the lack of smell; everyone was so clean, so neat. Seldom did she sense the sharp smell of sweaty labor, the dingy smell of lazy grubbiness, the soiled collar twice turned. The wilted look of Wilfred's shirts was nowhere in American sight, and the bright white T-shirt of young American males, a jolt of cleanliness.

Everything was new, bright, clean, and fresh. Almost unreal.

The quick easy friendliness. The informality, the smiles. Anybody could speak to anybody. Where did they draw the line? They didn't. Meryl soon decided; it simply was not there. Not the way she had always known it, separating, codifying, identifying, limiting, constraining. A sense of the possible seemed to pervade all areas of American life.

"Dad! Guess what! I sang duets with a taxi driver today! He had the radio going, and was humming, and then, just out of the blue, he asked me whether I liked music—and we sang! What a crazy place!"

"It's very different from B.A." Philipe agreed. "I'm glad you like it."

Meryl considered the subject.

"Oh, I do, I really do. But . . ."

"But?"

"There's something that makes me uneasy at times. I don't always feel it, but I guess it's always there, under the surface. It's as though there's nothing solid to stand on directly underneath."

One of the first people they got in touch with was Sal de Leo.

"So you finally made it up here to the land of the free. Welcome to America!" He raised the glass in his hand in toast to Meryl. "Welcome to your own land. Home at last. Did you remember any of it?"

She told him about the lobby steps.

"But of course, Dad keeps introducing me to people who say they knew me when I was a baby."

"And then they say intelligent things like 'My! How you've grown!'"

"Only the old ones."

He raised his glass again.

"And now let's drink to the future. What d'you plan on doing, Meryl? How about coming to work for me?"

"I was hoping you'd remember..."

"Remember? How could I forget? But I warn you, kiddo— I work hard, and I work my assistants even harder. D'you think you can take it? You have a great deal to learn—good as you are," he added.

Meryl nodded. "I understand."

"There's a hell of a lot of donkey work involved, too. Holding lights..."

"I remember from the museum..."

"...being a gofer..."

"A what?"

"A gofer. Someone who goes for things. Going for coffee when we need it. Or beer. Or supplies. A gofer. Don't you speak English?" he grinned.

"That's the trouble. I do."

"Forget it, kiddo. We'll learn you...."

But apart from a tour of Sal's studio, and an overall view of what her job would be, Meryl opted for a few more months of total freedom.

"...to get to know New York—and to help Dad...."

There was much to be done in the Park Avenue apartment. For one thing, it was technically hers, left in trust until she was thirty, and part of a larger trust that gave her a small income. The inheritance had come as a surprise to her; not so to Philipe. His mother, he explained, had long planned it that way, and told him about her will years before.

In contrast to the democratic and raucous bustle Meryl discovered and enjoyed outside, inside the building on Park Avenue all was patrician—discreet, cavernous, and quiet. Gloved doormen touched their caps when Meryl entered, the soft brogue of their voices an echo of their boyhoods in a distant land. Upstairs in the apartment itself, the last of a succession of dour housekeepers kept the dust at bay and the refrigerator stocked, and a cleaning woman arrived several times a week to help out.

Again in contrast to the newness Meryl found throughout the city, within the apartment she discovered clues and relics of the past. One of these lay in the drawers of the inlaid desk that had been her grandmother's, a delicately proportioned antique standing against the wall in the double-sectioned living room, a room where heavy leather armchairs were grouped around the fireplace, gros-point chairs and lighter antiques dominating the other half of the area.

Meryl, seeking a pencil, found all sorts of treasures in the inlaid wood drawers. Ancient nib holders, a silver inkstand, boxes of notepaper, old calling cards. They were yellowed with age, some bent and forgotten. There was sealing wax, and a mounted seal. But it was the cards that intrigued her most. She took one with her to the dinner table that night, and broached the subject when Philipe arrived.

"Dad, are you a baron?"

He looked at the card she handed him and nodded. "Technically."

"Then why don't you ever use the title?" Meryl gestured with the card. "Your mother and father obviously did."

"They lived in a different era. I don't believe in things like that." He slipped the silver ring off his napkin.

"But wouldn't it help at times?"

"Possibly," Philipe agreed. "But with all the wrong people. The old saying is true, you know: *Those who care, don't matter, and those who matter, don't care.*"

"Are you sure?"

"Yes—yes, I think I am. I've always found it to be so. Worth is intrinsic, an interior quality, not something you can tack onto the front of a name. Try and remember that as you get older. If you are somebody, you don't need to wear the fact like a hat. My father used to say that being is enough. Or should be," Philipe added with a rueful smile.

"That sounds almost more snobbish than using a title, Dad."

"You may be right. Perhaps it is."

As the weeks passed, she began looking at her father in a new light.

"You're such a shadowy person, Daddy. One always has to ask you—and then it turns out you've known about whatever it is all the time. Or been there. Or worked on it. Whatever it is." Meryl was at a loss for words. "Do you do it on purpose? I mean, consciously try, all the time, to be so unobtrusive?"

After reflecting for a moment, Philipe said, "Yes, I suppose

481

I do. But much of it seems to come naturally to me. Oh, I suppose it all started when I was a boy. My mother always felt I was in the way, so the only possibility of being around her was not to be a nuisance to her, not to be noticed." He smiled. "That probably explains a lot. And then, of course, later—well, later, that's what was required of me on the job."

"You've always been a spy, haven't you, Dad?"

"Not exactly. More of an information collector."

"What's the difference?"

Another smile. "I really don't know."

Yvonne thrust the trowel into the crumbly earth and enlarged the hole sufficiently for the rootball of the plant lying on its side on the lawn behind her. The longtime friends who had lived next door had given her several of their favorite plants when they moved away, and now at last she had them all accommodated and flourishing within the luxuriance of her own garden. She sighed, once again regretting her friend's departure; the new neighbors were nice enough, but not the sort of people she or Wilfred could every really get to know well. They weren't even very good with animals; there was their damn dog, barking at her through the fence again. She'd tried to make friends with him, but he was far too high-strung. So many terriers were, she knew. It was a pity, because his barking sometimes bothered poor Wilfred.

She frowned, partly with effort as she placed the plant into the hole and began packing it down, partly because Wilfred's condition was slowly getting worse. There wasn't anything serious yet, but there were numerous small signs; he was getting vague, and forgetting the simplest of things. However, it might pass.

The doctors had said as much.

". . . no use worrying, Mrs. Hume-Hawley . . . the arm isn't troubling him too much, and these cases are all very individual, you know. . . ."

Wilfred's just tired, Yvonne, so don't make a fuss about it. I've given him a tonic, and he'll soon be right as rain. . . ."

". . . got to remember Wilfred's in his fifties. . . . We all slow down at that age. . . ."

If only she could persuade him to travel to England; she knew it would do both of them a world of good. As always, she longed for London, longed to see it built up again, renewed. If only they could spend a year there; it would be marvelous for both of them. Wilfred would be able to see all the top British specialists; they knew far more about the problems of the limbless than the doctors out here.

But if Wilfred was vague and generally agreeable on most things, he was firmly adamant in his stand against a trip back home. He had no interest, he told her. And besides, his arm, the climate... He liked his doctors out here; splendid bunch of chaps. Couldn't ask for better, in his considered opinion. Besides, he liked it out here, and the quiet life suited him. London? London was a thing of the past—and was lunch ready now...?

Yvonne sighed, and focused her attention on the plant, replacing the excavated earth around its roots and tramping down the soil. The dog was still barking; she could see him on the other side of the fence, only a few yards away. He kept rushing up and down, directing his noisy protest at her. She hoped Wilfred was in the living room at the far side of the house; really, the dog was most annoying.

An answering bark from the area near the back door made her smile. That was Coco, on her parrot perch, exercising his voice and his variety of barks. He could still imitate the long-dead Taitai's surprisingly deep-chested, rolling series of barks, and his grasp of the phrases he'd learned in France was as firm as the grip of his scaly, taloned claws with their little fringe of tiny feathers down the outer side. He still liked to snuggle, too, and she would often take him on her arm, holding it close to her waist and letting him ruffle his feathers and cuddle close. If she sang, he had a selection of throaty sounds he used to sing along with her, sounds he would break with a screech or a whistle, usually in protest when she put him back on his stand.

The planting completed, Yvonne stood up, straightening her back slowly, aware of its ache. Leaving her gardening gloves and the trowel in the pot-cluttered tool shed, she went into the house, knowing she would just have time to get ready for the cocktail party they were going to that evening.

"That you, Yvonne? I can't find my shirt..."

At the party, Yvonne told a group of acquaintances, "Yes, I know, but we've changed our minds... Wilfred's arm, you know... and the climate..."

A chance remark later in the evening gave her the news that her mother had sailed for England earlier that day.

Yvonne heard of Edie's return in the same chance manner, for mother and daughter had not spoken since the cataclysmic row. They heard sifted versions of each other's lives and doings via their circles of friends, the gossipmongers who, in innocence or malice, held the family explosion to be a ninety-day wonder, and then went on to newer things.

"... a spoiled, selfish woman, but on the other hand, so is ..."

"... terrible pity ... always were problems there ..."

"... most peculiar, and they always have been ..."

There were also those who took stands and sides, the generational divide identified their positions.

"... headstrong daughter ..."

"... impossible mother ..."

"Poor Edie, coping with the *estancia*, all on her own ... and she's not getting any younger, you know ..."

"Poor Yvonne, coping with Wilfred, all on her own ... and he's not getting any better, you know ..."

Because of the unhealed breach between them, Yvonne did not witness Edie's saddened return to El Ombú. The voyage to England, so enthusiastically anticipated, had been a dismaying and dreary disappointment to her; everything felt different, so much had changed, the life she had lived there and remembered so vividly was nowhere to be seen. Oh, to be sure, there were friends in country houses, and the stretches of countryside were as lovely as before. But the side of life Edie had loved, the glitter, the excitement, the heady whirl of social encounters—that was gone.

A friend remarked, "My dear Edie, what do you expect? You're twenty years older, and you haven't got Maurice at your side anymore," and Edie had flinched under the statement's stark reality, but later, at the hotel, she pushed its message away. That was not the difference; the difference was England. England in its postwar mood and its Labour Government touch. No, no; it was they who had changed, not Edie, they who did not see what had happened to themselves and to the world. She changed her sailing back to B.A. and left a full month earlier, arriving back at the *estancia* in the middle of the spring planting and, despite the economic difficulties facing everyone raising beef in the crisscross of political chicanery and confusion. Edie breathed in the air of the *pampas* with relief. She was home, it was warm, and Raul had done a very good job of keeping everything going in her absence.

She slipped gratefully back into the harness of *estancia* life, attending to the accumulated papers on the desk. First came the bills and all the local correspondence. Then came a thorough checking of the *estancia* diary; Raul had done a good job there, too, although Edie saw he had enlisted Lala's help when she had apparently come down from Córdoba on a visit, for her handwriting covered the days of her stay. Wonderful to have such loyal people around.

Then came private correspondence. There was a long letter from Meryl in New York. She was apparently enjoying it, and working, too. She had sent some photographs of Central Park; Edie took out her airmail stationery and wrote back a long letter during the fading light of the lengthening evening until at last Rosita came in and started preparing the table for her dinner.

"I'm sorry *señora*. I'm late. I overslept my *siesta*, and now everything's delayed...."

Edie was surprised, as it was not like Rosita to sleep much in the afternoon. But it really didn't matter; the letter to Meryl had kept her busy and unaware of the passing time.

Much as she enjoyed getting letters from her grandmother and mother in Argentina, Meryl read their news and comments through a thickening veil of distance and, increasingly, time. She was completely immersed in her New York way of life, its freedoms changing her attitudes, its standards influencing her desires. Even her accent changed, became ambiguous, undefining. She acquired acquaintances, some friends, a few admirers, a lover. He proposed marriage, she turned him down; he went elsewhere, she went on working. Sal's studio became the hub of her life, the apartment, her refuge.

Philipe, his base of operations changed, traveled out of New York instead of B.A. He was home, however, most of the time, as the Washington office claimed his attention.

"My field days are probably over," he commented to Meryl.

"They want your opinions now, instead of observations."

"Something like that."

"Congrats, Dad—I guess you're an expert...."

And he continued his weekly visits to the capital, seldom

referring to anything there when he returned to New York. The apartment, modified and rearranged to suit their convenience, allowed each total privacy, and room to spare. Meryl had also had a small darkroom installed in an unused pantry, for she was now branching out on assignments of her own.

The solid commercial grounding she got at Sal's studio was one thing, her own particular vision and emerging talent another. They had merged and become obvious when she had been sent out on a job photographing a group of children.

"You might be able to make a career of it," Sal suggested on seeing the prints. "Taking natural pictures of kids in their homes, instead of the studio portrait stuff. . . ."

And so it began, first as a sideline, then becoming more important; Meryl's portraits of children held a charm all their own.

"It's the kids' themselves," she insisted. "All I'm doing is aiming the camera. . . ."

But there was more to it than that, and Meryl knew it, and kept quiet.

The first rule was: no parents in the area. Not in sight and not in earshot; no parents around. She'd discovered the rule the hard way, thinking when she first started that a child's shyness in front of the camera might ease with a mother nearby.

Out of the question.

"Smile, sweetheart—smile for the camera. . . smile for the nice lady . . . see? She wants you to smile . . . no, not like *that*, honey, smile nicely, like you smile at Mommy . . ."

Or:

"Push your bangs out of the way . . . you know Mommy doesn't like you to pucker up like that . . ."

Fathers could be even worse.

". . . I don't see why you can't sit still for a few seconds while she takes your picture . . . for Christ's sake, doesn't anybody around here know what they're doing? Let's get this show on the road . . ."

No. No parents anywhere near.

It meant spending time with the child before the shutter-clicking got going, gaining the child's confidence, putting them both at ease. It took time, and a gentle persistence, but the results were encouraging. Still working out of Sal's studio, Meryl's reputation grew.

In the land she had left behind her, two events occurred during the B.A. winter while Meryl herself was basking in New York's summer sun. The first made headlines around the world and plunged Argentina into mourning: Maria Eva Duarte de Perón, Evita to her adoring millions, died of cancer of the uterus at the age of thirty-three.

The second event, mentioned only in Buenos Aires, also made the papers there, on the social page. The engagement was announced of Dr. Jaime Julio Federico Casterán; a spring wedding would follow. On reading it, Meryl felt a stab inside her, and for the rest of the day, she was very quiet.

Late that night she searched through her closet until she found a dress on a hanger; removing its black folds from the wire, she hung it over her arm. Then she went out to the utility room where the incinerator chute received all the garbage. She stuffed the dress into the hopper, sending it plunging to flames and oblivion, closing the door on both its destruction and her past, in cold and silent rage.

Yvonne's letter, in which the engagement notice had been enclosed, was full of comment and jubilation on the more famous of the two events.

...everyone says he can't last without her...good riddance of bad rubbish...a lot of hysterical nonsense going on right now...sure to mean the beginning of the end for the whole regime...

Her only comment on Jimmy's engagement was that the girl was said to be older than he was, a recent arrival in Buenos Aires.

...she's Canadian, and is an artist of some kind...and has been married before...has two little girls, I'm told...it all sounds rather strange, but just the sort of thing Jimmy would do. I'm so glad you got out of that, darling, you'd never have been happy with him...far too unstable...

Alone in the apartment and unseen by anyone, Meryl tore up the letter and burst into tears. When she finally sat down to write, it was to Lala, not her mother, and she enclosed the letter in another, shorter one, to her grandmother, asking Edie to forward it to Córdoba for her.

Edie heard the prognosis and stiffened in the doctor's chair.

"Hopeless . . . quite hopeless . . . we did what we could, but . . . she waited far too long. If she'd come to us sooner . . . if we'd been able to operate right away . . . if the tumor were not so big . . . We have removed as much as possible. . . . She may last a year, perhaps a bit more, but eventually it will definitely grow again. . . ."

Edie looked out of the Rosario hospital's window and saw nothing but blankness. If . . . if . . . What did the ifs matter? Rosita was dying . . . would be dead. The doctor was still talking; they were doing everything possible . . . trying to make her comfortable . . . to ease the pain . . .

Edie turned to face him and the discipline of previous years and experience sustained her.

"Yes, of course . . . I understand . . . yes, all bills to come to me . . ."

After she rose and left the small office, she walked down the corridor. I must do one thing at a time, she thought. Today I can only tackle today.

There was little she could do for Rosita right that moment, as she would be unconscious for several more hours.

I know . . . I'll post the letter Meryl sent down for Lala—and I'll add a note asking Lala to come home right away. I can trust her, and tell her everything . . . but Rosita is never to know. . . .

2

In 1955, the government of Juan Domingo Perón was challenged by the military establishment, and a quick revolution ended with the president fleeing on a gunboat, upriver to Paraguay. After a brief period of jubilation and confusion, Argentina installed new leaders and regulations, and got down to the business of political reform.

Meryl read about it in the New York papers, and she also read her mother's outpourings of glee. But the distance was total: her life was disconnected from anything to do with the British community's actions or reactions.

"I don't think Mother realizes it's a whole other world up here. . . ."

488

Apart from which, a specific project was involving most of her time and interest: she and her father were planning a trip to Peru.

Originally, it was to be a vacation for her; then Sal suggested an assignment.

"It might be a terrific idea to work up a whole portfolio of kids' photographs... an international one, stressing how kids are kids, but also the differences..."

"Great. But that's only on-spec stuff."

"Moneygrubber." He grinned. "Okay—I'll get you work...."

It turned out to be the photographing of museum artifacts in Lima.

"Shades of my first job for you..."

"Except that this time, you can make someone else sweat and hold the lights...."

On the plane down to Lima, Meryl read portions of the latest letter she had received from Yvonne aloud to Philipe.

...glad to hear you're going to Peru. Will you be coming on down here? You'll find lots of things have changed. Do let me know, darling, if you'll be coming and, if so, when you plan to arrive and where you'll be staying...

"Obviously she doesn't want me staying with her," Meryl observed. The paragraphs following gave an inkling why; Yvonne's news was mostly about Wilfred.

...not at all well, and I'm learning rather a lot about nursing. It all has to do with his missing arm, of course; there's a form of creeping paralysis stopping the circulation on that side of his body...the veins stiffen...atrophy... doctors doing all they can, but...

Another letter Meryl was carrying in her handbag, written by Edie, gave a different viewpoint.

As to your mother, I have not seen her in years, and hardly hear from her at all. Everyone down in B.A. tells me she's playing nannie to that sinvergüenza husband of hers, who has no shame about using our money.

"The rest is all about Raul, and what a marvelous job he's doing—I'm so glad for him, after all that terrible mess.

489

... Grannie doesn't mention Harvey at all. I suppose he doesn't come near El Ombú with Raul in charge.... Grannie says Lala's still there. I wonder why? She's been there for ages—and after all that insistence on preferring Córdoba...."

Meryl put the letters away, her mood pensive. After a while, she said, "I wonder why Mother had to pick Wilfred. ... Surely she could've chosen someone more worthwhile."

"I doubt she chose him—I think he chose her," was Philipe's answer.

"Same thing, isn't it?"

"No, not really. You see, Yvonne never chooses anything—never has, as far as I can recall. Things choose *her*. She allows them to. Life has to happen to her. She is incapable of making things happen for herself."

He folded his newspaper and stuck it in the pocket on the seatback in front of him.

"I am much the same, I suppose, in certain ways. That's why it didn't work out. If only..." He stopped, turning to Meryl before he said, "I think *if only* is the saddest phrase I know."

"I'd never thought of it that way..."

"Never mind. Yvonne's doing all right. Things like looking after her present husband are what make her tick. She needs things like that to happen to her...."

As he kept talking, Meryl wondered: but what about me? I happened to her. And, as though he had tuned in on her thoughts, Philipe began talking of her own babyhood and early childhood, and how, when they had all lived in New York, Yvonne had blossomed.

"So then what happened?"

Her father smiled, his customary lighthearted attitude returning.

"You got upstaged by World War Two. Come on, Meryl, you can't complain; you didn't do too badly. I wasn't such a rotten parent to you, was I?"

"You were the nicest father in the whole world...." She said it slowly, soberly, meaning every word, and the moment of silence that followed was gold to both of them. Then the stewardesses came by to begin the meal service by installing the fitted trays in front of them. The dinner dishes followed.

They were already on their second cups of coffee when

Meryl asked, "Dad, did you ever love anybody? But I mean, really love them?"

"Oh, yes, I did. At least, I think so. You remember Sarita . . ."

Meryl nodded.

"I think I loved her . . . very much . . ."

"Then what happened?"

He shrugged. "Nothing much, really. It eventually petered out. I sort of lost touch after we moved to New York."

"But why didn't you marry her before that? Long before?"

"Well, when we first met, it all would have meant such an upheaval, divorcing your mother, and . . ."

"But eventually, she divorced you anyway."

Philipe sighed. "The truth is, Meryl, that there's much to that old saying about only the brave deserving the fair." He shrugged. "I don't believe I've ever been brave enough, or strong enough to face an argument. Or say no. Or stop. Point out that enough's enough."

Meryl took out a cigarette and accepted his light.

"Did you ever love Mother?"

There was a pause. Then: "I really don't know. I was attracted to her—obviously." He smiled at Meryl with warmth. "Otherwise, you wouldn't be here, would you?"

"But that wasn't my question."

"I know . . . and I'm trying to answer it as clearly as I can. As I told you long ago, everything happened so quickly. I knew at once what I felt was the right thing to do. There was so much fuss, and then we left England, and arrived in New York, and finally got married, and then you were born. . . . I hardly had time to think it all through, I suppose."

"But in the years since then . . ."

Philipe sighed.

"It was hard to know what your mother wanted. Other than England. And then, when she went there, and was happy—I could tell, at once, by her letters . . . do you remember them?"

"Yes."

"Well, then, there you are. And then, of course, the war . . ."

"Dad, you *still* haven't answered my question."

"No, I haven't, and I know it. The more I think about it, the more I wonder whether I can. Perhaps if I do it in a form of warning to you, a sort of *achtung*! *ojo*! and beware! message—I because I think you may be a bit like me in this respect."

He pushed away his coffee cup and turned in his seat.

"Meryl, always remember you tend to be a bit of a cold fish. Not through and through, perhaps, but in a thick, protective layer. At least, I think I see it in you at times. I know I recognize it in myself. First there is us, and then there's a long gap, and then—maybe—come all the others. . . ."

Meryl smiled in recognition and Philipe caught her expression.

"So you *do* know what I'm talking about. . . ."

She nodded. "And how. It's a relief to hear you say it out loud. Because I always thought I was—well, I thought it was something wrong in me, or something. At one point, I always seem to be able to look at me with whoever I'm with, from a distance . . . and then I'm not there anymore. I mean, next to them, but only where I'm looking from . . . and it's a long way away. . . ."

"Exactly." Philipe gestured in agreement. "And I never met anyone who made me forget that distance for more than brief moments at a time." He looked at her. "There you have it, Meryl. That's my answer, as best as I can give it. I've always been full of distance. No one has ever come close."

Lima was a revelation, a city like no other Meryl had ever seen before. Totally unlike Buenos Aires, it was a mix of colonial-baroque and cement-modern, filled with the tempo of Latin life as she knew it and Indian culture she had never experienced at all, Conquistador-brought overlays on indigenous craft and artifacts, clay pots and silver ornaments, Inca shards next to contemporary gold. A hodgepodge of huts clustered around parts of the tumbling, pebbled river that cleft the city in a fruitless attempt to divide its double ancestry. Subsequent influences had augmented and colored the intarsia of Lima: Indian markets, colonial churches, Chinese stores, and rising buildings all played their roles against the backdrop of the Andes.

Beyond the city's elegant suburbs lay the swathes of beaches and the current-cold sea, all shrouded in early morning mist and fog that rolled in from the ocean at night, to burn off again in the hot morning sunshine in preparation for another cloudless midsummer day.

The hotel, a blend of old-time courtesy and updated, efficient luxury, was right in the middle of town. It boasted not only a nightclub on its premises, but also a saloon known by its habitués as the Snakepit, and the two van Landens soon made it a ritual to meet there at the close of their individual days.

The car and driver assigned to Philipe called for him early every morning; Meryl, more independent, chose her own varying form of transportation every day.

"Let me get the museum job done first," she told Philipe, when he offered to hire a second car for her personal use. "When that's finished, I'll start exploring. Meanwhile, all I need is an occasional taxi..."

For the most part, she walked, having arranged with the museum to work set hours every morning. Lima, she discovered, closed down for a four-hour break every day, starting at lunchtime.

"Ah, yes *señorita*, it has always been so here in the summer," she was told. "It gives everybody the opportunity to rest, or go to the beach...."

And so Meryl headed out to the beaches, too, soon discovering the horseshoe-shaped cove that was the city's fashion, with its wide stretch of sand and summer eating shacks along the bordering road. Sometimes Philipe joined her for the midday swimming, and when he did, they were driven to the beach by his regular driver.

"Cholito scares the daylights out of me," Meryl said one day as they swerved around a corner on the way to the beach.

"But he knows all the roads—and the shortcuts, too...."

"I still think he drives too fast."

"Hey, lady—how come you're holding the camera sideways?"

The American voice, coming at her through the clatter of the open-air market, startled Meryl. She glanced up, annoyed, and found herself looking straight into the strikingly blue eyes of the pianist from the band that played at the Snakepit. He was grinning.

"Didn't mean to shake you up," he continued. "But I have one of those litle jobbies myself"—he gestured at her twin reflex camera—"so I couldn't help noticing..."

While he spoke, the trio of Indian women who had been squatting by the nearby stall rose gracefully and moved away, their multilayered skirts swaying over their bare feet.

"*That's* why." Meryl looked at the departing figures. "I got several shots of them because they thought I was aiming at the building over there. If they think you're pointing a camera at them, they often run away. You see, they believe the magic eye is going to steal their soul."

"No kidding. Well, what d'you know. . . . I'm glad I asked. Another question: what's your name? I'm Dan Horgan, and I've been watching you at the hotel."

Despite her momentary annoyance, Meryl smiled, and said, "I know." Then she introduced herself, adding, "I was considering going over to tell you how much I enjoyed your playing last night. I mean everybody's in your group. You all seemed to be extra good."

"Thank you kindly, ma'am. I'll have to tell the others. It's nice to know someone noticed. We figured we were hot, too. Here—let me help you with that." He took her camera bag. "It looks heavy." As he slung it over his shoulder, he said, "And it is. Mean to say you tote this around all the time?"

"Usually," Meryl found herself explaining her work as they walked along the pathway between the stalls toward the main street.

"If you're heading back to the hotel," said Horgan, hailing a taxi, "can I buy you a drink at the bar?"

Over peanuts and *pisco* sours, they matched up likes and likenesses in their lives: music and casual living and swimming and much of Gershwin. Dan Horgan was engaged.

"How nice," said Meryl, feeling safe.

He showed her pictures of his fiancée, taken down at the Jersey shore the previous summer.

". . . but of course, they're just snaps, not like the stuff you probably turn out every day. . . ."

"That's not true—they're pretty good. . . ."

"At least I didn't cut her head off." Dan put the pictures back in his wallet.

"I used to do that, too, when I first started. . . ."

They turned back to music.

"D'you ever sing?"

Meryl said, "Only in the shower. My mother used to play the piano for me and a friend of mine . . ." and she went on to describe the songs she and Lala had sung.

"Maybe you could join us in a set . . ."

"Oh, I don't think so . . ."

494

"...down in the nightclub, late in the evening. The guys'll love it. Everyone gets kind of mellow in the small hours ...nobody cares..."

A bellhop came over with a message for Meryl from Philipe; he would be back shortly. Meryl thanked the boy, and tipped him.

"How come you speak such good Spanish?"

More explanations, followed by further exchange of information. It was Dan's first trip to South America; he'd been to the Caribbean the previous year.

"With the same group. But this'll be my last adventure. My folks think it's time I settled down—and I guess I do, too."

He'd turned his hand to a variety of jobs, in between his piano playing.

"Any chance I'd get, I'd grab a gig with a group.... It isn't steady work...."

Out of school, he had missed fighting the war by a matter of months.

"There I was, all gussied up in a uniform, ready to go, and they rang down the curtain...."

Back in civilian life, he had traveled the forty-eight States at one time or another, mostly with a band.

"I'd just about had it, was all set to settle down, when this deal came through. So I figured, what the hell, one last fling, and then I'll give it up, get my teeth into something solid. Being a musician full time isn't steady. Not until you're in the big time—if you ever make it. And my chances are too damn slim. So I guess you can call this my farewell tour." He grinned, raising his glass, then catching the bartender's eye, he ordered another round.

He was easy to be with, Meryl found, and somehow, his company was a relief. Probably in contrast to all the formal gatherings she had been exposed to of late; interesting as many of them were, the stiffness attendant was tiring. Besides, Dan Horgan had the kind of good looks that became even more attractive with animation; he had an easy smile and very white teeth, and his tanned skin made the contrast of his blue eyes and black hair intense.

When Philipe arrived and came over to them at the bar, Meryl noticed Dan was considerably taller than her father.

"Dad, this is Dan—I guess it's Daniel—Horgan, from the band...."

The two men shook hands, and Horgan said, "Glad to meet you, sir." Then he added, "But it's not Daniel—it's Danilo...no, that's okay, everyone always makes that mistake, so I'm used to explaining. One name from each side, is the way my folks figured it, so Danilo for my mother...she's Italian from way back...."

Meeting Dan Horgan and the rest of the band changed the tenor of Meryl's days. She had finished her assignment at the museum; her photographic forays were now all her own. Essentially, her time was free and linking up with the musicians meant she was back in the fold of her own generation.

"...and far more fun for you than having to put up with me, and my fuddy-duddys.... I'd imagine you've had enough of 'em.... God knows I have...."

"That's not true, Dad—it's been fascinating at times..."

"But it's also nice to horse around on the beach with men who don't creak at the knees," said Philipe.

The musicians, for their part, were enchanted with the company of someone who knew and understood both languages, both worlds and a certain amount about music.

"You also make it easier for 'em to talk to the girls around here," Dan explained. "The guys look legit, with you around...."

Then came the nostalgia of Christmas away from home, and Meryl joined them singing carols when they played in the Snakepit on Christmas Eve. The next day Philipe took all of them to a Christmas feast given by a government official, where the food was Peruvian and the booze from the U.S. and the general atmosphere maudlin by the time the party drew to a close.

For New Year, the band, committed to play at the nightclub, reciprocated by inviting the van Landens to be their guests for the evening. Paper hats and champagne and noisemakers, international as air, made the scene indistinguishable from all the thousands of others taking place all over the world as the numbers and seconds slipped by for the count and another year sped away till the horns and bells and shouts and singing ushered in the invisible change.

As January began, Meryl decided to return to New York. Philipe, still using Lima as his temporary base, had several months of work ahead before he could go home.

"I'd rather deliver this work now, and then come back and join you again, Dad."

The idea suited Philipe, too.

"... and that way, we can go to Bolivia together—I'll only have to stay ten days or so, but that'll give you an idea of what it's like in La Paz...."

Meryl packed her photographic treasures with care, and said good-bye to the musicians that evening.

"Maybe we'll still be here when you come back.... There's talk they'll extend our contract...."

"I hope so... 'bye for now... see you soon..."

On the way to the airport, Philipe told her he would be doing longer out of town trips while she was away.

"Not out of Peru... but overnight or two-day journeys.... So by the time you come back, I should be ready to wrap things up here and we can take off any time...."

Meryl found New York to be cold and bleak and busy with its usual midwinter survival. Her tan looked incongruous in the blue-gray light of the short, hard days, and after delivering her work and spending a day at the studio, she retired to the warmth and solitude of her darkroom at home—her cocoon of yellow light a moth's protection against time and distance and life outside. All that mattered were the smudges getting stronger, the stark proud profile appearing here, a button-eyed child's smile flashing there, the hauteur of the Inca descendants amid their city squalor, children's faces beginning to reflect the wariness of the present while encased in the trappings of the bygone ages, their ancestry of grandeur and gold.

When the cable came, telling her that Philipe had been killed, along with the driver, in a one-car accident on the south road out of Lima, Meryl moved into a mist of white sound and cold tears and automatic responses while she got a ticket and flew straight down to Miami and then Panama and on to Lima the very next day. Dan was at the airport to meet her, staunch and monosyllabic, along with the embassy official, who was flanked by Peruvian authorities. And the impersonal necessities and motions continued until all the documents and papers had been signed and stamped and translated and recognized, by yet another governmental branch, a following authority, a counter-signing official.

In the midst of it all, Yvonne's telegram arrived.

RECEIVED YOUR CABLE VERY SORRY UNABLE TO TRAVEL DUE WILFRED UNWELL BUT AM CONFIDENT YOU WILL HANDLE EV-

ERYTHING IN BEST MANNER STOP AM WRITING LETTER TO NEW
YORK STOP PLEASE ADVISE WHEN YOU RETURN THERE

Meryl threw it out and kept going in a daze until at last the
searing sorrow burst through, and the hot tears spilled endlessly
on the comfort of Dan's shoulder. He was by her side every
minute she needed him there, his strong hand holding hers,
his steadfast presence her only support as the last of Philipe's
arrangements were made.

When it was all over, when to Meryl it felt as though
everything was over and nothing lay ahead, it seemed the
most natural thing in the world for the two of them to fly back
together to Miami. When they landed, instead of catching
the connecting flight to New York, they fell into bed together
at a local motel, and after a week's stay and the required
blood test, they got married at the Miami courthouse near
the rail tracks downtown.

Edie's hand moved across the paper, its fingers stiff around
the pen, and the steady ache a warning signal she would have
to stop soon.

*...so you have lost your father, and I have lost Rosita, the
best and dearest friend I ever had*, wrote Edie. *I shall miss
her for the rest of my life. Lala is here, of course, and says
she will stay until I feel better, because I caught an awful cold
at the funeral, and it doesn't seem to want to go away. Lala
really returned from Córdoba to help me here with Rosita's
illness, but we didn't tell anybody that because we didn't
want Rosita to find out what she had. And she never did, so
I'm glad we did it that way. Now Lala will go back to
Córdoba; she says the time spent here, helping me and
teaching at the pueblo school will only help her in returning
to her post up there. She is a dear child, and tells me to send
you her love. Raul also asks to be remembered. He is a tower
of strength.*

Edie put the pen down and stared into emptiness. Even
though Rosita had taken over two years to die, weakening and
wasting away as the cancer grew, the final loss had come with
shock: Rosita was no longer there. Nobody was there, except
Edie. The void inside her was limitless, unreachable. Everyone had gone.

With effort, she began writing again.

498

Your mother has not come near here. She sent me the news about your father, in her condolence letter to me about Rosita, and in it she also managed to tell me Wilfred is ill. But when I wrote back and asked what's wrong with him, I got no answer, only a quick note telling me of your marriage, which she had apparently only just heard about.

The pen slipped in Edie's grasp, and she acknowledged momentary defeat. She would finish the letter another time; perhaps tomorrow. Her arthritis had flared badly in recent weeks, and the pills weren't helping, but the doctor said what she needed to do was go away and rest for a week or so and take the salt-lake baths at Mar Chiquita as she had the previous year. Well, it had helped her then, so she would follow his orders as soon as she could get away. When her cold was better; Lala could take an extra week and stay at El Ombú while Edie was away.

She sat at the desk, motionless, rereading her letter to Meryl.

What a shame she didn't marry out here, thought Edie, wondering briefly who the young man was. Yvonne didn't seem to know anything about him, but then, Yvonne never did get a good grasp of things. Certainly the marriage seemed very sudden, but perhaps it had been planned all along, and Philipe's death had made the young couple opt for a quiet and private ceremony, which was understandable. Suddenly tired, Edie pushed the chair away from the desk and took off her glasses, placing them on the unfinished letter. Then she leaned back and closed her eyes.

I am getting old. . . .

The unbidden thought surfaced through her aching joints and burning eyes. Thus faced with it, Edie tried to stare it down. I'll be seventy next year, and I'm still doing splendidly. And after all, why shouldn't I be? Seventy isn't the grave . . .

That isn't the point.

Edie sighed, and gave in. Seventy was seventy, with eighty only ten years away. Running the *estancia* was already getting to be more tiring than she ever admitted to anyone. It was useless trying to hide from facts; she would have to think them through and make up her mind about what she planned doing. It was easy to see changes had to be made.

She sat in the lawyer's office and listened to his knowledge.
". . . but only one-fifth, *señora* O'Connor, that's all the law

499

allows. The rest of your estate must go to your immediate descendants—in your case, to your daughter."

"But she'll only make a mess of everything, and probably spend most of it on that *sinvergüenza* husband of hers. Yvonne is a fool. Always has been and always will be. And what's more..."

The lawyer knew better than to interrupt the *señora*. He waited for the familiar phrases to run their usual course. Eventually, he said, "But the allowed portion, that is, the one-fifth part of your total estate, that you may dispose of in any way you wish. And, of course, you may change your bequests at a later date, if you desire. After all, *señora*, although I admit neither of us is in the first blush of youth"— the lawyer was twenty years Edie's junior—"we are surely not old. There are many, many long years ahead for you...."

Edie smiled. "Nonetheless, I prefer having everything in order. And since there are many changes to be made, I'd like to get them all done now." She opened her capacious purse, taking from it her glasses and a sheaf of papers.

"Perhaps if you sit here at the desk, *señora*..."

"Thank you. Let's see, now. First of all, the *estancia*. I want a part of it divided off..."

She left the office well satisfied. He was an efficient lawyer; she had always been pleased with the way he worked things out. Look how much he'd been able to do for Raul. Not that the problems of La Chata and the inheritance were anywhere near resolved yet; *what* a mess Tim Casey had left behind! After all those years of being brought up together, Raul and Harvey did everything possible to avoid meeting, and everyone on the two *estancias* agreed it was better that way, for there was more than bad blood between them: there was blood in common. Edie did not see an end to the complications.

In the meantime, she was glad her own documents would be ready to sign before she left on the train back to El Ombú. Until then, she intended enjoying the change of being in Rosario; there were friends she could visit, and at the hotel she was treated like royalty. She felt quite at home.

Yvonne walked along the flagstone path near the dividing hedge, Coco on her arm. It had been a difficult day; Wilfred was worse than usual, and she blamed it on the late summer spell of heat. Even so, Wilfred's problem was very hard for her to deal with, as it was impossible to tell, right off the bat, whether he was aware of what he was saying and meaning whatever it was, or whether the arterial atrophy was acting up again, causing his mind to become fuzzy and confused.

At times, she was able to tell which was which by the effect her voice had on him. If he was totally rational and asking for something, he did not lose track of his immediate request when she responded.

But if it was the atrophy trouble stirring up some unreasonable longings in his mind, he would start staring blankly at her as she began to talk, and then, slowly, he would smile his vague, kind smile, and be quite content to follow whatever suggestion she made, his original question forgotten, the immediate past wiped completely away.

A sharp bark made her jump, and Coco fluttered and squawked, his talons slipping, then clinging to her arm. Damn that terrier; he was at it again, rushing up and down on his side of the fence, yapping and barking at her. Try as she might, there seemed to be no calming the dog. He always reacted the same way, every time he saw her, despite her many attempts to make friends with him in the years since he and his owners had lived next door. The people were exactly like their pet: noisy and common. She and Wilfred had often remarked on it, too. They were all right as neighbors, perfectly civil, but not the sort with whom one could become friends, even though they were English.

"Calm down, Coco... why not sign instead?" Yvonne began humming, trying to distract the bird, who was now barking in answer to the terrier, using Ming's voice and whistling in between. But as he heard the humming, he switched his voice and attention, turning his sounds to throaty imitations of Yvonne's.

Yvonne returned to her thoughts, walking across the lawn away from the barking dog. All she wanted was a quiet walk around the garden, partly to rest and relax on her own, partly to see what needed attending to over the weekend, as the gardener she sometimes used had promised to come in for a few hours. The lawns needed mowing... the back hedge needed a good clip... she could do the tidying up of the herbaceous border on her own... a broken branch, snapped in the last bad storm, really had to be cut loose and taken out of the way...

It was cool under the trees, and she stopped to enjoy their shade, wanting to make the most of her time in the garden, as she would have to return to the house very soon and try to finish her letter to Meryl before Wilfred needed her again. And then it would be dinner time and afterwards would be impossible; she would be too tired and anyway, Wilfred would probably want to go to the club for a short stroll and a chat with his friends. Yvonne didn't dare let him go on his own, not for the next few weeks, anyway. He might forget where he was again, and start wandering. It had been desperately difficult finding him last time it happened, but luckily a delivery boy, riding his bicycle along near the tracks, had sighted and recognized him and come to tell her right away.

Yvonne turned back toward the house, retracing her steps, her thoughts returning to the letter she wanted to finish. Pity Meryl hadn't married someone nice and English; Wilfred agreed on this point.

". . . rotten shame . . ."

The rapid burst of barking caught her by surprise, making her start. As she did so, Coco squawked in answering rage, flapping his wings with unexpected strength and screeching with fury. His talons left her arm; in horror, Yvonne saw the flapping bundle of color-daubed green feathers hurtle over the fence and fly directly into the dog's face.

"Coco!"

A yelp, a cry, and one last screech. Then it was over. Not even Wilfred protested about dinner being late that night, and the letter to Meryl, forgotten in the tears, never got finished until fall was in the air.

3

On her third wedding anniversary, Meryl sat opposite her mother-in-law at the decorated table; she smiled blankly, screening out the conversation going on around her and taking refuge in her thoughts. She knew, without having to listen, that Danny and his father were talking about their respective automobiles (Danny's sportscar, Edward Horgan's sedan) and that they would probably switch to power tools within a short while. After that, it would be back to business, and the new line in siding they had begun as their hardware store expanded into bigger items of do-it-yourself home building and repair merchandise. At some point, Ed Horgan would say, "Got a new sample to show you. Let's take a look at it now. Won't take us long, Mom"—with a glance at his wife as he rose—"I got it right here in the garage..."

Or the basement. Or the backyard. Or the driveway. Or... or... And as the two men left the room, Chiara Horgan would plump her face into her most satisfied smile and say to Meryl, "Those two... they're one of a kind...." And then give a lingering look of pride and self-accomplishment at the departing figures.

Meryl had long ago decided that her mother-in-law's judgment was on a par with her usage of the language. All Dan had inherited from his father was his height and his blue eyes. Danilo Horgan was essentially a taller version of his mother: the same smoldering, olive-skinned good looks, the same fleshy covering of the frame, the same dark, luxuriant hair—heavy-textured, wavy—the same thick lashes around similarly-shaped, large eyes. However, Chiara Horgan's eyes were the deep brown of her Italian ancestry, and middle-age had transformed youthful curves to solid, overabundant fat.

But if Danny had inherited his father's height, it was in tandem with his mother's fleshier surfaces and heavier bones. Even now, he was already beginnng to show signs of the shape he would become if he didn't watch it. Which he did—but then, so did Chiara.

"... the girls told me this scientist has written a monogram on the subject, and he says that if you throw the potato water away, there's not much starch left, and so you can eat them all you want..."

When the potato diet did not result in loss of weight, Chiara confided that, "... between you and I, Meryl, all that stuff that phony doctor wrote was a bald-faced lie...."

By and large, Mrs. Horgan was philosophical about her excess avoirdupois and her attempts to lessen it.

"... after all, Rome didn't fall in a day..."

And she would seize on each new diet with hungry cries of joy, cheating her way through it until the next one came along.

"Have some more pie, Meryl."

"No, thanks—it's delicious, but I honestly can't fit any more... maybe later..."

Meryl watched her mother-in-law serve herself again and gave silent thanks that everything had gone so well. So far, the sound barrier of family friction had not even been reached, let alone surpassed; the festive anniversary aspect of the Sunday dinner was no doubt the special amulet protecting the evening. Usually, it was too much to hope that the whole evening pass without friction of some sort.

Sundays. Always Sunday. Why Sunday?

"But everyone always gets together with their folks on Sundays." Danny had refused to understand her perplexity at the beginning. Later, he had counterquestioned, and attacked.

"At least my folks come visit us, invite us, take an interest in you. That's more than your goddamn family's ever done. Why, your mother doesn't even seem to want to meet me. . . ."

Meryl had tried to explain about Wilfred more times than she cared to remember. Yvonne had written to Dan, shortly after they got married. Danny had never answered.

"You know me, Meryl—I'm not the writing kind . . ."

"Well, maybe my mother's not the visiting kind."

It was a poor defense, and Meryl knew it, but to try and explain her family to Danilo Horgan and his parents was a waste of time.

"You'd think she'd show some interest . . ."

". . . figures her daughter's too good for you, Danny-boy—just because she went to college . . ."

"But I didn't go to college . . ."

It was useless to try. Geared up, the Horgans were off and running and fighting and shouting, their anger general and loud. No one was really listening to what anyone was saying.

". . . irregardless of the distance, you'd think family would count . . ."

But tonight, no irritant had come up. Her mother-in-law had gone to great lengths, decorating the table, making an elaborate meal, coordinating the food with the decor in an anniversary theme that Meryl found atrocious, but knew better than to say so anywhere in the neighborhood. The closest place in which she could speak and breathe freely was New York City—specifically, Manhattan and more specifically, Sal's studio—and that was a good two hours away.

Two hours. Manhattan might as well be as far as the moon.

". . . you're not listening, Meryl."

Chiara Horgan's voice reached her. Meryl blinked and automatically widened her smile.

"I'm sorry—I guess I was daydreaming... sent off by all the good food and..."

"I said I thought maybe you were getting heavier, putting on a little weight, filling out...."

Mrs. Horgan flashed one of her just-between-us-girls looks with a bright, questioning gleam. Meryl thought: oh, Christ, and refused to register understanding. Just then, Ed Horgan pushed back his chair and said, "If you girls'll excuse me, I just wanted to show Danny the new shears that came in on Friday. Got 'em right here in the garage..."

As the men left, and Chiara Horgan voiced her habitual opinion, the masked question remained unanswered, and temporarily forgotten.

But not by Meryl, who had heard it, overtly and covertly, many times before.

It was the baby question again.

When they got home that night, Dan said, "You know, Meryl—maybe Mom is right..."

Meryl finished pulling her sweater off over her head and dropped it on the bed.

"About what?"

Danny was standing by the window, staring out into the bleak night, his shoulders hunched, his hands in his pockets. He spoke without turning around.

"Maybe it's time we had a baby."

"A *baby*?" Meryl was aghast. It was one thing to get oblique looks from her mother-in-law, but Dan had never mentioned it. "What on earth for?"

He turned, and she saw his face was flushing to a deep and angry red.

"What d'you mean, what for? You don't have kids *for* anything. You just have 'em."

"Not necessarily."

Dan took a step toward her.

"Meryl—don't you *want* to have my baby? Wouldn't you like to bear my child?"

The brief stalemate of silence made Meryl's back stiffen.

"I don't want to have anybody's baby," she said quietly. "It would be my baby too, after all—and I don't want one. I never have."

"If you don't like kids, how come you're always taking their friggin' pictures? How come you were always tagging after those half-naked Indian brats with their whangers hanging out, while we were in Peru? And now, here, with that goddamn job of yours..."

"I never said I didn't like children..."

"Then if you like 'em, why don't you want to have a baby?"

"Because I don't want to have one of my own, that's all. It has nothing to do with liking or not liking children."

"Then what *does* it have to do with, Meryl?" Dan's voice began rising. "*Me*, maybe? Does it have to do with me? You think I'm not good enough to fuck you till you're pregnant?" He took another step toward her and glanced at the bed. "I've a goddamn good mind to lay you right here and now and keep on fucking the bejeepers out of you until..."

Meryl moved around to the other side. "It won't help right now. It's not my fertile time."

She saw the tension in his body relax, and his mood switched, along with the target for his questions.

"How come you didn't say anything about this before we got married? I mean, you never told me..."

"You never asked."

"But you'd think you'd have had enough sense to..."

"Danny, I was under the impression you wanted to marry *me*...that you loved *me*...not my possible children I might produce."

"But people get married to have a home and raise a family, don't they?"

"It's not a law that one has to do everything other people do, is it?"

"Then what did you get married for?"

Late that night, still lying awake in anger and confusion, Meryl thought: I'm beginning to wonder...

It had been a mess from the start, and the arguments began right away. After the brief courthouse ceremony—so brief that both Meryl and Dan smilingly confessed to each other they did not feel married—Dan said, "Let's call my folks. They'll be wild for you."

He crammed himself into a phone booth and began calling collect. Meryl went in search of cigarettes; as she came back, she could hear Dan saying, "Okay, okay, but I know you'll love her." He looked up, grinning. "And here she is: the brand new Mrs. Danilo Horgan..."

Putting his hand over the mouthpiece, he said, "They want to speak to you. Dad's just calling Mom to the phone."

Meryl took the receiver. A strident voice at the other end was saying, "Hello? Hello? Is that you, Danny? What've you done?"

"It's not Dan, Mrs. Horgan. It's me, Meryl..."

"What'd you kids do, for God's sake?"

"We...we got married..." Meryl looked to Dan for help, but he was still smiling at her, sitting on the wooden booth's bench inside. The voice on the line was still talking.

"I don't know what to say....It's such a shock...Danny never mentioned anything like this....He only wrote us twice...never said you two were planning to get married ...only wrote about the band..."

"We weren't—that is, I mean...well, we hardly realized it ourselves...everything's been so intense," Meryl faltered, aware of the weakness in her words against the outpourings coming from the other end.

"...always planned to give Danny's bride my poor dead mother's wedding ring, but it's too late now, and that poor girl...how will I face them next Sunday? That poor girl...I'm sure she'll put on widow's tweeds when she hears..."

"I'm sure you want to speak to Dan again," Meryl said, handing back the receiver. She leaned against the outside of the booth and lit a cigarette; her hands were shaking. Dan's voice wheedled through the open door, even though he had now lowered his pitch and had turned his back to Meryl.

"Ah, come on, Mom, don't be like that...then let me speak to Dad...yeah, now...yeah, Dad? Yeah, sure it's a surprise...no, don't you start in on me now, you hear? Yeah...maybe another week, sort of a short honeymoon....She just lost her own dad—sure I told you, in my letter...but we'll be home soon..."

Meryl moved away, twinges of unease pulling her earlier mood out of shape.

When they got to New York, they went straight to the apartment, and while Dan looked around, whistling in appreciation, Meryl called Sal.

It was di Leo who insisted that she get a lawyer.

"You'll need one, kid. Eventually, we all do...."

The three of them met for a strained, awkward dinner, during which Meryl's tears seeped through on several occasions.

"You'll have to forgive her." Dan put his arm around her shoulders and she quietened. "It's been a real rough time all around."

The photographer rose, "Take good care of her, Horgan. And see to it she gets an attorney. . . ."

The wisdom of his suggestion was proved at once; Philipe's estate proved to be an untidy affair, its largest assets, insurance policies, still in Yvonne's name. Apart from a minor sum of money, the one thing that now became Meryl's direct responsibility was the apartment; Philipe had always paid for it while he was alive.

"You could sell it," Dan suggested. "We won't be living in New York."

"No, I can't. Not till I'm thirty." Meryl had then explained.

"Boy—I never heard of anything like that. . . ."

"Haven't you?"

It was one of the first signs of the gap, but did not cause any immediate crisis. There were too many other things to do, too many things to decide; she wanted to rent the apartment, arrange to have the furniture stored . . .

"I'll have to call the folks soon, and tell 'em we're up here. . . ."

"Yes, why don't you?" Meryl was absorbed in the legal papers she was trying to understand. Dan wandered off down the hallway to the bedrooms; later she found him in bed, asleep.

Next morning he told her, "I didn't call my folks yet. I'd like to take one more crack at getting a decent gig with a band. . . ."

But it hadn't worked out, and the homecoming was to be total: Dan told Meryl his father was overjoyed he'd decided to join him at the store.

"He built it up from nothing . . . always wanted me in there . . . I guess it's only natural . . . getting too much for him these days, anyhow . . ."

If Edward Horgan's victory in having his son join him smoothed the immediate path of Meryl's entry into Horgan family life, it did not hold its effect for long. Meryl soon learned their angers were self-fueling, the arguments that raged in the family trio never resolved. There was no such thing as clearing the air; all argumentative elements were carefully retained and added to the next burst of ire. The

508

Horgans forgot nothing, resented everything, misunderstood a great deal, and took umbrage every day.

But in the first months of her move out of the apartment and into a small house in the suburbs, only a few blocks away from the senior Horgans' home, Meryl's cloud of grief and shock and excitement and total upheaval screened many of the realities from her perception. She was grateful for the warmth and kindness Dan represented to her, the one person who had stood by her, who had been there in the dark. As to his parents, well, no doubt she would get used to their ways.

It took some time for her to realize they might be incapable of getting used to hers.

It also took time to adjust to all the changes; not working began to emerge as a problem after a while. If she did not notice its lack at first, it was because there were so many other things to do. But Dan didn't want to hear of her working.

"No wife of mine needs to go out to work. . . ."

"But I'd like to . . ."

"Meryl, I need you here at home to help me for a while. This has been some change for me, too. . . ."

He was right, and Meryl fell silent; she knew how much he missed his former musical life on the road. Not that Dan complained, but she could see his deep resentment when his father brought up the subject of his joining the store.

"Finally saw the light, didn't you, Danny, my boy? And a smart thing, too . . . I thought I'd never get it through your head. . . ."

Danny. That was another change. The man she had married had been Dan, for Danilo Horgan; now, back in his home, he was Danny, or Danny-boy. Or, mostly, *my*-Danny—that was his mother. Or Ed's kid, or Old Man Horgan's son—but never again Dan. Even Meryl slipped into the habit of calling him Danny after a while, and once it struck her that, as they called him Danny, so Danny he began to be.

She tried to explain it to him one night.

"I don't see what difference it makes, Meryl—sure, the guys used to call me Dan . . ."

After he fell asleep, she found herself longing for her darkroom, and the peace and quiet and shelter it had afforded her, another lifetime ago.

Several months later, she again broached the subject of work.

"Don't you see, Danny—I haven't got anything to *do*."

"Nothing to do?" He was genuinely puzzled. "I don't see how you can say that, Meryl. I know this isn't a big house, but there's a lot of work in it, and I must say, you do a great job..."

"Oh, for God's sake!" Meryl was exasperated. Why didn't he understand what she meant? "Danny—*maids* can do that sort of work...."

"Oh. I see." His tone changed and hardened. "Forgive me, Miss Rich Bitch. I'd forgotten...housecleaning is beneath you, of course. And I, slob that I am, haven't been able to provide you with the correct household help...."

"That's not what I mean at all, Danny..."

But it was no use. Any attempt to go on explaining only made things worse.

If his father worked late at the store, Danny took to going over to his mother's—"...in case she needs some help with something..."

Chiara Horgan saw to it that she always did. The occasional chore grew to a weekly obligation and from there to an almost nightly visit. Meryl's discomfort with her own life worsened. Danny could not understand why.

"Well, maybe if you spent less time concerned about your mother and more time thinking about our own life, about how things are here in our own home..."

"What's wrong with our home?"

"Nothing. Everything." Meryl wept with rage.

Danny leaned back on the sofa and stared up at the ceiling in disgust, his arms spread out along the sofa's back.

"I don't understand you, Meryl—honestly, I don't. Here we are in a nice house, with everything anybody else in this neighborhood has..."

"If this kind of life is what it means to be an American woman, I'd rather be in a South American *jungle*...."

"What the fuck more do you want?" he roared, sitting upright in anger.

"It's not what I *want*, always. Sometimes it's what I *don't* want. And I don't want a damn mixer for my birthday. For God's sake, Danny, I can't even cook properly...."

"You could try to learn."

510

"Sure I can learn. And I will. But it doesn't mean I'm going to make it the big dream of my life—to sit around the kitchen all day making gooky green gelatin salad. Besides, any idiot can cook."

The room went hideously quiet. Then:

"Are you calling my mother an idiot?"

Meryl was nonplussed. "Who said anything about your mother?"

"You did."

"I didn't even mention her name!"

"But you implied..."

"I didn't imply anything. What *are* you talking about?"

"Meryl, don't pull that shit on me. You know very well you were thinking of her when you said..."

"Don't you tell me what I was thinking!"

"We both know my mother's a damn fine cook and loves cooking, and you mean to tell me you weren't referring to her when you said..."

"I was not."

Dan's manner changed fractionally. "Besides, you'll love cooking when you learn how. All women enjoy it."

"No, they don't."

"Around here they do...."

Meryl said nothing. It was an unarguable point. All the women in the neighborhood did profess to love cooking. And their lives: their tight, restricted circles of ceremonial ways of living. And having children.

"...and you really ought to have one, Meryl...You'll never know what you're missing until you have one of your own...."

But if it was true, why did so many of them behave so edgily? Why were the husbands going to seed? Why was the tightness seen as rightness? Why was the rest of the world seen as wrong? And why, at least in the Horgan family, was arguing and fighting a way of life?

Every new incident was used to lead back through the hoarded hurts of the past. A discussion that first flared over the younger Horgan's failure to give Chiara Horgan the birthday present she had hoped for soon wound up in the ancient injury of Danny's birth.

"...nearly lost my life giving life to him...could've went to my grave..."

"But Mom, I brought you a present..."

"If you really loved me you'd of known what I really wanted. . . ."

If the rows were difficult to understand, hard to believe, impossible to avoid, Meryl came to find the reconciliations even worse. They never lasted, only building false hopes with cloying sentimentality until the next friction's sparks rekindled the eternal flame.

Once, in the leaden aftermath of an unresolved row, Meryl and Dan went to the movies where, before the feature, a travelogue showed brief scenes of South America and some shots of B.A. That night, raw nerves and jagged memories fired Meryl before dawn, and the groping, gasping reconciliation that took place before either was truly awake rose to physical heights they had not experienced in months.

Danny held her for a long time afterwards.

"You're some woman, you know?" he murmured. "And you make me feel more of a man. . . . I love you, Meryl . . . you *know* that. . . . Let's try . . . hell, I know we can make it. . . . The rest of the crap is only garbage. . . ."

Spent, limp, Meryl agreed, pushing to one side the reminding truths, along with shadows from the distant past.

The idea came to Meryl one mid-afternoon. She was lying on the couch, leafing idly through the local paper, hardly seeing its pages, her mind stifled by inertia. The local rag, Danny called it, but the Horgans' hardware store counted on it for its most productive ads. A rag it might be, but a widely read rag.

A picture is worth a thousand words.

She explained her plan to Danny when he came home. The more she described her idea, the more he looked dubious.

"You think you can hack it?"

"I've just finished telling you . . ."

"I know, I know." He waved her words aside. "But can you really do the work?"

"Danny—I used to do it . . . did it for years . . ."

He shrugged. "That was different. It was all through connections. Hell, you even met di Leo through your dad, didn't you? Here, you don't know nobody—anybody," he hastily corected, casting a quick sidelong glance at her.

512

"I don't think that'll matter too much—and I don't understand why you immediately take the attitude you don't think I'll be able to make it. . . ."

"Because you're nothing but a lot of talk, you know that, Meryl? A big loudmouth about who you are and what you can do and your fancy background and all that jazz. And I'm just a skosh sick and goddamn tired of hearing all that crap—and so're my folks. . . . You think you know everything, but you fucking well don't. Just you wait and see, smart-ass, people out here aren't going to go for fancy-schmancy ideas. . . . Your type of photography don't mean doodley-squat around here. . . ."

The editor of the newspaper, a rumple-faced man in a loudly-checked jacket, thought otherwise.

"You won't get every Tom, Dick, and Sylvester," he said, the photographs Meryl had brought with her spread out in front of him over his desk. "But some ads should start you rolling—and yes, I think we can use you. On a free-lance basis, of course. . . ."

"And also," said Meryl, encouraged by his attitude, "I thought a child-of-the-week feature might be an idea—to run when you have some space to fill, perhaps. A two-column photo, a few lines under it . . ."

Meryl was bubbling with her good news that night. Danny listened, his face darkening.

"What the hell did you go and do that for?" he suddenly exploded. "Jeez—and in the *newspaper* . . . Now everyone'll think I can't keep up my payments, or something, and that you've been forced to help out. . . . You are such a ball-buster, Meryl. . . . Why d'you do these things to me? I'm earning decent enough money. . . . Dad'll let me have more soon. What the fuck d'you *want*, Meryl?"

"I told you. I want to go to work as a photographer again. And it's perfect—for you as well as for me. I'm freelancing . . . won't take any time away from anything to do with you . . ."

"Well, I don't think it's perfect. . . . I think it's a goddamn stupid idea. . . . Here I give you everything you need, everything you could want . . ." He waved his arm in an all-encompassing arc. "Decent furniture, coupla snazzy automobiles . . . I get you the latest in kitchen crap the moment it comes in the store. . . . And now this. From you, all I get is shit. What gives with you, anyway?"

Meryl closed her eyes, took a deep breath, and tried again.

"Danny, d'you really believe that simply living in this house is enough for me?"

"Well, whadda ya want? The White House? I told you—in another coupla years, we'll be able to build..."

"You still don't see what I mean."

"I sure as hell don't." He got up and strode over to the front entrance. "I'm going over to the folks' to eat. I've had enough of your shit for one day." He looked around the room before opening the door. "You're such an ungrateful bitch. ... When my Mom was your age, she had a hell of a lot less than you have here...."

By the time Meryl's third wedding anniversary rolled around, her photographic portraits of children were well known in the area and her work much sought after by families who sought safe sophistication and neighborly status, frequently through their children. Meryl's portraits were different; they were individual, at times almost austere. There was a likeness to the photographs seen in high fashion.

"...made our little Lisa look like she was stepping out of a page in *Vogue*..."

They were also expensive, which added to their value.

"The funny thing is," said the editor, "they're also damn good."

The child-of-the-week photo had grown into one of the newspaper's most popular features; a contest had grown out of it, then a series on children and their pets. It was all good local interest and helped circulation. Meryl's career was established, her name synonymous with her work.

But if her work life was flourishing, her marriage was teetering—not on the brink of rupture, but endless emptiness.

Neither she nor Dan admitted it; no one said anything. To admit failure would be to say they had been wrong from the start. Neither dared acknowledge the truth, because they instinctively sensed it; a replay of unsuited unhappiness was part of the Horgan code. Instead of facing the truth and dissecting the facts to arrive at a solution, the younger Horgans either battled or sulked over points peripheral to the basic flaw.

Anything and everything was grist for the grumbling mill.

"What say?" Danny, lying on the sofa, raised his head and looked over in Meryl's direction.

"I said it's crazy weather," Meryl repeated for him, realizing as she did so that she had spoken the phrase in Spanish the first time around.

"Then why didn't you say so in the first place?"

"I did."

"But in *Spanish*—in goddamn spic again. You do it on purpose, you know, Meryl? And I'm getting goddamn sick and tired of it. You may think it's fucking smart of you to speak so many languages, but let me tell you something. Here in America, *only English counts*. Capeesh?"

Meryl said no more, but as Danny ranted on, a small corner of her mind flashed: he's right, and you know it, you *do* do it on purpose; it's a way of fighting back. . . .

For a while she began wondering why she bothered to fight back. And then came the night she questioned why she bothered to stay.

During the exceptionally hot summer the tension between Meryl and Danny went from bad to worse. The fights became more frequent, triggered by the infinitesimal; the sulking periods were longer, the couplings only a truce. Meryl found refuge, as always, in her work hours; Danny, she suspected, honed his anger at the store, whetted against the similar strains that existed in his father, perfected in the years-long strife with Chiara.

She returned home late one evening to find Dan already there. "I thought you were going over to your parents'. . ."

"I did. We already ate. They went out visiting."

"I see." Meryl unslung her camera bag and put it on the table. "Well, sorry I'm late, but it turned out there were two kids instead of one, so I had double. . ."

Danny said, "Forget it," and turned on the television. Then he snapped it off again and looked around at Meryl. "It might be nice, though, if you were home when I got here. . . ."

"Danny, I said I was sorry. And I usually am here. . . just this time. . ."

"And another thing. The basement's a mess. . . ."

"It's just dusty. All that old stuff you brought over from the store. . ."

"Well, it wouldn't be a bad idea to clean up this house once in a while. . . ."

Meryl stopped in the middle of the room. "What's wrong with it now?"

515

"Nothing, I guess—it's perfect, just like you are." With an angry thrust, Danny pushed himself out of the chair and went into the kitchen. Meryl heard the refrigerator door open and slam closed. Danny appeared with a bottle of beer in his hand.

"What the hell kind of a refrigerator is that?" he demanded. "Jesus Christ, even when we were *poor* Mom had more stuff stocked in hers than you do in ours now. And she used to make me a goddamn *cake* once in a while."

"You said you wanted to watch your weight."

Danny turned the television back on and settled into his chair.

"You said . . ." Meryl began.

He turned around. "Bug off, will you? Just let me watch my program in peace. Discussing with you's no good, anyway. You always have a smart-ass answer for everything."

"But . . ."

"What I'm saying, Meryl, is that you're turning out to be a piss-poor wife . . ."

"I suppose you think you're a prize husband. . . ."

"Meryl, why don't you go take a flying fuck at a rolling doughnut?"

Despite herself, Meryl laughed.

She thought: there's too much distance. It's always been there, but now it's too much of a bother even to try getting across it.

Then she remembered where the words came from, and her father's warning.

And there were so many distances with Danny: background, attitudes, beliefs, desires. It certainly wasn't all his fault, but it wasn't hers alone.

At least he thinks he knows who he is and what he wants. I don't. But I do know what I don't want, and what I don't want is the American dream. It's not mine.

For the next few days, she worked diligently, finishing old assignments and refusing the news. She had a private talk with the editor, and made a call to New York City.

Then one morning, after Dan had left, she packed a small suitcase, took her camera bag and put both in her car, and drove permanently away.

"Sure I could've told you it wasn't going to work—but what would have been the use?" Sal shrugged. "I told you you'd need a lawyer—and in more ways than one."

Meryl said, "I'm sure I'd feel better about it if I could only work out what went wrong. Which one of us is really to blame, Sal? Did I goof so badly all the time?"

"Get it through your head, kiddo," Sal punched his palm with his fist for emphasis, "nothing *went* wrong, nothing at all. It *was* wrong, the whole marriage, right from the very beginning."

Meryl said, "Maybe if I'd tried to blend in more, joined his way of life, maybe that way it would have saved the marriage."

"That's crap, and what's more, you know it. It wouldn't have worked either. Let me tell you something, Meryl. In fact, this one you'd better learn by heart, or you'll ruin your chances again. A marriage that needs saving isn't worth being saved." He winked at her. "Keep it in mind, sweetheart—you'll see I'm right in the long run."

She smiled. "It's a pity we're not each other's types, Sal—then maybe I could catch up with you, between wives...."

"God forbid—it'd ruin a good friendship. And now, let's get down to it: are you coming back to work?"

"If you'll have me...."

"I need you. There's big plans cooking..."

And as the plans unfolded over lunchtime, Meryl saw her future for the first time in years.

X

Double Exposure
1962–1969

1

"... and when the *señora* O'Connor arrives," said the attorney, "bring her in immediately...."

As his secretary closed the door behind her, the lawyer took his glasses off, rubbed his eyes, and wondered what it was to be this time. A radical rewriting of her whole will? An addition or two? Or a long list of additions and subtractions and substitutions to be incorporated into the existing document he now had on the desk before him?

He replaced his glasses on his nose, ready for the onslaught. One thing about the *señora* O'Connor: she always knew exactly what she wanted—even if she changed her mind to something completely different the very next day.

His buzzer sounded. He rose and went to the door.

"*Señora*..." The Rosario lawyer held out both his hands. "What a great pleasure to see you... and to see you looking so well..."

When Edie returned to the hotel for lunch, she felt tired and she opted for the meal to be sent up to her room. It had been a busy morning, and she was well satisfied; now her will would be more in keeping with the changes that had occurred. It was pointless to leave so much to Meryl, who had inherited her other grandmother's estate on her thirtieth birthday; token jewelry had been substituted there. On the other hand, Lala was apparently not thinking of ever marrying, and since the girl was already thirty-two, a little more was needed to back her future.

Another deletion had been the brooch for Dollie Thaxter; she'd never be allowed to wear it, even if she did outlive Edie, which seemed increasingly doubtful. Of course, she must have begun to go funny years ago, only nobody had really noticed anything until last year. Robert had told Edie about it when she was down in B.A.; he had spoken in hushed tones, and it certainly was sad.

". . . but they look after her very well, and she'll never want for anything. . . . I've seen to that . . . but still . . . very sad . . . thinks I'm her long-lost Ted . . . calls me 'poor Ted' when I visit her . . ."

Which isn't very often, Edie had thought to herself, but then she hadn't gone to see Dollie, either.

Heaven only knows who she would have thought I was, Edie reflected, and there's no point in my going if it'll make things worse; they're quite bad enough already. . . .

It would be nice to get back to the *estancia* the next day; she was leaving on the early morning train and would be there shortly after noon. Even though many things were different there, it was still the most comfortable; El Ombú continued to be the showplace of the region.

But still . . .

It was lonely.

I'm lonely, and I'm getting old, thought Edie, settling down for a *siesta* on the comfortable bed. I'll be seventy-five next month, and I'm all alone. . . . No one will ever replace Rosita . . . I haven't seen Yvonne in years . . . Lala is a dear child, but it isn't the same . . . Meryl is so far away . . .

She thought of her granddaughter, now pursuing her photographic career in England. Edie was a bit vague as to how it had all come about, but apparently the marriage hadn't worked out at all, and Meryl had taken herself off to Europe and gone to work. She sounded happy enough in her occasional letters, and the places she mentioned evoked in Edie the scenes and shadows of her own happy past. Meryl had been to Paris. . . . Of course there were lots of changes in some ways, but basically, everything was still there. . . . Edie remembered going to the couture salons with Maurice . . . and the way he picked out the gowns that looked best on her . . . that embroidered jacket . . .

The remembered images of mirrored fittings and silken folds became superimposed as waves of sleep washed everything away.

Lala took another sheet of paper from the box and went on writing her letter to Meryl.

Teaching children is marvelous. All those terrible years at the Ladies Society School have really paid off. That's where I discovered how much I enjoyed showing the little ones their first letters and words, and teaching them how to read, and the shared enjoyment of their steps of discovery still thrills me to this day.

Apart from work, life in Córdoba City is fine, too. I like it here, even though I do miss the estancia. I'll be going down there next week, for your grandmother's seventy-fifth birthday. We have planned a little party for her, Raul and I, and everyone in the area has kept it a secret from her.

A visit there is not the same as living there, though, and, as I said, I miss it, and all the good times we had there together. But we were young then, and now the times are different . . .

Lala stopped typing and stared out of the window, continuing the phrase and thoughts only in her head.

You'd never guess how different, Meryl, and I cannot tell you . . . cannot write to you about all our plans and dreams, our hopes for a different future for the land. My group, and all the other groups . . . all of us working for change, for justice . . . none of us is able to speak out publicly at this time.

But the time will come: It has to. No civilized country can go on this way. It needs change and social justice, the correct distribution of its riches among its people, all of us, not only the landed and fortunate few, the powerful cliques of army and oligarchy that have ruled us so iniquitously for so long.

As you see, I dare not write of all these things.

Even if you were here, Meryl, and we could talk, I could not talk about it at all. Not unless you joined us, and you could not. You are not one of us.

Perhaps you are not really one of them, either, but you were born on their side. It makes it difficult to cross the fence between us, even though we can reach through it, and clasp real hands.

Turning back to the typewriter, Lala finished the letter with a few short phrases. Then she sealed it and put it in her purse, ready for mailing when she went out. She was longing to tell Meryl that Amelie was finally on the way—Lala did not doubt it would be a girl—but it was only fair to tell Raul first when she got to the *estancia* next week.

She wondered what his reaction would be when she told him they would be having a child in December. Would he insist on marriage? Probably, for the child's sake. Lala herself was not too sure how she felt about it; it would be a bit like having two children. Raul would always be her little boy, remembered from the long years past. But both she and he knew the problems of bastardy, the complications and dangers of illegitimate birth. To hand them on to the product of their own affection did not seem right, or in keeping with their views.

Lala smiled. Raul would be surprised. She knew that. But happy, too—at least partly so. Here she was less sure. All he was expecting from her was other information. And she had that, too. Names, numbers, figures. Projections. Phone contacts. Hidden caches. Locations, contents. Money available, future plans.

She knew it all by heart, the pages of figures and information. It was her excellent memory, honed by all those pages of prose and poetry memorized and repeated by rote in the classrooms of those many ugly years ago, that made her so valuable to the underground groups who relayed their messages, through her, knowing they would not be betrayed.

The birthday party was a resounding success. Edie had guessed nothing. The early winter weather, clear and calm, had made the midday *asado* a perfect meal, and afterwards everyone had retired for a *siesta*.

A smaller gathering, in the evening, shared drinks and supper in the fire-lit warmth of the house in the main room. Harvey Casey and other local *estancieros* and their families sang "Happy Birthday" as the cake was brought in, tiny candles glittering all around its decorated perimeter.

Lala placed it in front of Edie at the head of the long table.

"Now you have to blow out all the candles...."

"Make a wish, *señora*, make a wish..."

"Happy birthday to you..."

Edie stood up, looked smilingly around the table and then took a deep breath.

"That's it *señora*... in one puff..."

"Bravo!"

She blew out all the candles and again looked around at her guests, this time in triumph.

"There—you see? I did it. And all in one breath, too. I'm not such a decrepit old lady after all...."

"Whoever said..."

"What nonsense..."

"*Que viva la señora* Edie..."

"*Que viva!*"

Lala smiled over at Raul through the wisps of smoke coming from the extinguished candles, their shared secret lit between them. Then she turned to Edie again.

"Did you remember to wish, *Doña* Edie?"

"Indeed I did," said Edie in clear tones. "I wished for lots more birthdays."

Lala walked along the verandah toward the south wing. It was late; all the guests had gone home, and *Doña* Edie was probably fast asleep by now. The night was chill with rain, midwinter drear, and the tiles of the verandah glistened with damp in the moving spot of her flashlight.

Thank goodness it had been such a lovely sunny day, making it possible to have the *asado* exactly as they had planned and enabling the *señora* to get out and about. Spry and strong as she was for her age, the *patrona* showed the weight of her seventy-five years when the cold rains of winter set in. Her arthritis pained her, Lala knew, but one never heard her complain. Raul said that she merely became more impossible about work when the weather was bad.

"I don't mind her going over the books.... She's good at figures, even now ... but when she tries to tell me how to run the day-to-day work ... then, well, what can I do, Lala? I do what I have to do ... and I lie ..."

Lala had agreed with his tactics; they certainly worked where the *señora* Edie was concerned. To contradict her head-on was to cause further intransigence; far better to do it the softer way, and get the work done. If she remembered ... if she found out later ... those were bridges to be crossed when met. But she seldom did; the results of Raul's administrative work were too good for Edie to question afterwards.

And now the big birthday celebration was over. Lala, although tired, had not felt like sleeping, not even after all the dishes and glasses and debris had been cleared away. She had spent some time in the pantry, replacing the silver dishes in their cloth covers; the champagne bucket and its stand were among the pieces, and she decided to take them back to their usual storage place in a room of the now unused south wing.

She entered the wing's vestibule and switched on the light, extinguishing her flashlight and placing it on the table near the door. The rooms were still furnished with the old pieces, the dark brown surfaces cleaned and polished once a year,

Forgotten and unwanted items accumulated, lying in the back of the wardrobe or at the bottom of drawers. The window curtains, drawn against dust and sun alike, were threaded to the walls with cobwebs, and familiar smell of time-damp stillness made Lala's nostrils smart. The piano, neglected and out of tune, stood silent and dusty; the bookshelves' very neatness was evidence of their unused contents.

Lala set the bucket-stand in a corner and bent over to place the bucket beside it on the floor.

"Well! Isn't that charming . . . arse ready and in position for a really good screw. . . ."

She spun around too late. Harvey had already shut the door behind him, his mottled, besotted face flushed with alcohol and triumph.

"Why are you here? You left hours ago—get out, get out!"

"I didn't leave—I've been with the *peones,* sharing their *tinto* . . ." His fatuous grin shifted into a lopsided slant. "And no, I don't intend getting out—I intend to get you. . . ."

He lunged at her and gripped her arms, pinning them to her sides. With the bulk of his body, he shoved her against the wall.

"Don't bother to scream, bitch—no one can hear you. . . ."

It was true, and Lala knew it. The room they were in was far too remote from the center of the building and the kitchen quarters for any of the sleeping servants to be woken by her cries. *Doña* Edie's bedroom was even further away, on the far side of the main room.

Struggling, Lala wrenched her head from side to side, trying to avoid the florid mass of Harvey's face bearing down on her. But the sheer bulk and power of his body made escape impossible. His lips mashed hers; Lala clamped her teeth down, hard.

His knee jerked viciously into her crotch. Lala gasped. Harvey drew his face away.

"You rotten whore. . . . You hot, miserable bitch. . . . I'm going to give you a screwing you'll never forget . . . never . . ."

Lala pulled and struggled, knowing it was useless, yet desperate to try anything in an attempt to get away. Harvey jerked her around, twisting her arms behind her back and dragging her toward the doorway into the bedroom. He thrust her through with a shove toward the bed itself, and with one more step pushed her onto its faded counterpane.

The weight of his body sank onto hers at once; then, easing to one side, he wrenched her around so that he could force her back flat onto the bed. He heaved and kicked her legs onto the cover with his foot, leaning down on her as he climbed astride, his full weight crushing down on her hips.

Grappling and tearing, he ripped open the front of her dress, while his knees forced her legs apart. Lala managed to bite him again, this time in the arm. He reared up and slapped her back and forth across the face, his hand slamming down hard, palm and back.

"Don't try anything else, you cunt, or I'll smash your face in. . . ."

Lala's head drummed with horror, the sharp stars, seen as his hand slammed down, bursting with pain.

I can't escape. . . . I must do something. . . . I have to protect my child . . . Raul's child . . . nothing must happen to it. . . . No matter what happens to me, this force must not destroy . . .

Willing herself to courage, Lala forced herself to make her whole body go limp, trying to control her gasping breath, pulling her thoughts away from the brutality ravishing her. Harvey was threatening and tearing and assaulting all of her, invading her body, suffocating her being.

Silently she began to recite the rolling poems of her dreadful schoolday hours, the lines she had learned by heart to escape the injustices of the adult world.

In Xanadu did Kubla Khan . . .

She made the words flow and roll in the echoing chambers of her mind until their very resonance began obliterating the physical and the present. Line after line, poem followed poem, and Lala followed the images toward protective oblivion.

My name is Ozymandias . . .

Pain thrust, and she drew back once more, further than she had managed to escape, making the words come quicker and quicker in her desperate flight. Then, from a distance, she sensed the release of Harvey's venom, and felt the sudden dead weight of his quieting form. Still her inner voice declaimed, and the words rolled their fog, their curtain around her.

527

. . .Round the decay
Of that colossal wreck, boundless and bare,
The lone and level sands stretched far away.

The rush of words came to a standstill; the movements pinning her had stopped. There was silence, underscored only by dissonant breathing. She became aware of the rain; it was coming down much harder, noisy in the outside dark. The outside. . . but the outside was there . . . She could feel the cold . . . the draught . . . there was a shadow . . . a scraping sound moved . . .

The thin, flat whir of rawhide thong slicing through air cut across the rain-sound only a second before the whip slashed across Harvey's back. He seconded his grunted cry with a swiftly following scream, wrenching himself off her and landing on the floor at the far side of the bed.

"Quick, Lala—get out! Run!"

Raul's arm was snaking out again and again, the whip an extension of his power and his rage. Lala rolled over on her side and pushed herself up to a sitting position on the bed, her head reeling.

"Go, Lala . . . quickly . . ."

She ducked under the path of his arm and stumbled out of the room; the door to the verandah was wide open, the cold wet air reviving in itself. She cast a quick glance back; Raul was advancing still further, the whip swirling around and down again in frenzy, Harvey's form hidden from her by the door and the bed.

She closed the door and crept along the outdoor walkway, hobbling a few steps, clutching her stomach, then leaning against the wall, dizzy with pain and fear and hatred, knowing that this time she would demand revenge.

In the long and agonizing hours that followed, Lala swore and wept and swore again, lying on her own iron bed, getting up to pace up and down in her room until the aches and swellings rose above her anger and she was forced to rest again.

Sleep would not come; not even after Raul joined her, grim-faced and with smears of blood on his hands, did she even attempt to lie down and forget the night in sleep.

"You didn't kill him, did you?" she asked when Raul entered.

"No. But I should have. He is on his way home."

Raul washed his hands and brought in a basin and tended to Lala's bruises and pains. But her only worry was their unborn baby.

"It mustn't be allowed to hurt the child..."

"Then lie down and rest," Raul said reasonably. "If you try to lie still, it might help its chance...."

But Lala could not do so for more than a few minutes.

"Then at least sit there while I get something for you to have...."

He brought her hot *yerba*, and they talked in whispers; Lala's bruises grew darker and her swollen face showed clear. Raul made compresses, and gently applied them.

Lala said, "I don't care what I risk. I'm going to tell *Doña Edie*."

"Well, you'll have to tell her *something*. There's no use our thinking you can hide."

"I'm going to tell her the truth."

Raul watched her carefully, anxiety shading his eyes. He handed her another dampened cloth from the basin next to the bed.

"You do whatever you think best," he said. "I don't think she's ever liked Harvey, but because he's part of her family, she's defended him in the past. But the *señora* is known to be loyal to her own—and this time, I think her own will be you."

Lala's voice came through the cloth, muffled. "For me to go on being afraid... to lie, to try and hide... it's no use. It only means going on risking with Harvey, and with the risk being hidden from everyone else...."

After a few moments she removed the cloth and got off the bed. She looked at herself in the small mirror on the wall.

"As you said, I cannot hide... this...." Her fingers traced over the swellings. "I'd have to lie, to invent a story.... And for whose sake? Not for mine anymore. Only for his...." Her eyes closed and her already disfigured face became contorted. "And I would rather die than do anything that might help Harvey Casey... even in the smallest way...."

Raul came to stand behind her and put his hands gently on her shoulders, his hands trembling with anger and anguish, not wanting their touch to hurt her bruises even more.

"If he ever touches you again, I swear to you, Lala, I will kill him.... I swear it to you, for our love... and on my honor as a man."

"It's very simple, Harvey," Edie said, looking up at him from her desk chair. "All you have to do is sign these two documents."

She pushed the sheets of paper toward him. He was standing at the side of her desk, his broad-brimmed hat in his hand. Edie had not asked him to sit down.

"Whether or not you choose to be sensible and sign—I do not want you coming to El Ombú again," she continued. "But I warn you, if you do *not* sign—both the agreement to give up your legal claims against Raul's portion of La Chata, *and* your statement confirming the sum of money you are to give Lala, as I have specified..."

Edie peered forward at the two pieces of paper, as though checking for the last time all was in order there.

"... if you do not sign, then I shall immediately foreclose the mortgage on La Chata...."

Harvey made a motion, as though he were about to speak. Edie waved him silent.

"No, don't interrupt. It's useless for you to protest. I'm well aware of the precarious state of your finances. So you see, Harvey, it's all up to you: the papers are right there."

Harvey shifted his weight from one foot to the other, staring down at the floor as he did so. Then he cleared his throat several times, and when at last he began speaking, it was in a low mumble. Edie did not bother to tell him to speak up; she could hear him well enough, but was not much interested in anything he might have to say. Instead, she watched his hands, their thick fingers moving restlessly on the brim of his hat as he turned it ceaselessly round and round.

Finally, both Harvey's monologue and the hat's turning came to a stop. Edie knew the moment had arrived; she pushed a pen toward the edge of the desk.

"That's right, Harvey. You sign it down there, at the bottom... and the same thing on the next one..."

When she retired to bed late that night, Edie lay awake for ages, the ancient horror-images of Edgar lurking in all the dark corners of her room. She tossed and turned fitfully, tortured by the memories, all of them refreshed and vivid through the angers of the day.

At least she had the signed papers in her possession... at least there was nothing further that brute Harvey could do now. But the foul indignities had been committed, and the long-ago fears reacted within her, decrying the odious villainy of men against women, brute against queen...how dare they, how dare...

Eventually, her thoughts moved forward, until at last the balance of her life restored her calm, and she thought of La Maison, and her life then, and of Maurice...and now...they couldn't harm her...and at last Edie slept.

On Christmas day, shortly before evening, Lala gave birth to a baby girl.

"You don't need to tell me....I know it's Amelie," she murmured, hazed with anesthetic, as the doctor drew near.

Later, in her room, with Raul at her bedside, she smiled and held his hand for joy, and cried a little, too. And when they brought in the baby, she gazed at her in wonder.

"My Amelie...my little Amelie...I waited so long...and now you're here...."

The letter was lying on the desk, waiting, and had a January date on it.

Dear Dr. Casterán,

Even though we have never met, I believe my name will be familiar to you, from many years ago, through Meryl van Landen. I was a criada at her grandmother's estancia; Meryl and I shared many moments of our childhood and adolescent days.

The reason I am writing to you is that I gave birth to a daughter last Christmas Day. My husband and I wish to secure our little Amelie's future as best we can; Raul and I both suffered in childhood because of unknown parentage and lack of legal protection; we wish, therefore, to protect our daughter to the fullest extent of our capabilities. We are both well aware of the uncertainties of life; an accident could claim both our lives simultaneously. Illness, too, can destroy a home, to say nothing of unforeseen calamities which can occur. All of these matters have been discussed between us, which is why we now turn to you to help us safeguard our Amelie.

We would like to arrange for Meryl van Landen to be legally appointed as Amelie's guardian, should anything happen to either one of us, or both of us. And we appeal to you to help us in this matter, both because you knew Meryl when she lived in Buenos Aires and because of your respected name and standing in that city ...

The letter went on at some length, giving details of domicile, parental names and legal particulars; the mother of the child had obviously gone to great trouble to get all the necessary information to him at once. After he had finished reading the letter through, Jimmy leaned back in his chair and stared out of his office window.

The trees of the formal plaza across the street were at their deepest green, cool in their midsummer foliage, dark against the cloudless blue sky. Beyond them, down the slope leading to the central railway terminal on one side and the busy, ship-filled docks on the other, lay the gleaming waters of the River Plate. He remembered walking in the plaza with Meryl, the gravel crunching under their feet, its sound clean and satisfying in the companionable silence. There had been the background noise of B.A. traffic, exactly as there was now, muted through the double glass of the wide window. He looked back at the desk.

It was several minutes before he pressed the buzzer for his secretary, and when she came in to take the day's dictation, he started it by answering in the affirmative to the letter he was still holding in his hand.

2

The confusion at Schipol Airport was an admixture of delayed flights and building construction. Meryl found a semicircle of displaced seats behind one of the waiting area's many shops; as all the chairs were empty, she decided to spread out and make herself comfortable, placing her coat over one chair, her camera bag on the one next to it and sitting down on a third. She stretched her legs out in front of her, and closed her eyes.

If I see one more tulip, I'll scream....

Still, it had been a good assignment, one of Sal's. The specimens she had photographed would appear in a botanical society's report and yearbook, and the precision of her work might well bring in more assignments of like nature. She enjoyed an occasional departure from her usual portrait work.

Damn the flight being late. It would mean arriving in London smack in the middle of the rush hour, and that would mean taking ages to get to her flat in the West End.

The seat shook; Meryl opened her eyes and saw her coat tumbling to the floor.

"Ah, forgive me . . . your coat . . . here, allow me . . ."

The words were spoken in French; and the speaker wore a homburg; he was tanned and distinguished. In his fifties, Meryl guessed, taking the coat as he handed it to her and placing it across her lap.

"I'm sorry," the man repeated. "My briefcase caught it. . . ."

"That's all right. It's only dust . . ."

"And dust is everywhere," he replied, brushing off the chair the coat had been on and sitting down on it. "It is the way of airports—always bigger, better, louder . . . and above all, never finished. . . ."

Meryl smiled and agreed, exchanging pleasantries with the stranger on the generalities of air travel.

"Are you by any chance flying to Munich?"

Meryl shook her head. "No. London."

His look assessed her frankly. "What a pity. . . ."

She shrugged slightly, and smiled. Then the public address system began an announcement, and Meryl rose to go.

"That's my flight. . . ."

As she began putting on her coat, he also rose and helped her into it. Then he handed her the camera bag.

"*Bon voyage, mademoiselle . . . .*"

Meryl walked toward the boarding gate, picking her way through the crowd, wondering briefly where he came from. France, most likely; the accent, the air. Charming. Attractive, too. She shifted the camera-bag strap on her shoulder and held it with her hand.

The basket of roses arrived two weeks later. The card pinned to the enveloping cellophane read:

The address was on your case, and I have a good memory for things that interest me.
Would dinner tomorrow night be possible?

The engraved card read Jean-Luc Marcheret; he had drawn a pen line through the formality and signed the message, which was written in English, with his initials, under which his hotel was briefly scrawled.

Meryl looked from the roses to her telltale camera case; sure enough, its permanent tag had her name and address printed in bold black. Then she looked at the card in her hand again; there was no mistaking the unwritten message. And it was appealing; interesting indeed.

She was tired of trendy London and the hangers-on of the periphery. The center was beginning to move again, back to the U.S.A. Her own life was independent, and she enjoyed living in Europe, but London life had dimmed for Meryl, its glitter gone drab.

It's me, she realized; I'm tired of the mod world. It had been fun and new and challenging at first, and totally different from the stultifying marriage she had fled.

But now, she had outgrown it; other fields and fancies were probably calling. I'd hate to be an elderly trendy, she realized with a start. Now that I'm in my thirties, I want to keep on going forward. . . . Besides, he *was* attractive. . . .

Slowly, she dialed the hotel.

It was, above all, a most civilized affair, right from the very first evening, when they dined and talked and understood each other's eyes, and parted politely to meet the next day.

"I have a conference in the morning . . . but after that, my days here are my own. . . . Shall I send the car to collect you at, say, shortly after noon? I thought perhaps a drive out into the country, and lunch somewhere . . ."

A benignly sunny day darkened down to evening, changed into nightfall and night, became the first time. There were no fumblings, no gropings, no moments of awkward mishandling.

"The first—it is always the best, for people like us," he observed, lying next to her on the silk-smooth sheets of the hotel suite bed. "The initial urgency . . . that can never be recaptured . . . making it more precious, I suppose. . . ."

After a moment's pause, he said, "That is not to say, of course, that it will not be very good indeed the many other times I hope we are to have."

He was a charming conversationalist, a man of many interests and wide knowledge, a companion par excellence. Widely traveled, he preferred his native France to all other countries he had visited.

"...but of course it is well-known to be our fortunate blend of soil, climate, and geographical particulars..."

Thus the reason for the perfection of French food. Philosophy had similar safeguards: logic and pragmatism.

"All part of our national characteristics... in our history, you will find..."

He enjoyed England, was amused by America, found the Germans useful, the Swiss less so. When it came to the Spaniards, he offered no opinions.

"My forebears came from the Basque lands... and my prejudice would show...."

Jean-Luc Marcheret was, as Meryl had originally guessed, in his mid-fifties; for his age, he was well-muscled, the bodily armature produced by a lifetime of leisure sports. He no longer played tennis, but swam well, and skied.

"Competition bores me," he told her. "As the years passed, it becomes more difficult to win."

He was the keeper of inherited fortune and lands, monitoring the family investments and managing their affairs; his time, therefore, was completely his own. As Meryl was able to schedule her own work to suit her purposes, there were no obstacles between them.

If their relationship was free of mundane interference, it was also free of turmoil, its intensity contained within the passion of well-tuned sexuality, their senses given the free rein of the fully mature. It suited Meryl; she was tired of emotional fires she herself did not feel, and she knew she was no longer willing to put up with the behavior within the fires of others. With Jean-Luc, there was no room for the jealousies or the limiting barriers of possession she had experienced so often in liaisons of the past.

When she commented on it, Jean-Luc said, "There comes a level of experience, Meryl, which automatically eliminates all those strains."

He was, of course, married.

"What happened?"

"Nothing. Monotony, perhaps. We understand each other perfectly. Time changes many things."

"So I suppose you could say time happened."

He shrugged. "You could say it, yes. But only if you believe something has to *happen*. Happen in the active, or accident sense. That is a very American point of view."

Piqued, Meryl responded tartly that simply because something was American, it did not necessarily mean it was wrong.

"Of course not," he agreed. "Immature, perhaps. Often unrealistically idealistic. You think everything is possible."

"We think *possible* things are possible. In fact, there's even a saying about giving things a good old college try."

The conversation returned to the subject of marriage.

Jean-Luc said, "There is a saying, you know, that the first wife is the wife God sends you, but the second is the one you deserve. Well, not only God, but also my family were involved in the choosing of my wife—and perhaps I fear the one I might deserve. . . ." He smiled as he finished speaking.

"And you didn't ever think you might deserve someone who shares more of your life with you?"

He shook his head.

"No, Meryl, I know myself too well. Much as I appreciate the kindness of your thought, of course. But I am a compartmentalized man, and I choose to be that way. My interests, my family, my pursuits—they are all separate. That is the traditional way in my circles and I am, if nothing else, a traditional man."

Meryl smiled at him over her champagne glass.

"And am I an interest, or a pursuit?"

"Oh, a pursuit, Meryl!—definitely a pursuit. . . ."

They flew to Monte Carlo together, met in Paris, drove through the Rhineland, danced in Rome. Sometimes Meryl would fly to meet Marcheret at their destination; sometimes he would pick her up in London, and their journey would commence there. Often, Switzerland was the meeting point, either in Zurich or Geneva, and their weekend or weeklong trip would then get underway.

Their sparked sensuality, tempered by time, became inlaid with knowledge and intimacy's harvests; their conversations became more personal more often as mutual understanding grew. They talked as they traveled, flying or driving. They talked over leisurely meals, and while lying in the sun.

They did not sleep together; the hotel suites always had two bedrooms. He would leave her bed no matter how late at night it was, and go to his own. In the morning, when they breakfasted, he was already shaved and showered. Sometimes Meryl wondered whether he ever slept at all.

Their physical attraction deepened into friendship; uncommitted to each other, both could afford generosity of spirit; they met and parted to meet later, often on different ground.

Sometimes they traveled together, driving the roads of Europe. Then a month might pass, with only a phone call, and work the routine of each day.

"You're not getting married on me, are you, kiddo?" Sal demanded on a trans-Atlantic conversation, but Meryl assured him it was nothing like that.

"Okay, okay... just wanted to make sure..."

She handled his London office and assignments, did her portrait work when she had time. When she wanted time off, her assistant took over. Their free-lancing service had long established its worth.

Occasionally, an assignment coincided with a planned meeting. A Parisian get-together worked out that way.

"How amusing... I know them," was Jean-Luc's comment, when Meryl described the family whose children she had been commissioned to photograph. "It was only to be expected, of course...."

"Why?"

"Because of your style of working...."

She was flattered, and she said so.

"Flattery is for Italians. We do not approach craft that way in France."

Sometimes they argued—about the French, about the Americans. He did not know the Argentine, other than through its links to Europe. Often, they agreed—about life's vagaries and conceits. The gaps between them were always avoided—families, holidays, the seasonal calendar markings. By tacit agreement, their friendship left in limbo the subjects well-known to have no common ground.

They were in Vienna, about to attend a concert, when Jean-Luc remarked, "It seems absurb to have known you for a year." Later that night he returned to the theme, citing an old saying.

"I was once told that affairs last in threes: three days, three weeks, three months or three years. If it goes to the next division, that is to say, thirty, it is, of course, the classic case of the *petite amie*."

"Couldn't it also be a marriage?"

Looking dubious, Jean-Luc nonetheless conceded, "It could be, I suppose. There must be that rara avis somewhere, to disprove the rule."

"And we are already long past the three-month category. . . . Does it worry you in some way?"

"Not at all," he smiled. "Perhaps we'll achieve the three-year mark. Alas, the thirty is beyond me physically."

"Perhaps for us it's different," Meryl then suggested.

"My dear Meryl—it is *always* different. Everyone'll tell you so. That's what makes love so banal."

The limousine picked her up outside her flat and drove her to the airport. It was almost like traveling with Philipe again; with Jean-Luc, everything was always arranged. Meryl checked in her baggage and heard the flight's announcement.

". . . leaving for Cannes . . . boarding at Gate Five . . ."

He was there to meet her in the bright Riviera sunshine.

"How smashing. In London it's been doing nothing but raining for days. . . ."

They drove to his apartment, which was spacious and spectacular.

"We have an invitation, my dear . . . lunch at the home of friends. . . . Shall I accept?"

"Sounds lovely. . . ."

They took the road along the coast, its cliffs dropping to the rocks below, and the Mediterranean, streaked with sun and aquamarine, rippling out beyond.

"She's an old friend," said Marcheret, explaining their lunchtime hosts as he drove. "We met in early youth. He's her present lover. She gave up having husbands a long time ago. As to the gathering, it all has to do with showing off her new house."

They turned inland, climbing up through the rising terrain behind Cannes, then through a stone-pillared entrance up a curving driveway. They arrived at the colonnaded facade of the villa; their hostess, gray-haired, smiling, and warmly beautiful, came down the wide steps to greet them.

She reached out both her hands.

"Welcome to La Maison, Jean-Luc. . . . It's been far too long since I saw you last. . . ."

Marcheret took her hands in his and kissed the air above the jeweled rings. Then he introduced Meryl.

The two women smiled at each other, forming the invisible bond of instant recognition between those who, at different times, have shared the same man's attention, and his bed.

538

"Come. Let us get you drinks, and then I simply must show you the house. It is going to be the delight of the rest of my life. . . . I feel I have found my home at last. . . ."

Late in the evening, when they were returning to the apartment, Jean-Luc said, "You were very quiet today, Meryl. You are not ill, I trust?"

Meryl breathed in to explain, then held it with her thoughts. When she breathed out again, it was in a sigh of disguise, her mind already changed.

"Oh, no, I'm fine. Lazy, perhaps." She stretched convincingly, and covered a minor yawn. "I had a busy week, you know, and then the flight . . . perhaps all the fresh sea air. . . . I was busy drinking it all in. . . . I had a lovely time. . . ."

3

Yvonne spent long hours sitting by Wilfred's bedside in the hospital; sometimes she stayed there with him through the night as well. He slipped away by inches, mostly into the past; his conversation drifted to times and occurrences that meant nothing to her, and he began mentioning names and people of whom she had never heard.

One day he smiled with renewed life when she walked into the room. He was sitting up in bed—a good sign—and the pillows behind his back were fresh and neat.

"How nice to see you, Susan," he remarked. "You're looking very well, I must say. . . ."

As the months passed, so did his reason; the meaningless phrases turned into nonsense before they became babble. Then the silences stretched out longer, and so did his hours of sleep. Yvonne knitted a sweater and embroidered a tea-cosy for Christmas and started on a tablecloth with twelve matching serviettes, leaving her handwork in a basket that was always kept in his room.

After the festivities, when they told her the time of death was approaching, she developed a summer cold and had to stay at home, taking the cough mixture the doctor had given her and reading a book about the gardens of England as Wilfred slept and slipped away into forever at last.

Late at night, after hearing from the doctor that Wilfred

was gone, Yvonne went to sleep and dreamed of Cosunzué and the mountains, waking in terror of the void of darkness and lying there in fear until daylight came.

To Yvonne's surprise, her mother came down to B.A. for the funeral.

"I didn't mean you to bother, Mummy... really... there's nothing more anyone can do...."

But they stood together through the funeral's church service, and rode in the car behind the hearse.

Later, they talked, avoiding abrasions, and Yvonne told her mother her vague future plans.

"I think what I'd really like to do is get away for a while... maybe even to England.... Meryl's there.... I'd like to see her...." Her voice drifted away.

Edie nodded. "I think you should."

Yvonne looked up in amazement.

Edie said, "We're all too distant... all too far apart. And after you've been there, when you come back here again, we must get together and talk things over. We must work something out.... Keep in mind I'll be eighty next year... you'll have to help me...."

Impulsively, Yvonne said, "Yes, Mummy. I promise you I will." And even after Edie returned to her hotel, the mood of calm remained. At last Yvonne went up to bed, and that night she slept soundly.

Snow had drained the landscape of its energy and color and was still falling in faint, occasional flurries from the flat leaden sky. Meryl watched a tumble of white powder fall from a branch among the dense, dark trees, its slow-motion fall leaving another branch bare, a somber and accusing finger of winter against the white ground. Then she returned her attention to the letter in her hand, grateful for the cheery warmth of the French country inn's bedroom.

...and there wasn't anything any doctor could do, Yvonne had written. *I've known it for years. But he died peacefully, and I was with him every day, to the end. There was no point in my telling you it was going to happen; that's why I've waited until now to tell you about everything. The funeral service was well done and the flowers were lovely—none of*

540

*those awful arum-lily wreaths the Argentines are so fond of,
and lots and lots of mixed bouquets of pretty garden flowers.
Everyone was very sweet and kind to me . . .*

Meryl knew the letter's contents almost by heart, having
read it many times over since its arrival. Her grandmother's
letter had been in the same delivery, its basic news the same,
the perspective different.

*. . . has finally died, after all these years of being nothing
but a sponger and a chupa-medias . . .*

Meryl translated for Marcheret's benefit: "That's the Argentine equivalent of an ass-licker, literally, a sock-sucker."

"How vivid," the Frenchman murmured.

Meryl lit another cigarette. "She says she thinks my mother will probably make a trip here."

"From all you have told me about your family in the past,
I'd imagine that is highly likely. . . ."

When she got back to London, Meryl found another of the
familiar blue-and-white bordered airmail envelopes awaiting
her, her mother's handwriting bolder than on the previous
one.

*. . . and I'll be flying home this time—so nice and modern!
Do try to be in England when I arrive, and not off doing one
of your photographic jobs somewhere on the Continent . . .*

"You've changed," said Yvonne, handing her cup over to
Meryl who had the teapot on her side.

"We both have, Mother. After all, it's been almost sixteen
years . . ."

"I don't mean in appearance. I mean, you seem calmer . . .
thank you, darling, just one lump, please."

Meryl smiled as she handed back the tea-filled cup, and
changed the subject.

"D'you want to start right in doing things, Mother? Or
would you rather rest up from the trip for a few days . . . ?"

Beneath the banalities of small talk and the day's planned
routine, mother and daughter groped to meet each other
across the gap of years. There had been so much to talk
about, yet little to say, ever since Yvonne's arrival the day

before; this morning, they had filled the uneasy silences with other people's news and messages, and the snapshots of little Amelie enclosed in a package from Lala.

"Mummy told her I was coming over, and so she sent me a letter, asking me could I bring a parcel to you...."

Lala had also sent a package of *yerba* and a box of *alfajores*, and a short note apologising for not writing.

...but I really have very little spare time, as you can imagine, what with all the schoolwork and then our beautiful little Amelie....And she is beautiful; she has Raul's eyes, and she's going to be tall like him, the doctor says. I wish you could see her, but since you can't, I'm sending copies of all the photos we have taken of her lately. I'm also asking your mother to take some things for you so that you don't forget the taste of Argentina...

Meryl looked through the pictures again.

"My goddaughter," she remarked. "Lala says I'm also her guardian. I wish I could photograph her; she's a good subject. Perhaps I'll get to it someday."

Then she pushed the photos aside, and concentrated on her mother. Yvonne was looking through her address book.

"...must ring Lally...lives down in Sussex somewhere now..."

Later, Meryl heard Yvonne on the phone.

"Lally! Darling! Yes, it's really me....I know, I know...it's been simply ages....You got my letter, didn't you? Yes, that's right...."

Meryl went into the bathroom to have her shower and closed the door. When she reemerged, Yvonne was just getting off the phone.

"Well, that's settled," she announced. "I'm going to spend the weekend with her....She's told me what train to take, and everything. She'll meet me at the station, as she says her house is quite a long way from the village, too far to go by taxi....Oh, I'm *so* looking forward to seeing her...." Yvonne went over to the living room window and looked out at the tree-filled square beyond. "Is it going to rain, d'you think? I'd love to go for a short walk...."

Meryl smiled. "Don't you remember? It always rains....This is London in the spring...."

That evening, they spoke of loneliness and living alone and bereavement; the unexpected conversation closed the gap of years. Yvonne spoke of Wilfred; Meryl told about her father. And her brief, broken marriage, and the years between. She spoke of Marcheret.

"It's nice for now, and I'm not thinking ahead," she told Yvonne in the gentle twilight. They were sitting in front of the living room window, each with a drink in her hand. Meryl did not mention the visit to La Maison.

"Well, you're young yet. There's time to think things over."

"I don't think love has a time limit, do you?"

Yvonne shook her head. "No, I don't suppose so, really. Try not to get hurt, Meryl, or caught out again. Danny sounds as though he was a disaster."

Meryl, remembering Wilfred, paused before asking, "And you, Mother? How about you? Do you think, in the passage of time, you might marry again?"

Yvonne turned, her face lit by the mellow light of evening, beautiful in the softness of her late middle years. She put down her glass and smiled across at her daughter.

"Neither in the heights of happiness nor in the depths of despair would I ever consider marrying again."

In lighter moods over the next few days, Yvonne regaled Meryl with Buenos Aires gossip, mentioning names long-forgotten, evoking memories from the past. The past, too, returned to Yvonne, with every step she took around London.

"... and Harrods is *just* the way I remembered it. . . . I even sat in the bank for a moment. . . ."

"... used to have lunch with Philipe at a little place right around the corner from here. . . ."

Meryl suggested, "Let's go there now." But the building had changed, and the restaurant was gone.

"Oh, of course, how silly of me, it was bombed during the War. . . . Lally and I found that out when it happened. . . . I'm *so* looking forward to seeing her again. . . ."

Yvonne's war reminiscences filled much of the daytime; her tales of Buenos Aires came out at night.

"... so many of the children are marrying natives—I mean people who don't even speak English, let alone have English names. . . .

"Robert Thaxter died—but perhaps Grannie told you? No?

Well, he did, and his sister Dollie's on her last legs, too.... She was brought up with Grannie, you know...."

Meryl, remembering Lala's stories about Dollie Thaxter's command performance visits to the Ladies Society School in Córdoba, offered little comment on the news.

"And let me see what else has happened lately..." Yvonne frowned in effort to recall. "Oh, yes: Peggy Webb died. Peggy Webb that was Peggy Casterán. She'd been a widow for a long time. Her husband was so much older..."

Meryl, who had been clearing the dishes from the dinner table, stood quite still.

"Jimmy's mother," she said in a flat voice.

"Yes, that's right. The funeral was huge. Or so I was told, anyway. I didn't go, of course."

Meryl wondered: why of course? but only asked when Mrs. Casterán's death had occurred.

"Shortly before I came over. I remember I was already packing when I was told. She'd been ill—some sort of minor operation—and I think something went wrong and she never came out of the hospital. I remember her so well from my B.A. school days. She always let me have an extra pencil when I used to lose mine...."

And Yvonne was off on a tangent of early remembrance, with Meryl hardly listening to her words.

Close to noon the next day, after she had seen her mother off on a Sussex train from Victoria Station, Meryl did her weekend shopping and returned to the flat in a clouded mood. Her indecision lasted as she put away the groceries, automatically checking the augmented items in keeping with her mother's stay.

By the time she had finished, the cloud began lifting; she had reached her decision, for good or for ill. It only took brief moments to write the letter of condolence to Jimmy, and she addressed it to him at the old house in Palermo whose address she knew so well, taking a chance on the Casterán home still being in Jimmy's possession.

From the moment her mother walked in the door, Meryl could see something was the matter. Although Yvonne smiled and greeted her as she entered, it was clear from the older woman's stance and demeanor that something had gone terribly wrong.

Yvonne took her small suitcase through into the bedroom.

"I think I'll have a bath before dinner," she called out.

"Go ahead." Meryl retired into the kitchen, wondering.

Over dinner and wine, the visit's woes poured out.

"I hardly know where to begin... it was just too simply awful...." Yvonne closed her eyes, giving a little sigh. "I was so looking forward to it.... We used to have such fun, even during the war years... and now..." She opened her eyes again. "I hardly recognized Lally, for a start."

"Well, you know, the years..."

Yvonne waved the point aside. "It wasn't anything to do with age. *She* recognized *me* immediately. But—you should see her, Meryl—except of course, it wouldn't mean anything to you... you didn't know her before..."

"I remember photos," Meryl offered.

Yvonne leaned forward.

"That's right," she said eagerly. "I have some taken during the War. Remember the one of the two of us standing next to an official car?"

Meryl nodded.

"Well, Lally and I were more or less the same size and shape. Oh, she was always a little more buxom than I am..." Yvonne broke off. She sipped some wine before going on. "Well, you should see her now. She's *huge*. Vast. Completely out of proportion. And her face... I can hardly describe it, it's gone so strange...."

"But why...?"

"She drinks. I'd never have believed it. But she was tiddly when she came to pick me up at the station, and the first thing she did when we got to her cottage was pour us two very stiff whiskeys. After that, I'd had quite enough, but she kept on drinking all afternoon...."

Yvonne's description of Lally's house and style of living all fitted in to an alcoholic's way.

"... chaotic... never comes to town... looks like a char-woman... very kind, as she always was—but what a mess...."

And all, Yvonne told her daughter, because of the sad love affair that had ruined her life when she was still very young.

"... she never got over John...."

"And he never tried to divorce his wife and marry her?" Meryl asked.

"He couldn't. The wife was Catholic...."

Meryl's thoughts turned back to Philipe and his words

about only the brave being deserving after all. When she refocused on the present, her mother was rising from the table.

"I think I'll go to bed, Meryl... it's really been most upsetting...."

Meryl saw her mother had tears in her eyes, and rose to accompany her to her room.

"Never mind—we'll do something nice this week.... You'll feel better tomorrow," she tried, inadequately.

Yvonne smiled. "You know what'd be nice? We could take the train to Crestwood Close, and I could show you around...."

Yvonne leaned back against the cold pillar and looked across the Quadrangle, letting the past and its memories sweep along the stones. Late spring clouds scudded across her range of vision, puffy against the northern blue of the sky over the rolling hills.

A group of pupils clustered around the goal loops at the far end; any moment now they would start leaping, practising for Quad. They looked exactly like the girls she'd known in the former generation, history and facial features repeating themselves in the traditions of the place.

The Game.... her swimming triumphs, Podge Bartlett, the sneers... the cheers that had pulled her to her championship, the midnight feasts, the warmth, belonging...

A movement, caught by the corner of her eye, distracted her. It was Meryl; she was walking across the Quad, stopping to photograph something, aiming her camera against the sun.

Yvonne watched her daughter in speculation. It was funny the way some things worked out; in retrospect, she realized Meryl would not have fitted in at Crestwood Close. And yet, when the War had broken out, it had seemed such a shame the child couldn't be sent home for a decent education. Now, it didn't seem to matter, taking into consideration the sort of personality that was Meryl's, and her diffident ways.

She had always been a remote child; a bit like Philipe. She looked so like him, too. and nowadays, she was always hiding behind that camera of hers, and just as difficult to get close to as she had been as a small child, only more polite about it now as an adult, of course.

Meryl's slight figure moved against a band of sunlight, turning into a two-dimensional silhouette against the brightness beyond, a shadow in the setting of the old schooltime memories. Yvonne shivered, feeling the cold of the pillar seeping through her clothing, and she straightened up, adjusting her coat closer around her and looking forward to the warming cup of tea she knew awaited them in the refectory, where they would join visiting parents for the Saturday gathering with the girls.

On the train going back to London, Meryl said, "I'm so glad you went there, Mother—and I'm so glad I didn't."

Yvonne asked, "Why?" knowing.

"I'd have hated it," came the reply.

Meryl watched as her mother withdrew from the realities of contemporary England; the disappointments showed, the differences emerged, the years had forced their change. Yvonne never mentioned Lally again, seemingly forgetting her; other schoolfriends, met for lunch, made lesser impacts now.

But, Meryl noticed, her mother did not accept invitations to the country. There was always an excuse, a reason, a delay.

She's retreating from hurt, Meryl thought.

Only during the school visit had the past remained inviolate; elsewhere, all the changes were too marked to ignore.

"I think I'll fly back to be home for Grannie's birthday," Yvonne announced one morning. "She'll be seventy-nine next month...eighty next year, imagine...it must be weighing on her a bit. She mentioned it to me after poor Wilfred's funeral. . . ."

And so politeness and good manners and the factual side of matters orchestrated Yvonne's early return, disguising the truth. At the airport, on leaving, she turned to hug her daughter.

"I had a lovely time, darling. Thank you so much for everything. Do remember to cable my arrival to B.A. and write to me soon. . . ."

The handwriting on the blue-and-white edged envelope was painfully familiar. Meryl tore open the flap, her heart beating in her throat.

Memorable Meryl, Jimmy began.

Thank you for your letter. I hardly know what to say. Miss Peggy would have known. Exactly as you did.

Yes, she was an usual woman. Unique, as you put it. The funeral was so big you would have thought she was Rudolfo Valentino.

Did you know you were always her favorite? God knows why. It may have had something to do with her liking for your mother, when they knew each other at that reform school that passes, even today, as a Brrrrrrrritish educational institute.

Anyway, for whatever reason, I'd like to talk about her with you some day. When are you coming home?

It was signed *As ever,* followed by the slanted squiggle Meryl knew meant Jimmy.

When she looked at the envelope again, a long moment later, she noticed with a punch of shock that the stamp was upside down.

There were also letters from her mother and Edie. Yvonne had been to the *estancia* at last.

It was lovely going riding. Raul found a marvelous horse for me. But I'm dreadfully stiff, as you can imagine, after all these years!

Her grandmother's letter, written after Yvonne's departure, covered many more subjects and several themes.

Did you know about poor Dollie Thaxter? She died in her sleep in April. I didn't go down to the funeral. That was while your mother was with you, and I didn't feel up to it, somehow.

Your mother tells me you are doing well and looking very smart. She also mentioned you had a boyfriend on the Continent. Are you thinking of getting married again, by any chance? If so, do be careful, child. When one is young, one can marry any old thing, but later on, it matters . . .

Meryl noticed that her grandmother's letters tended more and more to contain fragments of life-collected observations and advice.

"She is no doubt reliving much of her past through you," observed Jean-Luc when Meryl mentioned it to him, and read him excerpts from time to time.

"There's a beauty in this letter—a French saying, Grannie says. Perhaps you know it." Meryl scanned the pages for the quotation. "Ah, here it is." She read aloud, "Until she's twenty, a girl needs her mother; from twenty to forty, she needs her looks—and after that, she needs her money!"

"It sounds to me," said Marcheret, "more like a universal ambition."

"But Grannie was happy with Granmaurice—and I don't care what my mother says, it wasn't just the money. At least, I don't think so. . . . Of course I wasn't there . . . but from what I've heard. . . ."

"I would imagine your grandmother and her second husband reached an equitable compromise, a reasonable quid pro quo. You've seen marriage for yourself, Meryl. Its so-called success has so much to do with social patterning, and acceptance. There are roles to fill, roles to accept."

"You mean set roles?"

"Usually."

Meryl shook her head. "I don't believe in that now. Not for myself, anyway. I could never accept the little wife at home bit—and what's more, I don't accept the theory that marriage has to be that way to work."

Marcheret shrugged. "Then you may have to consider that perhaps marriage is not for you. Remember Mary Queen of Scots, who was told she must choose whether to be a woman or a queen. She never could make up her mind, and because of it, lost her head."

Meryl considered this in silence for a while. Eventually she said, "Why can't one be both? I think I'd want to be both. . . ."

"In that case, my dear, you will have to marry a king," Marcheret smiled, and the matter rested there.

But later, after he had gone, she thought over his words.

A *queen*.

Meryl thought immediately of Edie.

Woman.

That was Yvonne.

To be both, you'll have to marry a king. . . .

The words echoed in the hollowness of silence; Meryl thought of Jimmy, and pushed the thought away.

4

In Argentina, the government kept changing: by coup, by fiat, sometimes by election, the men of state changed and changed again. A revolution returned the military to the center of attention; they issued statutes and instigated reforms, and for a while, there was quiet.

But splintered groups, disgruntled losers, and politicians from the past, all lurked directly beneath the surface, causing unease and unpublished concern. All over the Latin continent, the rumblings of change were rumored; a flare-up here, a repression there, unquenchable, ill-met.

In 1967, assassination took the limelight; the Argentine Ché Guevara was killed by Bolivian government troops. He met his death in that landlocked country's jungle hinterland; a frisson ran through Argentina. He'd been very close to home.

But it wasn't only there that the nervousness was kindled. The whole world began learning a new vocabulary, fueled by the headlines, day by day. Guerrilla groups were emerging, kidnapping was international, ransoms were the price of life, or freedom from jail. Subversive strands showed linkages from nation to nation; Japanese hands sprayed Russian bullets at a Middle Eastern airport, young women took to the air in hijacking cadres, revolutionary group names and slogans became international household words.

Ideologies fused and melded and muted, confusing the former establishment of rules. New orders were established, some as oppressive as the old ones, others different, hard to follow, seemingly hard to understand.

And everywhere, everywhere, even in the quietest neighborhoods, the voices of protest grew more youthful by the hour. In 1968, it was students in Paris, and hippies in California, the shootings of King and Kennedy, men orbiting the moon. And while they did, the carnage in Vietnam grew stronger, and the growing anger louder, as the world went on.

It's so difficult to tell who's who and what's what, wrote Edie, her handwriting getting untidier. *I don't understand much about it anymore, and I don't know that anyone does. I'm thankful I don't have to bother much, as Raul does everything here for me. Lala came last month, with their daughter, but then they went off to Córdoba again.*

Your mother's coming back, the letter continued. *She said she'd be here next month when the new foals are born. She thinks I should go down and live in Buenos Aires, but the doctor says I can still hold my own.*

It was the first inkling Meryl had had that her grandmother's health might be failing. Edie had always seemed quite indestructible; was there anything really wrong?

No, wrote Yvonne, in answer to Meryl's questions. *Basically Mummy is perfectly well. She has circulation problems; the doctor explained them all to me. But as long as she takes her pills, all should be well. You must remember, Meryl: Grannie is in her eighty-second year.*

Meryl read the letters, and she read the European newspapers, and both sources made her uneasy, in ways she found hard to define. She longed for news from Lala, who wrote seldom, but more realistically; Yvonne was still carping on the rise in price of everything, and Edie's understanding had dimmed with old age.

But even at a distance, Meryl could recognize the troubled changes, none turning into order, all changing yet again. And never to the satisfaction of the country as an entity; dissent split within its own ranks, to divide the split some more, spawning cliques within groups and cells within cells. Dissent was layered, diverse, opposing, fragmented, motivation often differing; for some, it was a rich boy's pleasure, parental fortune safe and secure. For others, it was the future's hope, a road to a better nation. For many, excitement seemed the key, a way out of boredom and dead ends. For all, it was dangerous; every group had the authorities to fear, and, most of them, each other. In an underpopulated country, with wealth both raw and inherited, the aims of insurgent theories were as varied as the land.

If only Jimmy would write again... He would know the political realities. But after that one short note, to which Meryl had answered eventually, no word from him had arrived. Of course, she knew her letter had not said much—

merely that she had no idea when she might travel to Buenos Aires, and how touched she was that he would want to reminisce about Miss Peggy with her, and perhaps if he ever came to Europe... And then there had been nothing more.

A kidnapping thrust Argentina into the international headlines. Meryl's London friends commented.

"They've got some bloody nerve...."

"Bet you're glad you're away from all that...."

"...never happen here..."

"...frightful lot..."

The ransom was paid. Immediately afterwards the round-up began; someone had been caught, made to talk, give a link. Headlines were vivid in the evening press: TORTURE SQUAD SUSPECTED and GUERRILLA ARMS FOUND.

The report that followed swiftly was equally garish; the full ferocity of the *gaucho* forebears emerged in the death squads' ways. For, no matter what group or contingent they belonged to, legal or illegal, government or clandestine, the terrorists and authorities shared their national heritage.

Castration by barbed wire, the electric *picana*, their methods of killing and torture harked back to generations past. Bodies were found staked out under the searing sun or near gigantic anthills, shapeless remains with shreds of flesh attached to the drying bones.

Corpses had also turned up in the vacant lots of cities or on the outskirts of one of the larger towns. But usually there was nothing, only rumors after silence; fear was the forerunner on the road of treacherous ends.

Under marital law, arrests multiplied the findings.

At last, pontificated a columnist, the law will be restored.

A week later, another series of kidnappings electrified Buenos Aires.

....right under the noses of the police, wrote Yvonne. *It's all very unsettling, so I'm going to stay with Grannie for a while. Fortunately, it's all quite calm there, away from cities and city problems. I'll write to you when I get to El Ombú, and tell you how everyone is. And yes, I've got a little camera, in answer to your question, so I'll be able to take lots of shots of Amelie, when she and her mother arrive ...*

It was not, however, a letter with pictures that Meryl received from the *estancia;* it was a cable sent by Yvonne to tell her Raul had disappeared.

A letter followed swiftly; Lala was also missing. She could not be found in Córdoba, where she lived during the school year. Her superiors had reported her absent, and a colleague was sent to fetch her; the rooming house landlady said she had gone. Her room looked undisturbed.

There was nothing from the authorities; no one had seen her leaving.

"Perhaps she has gone away with a friend," leered the uniformed policeman sent to search. "A boyfriend..."

Her colleagues denied it. Surely it wasn't possible....

The man winked with malice.

"With women... you never know..."

Then, burdened with official obligation, he reluctantly completed his task. His report, turned in to the station, turned up nothing of any consequence. The school applied to higher authorities; days passed, and nothing was found.

Yvonne's letter ended saying, *We still have no word on either of them. I'll let you know, darling, the moment anything comes through.*

Meryl thought: I must go there. Then she thought: It would be useless. Benumbed, she read the letter again, shivering inside. There was no one she could turn to; no one who could help them. She spent the rest of the day in a daze; in the evening, her telephone rang.

The speaker was from an embassy; was this the *señorita* van Landen? It was? He introduced himself.

"... and I have a message... that is to say, a written letter for you, entrusted to my care...."

He had arrived in London the previous evening, and apologized for not ringing.

"... official business to tend to first..."

Meryl listened, and made the appointment he suggested: tomorrow morning. In a hotel lobby. He would carry... She would wear...

And at 10 A.M. precisely, as they'd arranged on the telephone, Meryl was handed a sealed letter from Dr. Jamie Casterán.

Jimmy wrote:

*The news is bad, Meryl; there's no easy way to tell you.
Raul and Lala are both dead. I'm sorry but it's true. They
were picked up for interrogation; it's a very ugly story. And I
don't know all the details yet. Perhaps we never will.*

*Both had been involved, from years back. I doubt you
knew about it. No one else did either, for a long time, but
eventually, someone must have squealed. It always happens;
there are so many factions. In any case, with the crackdown,
they both got abducted. And I can tell you quite frankly that
that they never had a chance.*

*Harvey Casey is also dead. He was their interrogator. The
usual type of stunts were pulled—making Raul see Lala being
put through it, in order to break him down. Somewhere,
Casey miscalculated. Raul broke free and killed him before
guards burst in and blew Raul's head off. In the uproar, Lala
managed to grab a gun, but when she saw what had happened
to Raul, she put the barrel in her mouth and pulled the
trigger.*

*At least it is all over for them. Remember that, Meryl,
when you cry, as you are now crying.*

Meryl wiped her eyes to read through to the end.

*Their daughter is safe. She's been hidden at a friend's
house. Be careful when you write to your mother. Don't tell
her you know.*

Meryl cabled Jimmy:

GET ME LALA'S DAUGHTER

Jimmy cabled right back:

I ALREADY HAVE

XI

**El Refrán
1973–1974**

1

"You having one of your Argentine days?"

Meryl looked around, the spoon of *dulce de leche* still in her mouth. Amelie was standing in the kitchen doorway, reed-slim in her elfin elegance, her school bag in her hand.

Nodding, Meryl pushed the jar across the counter.

"Want some?"

"No, thanks." Amelie put her bag on the far chair and went toward the refrigerator. "I'd rather have a Coke."

Meryl went back to her task of pouring the *dulce de leche* from the high-sided pot into the glass jars lined up on the counter. They were occurring more frequently, her Argentine days, as Amelie termed them; they had started over a year before, and quite literally, out of the blue.

The blue sky. A dome of deep azure over Manhattan. She had been standing staring out of the window, not thinking of anything in particular, when she had noticed the clarity. Not a cloud anywhere in the highrise-notched sky. Meryl breathed in, savoring the air; it held the promise of summer warmth and sun—and suddenly she was far away, miles distant in space and years in time.

When Amelie asked her what she was doing, Meryl said, "I'm noticing the day. . . . It's a Buenos Aires day. . . ."

A few weeks later, it had been the taste of a peach. Not all the peaches of that peach season, but one particular peach. Meryl dreamed in mid-bite.

"It's going to drip onto the front of your dress. . . ."

Nine-year-old righteousness had brought her up with a start. Amelie was looking at her speculatively.

"You're having a Buenos Aires day. . . ."

"I was thinking of the *estancia*."

"Was it the peach?"

"Yes. How did you know?"

"Your face gets this look on it." Amelie began peeling a banana. "And you don't say much, and your eyes look away

557

and up to a corner where there isn't anything to see." She paused in mid-peel. "Meryl, can we go to the beach this weekend?"

"We *are* going. It's all arranged."

"Oh, goody. . . ."

But if Amelie's thoughts switched away from B.A., Meryl's did not.

I'm homesick, she thought, surprised; homesick for a home that isn't mine. And later, at the beach, Argentina returned again in the deep-hot feel of the clear summer sun and high heat and the silence of noon.

Next, it was a craving for *dulce de leche*, a foodstuff she hadn't thought of in years. But she wanted the real kind, not the substitute scattered Argentines used from time to time, an approximation reached by boiling a can of condensed milk for a couple of low and slow hours.

When a friend traveled up from Argentina, she remembered to ask for the recipe.

"Haven't a clue, my dear—but I understand you can boil a tin of. . ."

"Yes, yes, I know all about the condensed milk trick," Meryl said impatiently. "But I want to make the real McCoy."

"Well, *che*, you know how it is. Who wants to stand around boiling milk all day when you can buy it at the shop around the corner?"

When the craving hit again, Meryl thought: perhaps at the consulate. . .

She rang up.

"*Dulce de leche?* No, *señora*, I don't know, but perhaps our commercial attaché's secretary. . ."

Meryl put in a call to Washington. She got past the switchboard, the secretary, the next one.

"*Dulce de leche?* Certainly, *señora*. You take a can of condensed milk. . ."

Wearily, Meryl put down the phone.

She discovered an Argentine restaurant.

"Come on, Amelie, let's try it. . . ."

Over *empanadas* and memories, Meryl recounted some of her childhood days.

". . . and so your mother and I learned to swim there. Crazy, isn't it, learning to swim in a church. . . ."

"Weird," nodded Amelie, pushing aside the plate of *alfajores*.

558

"Meryl, do I *have* to have one of these? I'd rather have an ice cream on the way home."

"Okay." Meryl stifled her unreasonable disappointment. The psychiatrist had often gone over this ground.

The child will probably reject her background on numerous occasions . . . forcing her toward it will only exacerbate the already painful past . . .

"Meryl, can I go and look at the paintings over there?"

"May I," Meryl corrected automatically, and then gave Amelie permission to wander around. She finished her dessert of *dulce de leche* and sipped her coffee with enjoyment, feeling the distance of time.

Amelie reappeared at her elbow.

"I got it." She was waving a piece of paper in her hand. Then she put it down on the table in front of Meryl. "See? The real recipe for *dulce de leche*."

Meryl stared at the handwritten instructions.

"Where did this. . . ?" she began.

"From the lady at the cash register," said Amelie, looking pleased with herself. "She's the boss. I told her it was the first time I'd ever tasted the stuff, and what was it, and could it be made at home . . . so she wrote out the recipe for me."

Meryl looked at Amelie; the child's grin widened with glee.

"Of course," Meryl said, "you never mentioned Spanish. . ."

"Of course not."

". . . or knowing anything about B.A. . . ."

They both giggled, sharing the joke between them, Meryl savoring the moment of closeness and a sense of pride.

Truly, the child was not Lala's daughter for nothing. Amelie, when she wanted something, was definitely a *viva*.

Neither the bonds nor Amelie's inherited trait had been apparent right away.

Meryl's first glimpse of Amelie came at Kennedy Airport after hours of agitated waiting and weeks of tension and change. Jimmy's cable to London had been followed by a short letter, crossing Meryl's equally quick-written reply. Then her telephone rang, and Jimmy's voice came to her.

"This is a scrambler phone," he said. "You can say what you like—and so can I."

"All I need to say is that I want Amelie. . . . I promised Lala, years ago . . ."

"But she could stay at the *estancia*. Both your grandmother and your mother..."

"NO!" Meryl shouted. "I'll come to B.A. at once..."

"Don't do that. It'll make it more difficult. I'll get her to you...."

No, Yvonne and Edie didn't know anything yet. Yes, he had it cleared with the authorities. There were still some documents, some official signatures needed. It would take a couple of weeks, perhaps a month....

"...but then it'll be official, and no one'll be able to interfere or take her away from you," he concluded.

Meryl's thoughts whirled.

"Jimmy—I think I'll go back to New York in the meantime. Can you bring her to me there?"

"Of course. Keep in touch. I'll keep you posted from this end...."

And then their talk was over. Meryl put her head down on her arms.

After that, she had no more time for tears or second-guessing. Her mind made up, she got her plans in motion the next day. A call to Sal, one to her lawyer, arrangements about the apartment. The place in London had to be handed over; the photo service rearranged, her former assistant upgraded.

"Of course he can do it." This to Sal on the phone.

"If you say so, kiddo... let me know how things go, okay?"

They went quickly, double-quick nervous-time. Meryl found her energy aflame, her pace frenetic, the hours of sleep minimal and wracked by dreams. It was frantic, it was illogical, it was crazy, but she had to do it. She had promised Lala. It was that simple. Meryl knew where her drive and her acceptance lay.

The year-end festivities seemed such a mockery.

But next year there'll be Amelie to celebrate with....

She pushed the thought aside. It was too far in the future. Right now, there were things to be tackled and gotten through.

A brief note to Marcheret brought a quick reply.

You are tackling the impossible and I admire you for it. Bravo and bonne chance, Meryl, in this new life's adventure. I must tell you I suspect you will ultimately succeed, if only because you will either not see, or will simply ignore, the complexities.

The roses that accompanied his note were an exact replica of his original bouquet. Meryl smiled in full acceptance of the farewell gesture, and forgot, a moment later, that the flowers were even there.

She packed and flew westward. Sal met her at the airport.

"Your legal eagle called me yesterday," he said. "You're biting off a hell of a chunk, Meryl, in this deal. . . ."

"I know."

But somehow, the tasks had been accomplished, some of the furniture taken out of storage, a small apartment found. Later, she'd get the Park Avenue place back again, later, the finicky details could be resolved. Under pressure, the basics became obvious; when arrival data came from Jimmy, everything was as ready as it need be at the time.

Meryl went to the airport alone.

"Thank you Sal—but not this time. It's going to be rough on all three of us . . . and Amelie's the one who has to come first. . . ."

She arrived early, waiting for ages, had a cup of coffee, checked the arrival listing again. Then at last, there it was: ARRIVING FROM BUENOS AIRES . . .

Nervously, Meryl paced along the upper floor, looking down to the Customs' section below. Then, suddenly, she saw them, walking up to an inspection counter, a small child, huddled in a coat too big for her, clinging to the hand of a man darkly dressed in gray. He was bare-headed, narrow-bodied, his face not fully visible as he looked down at the little girl with the short-cropped hair and spoke to her, holding her head to his side. With a start, Meryl realized it was Jimmy. It had to be Jimmy—Jimmy and Amelie. There were no other small children around.

The man glanced up, his head turning to see all the upper floor windows. It was Jimmy; he looked haggard, alien, and alone. He saw her; then came his smile and a wave of recognition. He bent down to the child, and pointed upward, but she only hid her face against him. Meryl waved in understanding and turned on her heel; it would be better to regain her composure before meeting them downstairs when they came through the door.

The shocks came swiftly.
He was old, different, a stranger.

561

"Meryl." He spoke her name quietly, his voice unmistakable. It was Jimmy; he was the same. His hands touched her shoulders, and he kissed her forehead lightly.

"Meryl, this is Amelie.... She knows all about you, of course...."

Meryl crouched down onto her heels, bringing her face level with that of the seven-year-old child's.

"Hello, Amelie... I'm so glad you're here..."

The small, pinched face with the shadow-smudged eyes looked hesitant, uncertain. Meryl stretched out her arms; Amelie moved between them, still holding Jimmy's hand. Then, in a sudden dart forward, she was hugging her in greeting, her cold hands around Meryl's neck not nearly as chilling as the sudden realization that this wasn't Lala, and could not ever be.

Meryl remembered everything through a screening veil of panic. In the taxi going into Manhattan, the child had sat between her and Jimmy, her manner serious, her face drawn, her body shivering from time to time from the unaccustomed cold.

"She's very tired, Meryl...."

"I'm sure she is.... Here, why don't you put on my fur gloves...?"

It served as a distraction and a diversion, and somehow they arrived at the apartment after all. Then there were newnesses to be introduced to ("... and this'll be your room, Amelie... yes, all for your very own....") and food to prepare ("... even if it's only a small bite... try a little of it....") and the nerve-wracking tension of trying to make things easier, and smooth. But somehow, somehow, the hours moved on slowly, until Amelie, exhausted, fell asleep on Meryl's bed.

"You've changed," said Jimmy, sitting opposite on the sofa. Amelie was still asleep in bed beyond the open door. Meryl had just peeped in to see her, and the child was breathing deeply, relaxed at last after a day that had been emotionally wearing all around.

"That's what my mother said, when she came to London." Meryl dropped into the massive leather chair. "What's the matter with you people in B.A.? D'you think time stands

562

still? Of course I've changed. It's been—what?—twenty years, Jimmy...."

"I know, I know, I'm sorry." He grimaced. "I'm sorry, *che*—and I didn't even really mean it. You *haven't* changed, not really. They were just words, to cover up..."

His voice faded away.

We're tired, both of us, Meryl realized, tired and anxious and ripped to shreds. And now—how am I going to handle this? Amelie's a reality. It's so easy to make decisions ... and so hard to carry them through....

"I'm afraid," she said suddenly, sitting bolt upright. "Jimmy, how do I tackle this...? Suppose I can't cope with it...? really, I'm afraid."

He leaned forward, his elbows resting on his knees, his hands clasped together.

"You mustn't be," he said. "We'll talk it over together. It'll work out. You wait and see. I believe promises always do. Your kind, anyway."

Then he smiled at her, and winked, and the well-remembered gesture brought the past into the present, bridging the long-lost years until they seemed to snap together in the closeness of the moment.

"Right now, we're both exhausted. Let me get back to my hotel. Tomorrow, we'll get together, and talk, and get used to each other's faces ... the new ones that we're wearing with the twenty added years...."

During the week that followed, they spent their days arranging life and the future for Amelie. The child herself, docile and obedient, eagerly did everything she was told. She was quiet, seldom talking unless spoken to; she was obviously trying to please them both, yet wary of all that was new. The smudges of shadow began fading from under her eyes, whose green seemed to deepen; she did not, Meryl realized, look like either Lala or Raul, but was a blend of them both. Her rare smiles were a ray of sun, transforming her face into unique individuality.

When she gets used to being here, Meryl thought, I must try to capture that look on film.

In the meantime, she watched Amelie anxiously.

"Is she all right, do you think, Jimmy? Will she like it here?"

"Give her time, Meryl . . . and give yourself time, too. . . ."

In the evenings, out of Amelie's hearing, they spoke of the serious things. Of the death of her parents. The *estancia*. Yvonne. Edie.

"She has a better grasp of things than your mother."

"I know. It's always been like that."

They spoke of the inheritance laws that would eventually give La Chata to Amelie, of the political peculiarities involved where personal vendettas could be disguised as government.

"You must realize, Meryl, that Harvey was out for Lala and Raul, no matter what. . . ."

"But was he an official investigator?"

Jimmy shrugged. "Of his own little vigilante group, maybe . . ."

"And Lala didn't suspect him . . ."

"She probably did. We'll never know for sure. She certainly was a subversive—one of the guerrillas' top messengers. That much was proven. The police dossier is full."

Meryl sighed, and fell silent. Jimmy changed the subject back to Amelie herself, and the somber mood eased.

After a while, Meryl said, "I can see she's very fond of you. You're very good with her, you know . . . you handle her well. In a way, I suppose I'm surprised." She smiled at him. "It's something I hadn't associated with you . . . coping with children. . . ."

"Well, I've had lots of practise. I think you know I have two stepdaughters, twins."

"But you never had any of your own?"

"No."

Again, the conversation was switched back to the focal point of Amelie, but not before Meryl sensed the barrier of an invisible wall blocking any view of Jimmy's personal attitude toward his wife and home. Despite her twinge of curiosity, she let the matter pass; there were too many other pressing objectives to discuss.

A private school was chosen for Amelie, its authorities conferred with, special tuition arranged. After talking to the school's psychologist, a specializing analyst was sought.

"It is both usual and advisable, in all such cases, to work within a framework of therapy for a while. . . ."

It was suggested Meryl also take a series of sessions.

"You'll need to be prepared for the explosions. . . . Rebellion is sure to come—must come, if the child is to come to terms with the traumas she has undergone. . . ."

Late that evening, with Amelie sleeping, the talk became personal again. In contrast to his noncommittal attitude about his own life, Jimmy questioned Meryl about hers.

"What happened to your marriage?"

As briefly as he could, Meryl told him. When she finished, Jimmy said, "Well, it all goes to prove what I've said all along. . . ."

"What?"

He grinned. "That you can't make a sow's purse out of a silk ear."

The personal started emerging.

"Are your toes still nibbable?"

"You've gone different in the neck. . . ."

"I know." He touched his collar. "I know. . . . But *che.* How rude of you to notice. . . ."

She laughed. "I'm sagging, too . . . only with me, it's my knees. . . ."

"Your knees, eh? How about your tummy button? Some years ago, mine started *smiling.* . . ." He looked shocked. "Can you imagine the effrontery? One day it was as round as ever, and then—zas!—overnight, the bugger grinned. . . ."

Meryl giggled, and looked at Jimmy, but his pale eyes were changing. The laughter had gone out of them; intent was there instead.

"You know something, Meryl? I think I'd like to see them. Your knees, I mean. . . ."

She hedged. "Come to New York in the summer. I'll parade them for you on the beach. . . ."

"I didn't mean that."

Meryl sighed. "Jimmy, I know you didn't—but no."

"Why not?"

"Because as you said many long years ago, it's not worth boiling water unless you're going to make tea. One-night stands have never appealed."

He nodded. "Agreed." He stood up. "It's late, *che*—I must be going. . . ."

She had just slipped into her dressing gown when the doorman rang on the intercom.

"Mr. Casterán is here again. . . ."

She went to the door and waited for Jimmy. He knocked instead of ringing the bell.

"Is something wrong?"

He didn't answer, and then she saw the tea bag, suspended

on its string, wrapped around his finger, swinging through the silence of the midnight air.

The next day she was embarrassed, then angry, then mortified. What did he mean by tumbling her to bed like that? What did she mean by complying? By the time he arrived at the apartment, Meryl was being distant. The day was busy, spent on necessities for Amelie.

Only in the evening did the personal return.

"You're angry, Meryl."

"I guess I am. It wasn't clever."

"I wasn't trying to be clever. . . ."

"No—just taking advantage of a mood. . . ."

"If that's the way you take it . . ."

"What else can I think? I remember."

"Remember what?"

"The way you are."

There was a slight pause, and then Jimmy said, "Does it occur to you I might have changed?"

"You certainly hadn't changed last night."

"You hadn't, either."

"I never said I . . . but that's not the point. You've always had it your way . . . had *everything* your way . . . so why should you change?"

Jimmy strode over and grabbed her by the shoulders.

"Meryl, stop it. We're quarreling—and I don't believe either of us want to. Keep in mind we're both under great pressure . . ."

She wrenched away.

"Then leave me alone."

His hands dropped to his sides. "I will, I will, if that eases it for you. But first, let's finish all the things for Amelie. Only a couple more days, and I'll be going back to B.A. Until then, pax, Meryl, pax, as we used to say in school. . . . I don't want to quarrel or play games with you any more."

The truce held. When Jimmy left, Meryl didn't go to the airport.

"Amelie's had enough good-byes to last her for a while. . . ."

He agreed, and they parted as friends in the doorway. The child hugged him and returned to her new own room.

Late that night, as Meryl lay in bed, a long way from

sleeping, the ghosts of thought came back from the equally long-distant past.

Okay, Lala, I'm keeping my promise. . . . I've got Amelie, and here she stays. . . . But what I couldn't promise then, and don't know—am afraid to think about now is whether I'll be good for her . . . or she for me. . . .

The first blow-up, a screaming tantrum, occurred shortly after Jimmy had left, and the weeks following it became a time of strenuous adjustment for both woman and child. For Amelie, there was school plus tutoring in English and the newness of home and surrounding and country; for Meryl, there was the sudden and seemingly total curtailment of her freedom.

"It's not so much that Amelie has to be taken places, or that she needs clothes, or a dental appointment," Meryl said to the psychiatrist during one of the many sessions she took on her own. "It's that she's *there*. Always there. No matter what I want to do, or plan, or anything—I find it isn't just me involved. . . ."

"And do you see this as an imposition?"

"Frankly—yes . . . but . . ."

But: she had promised. *But:* she had to do it.

The psychiatrist suggested: "Perhaps you don't have to do it . . . possibly another way could be found. . . ."

"You mean—send Amelie somewhere else?" Electrified by the idea, Meryl responded with vigor. "Send her away? Now? Oh, no—I couldn't. . . ."

As the insights into her own feelings came further to light, so the means of handling Amelie's problems became easier to accept. During the analytic sessions, Meryl also derived the benefit of another point of view, and unexpected glimpses of progress began to emerge.

Then came a huge step forward, its concept born in the heat of battle. A tantrum was in full progress; Meryl despaired.

"I don't understand you, Amelie—last week, you wore this very same dress, and you said you liked it, and even yesterday, you said . . ."

"That was the yesterday me!" came the shouted answer.

Meryl stopped hanging the offending dress on its hanger.

"Oh?" She turned around, facing the red-faced, tear-stained child roaring at the foot of the bed. "Well, if that was the

567

yesterday you—who are you today? Let's see, now"—Meryl let her fantasy take over—"I know you were Amelie last night, because you answered to the name when I called you . . . and today you must be partly that . . ."

And the name game began.

Within minutes, the tantrum was subsiding, and the names were all-absorbing: Amelie was the whole child, Lia her tomboy side. Amie was, as a French, friendly: Mia—as the word indicated in Spanish—possessive; Lee was selfish; Melly, giggly; Lilly, grown-up and old. The fantasy invention went much further than solving the tantrum that spawned it; each name acquired its corresponding set of mannerisms and clothes.

The novel development was reported to the analyst at the next session.

"It won't turn her into a split personality, will it?" Meryl worried.

The analyst smiled. "Indeed not. She talks freely about it. She's well aware it's all a game, and it'll allow her to play out any number of emotions in harmless but highly revealing ways. . . ."

He elaborated further.

"You see, children who have suffered the sort of traumas Amelie has encountered take different paths—use differing roles, if you wish, to survive. Some remain infantile, trying to stay at the level at which they *were* safe. Others try to become their own parents, and appear to be amazingly mature for their age. Then there are those who aim to be model children—so good and so perfect that no one, nothing—not even fate—will ever reject or abandon them again.

"In Amelie's case, she is using the name game to act out all the different roles she perceives. You must remember she is extremely intelligent—all the tests we've taken have shown that—and her handling of her inner conflicts may well be in keeping with her high abilities."

"Perhaps she'll turn out to be an actress," Meryl speculated, and, motivated by the thought, and her desire to give Amelie as broad an education as possible, she enrolled the child in a dancing school that included classes in mime.

"Have you decided who you're going to be today?"

Meryl, ready for the onslaught, paused by the closet in

Amelie's room, waiting to hear the decision. Amelie, her growing hair pulled back into a spikey ponytail, balanced on one leg in the middle of the bedroom.

"Look, Meryl... I'm being a stork... we did it in dancing class yesterday...."

She held her hands behind her back and made her neck and head jut forward. Meryl, acknowledging the likeness, wondered privately whether a new ornithological personality was going to join in. But no.

"I think I'll be Lia—*you* know, with jeans and the stripeys...."

An hour later, Amelie left for school, her bag slung over the shoulder of her blue-and-brown striped T-shirt, her hair redone in pigtails, the rim of milk not quite wiped off around her mouth.

Meryl closed first the front door and then her eyes.

One day at a time, she told herself, recalling the psychiatrist's words for the umpteenth time. One day at a time...

And, one day at a time, it was more or less working. More or less. Certainly better than before. But there was still so much to face.

"Amelie's behavior patterns are understandable, in light of her background," the teacher had told her. "However, that doesn't prevent them from being antisocial...."

Fighting. Stealing. Lying to her schoolmates. Lying to Meryl. Testing everyone around. Pushing her luck, then buying, currying favor. The changing tactics were bewildering in their range and force.

Above all, patience... but certainly, firmness. Thus the shrink, and Meryl followed his course.

...was most surprised to hear from Mummy that Amelie is in New York with you, wrote Yvonne after months of silence. *I knew nothing about it, believing she would be returning to the estancia, as had been originally planned. But one of those new servants at El Ombú told your grandmother, and she wrote and told me. Is that why you went back to New York? I thought it was because of your work...*

And she doesn't even ask me how we're faring, Meryl noted, stuffing the letter back into its envelope and throwing it onto her desk. Just wait till she discovers it was Jimmy who brought Amelie up here....

There was a letter from him, too. A short one.

. . .glad to know the battles are decreasing. I know you can do it. Merely a question of time. Around here—well, che, life goes on, and that's about all I can tell you. Please sign the enclosed documents for my file . . .

The papers, still connected to her legal rights with Amelie, were signed and in the mail again by the evening postal pickup. Meryl knew better than to question Jimmy on the subject; whatever his methods had been, the results were the important thing. And he had achieved for her exactly the status that she wanted: no one could take Amelie from her.

"Well, well—here's the little mother herself," Sal greeted.

"Shut up," said Meryl pleasantly, sliding into the opposite bench of the restaurant booth. "I've had enough of it for a while. Have you any idea, Sal, what it costs to equip a kid for school?"

"None at all," came the prompt reply. "I'm an expert on wives, not children—and if you want to match costs, kiddo, I'll be happy to do so, and by the end of it, I'm sure you'll agree kids are a bargain . . . compared to *my* wives, anyway. . . ."

Over lunch, Meryl explained why she had rung to meet him.

"We're sort of settling down, Amelie and I, and I think we can now make the move back to my apartment. The people were going to leave anyway. I'll need some redoing, but then I think it'll be a good place for us."

Sal said, "And you'll have your darkroom again."

Meryl nodded.

"And you're thinking of going back to work. . . ."

"You get the prize cigar, Sal. . . ."

By the time winter rolled around, and the prospect of Christmas, the apartment on Park Avenue was once more Meryl's home. Amelie, her hair shoulder-length and shining, ran around the living room in excitement and glee.

". . . and when we have my party, we can all play in here . . . and have the tree over there . . ."

Christmas and birthday, all in one; almost a year since the child had arrived in New York. Meryl looked at her and wondered: was there a time she wasn't with me? She's changed. . . . *I've* changed. . . .

She smiled at her charge.

"Who are you going to be here, do you think?" she asked,

playing their daily fantasy. "You could match yourself to the rooms, you know—play Lily in the living room, and Lia in the hall, and..."

"Oh, no," Amelie was emphatic. "Here I'm going to be Amelie. And you know what else?"

She leapt onto the sofa, struck a pose, then jumped down again and rushed over to Meryl, grabbing and hugging her around the waist.

"Now I can be my pretend-people just for playing, and really be Amelie...and your little girl...."

2

...grown so much you'd hardly recognize her, Meryl wrote. *Her English is fluent; she avoids speaking Spanish unless we're alone. Her schoolwork is good. I think it stays that way because she's a show-off, though the shrink keeps insisting she's unusually bright. She's got Lala's facility for memorizing, too, which is why I suspect she only parrots much of the stuff she supposedly knows.... She's also showing an absolutely wicked gift for mimicry ...will either become an actress or a social outcast ...*

With a few more lines, she completed her letter to Jimmy; it joined the others—to her mother, to her grandmother—to be sent to B.A. She would mail them on her way to Sal's studio.

She found the housekeeper in the kitchen and gave instructions for Amelie's evening meal. Returning to the living room, she heard the front door open, and Amelie's voice saying excitedly, "I think she's home. Come on in," and then Jimmy was there.

"Jimmy! I was just writing...this is crazy...." Meryl reached for the letter, confused in the rush of blood to her face and the surprise.

Business had brought him to New York unexpectedly.

"I called you from the airport, but the line was busy, and I thought, what the hell—I'll give her a fright instead...."

Amelie was dancing around him, holding his hand, delighted he'd appeared.

"He didn't recognize me, Meryl—I had to pull at his jacket..."

"Of course I didn't—my God, how you've grown. . . ."

"Well, you haven't seen me for two years. . . ."

Grown and changed, prettier, gaining confidence, Amelie was beginning to show signs of aplomb.

"Let me take your coat, Jimmy—I can still call you Jimmy, can't I?—Would you like some coffee? I think there's cake today, too. . . ."

"Of course you can, yes, I would, and where did you learn to be such a lady?"

Giggling, Amelie ran off to hang his coat up.

"*Chupa-medias*," said Meryl, smiling.

"Which one of us?"

"Both of you. Oh, Jimmy—it's good to see you. How long are you staying?"

"Long enough to take you out to dinner, I hope. . . ."

Amelie came back into the room.

"Yes, there's cake—chocolate, my favorite. Jimmy, will you be here for Meryl's birthday next week?"

"That's enough, Amelie. . . ."

"Your birthday?" Jimmy turned to Meryl. "I'd forgotten . . . you do have birthdays, don't you? Even though you don't change."

The orchids arrived shortly after breakfast. A small package was attached to their pliable stems. The gold brooch inside was in the shape of a teacup, the spoon outlined on its saucer in a thin, diamond-chip line.

At dinner, Jimmy said, "I trust I make myself clear?" and Meryl, touching the pin with her finger, said nothing at all.

But later, in the after-stillness of her bedroom, she murmured, "Jimmy—why are you bothering to get mixed up with me again?"

He sat up and turned his back on her, silent for a moment. Eventually he moved around again and stared into her eyes. There was a new look in his expression, one she could not fathom.

"Does it strike you," he said at last, "that it's none of your business? Keep in mind that my life is my problem alone. . . ."

It was after he left, as the summer got started, that Meryl began experiencing the first of her Argentine days.

There was terrorist violence and skullduggery rampant in the world as the summer days went on. A burglary in Washington introduced the name Watergate; in Munich, at

572

the Olympics, a massacre took place. There were straws in the wind of political power returning to Argentina on the name of Perón; the elderly expatriate, sunning in Spain's capital, began making the moves to get himself welcomed back home.

The autumn winds came; President Nixon was reelected. And Jimmy Casterán arrived back in New York.

He came bearing records as an early Christmas present.

"Play this one first. It's got *Gabriela* on it. They're reissuing all the best old tunes."

Meryl said, "You remember...." half in wonder, half delighted.

"I spent too many years forgetting, and look at the horrible mess it got me into."

Jimmy turned on the stereo, and when the music started, he said, "Shall we dance?" and took Meryl by the hand to the open space beyond the chairs. They moved in time to the tango through the labyrinth of furniture; Meryl closed her eyes and leaned against the warmth of Jimmy's arm.

His cheek touched her and closed against it.

"You dance even better than before...."

"But I'm out of practise." As she spoke, she stumbled.

"Well, we'll have to do something about that, my girl, won't we?"

Among the many tunes Meryl discovered on the discs was a new recording of "*Adiós*, Buenos Aires, Good-bye."

They spent hours talking, over meals, across pillows. When she was with him Meryl felt time melted away. He spoke of his work, not in detail, but in concept.

"In all lawsuits, at some point, a mistake is made—and that's the hinge on which the outcome turns."

He was, he explained, a listener for that point. The flaw. The gap. The opening. The chink the armor showed.

"...so you see, that's why I talk so much when I'm with you—to make up for all my silences...."

She laughed. "I'll bet."

He agreed. "Of course I talk—to get them off-guard...."

She asked about B.A.

"Oh, yes. Perón's returning. No question about it."

She told him Yvonne's letters sounded afraid.

"I wouldn't worry about your mother. She's in no danger, I assure you."

"Is anyone?"

"Someone always is."

"I mean in general. . . ."

"No."

He took her away for Christmas, while Amelie vacationed at a schoolfriend's in Aspen. They went to a snowbound New England inn with a cuckoo clock in the hall. By the second day Jimmy was threatening to wrap up its beak in a bandanna.

". . . bloody bird interrupts thought itself. . . ."

"What you mean is you've had enough of the country. . . ."

"Bet your arse I have. Come on, let's go dancing in town. . . ."

With Amelie away and the housekeeper on vacation, they had the apartment all to themselves. One morning Meryl woke and Jimmy was not by her side. She rose and, in her dressing gown, went into the living room, to find him sitting, lost in thought, in the heavy leather chair.

"You look so pensive. . . ."

"Do I?" He smiled a morning greeting. "So early in the morning, too. I must be getting old. But it's pigeons coming home to roost, and I doubtless deserve 'em. About you, too."

"Why me?"

"Remember, all those years ago, how ungracious I was to you about being the first? Well, here comes my punishment, and hence my pensativity, because the trouble is, I now know . . . I would like to be the last. . . ."

Jimmy had already gone back to Buenos Aires when Amelie came home.

"When did he leave?"

"Last Friday."

"Oh." The sulking mood was obvious and, even though Meryl tried to ignore it, it permeated the atmosphere until she had to interfere.

"Might I ask what on earth's wrong with you? Didn't you enjoy Aspen?"

Amelie shrugged. "It was okay, I guess."

"But?"

"I'd rather have been here."

"I told you I was going away with Jimmy. . . ."

"I could've gone with you. . . ."

"I don't think you'd have enjoyed it."

"Why not? I like being with the two of you—and it *was* my birthday. . . ."

574

"Exactly—and I'd imagine most ten-year-olds would think it was wonderful to go on a skiing holiday for their birthdays—especially as your girlfriend had her tenth birthday, too...."

Underneath her words, Meryl knew, in suddenly discovered discomfort, where her real reasons lay: she had allowed the snow vacation so that she could be alone with Jimmy. But still...

"And *I'd* imagine," mimicked Amelie, in ugly imitation, "that most proper mothers would think it wonderful to be with their little girls for birthdays...."

Resisting the desire to slap her, Meryl was about to try opening full discussion when she saw Amelie's face go red in the deepening blush of the temper fits that had raged in the early days. In a second, the outburst came.

"Why can't I have proper parents? Why can't my home be normal?"

She was doing that awful roaring now, the terrible noise she used to do so long ago, but which Meryl had thought was a thing of the past. Its hideous sounds were at their peak; later, the sobs would start, and eventually block her words.

Meryl tightened down and made her own voice go as quiet as she could.

"Amelie, we've been through all that... and recognized its sadness... but that's the way things are. You know better than I that your mother and father..."

"I'm not *talking* about my dead parents!" Amelie interrupted with a heightened shriek. "I'm talking about *you*! It's about *you* I'm saying, why can't you be normal... a proper, normal mother.... Why can't you, Meryl? Why? And marry someone nice like Jimmy, and have a real home..." The sobs were beginning to break through now. "Why can't you marry Jimmy, so's I can have a dad...?"

Jimmy returned to New York in spring; Meryl was glad to see him. Amelie made it clear she was overjoyed.

"She saves her lousy moods for me," Meryl said when she and Jimmy were alone.

"That sounds normal enough. The twins used to do that." He seldom referred to his stepdaughters by name. Or at all, for that matter; Meryl waited and wondered.

Finally she asked, "Don't you ever see them?"

He looked surprised. "Of course I do. Why d'you ask?"

"Because you never mention them." Flustered, she pressed

the point still further. "You never mention *anything*... about your personal life. And... and it seems strange... almost unnatural...."

"Meryl, please listen to me: I come here to forget... the horrible mess it all is...."

She waited. Then: "But wouldn't it be better if you came out and talked of it?"

He looked out of the window. "I don't see why. It's all such a balls-up, it's almost comical. Except it isn't funny... it's all such a waste...."

He turned and faced Meryl. "All right. I'll tell you. Sonia and I live a life of empty formality—except for the moments when we rip each other apart. People said, when I married her, that the whole thing was nonsense...." He smiled ruefully. "And for once, they were absolutely correct."

"Does she know about me?"

"Not directly. She assumes there's someone. There always was."

"Yes. I remember."

Jimmy sat down and buried his face in his hands.

"No... no..." His voice was muffled. "That was entirely different. You and I were young... in a different world.... With Sonia... I have no marriage. Only the sharing of a household. And I'm very seldom there. It's easy for me, in a way. There's work, and business trips..."

"And women."

"There used to be," he acknowledged. "Now... well, one gets over that if one finds... something real. But with Sonia... it never was. She's an amateur professional. At everything. And the sad truth is she's not really very good at anything at all. Oh, I suppose she might be, if she did anything properly—but she's too much of a hysteric to get anything done. But she's an expert, make no mistake about it. The instant expert, by fiat. *Her* fiat, you understand."

He smiled. "I know it seems hard to believe, Meryl, but she's even more impossible than I am. One year it was painting, and the house full of artists and linseed oil. Then suddenly, it was plants. You needed a machete to get in through the front hall. Then it became the stage—the theatah, y'know." He struck a pose. "And with all these crazes came the crazy expenses—a gallery for the paintings, a greenhouse for the plants. With the stagestruck period, it was the absolute necessity of a theater and a professional, permanent company attached."

"In what language, might I ask?"

"Oh, English, of course, English...." He shuddered at the memory. "You have no idea of the slimy hangers-on you can attract that way.... But of course it didn't last, because nothing ever does. The next phase was psychology. She was going to set up a clinic. I thought I was going to have to shut her up in one...but it didn't come to that...."

"Jimmy, how on earth did you...?"

"Get tied up with her?" Jimmy supplied. "About as non-sensically as you did with Horgan, I'd imagine. The year I met her she was being a singer. In fact, that's how I met her—at a concert. You remember *Don* Julio's love of opera...."

"Of course."

"She was quite good, too. And, I thought, dedicated. She was also very beautiful." His voice softened. "To be fair, I must say she still is. But...Anyway, her singing career lasted a few months into our marriage and then, suddenly, no more singing. She was going to be an earth mother, and play pottery instead...."

He sighed.

"Oh, fuck it, Meryl, what's the use? I could go on and on complaining. Probably Sonia can do the same about me. I'll admit I've been no prize."

"And the girls?"

"The twins? They're puddings—sweet, but puddings. In clear contrast and rebellion against their mother, I've always thought. Actually, they're nice young women, and I'm very fond of both of them. We get on well together—survivors in the face of Sonia's constant creative storms."

Meryl observed, "So you seem to have managed reasonably well all these years. I don't quite see what's so different now."

Jimmy looked up. "Perhaps I am. Things changed when Miss Peggy died—at least, they did for me."

Meryl listened in silence. Jimmy talked on in memory.

"I think, when she died, that's when I finally realized...what life should really be...and that I was missing out. She had been lonely without *Don* Julio, but said it was worth it— because the years they had were worth it, and the price was the pain."

Jimmy looked away, and continued speaking.

577

"And I thought, here was I, more than halfway through my life, only just beginning to glimpse what my mother had known all along. And I'm sure she'd tried to tell me, many years earlier. But you know how it goes—or rather, how it didn't with me. How I didn't listen. I don't think I could hear. Not what she was really saying. Until she died, and I saw her death had taught me life...only I'd fucked it up so badly, there wasn't anything left anymore."

Until Meryl's note of condolence; a spark, he called it, in darkness.

"...and the thin, taut thread I held to you, through Lala's letters to me. And then, with the killings, and Amelie—you were back again...and ever since, in whatever way we live...I cannot let you go...."

At dinner, Amelie announced to Jimmy that Meryl had said she would take her to London.

"You mean now, to live?"

"No, no, after school. For my summer vacation," Amelie explained. "It's instead of camp, which means all those hot days here in the city, worse luck."

"You can always go out to the beaches...."

"But it's not the same as camp...."

Meryl told him later there was background on the discussion.

"I'd rather she got a glimpse of Europe, even if she hates it this time. But at least an inkling...of other people, how they really are, not just this know-it-all attitude of ethnic culture. Via restaurants, I might add. It really gets my goat. They eat a grape-leaf wrapped around mush and, whammo! they're Greek scholars."

"Have you considered moving back to London with her?"

"No, not really—I prefer basing my life here. I lived in London, as you know, and I tired of its style."

"Why?"

"It's rather difficult to explain...."

"I don't see why it should be."

"I'll tell you if I don't. Go on. Start talking...."

And Meryl did, speaking of the early Sixties, and the mood of the times.

"...eventually, it all grew tiresome...that awesome pressure to be trendy...to keep up with outmoded fashion.... I knew the center of things had moved on...."

"I see...."

"That's why I moved back here when I knew Amelie was to

join me. . . . I wanted to give her the best of all possible worlds. Oh, I know it isn't perfect. Nothing is. But at least she'll get a good smattering."

"I think it's working out, Meryl. The results look gratifying."

She stared at him in amazement.

"You really do understand what I mean, don't you?"

"Why shouldn't I?"

"No one else has, for years."

"How could they? They'd have to share all sort of things with you in your background. It's rather like telling jokes in two languages, the way we do in Spanish and English, with the joke in one and the punch line in the other. In order to understand it, you have to know both."

Meryl sat silently for a long moment, breaking the silence with a remembered sigh.

"I was just thinking how I once tried to tell Danny a joke like that, explaining the ending . . . and we eventually wound up in a rousing fight. . . ."

In midyear, the elderly Perón returned to Argentina. Jimmy arrived in New York the week after, with all the latest inside news and views. He didn't seem particularly concerned; Meryl was surprised at his insouciance.

"There's so much unrest, so much turmoil," she observed. "D'you think, in B.A., things'll straighten out?"

"Oh, come on, Meryl, stop sounding so English-pontifical. You're looking at changes that'll change again, and then come back to the same point. It isn't a question of a political problem, or phase, or insanity. It's merely that that's the way we are. The Argentine is unique."

"But right now . . ."

"Of course there are specific changes," he admitted. "Each man adds to his own regime. But the country remains the same. And so do its people—those who adapt. They blend in with it, and its particularity. And yet we're not a melting pot; look at our incredibly diverse communities. You and your Bowen Day School . . . the Goethe Schule for the krauts . . . we're full of the us-against-them strains, and finally Argentina, unique in the world. How many times have you heard the phrase: *I simply don't understand the place*—spoken by an outsider, of course?"

Meryl smiled in agreement. "I lost count long ago."

"And now they don't understand why we've got Perón back.

Well, I do—and so would you, if you'd stayed in B.A. Remember, it doesn't really matter who's currently in power. Basically, it's always the same network that runs the show."

"And," said Meryl, with deepening recognition, "you just happen to be one of the network's key lawyers...."

Jimmy made a small deprecating gesture. "If you want to put it that way."

She sat there looking at him; it explained so much. Why hadn't she guessed before?

"Shades of my late father...."

"Not really. He worked on an international scale, specifically, you told me, to gather information."

"That's true. But the likeness is this habit of appearing to do one thing while you're also involved in a secret other. Jimmy, why *do* you make these trips to New York?"

"I've told you: we have more and more American clients. In fact, if Texans keep on buying our land, we'll soon be singing 'Deep in the heart of Argentina...'"

But when after several weeks Meryl read in the newspapers of yet another huge sum of kidnapping ransom paid, she drew different conclusions.

Late that summer, Meryl took Amelie for the promised trip to Europe; combining photo-portraits and pleasure, she worked along the way. Assignments in London and Paris gave way to side trips into the country, and the last week was spent in the sun of Spain before flying home to New York.

"They don't talk like we do," Amelie observed, listening to the varied accents of Spanish, but, to Meryl's surprise, stopped pretending not to understand a word. It was a good sign, and Meryl returned to New York contented; the school year commenced, and the household's routine settled down once more.

In the world at large, frail structures were thrown off-balance; the mid-East erupted in the Yom Kippur War. The crisis marked a change in the globe's economic function.

"It's the end of an era..." was the phrase used by everyone watching.

"It's the start of a new one," said Jimmy Casterán. He arrived shortly after the actual shooting started. "It'll take time for people to realize it, perhaps, but all sorts of changes and surprises are most certainly in store."

580

As the Arab oil embargo gave birth to the energy crisis, their political conversations turned to the role of the Third World.

"Every dog has its day, and the same goes for groups of countries," Jimmy mentioned in passing. "And about time, too, that the Third Worlders got their share."

Meryl didn't answer. He looked at her carefully.

"Don't tell me you don't agree. . . ."

"Oh, no—of course I do," she said. "It's just that . . . well, what I was thinking was personal, not international. I'm trying to find my own vote, I suppose—the world in which to share my voice. But nothing seems to fit right. And never mind my passport. There's more in my mind than the American scene. But I don't feel I'm from the Third World, either."

"I know what you mean," Jimmy said in answer. "But actually, it's simple, you're a member of the Fourth World—the ones who belong nowhere—and can fit in anywhere at all."

She considered the question. "It sounds a bit outlandish."

"That's exactly what it is. Outlandish. No lands can claim you as theirs. And there are more and more Fourth Worlders as the world's people wander. They always did, but the difference now is the increasing number of those who don't try to become part of their new home. Or perhaps they can't. There are many variations. For example, those who leave and return again—only to find it doesn't work out."

" 'You can't go home again,' " Meryl quoted softly.

"Exactly. There was also the anonymous *paraguayo* who said one should never leave home at all, for the moment one does, one is never at home anywhere again. You can take your pick of quotations. But take an example: look at your father. Now there was a Fourth Worlder, through and through. . . ."

She nodded, remembering. "He fitted in everywhere."

"So he was a card-carrying member of it, all the way. Funnily enough, your mother is, too, but she'll never admit it. Yvonne's too busy clinging to her British passport—the one she got when she married old Dancourt—and closing her mind and eyes to anything else. Pity, 'cause she's lost out on so much. But there's her problem. Maybe it's more difficult for her generation to see."

"And you think we're Fourth Worlders also?"

"You, totally. I have only a touch of it. Just look at us: genealogical transplants and basically apolitical." He spun her around to face the mirror on the wall. Meryl looked at the reflection, at Jimmy's face peering over her shoulder, and she smiled at him through the mirror, and nodded, and said nothing, Jean-Luc's advice echoing to her from the distance of passing years.

If you would be both queen and woman, then you'll have to find a king of your own.

3

During the turmoiled years, there had been over five hundred kidnappings in Argentina, along with thirty political assassinations and countless skirmishes. Tens of millions had been paid to save lives held for ransom, and guards were standard equipment for high-echelon businessmen.

And ever since September, when Perón was elected president, it had been noticed. But not published, that a fully equipped ambulance followed his every motorcade.

Yvonne's letter arrived during the early part of December.

Grannie is doing very nicely, she wrote. *She fell and broke her hip last month, but it's mending very well. I didn't tell you at the time, because I didn't want to alarm you. Now she's much much better; the care at the British Hospital is really marvelous. Grannie insists she'll be going home very, very soon.*

Alarmed by the occurrence, Meryl wrote at once. Back came another letter.

No, darling, don't bother to come down. Grannie's doing splendidly; we're traveling tomorrow. She's been here at the house ever since she left the hospital, and now she wants to go home. I'm going to El Ombú with her, so write to me there.

"Jimmy, do me a favor. Call my mother and find out how Grannie is. . . ."

It gave them something to talk about, to cover the difficult good-bye.

"Next year, will you stay here for my birthday?" Amelie demanded.

"I'll try, funny-face, I'll try... remember your promise...."

"What was your promise?" Meryl asked as they returned to town from the airport.

"To keep an eye on you for him," came the composed answer. "Meryl, can we go skating tomorrow again?"

On Christmas Day, the figure skates glinted beneath the tree while Amelie whirled around the room in velvety red.

"Oh, it's beautiful, it's *beautiful*...." She spun to make the shaking skirt a wheel of color around her.

The telephone rang. Meryl answered. It was Jimmy.

"First let me speak to the birthday girl...."

Amelie bubbled on, until Meryl said, "That's enough," and took the receiver from her.

"Did you speak to my mother?"

"I did better," said Jimmy. "I spoke to the doctor—the one here at the hospital."

"And?"

After a brief hesitation, Jimmy's voice said, "Meryl, why don't you fly down? Nothing urgent, you understand, but... well, your grandmother's a very old lady...."

"But how is she?"

"The doctor says she did very well. She's walking again—with a cane, but walking. And she's back at the *estancia*.... She refused to stay in town."

"I know that...."

"Yes. Well. The thing is... she's an old lady... her heart's not totally in order.... Sometimes these accidents have later reactions...."

Meryl felt a sense of panic. I'm afraid of going down to B.A., she thought. And if it isn't really necessary...

"Jimmy, d'you really think I should go? I mean, there's Amelie, and school, and..."

"Bring her along. Stuff school," was the immediate answer. "And don't bother to mention work. I know you can switch that around."

"I wasn't going to...."

"Then get on with it, girl. Start packing. Remember it's warm here. Bloody hot, in fact."

"D'you really think...?"

"Yes, I do. Besides, I'd like to see you. And I can't go north again right now. Too much to do down here. Come down next month. That'll give you time for everything. If anything happens in the meantime, I'll call and let you know."

Leaving the thin light of a midwinter behind them, they took off for the south and the long flight ahead. Meryl felt light-headed, unreal, unbelieving. Beside her, Amelie fidgeted and frowned in her seat.

"You're sure they won't keep me?" She again repeated the question. It had arisen out of fright the moment she'd heard about the voyage and Meryl's plans. There had even been an additional visit to the psychoanalyst.

"I promise." Meryl smiled. "Remember, it's Jimmy who told you."

Amelie nodded, seemingly settled down. But later, in the darkness of the night flight's dimmed cabin, Meryl watched the child twitch under the soft blanket wrapped around her.

Meryl sat motionless, waiting and watching; sleep was too elusive; the aircraft droned on. So many years and happenings since she'd last seen Argentina; it had changed, everyone told her. Would she recognize her erstwhile land?

The sky changed color with a new day dawning; the direct flight, a twelve-hour marathon, began to draw to its close. She looked at the sleeping Amelie, now quiet in her slumber.

The green of the jungles slid away to the rivers; Meryl watched as Paraguay was left far behind. There were browns now, and roads, stretching fields, the *pampas*. A town here, another river. Rosario beneath them. And descent.

Amelie held her hand as they touched down and landed.

"Do you think," said the child, "that Jimmy'll be here?"

But as Meryl walked out to the early morning sunlight, all she could think was: *it's an Argentine day. . . .*

She stood at the top of the ramp for a moment, breathing in the air's moisture, twenty years vanishing in the space of one breath.

A real B.A. day . . . I am home in Argentina. . . .

Only then did she see Jimmy standing there, waiting. Meryl smiled and began to make her way down the steps.

"Your mother's still at El Ombú. I spoke to her yesterday. She says everything's ready for you at her house, and she'll be back here at the weekend."

Jimmy turned and spoke to the *changador* with the luggage.

"My driver's standing by the door . . . he'll bring the car over. . . ."

The limousine was air-conditioned.

"What luxury for here," Meryl commented.

"The Texans taught us how."

"I'll bet it's bulletproof, too," said Amelie.

Jimmy didn't answer. Instead, he took her hand in his.

"Welcome home," was all he said.

Amelie frowned. "It isn't."

"Not even when all three of us are together?"

She flashed a sudden smile at him. "If *you're* along. . . ."

Jimmy grinned at her. "Meryl is right. You *are* a *viva*. . . ."

"To say nothing of a *chupa-medias*. . . ." But Meryl was smiling, too. The worst was over; Amelie hadn't panicked. Now she was chatting to Jimmy and seemingly quite at ease.

And, Meryl realized, I didn't panic, either. I'm back . . . I never left . . . Jimmy's here by my side . . . even if it's only till we get to Mother's house. . . .

But when they reached the suburban home, there was a message waiting.

"The *señora* rang from El Ombú. . . . She says to come at once. . . ."

4

The frail figure on the bed had been still for hours. Now Edie stirred; Meryl saw her open her eyes.

"Yvonne . . ."

"Yes, Grannie," said Meryl, leaning forward. "Mother'll be back at once. She just went to get some tea."

Edie appeared not to hear.

"What time is it?"

Meryl checked her watch.

"Just after four. Are you thirsty, Grannie? Would you like something to drink?"

Edie faded further into the pillows.

"No, child . . . not now . . . perhaps later. . . ."

Her voice drifted off. She was sleeping again by the time Yvonne returned to the bedroom.

"Did she want something?"

"Only the time...."

"Then perhaps you'd like to go off for a while now."

The summer day's heat was still holding in the garden; Meryl went to the *gomero* tree and its remembered shade. There were so many shadows, past and present, on the *estancia*. Edie was dying; even the doctor had said it was only a matter of time.

"She is fading, *señora*. There is nothing we can do about it. The hip has mended as best it can. The trouble is her heart. Its strength is going. It could be a month, perhaps two, but eventually..."

A move back to the hospital had been under discussion when Meryl and Amelie arrived at the *estancia*.

"...but Mummy's absolutely set against it," said Yvonne. "I really don't know..."

Eventually, the doctor said, "*Señora*, to what purpose? We can care for the *señora* here, as best as we can...."

A nurse was brought from Rosario and additional servants from the *pueblo*, one of them specifically engaged to look after Amelie.

"But it's like being a *baby*...."

"Nonsense. I had a governess until I was much bigger than you are now."

"But that was in the *olden* days...."

"That's enough, miss," Meryl said sharply. "I don't want you wandering around here by yourself. And I can't go with you right now."

"When I lived here before..."

"When you lived here before, your father was in charge, or both your parents were here. Amelie, please don't go on about it. You know perfectly well..."

On the days Edie was lucid, Amelie was allowed in to see her. After her initial hesitancy, she reached out to the elderly wraith. They shared some long-ago memories.

"You used to love *alfajores*...and Rosita gave them to you...do you remember? Ah, how kind she was...."

And then it would be too tiring, and Edie would lie against the pillows, and someone would say, that's enough, isn't it, and Amelie would tiptoe away.

On one occasion Edie asked, "And does Meryl take good care of you?"

"Oh, yes, *Doña* Edie, we have a lovely time together...."

She was no longer listening. "Both your parents...so

sad . . . my Rosita, too . . ." The thin voice cracked and ended.

Her strength returned later in the evening, when Yvonne and Meryl were there.

". . . you must provide for the child . . . both of you . . . until La Chata becomes hers. . . ."

It had been a surprisingly lucid few hours, in retrospect; Meryl, sitting on the *gomero* branch, recalled their contents: Edie speaking of the two *estancias* and the heritage she was passing on.

". . . not today, perhaps . . . but I'll have to go, eventually. . . ."

Yvonne's eyes were tear-shiny and her nose was going red. Edie appeared not to notice it; Meryl kept her silence. At last, Edie slept again, and Yvonne said nothing more.

Jimmy's phone calls tended to come through in the morning.

"She's still much the same. . . . Mother and I take it in turns. . . ."

"D'you want me to get another nurse?"

But it was not necessary. Meryl said no.

"And how's Amelie?"

"Probably turning into the world's first female *gàucho*. I haven't seen her since dawn. All the old hands, the ones who knew Raul, spoil her rotten."

"Very good for her—far better, for the time being, anyway, than that New York den of iniquity she calls her school. Send her my love."

"I will."

They rang off. Meryl went on sitting at the desk for a while. The main room was quiet; no one else was about. Slowly, she rose and went over to the long dining room table. She dropped to her knees and crawled underneath it; her tears began as she slid her hands over its heavy wooden base. Her fingers found the ridges where time had darkened the work of two children so many years ago.

Moving closer, she saw the markings, the initials scratched and dug and deepened by pin and knife and determination. For a moment, she saw them clearly, the *L* and the *M*. Then her tears streamed and tumbled, splashing down her hands and clothing. Meryl clung to the wooden post and sobbed for the past.

The coolness of the *gomero* tree grew scented towards evening; the flowers of the nearby *dama-de-noche* bush became fragrant after dark.

"It's a lovely name, isn't it?" said Yvonne. "Lady of the evening...."

"Night lady...."

They talked of everything and nothing, she and Meryl, in the hours when Edie slept, remembering selected portions of the past, and the shapes of their lives in recent years.

"I so often think of England, and the lovely time I had there. With you," Yvonne added, after a momentary pause. "I'm sorry you gave up living in London. D'you think you might go back now?"

"It depends... on a lot of things...."

"You mean Amelie?"

Meryl nodded. "In part."

They shared their meals, if not their thoughts, and then returned to Edie's side.

"Rosita..."

"No, it's me, Mummy... Yvonne...."

The thin hand crept along the sheet fold.

"What time is it?"

"Very late at night, Mummy."

"But what time?"

Meryl said, "Ten past two."

Her mother, next to the bedside, sat back in a creaking of wicker. Edie sighed, and closed her eyes again.

"I think she's asleep."

Outside, the rustling sounds of the hushed, deep night stirred in the vacant breezes. Meryl sat and stared blankly at the low-lit scene in front of her; her mother sat immobile in the chair by the bed.

Meryl remembered the nurse's words of earlier:

Her skin is too salty.... The end is very close, señora. Don't leave her side.

And so they sat and waited, Edie's face sponged clean with water.

Another hour passed. Yvonne rose.

"I must get some sleep. Just a few hours...."

Meryl looked at her. "You heard what the nurse said."

Yvonne sat down again, looking uncomfortable. Edie stirred, grew restless.

"What... what is the time...?"

Toward the hours of dawn she woke, and her voice was stronger.

588

"Rosita," she said, whispering the name, "Rosita... I am here...."

But when she finally spoke again, Yvonne fled the room in panic. Edie's head rose fractionally off the pillow, her eyes wide open and clear.

"Mamma," she said distinctly, in her last moments of living, calling down the tunnel of time, "Mamma... Mamma..."

Jimmy stood next to Meryl all through the funeral, with Amelie on his other side, holding his hand. Yvonne stood alone, opposite the gravesite; the *gauchos* and the pueblo people stood behind the household staff. When the ceremony was over, they went back to the *estancia*. After everyone else had left, Yvonne and Meryl and Jimmy sat on the verandah and talked for hours.

"I feel numb.... I can't believe it...."

"At least the end was peaceful...."

Yvonne's eyes were dry and blank. "I've cried all my tears," she explained.

Meryl said, "I haven't," and accepted Jimmy's handkerchief.

Yvonne continued, "At least I was with her to the end...."

Meryl glanced up sharply, but Yvonne avoided her gaze, looking off into space. For the first time in her life, Meryl felt a stab of sympathy for the long-departed Wilfred.

Amelie appeared, and said she was tired.

"Then I'll help you get to bed...."

Meryl rose, and they walked off together. Yvonne turned to Jimmy.

"You're in love with her again, aren't you?"

"I always was... only before, I was too stupid to see...."

For a while, Yvonne said nothing, and then she said, "I've always known it. We're a strange trio, Jimmy—Meryl, my mother and I—I mean we were... before Mummy died...."

He waited for her to continue. Eventually, she did so.

"There are times we don't know where one of us ends and the other begins... but it never helped us understand. I think," she said, smiling, her face sad in the gesture, "I think we are a family best held together for being far apart."

Before Jimmy left, he and Meryl walked through the fields near the house together, and they stopped and rested a while near the old *ombú*.

"It's magnificent," said Jimmy.

"They always are. This one's an old, old tree. . . ."

"It isn't a tree, you know."

She looked at him in amazement, but he persisted.

"That's the only bit of interesting information I ever learned during Sonia's plant period—*Phytolacca Dioica*—technically, it's an herb."

After a while, he went on, saying, "It's such a symbol. Of the *pampas*, of this country. Majestic, magnificent—and not what it seems. Beneficial, too, for those who know how to use it."

"That's right." Meryl started remembering. "They used to use the leaves as soap, and there's something for rheumatism, I was once told. But most of all I remember all the giggles about the horrid habit of putting the leaves into *yerba*, and making someone sick with it. . . ."

"I'd say that represents our rather crude form of humor." He warmed to his theme. "I tell you, it's perfect. the *ombú* equals Argentina: solitary and proud. Beneficial in small doses, drastic in large ones. Misinterpreted, misunderstood—except by those of the land."

"You're saying it as though you were joking—but actually, you're quite serious."

Jimmy nodded. "Of course he is—just as Nixon's going to Argentine, too."

After a while, Meryl asked, "Jimmy, what's going to happen? Ever since I got here, people keep telling me Perón is going to die very soon."

Jimmy nodded. "Of course he is—just as Nixon's going to be ousted. The means are quite immaterial; the point is the end is in sight."

Meryl shivered. "There's going to be such a mess. . . ."

"No, there's not. There's going to be—nothing at all. Oh, sure, at the time, there'll be voices and confusion. In both cases, north and south. And then . . . ?" He gestured. "Nothing. It won't make any difference in the years ahead."

"But the governments . . ."

"In the long run, the governments *are* the people. Countries are ruled by what their people will endure."

Meryl stood up, breathing into the wind of the *pampas*.

"I don't know whether I agree," she said, "and I don't think I care. All I know is—this is my country, all of it . . . its sky, its sun, its grasses. And, yes—its sorrows. They're my tears, too."

They began walking back towards the main house of the *estancia*.

"It has nothing," she went on, "to do with the color of my passport. Or where I was born. It has nothing to do with loyalty, either. I don't plan fighting any wars, and anyway, I don't think the U.S, or B.A. plan to attack each other. What I *do* think—what I *know*, is that some deep chunk of me belongs here, stays here . . . no matter where I'm living, or what land I call my home."

On the train down to B.A., Amelie said, "I'm glad we're going. How much longer, Meryl, before we arrive?"

"Another two hours . . . perhaps a bit more. . . ."

Amelie sighed, spooning another mouthful of ice cream.

"If this was a plane, we'd be there by now."

Sitting across from her at the dining car table, Meryl smiled and offered no comment, the regular rhythm of the wheels' monotony filled with the past for her, and soothing to hear.

"Do we have to stay in B.A. for a long time?"

"No, not very." Meryl's eyes narrowed. "Why? Are you busting to get back to school?"

"Not exactly, but . . . I guess I'll just be glad to leave here." The ice cream finished, she put down her spoon. "I don't like it, Meryl. It makes me feel uncomfortable. Not because of my parents . . . somehow, it's because of me. . . ."

"It shouldn't, really. After all, you were born here, you speak the language . . ."

"But I don't belong here!"

The outburst was unmistakable; Meryl could see the girl's discomfiture; Amelie's fears tumbled out in a jumble of thoughts.

". . . I want to go home . . . to our home, where I like it . . . I'm tired of being here. . . . It makes me nervous inside, as though I don't know who I am. . . ."

"You're Amelie."

"Don't tease me, Meryl, I . . ."

"I'm not teasing. I'm trying to give you a point to start from," Meryl straightened up in her chair. "You are Amelie, and right now, you say you're homesick."

"It's more than that." The words were a mumble. "I don't know where I belong. . . ."

Meryl waited, sensing a struggle. After a while Amelie tried to explain further.

"Just because I was born here, does it mean I have to belong here, I mean, be an Argentine and live here, or call it my home? 'Cause I don't *feel* that way...."

"Can you tell me what you *do* feel?"

"I feel I want to go back to New York, and then, when I'm bigger, I can decide...."

"That sounds like a very sensible idea...."

But Amelie, with troubled eyes, looked across at Meryl.

"Meryl, do *you* know? Where *do* I belong?"

Meryl reached out her hand to place it over the child's for an instant.

"That's something you'll have to find out for yourself eventually. And it can take quite a while, you know, for those of us who have moved around..."

When at last they arrived in Retiro, Meryl told Amerlie she wanted to go and have some coffee.

"...and you can have more ice cream, if you want...."

The answer came in a mumble.

"No, thank you...I think I'd rather have an *alfajor*..."

Jimmy insisted on taking Meryl to the zoo.

"I want to buy you a balloon—a red one...."

"So you remember that, too...."

"Besides, it's time we revisited that hippo... the one with your toes...."

He parked the car and they walked along the tree-shaded sidewalk to the corner entrance. The balloon vendor was at his traditional post, and Jimmy tied the string around his own wrist.

"No, I'll give it to you later on...."

They strolled in the warmth of the late summer day along the gravel paths and past the tall trees.

"Just a minute...."

Jimmy stooped, turned aside, appeared to fumble with the balloon. When he turned back to Meryl, he handed its string to her, its end now wrapped around a small case.

"Here. It's for you."

She unwound the string and pushed the domed box open. A circle of diamonds glittered inside. Jimmy took the ring and slipped it over her finger.

"With this ring, I do thee love," he pronounced. Then he folded her fingers under his.

"Meryl, I don't know exactly what's going to be. But I do know what *isn't* to be: I won't be parted from you. Never again. And this time I mean it. In whatever way we can, we'll be together from now on. That's a promise."

"Except that on Friday I'm leaving for New York...."

"So am I," came the answer.

Meryl stared, not risking comment.

"I've left Sonia. She knows it. I'm out, and I'm through."

"But..."

"What's more—I have to go. To New York, I mean. We're opening an office. It's been planned for some time, and now's the time to go."

For a moment, she could say nothing; the balloon floated between them. The ring flashed on her finger. Meryl's voice returned.

All she could trust herself to say was, "Amelie... will be happy... will be so pleased when I tell her...."

"She already knows. I told her yesterday. Now let's go and fetch her. I promised we would... and that I'd take her out to dinner with us to celebrate tonight...."

XII

Coda

Meryl drove Jimmy's car through the parks of Palermo and onto the ribbon of the Costanera road. The mid-March day was bright with clear sunshine.

"We'll be able to have lunch outside."

"Uh-huh." Amelie fidgeted in the passenger seat beside her. "Meryl—is Jimmy really coming with us?"

"To have lunch? Of course. He invited us."

"No—I mean to New York."

Meryl frowned in slight impatience.

"That's what he said. You heard him."

"Will he stay?"

"He has to. He's setting up an office."

"I mean with *us*."

"I don't really know."

After a pause, Amelie asked, "Are you going to get married?"

"Not right now. We can't."

"But I mean *afterwards....*"

"*Amelie,*" said Meryl, her tone full of warning, "that's enough. Let's enjoy today, and the sunshine, and being here, okay? And please behave yourself at lunch. I don't want to hear an endless barrage of questions, and I'm sure Jimmy doesn't, either."

The line of *parrillada* restaurants was ahead along the roadway; the smell of charcoal grills began to tinge the air. Amelie fiddled with the knob of the radio. Familiar music filled the automobile. As the notes played on, she turned to Meryl.

"It sure isn't your theme song, is it? The words, I mean. You'll never say good-bye...."

A jet roared overhead, taking off from the aeropark by the water on its river-hopping flight over to Uruguay. The vibration rattled through the car, drowning out all other sound. As it faded, the music came through again.

> *...I say ciao*
> *And good-bye*

The road blurred. Meryl blinked hard behind her sunglasses, and the scene in front of her cleared. Her hand moved over to the radio; as the volume rose, Amelie began singing.

Meryl thought: no, no, I could never say good-bye and mean it.

"...*adiós* ...*good-bye* ..."

Not trusting her voice, she hummed along instead.

ABOUT THE AUTHOR

PIXIE BURGER was born in Surrey, England and grew up in France and in Argentina so she is truly A WOMAN OF TWO CONTINENTS.

Her first story was written at the age of six and was first published when she was twelve. The author of more than two dozen books, she has also been a teacher, a flight attendant, a model, and a photographer.

Pixie Burger currently divides her time between New York and Venice.

STEP OUT OF YOUR WORLD AND ENTER THE

CIRCLE OF LOVE

Step into the lives of men who are true men...and true loves. Step into another country—another world. Step into the Circle of Love. You'll find Circle of Love romances unlike any other romance novel you've read. They're beautifully written. The stories are more memorable. The characters, more genuine. And the romance, more satisfying from beginning to end.

Receive Six Books Each Month for the Price of Four

Dear Reader:

With all the romance novels available, finding consistently satisfying reading is still not easy.

In Circle of Love romances, you're assured better writing. The stories are more suspenseful and more realistic. The characters are more genuine. And the romance is more satisfying from beginning to end.

Now you can enter the Circle of Love each month with the convenience of this no-risk offer.

Cordially,

Mary Harding

Mary Harding for Circle of Love

Membership Application

☐ **YES.** Please send me the next Circle of Love romances without obligation. If I decide to keep all six, I'll pay $7.95—the cost of 4 books plus postage. Then each month, I will receive six new titles at this same price.

SIGNATURE_____

NAME_____

ADDRESS_____

CITY_____ STATE_____ ZIP_____

Payment Options: (check one)

☐ Charge each regular shipment to my: ☐ **Bill Me**

13029 ☐ **Mastercard**   ☐ **VISA**   11023

| | | | | | | | | | | | | | | | | | | |

(Credit Card Number)   *expiration date*

Send no money now—but mail today to

Circle of Love Reader's Service, Bantam Books, P.O. Box 994, Hicksville, N.Y. 11802

This offer is good only in the U.S. C

"The author of THE FAR PAVILIONS
has produced another winner,
tightly plotted, crammed with detail,
and irresistibly romantic."
—Cosmopolitan

Trade
Wind

M.M. Kaye

·· *Over two months on*
The New York Times *bestseller list* ··

M.M. Kaye's splendid new novel of love and
adventure sweeps us off to Zanzibar, a dangerous land drenched in languid, sensuous beauty. Into this lawless paradise comes Hero Athena
Hollis, a proud young woman whose noble
mission is to reform the savage. But she is
vulnerable to passion—and the insistent court-
ship of slave trader Captain Rory Frost sets her
afire. Now she faces the heartbreaking choice
between duty and love.

A few, precious novels arouse us, mesmerize
us, haunt our nights with visions that survive
long after the last page is turned. TRADE WIND
is such a novel.

0901-9 · $3.95)
    TRADE WIND, on sale July 1, 1982 wherever
    paperbacks are sold, or order directly from Bantam
       ng $1.00 for postage and handling and sending a
        tam Books, Dept. TW, 414 East Golf Road,
         llinois 60016. Allow 4-6 weeks for delivery.
       s 12/82.